THE
WANDERING
WAR

CINDY DEES
AND
BILL FLIPPIN

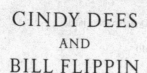

TOR®
fantasy

A TOM DOHERTY ASSOCIATES BOOK
NEW YORK

This is a work of fiction. All of the characters, organizations, and events
portrayed in this novel are either products of the authors' imaginations or
are used fictitiously.

THE WANDERING WAR

A Tor Book
Published by Tom Doherty Associates
175 Fifth Avenue
New York, NY 10010

www.tor-forge.com

Tor® is a registered trademark of Macmillan Publishing Group, LLC.

ISBN 978-0-7653-7032-7

Our books may be purchased in bulk for promotional, educational, or
business use. Please contact your local bookseller or the Macmillan Cor-
porate and Premium Sales Department at 1-800-221-7945, extension 5442,
or by e-mail at MacmillanSpecialMarkets@macmillan.com.

First Edition: February 2018

Printed in the United States of America

0 9 8 7 6 5 4 3 2 1

THE
WANDERING
WAR

CHAPTER

1

I t started with a prickle down Hemlocke's spine. Nothing much, but enough to cause the faintest spark of awareness in her sleeping mind. *Something was not right.*

Out of all her kind, she was the one who'd been created and empowered to act as a sentinel, exquisitely sensitive to the continent the humans called Haelos and to all its living creatures, aware even in the deepest of restorative slumbers when a threat stirred.

Slowly, slowly, blood began to seep through her veins, bringing a hint of warmth to her curled body and the beginning of thought to her dreamless mind. She'd been asleep a long time in her dark, watery lair. Her injuries at the hands of the Kothite invaders had been serious, and full healing could be measured in centuries. Her body might be nearly whole, but her spirit was still weak.

Not so weak, though, that she could not protect Haelos from its enemies. She waited patiently for her mind to come to sharp alertness, her claws to regain their deadly strength, her massive, scaled body to come to a fully active state, her great wings to unfurl. And when they did . . .

Then she would fly.

M adness! Unthinkable! Absolutely not!"
   Raina gazed sympathetically at the sputtering Heart patriarch and his equally agitated fellow matriarchs and patriarchs. Outrageous though it surely was, nonetheless, she had been raised to the rank of emissary in the White Heart by Lord Goldeneye, leader of the great Dominion

colony of changelings in the north of Haelos. He had no authority to do so, of course, but that had not stopped him.

High Matriarch Lenora had called this conclave of Heart leaders from across the settled lands of Haelos to discuss the matter, but the truth of it was that, no matter how much they blustered, their hands were tied. They needed the entrée to the heretofore impenetrable Dominion; hence they had no choice but to recognize her rank in the offshoot branch of the healer's guild, no matter how unorthodox it might be.

"She's a child!" a matriarch down the table spat in disgust. "The girl's hardly fit to be a White Heart initiate, let alone an emissary equal in rank to one of us."

The *girl* was sitting right here, hearing every word of their tirade. And she'd done a decent job of being a White Heart initiate, thank you very much. It hadn't always been easy, by the Lady. Even if she wouldn't be eighteen until springtime, age was not only measured in years but also in experience.

The Heart had three branches. The regular Heart to which most healers belonged. Then there was the White Heart, the pacifist branch of healers sworn to defend all life, to which Raina belonged, for better or worse. Lastly, there was the Royal Order of the Sun, the militaristic arm of the Heart, responsible for defending Heart chapters, their members, and the all-important resurrection Heartstones.

To Raina's vast relief, the Royal Order also took responsibility for protecting White Heart members from harm since she and her brethren were unable to protect themselves. Most of the Dominion's warriors had expressed a strong desire to kill her for being weak and spineless during her recent stint as a prisoner of that aggressive changeling army. They'd taught her to be abjectly grateful for the swords and shields that had hovered over her protectively since her return to Dupree.

At tonight's meeting, the Royal Order of the Sun was represented by Lord Justinius, knight commander of the entire order in Haelos. So far, he'd sat tense and taciturn at Lenora's right hand and not participated in the discussion. Raina suspected he saw the strategic necessity of letting her new rank stand and furthermore saw the advantage of finally having an emissary to the Dominion, her tender age notwithstanding.

Lenora patiently let the matriarchs and patriarchs belly-ache their fill, which took a while. Raina had taken just about as many insults to her age, intelligence, training, and skills as she could tolerate before their complaints finally wound down to a trickle and then ceased.

The high matriarch said with admirable calm from beside Raina, "Thank you for your comments. I appreciate your candor, but here's the thing. Never in the history of the Heart has *any* Dominion settlement, *anywhere*, allowed a member of the Heart to act as an envoy to it. We simply cannot turn down this opportunity."

"Agreed!" the sputtering patriarch from before exclaimed. "Let us send a more seasoned Heart member to Goldeneye with all due haste."

It was all Raina could do not to call him a fool for even suggesting such a thing. Lord Goldeneye would not stand for a substitute. They would be lucky to get their replacement emissary back alive, let alone with his or her mind intact.

She opened her mouth to tell the man so, but Lord Justinius sent her a brief, quelling look and a small shake of his head.

The big knight leaned forward ponderously, leather gambeson creaking under his chain mail, to weigh in at last. "Ladies and gentlemen. We are in full agreement that we have been presented with a rare opportunity, and we cannot turn away from it. However, I have met Lord Goldeneye, and he is not the sort to be trifled with. If this young lady is the one he chose, I guarantee you, he will accept no other. I shall send one of my most experienced knights to guard her, and he will be fully capable of advising her should she need guidance."

She studied Justinius while the others buzzed and Lenora tried unsuccessfully to quiet them. What was his game? Did Lord Justinius wish merely to plant an observer in his enemy's stronghold, perhaps co-opting control of her mission for his order?

Or did he aim higher? Did he dare hope for a rapprochement between the Royal Order of the Sun and the Dominion itself? The idea skirted perilously near treason. The Dominion's leaders openly declared themselves sworn enemies of Koth, nearly as openly as they declared their intent to conquer all the lands of Urth for themselves.

"*The enemy of my enemy?*" she murmured under the hubbub for Justinius's ears only.

"Silence!" he hissed in alarm.

Lord Justinius didn't deny her implication. But he did push abruptly to his feet, towering over them all in his armor and weapons while she stared at him in shock.

The others fell mostly silent, and his voice cut across the last few protests. "It is settled. I will send Sir Lakanos to Dupree to accompany her. He is a skilled warrior who will earn the respect of the Dominion and is subtle enough to help Raina manage the nuances of this assignment. When do you leave for the Great Den, Emissary?"

"Lord Goldeneye told me to return in the summer."

"Very well. When the days lengthen and the wheat ripens, look for my knight."

She bowed her head respectfully. "Yes, my lord."

D ownstairs in the big common room with its heavy-beamed ceilings and plenty of cots for the ill and injured, the Heart door opened to let in twilight's chill, and a crowd of drunken soldiers spilled inside loudly. The gypsy healer Rosana scowled as Will Cobb peeled away from his boisterous cronies, members of the elite Imperial Special Forces unit who called themselves the Talons of Koth. He wasn't a member of the unit, but they were recruiting him hard to join them. And to her chagrin, he was letting them.

"The lot of you are sloshed again?" she complained, hands planted in dragon wings of irritation on her hips.

"'Ey there, Rosie," Will called, overloud, his words slurring slightly. "We're here to get our blood purified so we can start drinking anew."

"What brilliant tactician thought up that idea?" she snapped.

"Me, of course." Will made an exaggerated bow in her general direction. "Will Cobb, tactical genius extraordinaire, at your service."

"I see your ego hasn't suffered any bruises after your training with Captain Krugar," she replied tartly.

Will had come to the Heart daily for the past two weeks for treatment of various contusions, cuts, and even a few cracked ribs after his sparring sessions with the Imperial Army officer. Unfortunately, Will's ego was growing right along with his prodigious combat skills.

Something had happened to him a few months back during the pitched fight to close a portal to the dream plane up in Dominion territory. He'd unlocked some sort of repressed memories of martial training from his childhood. He'd gone from being able to handle himself reasonably well in a fight to a highly skilled battle caster in the blink of an eye. Rumor had it he was actually beating Krugar on a semiregular basis in their weapons training now.

She ought to cut him some slack, forgive him for his abrupt surge of arrogant confidence, but it still rubbed her the wrong way. She preferred her humble cobbler's son from a tiny village in the Wylde Wold to this swaggering young man.

Maybe Will's attitude was influenced by the tree spirit trapped in the wooden disk that had grown onto his chest a year back. Bloodroot was the tree lord of death, destruction, and rage, after all. Ever since their unnatural union, Will had struggled against bouts of anger, jealousy, and quick temper.

Sometimes Rosana despaired of hanging on to the sweet lad who'd rescued her from an orc attack on a deserted road in the western woods over a year ago and won her heart in the process.

"C'mon, Rosie. Give us some potions," Will cajoled.

He opened his arms, and she scooted out of reach, swatting at his hands. "You know that is not how Heart resources are used."

Commander Thanon, leader of the Talons, threw an arm across Will's shoulder. "We'll pay for the potions. Twice—no, triple—their worth. I've got gold."

Rosana's scowl deepened. With triple the cost of the potions in gold, she could replace the ones she used on these fools with many more potions to heal the needy who poured through the Heart's front door in a never-ending stream. "Fine," she huffed. "But show me the gold first."

Raina heard a commotion downstairs and recognized the voices. Grabbing her white cloak boldly emblazoned with the royal blue symbol of the White Heart, she headed down to the big common room.

One of the men lolling about with Will spied her and peeled away from the others. She recognized the Imperial Army officer, a handsome young man entirely too cocky for his own good. He was a paxan, with a closed third eye in the middle of his forehead, and he made an exaggerated bow to her. "Greetings, my lady fair. Mine eyes rejoice at the sight of thy beauty."

She rolled her eyes. "Good evening, Commander Thanon. I see you and your friends have been celebrating again. Is there some occasion I am not aware of to warrant this revelry?"

"Merely the fact of being alive, my lovely Raina."

"I am not yours, sir," she replied a shade sharply. She turned to Will, her good friend and traveling companion of the past year. "I have some news to celebrate and was hoping you and Rosana could join me and our friends for a drink."

He frowned foggily, and she impatiently placed her glowing hand on his elbow, murmured an incant, and released magic that would purify his blood of the alcohol flowing through it.

Rosana stepped out into the main room holding a fistful of glass vials. "I've got the purification potions. Hand over the gold you promised."

"Take the gold, but keep the potions," Raina told her. "I'll take care of these louts."

"Hey!" A general cry went up from the soldiers, but they crowded around readily enough to accept her healing.

Irritated at their obnoxious behavior, Raina declined to trickle the healing slowly into the men to minimize discomfort. Rather, she slammed the healing into each man at combat speed, ensuring maximum pain as it did its work, coursing through their blood, cleansing the alcohol from it.

Thanon was last. Raina was tall, but Thanon was taller by nearly a head and smiled down at her entirely too intimately for her comfort. His attention zinged across her skin like a vibrating wire and made her more nervous than she liked to admit. He murmured low, "I shall relish the pain because it is you who causes it, my lady."

She really wished he would quit calling her that. Just to be contrary, she trickled his healing into him slowly enough not to cause the slightest discomfort. "I would not dream of hurting an important Imperial officer such as yourself, Commander. After all, I am but a lowly commoner."

He grinned broadly. "My dear, you are anything but common."

The twinkle in his eyes was hard to resist, but he was not the first handsome young man to flirt with her since her return from the Dominion lands. She stepped back and said formally, "I must go."

"Form up, men," Thanon ordered crisply, entirely sober now.

The Talons fell into a marching formation and departed the Heart with sharp efficiency.

"Shall we go find Eben, Rynn, and Sha'Li?" she asked Rosana and Will.

The three of them set out across Dupree, the capital city of the Imperial Kothite colony in Haelos, in search of their friends. Raina barely noticed the pair of Royal Order of the Sun guardians who fell in behind them, but she was still glad for their presence.

They arrived at what had been Landsgrave Hyland's residence until his permanent death. Leland's foster son and their friend, Eben, still lived there. The young jann, an elementally aligned humanoid, grabbed his cloak eagerly when he heard the plan to go out on the town and celebrate Raina's promotion in rank.

Rynn, a magnificently handsome paxan with golden hair and brilliant blue eyes—three *open* blue eyes, to be exact—was also pleased to join them, although his enthusiasm was more measured. He paused to don a filigree headband that covered the third eye in the middle of his forehead before sweeping on his cloak and pulling its deep hood far forward to hide his damningly illegal open eye.

All members of the paxan race had third eyes; it was just that most were permanently closed. Imperial law dictated that all open-eyed paxan were to be arrested on sight and turned over to the Empire. No one knew what happened to them once in Imperial custody, but it could not possibly be good.

The party, now numbering five, rang a great brass bell down by the dock and passed along an invitation for Sha'Li to join them to the lizardman who rose out of the water at their call. He knew who the black-scaled lizardman girl was and agreed to pass the message along to her.

Eben seemed relieved when Sha'Li didn't join them, which made Raina frown. Something had happened between him and Sha'Li in the Angor Swamp a few months back. Though they were once the best of friends, Eben refused to even speak of the lizardman girl now. It pained Raina to see two of her dearest friends so estranged.

They headed for the Hungry Horde Inn, a favorite watering hole of young artisans in Dupree. The ale was hearty, the food plentiful, and none of it too expensive. Tonight, Raina treated her friends to dinner and drinks, unaccustomed to having a bit of gold jingling around in her belt pouch. High Matriarch Lenora had given the coins to her before she left the Heart earlier, calling it her allowance as an emissary. Apparently, emissaries required spending money to conduct business in a manner commensurate with their rank.

"Look at you!" Will exclaimed. "All grown up and financially independent!"

She laughed. "I wouldn't go so far as to say I'm independent. The Heart provides me with my cash and resources. And I do have to earn it by doing a job."

Rynn looked concerned. "When must you return to the Dominion?"

"This summer. And Lord Justinius has offered to provide a knight escort for me."

"More like a babysitter," Rosana teased.

Raina rolled her eyes at the characterization but could not deny its truth.

They talked and laughed about nothing in particular through the evening. It was a welcome change after the stress and danger of the past few months. They'd sought, and ultimately found, another piece of the Sleeping King's regalia that they would need to wake the ancient elven king one day. Furthermore, they'd finally found their good friend Kendrick Hyland, who'd been kidnapped last year. Unfortunately, he'd chosen to stay with his captor, nature guardian Kerryl Moonrunner, and to retain the were-curse Kerryl had put upon him.

Raina worried about Kendrick and shared his grief at the permanent death of his father, Landsgrave Leland Hyland, who had been like a father to her since she arrived in Dupree.

Sha'Li, their lizardman friend, never showed up at the pub. Whether she didn't receive the invitation or simply chose to ignore it, Raina couldn't guess. Sha'Li spent most of her time underwater in the lizardman settlement near Dupree, rather than roaming the streets of the human city where most people eyed Sha'Li's kind with suspicion, if not outright hostility.

Not that the lizardmen had done anything to earn the enmity of the locals—or the Kothite regime, for that matter. They were just . . . alien. Technically, Raina supposed they were nothing more than simple animal changelings—part animal and part human, but their reptilian features and scaled bodies unsettled even Raina at a visceral level. Strange appearance aside, though, Sha'Li had been as loyal and supportive a friend as Raina had ever had. No matter how hard

Sha'Li would have protested if she said it aloud, Raina thought the girl had a deeply noble soul.

"Hey, look who's here!" a familiar voice boomed behind Raina, shaking her from her ruminations.

What was Thanon doing here? She swiveled on the bench, scowling to see the military officer and a half dozen of his men piling into the pub. Had they followed Will? Or worse, her?

"The hour grows late," Raina announced in disgust. "I'm going back to the Heart. Rosana, do you wish to come with me or have Will bring you back later?"

The other healer answered, "I'll come with you and your escort."

The two girls piled out of the corner of the pub, and Raina pressed a few coins into the hand of the bartender. "Keep the ales flowing for my friends, if you will."

"Consider it done," the fellow replied, grinning.

Raina stepped out into the evening, and two Royal Order of the Sun guardians emerged from the shadows beside the pub, falling in behind her. It had started to snow while they'd been in the pub, a fine, crystalline dusting coating every horizontal surface and hiding the usual mud and muck of the cobbled streets in early spring.

"Wait up!" Thanon called from the doorway of the pub. "I'll walk you home."

She sighed and summoned a smile. It was not as if she could tell him not to bother. He was a high-ranking Imperial officer, and the way she heard it, he was also the governess's favorite. He fell in beside her, sparing a nod and grin for the Royal Order guards.

"You're incorrigible," she muttered as he held out his forearm expectantly, forcing her to rest her hand on it or else be openly rude to the man.

"Irresistible, aren't I?"

"And modest, too," she replied dryly.

"My finest quality."

They walked in silence for a few minutes. Then Thanon commented, "In Koth, everybody talks about how squalid and filthy Haelos is, but seeing it like this, quiet and covered in a coat of new fallen snow, it's actually rather quaint. Pretty."

Raina considered the half-timbered buildings jostling for space on the cobblestone street. Dupree was by far the grandest place she'd ever been in her life, born and raised as she'd been at the very westernmost edge of civilization in Haelos. With Dupree sprawling up the sides of two great hills and sloping down to the expansive Bay of Dupree, close to five thousand people lived in the city's tall, narrow buildings and winding streets.

"Where's the most beautiful place you've ever been?" she asked Thanon, whose many badges and blazons on his uniform spoke of a long military career and travels all over Urth. No matter that the man looked to be no older than his mid- to late twenties. It must be nice to age at the rate of a long-lived race like the paxan.

He glanced down at her. "The most beautiful place I've seen is wherever you are," he answered. One corner of his mouth lifted in a grin.

She couldn't help but laugh. "Truly. Incorrigibility is your gift."

The slate roofs and black-painted timbers around them wore their fluffy coats of sparkling snow with quiet dignity. Their footsteps melted behind them, leaving a trail of footprints to mark their passing through the still streets. The evening was serene, as if a blanket of peace and calm lay over the entire world this night. The past several months of life-threatening danger and never-ending stress fell away, leaving her feeling as weightless as the flakes settling gently around her toward earthly rest.

The avenue they trod spilled into the large square in front of the towering House of the Healing Heart, a sprawling, four-story-tall structure taking up most of one side of the square. The tall dome of the central Heartstone tower in its private courtyard within the Heart headquarters peeked above the main building's roof. It was an elaborately carved and gilded rotunda as befitted a place where people could magically be restored from fully dead to alive.

Thanon escorted her across the broad expanse of pristine snow covering Heart Square and stopped at the foot of the wide, shallow steps leading up to the glowing front doors of the blond stone edifice.

"I shall leave you here and wish you sweet dreams, my lady."

"Safe travels and a good night to you, Commander Thanon," she replied formally.

"I have spent part of it with you. It is already a good night."

Stars, that man missed no opportunity to lay on the charm. Were all courtiers like that? She would not know. Funny, but the past year had taught her a great deal about just how much she did not know of the world. An urge to travel, to see more and learn more surged through her.

"C'mon. I'm cold," Rosana muttered, starting up the broad steps.

Raina followed the ever-practical Rosana inside, out of the snow and out of the night's quiet magic.

When the girls left the pub, Eben ordered a round of ales for himself, Will, and Rynn. He was surprised and pleased when the barkeep informed him that their White Heart friend had covered their tab for the rest of the evening. That was good of Raina. Beneath all that deep thinking and political maneuvering she lived for, she was a decent sort. Good heart.

"All right, boys. I need your advice," Will declared. "It's about Rosana."

"Give her whatever she wants and don't cross that gypsy temper of hers, man." Eben laughed.

Will punched him playfully in the upper arm. "No, you fool. I want to propose to her, but I have to figure out just the perfect way to do it."

Eben grinned. "About time you got around to it."

Everyone had known the pair was sweet on one another and would end up together for much longer than the two of them had known it. Rosana smoothed out the rough edges of Will's temper, and he helped her be braver and more confident.

Will turned to Rynn. "I figure a pretty fellow like you has lots of experience with women. How do girls like to be proposed to?"

Rynn squawked. "How should I know? I've never proposed to anyone!"

Will groaned, and Eben declared to him, "You're on your own on this one, my friend."

Rynn piped up jovially, "Good luck with it."

Will scowled and downed the entire contents of his mug, then stared morosely into the remnants of foam clinging to the sides of the tankard, which frankly amused Eben to no end. Not that he would tell Will that and risk rousing Will's formidable temper.

Rynn emptied his mug and slammed it down on the rough, board table. "A gift," he declared.

Will looked up, frowning.

"Give her a gift. Something significant to both of you. Something that will make her cry and feel all emotional. Then spring your proposal on her, and she'll be swept away and say yes."

Eben frowned. "Isn't that trickery?"

Rynn shrugged. "Either he wants the girl or he doesn't. All's fair in love and war."

The barkeep brought them three more brimming mugs, and Eben sipped this one a bit more temperately.

"What gift would make her cry?" Will wondered aloud.

Eben and Rynn both shrugged, their limited store of wedding proposal advice exhausted.

"What of you, Eben? Any young women in your near future?" Rynn asked.

This last mug of ale was hitting Eben hard all of a sudden, and he had to concentrate to form an answer to his friend's question. "No time for love. I have to help my sister, Marikeen. Get to the dream plane. Protect her from whatever goes on there." He asked Rynn abruptly, "Can you help me? You're good with all that dream plane stuff, right?"

Rynn nodded modestly.

"I know you can take me there. You did it when I first saw

my sister on the dream plane. Can we do that again? Watch me sleep or whatever it is you do, and take me to Marikeen." Whew. The pub's dirty plaster walls and low, blackened ceiling were starting to spin.

Rynn mumbled, "Sure, fine. Are you all right, Eben? You look like you want to pass out. Maybe we should go back to Hyland House . . ." The paxan started to push to his feet but collapsed back to the bench, blinking hard. "Whoa. I'm a little dizzy."

"Can't hold your booze?" Will teased, jabbing Rynn with an elbow, but half missing and tipping himself partway over.

Rynn gave Will a shove back upright and then grabbed Eben's hand across the table. "I'll help you find your sister. I promise, my friend."

"You're a good man. No matter how many eyes . . ." Why were words so hard to enunciate clearly all of a sudden?

"Thanks. Not so bad yourself for a jann," Rynn mumbled, frowning and appearing to work hard to focus on Eben's face.

Rynn's brilliant blue eyes whirled like a kaleidoscope, and Eben grinned stupidly. "Look . . . funny . . ."

"Feel . . . funny . . ." Rynn sighed back.

Eben felt himself starting to tip over and pulled against Rynn's hand to right himself. Rynn was leaning at an odd angle, too, and he did his best to prop up the paxan, not that it helped one whit.

A new voice intruded from somewhere above Eben's head. Eben squinted and made out the barkeep, flanked by two burly young men who looked like his sons. The fellow's words only sluggishly formed meaning in Eben's sotted brain. "Too bad the girls left, but ye three'll still bring me a pretty penny from Anton and his boys. He's got quite the bounty out on ye. Sweet dreams, then."

Eben glanced across the table at Rynn in dawning horror. The paxan stared back blearily, looking appalled. Will toppled sideways into Rynn just as Eben and Rynn fell forward in unison and passed out.

* * *

Raina hurried up the Heart's front steps behind Rosana. She loved how the broad stones were worn a little in the middle, testament to the thousands of feet that had trod these stones in search of healing over the years.

The glow around the front doors blinked out as someone inside removed the key from the wizard's lock for them. Raina followed Rosana inside, and the wizard's lock went back up behind them, the magically protected doors glowing once more.

Raina shook like a dog, giggling as Rosana did the same and they pelted each other with melted droplets of snow.

"A moment of your time, Emissary," High Matriarch Lenora said from near the big hearth across the room.

Raina crossed to where the woman sat in a deep armchair, a quilt spread across her lap. Raina sank into the matching chair, relieved that the common room was empty of sick or wounded supplicants for a change. She supposed most people stayed at home on a night like this, tucked into their warm beds, rather than venturing out and getting hurt.

"How may I serve you, High Matriarch?"

"I hear Commander Thanon and his men escorted you and your friends out this evening."

"They did."

"And that young Thanon brought you home?"

"He walked with me, yes." She did not correct Lenora for calling Thanon young. The high matriarch knew as well as anyone that a paxan could be hundreds of years old and look one-tenth his or her age.

"Tell me something, Raina. Why do you choose to move about Dupree in the company of Imperial soldiers rather than entrusting your safety to the Royal Order of the Sun?"

Caution surged through Raina. The high matriarch was as subtle as anyone she'd ever known. Even the simplest question had the potential to be fraught with layers of meaning.

"Has the Royal Order complained?" Raina asked.

"They would never dream of complaining about such a thing, but it does bother them that you do not seem to trust them."

Raina forced herself to take a moment to honestly consider the question. Clearly, there was import to the matter or else Lenora would not have brought it up. Perhaps Raina was unknowingly committing some grave breach of Heart etiquette and the high matriarch was too polite to say so outright. Or maybe the Royal Order of the Sun was embarrassed that the new emissary shunned them in favor of an elite military unit.

Or perhaps this was a deeper gambit by the Royal Order of the Sun to position itself as Raina's primary source of support and advice going forward. They had already managed to become her sole guardians and advisors once she went north to the Dominion.

She knew herself to be an extraordinary mage and was moving quickly into a position of unusual power compliments of her relationship with the Dominion. Of course, others would see her as a political tool to be possessed and wielded.

But as she considered the question, the truth was rawer and uglier than she'd realized. She was *afraid*.

Raina admitted reluctantly, "When the Dominion kidnapped me and my friends, I was utterly helpless. They gagged and bound me so I could not cast magic, and they did not acknowledge the neutrality of my colors. They showed me just how weak I truly am in hostile situations. I understand now that healers who wear White Heart colors are exquisitely vulnerable to the violence and cruelty of a wild place like Haelos."

"Make no mistake, child. Everywhere on Urth is rife with violence and cruelty. Haelos has no special claim to either."

"And because of my White Heart vows, I am as a babe in the woods, completely unable to defend myself should anyone wish me harm."

Lenora remained silent, studying Raina intently.

At length, Raina continued, "Thanon and his men make me feel safe. They're heavily armed, highly skilled warriors, and travel in packs. They display their lethality without apology. They're formidable soldiers whom others would do well not to cross."

"I would remind you that the reputation of the Royal Order of the Sun is no less formidable. You can trust the Order, Raina. Lord Justinius chooses and trains his men and women with great care. They will lay down their lives for you to the last one of them."

"But that's the problem! I don't want anyone to die for me!"

"Are you saying that you value Thanon and his men's lives less than Justinius's and his men's? Is that why you choose to travel with the Talons? You would rather see them die for you?"

Raina stared into the sluggish fire, shocked. Was that what she had been doing without even being aware of it? Stars, this business of being in the White Heart was hard. Apparently, she must give everyone around her an equal opportunity to die on her behalf in addition to healing those around her evenhandedly.

"It is the nature of your work that others will leap to protect you from harm, Raina. You may not like it, but you must not stop them."

"And yet my colors force me to try. It goes against everything I stand for to let others die protecting me."

"Then I must counsel you to do nothing nor go anywhere that will put your life at risk."

Hah. As if that was going to happen anytime soon. She and her friends still had to find a way to wake the Sleeping King. And that path was fraught with immense danger.

Her thoughts must have shown upon her face, for Lenora murmured, "You cannot have it both ways. There are consequences to all our decisions, all our actions. The course you have chosen is perilous in the extreme. You must be prepared to lead fine warriors to their deaths on behalf of your colors. And, I might add, on behalf of the quest you have chosen to undertake."

She got the feeling Lenora was warning her of more than a Royal Order guardian dying someday. Did the high matriarch know of some new threat to Raina and her friends as they searched for the means to wake the Sleeping King?

"Furthermore," Lenora continued, "you must accept that

those warriors freely chose their path. You must let them walk it."

Raina stared at the older healer, who stared back. She was missing some hidden message Lenora was trying to convey.

The high matriarch said soberly, "Sometimes the things we do are larger than our small lives."

Eben blinked awake and looked around, disoriented.
Why was it so smoky in the pub? No, not smoke. Fog.
White, choking fog everywhere. Thick enough that
he barely saw Rynn lying on the ground at his feet. He bent
over to help the paxan and was struck by the strange weight-
lessness of his body. As if he'd become a ghost or some other
noncorporeal being in the time he'd been passed out.

He shook the paxan, who thankfully woke quickly.

Rynn sat up and looked around curiously for a moment,
then his face took on a distinct look of disgust. "Of course,"
he grumbled.

"Where are we?" Eben asked.

"We're dreaming. And this is the dream realm. Where
else?" Rynn replied.

Ah. That explained why Will wasn't here, then. He hadn't
been hanging on to him or Rynn for dear life at the moment
they passed out. That ale had really packed a punch. Snuck
up on him, it had.

Something wasn't right about how they'd gotten here, but
Eben didn't much care. He was where he'd needed to go, and
Rynn was here to guide him. "How do I find my sister?"

Rynn sighed, sounding aggravated. "Think of her. Concentrate on some specific thing about her—the shape of her
face or the sound of her voice, or mayhap some small trinket
she always wears."

Eben knew all those things about his sister. They'd been
orphaned young and taken in by Leland Hyland, and it had
always been the two of them against the world, and they'd

been very close. He focused on Marikeen, and gradually the fog around them thinned, drifting away on unfelt currents of moving air.

A massive encampment sprawled away from him and Rynn in a long valley whose far end could barely be seen, so grand was the scale of this place. Rynn ducked sharply, yanking Eben down behind a rather scrawny bush.

Yet again, Eben was struck by the odd, weightless feeling of his body. When he looked down at himself, he appeared entirely like himself, though, solid and whole.

"She's down there?" he asked Rynn anxiously.

"Apparently. This is where your dream brought us when you thought of her." A pause. "Honestly, did you have to bring us to an army we did our best to destroy not too long ago?"

Oh. The elemental phantasm army that had tried to break through to the material plane using the gate in the Dominion stronghold. The same gate that Eben and his friends had helped the Dominion to close. It had been a bloody fight.

Eben muttered, "I don't think any phantasms made it back through the gate. I'm fairly certain we killed every one who came through to our side. Those soldiers down there won't have any idea that we were the instruments of slaughtering so many of their comrades."

"Still. Most of the creatures down there are powerful. They've been phantasms a long time. The forms we see them in now are merely recent personas they have adopted."

"So, what's the problem?" Eben asked, not understanding the accomplished warrior's sudden trepidation.

Rynn replied heavily, "I am not exactly unknown on the dream plane. Many of the phantasms down there will know who I am."

"And . . ."

"And will not take kindly to me barging into their midst as if I own the place."

Eben frowned. Did he own the place? None of them knew all that much about the secretive paxan. Sure, the guy had that open eye in the middle of his forehead that automatically made him a fugitive from the Empire. But what about here?

"Are you types"—Eben gestured at his own forehead—"unpopular here, too? Or illegal?"

Rynn answered reluctantly, "Not illegal. And not unpopular, exactly. More . . . feared."

Eben swiveled on his heels to stare at his friend. "Why?" He added hastily, "Don't get me wrong. You're a sight to see in combat, and it's an honor to fight beside you. But why are you so feared? Is it all that mental stuff you do?"

"Something like that," Rynn answered evasively. "Look. I can't go with you into yon encampment, but I'm fairly sure you will find your sister down there. You'll be fine. You're an elementally aligned being, and no one will think twice about you being there. You should be able to stroll right through the camp."

"You're not going with me? Won't I fall out of the dream or something?"

Rynn grinned. "No. You should be able to stay here and talk with your sister until you wake up. You might want to ask her where her physical body is located so you can go to her and rescue her, though."

"Good idea," he mumbled, staring intently at the city-sized settlement, learning its layout and trying to guess where Marikeen might be found. "You're sure you won't come with me?"

"Not into that place. I'll stand out even worse there than I usually do."

Eben sympathized. Being of a rare race in a sea of humans could be an exhausting and demeaning experience. "Wish me luck."

"Good luck." Rynn added, "And don't do anything stupid."

Eben snorted. The one thing he could be counted on to do with some regularity was the stupid thing.

Keeping an image of Marikeen firmly planted in his mind, Eben plunged down the hillside and into the maze of tents, huts, and more permanent structures. The place would have reminded him of the Dominion, except instead of teeming hordes of animal changelings, this place was crawling with elementally aligned beings.

Another difference between this place and the Dominion was the vaguely transparent nature of many of the denizens. He recalled Rynn saying that the more powerful and connected to a living being a phantasm was, the more corporeal the phantasm would appear. Eben strode farther in, seeking the most solid-looking beings. Marikeen would gravitate toward the center of power. She was a powerful mage herself and had never suffered fools lightly.

Walking through the camp was a strange experience. He fit right in, for a change. The colored striations across his caramel-colored skin that usually made him stand out like a freak blended in perfectly here. Elemental elves—pyresti, ikonesti, typhonesti, and other types of elves he did not recognize—were abundant. In his entire life, he'd seen maybe ten other jann, not counting his sister, and now he shoved through crowds of them. He felt like some lost creature who'd finally found his way home to his own kind.

Eagerly, he moved deeper into the encampment. He passed practice fields and healers' tents, heard barked orders and the grunts of drilling soldiers. This army definitely was training for some future attack. Had they found another way onto the material plane? It had been a monumental task to shut down the gate last fall and had taken the full might of the Dominion colony to contain the horde that had tried to pass through.

Marikeen was tangled up with this? She did, indeed, need her big brother to rescue her, then. He continued forward with no plan in mind other than to somehow infiltrate this army and extricate her from its coils.

He didn't know how long or how far he walked. Distance and time seemed to move strangely in this place. His dreaming body didn't seem to accumulate fatigue either. He kept a sharp eye out for his sister, who was strikingly beautiful, with shockingly pale skin and nearly white hair. Faint, pale blue striations played across her skin when she was agitated, and the rest of the time she looked like what he imagined a fairy snow queen to look like.

Eventually, he came to the far end of the crammed row of tents, and the ground rose before him into a beautiful copse of trees. There were tents here, too, but they were large and widely spaced, their skin walls extravagantly painted and silk ropes tying them to beautifully carved and inlaid tent poles.

"Who goes there?" a guard demanded as Eben approached the biggest tent of all in the center of the other dwellings. The fellow looked like an air elemental, his form not quite solid, not quite opaque. It was a little awkward being able to see through the fellow's head to the open tent flap beyond. Eben made out a group of people sitting in the tent's shadowed interior, eating and talking.

He spoke up strongly, "I am Eben of Hyland. I have come to see my sister, Marikeen."

Silence fell abruptly inside the tent.

A female voice, not his sister's, called out, "Bid him enter."

The crossed pikes in front of Eben lifted. With a polite nod to the pair of guards, he ducked his head through the opening and stepped into the darkness. His eyes gradually adjusted to the dim light, and he saw seated around a large table a group of elementals who exuded power as effortlessly as they exuded their various elemental alignments.

They all looked as dense and real as he was, and they studied him with alert curiosity.

"Thank you for seeing me," Eben started courteously. "I come in search of—"

"Yes, yes. We know. Your sister." The voice was high-pitched. Childish.

Eben peered toward the far end of the table and spied a little girl, aged maybe eight summers, sitting high on a pile of pillows in an adult-sized armchair. But her eyes. Heavens above, her eyes. They were older than time itself.

He remembered her vividly from his dream last fall. She was much more powerful than her youthful appearance let on. Curious, he searched the space behind the chair for her bodyguard from his last dream, a tall, lean warrior garbed in armor and wearing ancient gages on his forearms and hands. Someone, Eben couldn't remember who, had dubbed him the Gaged Man.

There he was. Standing still as a statue in the corner. Eben nodded respectfully in the bodyguard's direction, and not by even the tiniest flicker of an eyelid did the man acknowledge him. Nonetheless, Hyland had always taught his children that courtesy was never wasted.

The child's name came to him all of a sudden, and he blurted it out. "Vesper. That is your name, is it not?"

"Clever boy," Vesper murmured. "Come, Eben of Hyland. Sit by me," the little girl ordered. "Tell me all about yourself."

Although something in the back of his mind warned him against it, he met her dark, intense stare and found that he could not stop the flow of words once they started. He told her of his and Marikeen's childhoods and how lucky they'd been to land in Hyland's household.

She quizzed him on their education and training, their travels, and their ambitions. She was greatly interested in those, although Eben could not begin to fathom why. He ended with an account of how he'd been tricked in a business deal and he and his sister had been sold into slavery. Their foster brother, Kendrick, had managed to buy Eben's freedom, but not Marikeen's. He ended by saying regretfully that ever since, he had searched to no avail for his sister.

"You are alone, Eben. Do you not have friends?" she asked.

"I have many good friends," he disagreed. "They have helped me search for her."

"And this Kendrick who failed to buy Marikeen's freedom, does he help you?" Vesper asked keenly.

Smart girl. Eben reminded himself yet again not to be deceived by this female's youthful appearance. She was apparently hundreds or thousands of years old and fully as cunning and wise as any field general.

Eben glanced up at his hostess, and yet again, her dark, mesmerizing eyes captured his fascination. So much wisdom and pain in those eyes . . .

He jerked his attention back to the conversation at hand. "Um, no. Sadly, Kendrick is no longer with us."

"Did he die?" Vesper asked.

"No. He was kidnapped and taken from our search party.

And then he was transformed into a horrible, bestial creature by his captor."

Vesper's stare lit up, avid, almost greedy. "What sort of creature?"

Eben sighed. "A were-creature. He transforms into a great, hairy, tusked boar when ordered to do so by his captor or when he becomes very angry."

"A boar, you say?" Vesper blurted. Even the Gaged Man took a shocked, eager step forward.

"Aye," Eben answered cautiously.

"A tragic turn of events," Vesper said thoughtfully. "Have you and your friends given any thought to a cure for this terrible affliction of Kendrick's?"

"Indeed. We've given it a great deal of thought. One of my friends belongs to the Tribe of the Moon, and she was able to cure another friend of ours of a brand-new werecurse. Sha'Li does not believe she is powerful enough to remove Kendrick's curse, though."

Vesper tapped one of her front teeth with a small, pink-and-white fingernail, an adult gesture that looked strange on her childish frame. "What if I were to help you cure your friend Kendrick of his were-curse?"

Eben half rose out of his chair. "You could do that?" he exclaimed.

Vesper nodded slowly. "I believe I could."

"Why would you do such a generous thing for me and my friends?" Eben burst out. Surely there had to be a catch to this offer of hers.

"It is good to have friends, is it not?" Vesper asked sweetly. "Be my friend, and I will be yours. You help me, and I'll help you."

"How can I repay you for your generosity?" Eben asked promptly.

"I do not know, but mayhap, someday, some situation will arise wherein I need your assistance."

"And you shall have it," Eben declared. "Fix Kendrick, and I will be in your debt, my lady."

"We understand each other, then."

The Gaged Man stepped forward and leaned down to whisper in his mistress's ear.

She listened intently and then looked up at Eben. "I am given to understand that you find yourself in a bit of a predicament on the material plane."

He frowned. "I do not understand."

"Apparently, you have been recently drugged by agents of your enemy, one Anton Constantine."

Oh. Oh! Abrupt memory of that moment of appalled comprehension that he'd been drugged—they'd all three been drugged—slammed into him. The tent and its occupants started to fade as panic drew him toward the surface of his dream and wakefulness.

"Not so fast!" Vesper said strongly. Her black-upon-black-upon-black eyes dragged him back into the dream whether he willed it or not. "I can help you."

That got his attention. He stopped fighting the downward pull of her will and let her anchor him once more in this dreaming place. "How can you help me and my friends?"

"Even from this place, I have a certain influence on the people and events of the material plane. I do not know yet how I shall help you, but when you see it, you will know it. Do not hesitate when the moment comes to make your escape."

He nodded, oddly reassured that this strange child was on his side. She was supposed to be the enemy, yet she had turned out to be a generous benefactor. "My sister—"

"She is currently performing a small errand for me, but she will return soon. The next time you dream your way to us, I will see to it that she is here and waiting to speak with you."

"You are too kind." Eben stood and bowed formally to the child seated on the mound of pillows.

She nodded back regally—

—and the dream blinked out.

Queen Gabrielle of Haraland sat on a stump and looked around the heavily wooded margins of the clearing, a massive bonfire blazing up before her into the black night, a swirl of sparks rising to meet the heavy dusting of stars. Great, hulking mountains rose all around them, the Rignhall Ring of seven towering mountain peaks blotting out any far horizons.

The night was grand and cold, and she breathed deeply of its freedom, far away from the Imperial Court and her duties there.

The group of mostly dwarves around her was muddy and exhausted. The combination of the recent thunderstorm they'd summoned and the torrent of lightning and water they'd gathered and unleashed had been a messy affair.

But worthy. She glanced sidelong at the rokken dwarf seated next to her, roughly dressed in borrowed clothes and wrapped in a thick blanket. How strange it must be to him to have been magically released from a storm copper statue only to discover that *thousands* of years had passed since he'd been transformed to the rare metal.

He was big for a dwarf, nearly as tall as she, and wreathed in muscles that looked hard and capable even after all this time. She didn't know much about rokken. From what she gathered, they started as regular dwarves and then earned some special status through mastery of mining, metalworking, or weapons skill. Supposedly a few survived still, mostly in the Heartland, where they mined the priceless Heartstone. And her guide, Gunther Druumedar, had muttered something about rokken mining nullstone for Koth.

What must it be like to realize that everyone you'd ever known or loved has been dead for millennia? Mayhap this fellow had a few descendants alive, at least.

A hairy yeren, the very picture of an abominable snow monster and half again the size of a normal man, crouched across the great fire beside his mistress, a White Heart healer named Mina. At the moment, Mina massaged the stump of Gunther's leg. The dwarven miner had lost the limb above the knee some time back and apparently hadn't trusted the Heart enough to let a healer magically restore the limb before it was permanently lost. Gabrielle couldn't imagine voluntarily choosing to live without one of her legs.

But then, she couldn't imagine sitting here with this motley collection of rebels in a secret valley in the wilds of Groenn's Rest either. Yet here she was. This place could not be any more unlike the Imperial Seat of Koth or the luxurious palace she shared with her husband, King Regalo, in Haraland. In a way, the primitive camp and rugged demands of the past few months had been a refreshing break from all the pomp and ceremony of her otherwise caged life. Being Queen of Haraland might be a magnificently gilded cage, but it was a cage nonetheless.

Gunther spoke up, gesturing with the remains of a wild pheasant leg at the blanket-wrapped dwarf seated next to Gabrielle. "Ye feelin' up to speakin' yet, friend?"

The rokken beside her stirred, looking up from the fire as if startled to realize they were still there. "Sorry. It's disorienting to find out that so much time has passed."

Gabrielle shuddered. It was a minor miracle that he wasn't witless or insane after his ordeal. She moved over to join him on the long log he sat upon. "What shall we call you, good sir?"

"My name is Bekkan. Bekkan Kopathul, second guardian of the Septvardin, the Seven Guardians of the King."

"Which king would that be?" she asked.

"His Royal Highness, King Eitrik, also called Fireheart."

"Eitrik?" Gabrielle echoed. She was familiar with all the hundred kings of Koth, and she'd never heard of this one.

A look of intense grief passed across Bekkan's face as the loss of his liege and his comrades in arms apparently struck him. A heavy blow to bear all at once.

Gabrielle said gently, "Can you tell us of what was happening before your . . . long sleep . . . that we may help place you in time?"

"I do not know where to start."

"How far did the power of the Eternal Empire of Koth extend in your day?"

"The Kothites? Oh, them. They'd come. But their hold on Ymir is . . . was . . . tenuous. The giants rose up to oppose them, my king with them. When the other dwarven kings fell, Eitrik made a deal with Moten to hide him away."

"Moten, the giant?" Gunther blurted from across the fire. Shocked silence fell all around.

"Aye."

This man seated before her had lived in the Age of Giants? Had potentially seen and actually met one?

Gabrielle quelled her astonishment enough to murmur, "Pray, continue. What sort of deal did they make?"

"I do not know the details, of course, but Moten agreed to protect Eitrik, to change him so those filthy Kothites could not get their hands on him."

"To change him . . . like you?" Gabrielle asked into the hush.

"Yes. Like me. But not into storm copper, of course. I'm a coppervein, but my king is . . . was . . . an ironvein dwarf. He would've been transformed into ghardiin."

Gunther breathed, "These days, we call that adamant iron."

A hiss of indrawn breath among the oldest dwarves present made Gabrielle look up sharply. Thankfully, one of the younger dwarven smiths asked aloud what she was thinking.

"What's this adamant iron, then?"

A white-haired dwarf with a beard nearly to his knees answered solemnly. "'Tis said to come from the hearts of the great mountains of Ymir, from Thoris's Shield itself, pitch black in color and hard as diamond. Items forged from it are unbreakable by any means whatsoever. If our last great dwarven king rests in adamant iron, then he's sleeping undisturbed."

Gunther grunted and spoke up. "Can he be turned back to flesh from this adamant iron, same as Bekkan?"

The storm smiths exchanged looks among themselves, and Whitebeard spoke up reluctantly. "We have no knowledge of the working of adamant iron. But in theory, if someone still alive knows the working of it, the Dwarven King could possibly be unmade."

Gabrielle looked swiftly at Bekkan. "Do you know where to find your king?"

The rokken frowned. "I have an idea, but perchance this is not the place or time to speak of it."

His caution was probably wise. Many ears wagged in the clearing, and although their hearts might be willing to keep the secret, the Empire had ways of extracting information from even the most unwilling that did not bear thinking upon.

"Tell us more of your time," she asked eagerly. Rare, indeed, it was to hear of the far past of the Kothite Empire. "You were speaking of Koth."

"The Kothites came to Ymir, killed off the royal family, and took their thrones."

"What royal family?" she gasped. Koth had always ruled. The Empire was *eternal*.

"The etheri, of course," Bekkan answered.

Everyone stared at him, some with mouths agape in wonder, some in abject fear. A shiver passed across Gabrielle's skin as an unnaturally chilled breeze whisked through the clearing. At the very edge of her hearing, a scream started, so piercing and painful that she clapped her hands over her ears. Many others did the same.

Which was why precious few weapons were in hands when the oblivi, flesh-colored serpentine beasts without eyes or ears or limbs, came rushing into the light, attaching their suction-cup mouths to the necks and skulls of their prey. The fight was short-lived as a wave of the memory-stealing creatures rolled through the clearing. One by one, the creatures attached themselves to someone, taking away whatever memory had triggered their appearance, erasing awareness of themselves, and sucking away any impulse to fight against them.

She'd seen these creatures before, in the cave where they'd rescued the coppervein rokken. But this time, the clearing was brightly lit by the bonfire, and she saw markings upon the oblivi—black, burned brands in their pink flesh. And she *knew* that mark. It was Iolanthe's sigil. These creatures came from Maximillian's consort, the high perceptor herself? What if Iolanthe had some sort of mental link to these beasts of hers? Was Maximillian's closest advisor seeing this attack in her mind's eye? Did she see the Queen of Haraland consorting with rebellious dwarves?

Gabrielle had no more time to register the horrible rapid-fire questions in her mind, because the oblivi were converging on Bekkan. Her magical Octavium Pendant, a gift from her contact in the Eight, protected her from the forgetting effects of the oblivi, and she cast magic frantically into the one that came for her, blasting it into dust as she spun to protect Bekkan.

Nononononono. She raced forward as a huge serpentine oblivi wrapped itself around the rokken like a great, fleshy constrictor and greedily attached its rudimentary mouth to the rokken's temple as she ran.

Terrified that they would lose everything they'd worked so hard for with the coppervein, she gathered a huge ball of force damage and slammed it into the pink creature by hand. The oblivi screamed and exploded as Bekkan stumbled into her. She caught his hefty weight and staggered under it, barely managing to right them both.

"Where am I?" he demanded, a wild look in his eye.

"You're at the Great Storm Forge, where you were recently awakened," she said quickly. "Don't you remember? You were speaking of the etheri."

"The who?"

Panic tore through her. His ancient knowledge, his memories, were priceless treasures that must be protected at all costs! She yanked the long chain she'd worn for nearly twenty years from around her neck and shoved it over his head.

"Remember the etheri! And remember the mark of Iolanthe!" she cried as something bit into the back of her neck.

Blankly, he lifted the green-jeweled pendant with its eight compass points surrounding the central gem. "What is this?"

She blinked up at him. What had just happened, and why were they all standing up, wielding swords and axes as if they had come under attack? The clearing was still, filled only with her friends and the cadre of dwarves that had come together to . . .

. . . to do what?

A great forge filled the entire bowl of the valley they stood in. The whole forge, even up to its roof, was soaking wet, black and cold. Obviously, nothing had been worked there any time recently.

A really big dwarf stared at her. "Who are you?" she asked blankly.

"I an Bekkan Kopathul, a coppervein rokken," he answered impatiently. "All of you freed me from the statue I had become, using yon storm forge."

She frowned, but for the life of her, she could summon no memory of such a thing. She reached for her Octavium Pendant and lurched to find it not in its usual place nestled near her heart.

"Do you search for this necklace?" Bekkan asked, lifting her compass-shaped pendant from his jerkin.

She answered in dismay, "I have worn that for most of my adult life without once ever taking it off."

He started to lift it from around his neck, but she reached out hastily to stop him. His hands were rough and heavily calloused as a warrior's should be. "Nay. Keep it. I would only have given it to you for some imperative reason."

"You said I was to remember the etheri. Do you know what it means?"

The word slid off her comprehension as if a sheet of ice encased her mind. She shrugged. "I'm sorry. It means nothing to me."

"What about a mark of Iolanthe?" he queried.

An image of Iolanthe's distinctive sigil, a stylized letter *I* inside an eye-shaped design, came to mind immediately, along with a vague image of seeing it branded into pink flesh—the memory burst back into her mind all at once—Iolanthe's mark had been upon some creatures . . . stolen memories . . . forgetting beasts . . . *oblivi.*

Gabrielle sucked in a sharp breath of alarm as all her previous fears and questions came roaring back. How closely linked was the high perceptor to her oblivi? Did Maximillian's consort know that the Queen of Haraland conspired with the dwarven resistance against the Empire? If that was the case, not only was Regalo dead, but every single citizen of Haraland would be wiped out. Gabrielle's horror was so great she could not breathe. She collapsed to a log, gasping desperately as a great anvil of panic landed on her chest.

She fumbled for a small cloth bag in her belt pouch and placed it over her mouth and nose, breathing in and out of it to help calm her lungs. It took a while, but eventually, her breath calmed somewhat.

"What is this pendant?" Bekkan asked her curiously.

That, too, she remembered. "The central gem is made of octavium. At all costs, you must not take it off. Swear to me you will wear it without cease."

He looked up at her, confused.

"Swear to me!" she demanded.

"All right. I swear. I will wear this and never remove it. But . . . why?"

She stepped close to Bekkan to murmur urgently, "The Kothite Empire has ears everywhere. Do not speak of anything you know or remember to anyone, not even me. It is imperative that you keep to yourself whatever it is I gave you that pendant to protect."

"I merely spoke of events in my time—"

Frantically, she pressed her hand against his mouth. "Say no more. Do not speak of anything from your past for any reason. Not until I can take you to someone who can protect and preserve your memories. We cannot afford to lose what you know. Surely, that is the reason I gave you my most prized possession. Do you understand me?"

"Not really, but I will do as you ask."

She closed her eyes in profound relief.

"Who is this person who can protect and preserve my memories?"

"I have no idea, but I know where we must to go to find him or her."

CHAPTER

3

W ill woke, if that was what he could call the slow, groggy swim toward vague awareness of his surroundings. He registered dark first. Then cold. And wood pressed against his cheek. That made him crack one eyelid open. A rude wagon took shape around him.

He pressed his hands against the wagon bed, and something cold and hard bit painfully into his wrists. He tried to shake it off, and a telltale rattle of chains made him sit up in alarm.

Cold steel bit at his ankles, as well. He squinted at his feet in the gloom and was appalled to see that his boots were gone, which explained why his feet were freezing.

A canvas flap over the back of the arched wagon staves swung open, and Will instinctively cringed away from the blast of freezing cold air.

"Awake, are ye?" the big shadow in the doorway growled. "Our man said ye didn't seem as drunk as the others."

That would be Bloodroot's influence. He'd made Will somewhat less susceptible to poisons, including strong spirits. "Who are you?" Will demanded. He thought he caught a glimpse of facial fur. Some sort of changeling maybe?

"Ye don't know? Disappointed I am that my fame does not precede me."

The changeling's vowels were just slurred enough for Will to suspect he'd been taking a few too many nips from the flask hanging off his belt.

"Tell me of your fame, then," Will retorted.

"Why, I'm the warrior who put down your precious Leland

Hyland. And a broken-down old man he turned out to be, too."

Rage, bright and sharp, erupted in Will's chest. This was Hyland's killer? It took every ounce of discipline he possessed not to charge the man. But Will's tactical awareness informed him that the kidnapper prudently stood just out of range of the length of Will's chains.

"Oh, really?" Will asked lightly. "So then it took no great prowess on your part to kill Hyland. I will keep your lack of skill in mind when I take my revenge."

The fellow took an aggressive step forward, allowing Will to see him a little more clearly.

Rakasha. White tiger changeling. Male. Wearing no fewer than four edged weapons in his belt. Based on how he carried himself, Will judged him slow-footed but strong. He would rely on brute force and those thick bracers on his forearms to absorb and deflect any blows of fist or blade thrown at him. Not that smart. Braggart. *Keep him talking.*

The observations flashed through Will's mind in a fraction of a second. "How'd you kill Hyland, then? Surely you didn't take him down by yourself."

"I did so!" the changeling exclaimed, pulling a foot-long, bleached-looking deer antler from his belt. "Didn't even need a sword. I used this! Stabbed him in the throat and watched him bleed out like a stuck pig."

Will did charge then, all but dislocating his shoulders as the chains violently pulled him up short mere inches away from getting his hands around the murderer's throat.

The rakasha laughed, but Will noted with satisfaction that the whoreson did take a cautious step back.

"I've seen your face, and I will not forget it!" Will snarled. "You will pay for what you did to Leland Hyland, I swear it on the graves of my parents. You are a dead man. Enjoy each sunrise well, my friend, for one day soon, it will be your last. I and mine are coming for you."

The rakasha blustered, "You and yours are headed for torture and death at the hands of your greatest enemy. You should be afraid."

"Oh yeah? And who would that be?"

"Our true governor," the rakasha declared.

"Syreena Wingblade? She likes me very well and has offered me a position in her militia."

"No, you fool. Anton Constantine."

Will knew full well that the rakasha referred to the former, and now fugitive, governor, but attempted to goad the cat changeling into revealing more information.

"That buffoon?" Will snorted. "Nobody's afraid of him."

"They should be. He has plans. Big plans."

"Hah! Look where his big plans landed him the first time. Disgraced and deposed. He and his supporters are a bad joke for jesters to mock."

"Why, I oughta—" The rakasha started forward aggressively.

C'mon. Let me get in range of one of those blades in your belt . . .

"Gorath! Enough!" a voice growled from outside the wagon. "Leave the prisoners alone. Anton wants them unharmed."

The rakasha, Gorath, spit foul epithets in Will's direction as he retreated from sight.

At least two captors, then. But how many more there might be, he did not know.

He tried unsuccessfully to wake up Rynn and Eben, but neither showed any sign of rousing as he shook them. Frustrated, he curled up with his back to Rynn's to wait out the wearing off of the sleeping draught in his friends and share what meager warmth he could.

Princess Endellian looked around her father's opulent golden throne room, bored enough to wish for some random victim to torture. Next on the list of servitors summoned today to report to His Resplendent Majesty, Maximillian the Third, Emperor of the Eternal Empire of Koth, was Captain Kodo of the Black Ship *Victorious*. The poor man had been sailing back and forth between Koth and Haelos at maximum speed ever since the previous governor, Anton Constantine, had decamped and gone on the run last year.

Kodo looked exhausted as he made his respectful obeisance to her father, bowing until his nose nearly touched the black nullstone steps leading to her father's great nullstone throne carved in the shape of the Eternal Flame.

"Rise, Kodo," Maximillian intoned. "What news of our colony in Haelos?"

"It is quiet for the moment, Your Resplendent Majesty," Kodo replied.

She sensed he was pleased to be able to report that. And well he should be. It was he who had appointed the emergency governess to replace Anton and she who was responsible for any calm the previously turbulent colony experienced now.

"What do your spies report?" Max queried.

What had her father read in Kodo's mind to elicit that particular question? For the thousandth time, she wished she had been gifted with her father's keen ability to peer into the minds of everyone around him, discerning their thoughts and feelings before his subjects hardly knew they existed.

Only his fellow Kothite lords and ladies had any ability to shield their minds from Maximillian, not that any of them dared to defy him so openly. Even now, when she was merely acting as social secretary to her father, she was careful to think only thoughts she would not mind having her father pluck from her brain.

Kodo took a moment to formulate an answer, then said, "A spy in the north has brought me interesting news of an incursion into the Dominion colony in northeastern Haelos last winter."

Max waited patiently, not deigning to beg for more details. Kodo knew better than to hold out on her father.

The Black Ship captain continued, "An attacking force of elemental creatures came out of a planar gate of some kind and attacked the Dominion capital. The force was ultimately destroyed, but not before inflicting significant casualties upon the Dominion."

"Elementals?" Maximillian said alertly.

Endellian's attention swiveled sharply to her father. So forcefully was he thinking that she actually caught a brief image of her former lover, Maximillian's oldest and dearest friend, General Dikenn Tarses.

Stunned, she waited for more of her father's momentarily unguarded thoughts. Did he believe Tarses was behind the attack? Was the general on the move once more, in Haelos? To what end? The world believed Tarses to be long dead. He could never return to Koth. Surely, he did not attempt to restore himself to her father's good graces . . .

No. If anything, Tarses did the exact opposite, which was alarming to say the least. He had been her father's most successful general by far, so much so that his charisma and the loyalty he inspired in his troops had become a direct threat to Maximillian's throne.

"How large was this elemental force that passed through the gate?" Maximillian asked, his voice restored to bland indifference.

She was not fooled for a second by her father's bored tone.

"It numbered in the hundreds. Rumor has it that a much larger force was seen beyond the gate, though. Apparently, the Dominion forces were able to close the gate before the main body of the army came through."

"Too bad," her father murmured.

Indeed. An elemental army and a changeling army would be well matched to destroy each other. And why fight an enemy oneself if one could sic two of one's enemies upon each other instead?

"My liege," a new voice said from the other side of the throne. "If I might ask the captain a question or two?"

"By all means, Ammertus," her father answered.

As always, the underlying chaos in Ammertus's spirit grated on Endellian's nerves. One of her father's closest contemporaries, he was volatile and prone to fits of rage that made her cautious of him. No matter that his contrition and loyalty to her father came just as quickly as his outbursts.

"Tell me, Kodo, what news of Anton Constantine? Has he been seen? What is he up to?"

Of course, Ammertus would want to know of Anton, who had long been a protégé of his and was widely known as Ammertus's man.

"Rumors abound of the former governor, Your Dread Grace. If even half of them are true, it is fair to say that Anton is out and about, and he seems to be pursuing plans of his own."

"What plans?" Ammertus asked.

Kodo shrugged. "You would know better than I."

Ammertus's florid face flushed an ugly shade of radish pink that clashed with his carrot-orange hair. It was brash of Kodo to so openly provoke Ammertus by suggesting that he might be helping Anton work against the Empire's goals.

Kodo said in a more placating tone, "My spies tell me that Anton appears to be setting up in private business as a merchant. He continues to elude the Haelan legion and is thought to travel the wild lands west of the Estarran Sea. It is only a matter of time, though, before he makes a mistake and is caught. With construction of Maren's Belt well under way on the west coast of the Estarran Sea, the Imperial presence there increases. Someone will see Anton and apprehend him."

Maren's Belt was a great waestone highway being built all the way around the thousand-mile-long inland sea controlled by the underwater Merr nation. The Belt had a troubled history. Merr, bandits, and local peoples all opposed and hindered its construction. Nonetheless, Maximillian's will was inexorably prevailing, and Maren's Belt was nearly three-quarters completed.

Even the partially completed project was significantly reducing the economic and maritime power of the Merr who lived in the Estarran Sea's murky depths and controlled all shipping on its surface. The sea was isolated from the wider Abyssmal Sea by a great underwater obstacle across its narrow mouth called the Bone Reef. The Imperial Navy had tried—and failed—to find a safe route through the Bone Reef for large naval vessels, and hence, the Merr ruled their underwater kingdom of Estarra unimpeded.

Ammertus turned to Maximillian and murmured quietly enough so his words would not be picked up by the throne room's excellent acoustics, "Is there not some way that Anton Constantine can be brought back into the fold? After all, it is not as if he is guilty of treason. He merely engaged in some extracurricular commerce. At the end of the day, we all know such black-market activity to be necessary to the smooth working of the larger economy. Better that a loyal subject of yours capture that market than someone who would use it against you."

Maximillian considered Ammertus thoughtfully. Personally, Endellian thought her father indulged Ammertus far too much. The man was a spoiled, uncontrolled child. No matter that his first scion and only daughter, Vesper, had died tragically. That happened over a century ago. And it was Ammertus's son Tyviden Starfire's own fault that he'd been banished from court by her father. Tyviden had inherited his sire's unfortunate temper and had crossed swords with one of Maximillian's most powerful kings a few decades back. Tyviden and Ammertus had come out on the losing end of that little peccadillo with Regalo and Gabrielle of Haraland. Maximillian didn't owe Ammertus anything.

"What did you have in mind for Anton, my friend?" Maximillian asked.

Endellian mentally lurched. That last bit, calling Ammertus *friend*, had the feel of a barb aimed at her. She must guard her thoughts more carefully.

Ammertus answered obsequiously, "Surely there is something Anton can do to make amends. Payment of a fine. Renewal of his fealty vows to Empire and Throne. Perhaps a letter of censure. After all, Anton has proven himself over and over to be a capable administrator, and he did grow a fledgling colony into a thriving trade center."

"Indeed," Maximillian replied dryly. "And he used that thriving trade to line his pockets richly."

"But if those pockets serve you, where is the problem? All the gold ultimately advances the greater glory of Koth."

"You make a good point," Max allowed. "Still. He needs to understand his limits and learn not to overstep them."

"And if he provides you with proof that he has learned his lesson?"

"Some punishment will still be necessary as an example to all my governors to keep their fingers out of my treasure chests."

Ammertus bowed deeply. "Of course, my liege. But after that? Is redemption possible? Is there hope for Anton?"

"There is always hope, Ammertus."

A sentiment Endellian found highly ironic falling from her father's lips. His main goal had been forever, and would remain, to crush all hope from the spirits of his subjects. Where there was hope, there was anger, and in anger lay rebellion. Oh no. His Resplendent Majesty, Maximillian the Third, was having no part of tolerating hope among the subjects in his Eternal Empire.

Something big and dark moved slightly beside Will, waking him abruptly. He jerked away from it, heart pounding. Out of long habit, he reached behind his neck for his staff, but it was not slung across his back. The black shape resolved itself into Rynn, rolling over sluggishly, groaning a little. *Thank the Lady.* He let out a long sigh of relief. Until he remembered where he was and why. His pulse spiked up once more.

"Rynn," Will whispered urgently. "Wake up!"

To Will's immense relief, the paxan's three eyes blinked up at him, gaining awareness with admirable speed.

"We were drugged," Rynn said low.

"And kidnapped," Will added sourly. "Are you shackled as well?" He rattled his chains lightly.

"Aye. And stop doing that. We do not want to let our captors know we stir."

"Is that Eben behind you? We should wake him—"

Rynn answered equally quietly. "Nay. Let him sleep until

he wakes on his own. He has important business on the dream plane."

"More important than being kidnapped and hauled off into the wilds by rakasha slavers?"

"Rakasha slavers?"

"Aye," Will answered. "I woke earlier, and one of them came in to brag to me that he killed Leland Hyland."

Rynn growled in the back of his throat. "Which one?"

"White tiger changeling. Called Gorath. But I've got dibs on him."

Rynn scowled. "See to it you finish him off, or else I will."

He and Rynn traded grim nods of understanding. Gorath was a dead man.

"Have you attempted an escape, by any chance?" Rynn asked.

"Not yet. Until we're all awake, there's no sense trying anything."

"Where are we?"

"Good question. While you slept, I've been picking at the stitching that holds the canvas roof together. I think the rip in the seam is big enough to look out now."

Will pushed carefully to his knees, annoyed at the lingering weakness in his limbs from whatever drug had been slipped into their ale. The wagon swayed a bit, and he steadied himself against the sideboard.

The small tear he'd made in a roof seam admitted no light, but it did let in a bitter cold draft bearing tiny crystals of snow. A thin drift of it had formed on the wagon bed beside him. He peered cautiously through it.

Will reported in a whisper, "We're in light forest—mixed hardwoods, mostly. Dirt wagon path. I'd place us not far from Dupree. South and west, if I had to guess, into Hyland." He added, "Why would our captors take us into our greatest friends' lands?"

Rynn answered practically, "If they wish to take us across the Estarran Sea or put us on a ship bound for foreign lands, it's the fastest route to a deepwater port that's not Dupree."

Given that they were not resurrecting at the Heart this very minute, death was obviously not the plan for them. Will scowled. He would not go down easily into slavery or whatever else their captors had planned for them.

"Did they take your boots, too?" Will asked.

"Yes, but I have trained for many years barefoot. My feet are well toughened against injury or cold."

"Remind me to do the same once we are free of this mess," Will retorted grimly.

Rynn studied his chains. "If we can work our chains free of the wagon frame, we can use them as weapons."

Will examined his shackles and the bolt that attached them to the wagon. The bolt was the weak point. Using the chain for leverage, he began turning the bolt back and forth, attempting to strip the wood and pull it free. Rynn did the same beside him.

"Any idea how long Eben will be asleep?" Will asked as they worked.

Rynn glanced down at their friend. "None. No matter the import of Eben's dreams this night, we'll need to wake him soon, though, so he can get to work on his shackles, too."

As if uttering his name aloud summoned him, Eben blinked awake mere seconds later. He jerked against his chains in surprise and dismay.

"Easy, friend," Will muttered low. "We're trying not to make too much noise in here. We don't want to alert our captors that we are awake."

Eben nodded in understanding and joined in working at the bolt securing his chains.

"Did you find your sister?" Rynn whispered.

"No, but I did speak with that little girl we saw on the dream plane last fall."

"Vesper?" Will asked in surprise. They'd thought the being trapped in a child's body might have been behind the incursion into the Dominion lands from the dream plane. What was she doing talking with Eben?

"Yes. And her bodyguard, the Gaged Man, was there, along with a bunch of powerful elemental beings."

"Phantasms of elemental beings," Rynn corrected.

"Same difference," Eben muttered.

Rynn pulled a face. "Not many actual elementals could or would venture to the dream plane. It is not their native home and not their native source of power. A dream creature posing as an elemental would be vastly more powerful than an actual elemental on the dream plane."

"Fine," Will groused. "The difference is duly noted." He turned back to Eben. "What did Vesper want?"

"Nothing. She offered to help us fix Kendrick, and she also said she would help us escape our current predicament."

"Why would she do that?" Will asked suspiciously.

"Does it matter?" Eben retorted.

Rynn answered, "Yes. It matters a great deal. She is an extremely powerful being and could make our lives, even here, very difficult if we cross her."

"Well, she offered to help us," Eben replied defensively.

Will snorted. "Is she going to send someone to rescue us?"

"She did not say. She just said she would do what she could and that we would know when the moment had come to make our move."

Rynn grunted under his breath as he worked to free himself. "Fortune favors those who help themselves."

Eben caught up with them in their bolt-pulling efforts quickly. The jann was very strong and able to exert a lot of force upon the wood his shackles were attached to. His chains popped free first, followed quickly by Rynn's. Will was chagrined to be last to break free, but with the help of the other two men, his bolt pulled free in a few minutes.

"Now what?" Eben whispered.

"Now we wait for a bump in the road and sneak out the back of the wagon when they won't notice the shift from our weight leaving. I'll go first."

Will gathered his staff, which the rakasha had conveniently stowed in the front of the wagon bed, along with Eben's mace and sword, and Rynn's crystal gauntlets and greaves. He found their cloaks, as well, and passed those out, but there was no sign of their boots.

"Any sign of my headband?" Rynn breathed.

Will shook his head, and Rynn grimaced.

Holding his chains close against his chest, Will curled up close to the back of the wagon. Although it had high sides, it had no tailgate. The wagon jolted through a big rut, and Will rolled off the vehicle. He landed in a crouch that sent daggers of pain shooting through his chilled feet, then rolled again, this time off the rough path, into clumps of snow-covered dead grass.

Wet and muddy, he gained his feet in time to see Rynn roll off the back of the wagon and then Eben. Will danced on half-frozen feet as they ran back toward him. The pain in his feet was growing unbearable as the snow froze his flesh.

They moved away from the path into dark shadows, and Rynn tore long strips of cloth off the bottom of his cloak that Will and Eben wrapped around their feet and tied around their ankles.

They crept through the forest for close to an hour, with Rynn countertracking and Will using his Bloodroot-endowed ability to push leaves, vines, and branches out of their way and then closing the foliage back in behind them to cover their tracks. Finally, they stopped in the lee of a great black pine to confer.

"Where are we?" Eben whispered.

Will answered quickly, "Hyland. We can't be more than a few hours outside of Dupree. No poison works on me for very long."

"Where do we go now?" Rynn asked.

"Back to Dupree?" Will suggested. "My guildmaster will not be amused to hear of this." Not to mention said guildmaster, Aurelius Lightstar, was also his grandfather.

Eben added grimly, "Aurelius will want to hear what I saw of Vesper's army, too."

"As will I," Rynn added a shade sharply. The paxan continued, "If I am not mistaken, that is the first hint of dawn lightening the sky in that direction. And Dupree lies east of Hyland."

"Into the light, then," Will muttered. "With all due haste. Our captors will figure out soon enough that they've lost us. And apparently, there's a hefty bounty on our heads, compliments of Anton Constantine."

CHAPTER

4

Kadir studied the travel-weary man who took a seat at the table of proctors. He had come from the northeast reaches of Haelos, a journey of many weeks that had obviously taken its toll. The fellow's wrinkles looked permanently grouted with dust, and the insignia of rank on his navy blue cloak was stained nearly beyond recognition.

The windowless room in which they met was dim and damp, buried in its secret location for countless centuries. Oil torches guttered in their iron brackets at intervals along the walls between ancient tapestries of forgotten kings and queens, nameless even unto the Mages of Alchizzadon themselves.

High Proctor Albinus sat at the head of the table, little more than a collapsed pile of robes with a desiccated face peering out of them. Kadir spoke for the high proctor at whose right hand he sat. "Greetings, Claviger Angelico. I trust your journey from the Dominion lands was not too arduous."

"Greetings, Proctor Kadir, High Proctor Albinus, gentlemen. My journey was long but made less so by Maren's Belt. We were able to use a completed portion of the Imperial highway, and as promised by the Empire, the magic of its waestones sped our travel and increased our stamina greatly."

"Did you encounter bandits or brigands upon the Belt?"

"Nay. It was heavily patrolled by Imperial troops and workers making their way to the terminus of the Belt where construction continues."

Kadir nodded.

"And you had no trouble getting Lord Goldeneye to release you from your duties to come here?"

"He was well pleased to be rid of me. After I was possessed and caused such havoc among his people, he has no great love for me. In fact, one of my recommendations will be to replace me with a new claviger to tend the gate in his capital."

Proctor Elfonse, an arrogant turd of a man by Kadir's reckoning, spoke up. "Replacement clavigers are not easy to come by, Angelico."

Kadir reluctantly had to agree with Elfonse. Still, their relationship with the Dominion's leader was an important one to safeguard. If Goldeneye wanted a new claviger, he would get one.

The high proctor whispered in his direction, and Kadir's sharp ears picked up the command, which he repeated for all to hear. "Tell us everything, Angelico. From the beginning."

The claviger relayed how the gate had spontaneously opened, activated from the far side. The announcement caused a stir in the room, and Albinus assigned several proctors and their people to research how a gate had been opened without a key in *both* of the gate's matching tympans—the navigation and locking mechanisms that controlled a gate between the planes.

Kadir listened in dismay as Angelico described being mind-controlled by a powerful dream creature who had taken the form of a little girl. She had ordered huge phantasms in the guise of elementals to guard him. Angelico described advance scouts passing stealthily through the gate, and then an army of elementally based phantasms that had poured through the gate and attacked the Dominion. Kadir was particularly interested in how everyone who approached the open gate found themselves uncontrollably enraged and attacked every living being around them, including their own friends and allies.

He would hate to meet the being who could generate such a powerful mind effect over an entire area. Stars below, the danger of someone able to drive huge military forces mad. It sounded like something a Kothite might do, but then again, Kothites were not known to inhabit or even transit the dream plane. Creatures in that realm had defenses against the Kothites' mental powers that made the place particularly unappealing to the Emperor and his cronies.

The Council of Proctors agreed unanimously that word must be sent immediately to all the other clavigers who guarded and operated the various gates around Haelos to beware of incursions from the dream plane. For thousands of years, the mages had successfully protected the ancient gates, and they were not about to fail in their duty now.

While the others wrangled over instructions to the clavigers to stand guard over the gates in pairs and beware of spontaneous activations, Kadir considered why a being of such power as the little girl would build an army and then reach through to this plane.

The answer, when it hit him, brought him half out of his seat in alarm.

"What is it, Kadir?" Albinus asked.

"This child. Did she say anything of why she attempts to pass through to this plane from her own?" Kadir asked Angelico urgently.

"No. Why?"

Kadir looked grimly around the table at his fellow mages. "Why else would a powerful dream being come through to this plane if not to find and take over a material body?"

Blank looks met his declaration. They did not see the threat. He continued, "If you were a powerful dream creature and wanted to come to the material plane, what kind of body would you look for? Dream creatures are immortal, but fragile. If I were this child, I would want an immortal body of great strength and fortitude. One without a conscious spirit to fight my possessing it."

Mages rose out of their seats all around the table, making sounds of dismay.

Kadir pounded the point home mercilessly. "Our lord king and leader, Hadrian, is in grave danger. His physical body is exactly what this child needs."

Calls went up around the table for increased guards on Hadrian's resting place, for new magical protections to be put in place around the Great Mage that would defend him specifically against dream-based creatures. There were even calls for a complete moratorium on use of the gates until this childlike dream creature was destroyed.

Eventually, the panic subsided as layers of plans were put into place to safeguard Hadrian. Kadir looked down the table at Angelico and asked, "Is there anything else you need to report?"

"Indeed, there is. In the middle of the worst of the combat to close the gate, I heard a young woman shout our name. 'Alchizzadon!' she yelled. 'Raina of Tyrel has taken the field of battle!' The chit had the gall to announce herself to me at the top of her lungs, for all to hear!"

His full attention snapped to the claviger, whose tone had grown deeply indignant. Kadir suppressed a grin. Good for her.

"And then, at the victory feast following the battle, Lord Goldeneye named her his emissary to the Heart. And she actually accepted as if he had every right to do such a thing."

Elfonse rolled his eyes. "The Heart will never recognize her as an emissary. She does not even count eighteen summers in age."

"To add insult to injury," Angelico complained, "she's wearing White Heart colors as proud as you please."

Elfonse snorted. "As if those will protect her from us taking her and using her for the purpose she was born for."

Kadir suppressed his alarm at that sentiment. "Well, now," he drawled, "we do have to consider the Royal Order of the Sun. They are not entirely without ability to protect her."

"Bah," Elfonse retorted scornfully. "I could take down a dozen Royal Order of the Sun warriors with a single snap of my fingers."

"I'm sure you could," Kadir replied. "But what of the hundred Royal Order of the Sun warriors who would come back for you? Or the thousand who would come after you destroyed the hundred?"

Elfonse glared at him and did not deign to answer. Which was to say, the man had no answer for Kadir's logic. At the end of the day, the Heart was part of the Empire and could summon more might than they could ever hope to defeat. Not to mention Elfonse was talking about kidnapping an Imperial guild member of potentially considerable rank. There were only a handful of White Heart emissaries in all of Haelos.

Kadir leaned forward. "What if we invite Raina to come here to speak with us?"

A startled sound rose down both sides of the table. They did not know that she had reached out to their order last fall, writing a peace offering of sorts. Kadir had intercepted the missive, which offered, in return for the mages leaving her alone, her helping the Mages of Alchizzadon in their ancient goal of rousing the great human mage, Hadrian. Kadir had burned the letter to protect her whereabouts from Elfonse and his crowd of rabid hard-liners.

Something else he knew that his fellow mages did not was that Raina and a group of her friends had been attempting to wake another ancient being of legend. If he really existed, the mages should by all means help her find this sleeping king. Let the dream child and her elemental army take over that king's body instead of Hadrian's.

"Why do you attempt to coddle Raina, Kadir? It is of no matter whether she loves us or hates us, as long as we bring her here and possess her magic."

It took all of Kadir's self-discipline not to fume in visible rage. *No matter that "possessing" Raina's magic would drain her life energy and kill her permanently.*

Over his dead body would Elfonse do that to Raina.

The only person in the room who knew that she was, in fact, his own flesh-and-blood daughter was Albinus. And to his credit, the high proctor was not by a single look or word giving away any hint of that secret. Stars willing, the old man had forgotten the truth of Raina's parentage.

For longer than anyone had memory, the Mages of Alchizzadon had been lying with the women of the House of Tyrel in an effort to breed ever more powerful female mages who would one day be strong enough to rouse Hadrian.

The mages were close to that goal. So close. In fact, Raina might actually be the one powerful enough to do it. But now that she lived and breathed, his resolve to sacrifice her to wake some long-dead mage, who by rights ought to have been dust long ago, was not as ironclad as it had once been. She had his eyes, for stars' sake.

He mostly sat out of the spirited discussion of his suggestion that the mages try reaching out to her in friendship before they leaped to kidnap her and incur the wrath of the Royal Order of the Sun.

Elfonse hated the idea and argued that she would never accept the invitation. As his voice began to sway the others, Kadir was forced to speak up. "I will write her the letter. She knows me, and I know a little of her. I am best suited to draft words that will convince her to come to us of her own volition. And furthermore, I know just the person to deliver the message. I can personally guarantee that she will accept the invitation."

Albinus rasped in an onionskin voice, thin and dry, "So be it."

Elfonse shoved back from the table and stormed out of the chamber, torches guttering in the wake of his passing. For his part, Kadir retired to his own room to work out the logistics of not only inviting Raina to come here but how to get her here without revealing the secret of Alchizzadon's location.

Justin would have to be ritually marked with the rune that brought mages back to Alchizzadon and be taught how to use it. The young man had been Raina's best friend and childhood sweetheart before she left home. Of course, she would say yes to a personal request from him.

The last obstacle to be overcome would be crafting an invitation that appealed to her curiosity, sense of duty, and desire to be rid of the mages once and for all. The combination would be irresistible to her.

* * *

Will led Rynn and Eben through the forests of Hyland for most of the morning before they dared to emerge from the backwoods and travel the main eastbound highway to the capital. Crowded as it was with farmers, merchants, caravans, and soldiers, they felt safe joining the stream of travelers as they hurried back to Dupree.

The next challenge was to slip into Dupree without Rynn's open third eye being noticed. In the absence of his filigree headband to disguise it, he was vulnerable to arrest or worse. As they approached the city gates, Will traded cloaks with Rynn to give the paxan the most voluminous cloak with the deepest hood.

They attached themselves to a cluster of traveling merchants headed into the city with wares from distant shores. But it was not enough.

A guard called out to Will and his friends, "'Ey there! You three. Identify yourselves."

Will shoved his hood back and laced his voice with all the arrogance he could muster. "I am Will Cobb, battle mage of the Mage's Guild and apprentice to Guildmaster Aurelius Lightstar." He was stretching the truth a bit, but he wasn't technically lying. "And these are my traveling companions, a merchant and a monk."

Eben opened his cloak to show the Hyland colors and made a short half bow to the guard staring down at them from the parapet. Rynn made a low obeisance, flashing his crystal gauntlets and greaves as he made an intricate flourish with his hands over his outstretched leg.

"Go on, then!" the guard called down gruffly.

Will let out a relieved breath. They hurried through the familiar streets of Dupree directly to Hyland House. The residence was in the western quadrant of the city, close to the Great West Road that led to Hyland. The Mage's Guild was all the way across town, and they dared not risk hauling an open-eyed paxan through the streets of Dupree in broad daylight.

Will breathed another sigh of relief when they slipped

through the postern and into the small courtyard in front of Hyland House. Rynn expelled an even gustier sigh of relief.

"Now what?" Eben asked.

Will answered, "Now we send word to Aurelius of what happened, and we figure out some way to cover Rynn's eye so he's not hauled away in shackles by the Empire."

Rynn spoke up cautiously. "Do we know for certain that your grandfather is not the one who had us kidnapped?"

Will stared at the paxan in horror. "Of course we know!"

Rynn half bowed. "I meant no offense, but you know what they say. The Empire runs deeper than blood."

"Not in my family's case!" he snapped. "My grandfather has plenty of reason to—" He broke off. *Plenty of reason to hate Koth.* But those reasons were Aurelius's alone to share or not share.

Eben piped up. "I do not doubt the guildmaster, but Rynn makes a good point. We have no way of knowing who is or isn't our friend outside of our own small group."

Were they warning him off Thanon and his boys? Of course, Thanon's loyalties were perfectly clear: Empire first. Everything else second. In a way, it made Thanon singularly trustworthy. His motivations were wholly transparent and predictable.

"I'm hungry," Eben announced.

Will grinned. "You're always hungry, Eb."

Eben patted his muscular abdomen fondly. "I'm a growing lad."

Rynn joked, "Do not grow too much more, else you will be mistaken for a youngling giant."

"Hah! Throw no stones at me, Master Carnival Freak!"

Will chimed in, "If not a giant, you'll soon be taken for a suckling pig ready for a platter and an apple in its teeth."

Thus it was that they were still laughing and ribbing one another over a late lunch when Aurelius burst into Hyland's dining room. He was as discomposed as Will had ever seen him rushing in with hair mussed, arms akimbo, and cloak sideways.

"Are you all right?" Aurelius demanded.

"Yes, sir," Will answered quickly. "Thanks to my companions' quick thinking and our young legs, we were able to escape with relative ease."

"That, and my new friend on the dream plane agreed to help us escape," Eben declared. "I believe it is she who caused our captors not to notice us making our escape."

Will was skeptical. Why would a dream child with an army at her beck and call bother to aid them?

Aurelius answered sharply, "You should not have been taken at all. I will have the barkeep who drugged you arrested."

Will disagreed. "Anton will simply recruit some other local to do his dirty work for him. Better the minion we know and can avoid than the one we don't know about."

Aurelius fell heavily into a free chair at the long table, another sign of his unusual disquiet. "You are right, of course, but it infuriates me that Anton takes out his vendetta against me on you."

Will shrugged. "I have done plenty to draw the wrath of the former governor down upon my own head."

"Unfortunately, your escape last night will only infuriate him further. Next time, he will not come after you with a handful of rough brigands. You must be on your highest guard henceforth. You and your friends must leave Dupree. It is not safe for you here."

Rynn snorted rather inelegantly. "It is not safe for us anywhere."

The casual certainty in Rynn's voice sent a chill crawling down Will's spine. The paxan was right, of course. There would be no safe haven for them until they had woken the Sleeping King or died permanently, whichever came first.

"We need to make preparations with all possible haste for your departure. I will send for Selea to consult with us. And a jeweler."

"A jeweler?" Will asked.

"Rynn needs a new headband. Speaking of which, Rynn, could you draw up a sketch of your last headband so it may be copied?"

"Of course."

The never-ending necessity of watching over their shoulders in fear of discovery was beginning to wear on his nerves. Will wanted to find the perfect way to propose to Rosana and settle down to a quiet life somewhere out of the way. To his chagrin, his parents' choice to live in tiny Hickory Hollow, deep in the Wylde Wold, was finally beginning to make sense to him.

Aurelius said grimly, "Summon your traveling companions, Will. The time has come for you and your friends to continue your quest."

No matter how hard Gabrielle tried to remember what had happened to cause her to give her precious Octavium Pendant to the rokken, Bekkan, she could summon no memory to mind. She was still trying when a dwarf barged into the clearing, declaring loudly, "I come in search of Gunther Druumedar."

She nodded to Olivar Worbal, Stormcaller of the Achensberg, who had been traveling companion to her and Gunther these past weeks. In turn, Olivar gestured to his ogre-kin assistant, Jossa, who slipped away into the darkness.

Meanwhile, Gabrielle said in the pleasant version of her queen-giving-a-command voice, "Come, good sir, and have a seat. Warm yourself by the fire and chase away the night's chill from your bones."

"My bones be fine," he grumbled. But he did sit on an upended log and hold his rough hands out to the flames.

Gabrielle smiled into the collar of her cloak. She was growing genuinely fond of these dwarves and their prickly personalities. "I am Gabrielle. By what name should I call you?"

"Korgan. Korgan Druumedar."

"Any relation to my friend Gunther Druumedar, after whom you inquired?" she asked.

"Aye. His son. And plenty annoyed I am at having to come traipsing out here in the middle of nowhere to speak with him."

"Where is home for you?" she asked politely.

"Other end of Groenn's Rest near the finger lakes. A hellish long journey it has been to seek out my sire."

"Your news must be dire, indeed, for you to have undertaken such a taxing journey." She really shouldn't make fun of the grouchy dwarf, but his scowl was so fierce it bordered on comical. "Tell me, Korgan. What clan do you hail from?"

She'd discovered this was generally safe conversation territory with the dwarves, who delighted in their genealogy and never missed an opportunity to share long lists of ancestors, sometimes stretching back a dozen or more generations.

But to her surprise, the kelnor merely shrugged and looked away evasively.

Gunther stumped up to the fire, limping slightly on his mechanical leg. He took one look at her guest, and a ferocious glare overtook his expression.

"Korgan, I told ye to stay away from me and my business!"

"Your *business* came to the village dressed in a brace of Imperial Army tabards and asking a lot of questions about a certain helmet ye found," Korgan growled back. "I had to flee for my life and pray the soldiers did not kill everyone we know in their hunt for thee and me."

"Ye did not tell them anything about the helm, did ye?"

"I didn't know anything to tell."

Gunther threw up his hands. "Surely they followed thee. Why in the name of the great granite father did ye think it a wise course to lead them Imperials straight to me, boy?"

The beard of the "boy" came nearly to his waist, and he looked at least a hundred years old, if she was becoming any decent judge of dwarven age.

Korgan threw up his hands in disgust. "Bah! Ye never change, ye smelly old fart."

"Disrespectful whelp—"

Gabrielle interrupted smoothly, using her most diplomatic tone. "Perhaps the night would be better served by you telling us what brings you to the Valley of Storms with such urgency, young Master Druumedar." She smiled at the dwarf. It took a moment, but the hard edge of anger drained somewhat from his steely gaze.

He huffed and then said more temperately, "The Council of Elders sent me to give ye a message, old man. Do not come back to the village—ever—if ye wish for any of thy family and friends to live. The Empire be watching for ye, and they've orders to arrest thee and any who know thee. And I snuck away without any of them soldiers seein' me, ye old coot."

"Why would the Empire be ordering my arrest?" Gunther demanded.

"It has to do with that helmet of thine. Apparently, they're rounding up anyone who might have seen it. As of when I left, no one had come back to the village after being carted away."

"Sold into slavery, most likely," Jossa commented direly.

While she certainly knew slavery existed, Gabrielle's life did not include knowing anyone subjected directly to its horrors. She and Regalo always made a point of freeing any house servants who came to them as slaves, or at worst setting up a reasonable term of indenture if a slave was working off a crime.

Sadly, she did have personal knowledge of the Emperor completely erasing the existence of a man—what was his name again? Of a sudden, she could not remember it or conjure a face to put with the poor fellow who'd crossed Maximillian and been erased from the memories of all who'd ever known him.

She glanced over at the gleaming green gem winking on Bekkan's chest. Did memory of the forgotten one reside within its emerald depths? She could not remember, and something within her ached for the unnamed man. So many people simply erased by the Empire. So much loss. So much suffering.

Which was why she must protect Bekkan's memories and take him with utmost haste to the Eight. The ultra-secret group dared to conduct a glacially slow rebellion against Maximillian in the Imperial Seat itself, right under the Emperor's nose.

If soldiers were nosing around after Gunther, it was only

a matter of time before they stumbled across some connection between her and the one-legged dwarf.

She lowered her voice. "It is imperative that we see Bekkan safely to a friend of mine before the Empire gets its hands on him."

Korgan looked alarmed. "My father cannot leave this place."

"Why not?" Gunther asked quickly, his usual surliness absent.

"The Empire searches for you. Where else in all of Koth can a one-legged dwarf hide from the long arm of Koth but here, in a secret valley deep in the heart of terrakin country?"

The terrakin dwarves were infamous for stubbornly resisting the advance of Koth across their lands. Almost unanimously, the race of dwarves opposed Koth. And to hear it from Maximillian, they were an irritating thorn in his side. Given how many dwarves had materialized seemingly out of nowhere last night to operate the Great Storm Forge and transform Bekkan from a copper statue into a living, breathing man, she had no doubt there were plenty of hiding places and secret entrances and exits from this valley.

"Korgan is not wrong," she said regretfully. "If the Emperor has issued an order to find you, every citizen of the Empire is obligated to turn you over to the authorities on sight. You could not move two steps outside of this place without being apprehended."

"So I'm supposed to languish here for the rest of my days like a common criminal?"

Korgan snorted. "Not common, but a criminal in the eyes of Koth."

Gunther scowled fiercely enough that even his son looked taken aback. He demanded truculently, "Who'll take our rokken brother where he needs to go, if not me?"

"I'll do it!" Korgan snapped. "If you will promise to stay out of sight."

Gunther subsided on his log, abruptly looking well satisfied. The clever geezer had manipulated his son into making that offer. Gabrielle was reluctantly impressed. And frankly, she was glad Gunther would be staying here. His mechanical leg was cantankerous at best, and he rubbed his stump often in the evenings as if the long miles of travel bothered it.

"Where do we take this rokken fellow, then?" Korgan asked.

Gabrielle answered, "The Imperial Seat."

The young kelnor stared. "Are you mad? We'll all die, or worse!"

"Have a little faith, Korgan Druumedar. I would never risk the life of our rokken friend—or our lives, for that matter." Although as she said the words, foreboding washed over. She had no idea how she was going to sneak two dwarves, a human mage, and an ogre-kin into the Imperial capital unseen. And yet she must find a way.

"When do we leave?" the kelnor grumbled.

"At first light," she answered. "And we'll be traveling light and fast."

CHAPTER

5

Raina stepped out of the governor's council chamber, rolling her shoulders to release the tension of extreme boredom. Four hours that meeting had droned on. And not one person had said anything whatsoever of the slightest importance to the Heart. No wonder the high matriarch had passed down to her the onerous duty of sitting through the weekly guild council meeting with the governess.

Raina had kept herself awake mostly by studying Syreena Wingblade, the governess who had replaced Anton Constantine. She was petite of stature with a soft cap of white feathers where most humans would have hair. The governess didn't miss a thing that went on around her. Raina remembered hearing somewhere that Syreena was a falcon avarian, and she could see the resemblance in the predatory intensity with which Syreena regarded her guildmasters.

"A moment of your time, Emissary," a modulated voice said low behind her.

"How may I help you, Guildmaster Aurelius?" she responded courteously.

"I wish to invite you and your young friends to dine with me tonight. Hyland House. Seven o'clock?"

"That would be lovely, guildmaster. You do me great honor." She made a polite curtsy in the elven fashion.

His lips twitched in momentary humor at her exaggerated courtesy. While it might be appropriate among formal acquaintances, they were neither formal nor mere acquaintances.

She looked around for her usual Royal Order of the Sun guards and did not spy them. Maybe some threat had pulled them away, or perhaps they had ducked into the guard building to catch up with friends. Either way, it was midafternoon and perfectly safe for her to walk back to the Heart by herself. She relished the notion of having a few minutes entirely to herself for a change. How long had it been since she'd been that carefree girl back in Tyrel, hiking the forests and pastures around her home, lying by the bank of a stream, lazily fishing and not caring at all if anything nibbled at her hook?

It felt like decades, but not quite two years had passed since her sixteenth birthday, the day she'd run away from home rather than be made a virtual slave of the Mages of Alchizzadon.

She started out across the great square in front of the governor's palace. The temperature had risen above freezing, and everywhere water dripped off roofs as the blanket of snow melted, a teasing hint of the spring yet to come.

The mood in Dupree was buoyant, with children running and shouting, mothers stopping in clusters to gossip, and shopkeepers sweeping the granite cobblestones in front of their shops with gusto. She breathed deeply, relishing the freedom to stretch her legs and stride across the open space like she was on the road once more.

She looked up from stepping across a small cascade of runoff water and froze in shock. Blank disbelief flooded her as she stared at the dark blue cloak trimmed with a row of runes around its hem. Its owner was half turned away from her, but a heavy line of jaw was visible . . . with faint runes climbing the man's neck and spilling across that jaw.

Alchizzadon. One of the secret order's mages was here in Dupree. Standing out in the open, turning slowly in a circle, taking in everything and everyone in the square. In a few more seconds, he would turn and spot her—

Panic erupted in her belly, sickening and hot. Her legs trembled with need to run, and she gave in to their urgings. She spun blindly and stumbled away from the threat—

And fetched up hard against a wall of chain mail, boiled leather, and solid muscle. Strong arms went around her, steadying her. Trapping her.

"Let me go!" she gasped.

"Easy, Raina. I've got you. You're safe."

She looked up, and in her terror, it took her a moment to realize she was plastered against none other than Thanon himself. And he was grinning down at her lopsidedly.

"I've had women throw themselves at me before," he commented drolly, "but never one as beautiful and elusive as you, my lady."

"I have to go. Please. He'll see me."

"Who will see you?" Thanon asked quickly. "Who dares frighten you so?"

There was no time to explain. "He'll take me. They'll poison me. Do terrible things—"

Thanon cut her off sharply. "No man will harm you while I draw breath." His arms tightened protectively around her, drawing her deeper into the folds of his black cloak and even closer against his big, hard body.

As much as she wished to bury her head against his chest and hide like a child, the compulsion to stare at the mage who'd come for her was too much to resist. She turned her cheek against the tiny, cold links of steel mail and caught sight of the mage, who now faced her nearly fully.

A second shock, possibly even greater than the first one, coursed through her. Had Thanon not been holding her securely, her legs might very well have collapsed from under her entirely.

Surely not.

It could not be.

And yet she would know that face anywhere. The same . . . and yet not the same. The jaw heavier and more square. Brow thicker. Skin sallower. The suggestion of laughter at any moment gone from around his eyes . . .

Justin.

She tore free of Thanon's grasp and took off running, her own white-and-blue cloak billowing out behind her.

Justin spotted her coming and moved rapidly toward her as well. They collided as he wrapped her up in a bone-crushing hug, and she all but strangled the life out of his neck.

"Thank the Lady," he breathed into her ear. "I didn't think I would ever see you alive again. Why did you leave like that? I'd have gone with you—"

"Is all well here?" a stern voice said behind her.

She winced at Justin, then smoothed her facial features into calm and turned to face Thanon. "My humble apologies for worrying you before. I thought I saw an old enemy, but instead I found an even older friend. My lord Commander, this is Justin Morland of Tyrel, a dear family friend."

Thanon nodded tersely, looking Justin up and down suspiciously. "Have you need of me and my men to escort you back to the Heart, Emissary?"

"Nay, my lord. Truly, I do not. Next time I go out, I will send a message to you. We will stroll the long way to wherever I must go and I'll tell you all about the trouble Justin and I managed to get into as children. You'll be appalled."

Thanon looked appeased by the offer of a walk with her and even cracked a smile. "I shall look forward to hearing how disobedient a child you were." He bowed crisply and took his leave, looking every inch a dashing military officer.

As he strode away, Justin muttered out of one side of his mouth. "Who in stars' name was that?"

"Imperial Army officer. Not a man to anger if you wish to live."

"Good thing I didn't pick his pocket, then."

She swatted Justin on the shoulder, then tucked her hand in the crook of his elbow and began walking back toward the Heart. She had no doubt Thanon, and likely several of his men, were still surreptitiously watching her, so she was careful to observe strict propriety with Justin. But she did murmur, "What's happened to you? Are you all right? You look different."

"Oh. That. It's the magic. It changed me."

She pulled away a little, enough to frown at him. Up close, the changes in his face were even more apparent. And now that she took notice of it, his entire body was thicker, coarser, and more muscular than before. "Magic doesn't change people's appearances," she disagreed.

"It does when the bottled spirit of an ogre mage is stuffed into you."

She stopped and turned to stare at him, pushed him all the way back to arm's length. "Did the mages do this to you? How dare they! Why, I'll—"

"Is everything all right here?" a definitely threatening voice demanded from behind her.

Dregs. Thanon again. She turned to face the Imperial officer, who loomed menacingly, backed up by a half dozen of his men, weapons drawn, and black expressions spoiling for a fight.

Speaking quickly, she explained, "Justin gave me no offense. He merely shared some upsetting news from home. I'm sorry if I worried you, my lord. Thanks be to you for your vigilance on my behalf. I cannot tell you how much it means to me to know that you and your men are always looking out for me."

Thanon's thunderous scowl eased slightly as he glanced down at her hand resting on his forearm in supplication. "Always, Raina. You have but to call for me and I will come. My life is yours."

She stared, startled at the declaration. Speechless, she bowed her head and sank into a formal curtsy. Mailed hands lifted her by the shoulders, and Thanon stepped close enough that a low rumble came out of Justin's barrel chest.

Thanon murmured, his breath warm against her temple. "Never bow to me. I would that you see me as a man, not a soldier or an officer or an Imperial official. Give me that much hope at least that one day you will see me as more than a mere acquaintance."

Nonplussed, she stared at him as he released her, stepped back, swept into a flourishing bow, and then turned and strode away, his men in tow.

"Who in the name of the monsters below does he think he is?" Justin demanded.

She turned back to him and looped her hand around his forearm. "He's commander of the Talons of Koth, an elite Special Forces unit, and he's accustomed to getting his way. The fact that I am not falling all over myself to be with him has him a bit confused."

"He's sweet on you," Justin declared in disgust.

She laughed, relieved to hear her old friend, surrogate big brother, and childhood crush in that annoyed observation. "Whatever gave you that idea?" she replied gaily. "Now. Tell me everything. Start with the night I ran away from home."

They strolled across Dupree toward the Heart building with Justin filling her in on his months-long search for her, his return to Dupree, and his recruitment by Kadir of the Mages of Alchizzadon.

She stopped him short of the Heart steps. "Swear to me that he didn't coerce you in any way."

"I swear. He offered me magic and a chance to keep you safe. Those were all the incentive I needed."

She squeezed his arm affectionately. "Still. I would not have you caught in the clutches of those people if you did not wish it. You can tell me the truth. I have rank now and a measure of influence in the Heart. We can help you break free of the mages if you wish it."

"They would take back their magic," he responded with a sad smile.

"You can learn more magic in the Heart!"

"Yes, but taking my magic from me would kill me."

She spun to face him. "What exactly have they done to you? Not to put too fine a point on it, but you don't look entirely like yourself."

"Noticed that, did you?" he responded wryly. "Like I said, they placed another spirit inside me. Or more precisely, the essence of another spirit, distilled down mostly to just his knowledge of magic and capacity for shaping and using magic."

"He who?" she asked suspiciously. She knew Justin too well, and right now, he wasn't telling her something.

"An ogre mage who was once a powerful member of our . . . little group."

It pained her to hear Justin refer to himself as one of them. The Mages of Alchizzadon always had been and always would be her enemies. But then, the ramifications of the ritual he referred to distracted her. "Is this other person sentient? Does he possess you? Do you retain his memories?" She added in horror, "He does not control you, does he?"

"No. I'm still me. It's mostly just his magic they inserted into me."

"Did it hurt?"

Justin did not answer, but a fine ripple of memory passed across his skin. It had hurt. A lot.

"Here's the thing, Raina. Some of the mages want to do the same thing to you. Well, not what was done to me but what was done to the ogre mage. They want to take your magic from you and store it."

"For what purpose?" she exclaimed in dismay.

He pulled a face. "To place it in a more malleable and cooperative subject than you."

"Hah! No daughter of my house will ever cooperate with their unnatural schemes."

"Speaking of which, I'm sorry I did not believe you that night when you came to me and told me what they had planned for you."

She resumed walking, unwilling to go inside the confines of the Heart building just yet. "I didn't blame you for not believing me. I hardly believed myself. No one in their right mind would believe they wanted to use me as a broodmare to help them raise a super-mage."

"They still want you for that purpose," he said quietly. "But if you're not willing to help them, some of them are willing to simply steal your magic instead."

"Did you come to warn me? How did you slip away from them?"

"I did not slip away. They portaled me here magically and gave me this mark upon my arm to activate when I am ready to go home." He showed her an intricate mark on his left fore-arm.

"Home to Tyrel?"

"No, Raina. Home to Alchizzadon. I'm one of them now."

She shook her head in denial. It was not possible. Her best friend had joined her greatest enemy. It was the worst kind of betrayal, and yet she could not bring herself to hate Justin. He was the first friend from Tyrel that she had seen or spoken with since she left almost two years ago.

"What have they done to you?" She whispered past her constricted throat, "What have *I* done to you?"

"You've done nothing to me, muckling. All my choices have been my own."

She reeled at the use of his old nickname for her. The wash of fond memories of their childhood scraps and games together nearly undid her fragile composure.

Choosing to attack rather than burst into tears, she challenged, "So you did not join the mages in order to find me? You did not allow them to put another spirit into you so you could be closer to me? You are not here in hopes that you will be the Mage of Alchizzadon I choose to father my children for them?"

Justin's face might look different, but his eyes were exactly the same as she remembered. And right now, their azure depths swam with pain. "Kadir offered me a way out of Tyrel. A way to be more than just a peasant toiling for my tax money. In spite of your fondest wish for it to be so, I did not do any of this for you, Raina. I did it for me."

His words were a slap in the face to her. She'd always had her family's name and rank. Her extraordinary talent for magic. Her mother's inherited beauty. She had never been bound for an ordinary commoner's life—a life she now knew to be miserable and soul-destroying, a life of constant toil that ground a person down until he or she was no more than grit under the Empire's heel.

It had never occurred to her to wonder what Justin's fate would be. She had always assumed they would end up together, and he would live a life of comfort and ease, linked to hers. But when she'd left, she'd taken his future with her.

"I'm so sorry, Justin. I didn't know. I didn't think. I should have realized how my running away would affect you. I should have waited for you to believe me. We could have gone together—"

He pressed a finger to her lips, silencing her. "The past is finished and gone, muckling. We have only today to live."

When had he gotten so wise?

He shrugged. "Our decisions and choices have brought us to this moment, and we are both alive and well."

"And together again," she added.

He smiled at her, but it was no longer Justin's funny, crooked grin that invited a person to laugh along. It was the smile of that other spirit within him, serious and apparently a bit uncomfortable with her.

They completed their lap around Heart Square, and she noticed Sir Hrothgar standing on the steps of the Heart, staring down at her disapprovingly. At least he had the good grace to give her and Justin a pretense of privacy as they walked and talked.

She veered down a side street, her pace picking up considerably as she ditched her overseers. She hustled Justin into a tavern where they could get a bite to eat and continue their conversation in genuine privacy.

"Are we hiding from that Thanon fellow again?" he asked.

"Yes. And my other watchdogs."

"Do I want to know?"

She scowled at him as they sat down at a table in the back corner of the mostly empty space. "You might as well know. White Heart emissaries are guarded around the clock by members of the Royal Order of the Sun." She wagged a teasing finger at him. "Which is to say your kind had better not try to snatch my kind unless your kind plan to tangle with the knights who protect my kind."

Justin grinned. "I'm not here to kidnap you on behalf of my friends." He leaned forward and murmured conspiratorially,

"And if I were, I'd be much more afraid of Thanon and his men than a bunch of Heart types."

She snorted. "That's because you have not met Lord Justinius. He and his men make Thanon and his crew look like children playing at being soldiers."

"I'm glad," Justin said, his voice low and fierce. "You tell Justinius to keep a close eye on you. He'll answer to me if something bad happens to you."

She reached across the table and squeezed his hand. "Stars, I've missed you."

"And I you."

They ordered two plates of whatever the kitchen was serving and dug into steaks of fresh venison in a savory mushroom sauce and roasted root vegetables.

After the meal, they lingered over mugs of hot mulled cider, and Raina asked, "So if you did not come to kidnap me, why are you here? Not that I'm complaining," she added hastily.

"Ever the clever girl, you are. Nothing escapes your notice."

"Like the fact that you're avoiding answering me."

Justin smiled. "I'm here to invite you to visit Alchizzadon as the honored guest of the mages."

Her mug hit the table hard. "Are you mad?"

"I told them you would respond with exactly those words."

"And they sent you nonetheless?"

"Raina, you have neatly foiled their plans for you by joining the White Heart. They realize they cannot just do with you as they will. They wish, instead, to work with you. To share knowledge. To see if we and thee can be of mutual benefit to one another."

"I will *never* give them a new generation of daughters of Tyrel to manipulate."

"I believe they understand that," he replied dryly.

"Then what do we have to discuss?"

"There are . . . things . . . about the mages you do not know. Subjects they study. Goals they work to accomplish. Mutually beneficial aspirations we and you share."

"Like what?"

He glanced around the empty room and lowered his voice. "We have spent years beyond count working on ways to wake ancient beings who have fallen into magical torpors."

Her eyes widened. The mages could help her wake Gawaine? That might almost be worth the risk of talking to them.

"I see you are interested. I give you my word they will not harm you while you are there and that they will let you go without protest when you wish to leave. They only wish to talk."

"You cannot promise that all the mages will honor your word," she retorted.

"True. But I can promise you that mages powerful enough to protect you have sworn to do so. The high proctor himself—" Justin broke off.

She'd never heard the title before. So the mages had a hierarchical structure, did they? Just how many of them were there? She had always assumed they were a handful of crazies, a dozen at most, clinging to their fictional legends. But the way Justin spoke of them . . .

"What sorts of things do the mages study and goals do they pursue?"

Justin shrugged. "I don't know all of it, but they study magic in all its forms. Among other things, they study how to collect it and concentrate it. And of course, you know about the one whom they attempt to wake. I do not know what the third branch of the order does, but I see them moving in the halls from time to time. I have heard rumors among the other acolytes of a fourth order, but no one dares even guess what they might do."

Four entire orders? Dismay rolled through her. How big and powerful was this bunch, and what had Justin gotten himself embroiled in? Fear for his safety followed close on the heels of her dismay.

"When do they wish me to visit them?"

"Immediately. I am authorized to portal you back to Alchizzadon with me."

"No. Absolutely not," she declared forcefully. "I'm not por-taling anywhere!"

"Well, you can always walk to Alchizzadon. It will take you months, however."

"Better that I travel with my own two feet and know where I am, thank you very much." She did not add that with her own two feet, she could always turn around and run away from Alchizzadon, as well.

"They will not let you walk right up to the front door. Its location must remain secret. Surely, you understand the ne-cessity for that."

"Then I must refuse your invitation—"

He interrupted, "What if you were to travel on your own most of the way and then I were to meet you and guide you the rest of the way, but with a blindfold for the last portion of the journey?"

"What guarantee do I have that the mages will let me leave?"

"You have my word, and Kadir's word, and that of High Proctor Albinus. He may be ancient, but I'm telling you, I would not take on that man in mage's combat. His skin is so covered in runes you can barely see any flesh. He's a walk-ing bomb of potential magic."

"I will have to let the Royal Order of the Sun know where I am going and when I am due to return. They'll come look-ing for me if I am late."

"You don't need to threaten us," he replied mildly. "We un-derstand the immunity your colors grant you."

My, my, my. Look at Justin acting all grown up and po-litically savvy. He had, indeed, changed as much inside as outside. She tilted her chair back on two legs, studying him intently. "I have to say the changes suit you. Maybe you could use a little more sun so you look less yellow, but you look good."

"You're growing up well yourself. You look more like your mother than ever." He raised a hand as she drew breath to protest. "Never fear, you act nothing like her, muckling."

Her front chair legs thumped to the floor, and she grinned

widely. "You do realize that the Royal Order of the Sun would box your ears if they heard you call a White Heart emissary a baby pig, don't you?"

He met her grin with one of his own. "Who's going to tell them? You? I'll tell them how you earned the nickname."

"You wouldn't!"

"Don't test me . . . muckling."

"You're irredeemable."

"You'll come visit, then?"

She sighed, her smile fading. "Yes, Justin. For you, I will visit your precious mages, but I make no promise to cooperate with them. This one time, I will honor a temporary truce and listen to what they have to say."

He reached across the table and gave her hands an affectionate squeeze. "Thank you."

Her gaze narrowed menacingly. "And you can tell Kadir it was a dirty trick to send you to deliver the invitation to me."

Justin laughed heartily. "I will do so. With pleasure."

They stepped out of the tavern, and Raina was not the slightest bit surprised to see Hrothgar and three of his men standing guard, looking roundly annoyed with her.

Ignoring her bodyguards, she strolled with Justin back toward the Heart. They reached the steps, and she threw her arms around his neck, giving him a big hug.

"How will I find you?" she murmured into his ear.

"Head west into the Sorrow Wold, and I will find you."

W hat do you mean, they escaped?" Anton asked, his voice rising in disbelief.

"They somehow got free of their shackles and ran away," the one called Gorath explained, wincing as he spoke. For good reason.

"And why did you not give chase?"

"We did! But they were clever and quiet and left no tracks for us to follow," one of the others whined. "We ran and ran, but they must've been faster. They disappeared."

When he caught up with the spawn of Tiberius De'Vir, he was going to take great pleasure in torturing that boy slowly and painfully. Although, if he'd outwitted Kithmar slavers, Will Cobb was a boy no more. He would not make the mistake of underestimating Will and his friends again. Next time, he would see to them personally. He fingered the collection of glass globes in his pouch idly. Spirit deaths for Will and the other males. Enslavements for the females.

Oh yes. He pictured having a beautiful, young emissary of the White Heart groveling at his feet, mewling for his attention, and a slow grin spread across his face. This was going to be fun, indeed. He would crush them all. And then he would humiliate them the way they'd humiliated him.

Raina sighed as Sir Hrothgar nodded politely to her in front of Hyland House. "My men and I will wait here to see you safely home."

"Don't be ridiculous," she replied quickly. "It's freezing cold out here. Hyland's men will escort me back." Now that she'd accepted the invitation from the Mages of Alchizzadon, not a soul in Dupree worried her. Sure, the city had its fair share of thieves and brigands, but they were not likely to hurt her. They were much more likely to accost her and demand the free healing the White Heart dispensed to anyone who had need of it.

The front door opened behind her, and Guildmaster Aurelius said, "Thanks be for escorting my young friends to me in safety, Sir Hrothgar."

"I was not aware you had come back from Koth, Guildmaster. Congratulations on your safe return," Hrothgar responded.

Raina mentally snorted. Congratulations, indeed. It was a rare feat to be summoned to appear before the Emperor himself and return alive. Few managed it.

Thankfully, Hrothgar gave brisk orders to his men to move out, and she and her friends went inside the comfortably appointed home.

As Will and Eben related the tale of being briefly kidnapped and escaping their slaver captors, who claimed to work for Anton Constantine, she had abrupt second thoughts about having sent the Royal Order of the Sun men home without her.

An upset Rosana latched on to Will's arm and showed no inclination of letting go anytime soon. Raina smiled more charitably at their young love than she usually did. Perhaps her new attitude had something to do with an afternoon spent with Justin. It had been a shock to see him as changed as he was by the ogre mage's spirit within him, but he was still her Justin. If only she could figure out a way to convince him to come away from the Mages of Alchizzadon—

"Is there any word on a new landsgrave being appointed to the Hyland holding?" Rosana asked their host. Raina's attention snapped to the conversation at hand.

"The governess seems in no hurry to name anyone," Aurelius replied as they moved into Hyland's study, a big, messy room full of desks and shelves and maps and mechanical models. A half dozen comfortable chairs had been pulled into the chamber and arranged around the big stone hearth, in which a cheery fire burned.

Eben, foster son to Leland Hyland and nominal heir to his holdings until Leland's only son by birth, Kendrick, was recovered from his captor, was already seated before the fire. His caramel-colored skin shone warmly in the firelight, and faint swirls of gray, orange, and white were visible upon it. Notably absent were the blue tones of a water caster. Apparently, Eben had no affinity whatsoever for water magics.

"Will Rynn and Sha'Li be joining us?" Raina asked him.

Eben scowled and didn't deign to answer.

As if summoned by her question, the study door opened to admit a tall, cloaked form. The man pushed a deep hood back to reveal golden hair and three brilliant blue eyes. Ever the serene one, he made a slight bow in her direction. "Life as an emissary seems to agree with you," Rynn remarked. "You're looking well."

"Thanks be. The Heart is not the least bit pleased that Lord Goldeneye outmaneuvered them by granting my new rank to me. However, they hate my being an emissary slightly less than they love the idea of getting their hooks into the Dominion."

The nation of animal changelings was notoriously suspicious of anything or anyone Imperial. As for her, she was amused at the neat outflanking maneuver Goldeneye had pulled off. The appointment itself intimidated her immensely. The importance of it was not lost upon her, and frankly, she was relieved that Justinius would be sending a seasoned knight with her as both protector and advisor.

"Shall we wait for Sha'Li before you all tell me what you've been up to since I left?" Aurelius asked. "I look forward to hearing a full report from the lot of you."

Eben replied coldly, "Sha'Li may not show up."

What on Urth could have made him so resentful of her? Even Aurelius's golden-skinned brow puckered. He was a solinari, a sun elf, and his skin glittered as bright as a newly minted gold coin. Although Raina knew him to be several hundred years old, he had that annoyingly ageless look of all elves. All in all, he was rather dazzling to behold.

Aurelius said smoothly to cover the awkward moment, "Catch me up. Last I heard, the lot of you had gotten a lead on Kendrick Hyland and were heading west in search of him."

Will launched into the tale of their search for Hyland's kidnapped son. They'd found Kendrick, who'd been transformed into a were-boar and who ultimately chose to stay with his captor, a nature guardian, Kerryl Moonrunner. Along the way, they'd been accosted by Imperial hounds who seemed intent on devouring Eben, they'd freed a unicorn from magical bonds, and they'd been kidnapped by the Dominion.

Dinner was served, and they took a break in the telling of their tale. They had just adjourned back to the cozy study and were sipping on mugs of spiced wine when Raina noticed Sha'Li slipping unobtrusively into the shadows at the back of the room, well away from the fire. The lizardman girl had become an accomplished rogue in the two years Raina had known her. She noted that Sha'Li chose to stand directly behind Eben, out of sight of the jann.

Rosana took up the tale of their adventures. "So our captors took us to the Great Den of the Dominion and to

Goldeneye himself." She laughed ruefully. "I made the mistake of talking to him."

Aurelius groaned. "Let me guess. He enslaved you."

Will answered for her as she rolled her eyes. "Indeed, he did. Worse, he set us the task of taking back some vials of magical change water from Kentogen that Kerryl Moonrunner had stolen from him. So we were off again, chasing Kerryl."

Rosana took up the tale. "We caught him eventually and got back the water. We returned it to Goldeneye in the Dominion capital, Rahael."

"And that's when he declared you his emissary, Raina?" Aurelius asked.

"Well, not before we had a minor run-in with a gate to the dream plane, an elemental army streaming through it, and a possessed mage holding the gate open." She wasn't sure if Aurelius knew about the Mages of Alchizzadon, so she left out the part where the possessed mage was a member of the order that had long been trying to kidnap her for their own nefarious purposes. Her feud with the mages was personal.

"An open gate?" Aurelius exclaimed. "How on Urth did you shut it?"

Rosana answered proudly, "Will built a maze of magical walls of force, and Rynn ran the maze, dodging the elementals who came after him. We used the cover of the walls to get close to the mage holding the gate open, and I silenced him just as Will and Rynn attacked him. Then Eben used his mace as a makeshift key to turn a giant lock and close the gate."

Aurelius looked sharply at Will. "And where did you learn how to cast a wall of force? I don't recall teaching you that particular spell."

Will squirmed under his grandfather's scrutiny. "Something happened to me on that battlefield. Some sort of repressed memory broke through, and all of a sudden, I remembered how to cast the spell."

If Raina was not mistaken, he'd abruptly remembered a lot more than that. In an instant, he'd become a clever tactical leader, his combat prowess improved dramatically, and his spellcraft doubled or maybe even tripled. He claimed to have no idea where the knowledge had come from, but she suspected he knew full well and just wasn't saying.

Will and Aurelius shared a long, pregnant look. And then Aurelius broke into a grin, murmuring, "Clever whoreson did it, didn't he? Trained you to follow in his footsteps without anyone else finding out."

"Seems so," Will replied dryly.

Of whom did they speak? Perhaps Aurelius's missing son and Will's father?

"Tell me more of this gate," Aurelius said to the group.

Rynn took up the telling of the tale. "It's a permanent structure, guarded by a claviger—the same fellow who was possessed and whom we took down. The tympan, the lock, for this particular gate is intact, although the claviger threw the key to it through the gate in his temporary madness. Until someone can find or fashion a new key for the lock, the Dominion gate should remain closed."

Aurelius leaned forward. "And it led to the dream plane, you say? Where, then, did the elementals come from? They should be confined to their own respective elemental planes."

"They turned out to be dreaming constructs of elementals and not actual elementals," Rynn answered.

"Phantasms of elementals? Who would create such things?" Aurelius demanded. "For what purpose?"

Rynn and Eben exchanged a charged glance. Eben nodded slightly, and Rynn continued.

"Once the claviger was rendered unconscious, Lord Goldeneye attempted to remove whatever enslavement effect held the man in its thrall. He was unable to do it alone and asked for my assistance. When the two of us were working inside the claviger's mind, we"—he hesitated and then plunged on—"saw something. We glimpsed what lies beyond the gate."

"Tell me." Aurelius was tense. And for good reason. Raina had already heard some of what her friends had seen.

A shadow from the margins of the room stepped forward,

and Raina about jumped out of her skin. When had the master assassin Selea Rouge arrived? The tall dark elf must have slipped in sometime in the past few minutes, but so stealthy was he that she hadn't even noticed. Of course, his coal black nulvari skin helped him blend into the shadows. But still.

Raina caught Sha'Li's amused grin, a flash of white against the lizardman girl's black scales, as everyone else in the room jumped, too.

Eben had finally spied Sha'Li if his furious scowl was any indication. The next time Raina got either one of them alone, she was going to demand a full explanation of the rift between them.

"Go on," Selea urged Rynn.

Raina turned her attention back to the paxan's description of what he and Goldeneye had seen. "A vast army lies beyond the gate. Elementally aligned dream creatures of every size, shape, race, and form gather to attack."

"What is their target?" Selea asked tersely.

"Haelos," Rynn replied. "And then all of Urth if the claviger's thoughts are to be believed."

Aurelius sat back hard in his armchair, he and Selea exchanging worried stares.

"Who leads this army? Did you see?" Selea asked.

"We saw several figures clustered on a tall rock with the army at their feet as if they were the leaders. In that group were several large elemental figures. They looked entirely corporeal and not visibly phantasmal at all, which would make them extremely powerful dream creatures, indeed. Phantasms of elemental lords, if I had to guess. With them was a little girl. Close beside her stood a man—a warrior, by the looks of him, wearing full armor and distinctive armored gloves that extended up his arms. Their style was ancient."

"Gages?" Aurelius asked sharply.

"Yes. Gages on both hands and forearms."

Selea breathed, "The Gaged Man?"

Aurelius sucked in a shocked breath. "Surely not."

Although gages were gloves, a gage was also a promise to serve another. In which way did Selea mean the epithet?

Raina looked back and forth between the horrified elves. "What? Who is this man who alarms you so?" she asked.

"He is a bodyguard, sworn to death and beyond. But it is his mistress, the little girl, who alarms us," Aurelius answered grimly.

Selea added, "She was the daughter, scion, and heir of Ammertus."

"The Kothite archduke Ammertus?" Raina blurted, horrified.

"The very same," Selea replied.

"What's she doing on the dream plane?" Will asked.

Aurelius answered, "That's an excellent question. She was permanently destroyed long ago. Ammertus has never been quite the same. He still carries one of her braids in his belt as a token of grief and remembrance."

Rynn said slowly as if thinking his way through his words, "If her spirit was of sufficient power, it might survive being sundered from her body. Not for long, but long enough for someone to shunt it over to the dream realm. Once there, it might be possible for her spirit to survive as a disembodied being made of dream energy."

Raina responded, "So she is not actually a phantasm, then."

"Likely not," Rynn answered.

Aurelius said heavily, "What she would be is dangerous. Exceedingly so. As Ammertus's firstborn scion and heir, he would have imbued her with massive power at the time of her creation. She could be nearly as powerful as her sire."

Raina gulped. Ammertus was one of the most powerful Kothites of all, an immortal being of immense mental power. He was also rumored to feed on rage and be half-mad with lust for power.

Eben said reflectively, "She did not strike me as being especially dangerous when I spoke with her in my dream."

"You've been dreaming of her?" Aurelius exclaimed.

Eben squirmed a little. "I asked Rynn to help me visit the dream realm so I might search out my sister and speak with her."

"And did you?" Selea asked.

"I did not get to speak with Marikeen, although I did leave a message for her with Vesper."

"You left a message. With Vesper," Aurelius echoed. "What message, pray tell?"

"Simply that I worry about Marikeen and wish to speak with her," Eben said a shade defensively. "Vesper offered to help us escape our captors. It was she who distracted the rakasha slavers so we could get away."

Rynn responded, "You do not know that for certain, Eben."

"No, but she did offer to help us," Eben retorted. "And she said she would help us find Kendrick and fix him. She would have nothing to gain by doing that other than our friendship, would she?"

Aurelius and Selea exchanged worried looks again.

Aurelius answered grimly, "You can count on Vesper having something to gain by helping you. If she is even one-tenth—one-hundredth—as calculating and scheming as her sire, she wants something from you. Badly."

"But what?" Eben asked. "I have nothing to offer her."

It was Selea who answered grimly this time. "That's what worries me."

Will brought the conversation full circle by asking, "How can she conquer the material plane if she is but a spirit, or whatever disembodied thing she is, on the dream plane? And if that is the case, why does Vesper build an army and send it through to the material plane? What does she have to gain by doing that?"

"Besides dominion over all living things?" Rynn retorted. "My guess is she seeks a new body to inhabit."

Silence fell over the party. Raina suspected they were all thinking the same thing she was. Gawaine's body was somewhere in Haelos. It was immortal and at the moment inhabited by no spirit. It would be perfect for Vesper's purposes.

Into the silence, Eben said, "It is decided, then. I must go back to the dream plane and infiltrate this Vesper's army. I shall learn more about its goals and what she seeks."

Raina exclaimed, "You are no spy, Eben!" An able merchant and a fine warrior he might be, but the young jann was as direct, honest, and forthright as his foster father, Leland Hyland, had been.

He scowled at her. "We've already had this argument. Marikeen serves Vesper and trades favors with the elemental lords who appear to be Vesper's generals. If anyone of us can get close to Vesper and her cronies, it will be me. I will approach my sister and tell her I wish to stand at her side. That I have missed her and only want to protect her. Marikeen will believe me because it's the truth."

"What you propose is dangerous, Eben," Selea cautioned.

"Isn't everything we've done so far dangerous?" Eben retorted.

He had a point. Pursuing the awakening of the legendary Sleeping King, an ancient elf, so he might rise and throw off the shackles of Koth was beyond dangerous. It was suicidal. And yet, they'd spent the past year and more pursuing that very goal.

"Speaking of which, look at this," Raina said. She held out her right hand, showing Aurelius and Selea the carved ivory ring clasping her middle finger.

The Mage's Guildmaster examined it closely. "Unicorn horn?" he asked in no small wonder.

"Very good. It is, indeed, unicorn horn, and it is Gawaine's signet ring," she replied, smiling broadly.

"How can you be certain it is part of the Sleeping King's regalia?" Aurelius challenged.

"I dreamed of him again and visited his grove on the dream plane. He wears an identical version of this ring. He recognized mine as the physical version of his."

Like Vesper, the Sleeping King's disembodied spirit was trapped on the dream plane. However, unlike the Kothite girl, his actual body still rested somewhere on the continent of Haelos. When they found the pieces of his regalia and brought them to his body, they hoped to be able to rejoin Gawaine's spirit and physical form so he might awaken and lead them all to freedom. That was the plan, at least.

"While we are on the subject of dreams," Rynn said,

"Eben, you must tell our esteemed hosts about your dreams of late."

Raina sat up straighter, interested to see if Aurelius and Selea could shed any further light on Eben's strange visions of an ice lord rising in the east to stand against Vesper and her elemental lieutenants.

The two elves listened intently to Eben's description, their expressions freezing into polite masks as he spoke—a sure sign that both men were reacting more strongly to what they heard than they cared to let on.

Eben finished his recitation with, "So. Do you know what it all means? Who is the ice lord in the Heaves?"

The Heaves were a mountain range south and east of Dupree at the tip of the great peninsula where the colony made its home.

Aurelius and Selea exchanged another of those long looks they'd been sharing all evening. Except this time, both of them looked nothing short of aghast. Alarm spiked in Raina's belly. What did they know that they weren't saying?

Selea nodded ever so slightly, and Aurelius said, "Normally, elementals of different flavors would never deign to work with one another. Clearly, Vesper has some great hold over all of them and forces them to cooperate. This ice elemental you describe is behaving more as I would expect a powerful elemental to—posturing in protection of his own territory and challenging elementals of other alignments."

"Who is he?" Eben asked.

Aurelius winced. "That, my boy, is a question best answered in private."

Eben bristled. "These are my closest friends. I trust them with my life."

Raina couldn't help but wonder if he still included Sha'Li in that statement.

Apparently, he must, for he continued, "I have nothing to hide from them."

Dear, sweet Eben. So honest and decent. He lived his life as an open book. She envied him.

Yet another long look between the elves, and finally, Aurelius said, "The elemental ice lord you describe sounds a great deal like Dikenn Tarses."

Raina gaped. Tarses? As in General Tarses? The legendary battle leader of the Kothites, the one who conquered the elemental continent, Pan Orda, for the Empire? As she recalled, Tarses had been a jann just like Eben.

"Why on Urth would I dream of General Tarses?" Eben demanded. "I barely know the stories about him."

Aurelius opened his mouth. Closed it. Opened it again. Never before had Raina seen the solinari so visibly uncomfortable. Intrigued, she waited to hear what he was struggling so hard to say. Or not to say.

Finally, he said, "Eben, as you know, you and your sister were taken in by Leland Hyland shortly after the first Night of Green Fires two decades ago when your parents were killed."

"Yes, yes, I know," the jann answered impatiently.

"What you don't know is that your father was a prisoner of the first governor of Dupree. A very secret prisoner, held in a secret location. Your mother was allowed to stay with him, coming and going as she pleased along with their two small children."

"Marikeen and me?" Eben asked.

"The very same."

"Who, then, was my father?"

"His name was known only to the governor, but, son, I believe that prisoner was Dikenn Tarses."

"General Tarses is my father?" Eben exclaimed. "That's absurd."

Selea dived in. "Maybe not so absurd. There have been rumors over the years of a jann prisoner, stripped of his name and identity by the Emperor, locked up under orders never to be released. If you are his son, it might explain why you are dreaming of him in such vivid detail. And then there's the blazon you wear on your necklace that you say was your father's."

Eben fished the blazon out of his shirt and fingered the round medallion nervously. "What of it?"

Aurelius leaned forward. "It's a senior officer's medal from the Pan Orda campaign. Selea and I each have one. Only a handful of them were ever given out, and I know every man and woman who received one. The only blazon unaccounted for is the one given to General Tarses himself. It would also explain your sister's strong affinity for ice magic," Aurelius added. "She gets it from her father, who holds within him much of the spirit of the Hand of Winter, a great ice elemental lord."

"But every jann has an affinity of one kind or another," Eben protested. "Mine is for stone, and Marikeen's is for ice."

Will added, "And General Tarses is dead."

Aurelius retorted, "That's what Maximillian would have everybody believe, but that does not necessarily make it so."

Rynn spoke up, choosing his words carefully. "Scholars among my kind have long wondered if Maximillian actually fabricated Tarses's death. The general was said to be the Emperor's closest friend, and the story of Tarses's demise always seemed rather flimsy. The man was not only a great general but also an accomplished warrior personally. He would not have been easy to kill, particularly after he ingested the Hand of Winter. Not to mention, Maximillian would have carefully safeguarded such a useful tool."

Raina frowned. "Are you suggesting that the Emperor falsified the general's death and instead imprisoned him here in Dupree?"

Rynn shrugged. "Dupree was the remotest penal colony in the Empire until it was changed over to being a full colony. Where better to hide a prisoner you want the whole world to believe is dead?"

Selea said, "If we are correct about the identity of the prisoner and of your parentage, Eben, no one outside this room must ever know who you are. *No one.* Your father is supposed to be dead, which means *you are not supposed to exist.* The mere fact that you live is an affront to the Empire."

Aurelius added, "And believe me, the Emperor will be eager to rectify that mistake. Not only will he eradicate you, but he will eliminate everyone who has ever known you."

That, Raina could believe. The Kothite Empire was brutal and viewed life as entirely expendable, particularly the lives of commoners. In truth, the Empire stood for everything she was sworn to oppose as a White Heart member.

Eben looked shocked to his core. She didn't blame him.

Will came over to give the muscular jann a clap on the shoulder. "Welcome to the no-name, no-family club, my friend."

Raina snorted. Rosana already belonged to the club, having been orphaned the same night Eben had lost his parents, in the first great greenskin attack on the young colony of Dupree nearly twenty years ago.

Raina had voluntarily chosen to turn her back on her family and its plans for her. Instead, she had run away from home and ended up in the White Heart. She did not know if Sha'Li knew her family or stayed in touch, and Rynn never spoke of himself at all. Still. It was strange that four of them were, in effect, homeless and nameless. Even General Tarses could say the same.

Rosana broke the heavy silence. "It is late, and I am on duty in the Heart first thing in the morning."

The gathering broke up quickly after with Will and Selea offering to escort Raina and Rosana back to the Heart.

As Raina fastened her cloak, Aurelius stepped close to murmur, "I would speak with you in private at your earliest convenience, Emissary."

She blinked, startled at the use of her title, not to mention the deference with which he used it. "Of course, Guildmaster. I am at your disposal."

"I will send a note to arrange a time."

She nodded, shocked at being treated at something approaching equality by the solinari. She was not yet eighteen years old, and he was hundreds of years old and a powerful guildmaster to boot.

"Are you ready to depart?" Selea asked her politely.

"Yes, Master Selea. Lead the way." She'd learned in the past few weeks that her guards liked to go first.

The irony of a master assassin guarding a White Heart

member was not lost on her. Personally, she liked Selea and admired his deeply ingrained sense of honor, but she could not condone his chosen profession.

What on Urth did Aurelius wish to speak with her about? He'd used her title intentionally; was it White Heart business he wished to discuss, then? How exceedingly strange to suddenly be one of the top-ranking Heart members in all of Haelos. What had Goldeneye been thinking to do this to her? And what was Aurelius thinking of using her rank for? More than ever, she felt like a pawn on a great, invisible chessboard.

They stepped out into the night, and she drew up short, startled to see Commander Thanon and several of his men lounging in the street in front of Hyland House. "You haven't been waiting out here in this cold for long, have you?" she asked him, appalled.

He grinned. "Not long."

But the rolled eyes of his men gave lie to his words.

"Really, this is not necessary. Within Dupree, I am well known. No one here would harm me. They like the healing I give out far too much."

"Nonetheless, a little protection never hurts," Thanon responded.

"Let us not delay, then, so your men can return to their barracks and their warm beds."

The large party moved out, and Will joked and chatted with Thanon's men while Rosana scowled on Will's other side. As for Thanon, he fell in beside Raina, hovering protectively over her as if she were his own personal property. No doubt about it, he was a problem. The Empire—namely, Thanon himself—must not find out what she and her friends were really up to.

CHAPTER

7

E ben timed his departure from Hyland House to co-
    incide with Rynn's. He hurried out the postern door
    and lengthened his strides to catch up with the soli-
tary paxan. "A moment of your time, Rynn?"

"Of course."

"Share an ale with me?"

"As long as it's not served by one of Anton's flunkies and
it's a dark tavern," the paxan replied wryly, gesturing to his
forehead.

Eben nodded in understanding. At least Rynn's cloak had
a deep hood that he wore pulled well forward over his face
to cover his third eye. "I know a place where the proprietor
is fanatically loyal to Koth. I've heard him go on at length
singing Syreena Wingblade's praises."

Rynn grinned. "I can't believe I'm saying this, but the place
sounds perfect."

They ducked into an upscale but particularly dim tavern,
and Rynn made a point of sitting with his back to both hearth
and door, casting his face into black shadows. Two ales were
plunked down in front of them, and Eben flipped a silver coin
to the barman. "Keep 'em coming."

"Aye, sir."

Eben sipped the frothy, cold ale appreciatively.

"What can I do for you, my young friend?" Rynn asked
quietly.

"I have to get to the dream plane again."

"You are determined to go through with this plan of yours
to infiltrate Vesper's army, then?"

"Don't try to talk me out of it. My mind is made up."

"Fair enough." The paxan took a pull from his ale and grimaced. "Tell me this. Do you want to physically walk onto the dream plane like Will and Raina did when they found the echo of the Sleeping King, or do you want to sleep and go there only with your dreaming mind? Each method poses its own set of risks."

"I thought merely to dream my way there. Reaching the plane physically nearly killed all of us the last time we did it."

"When do you wish to make the journey?"

"As soon as possible. Can you help me?"

"I can, and I will. As for when, we can do it this very night if you wish."

Eben started. He'd expected a pitched argument from the paxan trying to talk him out of it, and Rynn's quick capitulation had taken him unawares. "Uh, that would be great. Tonight is perfect. The others won't expect me to move so soon."

"They really do care for you, you know. Even Sha'Li."

He scowled. "She betrayed me. Betrayed us all. I will not forgive that."

"Betrayed us how?"

Eben drained his mug and gestured for a refill. "She chose the Tribe of the Moon over her friends."

"How?"

"I do not wish to speak of it," he declared darkly.

"Fair enough." Rynn paused while the barman placed two fresh pints in front of them. The man retreated, and Rynn murmured, "All of us face dilemmas. Split loyalties, choices with no right answer. Sha'Li is not a bad person. She had to choose between two things, both important to her. She made the best decision she could in the circumstances. Don't condemn her for trying to do the right thing."

He leaned forward and ground out angrily, "She let Kerryl Moonrunner go. I *had* him, and she helped him escape me."

Rynn shrugged. "Mayhap she did you a favor. Perhaps in

years to come you will look back and be glad you did not murder the nature guardian. He may yet prove his worth to us all."

"Not bloody likely. He's mad as a hatter."

Rynn replied gently, "I have to agree with Sha'Li in that debate. He is most certainly not mad. I do not know why he does all that he does, but he is cunning and clever. He has a plan."

Eben scowled into his mug. Kerryl had kidnapped Kendrick Hyland and turned the youth into a were-creature against Kendrick's will. Kerryl was a bad guy. Period.

"We will need a private place where both of us can sleep undisturbed and in safety," Rynn said.

"Hyland House?" Eben suggested.

"Perfect. As soon as Aurelius clears out of there, we can go back and get to sleep. Tell me. How do you plan to convince Vesper that you sincerely want to betray your friends and work for her?"

Easy. He would tell the truth. He would speak of how Kendrick had betrayed him by choosing to stay with his captor. How Sha'Li had betrayed him by choosing Kerryl Moonrunner over him. How they all had betrayed him by taking Sha'Li's side.

"She has not asked me to betray my friends. To date, she has only offered to help me achieve my fondest wishes."

"Aurelius has the right of it. She is not helping you out of the goodness of her black heart. She wants something from you."

Then she could take a place in the long line of people who seemed to want something from him these days. All he wanted to do was get his family back together, safe and sound, and get on with his life. Was that too much to ask?

Eben glared bitterly into his ale and tossed down the last of it. "Let's go. I'm tired of waiting around doing nothing."

Rynn nodded silently and gestured at the door. "I'm ready when you are."

The hour had grown late, and a sharp wind had picked up. Bits of trash blew down the street on a gust of fine grit that stung Eben's skin. Shutters rattled, and the night buffeted him angrily. Head down, he leaned into the gale, holding his cloak closed as the wind tore at the wool.

Rynn drew up short beside him, making Eben look up sharply. Six men had stepped out of an alley in front of them and blocked their path.

"A foul night to be abroad, gentlemen," Rynn said evenly.

He knew that tone of voice from the paxan. Rynn had settled into the deep mental calm he used when he entered combat. Eben reassessed the men in front of them again. Now that he looked more closely, a certain predatory eagerness clung to the group. Hands hovered near knife hilts in belts, and they were spread out widely enough not to hinder one another in battle.

"What think you, Rynn? Shall we share them, or are you in the mood for a workout? I'll let you have them all if you wish."

Rynn released his cloak, and it flew back behind him, snagging on a large barrel standing in front of a general store. "I'm in a sharing mood. Shall we split them three and three?"

He replied casually, "It hardly seems fair to fight three on one against these amateurs, but the night is cold, and I'm eager to reach my warm bed. We might as well make this quick."

The brigands in front of them seemed momentarily taken aback, but then their gazes hardened.

One of them growled, "No need for violence, boys. Just hand over yer purses, swords, and them fancy gauntlets the pretty one is wearing, and we'll be on our way."

Eben grinned. "I'm fairly certain I speak for my friend as well when I say, if you want our possessions, come and take them." Although he suspected their possessions were not the goal at all. Surely these were more of Anton's boys in search of whatever fat bounty was being offered for them. At least the ex-governor had not made the mistake of making it an even fight this time.

The brigands rushed down the street, closing the distance

quickly. Eben supposed they thought to intimidate him and Rynn. Which was laughable after the foes they'd faced before. He drew his sword with his right hand and pulled his mace from its holder on his back with his left hand.

Rynn took a step away from Eben, giving each of them plenty of room to move. A good decision given the way Rynn could kick, punch, jump, and spin with lightning speed.

The fight was swift and brutal. Eben parried a blow with each of his weapons simultaneously, directing the parries in an X across the front of his body. He carried the momentum of his weapons in fast upward arcs, smashing the many-pointed mace into the side of one brigand's head and slashing his sword across the torso of a second one. The third fellow forced him to duck a wild sword swing, but a quick, brutal upward thrust of his own long sword into the belly of the swordsman made short work of him.

The guy he'd hit with his mace dropped to the ground unconscious or maybe dead. Sword guy number two staggered back swearing, and Eben stepped over his fallen companion, stalking his attacker aggressively. A flash of silver flew at him, and Eben batted the thrown knife out of the air with his mace, irritated now.

He feinted with his mace, a big upward swing that the brigand turned aside easily enough. But in so doing, the brigand turned slightly, opening up his side to attack. Eben chopped down into the fellow's hamstring with his sword. It wasn't an elegant blow, but it crippled his opponent and sent him to the ground, screaming.

Eben whirled to Rynn's assistance, but the paxan knelt beside one of his three prone attackers, his hand pressed against the brigand's temple. Eben bit out, "Did you kill them?"

Rynn looked up grimly. "Nay, they are not dead, but it is necessary to erase their memories of the fight."

"Because of your eye?"

"Just so."

"What about the other ones?"

"I've already cleansed their minds."

"That's a handy trick. Can you plant false memories at the same time you erase real ones?" Eben asked curiously.

"I can, but it's tricky to insert memories that fit seamlessly with a subject's actual experiences."

"Can all paxan do that, or is it an open-third-eye thing?"

Rynn rose to his full height, fetched his cloak, and returned to Eben, swinging the voluminous wool around his muscular frame. He pulled the hood up over his head, cloaking his offending eye in darkness. Only then did Rynn answer, "All paxan can influence others' minds with proper training, but doing so ethically is only allowed in limited circumstances. Such as this one."

Eben was impressed but also disturbed at the paxan's ability to alter another person's mind. Thankfully, he knew Rynn to be a man of ironclad personal morals. It was not hard to see, though, why the Empire despised his kind.

Rynn suggested, "What say we tie up these brigands and leave a note for the town guard that they are bandits and thieves?"

Eben grinned. "At this rate, we will reduce Anton's ranks of rascals to zero in no time."

They cut strips off the attackers' cloaks and used them to bind the unconscious men's wrists and ankles. While Rynn took care of the last man, Eben tore a page out of his trade journal and hastily scrawled a note declaring the men to be outlaws and thieves who had tried to rob lawful citizens of Dupree. He used one of the brigand's cloak brooches to pin the note prominently to the fellow's chest.

Eben and Rynn stood back to survey their work, grinning. Anton was going to be apoplectic when he heard about this.

"Shall we make our way to Hyland House before these miscreants awake or we run into any more unfortunate encounters?" Rynn asked.

"Aye. Let us be quit of this foul night. My sister—and Vesper—await."

Raw evenings like this made Marikeen grateful for her icy elemental alignment. It afforded her a certain comfort with cold and wet that most humans did not have. Still, she was annoyed to be kept from her bed by this late-night meeting. Anton Constantine was apparently up to his old tricks and hoped to recruit the Cabal, a secretive group of powerful magic users, to his nefarious purposes.

Anton believed that the Cabal's leader, Richard Layheart, was loyal to him, but Marikeen knew that not to be true. She'd heard Richard speak with disdain of his former superior, laughing about how easy it was to play upon Anton's greed and lust for revenge.

Of course, Richard was speaking in tones of utmost respect now to the former governor, droning on about what an honor and pleasure it was to be visited by the great Anton Constantine. For his part, the ex-governor preened at the praise.

Arrogant poppycock.

"And to what do we owe this delightful and wholly unexpected visit, Governor?" Richard asked.

"As you may know, I have spent the past months rebuilding my organization to be even stronger and more effective than before."

"Do you speak of retaking the palace in Dupree?" Richard asked in apparent surprise.

"Nothing so obvious as that. And furthermore, I do not need the palace to accomplish my goals. In fact, I can achieve my desired ends even more readily without the encumbrance of all that petty bureaucracy."

"Indeed?" Richard drawled. "I always thought you found all that bureaucracy extremely profitable."

"Oh, it was, but I can keep all the profits of my endeavors now and do not have to share any of them with my Imperial overlords. Anton Constantine is going into business for himself."

The way Marikeen had heard it, he'd been the head of the biggest underground crime ring in Haelos for years. The Coil apparently had connections across all the known continents, in fact.

"Can I assume, then, that your visit to us has something to do with this new enterprise of yours?" Richard asked.

"Indeed." Anton paced the length of the table they all sat around, gesturing grandly as he spoke and walked. "Although the bureaucracy was a millstone around my neck, it served its purpose. The guilds, for example, fulfilled a necessary function of resource harvesting and management. I still have need of such people, but working for me and not for that avarian impostor."

So. He wished to build a shadow government loyal to and reporting only to him, did he? She supposed if she were a criminal overlord, she would proceed in much the same fashion.

"How do you see our little group fitting into your larger scheme?" Richard asked shrewdly.

"I will have need of accomplished mages to marshal the resources necessary to use magic strategically in the further-ance of my goals."

He wanted to create a shadow Mage's Guild, in other words. What would Aurelius Lightstar have to say about that? She'd met the solinari guildmaster several times, and he struck her as a formidable foe.

Richard sat back at the head of the table, studying his guest closely. "Why should I believe you have the capacity to build this grand organization of which you speak?"

"Have I not decimated the Haelan legion by convincing men loyal to me to leave its ranks? Have I not gutted the guilds and the treasury with my departure? Is trade not cha-otic in my wake? Are my enemies not dead?"

He reached into his pouch and slammed an object onto the table in front of Richard. It took Marikeen a moment to iden-tify the foot-long, spiky object, but when she did, she rose to her feet with a gasp.

"Where did you get that?" she demanded.

"I got it from my man recently. He used it to kill Leland Hyland in his own home. There is no place in Haelos I can-not reach, no enemy I cannot kill."

The white antler lying on the table came from the Spirit Stag of Hyland, and she had stared at it on the wall of her foster father's trophy room for most of her childhood, ever since he caught the stag and, without killing it, removed a single antler to earn a boon from the magical stag.

His man had killed Leland? Anton was behind the death of the only father she'd ever known? Marikeen lifted her stare to Anton and memorized every last detail of his features so she could picture his bloated, smug face while she plotted his slow and painful demise. He thought he had an enemy in her little brother? He knew nothing of real enemies. She would utterly destroy him and everything he stood for.

"Give me that antler," she said coldly. "It is my right to have the weapon that killed my father."

Anton snorted in disdain. "Hyland was not your father, girl. I *know* who spawned you."

"Tell me," she demanded, her voice thick with rage.

"Enough, Marikeen," Richard said coldly. "Anton is our guest."

It took every ounce of self-discipline she possessed not to blast Anton into a pile of dust where he stood. She knew the magic to do it. Had the power.

"As a gesture of good faith, my friend, I respectfully request that you give my rather outspoken apprentice the item she requested."

Anton frowned, not pleased with the request, which, knowing Richard, was exactly why he'd made it. It was a subtle power play to force Anton into giving up a trophy he cherished.

The ex-governor hesitated a moment more and then looked up at Richard with a shrug and a smile. "Why not? My enemy is dead. That is what matters to me, not the toy that accomplished the deed."

Anton tossed the antler toward her. He aimed high, however, and it sailed over her head, clattering to the stone floor behind her. Infuriated at his intentional miss with the spirit antler, she nonetheless scrambled after it, clutching it tightly to her breast.

If she was right about it, the spirit stag's antler had more power than Anton knew. Much more. Power she would use to destroy the man who had destroyed Leland Hyland. She had no illusions that the assassin who had wielded the antler worked for anyone but Anton himself. The former governor had made an enemy tonight. An enemy he would live to regret making.

Her.

Hemlocke woke by slow degrees, coming into awareness of her body bit by bit, stretching deliciously as her senses came alive. There was something intensely satisfying about waking from a long winter's nap, feeling the distant approach of spring.

Not that she could see the earth waking up down here at the bottom of her deep, dark lake, encased in a magical bubble of air as she was. She could breathe water if she chose; she just preferred air with all its rich, lingering scents of green and growing things and drenched with the taste of emotions, human and animal, a spicy seasoning to flavor it.

Stretching her wings wide, testing their span, she rose to her haunches and, swinging her tail side to side, gave her spine a mighty crack. It was all right to confine herself to human form now and then, but she much preferred her massive draconic body to the puny bipedal existence of humans.

I would have music.

On command, the creatures of the lake, and the water of the lake itself, began to hum, serenading her with melodies older than time. Almost older than she. But not quite.

She expanded her awareness to take in the continent beneath her great claws. It was restless. Disturbed. Strange magics had come to it, tugging and distorting the natural ley lines of the land. The other planes crowded close, too close, their alien magics distorting the lush green magic of this land. It was these disturbances in the fabric of life on Haelos that had woken her, in fact.

She expanded her awareness further and felt living creatures scurrying across and under the land like so many busy ants, each intent upon its own petty business. Except . . .

Her sentinel's alertness zeroed in on a few of the tiny mortals in particular. Ignoring the boundaries of time, she looked back over the past few decades of human-measured time and found the disturbing pattern she sought.

She tsked to herself as she watched what they'd been up to.

A few of those scurrying humans were toying with forces well beyond their understanding. Irritation and a measure of curiosity coursed through her. So meddlesome, these short-lived humans.

She tested the greater winds of time, seeking intersections between past and future, mapping the effect of current actions by the young humans who'd caught her attention so sharply.

Oh my. The humans really were overreaching themselves this time. They thought to wake her brother, did they? Well, now. That was reason enough to rouse all the way. Soon now. Soon her body would heat and her green, fiery breath would burn. Soon she would fly.

CHAPTER

8

E ben was disappointed to see a lamp burning in Leland's office when he and Rynn entered Hyland House.
He'd assumed the guildmaster would be long gone by
now, returned to his guild house for the night.

"There you are, Eben. A word, if you please," Aurelius said
upon spying him.

Rynn murmured something about a midnight snack and
slipped out of the office silently.

"Yes, Guildmaster?"

"I would speak to you more of your birth father."

Eben sighed. He'd been trying hard to avoid thinking
about the revelation that General Tarses might, in fact, be
his father. "What of him? We are not even sure he is my
father."

Aurelius shook his head. "It all makes sense. Even your
sister's extreme affinity for ice and your total lack of it fit."

"Why, if my father was some great ice lord, would it make
sense that I got none of his ability with water and ice magic
at all?"

"The skill did not come to your father naturally. He attempted to absorb the essence of a great ice elemental and
nearly died in the process. Only my intervention and use of
my ability to capture and store magic saved both of us."

"You saved Tarses's life?" Eben blurted.

Aurelius shrugged modestly. "My point is that Dikenn's ice
magic was not his to grant to you. For some reason, the ice
lord within him attached to your sister, but not to you. Perhaps your spirit was too stubborn and strong for it to fight."

Eben smiled halfheartedly at the lame explanation. Personally, he had no great desire to hold part of some elemental lord within him. He'd watched Will struggle with the tree lord inside him, and it had all but killed Will. He could do without such drama, thank you.

"What is it you wish to discuss about my . . . father?" The word felt strange upon his tongue applied to a stranger he knew only from bardic tales of heroism.

"Selea did not overstate the danger to you if word of your parentage were to get out. The Emperor's credibility is at stake. He has declared his general dead, and dead he must stay. Maximillian will go to whatever lengths are necessary to wipe out any knowledge of Tarses's existence from tainting the common acceptance of his demise."

"I get it. I'm dead if anyone finds out."

"Oh, it's a fair sight worse than that, my boy. Everyone you've ever met will die. Your sister, your friends. Me, for that matter."

"You exaggerate. I've met hundreds of people in my lifetime. Thousands, maybe."

Aurelius said with quiet gravity, "Maximillian will kill every single person in Dupree, down to the last newborn babe, if necessary, to protect this secret."

Eben stared, shocked to his core to realize that Aurelius was serious.

The elf continued, "More is at stake than merely a lie told by the Emperor. Maximillian cannot afford for anyone to question his version of truth as he presents it. In that direction lies disaster. I have come to believe that the Empire is less substantial than Maximillian would have anyone know. I do not know the extent of his deception, but I am convinced that deception lies at the heart of his throne."

Eben frowned. Aurelius was alluding obliquely to something that lay just beyond his comprehension. He didn't like these mind games and layers of subtlety within subtlety. They were more Raina's delight than his.

The one fact he could latch on to was that, if he revealed who his father was, a lot of people could die. People he cared about. "All right, then," he declared. "I will never say anything to anybody about who you believe my father to be."

"I'm not wrong about him."

"Fine. I will not say anything to anybody about who my father is."

"Everything depends upon it, Eben."

"My lips are sealed!"

"Thank you." Aurelius's tone was conciliatory. "The good news is your father was able to have children at all. If the Hand of Winter did not stop your father from having children, then maybe he did not do the same to me."

Eben frowned. "I thought I heard something once of some curse upon solinari that makes them not have many children."

"It's called the Culling. As far as we can tell, a great wave of magic passed over the land, and in its wake, exceptionally long-lived races like the solinari and nulvari found reproducing to be much more difficult."

"Huh. That's too bad. Although on the other hand, if it were not so, we'd all be overrun with elves."

Aurelius's mouth twitched with humor. "You say that as if it's a bad thing."

Eben grinned. "No offense meant."

"None taken."

He stood up with the idea of going to bed.

But Aurelius forestalled him, saying, "I have one more thing for you before the bunch of you go haring off into the wilds again on your next adventure."

Eben replied, "We don't get into trouble intentionally, you know. It just has a way of coming to us."

"And it will keep doing so until you have completed your quest to wake the Sleeping King," Aurelius retorted. He rose from the desk and moved over to one of Leland's chests under a wall of bookshelves.

Eben watched him curiously as he opened a chest and rummaged around in it for a moment.

Aurelius straightened, and in his hands was a familiar suit of boiled leather armor, with a shirt of the finest chain mail sewn to it. The familiar White Stag of Hyland rose on its hind legs on a field of dark green. *Leland's armor.*

"We've been over this before!" Eben burst out. "It's *his* suit. I will not—"

"He would want you to have it. This armor isn't doing anyone any good gathering dust in a chest. He's gone, Eben. You would honor him by wearing his colors and letting his armor protect you."

For the first time since his foster father's death, he was able to seriously consider the idea of accepting Leland's armor. Still, he stared at the suit doubtfully.

"Wear it for Kendrick. You can give the suit to him once you rescue him, if you want. But you need the protection, and your friends need your protection. The further you go with this quest, the greater the danger you will face."

Eben hesitated one more second and then reached out to take the suit. It was lighter than he'd expected. But then, Leland would have worn only the very best armor.

"Put it on. I'll help you adjust it."

Eben was surprised to discover that his chest was larger around than Leland's. As a child, he'd always thought of his foster father as such a big, imposing man. He might fill the man's armor, but he doubted he would ever fill Leland's shoes.

Rynn smiled, his heart heavy, as Eben left the office wearing Leland Hyland's armor. "It looks good on you," he said gamely to his friend. The passing on of a person's weapons and armor was one of the most irrevocable and final symbols of death among his kind.

He stepped into the office in Eben's wake, bowing his head respectfully to Aurelius. The Oneiri had long believed the Mage's Guildmaster was one of the most intelligent and dangerous men in all of Haelos, and Rynn was coming to agree with the group of paxan scholars regarding him.

"There you are, Rynn. I have your new headband." Aurelius stood up and moved over to a chest under the window, emerging with a square, flattish box. "Of course, it is not nearly so finely made as your original one. Unfortunately, I do not have the resources of a paxan prince at hand to call upon the finest paxan artisans to make a replacement for you."

Rynn pursed his lips. He'd left that life far behind a long time ago and had no wish to resurrect it. "I'm sure this will be fine. Anything is better than roaming abroad with my eye totally uncovered for any chance passerby to see." He took the box and opened it. "This is an excellent facsimile. Thank you. What do I owe you for it?"

"Nothing. Consider it my way of thanking you for looking out for my young friends."

"It has been my honor. And honestly, they've looked out for me as much as I've looked out for them."

"They've accepted you as one of their company, then?"

"Yes."

"I have a favor to ask of you, Rynn."

"Anything, Guildmaster."

"Have you, in your dream travels, seen the child we believe to be Vesper and her guard, the Gaged Man, whom Eben speaks of?"

"I have."

"My request is this: Would you share with me a memory of what those two look like?"

"Of course. But . . . if I might ask . . . why?"

"I believe the day is coming sooner rather than later when one or both of them will figure out how to manifest themselves on this plane once more. If I do not miss my guess, we may have only a matter of seconds to react to them before they attack. I need to recognize them when I see them." He paused for a moment and then added, "Also, I would like you to share the images with Selea Rouge."

That made him pull back sharply. "I would not presume to enter his mind unless Master Selea wished it."

A small commotion in the hallway outside announced the arrival of some late visitor. Aurelius commented, "That would be Selea now. You may ask him his wishes in the matter directly."

"My wishes in what matter?" the nulvari asked as he entered the chamber.

"Whether or not you want me to insert a memory of what Vesper and her Gaged Man look like," Rynn answered.

"That would be acceptable," Selea replied. "Has he already done so for you, Aurelius?"

"He was about to."

"Carry on."

Rynn got the impression Selea wanted Aurelius to go first and make sure the paxan didn't blow up his brain or indulge in any other shenanigans. Privately amused, he moved over to Aurelius and reached for the elf's temple. "This won't hurt."

Rynn really did try to just insert the memory and get out, but Aurelius's thoughts were so vivid and moving so quickly that Rynn was not able to block them all. The elf's mind was all abuzz over the fact that General Tarses had children and what it might mean for his own ability to have a family. He caught a glimpse of Aurelius's raw worry over his . . . ah, grandson! He'd had no idea that Will was the guildmaster's adopted offspring. Interesting.

"You have the images?" Rynn murmured aloud.

"Clear as a sunny day."

Rynn turned to Selea. Stars only knew what chaff he would pick up in this one's mind. "Ready?" he asked.

Selea exhaled slowly, and his entire body went preternaturally still. "Go ahead."

Rynn touched Selea's temple, and the elf's mind was as still and silent as Aurelius's was bustling and loud. Shocked, Rynn summoned the memory to his own mind and offered it to the cold and dark that was the mind of Selea Rouge. The memory disappeared. He assumed it had been absorbed, but he had no way of telling. The man's mind was a dark, blank canvas.

Rynn jerked his hand away from the elf's warm skin. How a mind so cold could exist within living flesh, he could not fathom.

"Are you all right?" Aurelius asked in quick concern.

"Um, yes. I'm fine. Do you have the image, Master Selea?"

"Aye." A short half bow.

He bowed back out of long habit. In all the centuries he'd been doing mind touches, he had never experienced a presence so utterly still, not even in the greatest meditators of his kind. So. That was the mind of a master assassin, was it? No wonder Selea was so very good at what he did. No emotion whatsoever had rippled across that mental surface to disturb its glassy calm.

Selea turned to Aurelius. "How did your young protégés take the news that they must leave Dupree immediately?"

"Better than you might think."

"Speaking of which," Rynn offered up, "did Eben tell you that he and I were attacked by a half dozen bandits on our way back from the pub earlier?"

Both elves spun to face him. "How did you fare? Were either of you injured?"

Rynn pulled a face. "Surely you jest. Six common bandits stood no chance against myself and Eben. You should be inquiring after *their* injuries."

"But were they, indeed, common bandits?" Selea asked.

"I had to erase a few memories of the fight because my hood came off and revealed my third eye." Rynn grinned sheepishly. "I might have poked around a bit while I was inside their noggins."

"And?" Aurelius demanded.

"They were hired by a man I did not recognize. He had a distinctive tattoo on his right forearm, however. A serpent wrapped around it, terminating with its head upon the back of his hand. It was singularly ugly."

"Coil," Aurelius stated in disgust.

"Anton's thugs?" Rynn asked.

"One and the same," Selea answered dryly. "They all wear snake tattoos of one kind or another."

"You did warn us that Anton would come at us with more force after we made our escape. You were not wrong, Guildmaster."

"And now he will come at you with even more men and skilled fighters," Aurelius grumbled.

"We will handle the threats as they come," Rynn answered calmly. "We have yet to be tested to the limits of our ability."

"Take back those words!" Aurelius exclaimed. "You will jinx yourself and the party!"

Aurelius had a right to be nervous, he supposed. Will was his only living heir, and the sun elves took family legacies more seriously than most.

"Can they do it, Rynn?" Aurelius asked without warning.

"I beg your pardon?"

"Can Will and Raina and the rest of you wake the Sleeping King?"

Rynn hesitated, unsure of how to answer.

Selea stepped into the pause, commenting, "The forces lining up against them are formidable. We cannot put all our hopes upon them alone."

Rynn frowned, bringing all his many years of strategic and tactical training to bear upon the question. "Undoubtedly, the quest will become more difficult the closer they get to the goal. However, I think they may pull it off. After all, they have the greatest advantage on their side: they dare to try."

The First slipped into the room, content to stand in the shadows by the door and study the other seven conspirators gathered in the room. They were all powerful nobles in their own rights, sons and daughters of the Kothite archdukes and duchesses. Each of them had inherited immortality from their parents. However, due to the immortality of those same parents, none of these conspirators would ever inherit a throne or title. He, of course, was in the same predicament.

Not that lust for power motivated him. Not by a long shot. Abhorrence of what Maximillian did to the common people of Urth, grinding them slowly and inexorably into dust beneath his all-powerful heel, was his true motivator.

That, and maybe a little boredom.

After all, not only was he immortal, but through a strange quirk of great magics cast long ago, none who saw him or spoke with him had any capacity to remember him at all, except in the presence of a rare gem called octavium. The green stone protected the minds of its wearers from magical effects that erased memory.

"Ah, good. You are come," one of his co-conspirators said, spying him at last. "We have news from the east."

"You speak of the stormcopper rokken statue, I assume?"

"Can you imagine it? One of the Dwarven King's own guards captured for all time in metal? The things we could learn if only it could speak."

The First smiled broadly. "Funny you should say that. As it turns out, he can speak."

A minor furor erupted around the table. He waited for it to subside and then announced, "I have received word from a reliable source that the statue was successfully unmade. The Dwarven King's man lives and breathes once more. As we speak, he is being brought to us with all possible haste."

"To us?" one of the others exclaimed. "It is folly to bring him here so close to court!"

The First replied, "Where else would you hide such a man? Where is the very last place anyone will search for this ancient guard?" When no one ventured an answer to his questions, he supplied the entirely obvious answer. "Right here. Underneath the nose of the Emperor himself."

"Still. It's dangerous."

"I never said it wasn't. I merely said it was least dangerous here."

"What do you suppose he will tell us?" someone speculated.

The First answered grimly, "I hope he will tell us where to find the final resting place of the Dwarven King. Perchance we can find the body of the king and prove that he did, indeed, exist once upon a time. If we're lucky, the guard will also fill in some gaps in our knowledge of the rise of the Kothite Empire."

"And if we're very lucky, he'll hold the key to toppling the almighty Maximillian from his Black Throne once and for all," one of the younger members of the Eight, a hothead prone to grand statements, declared.

The First managed not to roll his eyes. The existence of a single key that could take down Maximillian was much to ask for. His own private hope was more modest: that the wakened rokken would help break down the great curse of forgetting that had held the people of Urth in its thrall for all these centuries.

He'd spent thousands of years researching the Great Forgetting, as he'd dubbed it, and as best he could tell, if enough irrefutable facts came to light that proved the Great Forgetting to be a lie, the curse itself would begin to break down. As that happened, Maximillian's creatures for erasing memories—the oblivi—would be overwhelmed by the sheer number of people beginning to remember the real history of their planet. Gradually, memory would win out over oblivion. And with memory he hoped would come anger. Enough anger to topple the eternal Empire.

It was as good a goal as any to a man with no dreams, no home, and no name.

"How soon will this rokken get here?" one of the others asked eagerly.

It could not be soon enough for him. He'd been patient for longer than any one person should have to be—lifetimes stacked upon lifetimes he'd waited for this.

Raina fingered the letter in her pocket as she hurried toward the Mage's Guild. A late-winter snowstorm had blown in overnight, and it howled around her this morning, flinging sharp crystals of snow against what little exposed skin she had, bundled up as she was against the cold.

The guard on duty at the Mage's Guild recognized her and let down the wizard's lock before she reached the door. She blew into the main foyer on a frigid gust, surprised as always by its formality and opulence in comparison to the humble comforts of the Heart building.

"What business brings you to our doorstep this blustery

day, Emissary?" a Celestial Order of the Dragon knight asked her courteously.

"Greetings, Sir Bruin. I believe the guildmaster is expecting me."

"I will announce you. Would you like to step into the salon and take a cup of hot tea while you wait?"

"That would be lovely." It had been a long time since she'd taken tea like a civilized person or sat in a formal salon, no less. Even her mother in Tyrel had not had such a space.

Her tea had barely cooled to a sippable temperature before Aurelius himself swept into the salon.

"Emissary. You do us great honor by gracing our halls with your lovely presence."

She smiled wryly. "Your halls are plenty lovely all by themselves."

Aurelius's eyes twinkled. He murmured under his breath as he escorted her upstairs to his private office, "One must put on a good show if one wishes to be taken at face value."

He escorted her into his office and activated a wizard's lock upon the space as she took a seat in front of his desk. She commented, "I sincerely doubt anyone who knows you would make the mistake of taking you at face value, Guildmaster."

"Too bad. The more superficial I seem, the less people really look at me."

"Like all members of your race, you are so dazzling to behold I suspect most do not see beyond that."

"One can hope." Abruptly dropping all pretense of formality, he said, "You sent me a note that we needed to have our meeting right away. What has changed?"

"I need to retrieve a certain item I left in your care some time ago."

"Indeed? You want Gawaine's crown back? Do you have reason to believe you will need it sooner than we anticipated?"

She twirled the unicorn ivory ring upon the middle finger of her right hand. "You're going to think me mad for saying this, but I think the crown is calling to me. Or rather, it's calling to this ring."

Aurelius stared at the intricately carved band that had magically shrunk to fit her finger exactly when she'd first put it on. "Do tell."

"I keep dreaming about the crown. And when I wake up in the morning, I have this overwhelming urge to come to you and get it."

"May I take a look at the ring?" he asked.

"It won't come off my finger, but you may certainly examine it."

"Do you mean that it fits too closely to come off easily or that it will not come off at all, in the same way Will's disk of Bloodroot's heartwood will not come off his chest?"

"Neither. This ring has definitely not grown onto my finger the same way Will's disk grew onto him. But no matter what actions we take in the Heart, we cannot get this ring to let go of my finger. It . . . clasps . . . my finger and refuses to let go."

Aurelius touched the ring with his fingertips and murmured a series of spells that would let him learn more about the ring. Eventually, he sat back. "Well, it seems to like being where it is."

"You say that as if it's sentient," she blurted.

"It is, after a fashion. A person could not have an intelligent conversation with it, but it has a thread of consciousness running through it, and it has definite opinions. I believe it experiences basic emotions."

She frowned, trying to understand. "Like a shard of a spirit? A piece of some greater awareness, perhaps?"

"That is as good a description as any," Aurelius allowed. He unlocked a drawer in his desk and reached inside. "Mayhap a small experiment is in order."

"What would that be?"

"I wonder what will happen if we put Gawaine's crown and his signet ring together."

Raina took the green garland with its perpetually living, gold-edged leaves. The gold filigree woven in among the living greens was warm in her hand. A few of the leaves brushed against the ring on her finger, and she cried out in surprise.

"Are you all right?" Aurelius asked quickly.

"I'm fine. It's just that they"—she searched for a word—"recognized each other. It was like the burst of excitement two great friends might feel upon seeing each other after a long separation."

"Interesting."

She stroked the delicate leaves of the crown, amazed at the vibrant life coursing through them. It reminded her of Gawaine himself. Given the warmth and energy of his dreaming echo, she had trouble imagining what the real man would be like. Assuming they managed to find his physical body and wake him up one day, of course.

"How soon can you be ready to leave Dupree, Raina? Will your duties as emissary delay you for long?"

She laughed. "They don't know what to do with my new rank over at the Heart. The high matriarch has been sending me to the hideously boring staff meetings at the governess's palace that she wishes to avoid."

He made a sympathetic sound. "I know those meetings all too well."

"I did get a letter from Lord Goldeneye this morning. It's a writ of safe passage through Dominion-held lands."

"Too bad Gawaine is not likely hidden up that way."

"In your quest with Selea and Leland, did you ever get any sense of where Gawaine's physical body might be resting?"

"None, but I can tell you powerful forces hide it and hide it well."

She gulped. "I was afraid you would say that."

Aurelius was quiet for a minute. Then he announced without warning, "Eben and Rynn were attacked again last night."

"What?" She rose out of her seat in alarm. "Are they all right?"

Aurelius smiled crookedly. "Oh, they're just fine. The ruffians who jumped them cannot say the same, apparently."

She subsided in her seat, deeply worried about how thick and fast the attacks upon them were becoming.

Aurelius was speaking again. "I believe it to be in all your best interests to leave this city immediately. It is a hotbed of Anton's spies and flunkies."

"You say that as if it will be better out in the countryside."

"There is less love for the Empire, and for our former governor, out among the common people."

"Perhaps," she said doubtfully.

"Your new rank will be both a boon and a hindrance when you travel henceforth. You may be able to use it to your advantage in public situations, but I fear it will draw a great deal of attention to you and your friends that may not always be friendly."

"I understand, but I cannot abandon my rank. A rapprochement with the Dominion is more important than my anonymity or my safety."

Aurelius replied with wry humor, "Ah. Politics has started to affect your choices. You are growing up, child."

Sometimes she wished the world were not as complicated a place as she was learning it to be. "In answer to your earlier question, I can be ready to leave on but a few hours' notice. My real problem will be in devising a way to ditch the Royal Order of the Sun."

"Why ditch them? Why not take one or two of them along? They will make your travels a great deal safer."

"Perhaps in the settled lands, Royal Order of the Sun colors would ensure us safe passage. But once we cross the Estarran Sea and venture into the west, I do not believe the same could be said of them. If anything, Royal Order of the Sun guardians would draw the ire and ill will of any locals who saw them."

He shrugged. "So let them take you to the edge of Estarra, then. Do not turn your back on safe passage through lands thick with Anton Constantine's people."

"I imagine he has some sort of bounty out on our heads."

Aurelius made a face. "The way I hear it, the bounty on Will's head alone is outrageous enough to cause every adventurer in Haelos to be on the hunt for him."

"I'm going to be disappointed if there's not a decent bounty out on me, too."

"Never fear. There are heavy pouches of gold being offered for all of you."

Well. Wasn't that just going to make their lives even more fun than usual. Not only would they have to dodge the forces trying to stop them from waking Gawaine, but they also were going to have to avoid all human contact with any outsiders while doing it, apparently.

Into the wilds it was, then. Now she could only hope that that was where the next piece of Gawaine's regalia waited to be found.

CHAPTER

9

Number One leaned against a cold boulder, his feet stretched out to the small fire they'd allowed themselves this late-winter night. He and his two companions had found a small shelter, more overhang than cave, actually, but it kept the snow off their backs and protected them from the worst of the wind driving the snow along at a sharp angle.

He'd been sitting watch for a while. Nothing was abroad on a foul night like this, and all was silent around him except for the ominous howl of the wind from time to time.

And yet, he did not hear the shadowy figure as it approached. One second the cloaked figure was not there, and the next, it was. He started to come to his feet, sword lifting, but the figure quickly sank to his or her haunches in front of the fire and pushed the cloak hood back. Female. Young. Jann. He registered peripherally that she was beautiful, and her white skin had pale blue striations upon it that reflected the hue of the snow around them.

He opened his mouth to ask her identity, but she lifted a warning hand at him. Instead, the sound of a musical female voice inserted itself directly into his head. Alarmed, he started to rise again, sword in hand.

"Be at ease, traveler," the voice said. "I mean you no harm. Sit."

Number One sank back down onto the cold stone, staring. How did she do that? He had been a practitioner of every conceivable kind of magic over the years, and he'd never seen such a trick.

He stared at her, and she gazed back at him steadily. Her eyes were the deepest pools of black he'd ever seen. The kind of dark a person could lose themselves in, swimming down, down . . .

The snow turned to fog around him, still cool and moist upon his skin, but abruptly lacking the bite of winter. Through the mist, an indistinct glow, as of moonlight shining down through the fog, illuminated the little cave.

"I know who you are," the young woman said.

"I am no one. I have no identity for you to know," he retorted.

"And yet, I know yours. You are—"

"Do not speak it!" He cut her off before she could utter the name he had forsaken long ago. After all, names had power. And true names had even more.

"I need you to do something for me," she said. "A small favor, really. Nothing difficult."

His gaze narrowed suspiciously. "I've had plenty of dealings with dryads over the years. If you're one of them in disguise, do not think to ensorcel me. I know your queen, and she would not be pleased."

The young woman laughed. "I am no dryad, but thank you for the compliment."

"Then who—"

"As I was saying," she interrupted, "I need you to do something for me. I need you to give me something that belongs to each of your companions. Something small that they will not even miss. A button off a shirt or a hairpin. And you must get these items without waking up your friends. Can you do that?"

"Of course I *can*," he answered scornfully. "But why would I?"

"Because I ask it of you," the woman responded persuasively.

"Nay. I will no—"

"You will do it." Her voice took on a note like steel, as hard and unyielding as his sword's edge.

Something deep within Number One recognized the tone

of command. Responded to it automatically. He nodded slowly. "I will do it."

What was this? Her request was ridiculous. What possible use could she have for a button and a hairpin? He stood up slowly and moved stealthily around the fire to where his two companions slept. After all, she'd said not to wake them. He reached into Number Two's pack and rummaged around, coming up with a length of hair cord. It was a simple leather strip she used sometimes to bind her hair behind her head.

"Will this do?" he asked his guest quietly.

"Perfect."

He nodded and moved on to Number Three's pack. What was something he would not miss? His fingers encountered several half-carved sticks in the bottom of the bag. Number Three was forever whittling on one or another of them to pass the time. He opened his fist and saw a large, curved tooth lying in his fist. Number Three hadn't carved this one. Perfect. It was the sort of object Number Three didn't use on a routine basis and wouldn't be likely to miss immediately. Later, he would likely assume he'd lost it.

Number One made his way back to the fire and the mysterious young woman. "Here." He held out the items to her. "Do you need something from me, too?" he asked.

Now why had those words come out of his mouth? He had no desire to help this intruder with whatever she was up to.

"No, thanks be. We already have something that once belonged to you. It was one of your most prized possessions, I hear."

He frowned. He'd lost nothing of great value in a while. Except his home. And his name, of course.

"Will I see you again?" he asked.

"You may hear from me again someday. And you will most certainly hear from my mistress, who is now your mistress, as well."

Surprise arced through him. "I have no mistress!"

"Ah, but you do."

He made a sound of disagreement, and she responded gently, "Why else did you give me exactly what I asked for, then? Your will is no longer yours alone to control, my friend. And the sooner you accept that, the easier it will go on you and your friends."

The young woman rose gracefully to her feet and drew the hood of her cloak over her sable hair and pale face. "Thank you for sharing the warmth of your fire this night. Sweet dreams to you and yours."

And with that strange blessing, she disappeared into the night as silently as she had appeared. He blinked, amazed at how she'd been there one second and simply been gone the next. When he opened his eyes, the fog was gone, and the snow was back, driven at an angle by a frigid wind that cut through his cloak and chilled him to the bone.

What bizarre dream was that? Had he dozed off for a minute and imagined that strange apparition? He got up, moved quickly around the fire, and stared down in shock. Dainty footprints disturbed the thin blanket of drifted snow. Horrified, he tried to track the prints out of the cave, but as he reached the edge of the overhang, they stopped. Simply stopped. There were no footprints at all in the deeper layer of snow over here. None into the cave. And none out.

What on Urth? Or rather, who on Urth?

He probably ought to wake the others. Tell them about his odd hallucination. Except they would think him touched in the head. And it was a brutally cold night. Both of his companions were hunkered down deep inside their bedrolls and cloaks, with nothing but their noses showing. They'd earned their rest, for they'd been traveling long and hard these many months now.

Let them stay warm in their beds. His dream visitor could wait until the morn in its telling. Although he suspected that with the coming of dawn's light would come a return of his common sense. By dawn, his vision would no doubt seem too ridiculous even to him to bother mentioning. He and his companions had more important things to think about. Like beating Anton Constantine to the one thing the ex-governor wanted worse than life itself.

* * *

Will tugged at his brand-new Mage's Guild tabard, royal blue with a gold, four-pointed star over his heart and a long comet tail stretching from the start to his right hip. Although he'd technically been an apprentice of the guild for a while, he'd never bothered wearing official colors before. Guild colors got in the way of blending in with regular people and traveling unnoticed and unremembered.

Of course, this garish procession they made now would hardly go unnoticed. Two Royal Order of the Sun knights led the way in their full white-and-red-trimmed, armed and armored glory. Raina paced behind them in her white clothing trimmed in blue. Then there was Eben in the purple and black of the Merchant's Guild, Rosana in her red-and-white Heart colors, and him in his Mage's Guild blue. Only Sha'Li and Rynn did not wear guild colors. But one was a black-scaled lizardman girl bristling with weapons all over her person, and the other a tall, spectacularly handsome paxan. They looked like a traveling circus.

Will had not been any more pleased than the others to find out that they were stuck with a Royal Order of the Sun escort as far as the Estarran Sea. Raina had explained that it was a compromise. She would let the order accompany her partway on their journey in return for the knights leaving them once they crossed Estarra into the west. Apparently, the Royal Order of the Sun knights were no happier about the arrangement than Will.

He had to admit, though, they made good time with the knights along. Everyone got out of their way upon the road, and rooms were always available for them at any inn they came across. Food was served hot and ale served cold. Their beds were comfortable and clean, and even fresh baths were forthcoming for them.

The week it took them to trek southwest through Hyland to the southern mouth of the Estarran Sea and the port of Seastar was honestly the most luxury Will had ever experienced in his young life. He supposed he could see how people got used to it, but he would still prefer a warm fire and a hard bedroll on the ground beneath the stars.

At least the long walk gave him plenty of time to think about how he was going to propose to Rosana. Rynn and Eben had the right of it. He had to come up with some gift, something of great personal meaning to both of them. And then he would need to find a beautiful place, a private moment with just the two of them . . .

But how? Out here on the road, they were always with their friends, looking over their shoulders for threats or running for their lives, it seemed. He had coins in his pouch these days thanks to his small salary as a Mage's Guild member, but he had no idea what to get for Rosana with them. He would ask Raina for advice, but he had no faith in her not to tell Rosana what was afoot. The two were thick as thieves with one another. Sha'Li was arguably the toughest fighter among them all. Not to mention she'd grown up in the heart of the Angor Swamp. No telling what she would consider to be a proper romantic gesture.

Raina spoke up from ahead of him on the dusty road. "Do you think we should spend the night in Seastar, or should we press on down to the docks and try to arrange passage immediately across the sea?"

Sir Hrothgar, who had been chosen to accompany Raina, answered quickly. "Please do not attempt the crossing of the Bone Reef at night, Emissary. It is dangerous enough in broad daylight with a skilled captain at the tiller."

"What makes it so dangerous?" Rosana asked.

Sha'Li answered, "It is the graveyard of the leviathans. Their great bones stick out in all directions and will tear a hole in an unwary boat. A coral reef has formed over them, making them even sharper and more dangerous. And then there are the difficult currents that swirl among them. A treacherous passage it makes for even a shallow-bottomed barge."

Will asked, "Is that why no Black Ships sail the Estarran Sea? They can't get into it?"

Rynn answered, "That, and there's the small matter of the Merr and their baron, Occyron the Six-Gilled, who claims Estarra for himself."

"It's true, then?" Will responded. "Even Koth does not challenge the Merr?"

"Not underwater," Hrothgar answered. "It would be like attacking a bear in its own cave."

Sha'Li remarked, "Too bad Kothites do not have gills."

Will stared at her. "You consider Kothites preferable to Merr, then?"

Raina cleared her throat gently, and he glanced up at her. Oh. Right. Royal Order of the Sun knights were within earshot. He was accustomed on the road to being able to speak freely with his companions, none of whom had much use for the Empire.

Sha'Li prudently did not answer his question, which had the potential to wander into treasonous territory. She did, however, roll her eyes at him behind the knights' backs, silently making her opinion of Merr crystal clear. Of course, lizardmen and Merr were known to compete over water territory the same way land walkers competed for control over countries and continents.

Will noted that, as they passed a public proclamation board in the town square of Seastar, Rynn reached out unobtrusively and tore down a sheet of parchment. It had the look of some sort of official proclamation. The paxan stuffed it in his pouch and said nothing about it. What was that all about?

Thanon and a company of his men, a hundred in total, arrived in Seastar in the late afternoon. Following the White Heart emissary and her entourage had been no hardship at all for his campaign-hardened men, accustomed to traveling much farther under much worse conditions carrying much more gear. He settled them in the local Imperial Army barracks with orders to go into town and drink their fill but not to draw any notice to themselves. Trained Special Forces troops one and all, they were adept at blending in with locals. And in the event any of them ran into trouble, all the men in this, his elite company, were paxan and fully capable of adjusting or erasing the odd memory here and there.

They left the barracks by twos and threes over the next

several hours, fanning out through the city quietly to reconnoiter where the emissary and her entourage had landed and to suss out what Raina planned to do next.

It made no sense for a brand-new emissary to hare off into the countryside like this. And the way his informants reported it, the Royal Order of the Sun was deeply irritated over this journey she made. The secrecy around it was enough to rouse Thanon to curiosity. And curiosity was a sensation he'd learned long ago to trust and investigate.

What matter was so pressing that Lord Justinius didn't forbid the White Heart emissary from making a dangerous foray into the untamed lands, if, indeed, that was where she was headed?

When two of his men reported back in the early evening that they'd found the emissary and her companions at a local inn, the Pour House, Thanon went there, hood pulled low over his face, and slipped into the common room unobtrusively to surveil Raina and her companions.

W ill couldn't complain about the accommodations on their journey so far. The inn Hrothgar took them to in Seastar was far more respectable than any place he and his friends would have stayed at on their own. As they relaxed in the Pour House's common room over supper, a call went up for a song among the patrons.

A wandrakin woman stood up from a tableful of merchants and sailors. "And what would you have me sing?" she asked the room at large.

"Sing 'The Lay of the Sleeping King'!" someone shouted.

Will's breath caught, and he glanced at his companions in quick alarm. Raina's face was frozen in a mask of a smile, and the others stared fixedly at the ceiling or down at the table boards.

The woman began to sing in a clear soprano that danced across his skin like a stream in springtime, "*In all my travels far and near, ne'er was a land so fair as Gandymere. A kingdom fine and full of grace, its king the noblest of his race . . .*"

The epic poem described a prosperous country ruled for a century by a young and handsome king. Peace reigned over the land, and it was the envy of all who did not live there. But in the way of all shining jewels, a neighboring king, the green troll Rudath, coveted it. He invaded Gandymere and laid waste to all in his path.

It seemed that Gawaine had made the mistake of believing that if he made all of his people happy, his kingdom would be secure. He did not realize that the very peace and prosperity he had given his people would also spell his doom. For it was not the way of man to be happy. According to the bard who wrote the tale, it was the way of man to be jealous and greedy, to want what his neighbor had, and to take it by force.

War came to Gandymere, and its green and verdant abundance was burned and slashed, the land left barren and wasted. Gawaine formed a great elven army and marched forth to do battle with the invader, Rudath. Blood flowed in rivers on both sides of the conflict. Exhausted, the two armies came together for one last battle that would decide the fate of Gandymere and its fair king.

The two kings agreed to do single combat, one with the other, and spare their badly depleted armies any more deaths.

The entire inn was hushed as the singer launched into the final verses. She described the two kings stepping out in front of their armies and engaging in a brutal, bloody duel that went on for an hour. They were evenly matched, Rudath and Gawaine. The troll was bigger and stronger, but Gawaine was quick and smart. Back and forth they fought, spilling each other's blood and testing each other's formidable wills.

Finally, in desperation, Rudath took a mighty swing with his great war axe. Gawaine could try to block the blow, or he could drop his defenses, step into the opening Rudath had created, and plunge his sword into the troll's heart. They would both die, but the war would be over.

Gawaine lunged with his sword as the axe swung down. The two kings traded mortal blows, pitching forward into each other's arms, dying as one, still locked in mortal combat.

Will let out the breath he realized he'd been holding as the martial melody shifted into a lament.

The elven army cried out as one as their fair king fell, and they rushed forward to retrieve his body. Each army laid its king tenderly upon his shield and carried their respective king back to his own battle lines. But as the elves laid down their fallen leader, a ghostly, glowing figure of a lady appeared at Gawaine's feet. It was his own mother, the Green Lady, come to fetch the spirit of her son home. As the soldiers looked on, Gawaine's spirit rose out of his body and took the hand she offered to him, and the two drifted beyond the Veil, disappearing into the land of spirits departed. There, the fair king Gawaine's spirit now walked in green meadows, forever young, feasting and participating in contests at arms with the spirits of his loyal soldiers who died for him and for lost Gandymere.

A deep silence fell over the crowd as the last, sad notes of the song floated away. Then, as one, Will and everybody else in the room burst into cheers and thunderous applause, pounding mugs on tables and stomping their feet in approval.

"Lady Hymner!" many of the voices shouted.

"Huzzah for the landsgrave!" others called.

That woman was a landsgrave? He leaned forward to ask where her lands lay, and Raina anticipated his question, murmuring, "She's landsgrave of Morassa. She rules from the city of Dumaw, across the Bone Reef on the western shore of the Estarran Sea."

"Well, she's a fine singer," Will declared.

Rynn smiled. "It doesn't hurt that she's a wandrakin. They have a special affinity for language and music. They give power to words that few others can."

Eben commented, "Beware of trading with wandrakin. They'll talk circles around you and end up getting the shirt off your back."

"A singing con artist. That should make for an interesting landsgrave," Will retorted.

Hrothgar sent him a quelling look down the table, and Will

heeded it. He didn't need any trouble with Raina's guards on this last night with them.

The next morning, however, Will did argue when the Royal Order of the Sun knights tried to put Raina on an expensive Merr longboat to cross the Estarran Sea. The sleek ship had a dozen oarsmen and great square sails to propel it, and if the stylized musical symbol on the chests of a dozen crates already aboard was any indication, Landsgrave Hymner would be taking the ship as well. The last thing they needed was to be cooped up with some Imperial noble for hours on end. While Raina might relish all that diplomatic stuff, he did not.

Besides, no commoner could afford passage on such a vessel. If they were to arrive on the far side of the sea in such a craft, at best they would be shunned as Imperial servants. At worst, they would be marked for robbery and murder by local brigands.

When he pointed that fact out to Sir Hrothgar, the knight retorted, "If the emissary is not going to be properly protected, we will not let her go at all—"

Raina cut him off. "That was not my deal with Lord Justinius. I allowed you to accompany me this far in return for you allowing me to continue across the sea without you."

Hrothgar scowled. "My duty forbids me from letting these children be your only protection."

Raina replied sternly, "And yet your honor requires you to abide by your promise. My friends may be young, but we are far from children. We've faced more and greater dangers than you can imagine."

"Like what?" Hrothgar challenged.

"I'm confident Lord Justinius did not send you here to argue with me, sir knight," Raina said in a voice so polite and chilly it sent frost down Will's spine. Wow. Where did she learn that tone of voice? Even his mother would have been hard pressed to achieve such an infusion of command, and she was an elf.

Scowling, the Royal Order of the Sun knights took their

leave quickly after that. Will sighed a great breath of relief as their white-clad backs retreated into the crowd at the docks. He immediately stripped off his Mage's Guild tabard and stuffed it in his pack while all the others except Raina did the same. She did, however, change out of her spotless, elegantly embroidered White Heart tunic bearing the emissary's badge and replaced it with a stained and rumpled White Heart tabard that had seen plenty of hard times. There. Now they looked like themselves again.

He gazed up and down the quay. "Looks like there's a barge loading passengers down that way. Want to see if there's room for us aboard?"

Eben and Rynn, who were tall enough to see over much of the crowd, looked where he pointed and nodded. The three fellows used their size to elbow a path through the crowd for the girls, and all six of them reached the dock just as the barge captain, a scarred and weathered-looking Merr, started to step from the dock to his vessel.

"Is there room for six more?" Will called to him.

The Merr turned. Looked them up and down. "Don't look like the types to cause trouble, I suppose. No food or water supplied on the crossing. A gold a head."

"A gold?" Rynn exclaimed. "That's highway robbery! Three silver will get a person passage here at the narrow end of the sea."

The captain shrugged. "Ever since our treaty with Anton collapsed, the price has gone up."

"What treaty is that?" Raina asked quickly.

"Treaty giving pinkskin vessels permission to cross Estarra. New treaty says no ship with more than twelve souls aboard may cross unless it's a Merr vessel, and no Kothite cargo ships at all may cross."

Huh. That had to be putting a crimp in the Empire's construction schedule for Maren's Belt. The way he heard it, all the magical waestones being used to build the road were being hauled from the Dupree harbor, where they arrived in Black Ships, carted overland to Seastar, and then sailed across the Estarran Sea to where the road was being built. It was the only practical way to move tons of stone over great distances.

Will commented, "Landsgrave Hymner can't be too happy about the new treaty."

The Merr grinned, a rather horrible grimace revealing sharply pointed teeth. "Way I hear it, she just found out about it. She's been in Dupree and no one bothered to tell her." He shrugged. "Good for us, though."

Eben dug six gold coins out of his pouch and passed them to the captain. Will, no lover of boats, felt sick the moment he set foot upon the gently heaving barge. It was a big, rectangular vessel, and he could discern no visible method of propulsion. Maybe Merr swimming underwater pushed it forward like the last Merr boat they'd ridden. This barge's broad deck was crowded with mostly farmers and merchants. He guessed they'd brought wares to Dupree to sell and now returned home.

The sky was heavy and gray as they set out from Seastar, and before long, nothing but black water and that ominous sky were visible around them. Will shoved his way to the rail and hung over it miserably, emptying his stomach explosively and dry heaving after that.

Rosana rubbed his back sympathetically. She might be able to heal his wounds or cure actual diseases, but there was no cure for a landlubber's stomach.

"How long will this journey take?" he groaned under his breath.

"Rynn says it should take about eight hours. Unless we hit bad weather, of course."

He heaved again at the mere thought of riding out a storm on this cumbersome, open-decked vessel. They were all going to die, swept overboard by the first big waves. Off to the south, he made out a few small landmasses jutting out of the choppy water. Those must be some of the peaks of the underwater reef that had grown up over the leviathan skeletons. If their captain misjudged and sailed too close to it, the bottom of this barge would be ripped apart and they would all drown and . . . he heaved again.

Rosana squinted up at the dark, pregnant clouds. "Not exactly auspicious weather for starting our journey, is it?"

He grunted, too miserable for words.

"Where do you suppose Raina's dragging us off to in such a hurry?"

There was no telling with her. He shrugged in answer to Rosana's question.

The gypsy continued gaily, apparently oblivious to the gently rolling deck beneath their feet, "Do you suppose Raina's ring, or her *friend*, has told her where to look for the next item we seek?"

That was an excellent question. He'd been surprised to find out that Raina apparently dreamed of Gawaine on a regular basis. Maybe it was because she wore Gawaine's signet ring continuously.

Speaking of rings, he asked Rosana, "Do you like jewelry?" He tried to sound casual, but ended up sounded nervous and lame. Hopefully, she would attribute any strangeness to his seasickness.

"I'm a girl," she teased. "I love jewelry. The shinier the better."

"Any particular kind? Necklaces? Bracelets? Rings?"

"Why? Are you planning on getting me one?"

He smiled, feeling even more lame. "I just noticed that you wear none. I didn't know if that was a Heart thing, or a gypsy thing, or a you thing."

She shrugged. "If I have coin to spend, I buy healing potions to pass out to those who cannot afford them."

And that was why he loved her. She had a giant heart filled with compassion. Why else would she put up with him? Hanging on to the rail for balance with one hand, he put his free arm around her shoulder. "You're too good for me, Rosie."

She laughed. "And don't you forget it."

"I'm serious."

"Oh." A pause. Then she replied seriously, "No, you've got it backward. You come from a fancy family. And you're a talented caster, an accomplished warrior. Everyone says you'll be a Celestial Order of the Dragon knight before long."

He stared down at her. "Who says that?"

"Everybody, behind your back. People say you can hold your own against Captain Krugar and even beat him sometimes. And he's thought to be the greatest warrior in Haelos."

That was because his father was dead. Tiberius had been the greatest warrior in the land in his day. A familiar wave of grief passed through him. To distract himself, Will said ruefully, "To hear Aurelius speak of it, you'd think I'll be lucky to end up cleaning the Mage's Guild latrines."

"He just wants you to work hard and achieve your potential." Another pause. "So do I, Will. If the day comes when you need to be with people of more social standing than our friends and I have, I'll understand."

He drew back sharply, appalled. "I would never forsake you or the others for status or appearing to be more than I am. I'm just a kid from Hickory Hollow."

"Will," she chided gently. "You're so much more than that now. You're becoming a formidable warrior and an important man. Why else do you think Thanon and the Talons of Koth are recruiting you?"

"Oh, him. We merely bonded over fighting Boki together."

"It's more than that. Almost all of them are paxan, but they still want you, and you're human. They know you're special."

This whole business of growing up and becoming the man his father had secretly trained him to be felt so strange. Like he was shedding the only skin he'd ever known and transforming into another creature altogether. Or maybe this feeling was Bloodroot's fault.

Although the tree lord's spirit was mostly quiet within him these days, every now and then that *other* consciousness made itself known in no uncertain terms. Sometimes he wondered if Bloodroot weren't merely biding his time, planning and plotting some new means of manipulating and generally torturing his human host.

A faint rumble of humor from deep in the back of his mind vibrated through his skull in response to that thought.

He cursed at the treant. Obviously, Bloodroot was not done with Will, or the sliver of heartwood containing the tree lord's spirit would have dropped off his chest already.

Scowling, he glared out across the dull, unpolished steel color of the sea. The next time Gawaine asked him if he'd like to keep Bloodroot's spirit or get rid of it, by the stars, he was dumping the unnatural wretch.

Raina sighed in relief when their barge made landfall in Dumaw, a dusty outpost in the process of building up around a new Imperial Army fort and an Imperial Navy contingent that had recently been assigned to the area. The town was being developed by the new governess as the trade terminus of an overland cargo route from Fleuran, outside the Bone Reef, to Dumaw, inside it.

Raina supposed Dumaw could prove strategic as well for keeping out invaders who thought to find a passage through the Bone Reef and enter the Estarran Sea. Of course, the naval contingent might be equally useful for keeping local Merr contained within Estarra and away from the port of Dupree. Either way, the completion of Maren's Belt around the Estarran Sea should render the Merr kingdom significantly less strategic.

For a few more silver apiece, they were able to stay on the barge and sail up the west coast of the sea to the Sorrow Wold. Her companions expressed alarm when she made it known that was where she wished to go. As if she were not fully aware of the dangers of the Sorrow Wold already. She'd grown up not far from its margins and had heard plenty of stories of the monsters and bandits who lurked within its murky boughs.

It was nearly dawn when the barge's prow ground against a pebbled strand. Raina roused with her friends, and they waded ashore, woken sharply by the cold water on their bare feet and legs. Shivering, she found a driftwood log to sit on and don her boots.

As the first pink of dawn reflected off the sea like a fine sheen of oil, she turned her back on it to study the dark and forbidding forest looming before her. It looked grim and black under the heavy canopy's gloom, like the gaping maw of a great beast about to swallow her whole. And somewhere in the belly of the beast was Justin, waiting for her.

"I don't like it," Eben declared.

"Me, neither," Rynn agreed.

Sha'Li shrugged, saying nothing. Raina moved up beside the lizardman girl. "Near this forest lies a place called the Scholl Swamp. It's said to contain black lizardmen, but I've never seen one myself."

Sha'Li's gaze lit up. "Really? Can we go there?"

Raina shrugged. "If my errand or Gawaine's ring leads us there, I don't see why not. With you among our number, I would feel perfectly safe going there."

Sha'Li's guarded expression softened for a moment. "There is no need to cheer me up."

"I've been worried about you. Ever since what happened between you and Eben—"

"It was my fault. Blame him not."

"What exactly happened?" Raina finally got a chance to ask directly after all these months.

"I betrayed his trust." She shrugged. "The blame is mine."

"I'm sure it's not that bad. If you two talk it out, he'll get over it. He's not the kind to hold grudges."

Sha'Li responded, "I let Kerryl go. Eben had him cornered and was going to kill him. I interfered so Moonrunner could escape. Eben will not forgive me that."

Ah. Understanding dawned. No wonder Eben had been so furious with her. "Why did you let him go?"

"He pursues some good goal even if his methods are dubious. Evil he is not. After all, Kendrick chose to stay with him. I could not let Eben kill him."

"I agree completely, White Heart or not," Raina said firmly. "You did the right thing."

"Tell Eben that," Sha'Li replied bitterly.

"He'll come around. Just give him a little time."

"Six months he's had!"

"By the way, is it me, or are you getting better at speaking the way pinkskins do?"

That earned her a great, glowering glare from Sha'Li. "I have been practicing."

"You're doing great."

"Among my people, the most important meaning or part of a sentence is spoken last. But your kind always says the person or thing, the word of action, and then what or who they did it to. Boring it—" She paused, correcting herself. "It is a boring way to speak."

Raina grinned. "That's us. Boring pinkskins who never say or do anything interesting."

"Huh!" The grunt was as close to laughter as Sha'Li usually came.

Raina took it as a small victory to have elicited any sign of humor from her dour friend.

"Any idea exactly where in this forsaken forest we're supposed to go?" Will asked from the edge of the trees. "I see no trail."

"There will be paths aplenty," Raina replied. "And no, I have no specific destination in mind."

Rosana turned around. "You're going to drag us into that nightmare forest just to wander around? What's going on here? Why are we here, and why are you leading us in there?"

Now that they were finally alone, she could afford to fill them in. "The Mages of Alchizzadon have invited me to visit them. They told me to meet their guide in the Sorrow Wold, and he will take me the rest of the way."

"We're going with you," Will declared.

Raina shook her head. "Not the terms of the invitation. I have to go alone."

Rosana protested, "Sweetie, you know what they plan to do to you."

"They promised they will let me go whenever I want. They just want to talk."

Rynn was frowning. "Didn't you shout something about

Alchizzadon when we were in the Dominion lands? During the fight to close the gate, was it not?"

"Correct. The claviger was one of them."

"Who are these mages exactly?" he pressed.

She sighed. "It's a long story. They've been interbreeding with the women of my family for a very long time in hopes of increasing our magical prowess."

"If you're any indication, I should say they succeeded." Rynn snorted.

Raina rolled her eyes. "Nonetheless, they're not nice people, and they have secret agendas of their own that they pursue, apparently. I need to find out what they're up to beyond trying to kidnap me and use me for their own purposes."

That sent Rynn's eyebrows sailing upward. "Do you really think it's a good idea to visit them?"

"No! I think it's a terrible idea, but if I don't make nice with them, they will kidnap me, drain my magic, and kill me permanently."

"That's it. You're not going alone," Will declared.

"Really, I appreciate your concern, but I have to do this."

"Is it a White Heart thing?" Sha'Li asked.

Rosana jumped in to declare, "No. It's not. It's a stupid Raina thing."

Raina sighed. They didn't understand. Justin was tangled up with the mages, who'd already performed some unnatural magic on him to make him part ogre mage. She had to make sure he was safe and rescue him if necessary. He would do the same for her; she could do no less for him.

She hefted her pack higher on her shoulders. "Let's do this."

Princess Endellian sat on the raised dais of the Imperial banquet table, looking out across the great feasting hall at dozens of long rows of tables holding the entirety of the assembled court. Her father, directly to her left, looked as disinterested as he usually did at these affairs, but even Maximillian understood the necessity of keeping the nobles and petty functionaries occupied with pomp, politics, parties, and of course alcohol. Lots and lots of that to dull their minds and distract them from the genuinely important matters of ruling the Empire.

The feast would go on for hours still. At least a dozen courses of lavish food had come and gone, and there were a dozen more to go. Everyone would be so gorged when they finally departed the tables in the wee hours of the morning that they would have barely the wherewithal to haul their bloated bodies to bed and collapse until sometime late tomorrow afternoon. And in the meantime, Maximillian would attend to the important affairs of state while they snored.

A commotion at the hall's entrance, at the base of the gigantic double doors made of solid gold and inlaid with every precious stone imaginable, caused her to look up sharply from her pâté of fatted quail's breast served with white truffles, a sauce made of five-hundred-year-old brandy, and garnished with edible gold tissue.

She spotted the source of the commotion and came half out of her seat she was so shocked. "He's back," she breathed. "Dread High Lord Tyviden is alive. He has returned."

Her father had sent Ammertus's hotheaded son across the

Bridge of Ice nearly twenty years previously to cool his heels and redeem himself after an embarrassing incident with King Regalo of Haraland. Of course, the catch to that was no one had ever successfully returned from the southern continent on the far side of the Sea of Glass, over which the Bridge of Ice crossed. For many years now, Tyviden had been presumed dead like all the others who'd ever attempted the crossing.

The bridge itself was not actually made of ice but of ancient titanwood. However, the southern sea that it crossed was horrendously stormy and cold, and the bridge was so often coated entirely in ice that it had become known as the Bridge of Ice.

"Indeed? Tyviden in the flesh?" Maximillian asked.

A rush of movement from down the high table turned out to be Ammertus leaping up from his seat and charging down to greet his long-lost son, his court robes sailing out behind him to reveal his trousers beneath. Always so impetuous, Ammertus was. No decorum whatsoever.

"Tyviden looks if not older, perhaps a bit wiser," she murmured to her father.

Maximillian's consort and Endellian's mother, Archduchess Iolanthe, heard Endellian's comment and laughed aloud. "If only wisdom and moderation in temperament went hand in hand in the line of Ammertus."

Even Maximillian smiled at that observation. From up here on the dais at the far side of the great feasting hall, Endellian still caught whiffs of the emotional reunion between father and son. It was sweet, if one was the sentimental sort, she supposed.

Maximillian folded his silken napkin beside his plate. "At least the whelp had the decency to interrupt this interminable affair and give me an excuse to leave."

"You can't leave," Iolanthe chided. "The meal's not even half over."

"I would hear of young Tyviden's adventures. As I recall, I ordered him to bring back something interesting. I should like to see what he managed."

And after all, it wasn't like he needed Iolanthe's permission to do anything.

"Korovo. Iolanthe. Endellian," her father murmured, "to my library, if you please."

When the Emperor rose from his seat, a hasty scraping of chairs and benches arose from the floor as everyone awkwardly leaped to their feet also, mouths full of food and glasses of wine in hand. Surprised as they were by her father's unexpected departure, the result was an indecorous scramble that she found more than a little amusing.

Rising somewhat more gracefully, she followed Maximillian and his closest advisors through the private exit behind the dais. They moved down a short hall and through a secret doorway into her father's library, a great, hulking chamber filled to bursting with treasures from all over Urth. Accumulated across thousands of years, the collection was awe-inspiring even to her.

He moved to the priceless desk made of wood from all the great tree lords felled over the millennia. An intricate inlaid pattern on its top depicted Maximillian chopping down the great trees and standing upon their great trunks brought low.

Ammertus and his son, Tyviden, were announced by the chamberlain and ushered into the room. Endellian was shocked at the changes in Tyviden. He was leaner, his face tanned and windburned into a leathery texture, his eyes permanently squinted as if against the glare of sun off snow. His hair was long and wild, and he wore a great fur coat all the way to his ankles. A deep fur hood was pushed back at the moment, and a long knitted scarf was wrapped round and round his neck. He was the very picture of a wild explorer returned from some icy wilderness.

"So, young Tyviden. Have you brought me a new bauble for my collection?" Maximillian asked pleasantly enough.

Clearly, her father was signaling his willingness to forgive and forget. Tyviden had been smart to time his arrival for the middle of an event Maximillian was known to despise.

"I have brought you several, Your Resplendent Majesty, in hopes that one of them might please you greatly enough to forgive my undeserving self for old indiscretions, for which I am abjectly apologetic."

A pretty enough speech. It would please her father.

"Let us see what you have brought me, then."

"If you would permit me to remove my coat, I fear I am not properly dressed for this warm climate."

Maximillian nodded, and Tyviden shed the greatcoat, revealing a heavy leather vest and thick, woolen sweater below. Just how cold was it where he had been?

Maximillian was leaning forward in his throne, more interested than she'd seen him in a long time. "You are the first person ever to return from across the Bridge of Ice. Tell me what lies beyond."

"As you know, Your Majesty, the bridge itself is made of ironwood. Great storms cover the bridge with seawater and snow, which freeze into a thick layer of ice. I walked for weeks upon the bridge, melting snow for water and fishing for food."

"How did you melt the water?" Maximillian asked.

"Fire magic. Without that, I would have perished in a matter of days."

"Continue."

"The bridge leads to the Sea of Glass, which is a great frozen wasteland of ice upon ice upon ice. I do not believe there is an actual continent there, but rather a massive, frozen ice cap resting upon the sea."

"Why do you think this?" her father asked.

"Because in the interior of that place, there are ranges of icy mountains crisscrossed by fault lines. When the seaquakes happen, instead of earth rising up out of them, seawater surges through the cracks. I believe massive sea currents and tidal forces beneath the ice cap fracture it and thrust up the ice mountains from below."

Endellian commented, "It sounds violent and uninhabitable."

"Violent, yes. Uninhabitable, no," Tyviden answered.

"Do tell," Maximillian responded quickly.

"Certain types of ice in the sea can support plant life.

These areas are called Beardlands and are said to be made from the beard of Hoardunn."

There was a name she hadn't heard in a long time. The Undine Jarl, Hoardunn, had been one of the great giants driven out of Koth by the coming of her father and his companions to the continent of Koth, which had been called Ymir in the Age of Giants.

Tyviden was speaking again. "Barbarian tribes of hydesmyn who call themselves Sudrekkar live throughout the Beardlands. I brought several Sudrekkar back with me, in fact. They are slaves I acquired in my travels. It would be my pleasure to gift them to you and your High Lord Inquisitor to examine their minds and memories."

"Excellent." Maximillian glanced over at her. "If you would let Laernan know I have several subjects for him to empty, Endellian? I want all the images, all the knowledge, all the information he can glean about this place and these people."

"Yes, Father." She dutifully made a note recording the order to her half brother, the High Lord Inquisitor Laernan.

"Continue, Tyviden."

Her father was using his first name and dropping titles. Maximillian was well pleased, indeed, with the report he was receiving.

Tyviden bowed his head and continued obediently, "Beyond the Beardlands lies a rift in the sea. It appears to be a bottomless hole of some kind. I was not able to enter it or examine it too closely, for great superstition surrounds it. The Sudrekkar call it Hoardunn's Hearth after the great gouts of heat that rise out of it nearly continuously. The area near this rift is constantly filled with a thick mist the locals call Hoardunn's Breath. I expect it comes from the meeting of heat and ice around the rift. Above this great rift is a continuous and magnificent display of a phenomenon . . ." He paused, obviously searching for words. "I can best describe it as skyfire. It is as if great waves of fire of every color swirl and dance across the sky. The Sudrekkar call it Glimrosud."

A vague visual image of spectacular colors swirling through

a black night sky reached her from Tyviden's vivid memory of it.

"It's hot." Tyviden continued, "When the Glimrosud burns, it warms everything and even melts the surface ice. The combination of heat from Hoardunn's Hearth and the skyfire causes everything to melt slightly. Then, when the Glimrosud ends, the layer of standing water freezes over everything into a perfectly smooth, clear layer of new ice that looks just like glass. And," he added ruefully, "it is just as slippery." He lifted one of his boots and showed how the bottom of it was studded with many sharp spikes designed to dig into ice. "I took more falls than I can count until I managed to take a pair of these off a Sudrekkar."

"Where do these natives live, if the land is a solid sheet of ice?" Endellian asked curiously.

"Do not mistake my description. The Sea of Glass is nothing like a great frozen lake. It is not flat at all. And there are many kinds of ice—it comes in all colors and hardnesses. It can be infused with any number of different substances or magics, and those change its color and composition greatly. It's actually quite a beautiful and varied landscape."

She caught the image he projected of an icy panorama tinted in many colors, much like a fiery white opal.

"In answer to your question, Princess, the Sudrekkar carve caves out of the ice and live in those. Some of the ice is exceedingly hard and requires significant heat to affect it at all. Alchemical and magical heat can be necessary to even chip the stuff. I brought back a piece of a particular kind of ice the natives call ever-ice. As its name suggests, it never melts. I've carried a piece of it around inside my coat for weeks to see if I could soften it or even make it wet to the touch, to no avail. You can throw a piece into a fire and it will not melt."

Tyviden rummaged around in the backpack he'd been wearing when he came into the room and pulled out a chunk of beautiful, pale blue ice nearly the length of his forearm. It was jagged and crystalline in shape. "I believe you've seen something similar before, Your Majesty, but this ever-ice does not require the spirit of an ice elemental to maintain its cold."

Of course. Tyviden referred to the ice helm that held a piece of the Hand of Winter, an elemental ice lord recovered from the solinari mage Aurelius. The rest of that spirit still resided in, doing who knew what to, General Tarses, her former lover. The helm sat on a table across the library, made of pale blue ice, never cracking, never melting because of the elemental trapped within it.

But this natural ever-ice of Tyviden's—she'd never heard of the like.

"Did you find any evidence of Hoardunn himself?" Maximillian asked.

"Nay, Your Majesty. And I searched most diligently. The natives believe he still lives, guarding his Hearth and breathing out the mist in which he hides. I did, however, create a map detailing my discoveries over the course of my travels. Perhaps my humble effort will be of some use to you or your servitors."

He pulled out a rolled piece of leather and opened it to show an impressively detailed and beautiful map of the Sea of Glass. He appeared to have traversed most of the southern ice cap, assuming his map was reasonably accurate.

"You may find that some of my slaves can fill in more details on this for you. Two, in particular, may be of value. The first one is an Undine Joten—a sea giant-kin—who is said to have served Hoardunn himself. My other slaves fear him, and he appears to have been a creature of no small status among the Sudrekkar if their reaction to him is any indication."

"And the other slave?" Maximillian asked.

"He is called the Hrimmut by the Sudrekkar. I believe him to be a scion of Alfang, the Great Mastiff of Canute."

That caused a gasp in the room. The Great Mastiff of Canute had been held captive and bred exclusively by the Emperor's master of hounds for many centuries. How had one of its offspring found its way south to the icy wastelands?

"Have the master of hounds examine this creature right away and report his findings to me," Maximillian murmured.

"So shall it be, Your Majesty," Endellian murmured, already writing down the order in the official record of the court.

"Did you find anything else of interest?" her father asked Tyviden.

"In my caravan are the bones of a giant, and a piece of septallum."

And there was another word she hadn't heard in a very long time. The dwarves of Ymir were said to believe the continent's heart was divided into seven individual metal portions, each composed of a different material. Septallum was a magically created hybrid containing all of the seven base metals infused into a single substance. It did not occur in nature and was said to be made only by giants. Personally, she'd never seen any of it before and had assumed it to be a myth concocted by dwarves as something to brag about.

Tyviden fell silent, and Maximillian stared down at his bowed head for a long time. At length, her father said, "You have done well, Dread High Lord Tyviden, son of Archduke Ammertus. I welcome you back into my presence and my court."

Ammertus exclaimed in relief and gratitude, and Endellian closed her mind against the great gust of emotion emanating from him.

"Do not abuse my hospitality again, Tyviden, lest my punishment be far worse the next time."

Endellian did not want to imagine what could be any worse than wandering a frozen wasteland for decades, but if such a thing existed, Maximillian would know of it and not hesitate to use it to his own advantage.

As a White Heart member, Raina wasn't supposed to fear going into new places considered dangerous by sane people. She was supposed to trust her colors and go forth where the bravest warriors feared to tread, offering healing and hope to everyone she met. At least, in theory.

The practical reality was that she found the Sorrow Wold eerie and frightening. The trees closed in around them as the morning sun rose, its wan light barely penetrating the thick canopy overheard. Patches of sickly moss grew here and there on the dank, black forest floor, and strange, twisted thornbushes reached out to pluck at their clothes. A foul stench of rotting vegetation—and worse—assaulted her nostrils. It was all she could do not to pull a fold of her hood across her nose to block it. And no matter how long she smelled it, her nose never became insensitive to the odor.

Twilight gloom hung over the place even at midday, and the deeper they hiked into the wold, the blacker and wetter it became. Faintly glowing slime streaked the contorted tree trunks, and long strings of moss hung from dead branches.

They found a path, but whether it was made by animal, human, or inhuman was anyone's guess. The weight of the gloom weighed more heavily upon Raina than her pack, and fatigue set in to her limbs much sooner than it should have. The walking was grueling, and yet she could not say why. The terrain was mostly flat, the path reasonably smooth, but she felt as if she struggled against the living will of the forest as it tried to expel her from this place.

"How long do you plan to wander around in here?" Will asked.

She sighed. "My contact told me to come here and said he would find me. So I guess we just wander until he does."

Rynn commented, "The way I hear it, this place is teeming with people and creatures. We're bound to run into somebody. After all, every path leads somewhere."

Will commented sarcastically, "And some paths lead to the lair of the great monster that will eat us all."

Who on Urth would voluntarily live in this miserable wood? How awful must their alternatives be to choose this instead?

"It's not that bad," Rosana intervened. "Sure, it's gloomy and damp, but it has probably just rained, and at the tops of the trees, the sun is shining brightly. As soon as we find a good-sized clearing, it'll dry out and brighten up."

It was a valiant effort to lighten the party's mood, but it fell flat, and they trudged on in grim silence. Everyone was edgy. But then, the Sorrow Wold was known to do that to un-welcome visitors in its midst.

They walked all day without stopping, ever deeper into the belly of the living, malignant beast that was the wold. The mood was tense, everyone jumpy, but her misery was noth-ing compared to what she felt when night fell. The tempera-ture dropped precipitously with the setting of the sun, and her damp clothing became icy cold, clinging clammily to her skin until her teeth chattered.

And then the creatures of the night came out.

If even half the monstrous shapes Raina glimpsed through the trees were pure imagination, the rest were enough to give her nightmares. Green-skinned beasts, walking on two legs but barely humanoid in any other sense, flitted in and out of the shadows. A grotesque, wolflike creature with a hairless, red face and gigantic, snarling fangs crouched not far from the path at one point.

They lit torches, which lent a hellish glow to the immedi-ate surroundings but did little to hold back the night or its monsters. Creatures darted at the edges of the dark, teasing them with glimpses of laughing, mad visages.

Worst of all was the almost subliminal moaning noise that was their constant companion. Will mumbled that it was likely the trees creaking, but it was unlike any creak of wood she'd ever heard of. It sounded more like a ghostly woman keening in grief.

They walked until every muscle in her body was beyond aching. She'd gotten little sleep the night before aboard the ship, and fatigue dragged at her every step like shack-les around her ankles. And yet, terror goaded at her, its sharps spurs digging deeply into her sides. The combina-tion was nigh unbearable.

Eben piped up. "I've had enough of this. As we do not ap-pear to be drawing near any kind of human civilization, I say we stop and make camp. A fire will dry us out and warm us up, at any rate."

Sha'Li rolled her eyes, showing the whites of them like a prey animal that senses a hunter stalking it.

Which worried Raina. The lizardman girl's instincts were usually spot-on.

Although there was wood aplenty for a fire, getting the damp wood lit ended up requiring magic from Will to, in effect, explode the wood into flame, but eventually, they sat around a larger-than-normal fire for them. It burned brightly, sending a spiral of sparks up into the blackness of the forest overhead.

"You're from near here, aren't you, Raina?" Will asked after they finished eating the dried meat and root vegetables they'd brought with them from Dupree and were sipping mugs of hot tea.

The cheery crackle of the fire seemed to have temporarily driven back the night and its monsters, and she breathed a sigh of relief. "I am. Tyrel lies just a little to the south and west of this forest's margins."

"Tell us a story or two of the Sorrow Wold," he urged.

"They're mostly horror tales meant to keep children from running away to or wandering into the forest."

Sha'Li grinned. "Excellent. Tell one."

Eben cracked a tiny smile, which warmed Raina's heart to see. Maybe there was hope for the two of them yet.

"Well, one of the most common hearth tales about this place is that it's the home of a giant spider. She has a huge web woven from tree to tree that she sits in the middle of, waiting for her prey to stumble into it and get stuck. Once they are ensnared, her magic web causes her victims to fall asleep and dream of being in a beautiful, peaceful place. So charmed are they by the dream that they do not wake up as she bites them, paralyzes them, wraps them in silk, and devours them."

Rynn responded thoughtfully, "I find there's generally a kernel of truth behind hearth tales, even old and outlandish ones. Have you ever heard tell of an actual giant spider in these woods?"

Raina shrugged. "There's a woman in these parts called the Black Widow. She's apparently a spider changeling of some kind. Oh, and before I forget to ask again," Raina continued, "what was that sheet of parchment you tore off the public notice wall in Seastar, Rynn? Anything we should know about?" She suspected it was some sort of cleverly worded offer by Anton to pay a bounty for their capture.

Rynn's scowl deepened, creasing his forehead around his uncovered third eye. The paxan always took off his headband the second they left civilization behind. He said the thing interfered with his vision and gave him headaches and dizzy spells. He answered, "It's an Imperial proclamation having to do with my race. It has been around a long time, but every now and then the Empire likes to remind people it exists."

"What does it say?" Rosana asked from across the fire.

Rynn pulled out the crumpled wad of parchment and spread it out on his thigh. He read aloud, "'For the protection of his Resplendent Majesty's people, all paxan with an open third eye shall be brought to an Imperial Hunter for cleansing by the Imperial Hounds or to an Imperial Censor to receive the Vexarum, a mark denoting the acceptance and protection of the Imperial Koths. Creatures of any race that demonstrate powers of Thought or Dream must also be presented to an Imperial Hunter or Censor for evaluation. Failure to report or present open-eyed paxan, or those who demonstrate powers of Thought or Dream, shall be considered Treason.'"

"Gee. I guess that makes us very bad citizens," Will commented.

Everyone chuckled, and Rynn continued, "It finishes with a quote from Archduchess Rahl. *'It is well known that paxan with an open third eye are extremely dangerous to those around them. Such beings manifest powers of the mind that they are incapable of fully controlling. Eventually, the physical transformation that begins with the opening of the third eye gives way to a mental and spiritual transformation that leaves them completely devoid of emotion, unable to control their emotions or maddened. Once a paxan reaches one of the later stages, no known magic, alchemy, or process has been able to cure the condition. Cleansing of the Imperial Hounds will remove the uncontrolled powers of the mind that accompany the condition, but the paxan remains changed, a shell of his or her former self.'"*

Silence fell after Rynn stopped reading. Into it, Sha'Li said, "And I thought the Empire hated my kind."

Rynn shrugged and smiled, but Raina didn't think the smile reached any of his eyes. She said stoutly, "Of course, that is all nonsense."

He nodded in gratitude.

Eben said drolly, "You will let us know when all that madness and loss of control happens, though, won't you? I would hate to have to try to subdue you. Your hands and feet scare me."

Everybody laughed heartily at that. Rynn crunched the ridiculous proclamation into a ball and tossed it into the blaze, where it caught fire and satisfyingly turned to ash.

"Tell us a real story, Raina," Eben asked.

Instead, she turned to Will. "Perhaps Bloodroot would tell us one. I've heard tales of a great willow tree who once lived in the wold. Its name was Moonshade. Something happened to it that destroyed it, and its ghost is said to haunt the wold now. Apparently, on a moonlit night in a clearing in the wold, a worthy person can catch a glimpse of the ghostly form of a magnificent, white willow tree."

"You do know Bloodroot doesn't actually speak to me, right?" Will replied. "I just get impressions and emotions from time to time."

"So how does he react to the name *Moonshade*?" Rosana asked.

Will frowned for a moment, concentrating. "Derision, mostly."

"Because the story isn't true?" Raina followed up.

Will was silent for a moment more. "No, I don't think that's it. I get the impression that his derision is aimed at Moonshade."

"As in Bloodroot didn't like Moonshade?" Raina asked curiously.

Will grunted. "It would make sense. The cranky old shrub dislikes most everybody."

Raina grinned. A shrub, huh? The great tree lord of rage, destruction, and death? Will was, indeed, getting confident in his old age.

The party fell silent, and her mind drifted to other tales of the Sorrow Wold from her childhood. Stories of misshapen monsters with hideous faces and forms, hordes of goblins, gangs of bandits, cutthroats, and killers. And then there were the tales of hauntings and madness, of the wold itself being sentient . . . and unfriendly to intruders. After watching Will struggle to get along with Bloodroot, she was more inclined now to believe the hearth tales of the wold having consciousness and of it having a bad attitude. Although she supposed anyone who lived long enough to watch the full scope of mankind's folly would likely develop a poor opinion of humankind.

The fire was burning low, and Eben was just stacking a pile of thick logs onto it for the night when she thought she saw a movement in the shadows just beyond the light of their fire. She peered into the darkness and for a fleeting second thought she saw a pair of glowing yellow eyes, but it could be a trick of the firelight on leaves. Or maybe a forest creature drawn to the light of their fire.

She glanced around and spied what looked like a wrinkled, half-human, half-canine face peering out from under a bush at knee level. She gasped and looked again, but the face was gone.

"Everything all right?" Rynn asked her quietly.

"For a second, I thought I saw something. It was nothing. Just my imagination working overtime after our talk of dream spiders and ghost trees."

Sha'Li looked up from where she was laying out her bedroll on an oilskin and took a long, slow look around the little copse. Will also appeared to be examining the forest, but he tilted his head as if listening to it. As one, Sha'Li and Will moved casually toward the fire.

They'd all been together long enough to know when their companions sensed a threat. Raina threw back the right side of her cloak to free her magic casting arm. "At least it's not as cold here as it was in Dupree. Sleeping outside won't be nearly so miserable as it would have been there."

Will pulled out his staff to use its metal-clad end to poke a log that had rolled free back into the fire. "As long as we can stay dry. It must rain a lot here for this place to be so pervasively damp."

And that was when a horde of green-skinned creatures the size of preadolescent humans charged into the circle of firelight, howling like banshees and swinging short, rusty swords.

Will and the others laid into them methodically. Although her companions made short work of every goblin they could reach, there were a lot of them. Wave after wave of the creatures charged the camp, and Raina spied her friends' arms growing battle weary and nicks and cuts beginning to blossom on their bodies and faces.

Eben was closest to her, so she laid her hand on his back. "We have no time to do this gently!" she shouted over a new wave of screeching goblins. She slammed a bolt of healing energy into him. He grunted in pain, but his various nicks and wounds disappeared. He nodded a quick thanks as he dived with renewed vigor into the fight.

One by one, she healed her friends. And eventually, the goblins began to dwindle. The sounds of the clashing metal and howled gibberish grew less deafening. They were going to make it.

But then, no fewer than twenty fast-moving, burly shapes rushed the clearing, screaming horrible, animalistic sounds in some sort of primitive battle cry.

Her relief evaporated in a rush of ice-cold terror. Those were *not* goblins.

She and her companions were in trouble now.

Raina backed up closer to the fire beside Rosana while Sha'Li and the boys formed an arc in front of her, weapons bristling.

The attackers were an assortment of creatures Raina had never seen before. Some looked frog-like, with great, bulging eyes set too wide in their faces. Others had bent spines and vaguely simian features. A few larger beasts, four-legged but with human intelligence shining from their eyes, charged through the trees, bellowing.

As the sheer numbers of attackers began to strain the party's ability to hold them off, Raina was forced to cast healing in a steady stream. The magic came up through the ground into her feet and flowed like warm sunlight through her body, bright and cleansing. Her entire body glowing, she not only healed her friends but spared bits of healing enough to keep their foes from dying. She didn't cast enough to allow the downed creatures to stand up and rejoin the fight, of course, but she did her best to keep everyone alive from her awkward position behind and blocked by her friends.

A steady stream of new creatures joined the fray as if they'd been drawn to the sounds of combat. How were they ever to hold off the entire population of this portion of the forest? For the first time, it entered her mind that they might not win this fight. Her friends' battle prowess notwithstanding, at some point sheer numbers of attackers would exhaust her and the others, and they would all die.

There was nowhere to flee, nowhere to hide. They were

surrounded by monsters, and more just kept coming. Desperation began to set in, and she tried a new healing spell she'd been experimenting with. Or rather a very old healing spell.

The last time she'd dreamed of Gawaine, he had mentioned such a spell existing in his day, and she'd been researching and trying to re-create it ever since.

The vitality spell not only healed all of a person's injuries or illnesses, but it also restored energy and overall health. It was very difficult for her to cast properly and took massive amounts of healing energy to cast, but her friends needed the boost. One by one, she cast the vitality spell upon them, and her friends returned to the fight fully refreshed. And just in the nick of time.

At long last, the end of the wave of attacking creatures seemed to come. No more greenskins or deformed monsters were forthcoming from the forest, and as the odds whittled down to nearly even, the last half dozen creatures abruptly disengaged from the fight, turned tail, and fled into the trees.

Rynn straightened from his fighting crouch, breathing hard. "Thank the stars that's over. They were relentless there for a while."

Will leaned against his staff, panting. "Well, that was more of a workout than I needed after a long day's walk."

Sha'Li helped Eben adjust his armor and rebuckle it where it had come loose under his sword arm during the fight. The lizardman's tough hide looked the worse for wear, nicked and bleeding in several spots. Raina moved over to her and began trickling more healing into her.

Without warning, perhaps three dozen men and women dropped out of the trees around them, one foot riding in a rope loop, the other taking off running the moment they reached the ground. Raina spied nooses draped around everyone's necks, and her blood ran cold. *The Hanged Men.* A gang of bandits whose requirement for membership was to have been executed at least once at the hands of the Kothite Empire. They were described as the worst of the worst brigands out here, completely without mercy.

They were the roughest, meanest-looking bunch she'd ever

laid eyes on. Only a few of them had full sets of teeth. Their hair hung in twisted, greasy ropes, and their skin was nearly black with ground-in grime. A few women mingled with the bandits, looking as tough and at ease with weapons as the men. Dying at the hands of brigands wasn't the end she'd have chosen for herself.

The Hanged Men attacked in complete silence, which made them all the more ominous. Only the grunts of effort, the clanging of swords, the dull thud of Will's staff, and the musical chiming of Rynn's crystal greaves and gauntlets marked the resumption of combat.

Raina began incanting healing spells aloud, and her voice provided the only soundtrack to the fight. She drew larger and larger balls of healing magic, slamming them into her friends' backs, having to restore nearly all their life energy with each touch of her hands. She began to feel like she was playing some oversized musical instrument, her hands flying in every direction, magic bursting from her fingers as fast as she could release it.

She had no time at all to check on their foes, so busy was she trying to keep the four fighters in front of her alive. It wasn't that she was unwilling to heal the Hanged Men. She just had no healing left over for them. Aurelius would be proud of Will and the others for boxing her in behind them and effectively hoarding her healing for themselves.

Even she could tell the fight wasn't going well. First, Eben went down, and then Sha'Li. Thankfully, the lizardman girl was able to get them back up in the nick of time before bandits leaped over them to attack Raina.

And then magic started to strike her. Raina was forced to throw up several magical shields in quick succession, which meant she was not healing her friends. She had to throw a life spell at Rynn and a big wad of healing after that to get him back up, and she barely got turned around in time to heal Will before he went down.

Another burst of magic hit her, silencing her. Thankfully, Rosana hit her fast with a spell to remove whatever curse had taken her voice, and Raina sprayed a fast round of healing at all four of her frontline fighters without stopping to see if any of them needed it. The technique was incredibly wasteful of magical energy, but she had no choice. She'd drawn and cast enough magic to heal a small village, and fatigue was beginning to set in. It wasn't as if she had any choice but to keep going, though.

She stumbled and took a step backward and then lurched forward as the smell of wool scorching announced that the hem of her cloak had strayed into the fire directly at her back. The bandits pressed the party hard, forcing them back closer and closer to the fire and into tighter and tighter proximity with each other.

Raina knew all too well that a moment would come when her friends would stop being combat effective with their weapons if they were crowded too tightly together. The bandits seemed to be counting on that, in fact.

But then Rynn executed a flying somersault all the way over the fire, and Sha'Li pulled a nifty duck-and-spin move that broke her out of their tight cluster. It left only Eben and Will holding position between Raina and Rosana and their attackers, but it also forced a portion of their attackers to turn away and face the new threats on their flanks.

It was a desperate move. Now Raina was forced to throw healing at Rynn and Sha'Li from several yards away, timing her bursts of magic to aim between dodging, spinning attackers at two rapidly moving targets. It was a questionable proposition at best.

One of the bandits charged directly through the fire, wrapping her in a crushing hold and slapping a hard, foul hand over her mouth. She struggled like mad, but the bandit overpowered her with ease.

With her mouth covered like this, she couldn't utter any incants. And without incants, she could cast no magic. Without magic, she was defenseless, and her friends would fall in a matter of seconds. Panicked, she looked around and saw that, indeed, all of her companions were either going down or already down on the ground. Various bandits sat on their chests or stood on their necks.

She knew defeat when she saw it. Now she could only hope that her White Heart colors meant something to these criminals. If she got lucky, she could heal the bandits and maybe even be allowed to save her friends.

Cautiously, the ruffian at her back lifted his hand away from her mouth. Of a sudden, all the bandits were climbing off her friends. One of the bandits, an elf, and Rynn pounded each other on the back, laughing. As fast as it has started, the fight was over.

Raina spied red, flame-shaped markings on the bandit's face. A pyresti. One of the fire elves. He was built powerfully for an elf, his hair black and long, his clothing strange. He wore black, pajama-like garments under a layer of armor that looked like hundreds of tiny pieces of bone drilled with holes and tied together with red cord. He turned toward her more fully, and she got a good look at his face.

She stared, stunned. She knew that man. Two years ago, he had helped Cicero break her out of her family's home in Tyrel on the night of her sixteenth birthday.

"Moto?" she asked in disbelief.

He stared back for a moment and then broke into a big grin. "Well, look at you. All grown up and a healer to boot."

"Speaking of which, may I please be set loose so I may heal everyone?"

Moto responded instantly, "For crying out loud, Klem, turn the White Heart healer loose and let her do her job."

She moved quickly around the clearing, checking everyone who was down on the ground to make sure no one was dying. Once she had everyone stabilized, she would go back and revive the unconscious and heal the badly wounded. She honestly didn't know how much healing capacity she had left, and this would be a very bad time to run out completely.

Rynn exclaimed, "Did your gang have to nearly kill us before you got around to recognizing me?"

"You couldn't handle a few flea-bitten gobbies by yourself?" Moto guffawed. "You should've let me know you'd be coming this way. I'd have sent a welcoming party."

Rynn grinned. "It seems as if you already did. Where in

the Great Void were you an hour ago? Those goblins and monstrous creatures nearly had us."

Moto laughed. "We were sitting up in the trees enjoying the show. I figured your crew could use the practice at sword-play, brother."

Brother? Elves did not use such terms lightly. Why hadn't Rynn told them that a close friend of his lived in these forests? What else wasn't the paxan telling them about himself?

The bandits repaired and stoked the fire that had been knocked apart in the combat and dragged more wood over beside it. A stew pot emerged from the Hanged Men's supplies, and the bandits pulled various bits of meat and herbs out of their pouches to drop in the pot.

While her friends and most of the bandits settled around the bonfire, Raina continued moving about, healing and listening to the conversation. Rynn was speaking.

"So, Moto. What news is there? What has transpired around here since the last time I passed this way?"

Raina couldn't wait to hear the answer to that. Perhaps Moto would have news of her dear friend, Cicero. And may-hap the pyresti would reveal why exactly Rynn was so famil-iar with this awful place.

Gabrielle was exhausted. Gunther Druumedar might have been grumpy and generally unpleasant to travel with, but at least his mechanical leg had slowed him to a reason-able pace on the road. Not so his energetic son. Korgan set a murderous pace up the steep, icy slopes through the thin mountain air so cold it burned her lungs.

The rokken, Bekkan, seemed none the worse for his long imprisonment in storm copper and readily kept pace with Korgan. Jossa, the ogre-kin apprentice stormcaller who'd come with them, also wasn't having any trouble keeping up in spite of the massive warstar she carried. The heavy shaft rested on her right shoulder, its two spiked metal balls clanging on their chains against her scaled armor. But then, she was tall-est in the party and had the longest stride.

This evening, they reached a good-sized village as dusk fell and a thin, crystalline snow began to drift down.

She panted, "What say you to the idea of renting rooms at the inn and sleeping in warm, soft beds for a change?"

Korgan shrugged, but Bekkan said courteously, "You must be exhausted, my lady. We have been moving fast and without pause for nearly a week."

She had no idea why he'd started calling her by a title. Someone must have told him who she was when she was not tromping around Groenn's Rest pretending to be a commoner. She responded to his remark with a grateful smile.

"Who's paying for these soft beds?" Korgan asked, even crankier than usual.

"My treat," she answered quickly. "I'm paying for all of us."

Korgan's attitude thawed considerably at that. At the inn, she engaged four rooms for the night and four steaming hot baths. The innkeeper said those would take about an hour to prepare, so in the meantime, they sat down in the common room to sup. A pot of melted cheese was set on their table, along with a platter of crusty bread and chopped vegetables to dip in the savory sauce. The meal was bracing and tasty, the sauce tangy and rich with wine.

They'd nearly finished a second pot of the stuff when a handsome avarian with a raven's glossy black feathers in place of hair ducked into the inn through its low front door. He looked around the room and, spying Gabrielle and her friends, made straight for them. Sharp alarm sounded in her belly as he stopped beside them.

"Well met, traveler," she said politely. "May we help you?"

"Gabrielle?" he asked low.

She blinked, startled. How did this stranger know her name? She surreptitiously searched his clothing and exposed skin for any sign of an eight-pointed compass. It was the symbol of the secret resistance group she worked in to bring down the Kothite Empire one day. "I am Gabrielle. And you are?"

Ignoring her question, he reached into his belt pouch and pulled out a leather parchment tube, handing it over to her.

Frowning, she fished out the letter and unrolled it. *Sasha's handwriting.* Her dearest friend and wife of the Heart's ambassador to the Imperial Seat, Sasha was also a member of the Eight, recruited by Gabrielle herself.

> *My dearest Gabby,*
> *I have sent Sir Valyri Nightfeather to accompany you on your journey. He has worked for my husband and me for many years. He is a Heart knight and a knight commander in the Graceful Order, an avarian group. He was trained by and has served under Lord Justinius, which is to say he's a highly accomplished warrior. I will feel better about all the traipsing around you're doing if you are guarded by someone like him. He is also exceedingly discreet, so anything he might hear or overhear while traveling with you will stay solely with him.*
>
> > *Safe travels to you,*
> > *Sasha*

Gabrielle looked up from the missive at the avarian. "Why do you not wear colors?"

"Sometimes the nature of the work I do requires a high level of discretion."

By discretion, he clearly meant disguise and subterfuge.

Curious, she asked, "Do you even carry colors with you?"

"No. Ofttimes, the danger of discovery makes doing so unwise."

She knew wherefore he spoke. She carried no proof of her identity either, although she did wear clothing of high enough quality and carry enough gold to be taken for a wealthy merchant or minor noble. It was generally enough to ensure that common bandits would steer clear of her and the Imperial repercussions to follow from messing with someone like her.

"Well, then, I suppose we should see to getting you a room

for the night," she announced. "And what should we call you?"

"Valyri is fine. My friends call me Val."

"Very well. I am, as you already know, Gabrielle. And my friends call me Gabby. And these are Korgan, Bekkan, and Jossa."

Val nodded politely, and Jossa smiled shyly at the handsome knight.

"Val has been highly recommended to me by my oldest and dearest friend. He is a seasoned warrior and is willing to travel as our guard escort. What say you to another sword in our party?"

Jossa's smile widened. She clearly approved of the idea.

Korgan, however, harrumphed. "The bigger our group, the more attention we'll draw."

Gabrielle shrugged. "If we look menacing enough, however, no one will bother us. And you must admit, Val, here, definitely looks menacing."

Unfortunately, Val chose that moment to look more amused than dangerous.

"Have you eaten?" she asked him.

"Nay. I've been trying to catch up with you for the past week and hardly stopped to eat or sleep. You've led me on quite the chase."

That made Korgan grunt in satisfaction. He declared, "Diamond season starts in a few months, and I have to get back home in time to sign up for the first tournaments of the year. Best gold of the season to be made knocking out the new crop of would-be gladiators."

"You fight in the Diamond?" Val asked, sliding in beside Korgan. "Have I bet on you?"

"They call me Ironhand. Won my fair share of tournaments."

Val's face lit up. "You fight with axe-hammer and shield? Tend to favor going in low on the attack?"

Korgan smiled broadly. "That'd be me."

"Well met, Ironhand. An honor. Let me buy you an ale."

Gabrielle mentally rolled her eyes. Male bonding was alive and well when it came to paid pugilists bashing each other's brains in. At least Korgan wasn't likely to protest Val traveling with them now.

As for Bekkan, he wasn't saying much about anything to anyone. Ever since the incident in the Valley of Storms that she could not remember, but which Bekkan solemnly vowed had happened, he'd been singularly untalkative. Not that she blamed him. This world he'd woken into must seem a passing strange place.

Raina peered into the stew pot, grimacing at the various skinned carcasses bobbing in the greasy water. She took a sniff and had no idea what was cooking. Frankly, she didn't want to know.

"I've got some cooking herbs. Would you like me to add them to the pot?" she asked the fellow tending to the stew.

"By all means." His enthusiasm worried her. Just how terrible tasting was whatever floated in the kettle?

She pulled out a bundle of thyme and shook some of its tiny leaves into the pot. A few bay laurel leaves, a handful of salt, and some peppercorns. That would do for now. Once it had cooked down a bit, she'd muster the courage to taste it and adjust the seasonings.

She asked Moto if he knew how his old friend Cicero fared, and the pyresti answered, "Last I saw of him, he was hale and well."

"Please give him my best when next you see him."

"That I will, and you've my word on it," Moto replied.

While Rynn filled in Moto on the latest gossip from Dupree, the elf filled them in on the goings-on in the Sorrow Wold. The big news, of course, was the imminent approach of Maren's Belt, which would cut through the eastern edge of the Sorrow Wold where it met the Estarran Sea.

Will asked, "Why would the Empire run the Belt so close to the water? The Merr will cause no end of problems for travelers on that stretch of the road."

Moto shrugged. "The creatures of the Sorrow Wold, and

the wold itself, will cause more trouble. I guess the Merr were the lesser of two evils."

The Hanged Men laughed loudly at that observation, seemingly delighted to be scarier than the Merr Empire.

Apparently, a number of Imperial patrols and scouting expeditions had been seen in the wold recently. Undoubtedly, they were survey crews and foresters getting ready to clear the way for Maren's Belt.

Moto also relayed that the governess had imposed production quotas on the guilds west of Estarra larger than any quotas seen in years. She was apparently determined to increase the region's productivity, including the Sorrow Wold. Both Moto and Rynn seemed amused at the idea. And after having spent a day here, Raina had to agree with them.

Even the Forest of Thorns, guarded as it was by the mighty Boki, was nowhere near as scary as this place. Raina highly doubted that Syreena had any concept of how forbidding a place the Sorrow Wold truly was.

These woods were a living, breathing entity. Raina highly doubted any army or collection of guilds could tame a beast that stretched for hundreds of leagues. She knew from her study of history that others had tried. They all had failed.

"White Heart!" Moto called, startling her out of her thoughts.

She turned and straightened.

"Have you any healing left after everything you just cast?"

"My hand is glowing, is it not?" she replied tartly.

His men guffawed.

"Then fix this if you can."

She cast her gaze downward. And blinked. A nasty, festering sore oozed on the inside of his calf, as big around as her palm. Red streaks traveled up and down from the raw, seeping wound. Alarmed, she squatted down to take a better look.

"How long have you had this?" she asked briskly.

"A couple of months."

"Months?" she echoed, alarmed. "How'd you get it?"

"You tell me."

"Looks like poison eating at your flesh. Did a venomous creature bite you, perchance?"

"Very good. Scorpion stung me. Big one. Regular healing hasn't worked on it. Cures for poison haven't worked either."

"You'll need enhanced healing, then. Lucky for you, I can cast that."

"What's that?"

"Regular magic enhanced with ritual magic."

She glanced up and made eye contact with Moto. His eyes were blacker than the night. "You want it fast or slow? It'll hurt either way, it's just a matter of how much or how long."

"I'll take the pain the long way."

She frowned. He sounded like he wanted the more drawn-out ordeal. An almost hypnotic look of concentration came over his face as he prepared himself to face her healing. Nonetheless, she pulled a hand-span length of thick leather out of her belt pouch and handed it to him.

"What's this for?" he asked suspiciously.

She grinned. "I give it to women in childbirth so they don't bite through their lips. You might want to put it between your teeth and chomp down."

Although she'd enjoy drawing out the man's apprehension after the scare he and his men had given her earlier, she wasn't that cruel. She summoned the magic quickly, forming a stream of crackling light between her fingers. She touched the wound with her fingertips, and the magic jumped from her hand into the center of the wound.

Moto's entire body jerked, arching into a taut bow of agony. Several of his men surged forward in alarm. Wincing, she bled the magic into him. Muscle by individual muscle, he gradually relaxed his body against the white-hot agony she must be causing him. Long before she had finished sending the magics into him, he'd achieved a state of trancelike relaxation. If anything, the expression on his face was akin to . . . peace. Joy.

She'd nearly finished the healing when he finally went limp and slumped over. It was probably for the best. The scrolls she'd been taught from said this magic took time to work its way through the bloodstream, seeking and destroying poisons throughout the body. And apparently, the process was excruciating.

She glanced down at Moto's leg. The wound already had a thin, semitransparent membrane of new flesh forming over it. In another three minutes or so, when she finally finished trickling healing into his leg, the wound was completely gone.

Moto roused sluggishly, mumbling in an odd, elvish cadence. She frowned, concentrating on his rantings, and they began to separate into words.

"Emerald jewel awakes, flashing. Flying. Devouring."

Raina frowned. A flying jewel?

"Kings rising, kings falling. Ah, the blood. The fire. The humanity . . ." His voice trailed off.

He'd done this exact same thing the last time she'd met him, prophesying then of sleeping kings and her power to destroy them all. And some of his vision had already come true. She worried that the rest of it, the part where she must wield her power with great care or else disaster would fall, might also come true. And now this? Blood, fire, and destruction as kings rose and fell?

Was this a pointed warning that the path they pursued would not turn out as they hoped?

Shivers of apprehension raced down her spine. She glanced up in dismay at the cluster of staring people around her and mumbled, "He's hallucinating."

Please let that be true. But the sick feeling in her belly proclaimed her wish to be a lie. Moto blinked a couple of times just then. Sat up, looking disoriented. Looked down at his leg. Looked up at her in surprised gratitude.

"Thanks be to thee," he said in a perfectly normal tone of voice.

"You're welcome." She stood up. "And now if you don't mind, I need to stir your supper. I'd hate to burn it after using my good herbs in it."

While the Hanged Men ate and swapped war stories, Raina cleaned off her bedroll as best she could. It had been trampled in the fighting and was muddy and wet.

One of the female bandits surprised her by offering a torn and flea-bitten bedroll. "It ain't much, but it be clean and dry. Lemme help you hang yours by the fire to dry overnight, then we'll beat it clean in the morn."

Surrounded by upward of thirty armed fighters, she finally felt safe enough to sleep and actually caught a few hours' rest.

As soon as she woke in the morning, a line formed in front of her, of brigands waiting to show her their various minor injuries and infections. She was shocked to realize that none of them had access to any sort of medical treatment at all. They had not a single potion maker among them. Were she to be out here for longer, she would've offered to teach one of them the brewing of the simplest healing potions.

As it was, she methodically worked her way through their aches and pains. Truth be told, the Hanged Men weren't so bad once she got to know them a little. A few of them told tales of being sold into slavery for unpaid taxes, others of being wrongly accused of crimes because they would not leave lands one of the Imperial guilds coveted. A few grinned and admitted that they'd deserved the hangings they'd gotten, but the majority seemed to be victims of the Empire rather than criminals out to harm it.

The Hanged Men invited Rynn and his friends to travel with them, and after a brief conference with her and the others, Rynn accepted the invitation.

They traveled fast and hard all that day and the next. The menace of the wood retreated somewhat but never fully went away. Raina couldn't ever shake the sensation that unseen eyes were watching her. Their malevolent stares crawled up her spine like spiders, cold and poisonous.

She ventured to strike up a conversation with the gypsy cook the fourth evening over the supper pot. "So how do all of you support yourselves in these woods?"

The young man shrugged. "Raiding caravans and robbing travelers, mostly."

Raina blinked. "Why didn't you rob us, then?"

"Rynn, he be different. He be one of us."

"A bandit?" Raina asked, surprised.

"No. Part of the—" The youth broke off abruptly, as if realizing belatedly that he'd almost said something he shouldn't.

"Part of the what?"

"Nothin'. Forget it," the gypsy mumbled.

Part of some group of some kind, she'd lay odds on it. Was there some greater union of brigands or something? She'd always pegged Rynn as a former noble, like herself, but likely of higher rank than she'd been born to.

"Is there such a thing as a Thief's Guild?" she asked, watching the gypsy's reaction carefully.

He looked genuinely startled and replied without hesitation, "Not as I know of."

Hmm. What group, then?

Late in the afternoon of the following day, the guard rotation was such that she found herself walking alongside Moto.

"How's your leg?" she questioned.

"Right as rain, thanks to thee."

She shrugged. "So tell me. How come you choose to live in this gloomy place? Last I saw, you were a prosperous merchant passing through Tyrel a few times per year."

He threw her a hard look. "I didn't choose this life. Most of us didn't."

"Then why are you here?"

Moto was silent a long time, walking reflectively. Then he said merely, "The Empire."

"I beg your pardon?"

"That's why we're all out here. We're avoiding the Empire. This is one of the few places left where the Kothites haven't wrapped their claws around the throat of every living creature and squeezed the life out of it. Yes, these woods are evil, but better them than slavery."

"I know exactly how you feel," she replied with a tinge of bitterness.

Moto looked at her with interest. "And yet you serve Koth."

"I had no choice but to put on these colors."

"Join us. We could use a healer like you."

She laughed. "I don't think I could keep up with you. Rynn says you're taking the pace easy because of me, yet I'm half-dead with exhaustion."

The bandit shrugged. "We are, but you'd shape up soon enough."

"I thank you for the offer. My situation is not yet so desperate that I need to take you up on it, but I'll keep it in mind."

One of the men walking point let out a cry, and the entire party jolted to full alert. Ululating, inhuman screams began to echo all around them, bouncing off the trees eerily. Raina's eyes went wide in alarm.

"Cursed kindari," Moto muttered. "We're coming into one of their villages. They don't mean us any harm. It's just their uncivilized way of saying hello."

The party halted.

"Here we are," Moto murmured. "Where you asked us to take you."

She looked around and saw nothing but black tree trunks and stunted undergrowth in the usual gloom. "Me? I made no such request. Where are we?"

He grinned, enjoying the apparent joke. "Look up. The kindari live in trees."

She looked up. And gasped. An entire village perched high in the limbs of the giant trees overhead. Wood and rope walkways extended between the round tree houses, and she glimpsed someone swinging on a long vine from one building to another.

"Will they come down to us, or are we supposed to go up to them?" she asked.

"Depends. Friends get invited up. Strangers and those they don't trust stay down here. With you and yours among us, who knows? Maybe they'll think you're a threat. Maybe not."

"Which way do they see you?"

He glanced over at her and smiled boyishly. "Haven't you figured out yet that I'm a pussycat?"

She grinned at him. "Now that you mention it, I was beginning to come to that very conclusion."

A delegation of a half dozen kindari dropped down out of

the trees and parlayed briefly with first Moto and then Rynn. Apparently, these wild elves were acquainted with the paxan, as well, and greeted him warmly.

In short order, a series of rope ladders unrolled out of the trees, clattering down to the ground. "Up we go," Rynn murmured to her and their companions. "It's a great honor to be invited into their homes, so behave yourselves."

Uh-oh. Her friends behave? This was not going to go well.

E ben fell into an exhausted sleep. The combination of a long day's hike and the strenuous fight had sapped his strength. He'd given no thought to his sister or to the child Vesper on the dream plane before he closed his eyes.

Hence, his dreaming mind was shocked when he was rudely and forcefully yanked through a white fog and popped out at the same giant encampment as before, except this time manifesting directly in front of Vesper's tent.

One of the dour armed guards holding a long pike intoned, "She wants you inside."

No discussion was necessary of who "she" was.

Eben nodded and ducked inside the dim tent.

"There you are," Vesper said in her high-pitched voice. "It's about time."

"Sorry," he muttered. "Had a horde of goblins and monsters to fight off before I could sleep."

"Are you injured?"

"No, but thanks be to you for asking," he replied with a courtesy he was far from feeling. He was tired and wanted his rest.

"Come with me. Your sister will arrive soon with a delivery for me. You wanted to see her, did you not?"

That surprised Eben. "Indeed. Thank you for remembering and arranging for us to meet." His gratitude was genuine this time.

Eben trailed along among the flunkies, unsure of what else

to do. One of the creatures, an earth elemental by the looks of his stony hide, stomped along beside him.

"Why you wear shoes?" the elemental demanded.

Eben answered, "To protect my feet from injury and extreme temperatures."

The creature lifted one massive foot and wiggled its toes comically. "But feel the earth be good. Connect to dirt. To your spirit."

The creature had accurately pegged him as being earth aligned. Interesting. "What are you?" he asked.

"Stone elemental. Duh."

Eben smirked. He wondered if the phantasms actually believed they were the entities whose identities they assumed. This one sounded like it did.

"You no connect to who you be. No feet on dirt, no skin in fresh air. No fingers in fire. How you know who you be under all them human clothes?"

That was a good question. Maybe he was too humanized. Maybe Leland Hyland hadn't understood his and Marikeen's need to connect to their core natures. Maybe that explained why he felt so at sea now, so . . . adrift.

He followed along in Vesper's wake, pondering whether he'd sold out on himself, whether or not he was traveling the right path in his life. But how to fix it? His friends were counting on him, and he was as deeply embroiled in the quest to wake the Sleeping King as any of them. He'd resurrected once, lost his foster brother, and lost his sister as a result of it.

At least he could correct one of those right now.

"Eben!"

He hurried his steps in response to Vesper's rather imperious summons. "Yes, my lady?"

"Marikeen approaches."

As soon as he heard the words, he felt a prickling across his skin that followed the colored striations of his jann tamgas—the marks that appeared on jann skin when a connection to a certain element was formed. He bore the brown and gray tamgas of earth and stone strongly with only hints of white as he worked on understanding air better.

With a whoosh of wind in the heavy fog, a figure materialized ahead of them, dark in the unending whiteness. The woman moved forward gracefully but broke into a run at the sight of him. "Brother!" she cried.

He ran forward as well, wrapping his sister in a giant bear hug. "What in the world are you up to now, Marikeen?" he muttered in her ear as he embraced her.

"Play along with everything I do or say and you will be safe enough." After the hasty warning, Marikeen stepped back, smiling widely. "It is so good to see you again at last, Eben. Where have you been, and what have you been up to all this time?"

"Searching for you," he answered.

"Well, now you've found me. What *will* you do?"

"Take you home," he declared stoutly.

Marikeen made a face and snorted derisively. "I am home. This is my home. And soon it will be yours, too. The things I can show you, the power you can have—"

"You do not need to recruit me, sister. I am here willingly, and Vesper has been most kind and helpful to me."

"Really? What has she done for you?" Marikeen blurted.

"She helped me and my friends escape when we were kidnapped by Kithmar slavers."

"Curse Anton Constantine," she spat. "One day I will bring him and his minions low and sing for joy while doing it." She scowled and pulled out a white deer antler from her belt. "Remember this?"

He stared. "How do you come by the Spirit Stag's antler from our foster father's trophy room?"

"One of your Kithmar friends used it to kill Leland."

Eben's gaze narrowed to angry slits. "The same tiger changeling was one of my captors. He bragged of killing Hyland."

"I'll give you him to kill if I can have Anton for myself," she replied icily.

"Deal."

"Come, brother. I must speak with Vesper. I have several items to deliver to her." Marikeen linked her hand around his elbow and strolled back toward their diminutive benefactress.

"How is it you can bring physical items onto the dream plane? Do you come here by some other means than dreaming?" Eben asked in surprise.

"Nay, I dreamed my way here this night, just like you."

"How can you tell I dreamed my way here?" he demanded.

"After a while in this realm, you will develop an eye for phantasms versus dreaming constructs of material people, and corporeal beings walking this plane."

"You did not answer my question. If you are a dreaming construct of yourself, how did you bring a physical object here?"

"I always was the more talented mage of the two of us. I have been learning new tricks since I left your side, little brother. My new friends know all kinds of clever things to do with magic. Some of them you would not believe if I showed you."

"What items did you bring for Vesper in this dream of yours, then?"

"Patience, Eben. They are for Vesper, and only to her will I reveal or relinquish them."

She always had been the secretive type. He rolled his eyes and walked beside her in silence as they approached Vesper.

"Do you have them?" the little girl demanded impatiently.

"Would I ever disappoint you, my lady?" Marikeen answered fondly.

"Nay. Not you. I am your favorite," Vesper replied.

Marikeen laughed a little. "Indeed, you are."

Eben stopped beside his sister just in front of Vesper. The Gaged Man tensed slightly, indicating his discomfort with the two of them approaching his mistress so closely. Keeping an eye on the warrior, Eben bowed low when his sister did.

"Well, hand them over!" Vesper cried impatiently.

Marikeen opened her pouch and pulled out a pair of completely innocuous baubles—a leather hair band and what looked like some sort of tooth or fang.

Vesper snatched the objects out of Marikeen's palm and closed her eyes, breathing deeply. "Ah, Marikeen, they are perfect. Well done. Well done, indeed!"

Vesper seemed barely aware of their presence. Eventually, she pulled a barrette out of her own pouch and tied the hair band to it, forming one hair adornment out of the two.

Eben leaned close to Marikeen to whisper, "Why is she so happy over a few bits of trash?"

"Because those bits of trash belong to people over whom she wishes to exert control," Marikeen muttered back sotto voce. "Watch and learn."

Vesper was rubbing the two objects continuously between her palms, round and round in slow, tiny circles. The child's lips moved, but if she made any sound aloud, it was too quiet for Eben to hear.

"Bring me three phantasms!" Vesper ordered abruptly. "Undifferentiated but powerful. As powerful as can be found."

One of the elementals floating along behind Vesper bowed gracefully. "So shall it be, Your Highness."

"She's a princess?" Eben whispered in shock. "Since when?"

"Since she was born," Marikeen answered back under her breath in exasperation.

It seemed to take but a few minutes for Vesper's order to be fulfilled, but Eben got a momentary sense of time not working the same way here as it did elsewhere. Three wispy white creatures drifted on currents of air to stand side by side in front of Vesper, wavering vaguely.

"Which one of you is the most accomplished warrior?" Vesper demanded.

Two of them pointed at the third. To that one, Vesper reached to her own hip and pulled out a magnificent white-bladed long sword. "By this object, shall you control your host. Give it to him, and guard it well when you control his mind. The blade is unbreakable by any human means. As long as it is whole, so shall your control of your host be complete."

"What a blade!" Eben muttered as Vesper handed over the gleaming, milky white weapon. He'd never seen a sword so gracefully shaped and yet deadly looking.

"That's Dragon's Tooth," Marikeen murmured back. "It once belonged to the greatest warrior in Haelos. And now that warrior will belong to Vesper."

To the other two phantasms, Vesper held out the claw and barrette. "Each one of you shall take one of these," she ordered.

The wraithlike beings did as instructed, and as Eben looked on, each one gradually began to take on the height and dimension of humanoids. One became a petite ghost of an elf—female, if he had to guess—but too insubstantial to be certain. And the other took on an older, slightly bent form that hinted of a rather grizzled humanoid male, maybe a hydesmyn. If Eben looked directly at them, he looked clear through the ghostly forms, but if he glimpsed them indirectly out of the corner of his eye, they looked very much like living people.

"Learn their skills, absorb their temperaments," Vesper ordered. "You will have need of both on the mission I have for you."

Eben stared, amazed, as first clothing and then gear took shape on all three phantasms. The creatures themselves began to transform even more. Their ghostly forms began to take on vague tints of color. The general curves of humanoids refined into recognizable individuals. Then facial features, hair, eyes, hands, and fingers began to take shape. It was as if he watched invisible hands mold a human being out of magical clay. The transparent quality of the morphing flesh gave way to firm, textured skin.

In a few minutes, three fully formed, totally real-looking adults dressed in the garb of adventurers stood before him, every freckle, wrinkle, and dimple in flesh, every button and thread in clothing faithfully reproduced. Had he not known they were phantasms, he would never have guessed it.

Which begged the question, could faked people like these get away with walking among the living for a time, spying on humans, and doing the work of this terrifying child?

Vesper said silkily, "Now learn their minds. Absorb their thoughts, their feelings, their gestures. Everything that makes them who they are. Become them."

Eben stared, shocked. She was talking about possession. That was among the most taboo of all known magics, an act universally reviled and feared. The taking over of another person's mind and thoughts, his or her actions and reactions—

The mere idea made him shudder in horror. And yet Vesper casually prepared to do that very thing.

For her part, Marikeen observed with deep, albeit academic-looking, interest. She asked, "So you fashion the phantasm first and then send it to inhabit the Urthbound body? And what of the actual spirits of the intended targets?"

Vesper answered in an offhand manner as if this was a thing she did every day, "I wait until they sleep and then trap their dreaming minds here in this realm. The objects you brought me will act as the lock on their dreaming prisons. As long as the object is intact, the prison remains intact. Once they're trapped here, the phantasms have no problem inhabiting and controlling the bodies."

"What if a target awakens or resists the phantasm?" Marikeen pressed.

Vesper shrugged. "A powerful phantasm can overwhelm the will of any sleeping human mind, but powerful phantasms are rare and difficult to bend to one's will, even here. Better to trap the target's sleeping mind and use weaker phantasms like these three who are biddable to my wishes."

Indeed, the three phantasms stood quietly, as docile and obedient as sheep.

"Won't people who know the three humans realize they're acting differently? That their personalities have changed?" Eben challenged.

Vesper shrugged. "Within a day or so, the phantasms will have absorbed enough of their hosts' memories, thought patterns, and tactile impressions that they will be nearly indistinguishable from the originals. Every one I've put in place so far has gone undetected."

Eben's jaw sagged. Just how many of these phantasmal recreations of human spirits were walking around possessing human hosts on her behalf? The notion made his skin crawl.

Marikeen leaned in close to murmur, "Never fear, brother. The magics required to create and control phantasmal doppelgängers are enormous. Very few beings alive on any plane have the skill to pull off such a thing."

And yet Vesper was one of those beings? He eyed the little girl with renewed caution. Just how powerful were the Kothites? If she was indeed the scion of her father, Archduke Ammertus, her abilities were but short shadows in comparison to his. And the Emperor was said to be vastly more powerful than any of his highest-ranking nobles.

One of the phantasms, the petite elven woman, said, "She sleeps. I feel it."

"Patience, my pet," Vesper murmured. "I would have you wait until the others sleep, as well."

"They will post a guard," the elf declared.

Vesper scowled in disgust. "Of course. It figures that this trio would be cautious. Fine. You may go now. And when it is your turn on the watch, let me know, and I will send your companions."

"Have you any other orders for me?"

"Indeed, I do. I have orders for all of you."

Eben shuddered as all three of those impassive, empty stares turned to lock on their mistress.

"Once you are firmly in control of your hosts, you are to use all their knowledge and skills to search out and seize any items that once belonged to an ancient king of these lands."

Eben's blood and bones turned to ice right where he stood. She knew about Gawaine? But how? And why did she search out his regalia? This could *not* be good. Impatience to wake up and report this alarming news to his friends coursed through him.

"Do you ail, brother?" Marikeen murmured.

"Nay, I am fine. Well, not exactly fine," he added hastily,

remembering how easily and well she could read him. "I am a little uncomfortable with the idea of possession in general."

Marikeen shrugged. "I've seen bigger and more impressive effects."

He didn't want to know what was more impressive than taking over an entire human being. "When we wake up, come join me and my friends, Mar."

"What are you up to now? Still wandering the wild lands?"

"Yes. We're exploring the Sorrow Wold and the western reaches beyond it."

"No, thank you. I like my warm bed, a roof, and nice clothes. I want my servants and little luxuries. You can keep your rough camping." She shuddered as she spoke.

"It's not that bad," he retorted, "and you always were a sissy."

"Hah."

"Hah!"

They glared at each other and then dissolved into laughter. It had been far too long since they'd argued with one another.

"I miss you, Marikeen."

"And I you, Eben. Come join me."

"Maybe I will when I get back from the west. Where will I find you?"

"At the moment, I am in the northern Lochlands. When you are ready to join me, I will give you exact directions to find me."

"I look forward to it."

Vesper moved off a little way, and Eben lowered his voice. "What is the child up to? Why this huge army?"

"Why do you think?" Marikeen asked.

"Obviously, she plans to invade the material plane. She has already tried once and failed."

"Ah, but did she fail?"

He frowned. "What do you mean?"

"She now is able to send agents and phantasms to the material plane at will. I and others are able to bring physical items to this plane. Her power has grown exponentially after the incursion through the gate, wouldn't you say?"

Eben tried not to stare but failed. "To what end?" he breathed.

"What end does every powerful being strive toward?" she asked cynically.

Leland Hyland had long taught them both that power begat lust for more power in all but the noblest and most disciplined of people. Their foster father had striven to raise them and his son, Kendrick, to be that noble and disciplined. And for that, Eben had loved and admired him without reservation.

He thought his sister had felt the same way, but here she was, bringing items to Vesper that allowed the child to possess other human beings. Had Leland failed with Marikeen? Had he, himself, somehow failed her?

"I know I lost touch with you for a while, Marikeen, and I feel terrible about failing to rescue you, but I promise I will not let you down again. Anytime you have need of me, you have but to ask, and I will be there. You are family."

She smiled, and he thought he saw genuine fondness in her eyes, but she was so difficult to read these days. So different. She had a hardness, an intense focus about her; that was new. He got the distinct impression she was not delivering items to Vesper out of the goodness of her heart. Marikeen pursued some agenda of her own, but he could not for the life of him fathom what it might be. And that worried him.

Will woke to the sounds of giggles, the likes of which he had not heard for upward of a year. He groaned and rolled over in his hammock, peeling one eyelid open just far enough to glare at a pair of dryads, heads together, whispering and giggling behind their hands.

"Yes, I'm Will Cobb," he grumbled. "And no, your charms won't work on me. Go away. I'm sleeping."

"But the sun is above the horizon, Will Cobb," one of them twittered.

"By how much?" he snapped.

"Almost a thumb's width."

"Go away or I'll throw my boot at you."

The pair scampered off, disappearing abruptly. He'd grown accustomed to the fae creatures' ability to walk into solid trees and pop out of them just as easily. At least he knew now that the Sorrow Wold had enough enchantment within it to support the magical groves necessary for dryads to survive. He'd begun to wonder as they'd walked through its dank, rotting, and dead depths yesterday. Even Lord Bloodroot had been put off by the wold's decay.

Although the tree spirit within him championed death and the completion of the cycle of life, apparently whatever was going on in the Sorrow Wold was well outside of that natural cycle.

Curse it. The dryads had woken him up enough that his brain had gotten going. Now he would never get back to sleep. Irritated, he rolled out of his hammock and stepped into the boots he'd threatened to toss at the dryads. He laced them up, stowed his staff in the sling across his back, and stepped out of the tree house in search of breakfast.

He smelled cook fires on the breeze but did not see any. Following his nose, he crossed a hair-raising rope and wood-slat bridge, and he entered a large, round house that seemed to mark the center of the village high in the trees. Up here, sunlight penetrated a lush canopy of green and vibrant leaves. No wonder the local kindari chose to live up here. So would he.

Moto and Raina looked up from where they sat beside the fire, chatting.

"You're looking none the worse for wear," Moto commented. "Most first timers get sick as dogs smoking kindari tobacco."

Will shrugged. "I'm forest born and bred. Me and the other lads in the hollow snuck tobacco out of our fathers' pouches all the time."

Raina passed him a bowl of some sort of grain-and-berry porridge. "Moto says he has a surprise for me in a day or two."

"Does that mean we're going to stay here in this pleasant, sunny place with dry beds and defenses against goblins, and let your guide find you?" he asked hopefully.

Raina laughed. "I don't know. I hope to speak with the local elders about that. Maybe they can advise me on how to go about finding my guide."

Given that Moto didn't ask for more details, he gathered Raina had already spoken to the pyresti about a Mage of Alchizzadon coming to fetch her. And given the disgusted look on Moto's face, Will gathered that perhaps Moto had some knowledge of the mages.

The other members of their party wandered into the common room over the next hour, save Eben. All the others were long done with breakfast and almost finished repairing their armor and sharpening weapons after last night's fight before the jann stumbled into the open space, rubbing his face.

"You look like death if it had a bad day," Will teased his friend.

"Are you in need of healing?" Raina asked quickly.

"I must look bad if you're offering healing," Eben replied groggily.

"Rough night's sleep?" Rynn asked.

"Unexpected dreams," Eben answered the paxan shortly.

"Ah." A pregnant pause, then Rynn asked, "Anything to report?"

"Yes, as a matter of fact." Eben's voice dropped. "It turns out we're not the only ones chasing the goals we've been pursuing."

Will noticed that Raina visibly paled. "*That* goal?" she asked.

"Yup."

"Who?" Raina breathed.

"Our very young-looking friend."

Rynn sucked in a breath. "If she gets to . . . the one we seek . . . first, I cannot imagine what would happen."

Rosana murmured reassuringly, "She's not even on this plane. Your dream of her could have been nothing more than a regular dream, made up in your imagination. For all we know, she's not doing anything to chase down old hearth tales or even to think about coming to this plane."

Rynn winced. "Actually, we do. My own dreams have been troubled of late, and powerful forces are moving in the Realm of Dreams."

"Yes, but she's just a little girl," Rosana protested.

Rynn retorted, "Consider Emperor Maximillian when he was a little boy, after all his mental powers manifested themselves and he had hundreds of years to learn how to use them. Would you dismiss him as a threat simply because of his age?"

Rosana scowled. "That's not a fair comparison. He's the most powerful Kothite of them all."

"Vesper is the scion of Ammertus. She is only one generation removed from the kind of power Maximillian wields. Given how devastated Ammertus was by her destruction, we can assume that he must have imbued her with a *lot* of his power. Her death was extremely costly to him."

"Still, she's only a child of a Kothite," Rosana insisted.

Rynn snorted. "Endellian's only a child of Kothites. And she's arguably the most vicious, dangerous one of them all at court."

Will neither knew nor cared much about the goings-on at the Imperial Seat. It was a world away from him and his life, and he planned to keep it that way.

Eben said fervently, "If Endellian's more powerful than Vesper, then I do not ever want to cross her path. I saw Vesper possess three people on this plane last night."

Rynn jolted. "How?"

"She got ahold of physical items belonging to them and created three exact phantasmal duplicates. Her phantasms were going to possess the people when they fell asleep, or something like that. I didn't understand the details, but she was definitely going to control them."

"To what end?" Raina asked.

"She told them to seek out any items that once belonged to an ancient king of these lands."

The group collectively gulped. Great. As if it wasn't bad

enough having Anton Constantine sending kidnappers and assassins after them, and Imperial hunters, Mages of Alchizzadon, and the Coil, now a powerful child Kothite was working against them.

Will said sourly, "Remind me again why it's so important that we risk our lives to complete this impossible quest?"

Of all people, it was Sha'Li who answered. "In the first place, impossible it is not. In the second place, many more people than we can see or know are depending on us. Common people. Simple people. Innocent people who cannot do this thing for themselves. We attempt the quest on their behalf."

"But why? What for?"

Sha'Li answered forcefully, "For freedom, Will Cobb. For hope. For restoring balance to nature. Think you the tree lord within you actually belongs inside you? Restored to his native home, he should be. Returned to a tree. The one we seek can make that happen."

He'd grown so accustomed to Bloodroot's alien, uncomfortable energy inside him, he had a hard time imagining life without the tree lord inside his head, draining life from his body.

Sha'Li continued, "We attempt the quest because it is the right thing to do. We are among a precious few with the courage and skill to stand up to evil among us. I speak not of laws but of justice. Of indignities against those who have done nothing to deserve them. Of prejudice and hate and small-mindedness. We dare to think bigger. We dare to think of a king worthy of his subjects. Of a world where dignity for all living beings is not a privilege but a right."

Will blinked, shocked. That was quite a speech for the taciturn lizardman girl. "I had no idea such passion burned within you," he murmured.

"I speak not of it often, but I agree with Kerryl Moonrunner. The world we live in is not right, and something must be done to fix it."

A powerful response stirred deep in Will's belly. Whether it was his own noble fervor or Bloodroot's, he could not tell.

At this point, he wasn't sure it much mattered. They had become one in more ways than he cared to contemplate. How was he ever going to let go of the tree lord's spirit when the time came? It would be like ripping out a piece of his own heart.

And this was why he needed to wake the Sleeping King. If anyone could safely and successfully disentangle his spirit from Bloodroot's, Gawaine could. As he was the greatest nature guardian of all time and the son of the Green Lady herself, no one else would have the knowledge, power, or skill to remove Bloodroot without destroying Will completely.

And he did want the treant removed eventually. Right? He still wanted a normal life. With Rosana. Settling down. Living out a quiet existence. Right?

Why, then, could he not conjure even the vaguest picture of a life lived thus that included him in the picture? Was he already becoming the vessel, totally controlled by his host, that Aurelius warned him about? Was he too far gone to Bloodroot?

CHAPTER

13

They spent two days at the kindari camp. On the third morning, Will, Eben, Rynn, and Sha'Li went out on a hunting expedition with a number of the Hanged Men and kindari while Raina stayed behind. Bored half to death, she turned to watch an elf nimbly free climb one of the great trees leading up to the village, eschewing the rope ladders entirely.

The fellow hopped over a railing not far from her, and Raina did a double take.

"Cicero?" she murmured in disbelief.

She flung herself forward to embrace the elf who had helped her escape Tyrel and then kept her alive in those early days after she'd fled her home. He'd been her stalwart protector and a true friend.

Cicero suffered her enthusiastic hug stoically, eventually muttering dryly, "If I say I'm glad to see you, too, will you let me go?"

Laughing, she took a step back from him.

"Please tell me you are not out here all by yourself in the middle of the Sorrow Wold."

"I'm not. Will, Rosana, Eben, and Sha'Li are here, along with our new friend, Rynn. You will like him. His sense of humor is nearly as dry as yours."

"I have no idea what you're speaking about."

"Ah, Cicero. I have missed you dearly. What brings you here?"

"I received a message from Moto that you were in the wold.

And knowing you, it won't be two minutes until you're in some terrible trouble and in dire need of a rescue."

"Have you so little faith in me?" she exclaimed.

"Nay. I merely know you."

They traded grins. He was not wrong about her.

She followed him across one of the precarious-looking rope bridges to the common hut, where Cicero took a long drink from a bucket of cool water and grabbed a handful of dried berries, nuts, and jerky from the communal bowl. They sat down beside the great, circular hearth and stretched their feet to the fire.

"Why are you out here, Raina?" Cicero asked plainly of her.

"I am supposed to meet a guide who will take me to visit the Mages of Alchizzadon."

"The Mages of Alchizzadon you ran away from home to avoid and who did their best to kidnap you?"

"Yes. Those mages."

"Are you mad?" he exclaimed in a rare display of emotion.

"Probably. They say they only want to talk with me. That they respect my colors and will let me leave whenever I want to go."

"And you believe them?"

"Why wouldn't I? The Royal Order of the Sun is very powerful."

"Oh, really? So you have a couple of Heart knights tucked away somewhere in the village where I haven't seen them yet?"

"No, I left my Royal Order of the Sun protectors back in Seastar."

Cicero shook his head in undisguised disgust. "I swear, you have a death wish."

"I've been told that before."

"What is wrong with you? Why would you agree to go with these mages? They're evil, Raina."

"We don't know that. Even if I disagree with their program of breeding powerful female mages, I still am the beneficiary of that. I can't very well revile them for making me into the healer that I am."

"They're evil. I'm telling you," he repeated stubbornly.

"And how do you know so much about them?" she challenged, a little frustrated with his insistence.

Cicero was silent for a minute and then muttered reluctantly, "I know someone who knows something about them."

She pounced on that. "Really? Who? Can I talk with him or her?"

"I don't know if she'd speak with you."

"Please? Can you ask? If they're evil like you say, the more I know about them before I go to them, the better off I'll be."

"You can't meet with them!"

"I gave my word."

He rolled his eyes, clearly expressing his opinion of that. "She lives some distance away. Is the mage supposed to meet you here in this village?"

"He said merely to come to the Sorrow Wold and he would find me."

Cicero grunted, sounding displeased. "If you've a few days before your guide is due, I can take you to her. Perhaps she can talk you out of this madness."

"Who is this friend of yours?" she asked curiously.

"She is no friend of mine!" Cicero replied sharply. "I merely said I know her. Not that I like her."

"Do you trust her?"

"Not particularly, but I do not believe she would harm you. At least not after she finds out how much you two have in common."

"What do you mean?"

Cicero merely scowled. "How soon can you leave to go meet her?"

"As soon as the others get back from hunting, we could be on our way, I suppose."

Cicero sighed. "The sooner the better. It's not wise to move in the wold at night. If we want to reach the next village before dark, we'll have to leave soon."

Fortunately, the hunting party came back within the hour, and her friends were willing to explore the wold further.

As they descended the great rope ladders to the dank, dark forest floor, Raina immediately began to regret agreeing to go with Cicero to meet this woman with information about the Mages of Alchizzadon. The sad, angry spirit pervading the wold weighed on her, so heavily that by suppertime she felt nearly unable to walk.

They spent the night in a kindari village nestled under a copse of massive pine trees and surrounded by a crude palisade. The sounds were awful as Raina huddled in her bedroll, wondering if the flimsy fence was enough to keep the creatures making the hisses, clicks, howls, and screams at bay.

It was a long night.

The next morning saw them traveling into deeper, darker, wetter, more dismal forest than they'd experienced so far. Even Cicero seemed jumpy as they made their slow, miserable way through the gloom.

"There it is," Cicero announced at around noon, if Raina had to guess. A cold rain dripped through the forest, impeding visibility.

She had to gasp at the beauty of the sight that met her as they reached the edge of a large clearing. But then her gasp turned to dismay as she realized what she was looking at.

A gigantic spiderweb stretched at waist height across the clearing, rising in the center to go over a low structure. Every gossamer strand of the massive web dripped with glistening droplets of water. It looked as if thousands of diamonds had been arranged in an intricate and delicate mosaic. They cast beautiful rainbows of color, painting the mosaic in brilliant, breathtaking hues.

A circular cottage squatted under the center of the web, its black sides coated in bright green moss and slime. It might have been a pleasant, even cheerful dwelling in another location with a fresh layer of whitewash. But here, it was nothing short of menacing. Was this the fabled dream spider's web?

Will asked low, "Who lives there, and is she a threat?"

Cicero retorted, "The Black Widow lives there, and she could kill us all without hardly lifting a hand. So be polite and don't stare at her." He picked up a stout stick and took a swing at the nearest strand of web silk. Bell-like sounds sparkled across the web as raindrops flew in all directions. Silently, ponderously, a great pole rose out of the center of the cottage, lifting the web up, a deadly parody of a children's maypole.

"Don't touch it," Cicero cautioned as he ducked under the low edge and made his way to the center of the tentlike space now beneath the web.

Gulping nervously, Raina did the same and followed him toward the dome. It did not help her trepidation that Cicero looked as apprehensive as she'd ever seen him—and she'd seen him proceed calmly into some pretty dangerous situations.

"Weapons out?" Will murmured under his breath.

"No!" Cicero said sharply. "The widow is guarded by a cadre of spider changeling fighters you do not want to tangle with. They all cast poisons that will kill you where you stand, not to mention they're big, strong, and *fast*."

"Thanks be to thee for the kind words about my companions," a raspy voice said from a deep shadow in the side of the cottage that turned out to be some sort of doorway.

Raina about jumped out of her skin. She'd heard no door open and seen no movement. An apparition glided into view, making an odd scuttling sound on the wooden boards of a porch that circled the dome. The Black Widow was a humpbacked humanoid draped in a wispy black cloak with a heavy black lace mantilla covering her head and partially concealing her face. But then she turned, and Raina had to bite back a gasp. The widow's skin was leathery and gray, and long fangs protruded from each side of her mouth. Her eyes were big and black and round, too widely set for a human face. Her forehead was too far back, her jaw too far forward, and the overall combination of arachnid and human was hideous.

"Who have you lured into my lair, Cicero?" the widow asked in a distinctly threatening tone.

"I have brought a young woman to see you, my lady. A daughter of Tyrel."

A sharp hiss of indrawn breath made Raina flinch.

The lace-covered head swung left and right as if examining every member of their party, but the widow's head didn't seem jointed to her body in an entirely human fashion.

Rosana edged closer to Will, and every scale on Sha'Li's body was standing up. Even Rynn was poised on his toes as if ready to leap into battle, or mayhap flee for his life. No wonder Cicero disliked this creature. She was the nightmare that lay beyond creepy.

"I would invite you to step into my parlor, but we would not want to be cliché, would we?" the Black Widow rasped.

Had that been humor? Did a human heart beat inside that monstrous, arachnid form? Raina took a hesitant step forward. This meeting had been her idea, after all.

"Greetings, madam. My name is Raina. I belong to the White Heart."

"Charlotte's girl. You're the mirror image of her at that age."

"You know my mother?"

"Of course I know my own great-niece."

Great-niece? Shock made Raina's mind go blank. This . . . thing . . . claimed kinship to *her*?

"I . . . I'm sorry, I'm afraid I don't . . . How are we . . ." Her voice trailed off. She had no idea how to ask this spider changeling why she called Charlotte of Tyrel her great-niece. Raina knew the family history backward and forward, and never, ever, had there been any mention of a spider changeling anywhere on the family tree.

The widow chuckled, a sandpaper-rough sound that did nothing to inspire confidence across Raina's cringing flesh. "I did not always look like this. In my day, I was considered a great beauty, like your mother."

Raina frowned. *Then how . . .*

"I gather you're a second daughter of Tyrel since you are

not walking to your death in the Arianna Plains. You're about the right age to be sent on the death march."

Raina frowned. "The Ariannas in my family leave to see the world and enjoy their freedom. They do not die."

The widow leaned forward, jabbing Raina angrily in the shoulder with a gloved finger. "They die, child. The Mages of Alchizzadon lie in wait for them and kill them. That is if the other Ariannas do not find her first and whisk her away to safe haven, hidden from those monsters."

"The mages *kill* them?"

The Black Widow shrugged. "They tried to kill me, but my beloved husband came across me fighting for my life against the mages and intervened to save me." Distant memory clouded the widow's expression for a moment, but then she shook it off, adding lightly, "My husband ate them all. It was most satisfying."

Raina had no idea what to say to that. At length, she circled back to the woman's previous statement. "What do you mean, the other Ariannas?"

"There is a daughter named Arianna in every generation, is there not?"

Raina nodded.

"That's one every eighteen to twenty years. Where do you think they all go? Why do not some of them come back home to Tyrel to be with their family? They're young, vital women when they leave, gifted mages all. What happens to them? Have you not secretly wondered when you lay in bed late at night all alone?"

"Of course I've wondered, but I assumed they found new places, started families . . ."

"Oh, the ones who live do. We've even formed a little enclave of our own—Ariannas and our descendants. As far as I know, at least three generations of Ariannas before you yet live, child."

Raina stared, stunned. "Why was I not told? Why could I not visit them?"

"The Mages of Alchizzadon would kill them all if they knew where to find them."

"But why? The Ariannas served them faithfully!"

"It's all about power, girl. Magic."

The word vibrated through Raina's brain like a dark prophecy. It always came down to her magic and who wanted to control it. Leland and Aurelius might have had noble reasons for manipulating her, but even they'd gently forced her into the White Heart and into the quest to wake Gawaine. Because of her magic.

The widow was speaking again. "The Mages of Alchizzadon have figured out how to take magic from people permanently and store it. Now they just have to figure out how to give it to their precious king and wake him."

Raina was half tempted to let the mages have her cursed magic. Her life would be so much simpler without it. But that was the point, wasn't it? Her magic allowed her to pursue goals that were not simple. That were important. That made a difference.

"Come, all of you. Sit. Tarant! Bring out a brace of chairs for our guests!" the widow called.

A burly spider changeling covered in bristly brown hair about the length of Raina's palm carried out four chairs, one in each arm. He went back inside and returned with four more. Eyeing him with abundant caution, Raina took a seat next to the widow, where their hostess indicated.

"Cicero says you know a fair bit about the Mages of Alchizzadon, madam," Raina said politely. "I would love to hear anything more you can tell me about them. They wish to meet with me, and Cicero is concerned that they will do me harm."

The Black Widow hissed again, and up close, it was one of the most menacing sounds Raina had ever heard. It sent shivers of primal horror down her spine.

"They have existed for many centuries, and as you know, have made free with the women of the House of Tyrel the whole time."

Raina nodded. "How many of them are there?"

"Oh, several hundred, I should think."

Shock reverberated through Raina's bones as if a giant bell

clapper had hit her. *Hundreds?* "Do you know where their tower is hidden?"

"South and west of Tyrel a little way. Mayhap somewhere in Fernel. My understanding is that it lies underground, out of sight. They hide like pale scorpions under their rock, never coming out into the light of day."

An ironic observation coming from a spider changeling, but Raina kept the thought to herself. "What do you know of their goals and purposes?"

"Of course, they work to increase the magical power of the daughters of Tyrel. To their detriment, I might add." The widow cackled. "When we finally started turning on them, we were formidable opponents."

"What else?" Raina prompted.

"They babysit the body of the Human King and think that if they wish hard enough, he will somehow come back to life, and they'll get credit for waking him. The fools think that, by holding his cold, lifeless hand for all these centuries, they'll somehow be his favorites when he wakes. They were flunkies and sycophants when he fell into his sleep, and they'll be no different when he awakes."

Raina didn't try to hide her smile. It was refreshing to hear someone take the fearsome mages so in vain.

"The mages guard the planar gates, of course. They train clavigers for the task. Although they're poor excuses for gate masters these days. In olden times, the clavigers could tune the gates to a pinpoint spot on any plane at will. Now, with so many gates broken and the ancient knowledge mostly lost, they're lucky to align one to the correct plane, let alone open or close it."

Raina responded, "We saw a claviger at a gate last fall. He was possessed by a creature on the other side of the gate and nearly let through an army of dream creatures."

"Fools," the widow spat. She was silent a moment and then turned the conversation without warning. "So tell me, child. Why do the mages wish to speak with thee?"

"I do not know, madam. And before you accuse me of being mad to accept their invitation, I will tell you that they recognize my membership and rank in the White Heart, and the Royal Order of the Sun does, indeed, know where I'm going and when I am expected to return. Should I fail to report back in on time, the Royal Order will come after me."

"Too late, they will come. The mages will destroy thee if they can. It's not the daughters of Tyrel they want, child. It's our magic. And if you're as powerful as your mother, the mages will want your power badly, indeed."

Raina ducked her head and said modestly, "I'm quite a bit more magically powerful than my mother."

The widow jolted, staring, which was more than a little disconcerting. "How much more?"

Raina shrugged. "I honestly don't know. I've never reached the end of my healing powers entirely."

Will piped up, "I've seen her heal six hundred of the simplest wounds before."

Rosana chimed in, "She can combat heal continuously for well over an hour and still have mana left to heal everyone on the field after battle ends."

The widow shook her head slowly in that odd, disjointed, side-to-side swing. "Mark my words. They will kill you for your magic."

"They have sworn not to harm me."

"Have *all* of them so sworn?" the widow demanded.

"My best friend from childhood, who is now one of them, and his mentor and the leader of the entire order have sworn it."

"If he is your best friend, get him out of there if you have any care for him."

"That is my plan," Raina answered grimly.

The widow rummaged under her filmy cloak and held out a gloved hand that was all bones and clawlike nails, even through the thin black leather. "Take this, child. It's a poison that will kill instantly."

"I thank you for the offer, but I cannot accept. I am White Heart."

"Bah! That shirt will get you killed!"

"It probably will," Raina allowed, "but I'm bound to up-hold the values it represents, nonetheless."

The widow rummaged again and came up with a handful of small glass globes. "Fine. Then take these sleeping gas poisons. When the mages turn ugly—and they will—drop a few of them for me. Long have I dreamed of such a moment. You are allowed to put people to sleep, aren't you?"

"Technically, yes. Although it's not entirely in the spirit of my order to—"

"Take the cursed potions, and do not be a foolish idealist. You are a *child*, and the mages you propose to visit are *not*. Heed me closely. This visit of yours will not end well."

E ndellian took the note from the chamberlain and
glanced down at it. Its contents would have to be important to interrupt her father while he sat in with the
Council of Kings. The hundred lesser rulers of Koth had
been kicking up their heels and complaining about the stiff
levies of men and supplies being demanded of them as her
father ramped up his armies for a new push onto the outly-
ing continents.

The note was from her half brother, Laernan, the Lord
High Inquisitor. She read it, and her eyebrows sailed sky-
ward. A young man had just walked into the grand reception
hall and announced himself to be a Child of Fate, come to
court to prophesy for the Emperor. Laernan had apparently
attempted a preliminary mental examination of the fellow's
talent and been sharply and curtly expelled from the prophet's mind.

It was Laernan's opinion that the young man was potentially the most powerful prophet since Oretia, Maximillian's
personal seer for centuries, had died. Ammertus murdered
her when she gave what was now called the Oretian Prophecy, foretelling the end of the line of Ammertus and the end
of the reign of Maximillian.

She looked up at her father, attempting to gauge his mood.
He wasn't even attempting to mask his impatience and disdain. She moved close behind his throne and leaned around
it discreetly, passing Laernan's note to Maximillian.

He glanced down at it, and a new wave of emotion, this
time of interest laced with suspicion, passed over her. His sus-

picion jolted her thinking to the next level of analysis. Who could have sent a talented seer to court, and for what purpose? Would the prophet see and report his visions truly, or was the young man here to sow discord and fear among gullible courtiers? Was he a spy? An assassin? A seer was one of the few commoners who might reasonably expect to have direct access to Maximillian at least once in his life.

Her father interrupted one of the kings to call a recess. She followed him across the vast palace complex to where Laernan did his work. She hoped there was no blood today. Some of the Children of Fate insisted on being tortured the old-fashioned way before they gave up their visions. Laernan obliged because he said it relieved their guilt at talking to him. Not to mention he got more complete revelations from the prophets once they fully capitulated to the suffering he caused them.

How her brother did his job and managed not to go mad, she hadn't the foggiest idea.

Maximillian paused outside Laernan's chamber to speak with the chief of his security contingent, the Hand. The fellow was a fearsome warrior and, like all her father's guards, deaf. They signed briefly, with Maximillian warning that the prisoner within might be planning to kill him. The guard bristled and nodded briskly, entering the chamber with several of his men while her father waited outside.

In a minute, her father's chamberlain opened the door, and Laernan personally stepped outside. "The prisoner is secured, Your Resplendent Majesty. My apologies for interrupting whatever else you were doing. This young man is . . . interesting."

A dozen shadings of meaning were packed into that single word. Primary among them were concern, fascination, and a hint of fear. Who or what could frighten Laernan after the horrors he saw and committed on a daily basis?

She followed Maximillian into a spacious, comfortable room outfitted like an office except for the wrist and ankle manacles on one stone wall and the drain in the floor beneath them. Laernan had no need of clumsy machines or gadgets to torture his prisoners. He could make them suffer ever so much more exquisitely by using his mental powers to stimulate their minds into feeling maximum pain. She'd seen people die over and over, cuffed to his wall. Laernan restored them to life only to torture them until their hearts stopped beating again under the duress of the agony he inflicted.

A shimmering field of magical energy encased Laernan's prisoner from the neck down, where he stood in front of the desk—a confinement spell that would prevent him from wielding a weapon or casting magic but still allowed him to speak.

The first thing she noticed was the bold tabard he wore, Darkadian in style, with a high collar and exaggeratedly long sleeves trailing nearly to the floor. Whereas Imperial fashion was gaudy to excess, the young man's black robe was severe to the point of asceticism. Darkadia was one of the wealthiest kingdoms in Koth, albeit one of the spookiest. Rumors of experiments to unnaturally extend life spans, blood drinking, infanticide, and other disturbing rituals circulated about the mysterious kingdom.

The lone decoration on the young man's robe was a large embroidered hourglass—the symbol of the Children of Fate. It was an arrogant declaration of who this young man was. The last half dozen Children of Fate had hidden tiny, furtive marks somewhere on their person where they would not be visible to the casual observer. But this man—he boldly declared his affiliation for all the world to see.

He was handsome in a dark, sinister way. Everything about him was narrow and severe. Tall and human, he was maybe in his mid-twenties. He had straight black hair that fell to his shoulders and pale skin stark in contrast. His face was lean, his cheeks hollow.

But what drew her attention most sharply were those black-within-black eyes of his. She couldn't tell where his pupils stopped and the irises began, if, in fact, his pupils stopped at all. He turned that strange, featureless stare on her, and she felt as if she were being sucked into a great, dark abyss of utter, hopeless nothingness. She looked away, shaking off the strange sensation. By the stars, looking into his eyes was like gazing into the Black Flame itself.

Yet again, her laggard suspicion was late arriving to the party. It dawned on her belatedly to wonder how he had gotten past her formidable mental defenses to influence her feelings at all. Alarmed, she consciously concentrated upon blocking whatever he was doing to her, and yet, the strange, tugging fascination remained.

"You say you came here to prophesy for me," her father said without introduction. "Here I am. So prophesy."

The young man's mouth curled into a sardonic smile, and he managed to bow his head so insolently she had to bite back a rebuke.

The young man declared in a rich, velvet voice, "One who stands within this chamber now will die within one sun cycle."

One sun cycle? A single day? Endellian's eyebrows shot up. That was a daring prediction, indeed. Furthermore, he hadn't bothered to wrap his prophecy in flowery phrases and cryptic double meanings that would give him an out when his prophecy didn't come true.

Someone in this room was going to die, was he? She looked over at Laernan, standing disapprovingly with his arms crossed on the other side of the room; a half dozen of her father's guards and chamberlains; her mother, Iolanthe, looking worried; and lastly, her father—who looked amused.

Maximillian remarked, "A clever prophecy, young man. For if one of my people does not die by this time tomorrow, it shall be you who dies. Thus, your prophecy will be fulfilled either way."

The seer looked blasé, as if he would have shrugged had his shoulders not been paralyzed. "I see more, Your Most Glorious and Resplendent Majesty. Much more. A great army launches from these shores into darkness. They will meet with disaster and fail in their mission."

That made Endellian stare. The directness and clarity with which this seer spoke was breathtaking. There was no mistaking his meaning. At all. He was absolutely prophesying that the Legion of the Vast, which was secretly bound for Tal'Shalloth even as they spoke, would be defeated and fail to conquer that strange and dangerous place deep in Inner Urth.

Maximillian wasn't so amused now.

The seer declared confidently, "A rebellion grows on distant shores and will unravel all that you have done there."

"Which shores?" Maximillian demanded.

"I do not yet see enough detail to identify a country or continent, but I will keep looking, and when I can answer you, I will."

"You are interesting," her father stated. To Laernan, Maximillian said, "He may live for today. Let us see what else he produces before I decide if he lives or dies on the morrow."

"So shall it be, Your Most Resplendent Majesty," Laernan murmured.

Maximillian swept out of the room, followed by his entourage. While Endellian waited her turn to leave, she heard the young man say to Laernan, "That went well, don't you think?"

"You still breathe. I should say it went exceedingly well for you," Laernan replied dryly.

"You will release me and show me to my quarters next," the seer announced.

"Not until you tell me the identity of who is going to die this day," Laernan replied.

Endellian halted and turned to hear the answer.

"If I tell you, you will take steps to prevent the event from happening. My prophecy will be undone, and the Emperor will put me to death."

"Undoing prophecy is the whole point of keeping creatures like you on a leash, performing your tricks for the Emperor!" Laernan snapped.

"Be at peace, my friend. The day is coming soon when you, too, will slip your leash. You will no longer have to destroy people's minds, Lord High Inquisitor of Koth. You will finally go home and rest."

"This is my home."

"Is it really? We both know where your heart yearns to be."

Endellian frowned as the two men shared a long, knowing look between them. Where else would her brother wish to live? If the two men shared some sort of telepathic moment of communication, she was not privy to it.

"As for you, Princess—"

She froze, infuriated that the Child of Fate would dare speak to her in so casual a tone. And truthfully, she was afraid. She did not want to hear what he had to say to her.

"Although the way shall be made clear for it to happen, in the end, your fondest wish will be denied to you."

She gasped. She couldn't help it. Glancing back over her shoulder at the insolent fellow, she stormed from the room. *How dare he.* He would be dead where he stood were it not for her father's order to let him live a while yet. He had no idea that her fondest wish was to have the Eternal Throne for herself with Tarses at her side. No one knew that, not even her father. And no matter what some arrogant seer said, she *would* have it one day.

No matter what she had to do to get it.

Will flinched as the Black Widow's inhuman stare left Raina and turned on him and the others. She rasped, "Who might the rest of you be, and why are you in my wold?"

Rynn usually spoke up in situations like this, but today the paxan stayed silent. He seemed distracted and focused inward.

Will reluctantly answered, "We are here to search for a friend of ours who has gone missing. Or rather, has been kidnapped." They'd decided that a search for Kendrick would be their cover story if anyone asked them why they were abroad, as opposed to the truth that they searched for Gawaine's regalia.

"By whom?" the widow demanded.

"By a nature guardian who calls himself Moonrunner."

"Ah. What trouble has Kerryl gotten himself into now?"

"You know him?" Eben interrupted.

The widow's black gaze turned to the jann. "Aye." Her

voice was flat and her tone not particularly friendly. Will gathered that she and Kerryl were not on the best of terms.

Eben said, "Kerryl Moonrunner kidnapped my foster brother, Kendrick Hyland. And then he turned Kendrick into a were-boar and commands him at will."

"Did he now?" The Black Widow made a noise that Will thought might be a chuckle, but it just as easily could have been a hiss of displeasure. Her inhuman features made reading her emotions nearly impossible.

"It's no joke!" Eben responded angrily. "We want our friend back!"

"I'm sure you do," the Black Widow replied blandly.

Will was reluctant to interact with this strange creature at all, but if she had information that could be of use to them, he had no choice. "Do you have any idea how Kerryl is controlling our friend?"

"Perhaps Kerryl has laid hands on the Band of Beasts or mayhap the Mantle of Beasts. They're said to give their wearer dominion over all the creatures of the wild."

Sha'Li, who rarely participated in these sorts of conversations, leaned forward, firelight dancing off the sheen of her scaled face. "Would these bands be leather bracers decorated with countless animals rendered so lifelike that they seem to move around the band?"

The widow looked sharply at her. "You've seen them, then? Where?"

"I helped Kerryl steal one of the bands a while back."

Eben exclaimed, "You're the reason Kerryl controls Kendrick? How could you?"

Sha'Li made a hissing sound before snapping, "I had no idea what it could do. He was my friend and said he needed it."

Eben made a sound of disgust, and Sha'Li added, "That night is when Kerryl gave me Will's disk. And where would we be without that? It led us to—"

She broke off, for which Will was extremely grateful. There was no need to reveal Gawaine's existence to this alarming woman who might or might not be trustworthy. One thing he did sense with certainty about the widow, she had an agenda of her own and wouldn't hesitate to use any who crossed her path to achieve it.

Eben said, "We would be grateful for any information you might be able to share with us about Kerryl."

The widow's gray mouth opened to reveal more long, curved fangs that made Will's skin crawl. "Well, now. What I know about Kerryl could take some time to tell."

Eben leaned forward expectantly.

"My beloved husband, rest his spirit in peace, was a Venerer in service to a child of Zinn, the Great Spider. Kerryl is—was—the Keeper of the Great Wolf."

Will frowned. "Who are these great creatures?"

"Bah. The old ways are broken and old knowings forgotten in you younglings," the widow grumbled. "First, there was the land. And it came to life, bursting with green and growing things. And the Great Circle of Tree Lords had dominion over it all. Then came the animals of land and sea and sky, and over them ruled the Great Beasts of Haelos. And last, there came life and death to the plants and animals, and over their spirits ruled the Great Totems. These three, the treants, beasts, and totems, worked together to protect us all until a terrible war came and broke their circle."

"What war?" Raina interjected.

Will knew she had studied history and read many books, but she asked the question as if she had no idea what war the widow spoke of.

"A forgotten war!" the widow snapped, sounding annoyed at the interruption. "And now that the circle of life is broken, a sickness has come upon the land. It is slowly dying because its balance is destroyed."

Something fierce surged in Will's chest. The widow's words were resonating strongly with Bloodroot.

"My husband should not have died, but Zinn was weakened and could not protect her children. Now she has no keeper to speak for her and spread her teachings. I do what I can, but I was never meant to be her speaker."

Was that how the widow had turned into a spider changeling?

"And Kerryl . . ." The widow's voice trailed off for a long moment. "And Kerryl lost his way. His wife and child were killed in the Forgotten War, his mind shattered. He sees dire threats where there are none and ignores the laws of nature." She shook her head and fell silent.

What Forgotten War? Aurelius had been trying to fill in Will's sketchy knowledge of Haelan history and had never mentioned anything about a war that broke the Great Circle.

"Kerryl ignored the law of nature forbidding turning humans who do not want it into were-creatures," Eben said bitterly.

"You fool!" the widow lashed out, her fangs abruptly extending several inches out of her mouth. "That is not his crime! He had to kill a scion of the Boar to change your friend! That is the crime! Do you have any idea how rare and precious such a creature is? The power to protect nature that was lost by killing that scion?"

"What about the power to do good that was lost by changing our friend?" Eben shot back.

The widow leaned back in her chair, her fangs retreating into her mouth. "Just so, boy. Just so."

Raina said thoughtfully, "So Kerryl had to kill a rat scion or two to make Pierre and Phillipe into were-rats, and an alligator scion to make our friend Tarryn into a were-alligator?"

"So many?" the Black Widow breathed. "What has he done?"

Will would take that as an affirmative answer to Raina's question. He would also take the widow's horror to mean that scions of Great Beasts were not plentiful. What *was* Kerryl thinking to kill so many of them? The man was a nature guardian after all and had to know what he was costing the Great Beasts. Sha'Li and Kendrick both insisted the man was not mad, but Will had to wonder.

He frowned. "Wouldn't this Great Wolf you spoke of do something to fix Kerryl if Kerryl is his speaker?"

"The Great Beasts expend all their energy trying to heal the land. Most of them are barely alive right now, let alone awake."

"And the tree lords?" Will asked. "What of them?"

She shrugged. "They do what they can for the land, but with the circle broken and Bloodroot destroyed, their balance, and their ability to restore balance, is gone."

"What if Bloodroot is not dead?" Will asked her cautiously.

The widow snorted. "I think we would all know if a greater bloodthorn tree had sprung up somewhere. They're gigantic. Impossible to miss."

Amusement bubbled up in his gut. What she didn't know wouldn't hurt her. "Tell us more of Kerryl," Will said aloud.

"The other nature guardians despise him. The Tribe of the Moon's Hunter in Green hates him for destroying Quinton, who was Kerryl's brother and her lover."

Sha'Li leaned forward, listening intently, as if she'd heard of this Hunter in Green before.

The widow continued, "As the war was lost, the Great Wolf was dying. Kerryl needed to bond its spirit to someone fast. Kerryl himself, as the Wolf Speaker, was the best candidate. But only Kerryl knew how to cast the magic, and he could not cast it on himself, so he snagged his brother, Quinton, and joined him with the Wolf instead."

"Why did that anger the Hunter in Green?" Sha'Li asked. "Quinton could still have been with her, couldn't he?"

"The joining was hasty and badly done. Both the Wolf and Quinton would have gone mad if Kerryl hadn't dived in to erase both of their memories. Afterward, Quinton had no memory of the Hunter in Green."

Will made a face. If someone took away Rosana's memory of ever having cared for him, he would be out for blood, too.

"At any rate," the widow continued, "the Hunter in Green despises Kerryl. She swears that if he'd given her time to try it, she could have taught the Wolf and Quinton to coexist in the same body."

Everyone in the party glanced at Will. To varying degrees, they all looked relieved and impressed that he had survived the joining with Bloodroot. It was a little late for that. He'd fought through the encroaching madness and loss of self mostly on his own. Raina and Rosana had helped him overcome the deathly poison to his body of hosting Lord Bloodroot, but he'd done the rest himself. Pride in his accomplishment surged through him.

"Why does Kerryl create these were-creatures?" Raina asked.

The Black Widow pulled her filmy cloak more closely around herself. "He creates an army."

"To fight what?" Raina followed up.

"You would have to ask him."

Will snorted. The next time they caught up with Kerryl Moonrunner, it would be to slit his throat, not to have tea and chat with him.

The Black Widow pinned Sha'Li with a piercing stare. "You're Tribe of the Moon. What say you about Kerryl?"

The lizardman answered carefully, "I do not speak for all of the tribe, but I believe Kerryl's heart to be in the right place, even if his mind is not. We are"—she paused as if searching for the right word—"concerned about his recent activities."

Will's eyebrows lifted. That was news to him. Sha'Li had been Kerryl's staunchest defender all along. But now she was expressing doubts? He might accuse her of being diplomatic for the sake of not angering the Widow, but Sha'Li didn't have a diplomatic bone in her body and always spoke the truth. Interesting. Eben looked thunderstruck at the change in position from Sha'Li.

Good. Maybe those two would quit giving each other the silent treatment. They made everyone in the party uncomfortable with their long, glowering glares directed at each other.

"Do you have any idea how we can find Kerryl?" Will asked.

"Of course," the widow replied.

When she didn't say any more, he prompted, "Can you share it with us?"

She grinned, a pointed, poisonous grimace that made him shudder. "Stay here a while, and he will come to thee."

* * *

Rynn was even less pleased than Cicero when the Black Widow proposed that their party spend the night with her. That giant web of hers worried him. A lot. Dream magics poured off of it, and he was having to fight for all he was worth not to be lured into its sleeping embrace, even now, while fully conscious and able to fend it off. Once they all fell asleep and their mental defenses were down, that thing would ensnare them all.

He cut off Raina as she opened her mouth to accept the invitation and said politely, "We must be on our way, I'm afraid. Thank you for your generosity and knowledge, Lady of the Wold."

The widow insisted on giving them dried rations for the trail, and it was nearly full dark before they finally stood in the door. Raina took the widow's clawlike hands and kissed that leathery cheek before they took their leave of the strange home and its equally strange occupant.

Behind him, ponderous squeaks announced that pole holding up the web was being lowered. A great sense of being summoned to the dreaming overcame Rynn. That dream web was giving off vibrations he could barely withstand. It took all his mental powers to hold off the dream.

They raced away from the clearing for perhaps a half hour, until Rosana finally huffed, "Can we stop for a moment and catch our breath?"

Rynn stopped apologetically.

"Why did we have to get out of there like that?" Raina asked him.

"The web. She was planning to capture our dreams."

"And you know this how?" Raina followed up.

"I could barely hold off the pull of the dream web, and I was wide awake. Asleep, we would have been defenseless. She could have taken all our dreams from our minds."

"But she had more information for us about Kerryl—"

He interrupted Raina, "Do you want her to see you dream of Gawaine? To let her know where exactly to find him?"

"No. Of course not."

"Or the rest of you?" Rynn demanded. "Do you want the

widow to see all your dreams? To know your most private wishes and aspirations and lay them bare?"

The other members of the party squirmed a little. As well they should. He tried hard to respect their privacy, but sometimes he caught glimpses of their dreams by accident. He knew that Raina visited Gawaine's grove in her dreams almost every night. That Rosana dreamed of Will, and Will dreamed of glory in battle. Sha'Li dreamed of returning home a hero, and Eben—

Ah, Eben. He so desperately wanted to prove himself that he would throw in his lot with a creature like Vesper and risk destroying himself. Rynn made a mental note to keep an eye on Eben. If Vesper could possess unwilling subjects, she could certainly possess a willing one.

Raina shuddered, her expression grim.

Cicero said urgently to her, "Look what the mages drove her to. What they've driven you to do already. This is what the Mages of Alchizzadon do to the women of your family. Why do you seek peace with them? You should be seeking their destruction."

Raina sighed. "They're not evil. They've merely lost their way. I can tell them what their original purpose was and help them find their way again."

Rynn had never met these mages, but he was compelled to ask, "Why would they believe you? In their eyes, you're but a silly, rebellious girl who's given them a lot of trouble."

"Thank you," Cicero said to him emphatically.

Raina shrugged. "I have to try. I owe it to my daughters and my daughters' daughters to try to make the mages understand where they have strayed from their intended path."

Rynn snorted. He wished her good luck with that.

Cicero said, "It is full dark, and this place is not safe at night."

Now there was a massive understatement.

"How do you suggest we proceed?" Rynn asked the kindari whose home this was.

"Let us find a tall tree and climb it. We're safer up there than down here where the monsters roam."

It took a while to get everyone high into the branches of a massive pine tree, and then to use an axe to chop off the lowest branches so no one else could easily climb up after them. But eventually, they were all settled on branches of their own, leaning against the trunk, and tied into place so they wouldn't fall out of the tree in their sleep. The night was cold and damp, but blessedly, there was no rain.

Rynn huddled deeply within his cloak and awkwardly draped bedroll, and at long last, he succumbed to sleep. He tentatively opened his mind to dreaming and was not surprised when the Black Widow's image crept into his mind with that weird, scrabbling gait of hers.

Wariness of her power and ruthlessness washed over him. He did not sense evil in her, exactly, but she was a predator—and extremely dangerous. If only he could sense her agenda more clearly. Like most paxan, when he was near people he could pick up emotional cues and bits of thoughts that gave him insight to people's true purposes, but the only emotions he got from the widow were grief and rage. Cold, implacable rage that would never diminish and never relent.

If he and his companions could focus her rage, channel it in a direction that suited their purposes, she could be a powerful ally in their quest to wake the Sleeping King, but in the absence of any clues to her real feelings and opinions, he had no idea how to go about shaping her rage constructively.

He would have to speak to Raina about that in the morning. Except when morning dawned, she was gone.

"W here am I?" Raina blurted, shocked by the abrupt change in her surroundings. One moment she was blinking awake in the dark of the Sorrow Wold with a hand over her mouth and Justin's shadowed face leaning over her, and the next she was standing here in this cavernous chamber, decorated with massive furniture carved from age-darkened wood, its walls hung with huge, faded tapestries. Iron torches guttered in brackets on the walls, casting hellish shadows over dozens of men looming ominously around her.

Runes on faces. Blue cloaks. *Alchizzadon*. The word exploded into her consciousness along with a burst of panic that brought magic surging defensively into her hands.

Justin answered from right beside her in a soothing voice, "Easy, Raina. We mean you no harm."

From her left, Cicero groaned, "Not again."

She whipped around to face him. "What have you done? Why are you here?"

"I saw him"—he pointed at Justin—"that kid from Tyrel you were friends with, sneaking up on you in your sleep. I waited to see what he would do. Didn't expect him to open a blasted portal." Cicero scowled past her at Justin.

"Let me guess. You were worried about me, so you jumped through after me. Again."

"Well, yes."

"Cicero, Cicero. You have to stop throwing yourself into harm's way on my behalf."

His glare turned on her. "You think I *want* to be here? I know who these guys are."

"How do you know that?" one of the mages demanded.

Cicero replied in disdain, "I've been to Tyrel many times. I see you mages come through, messing with the daughters of the house. No good ever comes of it. Shiftless bunch, you are."

Amusement coursed through her. She would lay odds it was the first time they'd ever been called shiftless. The shock of her abrupt relocation over, she powered down her magic. She asked Justin, "How did you find me?"

He continued, "I picked up your trail in the Sorrow Wold yesterday morning. After that, it was a simple matter of following you and your friends to the lair of that spider woman. When you left, I followed you and waited until you went to sleep for the night. It was not a simple matter to get up that tree to you, however. Clever trick chopping off the lower limbs. Took me nearly an hour to work my way up to you without waking your companions." He looked over in chagrin at Cicero. "Or at least most of them."

"How did I get here, and more to the point, where is *here*?"

He shrugged modestly. "I climbed the tree, cast a sleep spell on you to keep you asleep, then used a rune to open a gate and transport you and me—and unknowingly, yon elf—back here."

Yon elf looked rather smug that he'd managed to hitch a ride through the gate without being detected.

"And none of my companions woke up during this operation?" she asked.

Justin grinned. "Don't you remember how sneaky I can be?"

She did, indeed, remember how silently he could creep around her parents' keep, stealing cakes from the kitchen or spying on adult conversations not meant for their young ears. He'd been an excellent hunter, as well, as at home in the forest as in the keep.

A wash of fondness for him made her smile a little at him,

and he smiled back. They'd shared a more idyllic childhood than either of them had known at the time, but they knew that now, and it formed a connection between them that would never break.

She had to find a way to get him out of here and free of the clutches of these mages. For surely, they'd only used him as a tool to get at her. When they finally realized she would never, ever do their bidding, he would be of no more use to them.

But how? She had no idea where she was or where this place was. Surreptitiously, she examined the chamber into which they'd gated. It was large, crowded with at least fifty mages, but notably, the room had no windows. Only huge chandeliers crammed with candles lit the cavernous space.

The darkness crowding down from the ceiling and the heaviness of the stone walls closed in on her until she could hardly lift her chest to breathe beneath the combined weight of the place and of the stares boring into her from all sides.

That was when she became aware of a burning sensation on her left forearm. She looked down and was appalled to see one of the mages' infamous runes inscribed upon her wrist. Its navy whorls and lines were obscene against her fair skin.

"Take your mark off of me," she demanded to the group at large.

One of them, a weaselly looking fellow who was regarding her like a starving wolf at a Christmas feast, replied, "But if we remove it, we will not be able to return you to your companions."

"I'll walk!" she snapped.

A large man with iron-colored hair trying to go gray stepped forward. *Kadir.* This was the man who'd forced her to run away from home in the first place. Her mother's lover, and her father. Well, her parent by birth, not the man who'd raised her.

Kadir said gently, "Our tower is deep in the wild lands, Emissary. It would take you weeks or months to rejoin your friends on foot."

"Take it off, or I leave now," she declared, holding out her forearm.

"Go ahead," Weasel said. "Remove it if she so wishes."

Raina frowned. He sounded almost pleased that she'd insisted on losing their rune. As if she'd played into his hands and was now effectively trapped in this place, wherever it might be. Hating feeling outmaneuvered, she silently lectured herself to rein in her anger at these men and not let them use it against her again.

Kadir laid his hand on her mark, and one of his own runes, inscribed on the left side of his neck and disappearing down into the neck of his tunic, began to glow. She felt a surge of heat, a brief, painful sensation, and then nothing. He removed his big, gentle hand from her arm, and the mark was gone.

"Satisfied?" Weasel asked, almost, but not quite, gloating.

She ignored him and instead looked at Kadir. "Your invitation said you wished to speak with me. So speak."

"You've been woken and dragged from your rest. Perhaps you would like to finish your night's sleep? Or take a meal? Something to drink?"

She couldn't fault his hospitality, but he was stalling. "I'm wide awake, thank you. The work of a healer takes place around the clock, and I am accustomed to being woken when the last grains of sand trickle from the hourglasses."

"Our high proctor is not a young man, and he needs his sleep. I'm sure he will be pleased to speak with you in the morning."

With all these rune-marked mages staring at her like she was some sort of freak, she felt like an act at a bad circus. She was far too nervous to eat or sleep. "If I cannot speak to your leader, I would be pleased to speak with all of you. Tell me more about yourselves."

The instant pucker of reluctance throughout the group was tangible. Not interested in giving up their secrets, were they? Duly noted. They wanted something out of her, then. She would be happy to make them work for it if that was how they wanted to play this meeting.

Weasel turned out to have a name. Elfonse. And a rank. Proctor. The same rank Justin had murmured to Kadir in greeting as they blinked into this gathering.

Kadir said smoothly, not betraying any of the tension in the room, "As you know, we are an ancient order, dedicated to the study and preservation of magic."

Her mouth twitched as much in anger as in humor. "Is that what you call forcing the daughters of Tyrel to participate in your breeding program?"

Weasel-Elfonse responded sharply, "It's not as if you've suffered from being able to cast large quantities of magic."

She bit back a sarcastic rejoinder about enjoying using her magic to thwart the mages and, rather than rise to the bait, merely smiled serenely. "Indeed, I have not suffered from that." The rest of the sentence hung unspoken in the air. She had suffered greatly in other ways at their hands, however.

Uncomfortable silence settled over the room. Not only were they all men who acted as if they hadn't seen a woman in a while and had no idea what to do with one, but she gathered that they didn't get out in social situations much. She took pity and broke the silence.

"Tell me more about these runic marks you wear. Are they some sort of warding magic?"

The group latched on to her conversational lifeline and spoke eagerly of their research in how to create permanent, warding-like symbols on humans and make the symbols movable. It got too technical for her very quickly, but she did glean a few interesting tidbits from the mages' animated explanations.

The marks could apparently store anything from small, common spells to the largest ritual magics. Each mark had to correspond to a single magical effect, however, and the mage powered the mark with his own store of magical energy. Plus, there were apparently several subgroups within the Mages of Alchizzadon, each one studying something different from the others. One of the acolytes even let it slip casually that different types of Mages of Alchizzadon identified themselves with unique marks.

She let the remark pass and did her best to pretend she hadn't noticed it. The talkative acolyte was hushed, and the topic turned away to the difficulties in making runic marks portable.

Kadir and Justin both had a curly squiggle under their right ear. Was that the mark of their order? Weasel and several of the men clustered around him had tiny swords under their right ears. She looked around the room and saw no other marks. She cast back in her memory to the day she and her friends had closed the gate in Rahael. The keeper of the Dominion gate had a small star under his right ear. She'd mistaken it for an earring until she'd gotten a good look at the fellow after he was neutralized.

So. Three orders at a minimum, if she was correct about those being their identifying marks. The other runes on the mages' exposed skin were much larger and somewhat faded in color, like they got used a lot. Kadir's order—the Squiggles—were obviously involved with the daughters of Tyrel directly. What did the others do?

She had probably poked around enough for one night if she didn't want to raise suspicions regarding her motives in being here. She murmured, "Although I am used to late nights and little sleep, I suspect all of you are not. I will retire and let you gentlemen get some rest. There will be plenty of time to talk tomorrow."

Kadir and Justin ushered her and Cicero into a window-less hallway and down a steep, circular stair to a lower level and their rooms. Cicero's was several doors down the hall from hers. Was this place underground, like the Black Widow had said? It would explain the disconcerting lack of windows. It was lavishly furnished, but in an ancient style, and the walls were built of massive stones roughly hewn into rectangles the size of tables. Although her room was large, with tapestries covering the walls, well lit by lamps and candles, it still felt prisonlike.

"One of the acolytes will be just outside at all times should you need anything," Kadir murmured.

Which was to say she would be guarded and not be allowed

to wander the tower. Her sense of being a prisoner intensi-
fied. What in the world had she walked into? She gave herself
a little internal speech about how the Mages of Alchizzadon
wouldn't provoke the Royal Order of the Sun by harming
her, but she didn't believe herself for a minute.

Will helped Rosana climb down out of the tree as morning broke around them. How Raina had managed to get
out of the tree last night in her cumbersome skirts without
anyone hearing her was a mystery to him. Obviously, she'd
left to go off to her meeting and had taken Cicero with her.
Will was relieved that the stalwart kindari was with her. He'd
been her fierce protector last year in the Forest of Thorns and
would take good care of her this time, too. And as much of a
goody-goody as Raina could be, Will was genuinely fond of
her. She had grit beneath her prissy ways. Stars knew, she'd
saved his life more times than he could count with her seemingly endless well of healing.

Rosana picked the thought out of his brain as she often did.
"I'm glad she took Cicero with her. How do you suppose they
snuck away without us waking? I'll bet Raina cast sleep spells
on us."

"Could be," he replied. "Or the mages could have given her
an item that would let her portal to them directly."

"Such an item would be awfully expensive to make."

He shrugged. "I don't think money's an object where the
Mages of Alchizzadon are concerned."

Rosana sighed. "If only I had known about the perpetual
poverty of the Heart, I would have chosen my guild differently."

Will laughed and tweaked her nose gently. "No, you
wouldn't. You're a healer all the way down to your shoes."

She smiled up at him. "You're right, of course."

Rynn, ever practical, asked the party in general, "After we
grab a bite to eat, then what are we to do? Stay here and wait
for Raina's return? Or mayhap follow a lead and try to find
Kendrick?"

Sha'Li piped up. "We could try to find Eliassan's bow. If

the legends are correct, it's hidden somewhere in this part of Haelos."

"Haelos is a big place," Rynn replied. "You'll have to narrow down your search area quite a bit if you hope to find the bow."

Sha'Li reached into her belt pouch. "Maybe this will help." She held out a perfectly straight and beautifully fletched arrow. The head was gold, and the shaft was made of some rich, red wood inlaid with the finest threads of gold hammered flat.

"What is it?" Rosana asked.

Sha'Li replied dryly, "An arrow."

The party laughed, and Will commented, "It's quite a fancy arrow."

"I should hope so," Sha'Li replied. "It's said to be one of Gawaine's arrows."

"Where did you get that?" Will exclaimed.

"From the bronze lizardman. He thought it might help us one day."

Rosana said, "Even if that arrow can help us find Gawaine's bow, how will Raina find us if we move from this place?"

Rynn snorted. "You ask that as if the permanent residents of this wold don't know everything that goes on and where everyone is in these woods."

Will responded, "Are you willing to stake Raina's life, and maybe ours, on that?"

Rynn shrugged. "If we tell the locals to be on the watch for her, they'll find her. We can either leave a trail for her to follow or simply leave word as to where she should rendezvous with us."

Will didn't like that idea. A trail Raina could follow would be a trail Anton's thugs could follow. "We have too many enemies to leave trail sign that leads them right to us."

Eben piped up. "I do not need Imperial hounds on my trail ever again."

"Or Anton Constantine," Rosana added.

"Or Imperial soldiers," Rynn added fervently. "That Thanon fellow took far too much interest in Raina. If he hears she's gone missing, he'll come out here with his entire unit to track her down."

Will actually liked Thanon and his elite team of highly trained soldiers, but he could understand why an open-eyed paxan would think Thanon on their trail was a bad idea.

Sha'Li grinned. "We won't lay a trail down here. We'll lay it up there"—she pointed up toward the canopy of trees overhead—"where the local kindari can follow it and lead Raina to us."

Will returned the grin, impressed. Most soldiers did not think in the third, vertical dimension. He made a mental note to study it further when they got home. Although once again, home seemed far away, an unattainable dream.

Sha'Li changed subjects abruptly. "Eben, you're a dowser. Do you think you can use Gawaine's arrow as a dowsing rod and get it to point toward the king's bow?"

Eben frowned. "You're assuming that arrow is real and that Eliassan's bow was actually Gawaine's. We can't be certain of either. Furthermore, the arrow may have no link to the bow."

Sha'Li shoved the arrow into the jann's hand. "Just try."

Will watched with interest as Eben suspended the arrow shaft's balance point from a length of silk fishing thread. The horizontal arrow spun lazily, first one way, then the other, as Eben closed his eyes. Nothing happened. The arrow turned aimlessly like a magnet with no pole to seek.

But then Rynn put his hand on Eben's shoulder and closed his eyes as well. Will fancied that he actually felt a wave of mental power emanate from Rynn. Abruptly, the arrow stopped spinning with the golden arrowhead pointing to the northwest.

"How did you do that?" Will exclaimed.

Eben's and Rynn's eyes popped open, and the arrow went slack, twirling back and forth once more. "What? What happened?" Eben demanded.

Rosana declared, "Your dowsing gave us our direction of travel. What lies north and west of here?"

Rynn snorted. "Three quarters of Haelos."

Sha'Li asked practically, "With Cicero gone, who will guide us out of this wold?"

Will winced. The job would fall to him, and he could only hope that Bloodroot would somehow help him find their way. Although there were plenty of trails through this cursed forest, they seemed to go in circles and required a native to navigate them.

Eben murmured to Rynn, "I'm not sure what you did, but it helped. Thanks be."

"I but enhanced the power of your own mind," Rynn replied. "One day you will be able to do it without my help."

Will frowned. A paxan could enhance a person's mind power? Sometimes Rynn genuinely gave him the creeps.

They walked through the day, such as it was in the perpetual half night of the forest floor, stopping now and then to rest and eat. Will judged it was nearing sundown by the growling in his belly when Rynn, who'd taken a turn up front, froze abruptly, in the way of a soldier spotting an unexpected enemy.

It took Will a moment to spot what had caused Rynn to freeze like that. Flashes of light were flying back and forth in front of them from left to right. They resembled bolts of his yellow force magic when he threw it in combat, except these were green in tint. Faint shouts became audible. A pair of mages, and perhaps other warriors, were engaging in fierce combat in front of them.

Very slowly, Rynn sank to his haunches, and Will and the others followed suit. Crawling forward on hands and knees, they cautiously approached the fight.

Flat on his belly, Will stared in shock as he peeked out from under a dying sapling draped in thick, choking vines. Kerryl Moonrunner was under attack, and Kendrick, in human form but with his left eye glowing furious scarlet, was pacing behind him in frustration. Had Kerryl perhaps ordered Kendrick not to join the fight? How was it their friend had not transformed into his bestial were-form given how agitated he clearly was?

To Will's left, an aged but hardy man wearing a great,

hairy bear hide draped over his left shoulder and belted to his waist fired bolts of nature magic at Kerryl as fast as Kerryl fired the same type of magics back. To Will's knowledge, only the most powerful of hunters and nature guardians were able to master such magic.

Will noted the thick, long bear spear slung across the older man's back and the bear's claw he wielded in his off hand. From the belt that held down the bearskin hung a long braid of what looked like red human hair. Who was this new nature guardian, and why did he attack Kerryl?

Rynn gasped, and Will breathed into his ear, "Who's the bear guy?"

Rynn whispered back, "One of the People of the Hide. You call them hydesmyn. If I don't miss my guess, that's Berengar, an ancient and famous Tribe of the Moon hunter. He should be hibernating at this time of year, but something obviously brought him out of his winter's sleep."

"Why's he attacking Kerryl?" Will followed up.

"No idea."

From his other side, Sha'Li whispered, "Help him we must!" In her agitation, her speech had reverted to its old patterns.

"Help Berengar kill Kerryl?" Will responded.

"Nay! Help Kerryl we must."

Eben retorted, "Why would we help that scum? He kidnapped our friend and turned him into a monster."

"Were-creatures are not monsters!" Sha'Li hissed back. "Gifted servants of Lunimar they are. Kendrick trusts Kerryl enough to stay with him, and trust Kendrick we should."

Eben subsided scowling.

Rynn joined the whispers, saying, "We rescued Kendrick, but he chose Kerryl. That negates Kerryl's crime of kidnapping in my mind. And we think Kerryl led us to that cache in the Angor Swamp and then led us to the unicorn. He helped defend us when the Cabal attacked us. He is not our enemy, Eben. At least not anymore."

"He turned Kendrick into a were-boar. He is not our friend either," Eben growled back.

Will turned to Rynn. "What do you know of this Berengar?"

"He's a hunter. One of the Tribe of the Moon's protectors of nature. Hunters work closely with nature guardians."

"Then why is Berengar trying to kill Kerryl?" Will demanded.

Rynn shrugged.

Rosana cut in. "We must decide to help Kerryl or not quickly because his magic appears to be failing. And once that hunter closes on Kerryl with his claw and spear, Kerryl is done for."

Eben glared at Sha'Li, who glared back.

Will broke the stalemate by saying, "I have questions for Kerryl. I say we save him now, and if we don't like his answers, we kill him later."

Rosana shook her head. "We can't kill him—"

"You can't, but I can," Eben declared.

Will murmured, "We're decided, then? We save Kerryl?"

There were nods all around, some more reluctant than others, but nods.

He murmured, "Sha'Li, circle behind Berengar and do your rogue thing on him. Rynn, can you pass behind Berengar and come up on his left flank? Eben, you approach him from the front, and I will take the right. Rosana, you head for Kerryl and heal him as soon as you can. He looks badly hurt."

He gestured for them to go, and they all moved out swiftly and silently. Will could not believe the amount of magic he'd witnessed being used in this duel. Kerryl had shifted to throwing globes of poison gas at his foe, and Berengar was now casting some sort of protective spell on himself at high speed, one to replace each shield blown by Kerryl's poison gases.

When he judged that the others were in place, Will charged, shouting at the top of his lungs. He hoped to break Berengar's concentration and buy Sha'Li a moment to surprise the hunter from behind.

Now they had to hope that, in his futile rage, Kendrick

recognized them and did not identify them as new threats to Kerryl. Otherwise, Kendrick could still transform and kill them all.

Raina woke to a hard bed and total darkness that lay heavily upon her like a pile of quilts. Disoriented and afraid, she called magic to her hands, using its faint glow to illuminate the blackness. A bedroom. Ancient tapestries. Carved furniture. Her location came back to her. What time was it?

Using a lamp flint, she lit an oil lamp and then a half dozen candles around the spacious room. A mechanical clock took up an entire corner, and it indicated the hour to be a little after six o'clock. She hoped it meant six o'clock in the morning; otherwise, she had slept all night and all day.

She took care of her ablutions and dressed, donning the ceremonial White Heart tabard the high matriarch had given her for formal occasions, a gaudily embroidered silk and velvet affair.

She opened her door, and two guards came to immediate attention. She said politely, "Kadir told me last night that the high proctor would see me first thing this morning." It wasn't exactly true, but these two wouldn't know that. "If you could show me the way to his office, I'd be most grateful. I would hate to keep him waiting."

They didn't correct her on it not being morning. Now, to hope that High Proctor Albinus was awake at this early hour.

The guards strode down the hall, and she followed, taking in every detail of the décor. The tapestries depicted a number of scenes of life at a court long lost to the dust of time. Many of them showed a handsome man, human, wearing a crown. In some, he sat in judgment or hosted a feast. In others, he led hunting parties or parades of nobles. And in a few, he was shown wearing mage's armor at the head of a great army. Hadrian's time had not been entirely peaceful, apparently.

She was tempted to stop and study the man the mages had expected her sister to marry, but the guards were moving quickly, and she did not want to risk someone stopping them.

One tapestry, however, made her pause whether she willed it or not. Hadrian was depicted as a child in this picture, his distinctive crown identifying him as he knelt at the feet of a . . . being. The figure stroked the child Hadrian's hair fondly as a parent might do. The being was armored and cloaked in unrelieved black, but what made him remarkable was the lack of a face inside the hood of his cloak. Instead, a starry night was depicted within it. The Star Lord himself? Ruler of the Outer Planes and Sentinel of the Aether Gates? He was supposed to be one of the twelve greater beings who watched over Haelos, along with the Green Lady and other mythic figures. If she read it right, that tapestry suggested Hadrian was the Star Lord's son.

She lurched into motion, hurrying to catch up with her guards. As she lengthened her stride to catch the retreating pair, she noticed a man coming toward her down the hall. He was unkempt and wore dusty, torn clothing as if he'd recently returned from hard travels. Most notably, he did not wear the dark blue robes of the mages. He was a big man, bearded and fearsome-looking, but it was the look in his eyes that arrested her attention. An almost feverish light shone in them.

As he drew level with her, glaring at her as if he would incinerate her, she paused, reaching out to rest her hand on his forearm. She was surprised to feel rock-hard muscle beneath her fingers before he jerked away from her. "Are you ill, sir? May I offer you any healing you might need?"

A brief look of confusion passed through the man's expression, perhaps tinged with suspicion.

She said gently, "I am a healer, sworn to harm none and defend all life. It would be my pleasure to help you."

She reached for him once more, but the man pulled away just as her guards arrived behind him. They must have doubled back to collect her.

"Move along, prisoner, and quit bothering her. She's no concern of yours!" one of the guards snapped.

"I stopped him," Raina explained. "He was not bothering me in the least." Her guards shooed the man away and continued walking, this time on either side of her.

"I was not aware the mages took prisoners," she commented mildly.

"Now and again, someone discovers our location. If we're to keep the secret of our tower, we have to hold them until we can erase their memories of this place."

Although startled by the revelation, she still managed to ask casually, "I suppose you use ritual magic to erase memories?"

"Aye. We're no Kothites."

The capacity of the most powerful Kothites to control and manipulate people's minds was well known.

She nodded, relieved that she need not worry about the mages wiping her mind clean by merely willing it so. "How long does it take to erase a memory? I would think that's a relatively simple ritual."

"Oh, it is," the chatty guard answered. "But ritual components don't grow on trees, you know. At least not most of them," he joked.

Interesting. She was relieved to hear that there were limits to the mages' resources. She commented, "I imagine you go through quite a few components around here. We go through them like we go through bandages at the Heart."

"Oh yes—"

"You talk too much," the other guard interrupted. "The emissary is an outsider and not privy to our business."

"Elfonse is just angry he didn't get his way and she's here!" Chatty snapped back.

Raina took note of the mark under Chatty's ear. The same as Kadir's and Justin's. She couldn't see the surly guard's mark, but she would lay odds it was the same one Elfonse, the grumpy proctor, wore.

She thought she'd sensed tension between the factions last night, and this little exchange confirmed it.

"Here we are, Emissary," Surly announced. "Shall I announce you to the high proctor?"

"Please."

The guard knocked on the door, and a thin voice bid him to enter. Thank goodness. Albinus was awake.

She listened as the guard made the formal announcement. Albinus cut the fellow off midsentence with, "Yes, yes. I know who the girl is. Let me speak with her before I expire of old age."

Oh, she was going to like this fellow. Smiling a little, she stepped inside and saw a tiny old man swathed in ornate blue robes that seemed overlarge for his frail frame. His skin was transparent and dry with age, and only a few wisps of silver hair clung to his age-spotted pate, but his eyes danced like a child's, bright and curious. She curtsied low to him, granting him full diplomatic honors with the gesture.

"Let us dispense with this formality," he rasped. To the guards, he waved a hand made solely of skin, bones, and veins, dismissing them.

The door closed, and the two of them were alone. She moved closer to the desk that swallowed him and noted that every single inch of the high proctor's slender arms, face, and neck was covered in faded runes.

"It's an honor to meet you, High Proctor. I apologize for coming to your study uninvited—"

"Cease, child. I'm pleased that you skipped all the protocols. If you will help me over to the fire, we can sit and have a nice talk."

He felt as light as a bird as she steadied him. Depositing him in a chair, she sank into the matching seat.

"Well, child, you've certainly led us a merry chase these past few years."

"I'm sorry about that—"

He waved a hand, stopping her. "It is I who owe you the apology. What the Preservators have done to the daughters of Tyrel in the name of rousing the Great Mage is unfortunate at best."

"On that we are agreed."

He nodded slowly, as if to himself. At length, he said, "I hear you have been doing well for yourself."

"If you define doing well as attaining rank in the Heart, then yes, I am doing very well."

"And if I define doing well as learning what you can do to

help us wake the great king, Hadrian, what would you say then?"

Direct, this high proctor. She chose, however, to be obtuse. "Who exactly is this Hadrian? I was taught that the daughters of Tyrel were linked to a being called the Great Mage."

"Hadrian is the Great Mage's given name. His title was High Lord King Hadrian of Haelos, and he was also a great mage. In his day, some called him the Human King. A great elven king and a great dwarven king lived in the same era, and the three were often distinguished by race."

She chose her words carefully. "My studies have revealed that one must first find where the spirit of Hadrian rests and then find a way to rejoin it to his body."

"And if his spirit is no longer on this plane?"

She shrugged. "Like I said. You must find it wherever it resides."

"Interesting. So you recommend travel to other planes of existence for our research?"

"You do control the planar gates, do you not?" she shot back.

Albinus leaned back, studying her intently, his gaze piercing. So, the feeble-old-man thing was an act, after all. His mind was obviously as sharp as it had ever been. At length, he murmured, "You have done your homework on us, haven't you? I understand you became acquainted with one of our clavigers last fall."

"I doubt that he would characterize our attacking him, dropping him, and invading his mind to repair it as making his acquaintance."

Albinus chuckled, a sound of childish delight issuing from ancient lungs. He turned to gaze into the fire, and Raina noticed a small flower marking under his right ear. *A fourth order within this bunch? Or was that a mark of leadership?*

"Tell me something, High Proctor. I noticed a fine tapestry not far from your door that seems to indicate the Star Lord was Hadrian's father. Was that a figurative depiction or a literal one?"

"Oh, it's literal. Hadrian is the Star Lord's son."

"So Hadrian is a scion of one of the Twelve of Haelos, then?" The Twelve were mythological beings purported to watch over the continent and its people. Mostly, they were the stuff of hearth tales and bards' songs, but as she was coming to know, the songs and tales were laced with more truth than she'd ever guessed.

"This is not something we discuss, child."

And yet, Hadrian was called the Great Mage. All scions were said to be given a portion of their immortal parent's powers. It would explain why the Mages of Alchizzadon were associated with the planar gates. The Star Lord was said to be the defender of the planes, keeping them separate from one another—

Wait. Were *those* the Aether Gates?

She'd heard the title in stories before but had never realized exactly which gates the tales referred to. She doubted anyone who told the legends of the Star Lord knew. The Aether Gates were always described as a set of black iron gates that guarded a mythical castle where the greater beings feasted and slumbered. But were they, in fact, the gates keeping the planes apart and at the same time connecting them?

"What can you tell me of the Aether Gates?" she asked.

"Nothing that you have not seen with your own eyes. They align the planes with one another."

She reeled mentally. The planar gates *were* the Aether Gates, and they were real. Furthermore, she'd seen one in action last fall in Rahael. "How do the gates connect the planes?"

Albinus studied her for a moment, appearing to weigh some sort of choice in his head, and then he answered frankly, "The story goes that when the separate planes were created, they were identical to this one. The gates allowed travel to and from corresponding identical points between planes. However, as the different creatures who inhabited the planes began to alter them to reflect their essences, the matching points on the planes started not to match so exactly. The tympans were created to realign the travel nexuses and keep planar travel possible, but even those are very old and falling into disrepair."

She was amused at his choice of words. The tympans—the mechanisms that aligned these nexuses of which he spoke—were not merely old and in disrepair. They had been broken and scattered intentionally.

And although he did not say it, the other planes were probably continuing to diverge from the material plane, too. She was not sorry to hear that travel to other planes was becoming difficult, if not nearly impossible. As long as she and her friends could bring Gawaine's spirit from the dream realm to this one, she never needed to visit—or fight off an invasion from—another plane as long as she lived.

A silence fell between them, and Albinus said, "Surely you must have questions for me, else why would you have accepted our invitation?"

This time, she chose directness. "Will you fix my friend Justin? Or if not, how do I fix him?"

"I was not aware he was broken."

"He is part ogre now. That is not his natural state."

"Young Justin agreed to accept the spirit of an ogre mage into himself. The way I hear it, he wished to learn to cast magic. The least painful and most expeditious way to do that was to give him the spirit of a magic caster."

"And how exactly did you come into possession of this spirit?" she asked. "I would warn you that I'm asking in my official capacity as a White Heart emissary."

Albinus's mouth twitched in humor. "Duly noted . . . Emissary. An ogre mage of our order volunteered to surrender a portion of his magical energy as his life waned from old age into death. I imagine I shall do the same one day."

She frowned a little. "The way I understand bottling to work, once a person dies permanently, any magics stored in the bottle pass away beyond the Veil into the spirit realm, also."

"Which is why we maintain the bodies of those who have volunteered for the procedure in an indefinite stasis."

She leaned back hard in her seat. "So you know how to put people into stasis? The same kind of stasis your Hadrian exists in? And do you know how to remove people from this state?"

"These matters are private to my order and do not concern you."

"If you are killing people and stealing their spirits, I assure you it does concern me. Greatly."

"We kill no one. And we steal nothing."

She didn't believe him, not on either count, but she was not in a position to make any further accusations or to call in the Royal Order of the Sun to investigate the matter and take punitive action against the mages.

Albinus offered her tea, and she busied herself making it for both of them at a small cart beside his desk. It took several minutes to steep the tea, and by the time she carried mugs of the hot drink around to him, the elderly proctor had dozed off.

She tiptoed back to the tea cart to set down the mugs, and her glance strayed to his desk. Papers were scattered across it, and rows of ancient-looking books lined the wall behind it. A large leather map book lay on a tall drafting table to her left.

She looked over at the back of Albinus's head. It lolled to one side, and a gentle snore emanated from the chair. It wasn't nice to snoop, but how could she not take the opportunity to learn all she could about her nemeses?

She quickly skimmed the papers on his desk and spotted nothing of interest in the administrative correspondence. She headed for the map case next, rolling back the large leather cover, which was as tall as her arm and half again as long.

On top was a map of the entire continent of Haelos, depicted in more detail than she'd ever seen on any map before. Plentiful information about the interior leaped up at her—lakes and rivers and mountain ranges she'd never heard of before. And then she spied a network of stylized ovals drawn across the map. The Aether Gates, perhaps?

Eagerly, she turned the page. And gasped. *A map of the*

planes. The vellum sheet was covered with spherical shapes, each labeled with a name, its interior filled with intricate runic shapes.

Shocked, she realized she'd seen some of those shapes before. The wedge-shaped piece of black nullstone that Lord Goldeneye had given Eben last fall had at least two of these shapes inscribed on it. And Will had drawn a rough shape of a third rune that he'd glimpsed on another nullstone piece the Boki had stolen from the Haelan legion's armory in Dupree last summer.

Were these the tympan coordinates to each of the planes? Stealthily, she lifted a piece of parchment off Albinus's desk and dipped his pen in ink. Glancing at him furtively, she quickly copied the circles and runes. Her work wasn't neat, but she finished the copy, blew it dry, and stuffed it inside her shirt without him waking. Closing the map case carefully, she moved over to the bookcase and browsed the titles.

Most were innocuous, various histories and collections of poems or stories, but a few words of note jumped out at her. *Preservators. Collectors. Servitors. Magia.* Were those the four orders within the Mages of Alchizzadon? She was just reaching for a thin volume on Magia when Albinus stirred and coughed.

Quickly, she jumped back from the books and snatched up the cups of tea. Hopefully, he wouldn't notice how much the drinks had cooled.

"Here we go, High Proctor. Tea for two." She pretended that he hadn't dozed off at all and that a few seconds had passed and not many minutes.

Frowning slightly, he took the cup of tea and sipped it.

"What can you tell me of the previous women in my family? Do you and yours follow where they end up when they are released from their duties as Ariannas?"

The eldest daughters in her family were each raised and trained to be brides for Hadrian, should he awaken in their lifetime. When the next Arianna was fully trained and of marriageable age, the previous one was free to leave Tyrel and pursue a life of her own. Or at least that was how the story went.

But knowing the mages, she wouldn't put it past them to kidnap her ancestors or worse, as the Black Widow had accused them of doing.

"I'm sure they end up doing productive work," he answered smoothly.

Riiight. "I'm sure you're correct," she replied just as smoothly. The mages *were* doing something to the other Ariannas. The Black Widow's accusations suddenly seemed a great deal more credible, and for the first time since she'd been given them, Raina was grateful for the sleep gas poisons the widow had insisted she take.

The map stuck to her skin inside her shirt, and she needed to wrap it and figure out a place to hide it before the ink ran and was ruined. She drank down her tea quickly and rose to her feet. "Thanks be to thee for your hospitality, High Proctor. It has been an honor to meet you. I have occupied too much of your precious time and will take my leave now. I hope we may speak again before I leave."

He patted her hand. "You're a lovely young woman, and I wish you well in your endeavors."

Guilt speared her right in the place her copied map lay, but not enough to consider destroying it or giving it back. They'd taken her family and all her dreams of a normal life from her. They owed her much more than a map.

Will ducked an incoming gas globe as Rosana hit Kerryl with a healing spell. They had to close in fast on the caster, Berengar, neutralize his advantage of distance, and pound through his light mage armor before they all died.

He was acutely aware of Raina not being at his back, able to pour massive healing into him for as long as any fight could hope to last. He felt naked without her on his heels. With her behind them, they could fight indefinitely, which made them nigh unto unbeatable. He'd never realized how completely she dominated battlefields until this exact moment. The pacifist White Heart healer was the ultimate combat weapon.

A dark shape leaped out behind Berengar. *Sha'Li*. She swung hard with the flat of her claw at the back of his head. Startled, the hydesmyn turned around to face this new threat, and that was when Will and the others charged from all sides. Surrounded by five attacking warriors swinging weapons in a devastating flurry, Berengar cast one last magic spell, this time upon himself, and abruptly popped out of sight.

Will cursed under his breath and fetched up his staff hard, barely missing clocking Rynn in the head without Berengar in front of him to catch the blow.

"He spirit formed," Rosana declared in disgust. "And I don't know the spell to anchor spirits. He'll be able to flee from here invisibly, and we'll never find him."

Sha'Li added, "I cannot yet track a spirit either. Rosana is right. We'll never find him."

Will turned sharply to face Kerryl. The nature guardian was backing up, brandishing a fistful of evil-looking poisons. "Who are you?" he demanded. "Get back! I'll kill you all!"

"They're friends! They mean you no harm!" Kendrick yelled.

Kerryl lifted his arm and threw a gas globe at Rynn, who batted the globe down with his hand even as a golden sparkle across the paxan's body indicated that a magical shield of some kind had been blown by the incoming alchemy.

Rynn dropped into a fighting stance, and Will stepped up beside him, brandishing his staff. Kerryl might not be their enemy, but Will had no problem with taking down the nature guardian if the fellow wanted a fight.

Eben stepped forward, mace in hand. "Let me have him. I've wanted this for a long time."

"No!" Kendrick shouted from behind Kerryl.

Kerryl threw another globe, but it came in high enough that Eben and Will were able to duck under it. It passed behind them and crashed into a tree. Eben charged, and Will and Rynn followed closely behind. As always, the key to defeating a ranged attack with hand weapons was to close in as fast as possible on the caster.

Will heard the bellow before he saw the boar charging at them. Kendrick had transformed. *Not good.*

Eben raised his mace and was mid-shout and mid-swing of his deadly weapon when Kendrick smashed into him, head down, with one heavy, bristled shoulder. Eben went flying, and Rynn dived left as Will dived right out of the path of Kendrick's charge. Kendrick altered course just enough to graze Kerryl with his right shoulder and sent him to the ground, as well.

The great, chest-high boar skidded to a stop on his short, powerful haunches and shook his giant, tusked head, sending spittle and foam flying in wide arcs. His eyes glowed brilliant red as he glared at all of them sprawled on the ground, his huge body physically blocking them from reaching Kerryl and vice versa.

Will braced to leap aside should Kendrick charge again, but instead, the great were-beast went down to his knees and then to his belly with a grunt. And then, in arguably the most revolting sight Will had ever witnessed, he transformed from boar to human. Bones and hide melted away, and for a moment, the innards of the beast were visible. But then they morphed and melted, the goo re-forming into a vaguely human shape. Skin, hair, and human features formed, and where the great boar had lain but moments before now lay a naked, trembling human.

In truth, the whole transformation had taken maybe a second or two, but Will would never forget the sight of it.

Eben rushed forward, doffing his cloak and wrapping it around his brother. "Gads, that looked like it hurt," the jann declared.

"It did," Kendrick ground out. He climbed unsteadily to his feet. "It's always hard to get the hang of balance on two legs again, even if I'm in boar form for only a few seconds."

Will shuddered. And he thought it was hard to have a tree spirit inside him. It was nothing compared to what Kendrick lived with. Behind their friend, Kerryl was swaying, clinging to a tree for support. He didn't look too good.

Will murmured, "Uh, Rosie, any chance you could give Kerryl a little healing? He looks ready to fall over."

"I've got a potion, but I'm out of mana." She moved forward hesitantly and offered a small bottle to the nature guardian. He took it with equal caution, giving it a long sniff before drinking it down. Kerryl carefully turned the tree loose. He wavered a little but could stand upright on his own.

Will asked him, "Can you track Berengar in his current spirit form?"

"Possibly," the nature guardian replied thinly, "but I'm in no condition to run around in the woods tracking a foe I cannot defeat when I'm half-dead myself. Thanks be for your assistance, young lady."

Rosana nodded.

Sha'Li spoke up. "Why did that man attack you, Guardian Moonrunner?"

"Ah, Sha'Li. Well met. It has been a long time since our paths ran together, my young friend. As for Berengar, that's a long story."

Will responded, "We've got time." He noticed that Eben was speaking to his foster brother in low tones. Kendrick's human eyes were glowing less brightly now, becoming more hazel than scarlet.

Sha'Li asked Kerryl, "Where do you sleep this night?"

Rosana answered for him, saying tartly, "He's sleeping right here with us, by a nice, warm fire. I was able to heal him a little, but he's nowhere near full strength. He needs to rest."

Will and Rynn traded alarmed glances. This man was only marginally not their enemy, and a formidable one, even badly injured.

They set about making camp, and using a bit of magic, Will soon had Rosana's nice, warm fire going. The mood was cautious as they eyed Kerryl and he eyed them back. Only Kendrick seemed at ease as they settled around the fire to eat.

It was almost like old times when they'd traveled the Forest of Thorns in search of a clue to the whereabouts of the Sleeping King. Will found it hard to believe how much more they knew now, how much closer they were to the end goal. And, he added to himself wryly, how much more worrisome and numerous their enemies were. It was amazing to realize that Kerryl no longer ranked as even a serious threat in their world. How much had changed in the span of less than two years.

As Kerryl looked down at the tied napkin of dried food Sha'Li passed to him, he fingered the black silk and smiled a little. "I gather you've been to see the Bride of Quetaryn. How does the Black Widow fare these days?"

When no one else spoke up, Will answered, "Fine, as far as I can tell, but how would I know, given how she, um, looks?"

Kerryl grinned. "She does tend to look rather more pre-served than alive, does she not?"

Rosana asked curiously, "How did she join the spirits of her husband and the spider scion to her own spirit? Was it ritual magic?"

Kerryl nodded. "A ritual of her own invention. It's a mir-acle she did not kill them all."

Indeed. From his studies of ritual magics, Will knew a sin-gle ritual could take scholars centuries to perfect. Speaking of centuries, he asked, "What can you tell us of the war that broke the Great Circle?"

Kerryl's entire body twitched, like Will had poked an in-credibly painful nerve. The nature guardian stared into the fire for a long time as if reliving memories triggered by the question. He continued to twitch from time to time.

Will was on the verge of prodding him for an answer when Kerryl looked up, his gaze on Will but his stare fixed on the distant past. The nature guardian muttered, "And the great destroyer came, annihilating all in his path. His army stripped the land . . . stripped the people . . . made them hollow. Starv-ing shells of people . . . took everything . . . no memories . . . no hope."

Will glanced at the others, and they looked as confused as he. Rynn, however, seemed to be concentrating fiercely on

Kerryl. Will sincerely hoped the paxan was reading the nature guardian's mind and stealing all his secrets.

"Who was this great destroyer?" Will asked.

"And they shall come as babes in the woods. One to save, one to destroy. That's what she said, my dear wife. And she was right. By the Lady, she was right . . ."

Will frowned, lost. That almost sounded like a seer's prophecy. And everybody knew how inaccurate those were. All mumbo jumbo and dire warnings that added up to nothing.

Rosana said gently, "Tell us of your wi—"

"No!" Kendrick said sharply. "Do not ask that. He will not be sane for days if you do."

This twitching man mumbling nonsense was the sane version of Kerryl? And Sha'Li insisted he was not mad? Hah!

Will glanced over at Kendrick, who'd been mostly silent as they'd set up camp and eaten. In a bid to give Kerryl a moment to recover from whatever grief-induced madness encroached upon his mind, Will asked Kendrick, "How do you fare these days, my friend?"

"Well enough. Kerryl and I have made our peace. He does not often do as he did today and use the Band of Beasts to give me orders."

"So he did order you to stay out of the fight with Berengar?"

Kendrick scowled. "Aye. Worse, he ordered me not to change to help him against Berengar. He forced me to stay human."

"How is it you changed to attack us, then?" Will demanded.

"I did not attack you," Kendrick answered quietly, "else you would be dead now and not eating your supper. I was given no orders regarding protecting you from him or him from you. Hence, I was free to change."

Rynn asked, "Why didn't you attack us? You showed excellent self-control while you were in your other form."

Kendrick shrugged modestly. "I've been working on it. Kerryl has been helping me gain control of my were-form."

"Why wouldn't Kerryl let you help him in his fight?" Eben asked. "You're a formidable foe in . . . your other form."

"He said it was between him and the Bear hunter."

Will interjected, "The way we hear it, others who look out for nature aren't fond of your mentor."

Said mentor was fiddling with his fingers now, staring down at them as he twined and untwined them, muttering disjointed words under his breath, things about mad armies, pink, mind-sucking monsters; nightmares made real; and who knew what other nonsense.

Kendrick shook his head. "The others do not understand. Threats loom on the horizon bigger than anything they can imagine."

"What threats?" Will asked urgently.

Kendrick shook his head, but a haunted look entered his hazel eyes. He knew something of the threats Kerryl so feared, and they frightened Kendrick, too. Either that, or their friend had been affected by the same madness that gripped Kerryl.

Will reached out to grip Kendrick's forearm. "Please. We need to know. Help us to believe you and trust him."

Kendrick murmured low, "Wake he whom you seek, Will. Wake him soon. He needs time to build an army, consolidate his forces before . . ."

"Before what?" Will asked in supreme frustration. "Why are we doing all this, risking our lives, risking more than our lives? Of all people, we have a right to know."

Rynn, who was staring intently at Kerryl, burst out, "Do not answer that, Kendrick."

Will turned in fury on the paxan. "How dare you. We've been out here for nigh unto two years under constant threat of death, trying to save the cursed world. We've earned the right to know exactly what threats we face!"

Rynn said evenly, without any hint of anger, "I understand your anger and impatience, but trust me, there are things . . . monsters . . . in this world that it is best you know nothing of. Look at what the knowing of them has done to Kerryl Moonrunner. He is a powerful magician, a nature guardian, closely linked to the Great Wolf, and still the knowledge was too much for his mind to grasp. It broke him."

Will subsided, but not happily. Rynn's logic was sound, but it did nothing to lessen Will's burning need to know.

Kendrick chimed in. "You are doing what needs to be done. It is vital that Gawaine be raised up and Koth defeated before the real danger arrives."

Will's jaw actually sagged. "There's something worse in this world than the Kothites?"

Kendrick's entire being tightened, the skin across his forehead, his shoulders, even his knees pressed more tightly together. He did not answer Will's horrified question, but every bit of his body language shouted that Kothites were far from the worst there was. What could possibly be worse than an empire that crushed the hope, the breath, the very life out of every living thing?

Kerryl said without warning, "Gawaine? The Mythar? Is he nigh? Where? I must speak with him urgently. The Circle is broken. We need him to restore it. Bloodroot gone. Destroyed. The Beasts attacked. No idea how many dead. The Totems in disarray, torn from their realm . . ." He descended into incoherent mumblings once more.

Will leaned forward. "If the two of you would restore the Great Circle, come with us. Help us wake Gawaine."

Kendrick frowned, glancing over at Kerryl doubtfully.

Eben chimed in. "There is safety in numbers. Travel with us a while. Have you any specific destination you go to?"

"Kerryl's looking for a spider scion and someone whom he can bond to it. Since the Sorrow Wold is home to the Great Spider, he thought this would be the best place to look."

Will frowned. "How can you support Kerryl's efforts to do to another what was done to you?"

"Sometimes the ends justify the means," Kendrick answered defensively.

"He took your life from you. Your freedom," Rosana objected.

"His ends justify his means," Kendrick repeated stubbornly.

Will wished their friend would elaborate. Share the details of what Kerryl planned. But instead, Kendrick had become as stubbornly silent as his mentor. Rynn glanced up, caught Will's stare, and gave him a hollow, horrifying parody of a smile. Stars above, what had Rynn seen in Kerryl's mind to put that ravaged expression in the paxan's eyes?

Kendrick murmured, "There is something else Kerryl seeks. Mayhap you've run across it or heard of it."

"What's that?" Will asked suspiciously.

"A gate of some kind. It's said to lead to the dream plane."

They all lurched at that, but it was Eben who collected himself first to demand, "Where is it? What does Kerryl know of it? Is it open? Do creatures pass through it?"

Kendrick looked taken aback. "I don't know. You'd have to ask Kerryl when he's in a more lucid state. My impression is that the gate is broken and its operating mechanism destroyed and scattered."

Will exhaled the breath he'd been holding. Thanks be to the Lady. They didn't need to face more armies of elemental phantasms anytime soon. "Any idea when he'll be able to answer questions?"

Kendrick glanced over at Kerryl and shrugged. "Mayhap in the morning, after he sleeps."

To that end, Rosana and Sha'Li led the mumbling nature guardian to the bedroll Kendrick had spread for him and coaxed him into lying down. Eventually, the two girls returned to the circle around the fire.

Kendrick took an appreciative puff from the pipe Rynn passed him. "Last I heard, you were on the hunt for the Sleeping King's regalia. How goes the search?"

Will shrugged. "Raina's gone off to visit some mages she's tangled up with. Without her, we're without many trails to follow." He didn't trust Kerryl and, by extension, wasn't willing to give up their secrets to Kendrick, friend or no.

Kendrick asked, "Does anybody know how the Sleeping King went to sleep, anyway?"

"Yes," Sha'Li responded, to Will's surprise.

Everyone stared at her, but it was Will who finally asked, "How do you know?"

"A while back," she said carefully, "when we visited the cave of the Bronze . . . do you remember it?"

Will responded, "You mean the bronze lizardman in the cliffs above the Estarran Sea?"

"The Bronze I refer to is the bronze dragon, but yes, that is the cave I meant."

"Dragon?" Will echoed in shock. "That was a dragon's cave?"

Sha'Li frowned. "Where did you think all the nullstone lining it came from? Dragon's breath is what forms nullstone."

"Okay, then," Will responded in minor shock. He'd sat in a dragon's lair?

"At any rate," Sha'Li continued impatiently, "the old bronze lizardman told me a story. Mayhap you remember seeing a carving upon the wall there of an elf wielding a bow and arrows in battle against a great boar. Sorry, Kendrick."

"No apologies required. Continue," Kendrick murmured.

"Let me see if I can remember it in full." She paused, gathering her thoughts, and then continued, "When Gawaine and Rudath battled, they traded blows for a long time, shredding each other's armor and bodies. Eventually, Gawaine used his bow to fire an arrow imbued with killing power from the path of light magics at Rudath, mortally wounding the troll king. Rudath, knowing he was dying, charged Gawaine and let down his defenses to swing one final, mighty blow. Gawaine finished the job of his arrow by nearly severing Rudath's head from his neck with his sword, Lightbringer. But Rudath cleaved Gawaine from shoulder to opposite hip with his battle-ax.

"After Gawaine and Rudath felled one another, Rudath's Night Reavers took his body away for burial, and Hemlocke took Gawaine's body away from the battlefield to put him to rest."

Will remembered well his own dream about that sad battle and its aftermath when he first joined spirits with Bloodroot. It had not been a pretty sight.

Sha'Li continued, "The zinnzari believed Bloodroot to be responsible for inciting Rudath to kill Gawaine. In their grief and rage, they attacked Bloodroot, trapping him in his heart-wood and scattering the pieces of him far and wide. For their part, the Night Reavers stole Gawaine's crown and ring from the field where they fell, sword and shield, and of course, the bow that dealt the fatal wound unto their king."

Will exclaimed, "So that's how Gawaine's crown came to be in the hands of the Boki! They're the descendants of the Night Reavers, aren't they?"

"Aye," Sha'Li answered, looking pleased that he was following her tale.

"Go on," he said with interest.

"Then followed a time of unrest and fighting with the Night Reavers and Gawaine's army struggling for power."

"And the zinnzari?" Rynn asked.

"Bound to Hemlocke and gone away to serve her in return for being allowed to stay close to their fallen king," Sha'Li answered.

"Bound to Hemlocke how?" Rosana asked.

"I do not know." Sha'Li picked up her tale once more. "The Night Reavers looked for ways to gain more power and break the stalemate against the elven armies. The leader of the Night Reavers built a portal to the Court of Night—"

Rynn interrupted, exclaiming, "The fae Court of Night?"

"Aye!" Sha'Li snapped. She obviously didn't like being interrupted in her story. She continued, "The fae Lord of the Black Boar came through the portal and began attacking elven settlements in acts of terror and revenge, hoping to take control of the fane."

"Fane?" Rosana asked.

"An ancient shrine of significance to the fae, left in this realm when they were ejected from Urth." She continued, "An elven warrior, Eliassan, set out to find Gawaine's bow, which was said to enhance the skills of its user. The bronze lizardman I spoke with did not know if Eliassan found Gawaine's quiver and arrows or not. The arrows were said to take on whatever magical quality was needed to harm their target the most."

Will was impressed. He'd like to have a weapon that could do such a thing.

Sha'Li was still speaking. "Eliassan supposedly used the bow to vanquish the Lord of the Black Boar and send him back through the portal from whence he came. Unto his passing, Eliassan used the bow to protect the remains of Gandymere."

Will frowned. "Where exactly was Gandymere?" He recalled hearing the wandrakin landsgrave sing of the place in her song about the Sleeping King, but she hadn't described where it was.

Rynn answered, "It once spanned most of this continent. Gawaine was the last king of Gandymere."

"Where's the bow now?" Will asked.

Sha'Li shrugged. "The lizardmen do not know. An elven secret this is." She added, "This the lizardman did know. Eliassan was zinnzari, and in the Valelands lies the last known zinnzari fane."

Will sighed. "It sounds like we need to find some zinnzari and talk to them. Not only do we need them to tell us where Gawaine's body is, but now we need to know where his bow and quiver are hidden, too." He looked around the circle at his friends. "Anyone have an idea where we can find some?"

Rynn asked Sha'Li, "Do the lizardmen believe any zinnzari are still alive?"

"They have no idea," Sha'Li answered.

Will frowned. "If the fane thing that Eliassan protected was in the Valelands, he might have retired close to it in his old age, in case the fae came back for it. Perhaps that is where we should start searching for his bow."

"What about Raina?" Rosana asked. "Do we wait for her here or move on in search of the bow?"

Will responded, "Did she give anyone an idea how long she might be gone speaking to those mages of hers?"

There were head shakes all around.

Rosana said reluctantly, "She did say not to stop the quest on her account. If we found a lead, we were to continue on. She said she would catch up to us if needed."

Kendrick suggested, "You can leave word with the local villagers of where you've gone. They can relay the information to her, and she can follow you."

"Why are you in such a hurry to move us along?" Will asked Kendrick, suspicion blooming in his gut. Did Kendrick and Kerryl have secret plans they did not share with the group? Or maybe the pair had other enemies hot on their trail besides Berengar. For all they knew, Berengar would be back to finish what he'd started as soon as he healed from his injuries.

"Time grows short for your quest," Kendrick said soberly. "I know it will infuriate you to hear me say it, but I cannot tell you why time is short or what comes this way. Merely that it does. If Gawaine is ever to wake, now is the time."

Will glanced into the dank, moss-festooned forest. A mist was starting to rise in the dark, shadowed and wispy, drifting ghostlike among the black trees.

Rosana asked Kendrick, "Can we leave word with the kindari of the wold of where we've gone? They'll pass the information to Raina?"

"Of course. She's White Heart. People may live simply out here, but they're not barbarians. They respect the White Heart."

Rosana nodded. "All right, then. I'm in agreement if the rest of you wish to go. Let's head for the Valelands and find Eliassan's bow."

D uring the day, Raina was given a careful guided tour of the mages' tower. It was an impressive place, sprawling in all directions and on many levels. Were it not for her escorts, she would be hopelessly lost in here. Not once did she spy any hint of natural light, lending credence to the notion that this enclave was underground.

Although it was carefully masked, she glimpsed tiny hints of discord between the factions of mages. In particular, Kadir's devotees and Elfonse's had a tendency to snap at one another. More alarming, though, was the smug way in which Elfonse's people tended to look at her whenever Kadir's people were not present.

From what she gathered, it was Elfonse and his faction who studied methods of gathering and storing magic, meaning they must be in charge of bottling spirits. As much as she would like to challenge him and his practices, she sensed that he was already hostile enough toward her. No need to kick an already angry hornet's nest.

Supper was a formal affair that dragged on so long she thought she might fall asleep in her plate of food. At long last, people stopped making speeches and singing dirgelike songs that went on for verse after verse. These guys seriously needed to get out more.

She stumbled back to her room, barely able to keep her eyes open or place one foot in front of the other. She fell across her bed, exhausted, resolved to rest her eyes for just a few minutes before she got ready for bed.

When she blinked awake, she was still lying down, but

torches guttered around her, and her bedroom had disappeared, replaced by a circular chamber filled with hooded and cloaked figures. It looked like a scene straight out of her worst nightmares, Mages of Alchizzadon surrounding her, glaring at her in malice.

Wait. She was *awake*. This was no dream!

She sat up, or tried to, but ran into leather straps across her torso and pinning her arms and legs down. Panic surged through her, but she shoved it down by force of will. They hadn't bested her before, and they wouldn't best her now. She looked around the room for the bulk of Kadir's form. No one of his build was in here. Time. She needed to buy time for someone or something to rescue her.

"Elfonse. Why am I not surprised you're behind this kidnapping? You couldn't stand the fact that Albinus gave me his word I would be safe here, could you?"

The mage didn't respond, but he scowled darkly.

She poked a little harder. "It must gall you to no end to know how much more talented a mage I am than any of you. For longer than anyone has memory, you've dreamed of creating an arch-mage, and now that you've finally done it, I refuse to be your puppet. The irony is rich, isn't it?"

That did the trick. Elfonse sputtered, "Arrogant, selfish child. After all we've done for you—"

"Done for me?" she interrupted. "I can't wait to hear what you think you've done for me."

Where was Kadir? Justin? Albinus? Had they been drugged, too? For surely that was how these men had been able to remove her from her room and bring her to this chamber of horrors. She silently begged them to rouse from whatever drug had been in their food. It had worn off of her; hopefully, it would wear off soon for them, as well. But would they even realize she was in trouble?

While Elfonse ranted about what a pain in the arse she'd been and how much trouble she'd caused them and how many generations she was going to set back their breeding program, she eyed the walls in dismay. They were made of the same thick stone as the rest of this pile of rocks. No one would hear her outside this room even if she screamed her head off.

She craned her head from side to side and spied thick braided silk ropes lying in a groove in the floor, forming a perfect circle around her. It was a high-magic ritual they had planned for her, then. She spotted a small table with a half dozen recognizable ritual components on it and a few more she didn't recognize. A major ritual, then, to require so many power sources.

Then she spotted a tall rose-colored glass bottle, wider at the base than a wine bottle, but nearly as tall. It was decorated with jewels and enclosed in a cage of wire. She frowned for a moment, and then it hit her. They were planning to take her spirit from her. All of it. To bottle it and put her in permanent stasis. Oh, this was bad. Very bad, indeed.

Y our time is up, seer. A day has passed with no deaths. You are summoned into the presence of my father for sentencing and punishment," Endellian announced in satisfaction.

The Darkadian seer, Vlador Noss, looked up at her, seemingly unconcerned and without even bothering to rise to his feet. The affront of it stole her breath away. "In point of technical fact, the sun will not set for another hour or so. And I did say the death would occur within this sun cycle."

Laernan and the seer shared an intimate smile. Weren't those two just getting all kinds of cozy with one another? She logged that bit of information for future use as a weapon against one or both of them.

Vlador sighed. "Princess, you need to stop trying so hard. Relax. Your time will come."

She gasped at the man's effrontery.

"I mean no offense, my lady. One day, you and I will work very closely together and, between us, shape an empire even you can be satisfied with. I do not prophesy to anger you but rather to prove to you my usefulness."

Eyes narrowed, she replied, "First, you must survive your imminent appointment with my father, which will be no mean feat. He is set on putting you to the Flame." When the Eternal Flame consumed its victims, it sent them to the Void permanently.

"Never fear, my lady of the raven locks."

She jolted. That was what Tarses used to call her after her long, dark hair, which she often wore loose and flowing around her.

"All will be as I have said, Princess."

"We shall see about that, dark Child of Fate."

He laughed aloud at the sobriquet and bowed deeply, with an elaborate sweep of his arms and a saucy grin up at her.

He was impudent, to say the least, but she had to admit she rather enjoyed the verbal sparring. Few at court would dare speak to her so familiarly, and she found it . . . stimulating.

They paced down a long, broad hallway to the great double doors leading to her father's trophy room. A pair of guards opened the ironclad portals, and she swept inside, leading the way across the cavernous space crammed with treasures from the length and breadth of the Empire.

She spied her father's chamberlain standing before the tall golden doors leading into Maximillian's private throne room, the one he used for conducting official business that did not require open court.

"He is not ready for us yet, I gather?" she asked the fellow.

"The report from Archduke Korovo's messenger is taking longer than expected."

She nodded and took a seat in an intricately carved chair once said to be the throne of a fae king. Idly, she studied the Child of Fate, who was studying the Man in Amber beside the entrance to the throne room.

"Who's this fellow?" Vlador asked no one in particular.

She answered, "Someone who once got in the way of my father. The Emperor had the Amber Mages encase him in amber many centuries ago."

"And he's stood here ever since, watching the comings and goings from your father's throne room?" Vlador added, "The stories he could tell if he lived."

"I am told he does live," she replied.

"An apt last reminder to those who are about to enter yon throne room and face the Emperor. Step carefully or end up like this poor sod."

She had no doubt that was her father's intent in placing the Man in Amber just outside his door.

The seer reached out to touch the amber, which she knew to feel smooth and warm to the touch. "Ah!" Vlador exclaimed in surprise. "Not only does he live, but he sees and hears, as well."

Endellian was startled. She'd always thought the amber man's open eyes looked eerily conscious, but to know the man really was wide awake in his golden prison—

"He must be stark raving mad by now," she commented.

Vlador laid his palm flat on the amber casing and closed his eyes. After a few moments, he murmured, "*Mad* is not the word I would use. *Maddened with rage* is the description that comes to mind. By the Mistress, the power of it . . ." His voice trailed off.

"Do not touch that!" the chamberlain snapped, swatting away Vlador's hand from the amber.

The seer grabbed the chamberlain's wrist and forced the smaller, older man's hand flat upon the amber. "Feel what you have done to him." Vlador pressed his hand over the chamberlain's, holding it in place.

Something happened inside the amber prison. Although the Man in Amber did not—could not—move so much as a muscle, something hot flared in his perpetually open eyes. Awareness. Consciousness. And rage. Layer upon layer of rage, rolling forth from his resin sarcophagus in waves so violent Endellian had to throw up every mental defense she possessed to shield herself from it. The only time she'd ever felt such fury before had been the day Ammertus had killed nearly everyone in the golden throne room over the Prophecy of the End. The prophecy, given some twenty years ago, had forecast the end of both the Kothite Empire and the line of Ammertus.

Something not quite visible—but not quite invisible either—flashed from the Man in Amber, through his prison, into the chamberlain. Immediately, the chamberlain went limp and fell to the floor in a faint.

For his part, Vlador Noss stepped back in satisfaction. "There you have it. My prophecy fulfilled."

"You killed him?" Endellian demanded in outrage.

"Not me. Him." Vlador nodded at the Man in Amber. "I merely opened a conduit between his mind and that of the chamberlain. The man in the golden prison did the rest."

Endellian stared at the Man in Amber in shock. A man who could kill with his mind? Only her father had such power. Who—*what*—was the Man in Amber?

She gestured her father's deaf guards forward to tend to the chamberlain. One of them poured a potion down the man's throat, but nothing happened in response. She strode across the trophy room and poked her head out into the hallway. "Send for a healer, and quickly."

Within two minutes, a healer wearing the white tabard and red-and-yellow sunburst of the Heart all askew came running into the room. He stopped panting before her and gave a messy bow.

"Heal the chamberlain," she ordered.

The healer knelt down and announced immediately, "This man is dead. Do I have permission to restore him to life?"

"Do it!" she snapped.

The healer incanted the magic and cast the white light from his hand into the dead chamberlain.

Nothing happened.

What was this? The spell failed?

"Do it again," she ordered.

The healer obliged frantically. Still nothing.

"I am sorry, Your Highness. But this man has already passed beyond the usefulness of a life spell. He will have to resurrect . . ." The healer trailed off, frowning.

"What?" she demanded.

"If this man has just died, which I gather he has, his spirit should hover close by his physical form for some minutes before moving off toward a Glow in search of renewal, and yet, I do not sense a spirit nearby."

Vlador spoke up. "That is because he is permanently dead."

Endellian stepped over to the tall seer and grabbed a fistful of his tunic. She asked in cold fury, "What did you do to him?"

"Truly, my lady, I did nothing but open a mental channel between the chamberlain and the Man in Amber."

She spun and snapped over her shoulder to a hovering courtier, "Fetch Laernan! Now!"

She glared in silence at the Child of Fate, who took the opportunity to stroll about the trophy room, examining various priceless artifacts, unconcerned. He certainly didn't act like a man who had just murdered another in cold blood in front of a dozen witnesses.

Laernan swept into the trophy room, looking alarmed. "Is aught amiss, sister?" he asked her quickly.

"Your toy seer has done something to get the chamberlain killed. Yon healer says the spirit has departed already beyond the Veil. Call it back."

Laernan frowned. "I can force a spirit back into a body if it is nearby and yet wishes to live. I may not be able to help in this case."

"Try."

"As you wish."

Her half brother knelt down beside the chamberlain's body and laid his hands on either side of the man's head. He closed his eyes. She felt Laernan's concentration, his will, reaching out for the spirit to force it back into the chamberlain's corpse. She didn't understand her brother's capacity for reaching beyond veils—the Veil of Time, the Veil of Death—but she knew him to be gifted at it.

Laernan stood up shaking his head. "The healer was correct. His spirit is, indeed, departed."

"Departed to where?" she demanded in frustration.

"Beyond the Eternal Flame, sister. He is dead, and nothing will bring him back."

She spun to glare first at the Man in Amber, who she swore stared back at her in smug satisfaction, and then at the cause of this mess, Vlador Noss. "Is this the death you foretold yestereve, seer?"

"Of course it is, my lady."

"You have no other murders planned this day?"

"I swear upon my sacred power, I do not."

"Do not lie to me," she threatened.

"Never, my princess. I vow it upon my life."

The golden doors to Maximillian's throne room swung open, and she turned in trepidation to face the wrath of her father.

Raina listened in dismay as Elfonse began to read the ritual magic scroll, summoning magics first to build the circle to contain the magic and then to summon bottling magic. If only she weren't White Heart! She had more magic than all these men combined, and if it she channeled it as damage, she could kill them all where they stood.

For an instant, it was tempting to abandon her vows. To summon magic and shape it to do harm. To blow all these men beyond the Veil and wipe them out as a threat to her and her sisters and daughters once and for all.

But she was better than that. Better than them. She would not break her vows or shame her tabard. She was White Heart. She would find a way through this to a solution that did not involve bloodshed even if it killed her.

At first, the ritual's power was a tingling across her skin, and then it grew to an itch of all over, unbearable torture. That was when the voices began. The whispers she'd worked so hard to learn to control broke free in her mind, muttering in an unintelligible cacophony that grew louder and louder as the ritual did its work upon her, tearing her spirit free of her body bit by bit.

She must stop this! But how? She could not speak, gagged as she was. She could not cast magic, her hands bound down as they were.

The voices became screams in her head. Or maybe that

was her screaming inside her own mind. The piercing noise of it was unbearable, ripping apart her mind by slow, agonizing degrees. *Must. Not. Give. In.*

And then the emotions came. All of them. From every throat screaming in her head poured forth everything they'd ever felt. Joy. Rage. Grief. Frustration. Terror. The onslaught was completely overwhelming, and she felt her own sanity giving way before the deluge.

Too much. She couldn't absorb it. Couldn't hold it within her mind and heart without exploding. The mages and their ritual were destroying her body from the outside in and her spirit from the inside out. Tearing her magic from her spirit and her spirit from her body.

They'd lied to her. Lied to Justin so he would lie to her. This had been their plan all along. They couldn't have their docile, obedient broodmare, so they were going to kill her instead.

How dare they. She was a daughter of Tyrel, by the Lady. Of all people, they should know what she was capable of.

Think, Raina. Think. There had to be a way out of this . . .

More furious than frightened, although she was terrified, she commenced summoning her own magic. It was nigh impossible to hear her thoughts over the screaming rampage in her mind or to summon energy to herself through the agony of her dissolving flesh and the onslaught of emotions suffocating her.

Even though they'd gagged her after she'd taunted Elfonse, she did not need to speak to summon great crackling balls of unshaped magic to her hands. Experimentally, she sent a bolt of magical energy up toward the ritual circle where it arced upward less than a foot away from her shoulder. Her magic crackled against the ritual shell, and the shell waivered, dimming for a moment.

Hah! She could mess with Elfonse's circle!

She sent a big bolt of unshaped, chaotic magic toward the ritual shell again. She couldn't throw it with any force; she would have to rely on the power and volume of magical energy to do the work for her. She sent more magic outward. This time the shell nearly failed.

Elfonse snarled, and a pair of his acolytes jumped toward her. She opened wide the gates of her magic and let a huge burst of it envelop her entire body. The acolytes jumped back, startled.

Quickly, she willed the entire mass of energy she'd just summoned into the spot in the ritual circle beside her that was still dim. The ritual shell broke with the noise of a thunderclap, deafening in the enclosed room. The cot she lay on toppled over with the force of it, and had she not been strapped onto it, she would have taken a hard fall. As it was, she shifted in her bonds, and her bonds themselves shifted, sliding to one side enough so she could slip her right hand free of its buckled strap.

Shouting erupted, and feet raced all around her. Plunging her freed hand into her belt pouch, she was relieved to feel the cluster of small glass globes from the Black Widow inside. The mages hadn't searched her before they'd strapped her down to drain her spirit and kill her. A mistake, that.

She grabbed several of the globes and threw them up at the men leaning over her. The tinkles of shattering glass were not audible over the din of shouting men trying to relight torches and contain the ricocheting magic of the failed ritual circle and the loose ritual magic flying about the chamber, bouncing from wall to wall in search of a target.

The three acolytes dropped to the ground beside her. She wriggled frantically out from under one of them and tore loose the gag from her mouth. She cast a quick spirit form on herself, which would make her temporarily invisible and noncorporeal.

"Where is she?" Elfonse shouted in the darkness. "She's got to be in here. The door is still barred."

A few torches sputtered to life.

She moved as quickly as she could in the invisible, drifting state of a spirit form toward the door, dodging mages and scooting around them as they raced around the chamber doing damage control and seeking her.

Crouching low, she got down beside the fellow guarding the door and reached for the latch.

"Somebody cast an area-of-effect spirit anchor!" Elfonse shouted.

The anchor spell would force her spirit form to drop. Not waiting for that, she dropped her own spirit form at the same second she lunged for the latch. Her body popped back into existence in its physical form, heavy and awkward, but she managed to grasp the latch and yank it down as the guard beside her lurched and grabbed for her. She rolled below his reaching arms and slammed against the door panel. It flew outward into the hallway, and she tumbled after it.

She did scream then—at the top of her healthy, young lungs. Ironically, it had been her older sister, Arianna, who had taught her how to "scream like a proper female" some years ago, a piercing shriek fit to wake the dead.

Someone threw a silence spell at her, and she incanted a magic shield just before the silence spell arrived. That shield dropped, and as fast as she could say the words, she put up another one. She resumed screaming for all she was worth.

But then they were all casting at her at once, and she couldn't put up shields on herself as fast as two dozen or more mages could pepper her with silencing spells.

Her scream cut off abruptly, her throat paralyzed, no more sound coming out. She could only hope it had been enough. Rough hands grabbed her and dragged her back inside the ritual chamber, shoving her into the circle and down to her knees.

She glared up at Elfonse in defiance, daring him to do his worst to her, silently vowing not to go down without a fight.

"That was costly, you wretched child!" he snarled. "Now we'll have to cast a new circle and start the whole ritual over again with new components."

She summoned a glow of magic to both hands menacingly, as if to say she was willing to start the fight over as well.

"Knock her out, you fools!" Elfonse snarled.

Raina glanced back over her shoulder and saw a pair of acolytes with the butts of their daggers raised, hesitating to strike her. She mouthed the words *White Heart* as both a warning and a threat.

Memorizing their faces so she could recognize them the next time she saw them, she would take pleasure in pointing them out to the Royal Order of the Sun as the men who'd struck down a White Heart member.

They seemed to read her intent in her eyes, for both of them paused, frowning, and failed to swing their short swords at her.

"Oh, for the love of Hadrian, I'll do it," Elfonse growled.

Something hard smashed into her temple, and everything went dark.

With the death of the chamberlain, there was no one to announce their entrance to the throne room, and Endellian was forced to step inside herself, calling out, "Princess Endellian and the Child of Fate, Vlador Noss, answer the summons of His Most Resplendent Majesty, Maximillian the Third, Emperor of the Eternal Empire of Koth." She added a little desperately, "May he ever rule in prosperity and peace."

"What's this?" her father asked. "Where's my chamberlain?"

Endellian stepped fully into the room, bowing her forehead to the first golden step leading up to her father seated in his black nullstone throne in the shape of a rising flame. It was the full obeisance of a commoner and one she never, ever used. "I am sorry to say he is dead, Your Most Resplendent Majesty."

"Rise, for pity's sake, daughter!" Maximillian snapped. "What's this about my chamberlain being dead?"

"Something happened with the Man in Amber. The Child of Fate claims to have opened some sort of mental conduit from the Man in Amber to the chamberlain that the Man in Amber used to . . . kill him . . ." The explanation sounded lame even to her ears, and her words trailed off uncertainly.

"This would be why I encased that whoreson in amber in the first place!" her father snapped. "Has the chamberlain gone to resurrect, then?"

"I'm sorry to say his spirit has departed," she replied reluctantly.

"Laernan? Why did you not anchor his spirit back in his body?"

"By the time I reached the chamberlain, his spirit had already departed too far beyond the Veil for me to retrieve it."

Maximillian frowned. "How long ago did the chamberlain die?"

"No more than five minutes, Father," Endellian answered, cautiously adding the familiar term as a gentle reminder to Maximillian that she was more than a regular courtier to him.

"And you cannot reach his spirit?" Maximillian questioned Laernan.

"I cannot. It must have flown from his body directly to the flame and beyond, at high speed."

"Enhanced speed?" Maximillian queried.

"Just so, Your Majesty," Laernan answered solemnly.

"Well, well. How very interesting. Step forward, Child of Fate."

Vlador did so, bowing in the same manner Endellian had. Maximillian let the seer remain bent double for somewhat longer than he had her before finally granting permission for Vlador to rise.

"What did you do to my chamberlain?" Maximillian asked mildly enough.

The question was accompanied by a wave of mental power from her father that stripped bare all deception, cut through evasion, and tore the truth directly from the mind of the one he interrogated. It was this exact power of her father's that made him so formidable. None could deceive him, and none could hide even their deepest, innermost, secret thoughts from Maximillian when he chose to pry into someone's mind.

Vlador Noss answered easily, "Upon my word of honor, Your Majesty, I did nothing to your chamberlain. I merely . . . enabled . . . mental communication between the Man in Amber and your servant."

"Did you hear or feel the nature of this communication?" Maximillian asked.

"I did."

"Describe it."

Vlador frowned for a moment. "It felt almost psionic in nature. And yet, not. It was not a skill the Man in Amber called upon, but rather a mind power intrinsic to his being."

Maximillian planted an elbow on the arm of his throne and his chin in his fist. He sat thus for a long minute, thinking. The emanations of his mind rippled out across the room, although Endellian could discern nothing of his actual thoughts. Sometimes she forgot just how powerful her father truly was. But in an unguarded moment like this, when he did not bother to channel or contain his mental powers, the display was fearsome, even to her, and she was closer to him in power than anyone else alive in the Empire.

At length, he said, "You may live, seer. For now."

The rush of relief she felt at that pronouncement surprised Endellian.

Her father said to Vlador, "Tell me more about this rebellion you see brewing, specifically where it grows and who is behind it."

"Of course, Your Majesty. I see a person with no name standing in a wild land . . ."

Raina blinked awake to the sounds of fighting. Painful magic coursed through her body. Someone had cast some sort of healing spell at her, apparently. Her face rested on something cold and hard. Stone. A floor. Feet stomped perilously close to her face.

"Get up, Raina!" a familiar voice shouted. *Cicero.*

Startled, she pushed upright and saw a wild mêlée before her, a tangle of dark blue robes with fists and swords and bolts of magic flying wildly. She had no idea where to wade into the fight, who to help, or who to hinder.

Then she spied a familiar face. Justin. Standing back-to-back with a big figure. That must be Kadir. And they were losing. In spite of both of them spraying magic like mad, they were outnumbered and out-cast by a factor of at least twelve to one. A third man joined them, his sword flickering in and out among the robes almost too fast to follow. Cicero always had been a fine swordsman.

Still, she knew a losing fight when she saw one. Pulling an abandoned blue cloak over her like a sheepskin, she crawled forward on her hands and knees until she could pop up to her feet beside her defenders.

She tossed all her remaining sleep gases toward the exit door, trying to create some sort of corridor for them to escape through. Shocked mages fell over one after another as she mowed them down with the Black Widow's sleep gas globes. Because she did not have to incant a spell and gather magic before throwing each gas globe, the alchemy was extremely fast at knocking down their foes.

"This way!" she shouted to Cicero, Justin, and Kadir. The three of them moved in a tight cluster, backs pressed together, as she fired off silence spells and sleep spells as fast as she could cast them.

The screaming from before resumed in her head, nearly splitting her skull in twain, nearly driving her to her knees in agony. A horrendous rush of fear and rage filled her mind until she could barely shape magic, but she kept on casting grimly.

They'd nearly made it to the door when at least a dozen more men charged through the doorway, weapons raised and hands glowing.

"Get them!" Elfonse screamed, pointing at her and her companions.

Raina braced to go down, but of a sudden, the men in front of her started turning around. Casting magic away from her. What on Urth? Someone was attacking them from outside in the hallway.

Without stopping to see who it might be, she took advantage of the backs of her foes and nailed them with more sleep spells. They toppled over like pins in a lawn bowling game. She leaped over their prostrate forms, yelling for Cicero, Kadir, and Justin to follow her.

The entire fight poured out into the hallway, lit by torches guttering wildly in the air currents stirred up by the combat.

She was stunned to see the prisoner brandishing a shield

and sword, dropping the last pair of mages who fought against him.

"To me, White Heart!" he shouted. "I am Royal Order of the Sun!"

He wore no colors, but she didn't care one whit. She bolted forward, praying that her companions were still on their feet and close behind her.

The prisoner turned and sprinted down the hallway, leading Raina around a corner. He ducked into a small room, and she charged in after him. As he began to slam the door shut, she grabbed his arm frantically.

"Those three are with us!"

Cicero, Kadir, and Justin screeched through the opening, and the prisoner shoved the door closed behind them, dropping a stout wooden bar into place to bar it. Total darkness enveloped them.

"Where are we?" Raina whispered.

Kadir's voice floated out of the darkness, out of breath but disgusted. "A storeroom filled with casks of wine. There's no other way out."

A glow from Kadir's hand illuminated what was, indeed, a small, low-ceilinged chamber mostly filled with barrels and casks. He murmured the incant for a wizard's lock, and a protective glow abruptly encased the wooden panel.

The prisoner said, "I have a magic item. It will transport one person out of here. Take it, Emissary."

"No, thank you."

"I'm not going to debate this with you. It is my duty to protect you—"

She cut him off. "I have a better idea. Let's all get out of here."

Pounding commenced on the door at her back. The portal glowed brightly for a moment, accompanied by a sizzling sound, as the wizard's lock spell Kadir had just cast upon it met the dispelling magics being cast upon it from the other side.

Kadir quickly cast another wizard's lock as Raina fished

frantically in her pouch. She found and pulled out a bumpy stick of wood, about the length of her forearm and slightly tapered on one end. "I don't know how to use this, Kadir, but perhaps you could do the honors?"

"Bless you for your stubborn, willful ways, and for stealing that from me long ago," Kadir muttered as she held out the Wand of Rowan to him. He took the powerful magic item and ordered, "Everyone grab onto me. Not my cloak. My skin."

Raina grabbed onto Kadir's forearm as he uttered a complicated command word.

The door to the wine cellar exploded behind them, and Elfonse raised his hands to cast a gigantic bolt of magic at them—

—and then it all blinked out of existence.

In the enraged mage's place stood a young, beautiful, green-skinned woman, clothed only in woven leaves and artfully draped vines, staring at them curiously.

In a sweet, trilling voice, she asked, "I'm Callisia. Who are you?"

Thanon looked around in the damp and gloom of the Sorrow Wold in disgust. Even his best trackers could barely tell where they were, let alone reacquire the trail of Raina and her companions through this light-forsaken place. He could not believe that a young girl and a handful of her friends had slipped away from the Talons of Koth, one of the most elite units in Maximillian's entire army.

A commotion at the edge of their camp drew his attention away from the roughly sketched map of the Sorrow Wold his scouts had assembled for him over the past few days. Not that it had done them one bit of good when it came to tracking the emissary.

A pair of his scouts escorted a rough-looking fellow forward toward him. The bearded hydesmyn was dressed in little more than bear skins and looked half-crazed. "And who might you be, sir?" Thanon asked pleasantly enough.

"Get your hands off me, you filthy soldiers!" the prisoner

shouted, tearing free of his escort and charging toward Thanon with a ferocious-looking battle-axe raised aggressively.

That, of course, earned the man a quick tackle and a foursome of soldiers sitting on top of his limbs. Thanon approached the cursing wild man and crouched beside him. He laid his hand on the man's head and used a mind touch to force his way past the fellow's resistance to his mental invasion.

Once inside the man's mind, Thanon casually ripped through the fellow's recent memories—ah hah! Will Cobb, the black lizardman girl he ran with sometimes, the big jann—

And then Thanon became aware of a subtle alteration to the hydesmyn's mind. He reached out to probe it and recoiled, stunned. He yanked his hand away from the man's head and lurched to his feet, taking a few stumbling steps backward, staring down at the prisoner in shock.

"Is aught amiss, sir?" one of his lieutenants asked quickly.

"This man. He's been touched by one whom I recognize." He ordered quickly, "Let him up. Get him food and bind his wounds. And for stars' sake, get him a basin of water and some soap."

"Who is he?" the lieutenant asked as several men hurried to follow Thanon's orders.

"One we would do well to leave alone."

Thanon had experienced that chaotic mental vibration once before, many years ago. It was not a thing a paxan ever forgot, to touch a mind so consumed by ambition, lust, and rage. How—and *why*—was a filthy barbarian out here in the untamed lands touched by a Kothite? Ammertus, no less? Maybe not Ammertus directly, but certainly the familial signature was unmistakable.

A little while later, a considerably cleaner, bandaged, and well-fed hydesmyn was brought to Thanon.

"We did not get off to a good start. Let us begin again. I am Commander Thanon of the Talons of Koth. And who might you be, sir?"

"Berengar's the name. I'm a hunter from way back. What brings a fancy gent like thee to these parts?"

Amused, Thanon answered, "I'm also a hunter. And my prey is a young woman wearing white as well as a half dozen of her friends."

"Ain't seen no woman in white. Ran into a bunch of kids a few nights back, though. Brats stole my kill from me and left me half-dead."

Thanon had, of course, seen the encounter in Berengar's memory. He was pleased that the man was being honest with him. It would make this interview so much easier. And no way was he touching the man's mind again. Whatever Imperial machinations this fellow was involved in were above Thanon's pay grade to interfere with.

"Tell me, Berengar. Where did this attack upon you occur?"

"About a day's walk east of here," the surly hydesman replied.

"Could you show me and my men the place?"

A snort. "Wouldn't be much of a tracker if I couldn't back-track my own cursed trail, now would I?"

"I suppose not," Thanon replied, smiling. "Did you happen to see what direction this pack of youths was heading when they left you?"

"Of course, I tracked them for a solid day, but I didn't want to mess with that cursed boar-man they had with them. Once the rage came over him, he was something fierce, I tell you."

A boar-man? A boar changeling, huh? Thanon had personally never seen one, but he could imagine such a man would be strong and aggressive. He ordered his troops to prepare to move out.

What in the world was Raina tangled up in out here? More curious than ever about what she was up to and why a powerful Kothite was influencing people in this region, Thanon formed up his men. He gave the order to move out, and they followed the hunter east, marching fast.

I f there was a more miserable place than the Sorrow Wold, Will surely had never seen it. Their path was blocked by webwillows—trees with long, trailing branches, and leaves coated in a milky substance. When brushed against, they wrapped tightly around a soul like spider silk and left behind a sticky residue that no amount of scrubbing would remove. Not to mention the biting spiders that dropped down out of the willows to suck one's blood while a person's friends swatted them away and tried to cut the trapped person free.

As if that were not enough, the party was attacked by a swarm of giant wasps, each insect the size of his hand and the stings of which took almost all of Rosana's magic to heal. And it was not even noon yet.

By midafternoon, it had poured rain on them for a half hour and then grew so cold Will swore his clothing had frozen to his back. Drenched and shivering, they slogged onward in the gathering gloom.

A dozen bipedal creatures vaguely the size and shape of men—but made entirely of twisted, growing vines—attacked them at a spot where the path narrowed to a single person wide and was crowded on all sides by thick brambles. Will was in the lead and slammed his staff into the closest one.

"Vinemen!" he shouted.

The rest of the party crowded close together, alternating who faced left or right. For his part, Kerryl Moonrunner merely stood in the middle of the path and stared vaguely at the vineman, who ignored him in return.

The vinemen waved their sinewy, green arm-appendages,

brandishing long thorns at the end of each, and Will and the others dodged and slashed at the creatures. When an appendage was cut off, it oozed a bright green, foul-smelling slime.

"Their blood is poison!" Sha'Li called.

Will seriously did not feel like sparring with some poisonous weed. Every blow his foes got in on him stung like frozen fire against his chilled flesh.

So short-tempered he didn't even bother to warn his friends to stand back, he blasted the vinemen with bolts of force damage channeled through his staff. It was tremendously wasteful of magic, but he was too cold and tired and out of sorts to care. And besides, his magic would reset at sunset or thereabouts.

The rest of the party, who'd had to duck for their lives to avoid his blasts, straightened cautiously behind him to catch their breaths and adjust their armor, making a few minor repairs and wiping off the slime the creatures had left behind.

Rynn asked cautiously, "Do you have a particular dislike for vinemen that we should know about?"

Will scowled. "Not particularly. But what's the point of having all these combat skills if I never use them? I didn't feel like wasting my time in a training session against a bunch of plants."

Rosana sidled past Eben to stand close beside Will. She put a soft hand on his forearm. "Patience, Will. We're all uncomfortable, but this day will pass."

He scowled a bit more but allowed silently that she was right.

They resumed walking, and Rynn said from the back of the line, "While I'm grateful that you obliterated those vinemen, in general, it might be wise to preserve the tide-turning power of your magics for times when we have need of it to stay alive."

Will made an irritated face at the forest ahead of him. He knew that. His father had drilled the lesson into him from the day he'd first learned to cast magic. Save his precious and finite magic for when it was really needed. Rely on the infinite number of swings in his sword the rest of the time. He didn't need some smug paxan monk telling him how to use his magic.

Eben spoke up. "I sense something. If we could stop for a moment, mayhap it is a thread of water . . ."

Will stopped with alacrity. Eben had discovered a talent for dowsing last fall, and it had saved their lives more than once. "If you can find us water, my friend, I will be in your debt for life."

Eben grinned. "I'll hold you to that. It's over this way."

The jann took the lead, slashing his way through thick brush with his sword at right angles to the path.

If Will thought the wold was awful while walking a path, it was nothing compared to the horror of it once they had to fight their way through nigh impassable brush, poison ivy with stems as thick as Will's wrist snaking up the tree trunks, and face-height spiderwebs that made instant paxan fist fighters of any who walked into one.

"It has to be right around here," Eben muttered, walking in a tight circle in a small gap between several sickly trees with thin trunks, straining upward among their bigger cousins for scraps of light.

Frowning, Eben bent down and pushed back a cluster of weeds. Will was disgusted when only black dirt showed and no upwelling of water. But Eben gasped and fell to his knees, digging eagerly with his hands and belt dagger.

The jann lifted a muddy stone in triumph. "Look at that!"

"It's a rock," Will declared. "A muddy one."

"Can't you see it glowing?" Eben asked, enthralled with his find.

"Nope. It's just a rock."

"Cast some magic at it," Eben challenged him.

It was Will's turn to frown. "Rynn just chastised me for wasting my magic, and now you want me to cast it at a *rock*?"

"Just a little," Eben urged.

Huffing, Will cast the simplest magic he knew, a light spell, at the rock. The magic struck the dirt-smeared surface and disappeared. Completely. The stone absorbed the magic like a dry sponge took up water. "What the—" Will blurted.

Sha'Li cut him off, breathing, "Nullstone." She added in confusion, "How did that get here? It comes only from dragon-touched places. I see nowhere around here that could be the lair of a dragon."

Rosana asked, "What does nullstone do, exactly?"

Rynn answered, "It absorbs magic and is impervious to magical damage. It's so hard that it's nearly impossible to mine or work. It takes special tools and training to cut or carve it."

Eben used his sleeve to wipe the dirt off his find. "This side of the stone is worked. And this line across it, here"—he traced a smoothly arcing groove across its face—"is man-made. I'll wager this stone was a piece of something larger at one time. This other edge, here, is jagged like the stone was split by some sort of impact."

Will stood back as the others exclaimed over the stone like it was a nugget of gold. Finally, when they'd fawned over Eben's find until his nerves grated, he grumbled, "Yes, but we can't drink that stone or wash with it."

Eben rolled his eyes. "Fine. Step back, Grouchy Pants, and let me look for some water."

He was not grouchy! He was simply looking out for the good of the group. Glaring, he moved back a few steps so Eben could stretch out face-first on the ground, his fists clutching at the moist dirt.

It took only a few seconds for the jann to hop to his feet. "This way. There's a creek close by."

After he drank his fill and wiped the noxious slime off his clothing and armor, Will's mood improved somewhat. He led the party along the creek, using his Bloodroot-inspired affinity for trees and plants to move branches aside and make their travel easier. He led the way until they came across another path heading roughly west. Rynn took the lead once more, declaring that Will could use a break. He didn't need a break, curse it!

Rynn set a blistering pace, while Kerryl muttered direly of ghosts in the wold and dreamweaver spiders that came out after dark. As the perpetual twilight deepened into a colorless gloaming made up of monstrous silhouettes, the path spilled into a large clearing littered with broken boulders. It looked like a ruin of some kind.

"Who lived here when this place was whole?" Rosana asked curiously.

Rynn looked around, frowning. "This must be a forgotten place, and very old, for I have no knowledge of it."

Will turned to Kerryl. "Do you know this place?"

The nature guardian was still not in his right mind and muttered of doorways with monsters pouring out of them, a great army of creatures that stole the minds of their attackers.

Eben, who was examining one of the boulders, said over his shoulder, "The damage to these stones did not happen that long ago. No more than a few hundred years at most."

Rynn's frown deepened. "I've been alive that long and traveled this wold many times, yet I have no memory of a village—or a structure, for that matter—of this size or in this place."

Will looked around with interest. He never could resist a mystery. In the last of the light, they gathered wood and built a fire, eating rations left over from the Black Widow rather than trying to hunt this late. After the rough meal, he fashioned a torch out of twisted grass and a stout stick and thrust it into the fire. Using it for light, he explored the ruin further.

He found a pair of square stones mostly sunk into the ground, but sheared off only a few finger spans above the dirt. They were placed slightly wider than both his outstretched arms apart. Studying the broken stones around them, he spotted several with arcing sides. An archway of some kind might have stood here once, but strangely, he saw no sign of a foundation or debris on either side of the arch that might have indicated that it had once been a doorway to a building. Odd. Shrugging, he made his way back to the fire.

"Who wants first watch tonight?" he asked.

"You take it," Rynn said. "I took it last night. I'll take middle watch tonight."

The middle watch was least desirable because it meant a night's sleep had to get broken into two parts.

"Done," Will said briskly. He found a sturdy boulder about the right height to sit on and made himself comfortable, staring out across the clearing as the others settled down behind him.

Kendrick commented, "If you see a ghostly woman moaning and sobbing, it's only the Lady of the Wood. Don't attack her and she won't attack you."

Will snorted. "There's no such thing as ghosts."

Rosana laughed. "I'll bet two years ago you thought there were no such things as tree lords or dryads or dragons either."

With that discomforting thought foremost in his mind, he commenced sitting the night watch.

A bulging gibbous moon glowed sullenly from behind a thin layer of scudding clouds. The day's chill turned into a night so cold that it pierced all his clothing as easily as needles. He shivered in his cloak as the darkness deepened.

A sudden break in the night sounds caught his attention. He thought he spied a figure lurking in the trees at the far edge of the clearing. He stood up, throwing back his cloak and taking up his staff. "Show yourself!" he called.

As he knew it would, his voice precipitated sounds of quick stirring behind him as the others jumped up and grabbed weapons.

Simultaneously, a half dozen humanoids stepped out of the trees. They came from all directions, and Will retreated into the tight defensive circle his friends had already formed. The attackers were completely silent, not communicating with one another by any visible means. Although they advanced slowly, their hands, and hence their weapons, were *fast*.

Will was no slouch as a fighter, but it was all he could do to block the barrage of incoming blows that peppered him from the front and both sides. His attackers appeared human, but they stared blankly at him, never blinking, never showing the slightest reaction or emotion when he landed a smart blow with his staff.

Even the most stoic of warriors winced when he hit them sharply enough. Given how hard he was swinging his metal-clad staff now, these fellows ought to be howling in pain every time he clocked one of them, but they didn't make a single sound and fought on in eerie silence.

Behind him, he heard a low grumble that grew into a roar.

Over the sound of it, Eben shouted, "Kendrick, no!"

Will dared not turn or even look over his shoulder for fear of being skewered immediately, but he knew well enough what he would see if he looked. Kendrick had transformed into a were-boar. Now he could only pray that Kendrick had enough control, or Kerryl had enough control over him, to target their attackers and not his own friends.

Another shout from Eben, something along the lines of "What are you doing?"

Without warning or visible cause, Will's attackers disengaged from their assault and moved purposefully around him and his friends, heading for the trees.

"They're chasing Kendrick!" Eben called, racing after the pack of retreating humans.

Swearing under his breath, Will shouted at Kerryl, who was still badly injured, to stay by the fire. Will took off after Eben, and Rynn joined him. Sha'Li was nowhere to be seen, but he had faith she was racing through the trees in the dark close by, paralleling their course and positioning herself for some sort of stealth attack when their prey finally slowed. Forced to pay close attention to his footing while ducking vines and leaping over brambles, he couldn't look back to see if Rosana was keeping up with them. He just had to hope she was. They would likely have need of her healing skills before this ended.

As the silent humans spread out in front of them, Rynn peeled off to the right and Eben to the left. Will hesitated, unsure which way to go. The last thing they needed was to get lost and separated out here in this infernal forest. He caught a glimpse of Eben darting ahead of him and gave chase since he was likely following Kendrick and the silent humans.

A pair of the silent men stopped in front of Eben, turned, and assumed fighting stances. Will, close on Eben's heels, barreled into them.

Eben, a strong man and a skilled swordsman, dropped his opponent in under a minute. Will, using a staff, took less time to stagger his man, but longer to drop him. Sometimes he considered shifting to a long sword, or maybe an edged pike, but he'd grown up staff fighting, and it was by far his most comfortable weapon. And besides . . .

He incanted and gathered force damage, channeling it down his staff like a miniature lightning bolt at his foe. His opponent dropped to the ground, dying.

. . . he could do magic with his staff.

As a rule, Will tried not to kill his opponents. Not only did Raina squawk when he killed anyone, but Rosana didn't like it either. For her, he usually refrained from using lethal force.

But these assailants were not usual. In addition to their terrible speed, they were highly skilled fighters and severely creeped him out.

A momentary lull fell around him and Eben with only their panting disturbing the quiet. The jann lifted a hand and signaled for silence, and Will held his breath. He tilted his head, listening, too.

"Over that way," Will murmured. "Do you hear it?"

Eben nodded, and they took off running, bursting onto a pitched fight between several more of the silent men against Rynn and Sha'Li, with Rosana casting battle magic over their shoulders in between healing her friends.

Will and Eben plowed into the backs of the attackers. Once surrounded, the silent men fell into disarray and went down quickly enough.

"Any sign of Kendrick?" Rynn asked, impressively not out of breath.

"Hush, everyone," Eben ordered.

They froze for a moment, and simultaneously, Sha'Li and Rynn pointed in the same direction. The group took off running again, stretching out into a line as the fastest pulled ahead and the slowest fell back.

They ran into two more pairs of the silent humans, who seemed more interested in retreating than fighting, a change in tactics for them. Steadily, the silent men led them in a concerted direction. Will couldn't tell if they led the party toward some ambush or away from something else entirely. The silent men would engage a little, then fall back, engage for a few seconds, then fall back.

After defeating one such frustrating retreat, Rosana asked worriedly, "Where could Kendrick be? In his boar form, he's faster than all of us."

Will hadn't paid a lot of attention to where they had gone in the running combat, and he looked around in the tangle of black tree limbs and dark shadows in confusion. "I have no idea where *we* are, let alone where he is."

Rynn commented, "I think we've more or less traveled in a big circle."

Rosana asked worriedly, "Any sign or sound of Kendrick?"

Everyone shook their heads.

It took Rynn a while to find elfsign carved on a tree beside a narrow trail they stumbled across and for him to decipher its worn runes in the dark. Will cast a bit of his remaining magic to make a light spell that danced at the ends of his fingertips for a few minutes—long enough for Rynn to figure out where they were and which direction they needed to go to return to their camp.

It took another ten minutes or so to trudge along in a single-file line on the path, which looked like little more than a deer trail, before Will spotted a speck of light through the trees, low to the ground and flickering. Their campfire.

Relieved, he followed Rynn until the paxan stopped abruptly, and Will nearly plowed into him. "What the—"

Rynn cut him off with a sharp hand gesture, but the damage was done. The small figure crouching next to the fire looked up in alarm.

Will took in the scene in dismay. Kerryl sprawled unconscious or dead beside the fire. Another figure lay barely visible on the other side of the fire on the ground, and a little girl was kneeling beside that person. In each of her hands, a tiny brazier rested, with flames rising out of each. Red flames from her right hand and misty gray flames from her left hand. A faint nimbus of magical energy surrounded her like glowing fog.

She stood up. The fog detached from whoever lay on the ground and whooshed into the little girl all at once. She inhaled a deep, delighted breath.

"Too late!" she cried out in a high, musical voice. "I got what I came for." She scampered away from them, beyond the circle of bedrolls, dodging and jumping so lightly between and over the fallen stones it was as if her body had no weight.

Will spied the membranous glow of a planar gate between the pair of boulders he'd examined earlier. The gate was fluctuating, opening and closing like a spasming sphincter. He darted toward the girl to stop her, to ask who she was and demand to know where the gate had come from, but even as he jumped toward it and her, the gate blinked out of existence with a crash of sound and a blast of magical force that knocked him backward off his feet.

He slammed to the ground hard. He rolled and painfully pressed himself upright, aching from head to foot. Tonight, he could have used a good dose of Raina's healing.

"Will!" Rosana cried out.

He turned quickly, his staff coming up defensively. Rynn was on his knees beside a naked man, who was beginning to moan in terrible agony. A movement in the long grass behind Rynn made Will cry out and jump forward to cover the paxan's back. But it was another downed man, beginning to groan and regain consciousness. This time, it was Eben.

Will knelt beside the jann, helping him sit upright. "Are you okay? What happened?"

"Got jumped. Hit over the head and knocked out." He rubbed his skull and then cried out suddenly, "Kendrick! Is he all right? Something attacked him and Kerryl."

"Kendrick's in human form and making noise, so he lives. I don't know about Kerryl."

Will called, "Rosie, could you check Kerryl and make sure he lives?"

The gypsy darted forward and commenced performing first aid on the nature guardian. In a few seconds, she announced, "He has sustained more injuries. I've given him the last of my healing, and it's enough to stabilize him overnight and keep him alive, but I'm going to need help sewing shut a nasty cut on his thigh and bandaging his other wounds."

"I'll help," Rynn offered.

Will gnashed his teeth. It seemed like that cursed paxan was always hovering around Rosie these days, jumping to help her lift a heavy basket or taking her pack from her when she got tired on the road. Even tonight, he'd stayed in front of Rosie like he was her personal bodyguard.

"I'll help her with Kerryl," Will growled, shouldering past the paxan. Will hadn't the slightest bit of first-aid training, but he'd be cursed if he let Rynn rub shoulders with her and work forehead to forehead over the patient, trading smiles and whispers.

"Are you all right?" Rosana murmured as he dropped to his knees at Kerryl's side. "You seem tense." That was Rosana-speak for he was being a jerk and she was trying not to be a nag about it.

"I'm fine!" he snapped. "What do I do?"

"Hold up a torch for me so I can see to sew this wound closed."

He grimaced and looked away in distaste as Rosana commenced sewing the nature guardian's flesh like it was cloth, poking a needle through it and drawing the edges of the long cut together.

He must have made some sound of revulsion, because Rosana asked, grinning, "How can you be squeamish? You're the fighter who makes these messes we healers have to deal with."

He didn't mind seeing blood or guts in the heat of battle, but this was disgusting. "I don't generally slow down to study the results of my handiwork. I drop 'em and move on."

"Welcome to my world, cleaning up after the likes of you."

"You're starting to sound like Raina."

Rosana shrugged. "I considered going White Heart, but the

high matriarch said I have too big a temper and would get in trouble."

Will grinned. "Wise woman."

Rosana stuck her tongue out at him and commenced wrapping a cloth bandage around a gash on Kerryl's arm.

Eventually, everyone's cuts and bruises were salved or bandaged as required. Sha'Li gathered all of Kerryl and Kendrick's gear and laid out their bedrolls for them. Kerryl fell asleep immediately and heavily, but Kendrick twitched and thrashed as if captured in the throes of some terrible nightmare.

Although it privately galled Will, he made no protest when Rosana finally asked Rynn to do a mind touch on Kendrick and make sure their friend was all right.

The paxan knelt beside the human. He touched Kendrick's temple for no more than a second before he drew back his fingers sharply. Cautiously, he touched Kendrick's face again, this time murmuring something under his breath, almost like a magic spell.

Kendrick's eyes fluttered open. Will had never seen such anguish in anyone's expression. Kendrick threw back his head and let out a keening cry of grief that hurt to even hear.

Rosana rushed over to him, and even Sha'Li took a step toward Kendrick.

Eben cried, "What is amiss, brother?"

"It's gone! My gift is no more!" Kendrick wailed.

Everyone stared at him, but it was Will who muttered, "We'd better wake Kerryl."

The nature guardian was nearly as distraught as Kendrick, and the pair huddled together, alternately grieving and ranting.

For his part, Eben seemed thrilled. He'd long wanted Kendrick to leave Kerryl and get rid of his were-curse. After Sha'Li and Raina, with help from a unicorn, had successfully rid Hyland's scout, Tarryn, of the were-curse last fall, Eben had been fretting about how to convince Kendrick to do the same.

Will understood Kendrick's position, though. He knew how conflicted he would be if someone took Bloodroot from him. He'd lived with the spirit for so long that it was almost a part of him and he a part of it. It would feel like part of him had been amputated if someone took away the tree lord.

Speaking of which, "Who was that child earlier?" he asked no one in particular.

Rynn and Eben both whipped around to stare at him. "What child?" they demanded in unison.

"The one who was kneeling over Kendrick before. As soon as she saw me, she ran away and left through a planar gate of some kind."

The others stared at him as if he'd grown a second head. Hadn't they seen her? It dawned on him that he must have outpaced the others by a good bit in running back to the clearing. He'd have been the only one to see her, then.

"Why didn't you mention this before?" Rosana asked.

"It didn't come up. We've been busy getting everyone stabilized and patched up. This is the first time I've stopped to think about it, and I assumed everyone had seen her."

Rynn said, "It must have been the child from the dream plane. Vesper. How did she take Kendrick's power?"

Will answered, "It looked like she was performing some sort of magic ritual. She held two small, hand-sized braziers with flames in each. A fog of some kind hung between her and Kendrick. When she fled, the fog followed her and disappeared into her."

Rynn sucked in a sharp breath. "Do you have any idea what it means if she's found a way to come to this plane, even temporarily? Stars, the power she'll have if she has managed to absorb Kendrick's were-curse into herself." It was the most distraught Will had ever seen Rynn. The paxan paced round and round the fire, muttering to himself about the repercussions of this disaster.

After a while, Eben finally stood up, blocking Rynn's agitated path. "Be at ease, friend. Vesper's on our side."

Rynn made a sound of incredulity.

Eben argued, "She kept her word and helped us fix Kendrick, didn't she?"

"I didn't want to be fixed!" Kendrick exclaimed.

"Nonetheless, brother, she promised to help me fix you, and she did. What's wrong with that?"

"How do I get it back?" Kendrick interrupted. "Make her help us with that."

"You won't get your curse back. Not from her," Rynn interjected.

Eben retorted hotly, "You always see the worst in people, Rynn!"

The paxan snorted. "And you are naïve to a fault, Eben. It's high time you grew up and saw the world as it really is. Vesper is dangerous. She's more powerful than all of us combined, and we do not know what she schemes at. One thing I do know—she did not take Kendrick's curse out of the goodness of her heart. And although I don't know the whole reason why she took that specifically, she unquestionably made herself stronger in the process."

Kerryl offered, "I know why she took it."

They all looked at him expectantly.

Raina, no stranger to dryads and their effect on men, leaped forward to speak for the four men with her. "Well met, Lady Callisia. We are friends of Rowan. She gave us a wand from her own tree to use if we ever got into trouble."

Kadir muttered from behind her, "How did you know what it was and where it came from?"

Gawaine had recognized the wand in one of her dreaming visits to him and regaled her with hilarious tales of Rowan and her fellow dryads bringing low great, tough male warriors who thought themselves immune to the charms of mere forest sprites.

Raina explained, "We just escaped someone who was trying to kill us and used the wand rather haphazardly. Can you tell us where we are, exactly?"

"I've heard your kind call this place the Machaira."

Raina stared at the dryad. The wand had taken them from Alchizzadon, which she believed to be somewhere to the south and west of the Sorrow Wold, all the way to the northern shore of the Estarran Sea? It was going to take her *months* to make her way back to the Sorrow Wold. Worse, she'd left it with her friends that, if she had not returned from Alchizzadon in a few days, they should continue on without her. How she would find them now, she had no idea.

In the meantime, she had a dryad to make nice with. Raina knew from previous experience with them that the forest creatures were partial to men and could get very touchy with human females who said the wrong thing.

"You've been kind enough to introduce yourself, Lady Callisia, and we should do the same," Raina said courteously. "My name is Raina, and I'm a healer. This gentleman is Proctor Kadir. He's a very important mage and the keeper of the Wand of Rowan. This is my longtime friend and also a mage, Justin Morland. This elf is Cicero, a kindari warrior. And this gentleman"—she gestured at the bearded, filthy, alleged Royal Order of the Heart member in rags—"is . . ."

She didn't actually know the prisoner's name.

He bowed gracefully, surprising Raina. He was a big, burly man, every bit as large in stature as Kadir, and spoke in a deep, mellifluous voice. "Sir Lakanos of the Fen, Knight of the Royal Order of the Sun, at your service, my lady."

A knight? Raina was shocked speechless. Everyone stared at him, and he fingered his beard ruefully.

"You are Royal Order of the Sun?" Kadir exclaimed. "How on Urth did you manage to gain entrance to the mages' tower?"

The knight, Sir Lakanos, shrugged. "I was taken there as a prisoner and being held until someone got around to stealing my spirit or killing me, I expect."

Raina wondered if there wasn't more to the story than that. How had he known the mages existed or crossed paths with them in the first place? Was he some sort of spy, put there by Lord Justinius? Or had it really been sheer luck that placed him in the tower when she'd arrived? Knowing Justinius, he'd engineered his knight's capture to make sure Raina had his order's protection while she was there or had known Lakanos was already there. It would explain why the Royal Order of the Sun had agreed to let her visit Alchizzadon without a knight escort in the first place.

Lakanos was speaking again. "Then you came to the tower, Emissary, and my duty required me to protect you. I am only sorry I did not realize Elfonse and his cronies would move so quickly to destroy you, else I would have found a way to stay closer to you."

"You got there in time to help us escape alive, sir knight.

You were close enough. And thanks be for that," Raina said gratefully.

Callisia purred a little as she sidled up to Lakanos. "You need a bath. And a shave. But you're pretty underneath all that dirt and hair."

"I would not say no to a bath," Lakanos said politely. "But I beg of you, please do not test my willpower. In the hands of one as beautiful as you, I would be as helpless as a babe."

Callisia giggled in the musical tones Raina remembered all too well from two years ago. Without Will present—he was immune to the charms of dryads, much to their chagrin—it would fall to her to rescue her male companions should the dryad get a notion to play games with any of them.

Raina looked around the beautiful and otherworldly grove in which they stood. "I have a pouch full of tasty herbs. I would be delighted to cook something wonderful for you to show our gratitude for your kindness, Lady Callisia."

The dryad trailed delicate fingers down Raina's cheek. "I like you, human Rain child. You may cook while I see to these delicious men."

As Raina had expected. If she offered to play servant and stay out of the way, the dryad wouldn't bother her. She asked politely after a kettle, and another dryad appeared from behind a large tree, pot in hand. Some sort of vegetable broth was already inside it, and Raina gave it an experimental taste. It was cold and bland, both of which she could remedy.

With the new dryad's help, she had a fire going in a few minutes and the broth seasoned. Raina sat down by the fire to contemplate her next move. And that was when she became aware of the voices in her head forming words just beyond her understanding. She'd heard them like this when her magics were just coming into their own. Gawaine told her they were echoes of spirits tied to Haelos, from whom she drew her magical energy.

She performed the technique Gawaine had shown her to quiet the voices. Except tonight, it did the opposite. A flood of many different emotions, all jumbled together, rolled over her. She got the distinct impression the emotions belonged to the disembodied spirits chattering in her head. So overwhelmed was she that a tear slipped down her cheek, startling her. Raina swatted it away impatiently.

She had nothing to cry about. She, Justin, and Cicero had escaped Alchizzadon, and Kadir and Lakanos were safe to boot. It had been a good day's work. Then why did she feel on the verge of a total breakdown and sobbing fit?

Justin came to sit beside her, his hair still damp from his bath. "You okay, muckling? You look like someone just took your mud pit away."

She made a face at him, and he grinned at her. She confessed, "Truth be told, I'm feeling a little down. And I don't know why. I've finally got you all to myself out here in the wilds and can have my wicked way with you."

Justin's grin widened. "You sound like Callisia. She suggested several utterly scandalous things to me while she scrubbed my back."

"She attended your bath?"

"No need for jealousy. It wasn't like I could keep her out, the way she just walked in and out of that tree of hers. Takes a little getting used to seeing a person tree walk like that."

Raina ladled up a bowl of broth for him. "Yes. It does. Wait till they drape themselves all over you and purr in your ear. I've seen Cicero sweat until streams of perspiration ran down his face trying to resist them. You do know not to gaze directly into any dryad's eyes, lest she charm and enslave you, right?"

"I'm not that fresh off the farm. I do know a thing or two about the world."

She stuck out her tongue at him and passed him the soup.

Kadir joined them in a few minutes, also freshly bathed. As Raina passed him some of the rich broth, she asked, "What's the fastest way back to the Sorrow Wold or thereabouts?"

"If Maren's Belt were finished, I would say that. But the waestones that will enhance speed of travel along it are not yet installed, according to my sources. Barring that, I suppose cutting across the Thirst and then traveling south through the Valelands and Meadowlands would be the fastest way back to your home."

"I'm not going back to Tyrel," she replied quickly. "I left my traveling companions in the Sorrow Wold and hope to rejoin them somewhere in the untamed lands."

Justin snorted. "Good luck with that. Do you have any idea how big the untamed lands are?"

"No, but I'm about to find out—"

She would have gone on to tell him what he could do with his rolled eyes, but a massive wave of noise rolled through her head along with an overwhelming sense of despair. So much so that she barely got her bowl set on the ground beside her before she rolled off the log and into a tight ball, hands plastered uselessly over her ears. Someone was making horrible, choked, gasping noises, a scream not quite making it past paralyzed throat muscles. Oh, wait. That was her.

She was vaguely aware of Kadir, Justin, and Lakanos bending over her in concern. But the pain, both physical and emotional, was so intense she could hardly bear it.

Somebody, maybe Cicero, demanded, "What did you people do to her?"

Somebody else—Kadir, maybe—replied, "The ritual to drain her spirit must have gotten started before she broke free of the circle. There's been some damage to her."

That was definitely Lakanos asking in a deep, angry voice, "What kind of damage?"

Justin snapped, "The first order of business is to ease her pain and not stand here arguing over who did what!"

Someone incanted a sleep spell, and that was the last she remembered before blackness, and blessed silence, engulfed her.

"Well?" Will demanded.

Kerryl sighed. "Vesper wanted to take back the part of her spirit trapped within Kendrick."

Kendrick started. "How was part of her inside me?"

Kerryl opened his mouth, but no sound came out. It looked to Will as if he was genuinely trying to answer, but to no avail. Finally, Kerryl stopped, swallowed, and said, "The spirit was not in you, boy, but in the boar."

"What boar?" Rosana asked.

Kendrick groaned. "The boar scion that he used to create me."

Abrupt rage bubbled up hard and fast inside Will. Whoops. Bloodroot hadn't liked that bit of news. "Used?" Will asked ominously. "Used how?"

"I wasn't conscious for most of it, but I believe Kerryl used a magical boar to transform me in the ritual."

"And what happened to the boar?" Will asked.

"He was . . . merged . . . with me."

"You mean destroyed," Will accused, barely able to contain Bloodroot's rage within his body. An urge to take up his staff and blast Kerryl to smithereens nearly overwhelmed him.

Thankfully, Rosana placed a steadying hand on his forearm, distracting him enough from his fury to gain the upper hand over his treant symbiont.

Kendrick winced. "He's not destroyed, exactly. I carried around his spirit within me. But now that shard of the boar spirit is with this Vesper person you speak of."

Rynn interjected, "And she will control it and steal its strength for herself."

Kerryl said heavily, "The Great Boar was present when she died. It and the other animal lords absorbed pieces of her spirit as it disintegrated."

Kendrick whirled to face his mentor. "Then she will go after all the other animal lords and scions to get back the pieces of herself. We must warn them!"

Rynn added, "And with each piece of her spirit that she gets back, she'll be one step closer to returning to this plane and wreaking havoc."

Will commented sarcastically, "Luckily for us, she's Eben's friend."

The jann scowled furiously at him and then sulked, silent by the fire.

Every instinct Will possessed shouted that trouble was

brewing with Eben. If the jann had fallen under the thrall of Vesper, they were all in mortal danger.

Raina woke, more rested than she'd been in weeks. But dryad groves were known to have that effect upon a soul. Thankfully, the screaming voices from last night and the splitting head pain that had come with them had abated this morning. She did not know who had laid hands on her skull and cast magic into her last night to put her to sleep, but she was grateful for it.

Her companions were already awake, seated by a cook fire, chatting companionably with several dryads. Uh-oh. Were all three men ensorceled?

"Morning, muckling," Justin said cheerfully. "How're you feeling today?"

She made a face at him out of general principles as she approached the fire. "I'm fine, thank you." To Kadir and Lakanos, she said, "And how did you gentlemen sleep?"

The dryads giggled, and both men grinned crookedly.

But it was Justin who replied, "We all slept well enough, considering the, um, evocative dreams our hostesses shared with us."

Raina's eyebrows shot up. "I don't want to know." She ladled some porridge into her bowl and sat down on an upended log. "So, do we know yet exactly where we are?"

"As Callisia said," Sir Lakanos answered, "we are in the Machaira. That wand of yours packs a wallop."

"Actually, it's his wand," Raina replied, nodding at Kadir. "I borrowed it from him a while back."

Both Kadir and Justin snorted at that, but neither elected to share the tale of her running away from home and snatching Kadir's wand to teleport away from Tyrel.

"Where will you go with our Lady Rowan's wand, now that you have it back?" one of the dryads cooed at Kadir, all but climbing into his lap while asking.

He pushed her away gently. "That is up to the emissary. Where do you go from here, Raina?"

She studied her cereal intently. She needed to rejoin her

friends or, barring that, to continue her quest to wake Gawaine. Did she dare speak of that to these men? It would take her weeks or months to rejoin her friends if she was even able to find them out here in the wilds. And time was the one thing Gawaine was running short of.

Frowning, she looked up at Kadir. "Where do you stand with the Mages of Alchizzadon after rescuing me last night?"

He made an inelegant sound in his throat. "To say I am persona non grata would be an understatement, I should think."

"And Justin?"

Kadir answered, "Same. If they catch us, they will do to Justin and me what they tried to do to you. You may safely consider us fugitives from them along with you."

The bitterness with which he spoke did wonders to calm her fears about his loyalties. "What will you do now?" she asked.

He shrugged. "I have magical skills. I suppose I shall find work somewhere."

"I know the Mage's guildmaster. I can put in a good word for—"

Kadir cut her off firmly. "No, thank you. I have no desire to serve the Empire." He glanced over at the Heart knight nervously. "Not that I have anything against the Empire, of course—"

It was Lakanos's turn to cut him off. "My duty is to the Heart first and foremost. Who you choose to work for is purely up to you."

What of Lakanos? Could she trust him with knowledge of Gawaine? "Is there more than one knight by your name in the Heart, Sir Lakanos?"

"Not that I am aware of. Why do you ask?"

"Did you know that Lord Justinius plans to send you with me to the Great Den of the Dominion this summer to act as my bodyguard and advisor?" Even as she asked the question, the coincidence of that selfsame knight being inside Alchizzadon when she arrived suddenly seemed like no coincidence at all.

"Is that so?" Lakanos replied mildly.

"Yes, indeed."

He nodded politely over his porridge bowl. "It will be my honor to serve and protect you, Emissary."

"Mmm-hmm," she responded skeptically. How Lord Justinius had managed to outmaneuver her so adroitly, she did not know, but she was reluctantly grateful that his man had been present to save her.

"Perhaps, sir knight, you can enlighten me more on the relationship that your order and mine share."

Lakanos set aside his empty bowl and studied her intently. "Are you asking in general, or do you wish to know specifically what my responsibility to you shall be?"

All right, then. Apparently, this knight was as subtle as Lord Justinius had indicated he would be.

"The latter, if you please. How much or little are you required to support my activities on behalf of the White Heart? Or is your duty purely to protect my life?"

Lakanos said slowly, "If you're asking where my loyalties lie, they are and always will be with doing the right thing. I am a knight before all else and sworn to my code of chivalry first and foremost. I serve the Heart, I serve my lord, Justinius, and I serve you because they are the right things to do."

A wave of grief washed over her. That was the sort of thing Leland Hyland would have said. She'd admired Hyland greatly and, more than once, had secretly wished he'd been her father.

"Do you place doing right over following the law?" she asked carefully.

One of the knight's eyebrows arched upward. "Are you planning to break any law in particular?"

"I'm planning to break a number of them," she answered bluntly.

All three men were staring at her now.

"Please elaborate," Lakanos said cautiously.

"I would rather not involve any of you and put you at risk, but I did not feel it was ethical to ask you to travel with me without being aware that I am up to no good."

Justin guffawed. "You? Into mischief? Why am I not surprised?"

Kadir smiled, as well. "You never have been one to do as you were told. If you think to shock me with your declaration, I am sorry to say you do not."

Lakanos, however, was more sober. "Do you plan to break your vows or ask me to break mine—either Heart or knightly vows?"

"Good heavens, no!" she exclaimed.

"Then what?"

"In the name of upholding my White Heart vows, I plan to commit treason."

Lakanos stood up, settling his long sword on his hip. "Ah. In that case, what shall we do first?"

Eben huddled in his cloak, staring at the morning cook fire morosely. The worst of the night's mist had yet to abate, and the new sun shone through it anemically. He'd spent hours last night arguing with his brother, trying to convince Kendrick to come away from Kerryl Moonrunner and travel with their party or at least to return home to Hyland and take over running their father's holding.

But Kendrick had refused to do either. He was determined to stay with Kerryl and help the nature guardian along his mad path toward fighting some unknown evil that was supposedly approaching.

Of course, both Kerryl and Kendrick refused to name this evil or even to suggest a rough date when it would arrive. No matter how hard he fought with Kendrick, his brother had remained steadfast in his intention to aid Kerryl.

It was utter madness, and there wasn't a cursed thing he could do about it.

Sha'Li sat down on the log beside Eben, startling him. They hadn't been close since she'd betrayed his trust last fall and helped Kerryl Moonrunner escape his sword. She declared without preamble, "Neither of them is insane. You must trust their reasons for what they do."

"Now they've got you ensorceled, too?" he snapped.

"Nay. My feet are planted firmly on the earth, but I am worried about you."

"Why me?"

"You have worked very hard to save your brother, but he turns you down. You work very hard to save your sister, and she turns down your help, also. It is time you quit saving others and save yourself."

From what?

A new voice spoke from behind him. "What's this about Marikeen turning down your help?" It was Kendrick, sitting up in his bedroll.

Eben replied sourly, "She is in league with a group of powerful magicians and refuses to leave them. The only way I can see or speak with her is to find her on the dream plane from time to time."

"Is she in need of rescue?" Kendrick asked.

Eben half turned on his log. "Why do you care? You're set on running around the countryside with your hero. The man who enslaved you and turned you into a monster."

"Don't be bitter, Eben. You're a better man than that," Kendrick said gently. "Anger and petty jealousy are not worthy of you."

"You're a fine one to speak of worthiness when you refuse to take up any of the responsibilities our father left to you."

"My responsibility is to all the people of Haelos, not just those in Hyland. I work to defend everyone from that which comes."

"That which you will not name or even describe," Eben retorted.

"Exactly so."

Eben threw up his hands in exasperation. And they had circled back to the same old argument.

Kerryl spoke up from the other side of the small cook fire. "I shall have to find a new way to pursue my goals, Kendrick. I managed before you joined me, and I will manage after you go. If you need to be with your friends and see to your sister, go."

"What will you do?" Kendrick asked.

"A way must be found to restore the Great Circle. The Great Beasts must heal and wake. The Great Totems that were destroyed must be replaced. And as for the treants, he who betrayed the Circle must be replaced."

Not restored but replaced. Eben glanced over at Will in alarm. But for his part, Will merely studied the nature guardian impassively and held his tongue. Eben had long suspected Will knew more about the workings of the great treants than he was letting on, and this moment confirmed it.

"How will you restore the circle?" Sha'Li asked. She was as eager as a puppy around her old mentor, Kerryl, and Eben mentally turned his nose up in disdain.

"Old forces are made new and prepare to act. The forgotten return, and those of us who still remember will call them by name."

Eben hated prophetic mumbo jumbo, but he gathered turmoil was on its way as forces from the past came into play once more. No surprise there.

"You saved my life last eve. How may I repay my debt to you?" the nature guardian asked them all.

Kerryl's offer surprised Eben. As did Will's reply.

"We seek one of those forces from the past of which you speak. The Children of Zinn."

"There is a name I have not heard in a very long time." Kerryl stared off into space for a moment. "Some years ago, I heard rumors that one of Zinn's children attempted to live away from the wake tree."

"The what?" Will asked.

"That information is not mine to give. It belongs to the very children of whom you ask. Find one who lives away from the others, and mayhap he or she will tell you of it."

Gah. Kerryl and his cursed secrets.

The nature guardian asked curiously, "How do you know this forgotten name?"

Again, Will answered. "The Black Widow spoke of them. And we have heard from elsewhere that the zinnzari still exist."

That "elsewhere" was Gawaine himself. The echo of the

Sleeping King had told Will and Raina in their visit to his grove on the dream plane that the zinnzari guarded his physical body on the mortal realm. Find the zinnzari, and they would find him.

"Where does the rest of the clan of Zinn live?" Sha'Li asked Kerryl.

"Let me see. That would be a ways north of here. In the Thirst, if memory serves."

"Where in the Thirst?" Rynn asked. "It is not the sort of place one wanders around in searching for a tribe of elves."

"In the Drifts, mayhap," Kerryl answered uncertainly. "Or perhaps the Silver Sands."

Rynn sucked in a sharp breath. Eben threw him a questioning look, and the kindari muttered, "Many are the legends of the wild magics in the Silver Sands."

Sha'Li asked, "How will we know these zinnzari when we meet them?"

Kerryl answered, "You will know them by the markings on their faces. They wear the magical web of Zinn across their skin."

Cicero's facial tattoos were spiderlike in nature but reminded Eben more of the eyes and mandibles of a spider than of one's web. Perhaps that was the difference between arachnari and zinnzari.

Rosana asked, "How long does it take to travel to the Thirst from here?"

Kerryl smiled kindly at her. He'd taken a liking to her after she healed him yesterday and again this morning. "To walk there will take two months or more if the weather holds and water isn't scarce, but if you were to go by sea, the journey up the coast would take a few days, and then maybe a week inland on foot to reach the first of the sands. To see all of the Thirst would take years. It is a vast land, full of wonder and desolation. Only the smart and tough survive there."

What little Eben knew of the Thirst was that it consisted mostly of desert and few merchants ventured there. Bandits were plentiful, food and water scarce, valuable resources scarcer, and the local population disinterested in trading with outsiders.

Rosana looked dubious. "I'm worried about going so far away without Raina. How will she find us?"

Rynn answered, "She's an adult and has all the resources she needs to find us or continue forward on her own."

Huh. Eben had never thought of her in that way. Because of her White Heart vows and because she neither used a weapon nor defended herself when attacked, he'd always thought of her as the most vulnerable of their group.

Will said briskly, "Are we agreed, then? We head for the coast and seek a ship bound north toward the Valelands, and then we proceed on to the Thirst?"

With varying degrees of speed and reluctance, everyone nodded, including Eben. He didn't know about the others, but he was more than ready to be quit of this dark and dank forest of sorrow.

"What say you, Kendrick?" Will asked. "Will you come with us and lend your sword to our cause?"

Kerryl answered for him. "Yes. He will. Go, boy. Be with your friends. They need your help, and their quest is worthy. When I have need of you again, I will send for you."

Kendrick scowled long and hard at his mentor, and Kerryl scowled back, finally growling, "Don't make me order you to do this."

Kendrick threw up his hands in disgust and, to Eben's immense joy, surrender.

Will laughed. "Excellent. Mayhap you can show us the fastest route out of this interminable wold."

Kendrick jerked his chin toward Kerryl. "He's the one to show you the quickest way out."

"And it will be my pleasure to do so," Kerryl declared.

Eben got the impression Kerryl was as eager to have them out of the Sorrow Wold as they were to be quit of this foul place. The nature guardian was up to something, but he could not fathom what, and he wasn't sure he cared as long as Kendrick was not part of Kerryl's plans.

* * *

G abrielle took the party to an inn nestled on the banks of the Crystal River, a half day's float upstream of the Imperial Seat, and engaged rooms for all of them. For herself, she rented a luxurious suite and ordered a perfumed bath and a hairdresser for the following morning. Her adventures roaming about Koth incognito must end, and it was time for her to transform back into the queen she was.

The next order of business was to send word to Talissar, her primary contact within the Eight, and ask for a meeting here, away from the Imperial Seat. She dared not march Bekkan through the front gates of the palace and risk all he knew upon the power of a single Octavium Pendant against the mental might of the Emperor and his Kothite cronies.

She drafted a quick note to Talissar suggesting that if he wished her help in planning a surprise birthday party for his wife and queen, Lyssandra, she should not be seen at court. Then she pressed a gold coin into the hand of the innkeeper's eldest son, asking him to sneak her note to Talissar in utmost secrecy. The youth was happy to participate in the conspiracy, particularly when it involved such extravagant compensation. He trotted off toward the pier to catch a barge bound for the palace.

The innkeeper's son returned late in the afternoon in the company of an Imperial runner. The messenger was a handsome young man with dark hair and piercing blue eyes. His face looked familiar for an instant, but then recognition slipped away. He bowed pleasantly enough and delivered a verbal message that Talissar would arrive late in the evening, and he greatly appreciated her help in planning his wife's birthday party.

The ruse of a surprise party had to hold long enough to protect both her and Talissar from rumors of a dalliance between them. She had no illusions that even here, many miles from the palace, they would be safe from prying eyes and wagging tongues. Rumor and innuendo were the stuff and trade of the Imperial Court, and the last thing she and Talissar needed was to draw attention to themselves at this critical moment.

The runner bowed himself out of her room. She ordered supper in her chambers and invited Bekkan to join her for tea after the meal. The other members of their party stayed downstairs, ostensibly listening to a local storyteller, but actually standing watch to warn her should an uninvited guest—or a military squad—show up.

It was nearing midnight, and the common room had grown raucous below with people well into their cups when a quiet knock on her door made Gabrielle nearly jump out of her skin.

She opened it, and two cloaked and hooded men slipped inside quickly. As they swept off their concealing garments, she recognized Talissar's pale beauty instantly. The man never aged. Lucky Lyssandra.

The second guest was a handsome young man with dark hair and piercing blue eyes. His face looked familiar for an instant, but then recognition slipped away.

Bekkan, however, gasped audibly at the sight of the young man, lurching forward for a moment as if to embrace an old friend, and then lurching back in confusion, his brows slamming together. His sword whipped out of its sheath, and he backed into a corner defensively. "I am betrayed," he growled.

Talissar's reflexes were equally fast, and before she could blink, he, too, had a sword in hand and had leaped defensively in front of the young man.

For her part, Gabrielle jumped between both armed men, her hands up in supplication. "Stop!" she cried. "We are all friends here!"

"You summoned one of those cursed, body-stealing Kothite scum to kill me!" Bekkan accused.

She looked over her shoulder at the young man in shock. A look of intense chagrin was breaking across his handsome features. "Of course! I should have known you would recognize my face." He actually smacked his forehead with his palm in disgust before saying, "You are correct, sir knight protector. I do inhabit a body you recognize, but I am not one of them. Well, technically, I am a Kothite, but I am not *with* them. I seek to bring down the Kothite scum you so despise."

The runner bowed himself out of her room. She ordered supper in her chambers and invited Bekkan to join her for tea after the meal. The other members of their party stayed downstairs, ostensibly listening to a local storyteller, but actually standing watch to warn her should an uninvited guest—or a military squad—show up.

It was nearing midnight, and the common room had grown raucous below with people well into their cups when a quiet knock on her door made Gabrielle nearly jump out of her skin.

She opened it, and two cloaked and hooded men slipped inside quickly. As they swept off their concealing garments, she recognized Talissar's pale beauty instantly. The man never aged. Lucky Lyssandra.

The second guest was a handsome young man with dark hair and piercing blue eyes. His face looked familiar for an instant, but then recognition slipped away.

Bekkan, however, gasped audibly at the sight of the young man, lurching forward for a moment as if to embrace an old friend, and then lurching back in confusion, his brows slamming together. His sword whipped out of its sheath, and he backed into a corner defensively. "I am betrayed," he growled.

Talissar's reflexes were equally fast, and before she could blink, he, too, had a sword in hand and had leaped defensively in front of the young man.

For her part, Gabrielle jumped between both armed men, her hands up in supplication. "Stop!" she cried. "We are all friends here!"

"You summoned one of those cursed, body-stealing Kothite scum to kill me!" Bekkan accused.

She looked over her shoulder at the young man in shock. A look of intense chagrin was breaking across his handsome features. "Of course! I should have known you would recognize my face." He actually smacked his forehead with his palm in disgust before saying, "You are correct, sir knight protector. I do inhabit a body you recognize, but I am not one of them. Well, technically, I am a Kothite, but I am not *with* them. I seek to bring down the Kothite scum you so despise."

Sleeping King had told Will and Raina in their visit to his grove on the dream plane that the zinnzari guarded his physical body on the mortal realm. Find the zinnzari, and they would find him.

"Where does the rest of the clan of Zinn live?" Sha'Li asked Kerryl.

"Let me see. That would be a ways north of here. In the Thirst, if memory serves."

"Where in the Thirst?" Rynn asked. "It is not the sort of place one wanders around in searching for a tribe of elves."

"In the Drifts, mayhap," Kerryl answered uncertainly. "Or perhaps the Silver Sands."

Rynn sucked in a sharp breath. Eben threw him a questioning look, and the kindari muttered, "Many are the legends of the wild magics in the Silver Sands."

Sha'Li asked, "How will we know these zinnzari when we meet them?"

Kerryl answered, "You will know them by the markings on their faces. They wear the magical web of Zinn across their skin."

Cicero's facial tattoos were spiderlike in nature but reminded Eben more of the eyes and mandibles of a spider than of one's web. Perhaps that was the difference between arachnari and zinnzari.

Rosana asked, "How long does it take to travel to the Thirst from here?"

Kerryl smiled kindly at her. He'd taken a liking to her after she healed him yesterday and again this morning. "To walk there will take two months or more if the weather holds and water isn't scarce, but if you were to go by sea, the journey up the coast would take a few days, and then maybe a week inland on foot to reach the first of the sands. To see all of the Thirst would take years. It is a vast land, full of wonder and desolation. Only the smart and tough survive there."

What little Eben knew of the Thirst was that it consisted mostly of desert and few merchants ventured there. Bandits were plentiful, food and water scarce, valuable resources scarcer, and the local population disinterested in trading with outsiders.

Rosana looked dubious. "I'm worried about going so far away without Raina. How will she find us?"

Rynn answered, "She's an adult and has all the resources she needs to find us or continue forward on her own."

Huh. Eben had never thought of her in that way. Because of her White Heart vows and because she neither used a weapon nor defended herself when attacked, he'd always thought of her as the most vulnerable of their group.

Will said briskly, "Are we agreed, then? We head for the coast and seek a ship bound north toward the Valelands, and then we proceed on to the Thirst?"

With varying degrees of speed and reluctance, everyone nodded, including Eben. He didn't know about the others, but he was more than ready to be quit of this dark and dank forest of sorrow.

"What say you, Kendrick?" Will asked. "Will you come with us and lend your sword to our cause?"

Kerryl answered for him. "Yes. He will. Go, boy. Be with your friends. They need your help, and their quest is worthy. When I have need of you again, I will send for you."

Kendrick scowled long and hard at his mentor, and Kerryl scowled back, finally growling, "Don't make me order you to do this."

Kendrick threw up his hands in disgust and, to Eben's immense joy, surrender.

Will laughed. "Excellent. Mayhap you can show us the fastest route out of this interminable wold."

Kendrick jerked his chin toward Kerryl. "He's the one to show you the quickest way out."

"And it will be my pleasure to do so," Kerryl declared.

Eben got the impression Kerryl was as eager to have them out of the Sorrow Wold as they were to be quit of this foul place. The nature guardian was up to something, but he could not fathom what, and he wasn't sure he cared as long as Kendrick was not part of Kerryl's plans.

* * *

Gabrielle took the party to an inn nestled on the banks of the Crystal River, a half day's float upstream of the Imperial Seat, and engaged rooms for all of them. For herself, she rented a luxurious suite and ordered a perfumed bath and a hairdresser for the following morning. Her adventures roaming about Koth incognito must end, and it was time for her to transform back into the queen she was.

The next order of business was to send word to Talissar, her primary contact within the Eight, and ask for a meeting here, away from the Imperial Seat. She dared not march Bekkan through the front gates of the palace and risk all he knew upon the power of a single Octavium Pendant against the mental might of the Emperor and his Kothite cronies.

She drafted a quick note to Talissar suggesting that if he wished her help in planning a surprise birthday party for his wife and queen, Lyssandra, she should not be seen at court. Then she pressed a gold coin into the hand of the innkeeper's eldest son, asking him to sneak her note to Talissar in utmost secrecy. The youth was happy to participate in the conspiracy, particularly when it involved such extravagant compensation. He trotted off toward the pier to catch a barge bound for the palace.

The innkeeper's son returned late in the afternoon in the company of an Imperial runner. The messenger was a handsome young man with dark hair and piercing blue eyes. His face looked familiar for an instant, but then recognition slipped away. He bowed pleasantly enough and delivered a verbal message that Talissar would arrive late in the evening, and he greatly appreciated her help in planning his wife's birthday party.

The ruse of a surprise party had to hold long enough to protect both her and Talissar from rumors of a dalliance between them. She had no illusions that even here, many miles from the palace, they would be safe from prying eyes and wagging tongues. Rumor and innuendo were the stuff and trade of the Imperial Court, and the last thing she and Talissar needed was to draw attention to themselves at this critical moment.

Bekkan snorted.

Gabrielle was missing something important here. "I don't understand."

The handsome young man spoke calmly. Soothingly. "I am an offspring of the original Kothites who invaded this land and destroyed its rulers."

"They had a name," Bekkan spat. "They were the royal family of the etheri people. His Majesty King Notarka Domitrin, Queen Elena, Prince Nicos, and Princess Raisa. And you. That body belongs—belonged—to Lord Pavel Romaya, cousin to Nicos and Raisa." Bekkan ground out in tightly contained fury to the young man, "It's. Not. Yours."

The young man said simply, "You are correct."

His complete lack of ire in response to Bekkan's attack seemed to disarm a tiny bit of the dwarf's fury.

"You may kill me if you like, sir," the young man said. "I will not defend myself or attack you. But in killing me, you also kill my host, and no chance would remain to restore Pavel's spirit to this body."

"That's what the Kothite scum said when they took over the etheri royals' bodies to prevent the people from slaughtering the possessed etheri where they stood."

"It was true then. It remains true now." The young man shrugged. "Kill me; kill the host. I did not choose to take over this body. My spirit was created and forced into it. Not that this fact makes my existence any less of an abomination."

That gave Bekkan pause. He frowned, looking confounded at the young man's ready agreement with his accusations.

The young man continued, "I am, indeed, a Kothite. Full scion of the two most powerful Kothites of all, as a matter of fact. I have the ability to strip from your mind everything I wish to know, the ability to kill you simply by willing it so. However, to prove the sincerity of my wish to destroy the Kothite Empire, I give you my word of honor that I will not touch you in any way. I will not even look into your mind, let alone tamper with it. You shall choose exactly how little or how much you share with me and my co-conspirators."

Gabrielle barely heard most of his speech, for she was

stuck on his first sentence. The two most powerful Kothites of all would be Maximillian and Iolanthe. And yet, those two had only one child—Princess Endellian. How on Urth could they have had a second child, a son, and *no one had ever heard of him*?

"Since he is already acquainted with my companion, perhaps you would like to introduce your friend to me?" Talissar said to her, sheathing his sword as he spoke.

Startled out of her shocking thoughts, she mumbled, "Bekkan Kopathul, second guardian of the Septvardin—the Seven Guardians of His Royal Highness, King Eitrik of the Mountain Dwarves, also called Fireheart—may I present you to Prince Talissar of Quantaine."

To her vast relief, Bekkan put away his weapon, executing a terse, short bow.

Talissar lurched forward suddenly, swiftly grasping the Octavium Pendant swinging on its long chain from Bekkan's neck. "Where did you get this?"

Gabrielle jumped forward. "I gave it to him. He has more need of it than I."

The dark-haired young man asked, "Why is that?"

Gabrielle glanced questioningly at Talissar. She wasn't about to let Bekkan tell his full tale until the elf vouched for his companion. Bekkan might recognize him, but she did not.

"He is one of us," Talissar said quietly to her. "I trust him with my life."

She explained to the young man, "Bekkan has certain ancient memories. When he speaks of them, everyone who hears them . . . forgets them. I know that sounds passing strange, but it's true."

"Not strange at all," the young man said. "If you would indulge me, Bekkan, perhaps you could give Her Highness her necklace back? The piece is well known to belong to her and would raise questions if seen upon your person. Perhaps you will consent to wear this instead?"

She stared as he removed a wide cuff from his wrist and held it out to Bekkan. Its beaten gold clasped a green cabochon gem, not as big or bright as the one in her necklace, but octavium nonetheless. Bekkan slipped the cuff on his wrist and then lifted the long necklace over his head. She took it with a nod of thanks and sighed in relief to place it back in its familiar place around her neck.

Within seconds, a host of memories came flooding back to her. Of a cave high in the mountains where Bekkan had been trapped in copper, a desperate fight to stave off a wave of creatures who would have erased their memory of seeing him. And another fight with oblivi the night they'd unmade him from storm copper back to dwarf.

Was that how Maximillian's son had been forgotten? Had the Emperor for some reason destroyed all memory of him? She blurted, "Why did Maximillian erase you?"

The young man looked at her keenly. "She's as good at leaps of logic as you said she was, Tal."

"And she is as persistent as I warned you she would be," the elf responded dryly.

The young man sighed. "Maximillian did not erase me. An unfortunate incident with Maximillian the Second required an entire period of time to be erased from living memory. I was born during that period, and I was erased along with it. For a time, I was bitter, but then I realized it would work to my advantage. Only people who wear octavium to protect themselves from the effects of the Second Forgetting can retain any memory of me at all."

"Second Forgetting? There was a First Forgetting?"

"How do you think all history prior to the coming of Koth was erased and replaced with the belief that Koth has always been here? That was the First Great Forgetting."

Koth was *not* eternal? Her mind could hardly absorb the idea. Only decades of despising the Empire and wishing that it wasn't eternal made it even possible for her to entertain the notion.

"How many of these forgettings have there been?" she asked, on fire with curiosity to know what had been taken from her. From everyone.

"Three big ones that I'm aware of. The first one erased the past history of Urth and stripped all knowledge of the existence of etheri. Then the second one covered up Maximillian the Second going mad and the reign of Ammertus in his stead. A third, more recent one undid the mess Ammertus made in Haelos. And, of course, Maximillian occasionally uses his priori for smaller forgettings—against the advice of his closest advisors, I might add."

Maximillian the Second? Mad? A mess in Haelos? Just how much history had been lost? "Priori?" she mumbled, overwhelmed. "What are those?"

"Primordial creatures who exist outside of time, space, or form. You can think of them as the embodiments of ideas. Love. Hate. Life. Death. Memory. Forgetting. Maximillian managed to trap the priori of forgetting, and it is with that being's help he maintains his choke hold on the Empire."

She could feel her sanity beginning to slip. An urge to laugh hysterically at these revelations nearly overcame her.

She was grateful when the young man turned the conversation away from this madness, saying to Bekkan, "All of us in this room are protected by the magical properties of octavium. You may speak freely of your memories without fear of oblivi coming to strip your memories."

Bekkan tilted his head in her direction. "She bade me to remember that word. *Oblivi*. What is it?"

"They are creatures who attack the mind. Their purpose is to strip memories and knowledge from people. They serve the priori of forgetting that serves Maximillian."

Talissar turned to the rokken. "If you would do us the honor, we would like to hear what you can tell us of a past that you remember but the rest of us have entirely lost."

Bekkan frowned. "It is still coming back to me—in bits and pieces mostly, but sometimes whole chunks of my life come back all at once. I will tell you what I remember, and mayhap you will ask questions that jog other memories loose from wherever they are rusted away inside my mind."

"Start at the beginning. When and where are you from?"

Bekkan chose his words cautiously. "As best as I can tell, upward of five thousand years have passed since I last drew breath. As for where I'm from? That would be here. Except when I lived here, Ymir was home to many races who lived in peace and prosperity."

"In the time of Maximillian the First?" Talissar asked.

"Before that," Bekkan answered scornfully. "Before the coming of Maximillian and Koth."

Gabrielle frowned. "When exactly did they come?"

The young man intervened to answer, "About five thousand years ago."

Bekkan snorted in disdain and continued, "The Kothites were upstart usurpers. The real rulers of Ymir back then were the giants. They ultimately ruled the entire continent, allowing the etheri to rule the surface and my king to rule that part of Under Urth lying below Ymir."

Something powerful rippled through Gabrielle. A chill without cause. Or maybe the cause of the chill was hearing truth that she recognized deep down in her bones. Who had these etheri been? She'd never heard of such a race before tonight. And what place was Ymir?

Talissar voiced the question aloud for her.

Bekkan answered soberly, "Ymir is the old name, the giant name, for this continent that you call Koth. As for the etheri, they are—were—a race of humanoids specializing in spiritual magics. Not just healing but also curse magics and void magics. In my day, they were the kings and queens of Ymir."

Gabrielle exchanged awed looks with Talissar. Then she said, "Tell us of the coming of Koth."

"The Kothites were few in number but impressive in power. They used their psionic abilities to enslave armies and attack the etheri capital. Instead of killing the members of the royal family and important courtiers, the Kothites possessed their bodies." He jerked his chin in the young man's direction. "Like him. That's the body of a member of the etheri royal family. The common people did not have a way to fight back.

If they killed the usurpers, they would kill their own beloved nobles."

Stunned silence filled the room. Gabrielle's mind felt full to bursting, as if it struggled to contain the information she was hearing.

The dark-haired man raised a hand to stop Bekkan's story. "My lady, how do you feel?"

She blinked, startled at the question. "Shocked. Overwhelmed. Why?"

"Some people, when exposed to these lost truths, lose their way. Their minds rebel against the evidence of their eyes and ears and they suffer . . . a break. In here." He tapped the side of his head with a finger.

"You mean they go insane?" she asked.

"That. Or worse. Some die. Some try to convince others of what they have learned and end up accused of being mad. The frustration of not being believed ultimately strips what sanity they have left."

"I don't understand," she confessed.

"The Emperor's forgetting priori is capable of stripping memories from everyone."

"Everyone on Urth?" she asked, appalled.

"Just so. And when some piece of information or evidence surfaces to contradict history as Maximillian has rewritten it, his oblivi arrive to rectify the paradox."

"That's *horrible*!"

The young man shrugged. "In many cases, the oblivi are preferable to the madness that undone forgettings cause. In a way, the Emperor does his subjects a favor by keeping them all blissfully ignorant."

She declared angrily, "How can it ever be a kindness to erase a person's memories?"

Talissar said grimly, "We're not talking about a single person's memories, my lady. Maximillian has tampered with the mind of every soul living on Urth today, and of every soul yet to be born."

"How is he so powerful?" she breathed in dread.

"He has help," the young man declared. "Not only from

his priori but also from his fellow Kothites. They're all in on the conspiracy to keep people in the dark."

Now that she looked at him, she recognized him as the messenger from this afternoon, the one who'd brought her Talissar's reply. In fact, now that she thought about it, she realized she'd seen him around the palace any number of times in the past.

"Why didn't I remember you before now?" she asked him.

He smiled enigmatically. "That, my lady, is a story for another day. Right now, I would hear more of what our guest can tell us of his former life, if you think you can hear it without growing confused."

"Confusion is one trait I am rarely accused of," she said lightly. Indeed, she had a reputation for being one of the smartest consorts at court, along with Talissar. Both of them were known to provide wise counsel to their powerful spouses.

The young man turned back to Bekkan. "When the Kothites came, what happened to the giants and dwarves who shared Ymir with the etheri people?"

"The giants did not take the Kothites seriously enough at first. One by one, the Kothites killed and enslaved the giants until the few who were left fled Ymir or went into hiding."

"And the dwarves?" Gabrielle asked breathlessly. "What of them?"

"Initially, we stayed inside our mountains and under our hills, thinking ourselves well clear of the invaders. But then they came for Under Urth, and we, too, were overrun and overwhelmed. Without the might of the giants to aid us, we were not able to hold off the Kothite scourge."

"And your king?" the young man asked urgently. "What happened to him?"

"As a last resort to save him from the mind control of the Kothites, the giant Hoardunn transformed my king into stone."

"Like you?" Gabrielle asked.

"I was transformed into storm copper—for I am a copper-vein dwarf—to protect me and the knowledge I held. My lord king is an ironvein, and it was into iron he was changed. Septallum, to be specific."

Talissar asked, "Where is your king hidden? It is our intent to find him and wake him. The time of the Three Kings draws nigh."

"Three Kings?" Bekkan echoed.

Talissar explained, "Prophecies speak of a time when three ancient kings will rise up and reclaim their ancestral lands. We believe that time is now, and a small cadre of people with memory of them seek out these kings."

"The three dwarven kings?" Bekkan asked eagerly.

The young man answered sorrowfully, "Among the dwarven royalty of your day, only your king survived the Kothite conquest. And even now, he is lost, hidden away for millennia, the knowing of how to wake him long lost in the dust of time. *If* we can find him, *maybe* we can wake him."

"You woke me," Bekkan declared. "The knowledge to do the same for him must still exist somewhere."

"We were lucky with you," Talissar replied. "The Kothites never found the Great Storm Forge."

The young man leaned forward, clutching the arms of his chair intently. "Please tell us, Bekkan. Where is your king hidden?"

Raina considered Lakanos's question. What *did* she need to do first? "I need to rejoin my friends as quickly as possible. And as we travel, I shall make inquiries as to the location of an elven clan known as the zinnzari."

Kadir said, "As for me, I rather urgently need to find a man. I could scry the mark upon him if I had access to ritual components—"

The dryad Callisia purred, "Components, you say? I have lots of those."

Kadir looked at her in interest. "Perhaps we could come to some sort of mutually beneficial trade?" He moved off out of Raina's hearing to barter with the dryad, which she frankly thought was an exercise in folly, but good luck to him.

Apparently, Kadir struck a deal with the dryad because in

a few minutes, Raina spied him laying out a ritual circle on the ground with the rope from his belt. She would have liked to watch him cast the scrying ritual, but Lakanos insisted that she stand well back from the circle, clear of any possible blast zone.

She'd already been hit by one magical backlash in the past day. She supposed she didn't need to risk another. Particularly since she still had a smashing headache from the first and the voices were back, lurking at the edge of her hearing.

Justin joined his master in the circle, and jealousy speared through her. Not because he served Kadir or because he could now perform ritual magic but because he'd changed and grown without her. He'd become a man in the two years they'd been apart, and she didn't know this new person he'd become.

Eventually, Kadir ended the ritual and smoothly let down the iridescent dome of ritual magic, announcing, "The man I seek is well south and east of here in mountains."

Lakanos, lazily sharpening a magnificent sword, commented, "That would place him in the Heaves."

"Just so," Kadir agreed. "What of you, Justin? Will you come with me?"

Raina met Justin's conflicted gaze with one of her own. She hated to part with him again after having just found him. He was her best friend, and he reminded her of what it felt like to be a seventeen-year-old girl. But they both had places to go now, their own paths to pursue. As much as she wished to be with him, and as much as he seemed to return the feeling, now was not their time.

He drew her into a hug. She burrowed against his chest just like old times. A deep sense of comfort unlike any she'd experienced since she left home draped over her like a comforting blanket. How was she supposed to let him go?

"One day, muckling," he murmured. "We'll find a way for the timing to be right for both of us."

Hot tears burned in her eyes and throat. Would she never have the home and family she craved? Was she doomed to always leave behind the people she loved? Just once, she would like to do what made her happy and not be forced to do what duty demanded of her. Was that so much to ask for?

A premonition that they would never end up together swept over her, crushing her in a loss so heavy and deep she could not see any light at all in her future. When he left her this time, he was never coming back.

Kerryl led them quickly through the Sorrow Wold. Will took much of Rosana's gear into his pack so she could keep up. He had to give her credit. She was small, but she was tough. She kept up with the fast-moving party and still had energy to help set up camp and cook the greens and small game animals the rest of them hunted and gathered.

On the evening of the third day, they burst out of the forest without warning, and the expanse of the Estarran Sea stretched before them, tinted orange as the sun set behind them in the west.

Thank the Lady. He was more than ready to be quit of the cloying misery of the Sorrow Wold. The place had weighed upon his spirit until he could hardly breathe. Well named it was.

Kerryl announced, "We separate here. Good luck, and may the Lady watch over you and your quest." He traded short, hard hugs with Kendrick, muttered a gruff good luck to his protégé, and disappeared swiftly back into the forest.

Sha'Li suggested, "To the north, the shore looks more open. With the last light, let us proceed that way and look for a bell to summon a Merr vessel. Failing that, mayhap we will find a likely camping spot."

They hiked the pebbled strand into the twilight. The sea turned black to their right, and the forest turned blacker to their left. But then the trees gave way to a massive stone outcropping. A silver-gray strip of sand arced around it and disappeared.

Sha'Li pointed up the bluff. "I see a cave."

"What if there's a bear in it?" Rosana asked nervously.

Will laughed. "We'll evict it. It's getting cold out here, and I, for one, am ready to sleep on dry ground next to a warm fire."

The past few days had hinted at spring to come, but the weather today had turned cold, bringing frigid air on stiff northern winds. Low gray clouds scudded across the sky, with only that one short break in the cloud cover at sunset. Wind whipped around them now, tearing at their clothing and hair. If he didn't know better, he would say snow was on the way.

Eben piped up. "I vote for the cave as well. I feel wetness, and lots of it, in the clouds."

"Stay here," the lizardman announced. "I will scout the cave."

In a few minutes, Sha'Li emerged from the cave entrance, waving at them to join her. It wasn't a long climb or particularly difficult, but the rocks were damp with sea spray and coated in green sea slime that made them slippery.

Will helped Rosana up the outcropping to join Sha'Li.

"Is it empty?" Rosana asked her, breathing hard.

Sha'Li grinned. "No. It's not."

Will and Eben reached for their weapons.

"No blades necessary," Sha'Li announced, clearly enjoying herself.

Frowning, he moved in front of Rosana protectively and followed Sha'Li into the narrow opening. A dozen lizardmen sat around a blazing fire in the middle of the large, warm chamber, and the smell of fish cooking filled the space.

Honestly, most lizardmen looked pretty much the same to Will unless they were colored differently from one another, Sha'Li's black compared to the olive green scales of these other lizardmen, for example. But as Will spied an aged bronze lizardman across the big fire, he could swear he'd seen that one last year in the cliffs of the eastern shore of the Estarran Sea.

Will sidled up next to Sha'Li to mutter, "Is that the same bronze lizardman from last fall? What was his name again?"

"Brozhen. And yes, it is," she answered under her breath.

"What's he doing here?"

"Eating supper."

Will huffed. "No, I mean what's he doing on this side of the Estarran Sea?"

"I do not know. I have not had time to talk with him. He recognized me and invited us to share their fire. Be polite—he does us great honor."

His mother hadn't been an elf for nothing. She had been a stickler for etiquette and polite comportment, and he'd been trained to be courteous to everyone.

Their hosts made room for them around the fire. The lizardmen spoke rapidly in their odd syntax, trading stories and jokes almost too fast for Will to follow. Thankfully, he'd had experience listening to Sha'Li when she'd been fresh come from her swamp two years ago.

The lizardmen shared the delicious fish, and a skin of some fermented liquor was passed around. Will tilted it cautiously, but the lizardman on his right intentionally bumped Will's elbow, tipping the skin up and sending a gush of the stuff down his throat. The liquor was so strong it made him cough, and it burned all the way down to his belly. His face got hot, and he began to feel light-headed in a matter of seconds.

"What's in that stuff?" he gasped.

Sha'Li laughed. "Most lizardmen are resistant to simple poisons, so our liquor has to be very strong to have an effect on us. Be careful, pinkskin, or you will end up flat on your back."

"It's a little late for the warning," he wheezed. Gads, the cave was already spinning around him. The other members of the party seemed similarly knocked on their behinds by the liquor. All of them were leaning a little off-kilter or grinning stupidly.

"Hey, Sha'Li," he slurred. By the stars, his tongue was twice its normal size. "Ask the old one about the bow. Maybe he knows where to find it."

Brozhen stared at him across the fire and then turned his glittering golden stare on Sha'Li. "You told them of the bow?" the bronze lizardman demanded.

"I trust my companions," she replied defensively. "We seek Eliassan's bow together."

Will noticed that all the lizardmen had gone silent, staring at him and his friends.

"Why?" Brozhen demanded.

"We seek to wake the Sleeping King," Sha'Li answered. "He will need his bow when he wakes."

Now even Brozhen seemed shocked silent, studying Will and the others.

Will blinked hard and shook his head a little to clear it. This conversation was important, and he needed not to be too drunk to remember it on the morrow.

"Who are you?" the bronze one asked. The question was not aimed at Sha'Li but rather at her friends.

Rynn spoke up first, and Will was impressed at how well the paxan was enunciating his words. "We are a party of like-minded friends. We near completion in our quest and lack only the last pieces of the Sleeping King's regalia to wake him."

It was an exaggeration. They didn't know where Gawaine's physical body rested or whether those who guarded it would let them even attempt to wake him. But those were minor details in the grand scheme of things.

Brozhen surprised him by saying, "Eliassan's bow is said to rest in his final home."

"Where's that?" Will managed to ask him without slobbering down his own chin.

"The Wychwold. That was where Eliassan is said to have spent his latter days."

"Where's that?" Eben asked.

Rynn answered, "Western Valelands. At the headwaters of the Lance."

"The Lance?" Will echoed.

Rynn nodded and then winced as if moving his head rapidly had been a bad idea. "It's a river. Runs east through the Vale to the Estarran Sea."

Rosana listed to one side, and Will grabbed her arm as she nearly fell off her seat. He propped her back upright, and she nodded her thanks as she asked their hosts, "If the Lance goes to the sea, can we take a boat up the coast, then up the river, then into the Wychwold? I'm tired of walking."

Brozhen shrugged. "Merr control Estarra. You will have to obtain passage from them. When you get to Lifton, the port where the Lance meets the sea, you will have to transfer to an inland vessel. Humans control the Lance."

The firelight wavered wildly as the liquor overwhelmed what little sense Will had left. The last words he heard before the ground came up in slow motion to meet his face were the bronze lizardman saying, "Nearest Merr bell's a day's walk north along the coast. At a human settlement called Bannockburn."

Gabrielle held her breath as Bekkan considered the two men seated before him.

Talissar urged the rokken, "I am sorry to push you, but events are accelerating quickly at court, and we need your answer."

"What has happened at court?" Gabrielle asked quickly.

"Tyviden Starfire has returned from his exile."

She sucked in a sharp breath. He was the infuriating Kothite lord who'd gotten her knight exiled many years ago and started her down the path to rebellion against the Empire.

"In typical Tyviden fashion, he has been bragging that he brought back great treasures from the Sea of Glass along with knowledge of how to cross the Ice Bridge."

The young man spoke up. "I have caught whispers that Maximillian is elated at whatever Tyviden brought back and believes it will solidify the Emperor's hold over his subjects. Particularly the dwarves."

She said, "You think Tyviden found something to do with the Dwarven King?"

The young man answered, "He is the last and only remaining true king of the dwarves. Destroying him would eliminate any hope the dwarves have for a revolt against Koth and a return to freedom. Worse," the young man continued, "we have received news that Tyviden departs very soon on some secret journey at the bequest of the Emperor. It makes sense that Tyviden follows up on whatever he discovered in the Sea of Glass."

Gabrielle looked over at Bekkan. It all came down to this. Would he share with these relative strangers the information he'd protected for the past five thousand years or not?

"Why should I trust you?" he finally asked them.

Talissar answered soberly, "You have no reason at all to trust us, other than the fact that we are the ones who found you and freed you from your copper prison. At great risk to ourselves, we have not turned you over to the Empire. We risk not only our own lives but the lives of thousands of other people to ask you this one question."

Bekkan frowned. "How are thousands of lives at risk if only four of us sit in this room?"

Talissar answered candidly, "Her Highness Queen Gabrielle and I, a prince in my kingdom, have conspired against the Emperor in freeing you. Should either of us be caught, not only we but our families, our friends, our subjects, anyone who's ever met us would be put to death. I wouldn't put it past Maximillian to wage war on our respective kingdoms and wipe out the populations of both in punishment for our crimes."

Gabrielle gulped. It was an inconvenient truth she tried hard to avoid thinking about, and not surprisingly, an iron band around her chest began to tighten. She tried to calm herself and her breathing, but it didn't do any good. She had betrayed everyone she loved, everyone she served by bringing Bekkan to court. She had stepped across the unforgivable line of treason.

At length, Bekkan nodded slowly. "Kothites were a pestilence when they came, and I see that five thousand years have not changed them."

Talissar and the young man held their tongues, waiting, and Gabrielle did the same, even though she had to bite back an urge to plead with him not to make her sacrifice be in vain.

Not to let what she had done and everything she had risked mean nothing.

She could never come back to court. She must avoid Maximillian for the rest of her life lest he look into her mind and see her crime. She could no longer support her husband, could no longer work on behalf of the people of Haraland at court. She had thrown all of that away.

Although how she was going to explain it to Regalo, she hadn't the slightest idea. He would insist she join him at court, and he would believe he had failed her as a husband in some way if she refused. Her heart ached at the idea of being apart from him, but it ached even more at the idea of him believing less of himself when it was all her fault.

Bekkan took a long, deep breath. Released it slowly. "Funny how I never considered the pleasure of breathing until I was encased in metal and could no longer do it."

He was stalling. Not good.

She could not hold her tongue one second longer. She blurted, "Bekkan, you and I have traveled together for weeks now. I would like to think you've seen a fair sampling of my character and of those who rescued you. We are decent people trying to do the right thing. We stand against an all-powerful foe, and we must move with extreme caution. You are the culmination of centuries' worth of work."

Bekkan looked a bit taken aback at that.

She pressed the point. "You may walk out of here and keep your secret. But understand this: there is no other opposition to Koth. We're it. We are your only chance for help finding your king and setting him free before Tyviden finds him and destroys him."

Bekkan's frown deepened.

"If you choose not to trust us, which is, indeed, your right, I beg of you, do not abandon your quest. Please find a way to wake the Dwarven King and do so with all possible haste. Koth is strangling the life out of the people of Urth slowly but surely."

The young man interjected, "Koth is strangling the life out of Urth itself. The Kothites have upset the balance of nature until it cannot recover from them. Urth is dying, and everyone upon it and within it, too."

Bekkan looked stricken. "At the time I was encased, nobody gave me any instructions on who to tell what when I awoke. My transformation was performed in secret and in haste as Kothite forces literally banged on the doors of the chamber in which I was changed. My king told me only that he trusted me with his life to do the right thing."

Again, a waiting silence fell between them. It was a momentous decision, and they could not rush the dwarf. Not to mention, if they pushed too hard, he would push back out of general principles. In her experience, dwarves and goats had that trait entirely in common.

Bekkan nodded abruptly, once, curtly. "So be it. I will tell you what I know of the fate of my king under one condition."

"Which is?" Talissar asked quickly.

"You plan to send a party to Fireheart and free him, do you not?" Bekkan countered.

The young man answered, "That is correct."

"I must have your word of honor that I will be part of the party sent to rescue him."

"Of course!" Talissar and the young man exclaimed in unison.

Talissar added, "We would have it no other way."

"Very well. When it became clear the Kothites were too powerful to stop and they would soon overrun the halls of the Mountain Kings, King Eitrik and a few of his most loyal followers fled to the south, across the Ice Bridge. There, they begged Hoardunn for protection. But even he was no match for the might of Koth. The best he could do was to encase my king in the magical metal we called septallum."

"And did Hoardunn hide the Dwarven King there?" Talissar asked.

"I do not know," Bekkan answered heavily. "I was encased myself before that decision was made."

The young man said thoughtfully, "Tyviden has spent the past twenty years traversing the width and breadth of the Sea of Glass. If the Dwarven King's entombed body was there to be found, my guess is he would have located it."

Bekkan responded, "Hoardunn is a canny old goat. I do not believe he would hide the Dwarven King anywhere so obvious as his own refuge in the south. My guess is the giant had my king moved somewhere obscure, somewhere unexpected, and secreted him away where he would quickly be forgotten, safe from the prying eyes of Koth."

Talissar and the young man traded looks of alarm. "So you do not know where the Dwarven King is hidden?"

"Nay," the young man replied.

"What is it?" Bekkan asked forcefully. "Why do you look at each other like that?"

The young man answered, "That must be what Tyviden is setting out to find. The body of the Dwarven King."

"To what end?" Bekkan asked sharply.

"To destroy him, of course."

"We must find my king first!" Bekkan's face creased in lines of dismay. "But I have no idea where to search. What are we to do?"

Talissar stood up. "We must move quickly."

"When do we leave?" Bekkan asked. "I can be ready to go within the hour."

The young one laughed. "It will not be quite as soon as that. First, we must attempt to discover what Tyviden brought back from the Sea of Glass that has Maximillian so excited and which is setting Tyviden on what I am certain is a hunt for the Dwarven King."

Gabrielle wondered if the young man could read Tyviden's mind. He sounded so sure of himself when he spoke of Tyviden's goal.

"How shall we discover what Tyviden brought back?" Bekkan asked.

"Easy. We'll break into the trophy room and find it."

"You mean to break into the treasure trove of Maximillian himself?" Gabrielle blurted in amazement.

"Have you a better idea?"

She snorted. "Casting ourselves into the Eternal Flame sounds like a better idea than that. At least our permanent deaths would be swift."

The young man merely said, "I have given this a great deal of thought, and unfortunately, I see no way to pull off a break-in without your help, Your Highness. You have already risked much, but I must ask you to risk even more. Will you help us find out what Tyviden brought back?"

She gulped. What was it Regalo always said of starting down the path of wrong? *In for a copper, in for a gold.* She added wryly to herself, *And before long, in for a kingdom.*

"I do not see how I can help. And if I were to be discovered, all would be lost."

"All will be lost if we do not do this," the young man said grimly. "The crisis is approaching quickly now. The stars are aligning, and in a matter of weeks or months, we will arrive at the crossroads. We will make our move to overthrow Maximillian, or he will become so powerful no one will ever dislodge him."

"I cannot go back to court," she wailed in a whisper. "I do not even dare go home."

"You must go home. Even if you do not help with this heist, dark times are coming. Your husband, and the people of Haraland, will need your support as you all try to find an honorable path forward through what lies ahead."

The young man's words had a prophetic ring to them, and she did not like the dire undertones she sensed. She asked cautiously, "What lies ahead?"

"You do not think Maximillian will go down quietly, do you? He will die like a dragon, spewing fire and destruction in every direction. It will be a bloodbath when he falls."

The iron band was back around her ribs once more, and no amount of calming breaths eased it this time.

B annockburn was a dusty frontier town with more
shifty adventuring types in it than Will liked. He stuck
close to Rosana's side as they made their way through
the generally ramshackle buildings toward the pier. He was
surprised to spot a few guildhalls with peeling paint and
derelict-looking members lounging about. The Imperial presence out here in the hinterlands was quite a bit more casual
than it was nearer to Dupree.

"There's the bell," Rynn announced.

Eben picked up the hammer hanging from a chain beside
the big brass bell and gave it a hefty blow. The sound rang
out across the docks and vibrated through Will's feet into the
pier itself.

Someone had helpfully provided benches next to the bell,
which didn't bode well for a speedy response. But within a
quarter turn of an hour, a blue-scaled Merr climbed the lad-
der beside the bell pole and said as dry as dust, "You rang?"

Will grinned, amused, as Rynn stepped forward to inquire
after passage north along the coast to Lifton.

"Sure, if you're willing to share passage," the Merr responded. "Got a cargo vessel headed up that way on the
outbound tide. Already has a few passengers. No covered
quarters. You'd be camping on deck. Five silver a head all
the way to Lifton. Paid in advance."

"Food and drink provided?" Rynn asked.

"You'll be needing fresh water for the whole voyage?"

"Correct."

"Silver apiece extra for food and fresh water," the Merr said.

"Done." Rynn fished out the necessary coins and handed them over.

"Tide goes out in six hours. The *Karolus* will dock at the end of this pier in a few hours. Don't be late. She'll sail with or without you."

The dryads left Raina to wash the dishes after breakfast, which amused her. She was just finishing stacking their breakfast bowls when Kadir asked one of the green females, "Do you have a large basin, preferably a shiny one, that I could borrow for a little while?"

"Like a fortune-teller's bowl?" the dryad Callisia replied.

"Exactly."

Callisia giggled. "When we wish to gaze into the past or future, we use a pool over there." She pointed to the far side of the grove. "In the morning, the sunlight hits it just so and makes a mirror of it."

"Does the sun strike it just so now?" Kadir asked.

"Aye."

Raina trailed after Kadir, Justin, and the dryads who led both men by the hands toward a little pool in the lee of a lovely rowan tree. The sun was, indeed, shining down upon it, turning its surface into a silvery, lightly rippling mirror.

Kadir knelt beside the pool and spread his hands out above the surface. Raina watched with interest as he drew magical energy and a pair of the runes on the backs of his hands began to glow.

"What's he doing?" she muttered to Justin.

"No idea."

"I'm scrying by another method," Kadir answered. "I have marked several places within the Tower of Alchizzadon with a mark identical to this one on my arm. I can use my mark to look through those marks and see what transpires. Elfonse and his cronies will find them sooner or later, so I thought to check in now, before they're discovered and erased."

She'd heard of the art of seeing through ritual marks, of

course, but she'd never seen it in action since the Heart did not make a common practice of spying on others.

A wavery image of an office formed on the surface of the pool. The view was from a perspective high in a corner of the room looking out and down across the space.

Raina exclaimed, "That's High Proctor Albinus's office!"

A shadow moved across the image, resolving after a moment into a man.

"Elfonse," Kadir growled in disgust. "He's probably bending Albinus's ear and telling him all sorts of lies about how you asked to be spirit-bottled and how I am an evil schemer for stopping him from doing as you asked."

Several more men moved across the office toward the fireplace. They bent down and among them lifted something heavy and lumpy. As they carried their burden toward the scrying mark, Kadir gasped first.

An instant later, Raina did the same. The men were carrying a body. An elderly, emaciated body wrapped in blue robes too big for it. *Albinus.*

"Surely, he'll resurrect," she said hopefully.

"He was very old and weak. He said for a while that his next death would be his last. Even if he still had the strength of spirit to resurrect, he had no desire to do so."

Sadness swept over her. She'd liked him in spite of his order's offenses against her. She became aware of Kadir's shoulders bowing in grief, and she placed a sympathetic hand on one of them. "I'm sorry for your loss."

Kadir said heavily, "Any chance I might have had at forgiveness, or at least for clemency, died with Albinus." He looked up at Justin. "I'm sorry. You were just starting your journey in the order, and I've cut it short."

"All I ever really wanted was to find Raina and make sure she was safe. I've done that. And as a bonus, now I can cast magic."

He was putting a brave face on having had the bottled spirit of an ogre mage forced into him, and she was grateful for that.

In the scrying pool, Elfonse moved over to Albinus's desk

and ran his hands covetously over the surface. He sat down in the big desk chair, and a look of immense satisfaction crossed his features. Raina was surprised to actually hear his voice when his lips moved.

"Good riddance," he muttered. "Old sack of bones didn't think I had it in me to take him out. Hah!"

Raina's jaw dropped. Elfonse had killed Albinus? Surely not! But there was no other way to interpret his words. A low rumble of rage emanated from Kadir. He was interpreting Elfonse's words the same way she was.

Albinus's office door opened, and a man Raina vaguely recognized as having hovered around Elfonse while she'd been at Alchizzadon stepped inside. "You summoned me, High Proctor?"

Raina gasped. Elfonse had not only killed Albinus but had usurped the older man's position, too?

Kadir rose to his feet on a roar of fury. The surface of the pool rippled violently, and the view of Albinus's office was shattered into a thousand ripples of disturbed water. "I'll kill him!" he shouted.

She interrupted abruptly, pointing down at the water. "Look. Who's that?"

Everyone turned back to face the pool. An image of a man was coming into view as the water in the seeing pool stilled. Albinus's office was gone, replaced by this man. A jann based on the colored tamgas marking his skin. He wore a suit of pale armor and had a very impressive bearing. Like a noble or a knight.

Justin jolted. "He's the one you sought earlier!"

"Who is he?" Raina asked.

"Why is the man you just scryed showing up again like this?" Justin asked.

Lakanos answered, "Apparently, someone really wants you to find this gentleman."

Kadir frowned. "He visited Alchizzadon last year. I was shocked because we never allow outsiders to come into the tower."

Lakanos retorted dryly, "So you were planning to kill me after all?"

Kadir snorted. "I was not personally planning to kill you, but no, you were never getting out of there alive." He added curiously, "Did you discover where the tower is when you were brought there?"

"No. I was portaled in, same as the emissary."

"Then mayhap they will let you live. Your colors will prove a thorn in their sides. Murdering a Heart knight is likely to provoke the sort of response they would rather avoid."

"If, by that response, you mean all-out war upon Alchizzadon by the Heart, you would be correct," Lakanos replied. "We may exist to serve others in peace, but we do not take kindly to the killing of our own. Only by responding forcefully to the murder of our members are the rest kept safe from harm."

Although his words were delivered quietly, Raina was startled at the steel beneath them. This was clearly not a man to trifle with when it came to defending the Heart. She warmed to him even more as the residual terror of her narrow escape from permanent death last night receded a little further in the face of his protectiveness toward her and the Heart.

"Why is that jann in the pool?" Justin asked practically. "Is that vision meant for you or for our hostesses?"

The dryads leaned in, cooing over how manly and handsome the man in the pool was. But they also declared that they did not recognize him.

Kadir said, "He was at Alchizzadon to investigate ways to remove partial spirits from a person and store them."

"Why?" Raina asked. "That's a pretty obscure question."

"My impression was that he was holding part of a spirit inside himself that he wished to be rid of. But he was also concerned that he not lose its power. He wanted it out of him but still wanted to control it."

Raina asked, "Where does the image come from, then? And why?"

Callisia knelt beside the pool and passed her mint green

hands over the surface without touching the water. "It is a gift," she murmured. "From the faerie of the pool."

"The who?" Raina asked. "What faerie?"

Callisia shrugged. "She does not wish to reveal herself. The seer is bidden to remember this face and find this man. With him lies your fate, man of runes."

Man of runes? Surely that meant Kadir.

Raina leaned in closer to stare at the jann in the pool. His skin was the palest blue, just shy of being white. "What's his armor made of?"

"Ice," the dryad answered promptly.

"Wouldn't that shatter easily or, oh, freeze him?" Raina responded.

"Obviously not!" Callisia snapped, sounding miffed.

"What's his name?" Kadir asked.

Callisia was more congenial with him and passed her hands over the image again. "No name has he. It was lost long ago. But he was a soldier . . . a leader . . . ah . . ." A long sigh. "He was a general in his day. But that was long ago."

Raina stared. *Surely not.* "Does he have the feel of a Kothite to you, Callisia?"

The dryad hissed at the word but turned her attention back to the pool. "The stink of the Circle breakers clings to him . . . but also I sense anger in him toward his masters."

"I think I know who that is," Raina announced. Every gaze turned on her. "That's General Tarses. I heard not long ago that he lives, and furthermore, that he roams the wild lands of Haelos."

"For what purpose?" Lakanos asked sharply.

She shrugged. "Perhaps Kadir should follow the advice of the faerie of the pool and find the general to ask him what he's up to."

"Such was already my intent." Kadir rose to his feet, and as he did so, the image of Tarses faded away, leaving behind a shallow pool with a few stray leaves floating idly on its surface.

"When you find him," Raina added, "tell him his son and daughter live."

Kadir's eyebrows shot up. "Tarses has children? Where? Who?"

"I am not at liberty to reveal that. If Tarses wishes to speak with me directly, I will be happy to tell him where to find his family," she replied.

Kadir nodded thoughtfully. "I will pass the message to him. Are you ready to go, Justin?"

Justin looked back and forth between her and his mentor in indecision. Raina said gamely, "You know you want to meet the great general who brought entire continents to their knees. I'm safe and under the able protection of Sir Lakanos. Don't worry about me. Go, Justin." They were the hardest two words she'd ever had to say.

Justin took her by the arm and led her a little way away from the others. "Once, a long time ago, you offered to run away with me. To make a child and marry me. I have long regretted not taking you up on that offer."

She smiled up at him sadly. "Once upon a time, I wished for nothing more than that with you. I would still love to settle down and have a family and be . . . normal. But my fate has not led me in that direction, and neither, it seems, has yours. Mayhap we will still find a way to be together and make that dream come true. But for now, both of us have other work to do. Go with Kadir and know you have my blessing."

Justin let out what she interpreted as a sigh of relief. He said, "We're both young yet. We have plenty of time to settle down and have that family we talked about. Know you take my heart with you wherever you go. If you ever have need of me, you have but to call me."

"How will I go about doing that?"

"If you're willing, Kadir can put a mark on you. A small one. A simple rune you can activate to summon me. The mark will act as a homing beacon I can follow to wherever you are."

As hesitant as she was to wear any mark from a Mage of Alchizzadon—even if he was a former mage—she nodded in agreement. She could only hope the mark wouldn't give

Kadir some other power over her. It was a calculated risk, but if it meant keeping in touch with Justin, she was willing to take it.

"Where will you go, Raina?" he asked as the two of them strolled back toward the others.

"I need to find a zinnzari," she replied. "They're a type of elf widely thought to be extinct, but I'm sincerely hoping they're not."

Callisia commented casually, "The zinnzari are not extinct. They are bound to a tree."

Raina was shocked. Carefully, hiding her eagerness lest she put off the dryad, she asked, "Do you know where to find them?"

"Of course. At their tree."

"Where is their tree?"

"In the desert."

Raina frowned. "I did not know trees grew in deserts."

"Tetrakis trees form their own oases and can grow anywhere," Callisia explained impatiently as if every child knew that. "And there are places, even in deserts, with water that nourishes other types of trees."

"Are the zinnzari bound to their tree in the same way you're bound to yours?" Raina asked. Not that she understood how dryads were bound to their trees either.

"No, silly human. The zinnzari were bound by Hemlocke."

"Hemlocke?" she echoed.

"The green dragon." A shrug from the dryad. "The zinnzari must return to their tree to resurrect."

"Ah." She made a sound as if she understood, but she didn't at all. Dragons? Trees that could resurrect elves? And since when did any spirit have no choice in where it resurrected? Aloud, she asked, "Is it a tetrakis tree?"

This sent all the dryads into gales of laughter. Eventually, Callisia calmed enough to giggle, "No, silly. It's a wake tree, of course."

"A wake tree?"

Lakanos murmured, "They're trees tied to the spirit realm. Near a wake tree, a person can sometimes see or hear a departed loved one and speak across the Veil with him or her. Hence the name *wake tree*."

Ah. *Wake* as in a vigil for a loved one recently dead. She asked the dryads in general, "Where is this wake tree and its zinnzari?"

Callisia answered solemnly, "They abide in the bosom of the Wust."

She knew dryads gloried in speaking in riddles, but this was getting annoying. Patiently, Raina asked, "The who?"

"I will speak no more of it. Terrible and fearsome is the Wust, and anger it I would not."

Raina frowned and would have pressed further, but Lakanos caught her eye over Callisia's shoulder and gave Raina a small shake of his head. Respecting his judgment, she bowed her head and said respectfully, "I thank you for your help and hospitality, Lady Callisia. You have done me and my friends a great honor."

A trilling giggle. "I have, haven't I?"

Their first night aboard the *Karolus* passed uneventfully, and morning dawned warm and sunny. Better, Will's seasickness had abated.

As the sun rose in the sky, reflecting off the blessedly smooth sea, he shed first his cloak and then his armor, tabard, and outer shirt. The Merr crew stripped down to their bare chests, which glittered brightly in the sunshine. Whereas Sha'Li's fine scales had a bit of raised texture to them, the Merr's were larger and lay flat, more like fish scales.

Rosana also shed her outer layers of clothing, stripping down to a white linen camisole held up by thin straps. Will tried to keep his gaze off her shoulders, but failed. Her rose tattoos were prominent against her winter-pale skin, each of the four roses so delicately etched as to appear real. One was white, one red, one black, and the last, newest one was green. Rosana swore the green rose had just appeared on her skin when she'd touched a magical staff Aurelius had handed her. But Will had a hard time crediting that, and his grandfather refused to speak of it.

Will studied the mark as Rosana closed her eyes and tilted her face up to the sun. He'd never seen skin ink so finely drawn and could not imagine any artist being capable of such realistic detail.

They'd been soaking up the sun's rays for a lazy hour when one of the other passengers, a shifty-looking man of middling age wearing a lot of jewelry and carrying a wicked, sharp-looking dagger in his belt, strolled past.

He stopped abruptly, staring at Rosana's left shoulder.

Will reached for his staff, gathering a fistful of magic. "Move along, sir," he said sternly.

"Don't get your breeches in a wad," the man said casually. "I was just looking at the roses. I haven't seen the like in a long time."

Will's scowl deepened, and he came lightly to his feet, silently announcing his fitness and skill in combat.

Rosana pulled her long-sleeved blouse on as she stood up, too. "Where have you seen such roses before, sir?"

"Ah. You're gypsy, then?" the man asked, sounding startled.

"Aye. And thee also?" she responded cautiously.

The man swept his hat off and made a grand bow to her, nose nearly at his knee. "My name is Luka, and I am a wandering gypsy soul. To whom do I have the pleasure of speaking?"

"I'm Sister Rosana of the Dupree Heart, and this is my good friend Will Cobb. Our other friends are lurking around here somewhere."

He wished she would call him her beau or, better, her fiancé. That would back the flirtatious gypsy scoundrel off. *Good friend* sounded so . . . platonic. Cursing under his breath, he spied Rynn and gestured the paxan to come over. Sha'Li sidled closer, as well, although she stayed tucked behind a pile of barrels, mostly out of sight.

"Tell me where you've seen similar roses to mine," Rosana asked eagerly.

"To answer that question properly, Sister Rosana of the fair cheeks and raven locks, I must introduce you to my traveling companion. Will you wait here while I fetch her?"

Her? Luka had a female companion? That was more like it. Will relaxed his death grip on his staff. The gypsy hurried away, and Will pulled on his shirt and buttoned it up.

Rosana was bubbly. "I've never met anyone with a marking like mine. A few people have heard of spontaneous roses, but this is so exciting! Maybe they can tell me which clan of gypsies I might belong to."

"You know nothing of your origin at all?" They'd never talked about her family, or lack thereof, and he'd never given it much thought. She was simply his Rosana.

"Nothing. I came to the Heart as an infant after the first Night of Green Fires. I always guessed my parents were killed by the Boki in the raids of that incursion. And I know I'm gypsy. That's all I have of my past."

As alone in the world as he might feel now, at least he knew who his parents had been. That they'd loved him unconditionally. What their faces looked like and their voices sounded like. He had a mental treasure chest of tiny memories that added up to a complete picture.

For Rosana's sake, he pasted a smile on his face when he spied Luka coming back toward them. But the smile slipped as Will spied Luka's companion. The woman had to be approaching a hundred years old. She looked like a fully dehydrated version of a human beneath that multihued scarf enveloping her head and upper body. A faint jingle of coins around the old woman's waist declared her to be gypsy as well. Her eyes were dark and hard as if she'd seen the worst that life had to offer, yet had survived.

"Sister Rosana, Will Cobb, this is Baba Razlet, my traveling companion."

"Well met," Will mumbled as Rosana dipped into a deep curtsy.

For her part, the old lady chuckled. "Gor, don't go bowing to me, child. I'm lucky I'm not in slavery or prison. I'm not of high enough station to merit being curtsied to."

Rosana smiled up at the woman, her young eyes sparkling. "It is rare that I meet an elder of my own kind. Please forgive my enthusiasm."

"It does my heart good, child, to see a young gypsy face. Our kind keep their heads low these days and rarely go abroad or congregate." Baba Razlet eased down onto a burlap bag filled with some grain-like substance, and Rosana leaped forward to take Baba's right arm as Luka eased her down by the left. Once the elderly woman was situated, Rosana sank down at her feet like an excited child. Will couldn't fault her. This was the first time Rosana had likely even seen a grandmotherly figure of her own race, let alone gotten to sit and talk with one.

"Show me your roses, child," Baba rasped.

Rosana pulled back the collar of her blouse to expose the four roses.

"Four?" Baba Razlet exclaimed.

Luka spoke up apologetically. "I thought you would accuse me of lying if I told you there were four."

"I would have, you scoundrel." She shook a crooked, bony finger at him reprovingly. Using that same finger, she reached out and touched Rosana's red rose lightly.

Rosana lurched as the rose abruptly glowed a little, a faint red aura that made the mark seem more three-dimensional than two. The woman touched the white rose next, and a faint white aura glowed for a moment. Hesitantly, the woman touched the green rose, and a bright green aura rose from Rosana's skin.

"So beautiful," Baba Razlet breathed. "Never have I seen the green rose come to life." Almost as an afterthought, the woman touched the final rose, the black one.

It, too, came to life, but with a dark energy that traced the black petals across Rosana's skin.

Baba Razlet yanked her finger back hard. "It's like that, then, is it? Where did you get the black rose, and how did you wake it?"

Rosana stared up at the woman. If Will wasn't mistaken, that was fear glinting in her eyes. "I've always had it. As long as I can remember. As for waking it up, I don't know what you're talking about."

Will's brows twitched toward one another. That sounded

like deception in Rosana's voice. The old woman harrumphed as if she didn't believe Rosana's answer either.

"Where do you know the roses from?" Rosana asked.

"Certain members of the gypsy race bear them as marks. Among our kind, they are known as the old ones and are thought to have the purest gypsy blood. There are precious few of you left."

Luka piped up. "I haven't seen the roses since my brother's wife died, and that was nearly twenty years ago."

Baba Razlet asked Rosana, "How old are you, child?"

"I'm twenty summers old."

Luka interjected, "That would have made you a babe during the first Night of Green Fires."

Rosana nodded. "That's correct. My parents were killed, and I was given to the Heart to raise."

Will noted that a strange look passed across Luka's face, and the gypsy man tilted his head, staring intently at Rosana. Will edged a little closer to her side.

Baba scowled at Rosana's tabard. "You should have been raised by your own kind. Them Heart types know nothing about being gypsy. They couldn't teach you all you need to know."

"Like what?" Rosana asked.

"Like the importance of family. The name of your clan. Your place in the world."

Will suspected Rosana's place in the world was considerably better as a Heart member than as a gypsy, but he refrained from saying so aloud.

"Do you know your exact day of birth?" Luka asked abruptly.

"The high matriarch told me I was born in March."

"On the tenth day of the month, perchance?" Luka asked.

Will started along with Rosana, who said, "That's correct! How did you guess?"

"My brother had a daughter born on that date. His wife and baby daughter were said to have died in the first Boki Insurrection. And you are the living image of his wife."

Will stared. This man knew Rosana's mother? And furthermore was brother to Rosana's father?

"Who?" Rosana choked. "Who were my parents?"

"You have to understand," Luka said cautiously. "Certain people would love to find me and send me to an Imperial prison. I must be careful to whom I reveal my identity."

Will blurted, "For the love of the Lady, tell the girl who she is. If you are, indeed, family, she will certainly not turn you over to the Empire."

"What about the rest of you?" Luka challenged.

Rynn spoke up soberly. "I think I speak for all of us when I say we have no great love for the Empire."

"How am I to believe you?" Luka asked suspiciously.

"If we convince you we are enemies of the Empire, will you tell Rosana who her parents are?" Rynn countered.

"Aye."

To Will's shock, Rynn reached up and removed his headband, revealing his third eye. Baba Razlet and Luka both sucked in their breath. Obviously, they understood the implications of it.

"Very well, then," Luka said, his voice pitched low to carry only a few feet. "My name is Luka Beltane, and my brother was Landsgrave Gregor Beltane. He and his wife, Lillianna, were your parents."

Rynn snapped his fingers. "That's it! I knew I had seen Rosana's face before." The paxan turned to her. "I met Gregor and Lillianna once, just after they were married. Luka is correct. You are the very image of her."

Rosana threw her arms around Rynn's neck in a hug, and jealousy flared in Will's gut like a gout of acid. Cursed paxan had better not try to steal her from him, or blood would spill.

Rynn gently set Rosana away from him, which mollified Will only slightly. "This explains a great deal."

"Like what?" Will asked suspiciously.

"Like why my mentor told me to protect Rosana's life at all costs."

Luka demanded, "Who is this mentor?"

Rynn replied smoothly, "No enemy of yours. He told me it was of utmost importance to protect Rosana's blood. Now

I understand what he meant." Rynn turned to Rosana. "You hail from one of the oldest known gypsy bloodlines."

Baba Razlet added, "And one of the purest."

Suddenly, Rosana looked stricken. "All those years, my father was alive. If only I had known . . ." Her voice trailed off, thick with tears.

Will said gently, "At least you knew him a little, if only from a distance."

"Gregor was a fine man. The best in our family," Luka said sadly.

Will murmured, "When we get home, you should speak with my grandfather. He knew your father—and mother, for that matter—very well. He will tell you all you wish to know about them."

Rosana dashed tears off her cheeks. "It is not the same as knowing them myself."

"It's better than nothing. I take comfort in hearing stories of my parents from him."

"You knew your parents!" Rosana snapped.

Stung, he moved away from her to lean over the rail and stare into the black waters of the sea. It wasn't his fault his parents had died. He'd tried to get them to run away with him, but they'd refused. They'd insisted he continue their quest, and that waking the Sleeping King was more important than their lives. It was the only reason he continued this madness and didn't walk away from it this minute. He had sworn a vow not to let their deaths be in vain, and he would not go back on it.

Startled to be awake and seemingly back in control of his body, Number One blinked. A voice whispered in his mind, *Those whom you seek flee from you. Follow them, warrior.*

Of course he would follow his quarry. It made perfect sense to do so. He gripped his white-bladed sword more tightly and strode out of the woods into the village, his two companions in tow.

He shook his head to clear it of the cobwebby feeling. Where was he? It looked like the worst sort of frontier town, rife with smugglers, mercenaries, and just enough Imperials to cause trouble.

"Where are we?" Three murmured fuzzily.

For a moment, it struck him as odd that they weren't sure where they were. But then the uncertainty evaporated, replaced by that whisper urging him to move with haste and not let his prey slip away.

He looked down at Three and mumbled, "Do you know who I am?"

"Of course I do. You're our leader."

"And me?" Two mumbled. "Who am I?"

"You're my biggest pain in the neck," Three quipped.

"Where are we?" Two echoed.

"You tell me. You're the scout," One replied.

It was actually Three who piped up. "Yon massive body of water looks like the Estarran Sea. The sun is going down, and it's behind us, which means we're on the west coast."

"How did we get *there*?" One exclaimed.

Two was frowning. "Forgive me if I sound mad, but I could swear I heard a voice tell me to follow someone."

One matched her frown. "I thought I heard something similar a moment ago."

"Me, as well," Three added. "Let's have a look around."

It didn't take Two's outstanding scouting skills or Three's equally outstanding tracking skills to spot the docks, or for One to be sure that whoever they were supposed to be following had left these selfsame docks by boat very recently. Now why would he be so sure of that?

But like so many questions that came to his mind these days, this one also drifted away as lazily as sunshine riding a current of warm air.

They walked the length of the docks and spied a likely looking gent with great white muttonchops covering most of his cheeks. More importantly, he acted like the harbor supervisor, yelling instructions and epithets at the sailors bringing in a small barge badly and banging into the vessels on each side of it before slamming into the dock itself.

One waited until the harbor master's face wasn't an apoplectic shade of red and then approached him. "Excuse me, sir. We're looking for a friend of ours. We were supposed to sail out together, but we were late getting here, and he seems to have sailed already."

"Only ship that left in the past two days with passengers was the *Karolus*, last night. Merr vessel."

"Where's she headed?" Two asked politely.

The harbor master smiled at her more lasciviously than One liked, although he wasn't sure why it should bother him so. "She'll be making port up at Lifton to unload her cargo."

Two asked worriedly, "Is there any chance the vessel could put ashore along the way to let off passengers?"

The harbor master tucked his thumbs in his generous waistband. "Oh, there's a chance, little lady. But not much o' one. The *Karolus* is carrying supplies for the construction crews working on Maren's Belt. Them Imperials is in an all-fired hurry to get new supplies, you see. Ever since the treaty with Anton Constantine and the Merr collapsed, only way to move cargo on the Estarran Sea is on Merr ships. And them Merr ain't stupid. They's runnin' everything at half speed and charging twice the going price for passage."

"Thank you for the information," Two replied.

"You busy tonight, little la—"

One cut him off, snarling, "Yes. She is." His sword lifted in his hand, and his hand grasping it began to glow.

"Easy now!" The harbor master threw up his hands and took a step back. "I was just inquiring. No need to get violent or nothin'."

Three interjected soothingly, "If you could just tell us when the next ship bound for Lifton leaves, we'd be in your debt, sir."

"That would be day after the morrow. On the morning tide."

One scowled. The pressure to stay moving, to keep their quarry in sight, built up in his head until he thought it might explode. Two and Three were wincing as if pained also.

"We've got no choice," he muttered to the searing agony in his brain. "We must wait for a boat."

The pain subsided a little, and he breathed a sigh of relief. Two days. And then they'd be on the move again. A surge of triumph at closing in on their final target rushed through him.

What target?

But then those words wafted away on the evening air along with every other question his mind might have formed.

Raina was grateful that Lakanos seemed to have taken control of their trio's journey. He set a reasonable pace that she could readily keep up with. She still remembered the breakneck pace at which Cicero had dragged her to Dupree the first time. She'd thought to die of exhaustion before they'd reached the capital.

She missed Justin nearly as badly as she had the first time she'd left him, that night when she'd run away from home two years ago. But he and Kadir had set out for the coast to hire a fast boat to take them to the southern end of the Estarran Sea and the western tip of the Heaves.

Lakanos led her and Cicero south toward the eastern Vale-lands, from whence they would turn southwest into the heart of the Thirst. They camped on the road at night, using gear they'd gotten from the dryads in return for Raina casting as much healing magic into an ancient rowan tree as her head could stand before the pain made her nearly pass out. She had no idea if it had done any good or not, but the dryads had been delighted. Strange creatures, those women.

In the late morning of the fourth day, Cicero left them to hunt, and it was just her walking in one dusty wagon rut, and Lakanos walking beside her in the other.

"You're sure you do not wish to go east for a day and walk Maren's Belt, Emissary?"

"Please. Call me Raina." It was at least the tenth time she'd said that.

"Sorry. Old habits die hard."

"I would rather not be seen by anyone," she answered.

Lakanos shrugged, accepting her wish for secrecy without question, for which she was immensely grateful. As they walked on, she considered the massive construction project necessary to create a two-thousand-mile-long road.

"Tell me something," she said a little while later. "Is construction of Maren's Belt a prelude to invasion by the Empire?"

He glanced at her in alarm. "I've heard no such thing."

She sighed. "Let me be frank with you, Sir Lakanos. I am no great fan of the Empire. It is impossible to wear these colors and be fond of its treatment of its subjects. My loyalty lies first and foremost with the Heart. I would never turn you in to the Empire for criticizing Koth. We are alone in the middle of nowhere, and I beg of you, please feel free to speak your mind freely and honestly with me."

He smiled gently at her. "It is neither noble nor honorable to rant against the law of the land. I may not be fond of the methods the Emperor and his nobles employ, but it is not my place to criticize."

"You consider yourself a loyal subject of the Empire first and the Heart second, then?" She was dismayed at the prospect.

He answered firmly and without hesitation. "Absolutely not."

Whew. They walked in silence for a little while, and the bumps of the waestones resolved themselves into stocky pillars. Although they still seemed far away.

"What's it like working for Lord Justinius?"

Lakanos smiled fondly. "It is a great honor and pleasure to work for such a man. He is a remarkable leader and the noblest soul I have ever met."

High praise, indeed.

"Does he think war is coming to Haelos?"

Lakanos grunted. "You are blunt, aren't you?"

"My tabard often requires me to be diplomatic. Subtle to the point of being obtuse. However, with you I shall always endeavor to be honest and forthright. Assuming no one else is about to hear me."

"Thanks be for that. I shall endeavor to do the same with you." They walked for a minute or two in silence, and then Lakanos asked, "What of the kindari, Cicero? Why do you wait until he is gone to have this conversation with me? Is there reason not to trust him fully?"

"On the contrary. I trust him with my life, and he has even less love for the Empire than I."

"Be careful where you utter such words. I have seen good people put to death for less."

"Thank you for the warning. I assure you, I have no death wish."

He laughed a little. "That's not the way I hear it."

Raina reveled in the perfect traveling weather as spring came to Haelos. The grasslands of the southwestern Machaira gave way to the forests of the Valelands. They caught a ride on a barge down a small canal barely wider than their vessel and made fast time across the Valelands. Gradually, its lush forests gave way to the arid holding of Amadyr, the easternmost portion of a region known as the Thirst.

Ever larger drifts of sand spread before them until great dunes rose high on either side of them. They trudged along in the rifts, somewhat protected from the worst of the buffeting from what Lakanos called the Dragon's Breath Winds.

They slogged through one such valley as the sun dipped low in their faces, a pulsating ball of liquid fire presaging the freezing night to come. Without warning, a dozen beige-robed figures flew down the dunes on toboggans, coming at them from both sides, long veils streaming out behind them like horses' manes. In a matter of seconds, Raina and her companions were surrounded by a menacing phalanx of bone spears.

Lakanos whipped out his sword in front of her, and Cicero did the same behind her. For her part, she summoned magic to her hands, and almost went down to her knees as searing pain exploded in her skull. Only fear and sheer force of will kept her upright.

The veiled bandits flowed out of the way of Lakanos's and Cicero's swords like water. As one opponent slid out of the way, another would slide into his place. It was like fighting the wind, and just about as effective.

Many of their attackers cast magic, some using glamours, others using water magic, while several were healers. Raina did her best to keep magical shields up on Lakanos and Cicero and to heal their nicks and cuts as they happened. But with each spell she cast, the pressure in her skull built up more, and waves of overwhelming emotion—every type and flavor—drowned out her ability to think. She gasped out the incants, barely able to shape the magic into useful spells.

After many futile minutes, Lakanos and Cicero both broke off attacking to catch their breaths.

The assailants apparently mistook the pause for a surrender, however, and one of them demanded in a strangely high-pitched rasp, "Hand over your packs."

Lakanos answered evenly, "You might as well kill us now. If we hand over our gear, we'll die out here far more slowly and painfully than if you slaughter us with your weapons." He added, "And as you can see by my Royal Order of the Sun colors, I am the sworn guardian of this White Heart emissary. I will fight to the death to defend her."

Raina said past the daggers stabbing her eyeballs, "Greetings, friends. Are you familiar with the markings of my tabard and what they mean? I am sworn to defend all life. I will gladly share my healing skills with you and yours. Are any among you sick? Injured? How about your families? Your children? I will even heal your animals. I have enough magic for all of you." To illustrate that point, she summoned more energy to her fingers. The pain increased apace inside her skull. She wavered but managed to stay on her feet. Curse the Mages of Alchizzadon and whatever their backlashed ritual had done to her!

"We know the White Heart. Healer or no, you are nonetheless an Imperial lackey."

Cicero spoke up. "She heals the enemies of the Empire as readily as she heals anyone else." As he spoke, he unwound the cloth from around his head, no doubt to improve his vision and mobility when the lopsided fight resumed.

A gasp went up around them.

"You are Spider Clan?" the one with the high-pitched voice demanded.

"I am arachnari," Cicero answered cautiously.

"From whence come you, spider elf?"

"I hail from the Sorrow Wold."

Another gasp. "Did the Black Widow send you to us, then? Have you a message for us?"

Cicero sent Raina a questioning look, and she nodded slightly.

"Aye," he answered. "We have news of the widow."

The sharpened bone tips of the spears lifted away from them. "Welcome be unto thee, servant of our sister. It has been too long since we have heard from the Bride of Quetaryn, and we are pleased to do so now."

The bandits led Cicero up a dune face, and Raina and Lakanos were left to trail along in his wake. She traded shrugs with her knight and followed along behind the entourage.

She gasped as she topped the wind-creased crest of the dune and spied a sprawling oasis in a wide valley beyond.

How could they have passed so close to such a large encampment and had no idea it was there?

Lakanos murmured, "Such is the expanse of the Thirst. One may pass right by another man and never see him."

Raina asked, "What is this place called?"

"This is the great eastern oasis of Nefiwah," one of their veiled escorts answered.

In the middle of the sprawling collection of tents stood a huge tree unlike any Raina had ever seen before. Its trunk, although not particularly thick, was covered in scarred, gnarled bark, and bore the curve of a spine bent with great age. A wide canopy of branches spread outward overhead, its tangled junctions creating a maze of strangely angular forms. She realized with a start that hexagons seemed to be repeated over and over in the shapes of the branches.

"What is that?" she asked.

"A tetrakis tree," one of their escorts answered.

Which explained the oasis. Apparently, this species of tree could store vast amounts of water in its roots and release the water slowly in dry times to nourish itself. Clusters of animals, people, and plants were able to live off that secreted moisture, as well.

They slipped and slid their way down the dune face into the valley below, and Raina filled her boots with sand in the process. The parade, with Cicero at its head, wended its way through several dozen small tents to a large, open-sided tent.

The natives, a mix of women and children, stared and muttered as Raina and her companions passed. Men were notably absent from the encampment.

Cicero was seated on cushions near a brass brazier filled with blazing bricks of something akin to peat, or perhaps animal dung, given the ripe odor of the smoke. Raina and Lakanos were waved to a plain wooden bench farther from the fire.

"This is a bit of a switch," the knight murmured.

She muttered back in good humor, "I'm rather enjoying being the lackey and not the center of attention."

"Let's hope their fascination with our friend holds,"

Lakanos replied. "I do not relish fighting an entire encampment of these warrior women. A single scouting party was more than Cicero and I could handle."

One stood in front of the cave, with Two and Three peering over his shoulder. He announced, "I'll go first."

They charged into the space, which turned out to be deserted, as he'd expected. The cliff they'd had to scale to get here would have put off all but the most-skilled climbers, human or animal. Thankfully, Three had as much experience at climbing as he did, and Two was light and agile enough to make up for what she lacked in climbing experience.

He hated to break off tracking their quarry to explore this place, but all three of them had dreamed of this exact cave. When they'd passed by it on their way inland into the Valelands, they had to take a look.

Below them stretched miles of verdant woodlands with the thin silver line of the Lance cutting east in the distance.

"Quit gawking at the view and help us search the cave," Three complained from behind him.

No sooner had he turned around, though, than Two exclaimed in surprise. They had to pour water on the wall to reveal the ancient markings hidden under a layer of dust, but eventually the writing became legible.

"What's this doing way up here?" Two breathed.

"What is *this*, exactly?" One asked, irritated that he couldn't read the words.

"Ancient writings of the pastors," Two answered.

Pastors? The people who looked after and protected the trees of the Great Circle?

Tracing the writings with one finger, Two pointed at a set of markings on the back wall. "See that picture of a spear carved on the raised rock near the right end? Push on it."

Three shoved at the fist-sized rock. It moved inward with a scraping sound of stone on stone.

"Now the one with the squiggly lines," Two ordered pointing at a raised rock in the lower center of the wall.

One realized with a start that the entire back wall of the

cave was covered in those protruding little stones. One by one, Two talked them through the correct order to press the stones. How she knew which symbols to skip and which to use, he had no idea. It must be pastor stuff. Even if she'd never become one herself, she did come from a long line of Hickory pastors, after all.

It took many long minutes to decipher the code to the lock, but at long last, a great slabbed portion of the back wall swung inward. Two moved toward it, but One snagged her arm. "Let me go first. We cannot be too careful."

It turned out he'd made the right call, for a many-limbed creature made of dried wood came at him as soon as he raised his torch to light the inner cave.

"What is a wolden doing here?" Three gasped.

One grunted as he fended off multiple shockingly fast attacks, "What's a wolden?"

"They're called the sons of treants, somewhat like dryads are called the daughters of treants. But the wolden are more plantlike and do not speak like humanoids."

"They blasted well fight like humanoids," One complained as he was forced to retreat from the onslaught of slashing limbs.

Quickly assessing his foe, he used a combination of sword and torch to make short work of the wolden. Normal warriors would have had a difficult time with the multilimbed creature whose arms whipped back and forth with incredible speed and strength. Fortunately, he was not a normal warrior.

There seemed to be only the one active wolden in the cave. While One stood by watchfully in case more appeared, Two and Three searched the inner cave to find whatever treasure was guarded by such a powerful creature. Tucked away in a dark corner, covered by dust, they found only a small, plain wooden box, not much larger than his hand.

"Take it to the outer chamber where there's more light," One directed. He was as curious as the others to know what was hidden in such an out-of-the-way spot and so well defended.

It took Two nearly a half hour to disarm a very clever trap

inside the box that would have spilled acid on the box's contents had it not been properly opened. At last, Two carefully lifted the lid to reveal what looked like a fist-sized walnut. The wooden orb was bumpy on the outside and ovoid in shape, and as Three lifted it from the box, its surface gleamed a deep, rich burgundy brown like highly polished mahogany.

"What is it?" One asked.

"A seed," Two answered reverently.

"That's the biggest seed I've ever seen!" Three exclaimed.

"What's it a seed of?" One asked skeptically.

Two shrugged. "No idea. But it's beautiful. And the energy of it . . ." She trailed off, rubbing her fingers gently across its irregular surface. "I can practically hear it singing to me."

"A singing seed," One responded in disgust. "We went off course for this?"

Two tucked the seed lovingly in her pouch, nesting it in a woolen scarf like a fragile egg.

"Are you ready to get back to the business at hand of tracking our prey?" he asked impatiently.

Two nodded, and they turned their attention to descending the cliff, which, though less strenuous, proved nearly as tricky as climbing it. They'd lost at least two hours on their quarry and would have to hurry through the afternoon and march into the evening to make up for lost time.

But a driving compulsion to get back on the scent of their prey drove him mercilessly, and he'd learned not even to try to fight it.

Raina grinned as Lakanos asked drolly, "Should we offer to serve Cicero his dinner? It has been a long time since I was a page, but I think I could pull it off."

She replied, "I draw the line at peeling grapes."

Their escorts lifted away their veils and set them aside, revealing themselves to be women. Lakanos's face reflected surprise, perhaps that he'd been fought to a draw by a group of females.

Raina unwound her own head wrap with a sigh of relief as

a breeze cooled the sweat on her skin, granting her a moment's relief from the day's stifling heat. She knew from experience that the evening would not cool until the sun fully set, and then the temperature would drop precipitously. She could not imagine what this place would be like in the height of summer. It was barely spring and already nigh unbearable.

They were offered skins of water lightly flavored with what tasted like a cross between green tea and some fruit akin to a fig. Either way, it soothed her parched throat and eased her headache somewhat. She nodded her thanks to the woman who'd given the skin to her.

They were served rounds of flat bread, charred black on the outside but soft and chewy on the inside. A paste of some kind was provided to spread on torn pieces of the bread. It was salty in taste, gritty in texture. She did not ask what it was; she didn't want to know. After choking it down, she was happy to accept a cup of some hot, bitter liquid that cleansed her mouth.

When the simple repast had concluded, a trio of woman approached Cicero. Together, they looked older than time, their skin dry and deeply wrinkled. Pale lines of dust seemed permanently inlaid in their facial creases.

"You are the messenger from our cousin in the Sorrow Wold?" one of them asked. "What news is there?"

Raina and Cicero had not had a single second to themselves to discuss what he would say in response to this expected question. She gulped. He was on his own.

"The Widow of the Wold lives and prospers. She hopes her cousins in the Thirst do the same."

"We of the Veils prosper, as well," one of them intoned solemnly.

The Veils? Raina gaped. They were a notorious outlaw group, said to be ruthless in protecting their territories and exceedingly unfriendly to outsiders of any kind. The Veils ruled the deserts of the Thirst, no matter what the Empire might claim to the contrary.

"My mistress wishes to inquire how you fare. It has been

too long since she has heard from you," Cicero intoned formally.

Ah, well played.

"The Wust is restless," one of them replied as if that explained everything.

"The Wust?" Raina intervened to ask, curious after the dryads had refused to talk about it.

"Aye. The living embodiment of this land. It is the fearsome spirit and heart of the Thirst. It takes the blood we offer to slake its great and terrible thirst, and in return, it grants the land water, thus granting life."

Raina was startled. In her short time in the Thirst, the region had struck her as dead and barren.

The woman who had answered her snorted. "You see no green and assume the Thirst is dead. Yet does not yon tree live? Do we not thrive? When night has fallen, do not the creatures of the desert sing?"

Raina nodded, conceding the point. But she couldn't resist asking, "You say you offer the Wust blood. Do you do this in the form of sacrifices?" As a White Heart member, she opposed such practices, but it was also not her place to tell the people of a place that their culture and traditions were wrong.

"Food is too precious to waste in the way you suggest, White Heart. But marauders and intruders aplenty come here, eager to spill their blood upon our spears."

While she abhorred bloodshed, she also couldn't fault these people for defending themselves.

After dinner, more women came to the open tent, gathering to talk and laugh and stare curiously at the visitors. Elders arrived, and one of them stood up to speak.

"When the first daughter of the sand was exiled from her people, she walked into the Wust expecting to die. But instead, she found life in the branches of Bastion, the great father of all the tetrakis trees."

As the woman described the dimensions and powers of Bastion, Raina guessed he must be a treant.

The storyteller continued, "Bastion and the Wust lived in

harmony, and because Bastion accepted the lost daughter unto himself, so did the Wust. Bastion changed as the seasons changed, and the daughter learned the ways of the land and the rhythm of its seasons."

As far as Raina could tell, the Thirst had two seasons. Hot and hotter.

"Many years passed, and another daughter of the sand came unto this land, parched and nearly dead from her long journey, cast out of Tyrel to die."

Raina jolted. "Tyrel?" she blurted. "Are you certain?"

The storyteller turned on her. "I know where I was born, girl. And I know from whence I was cast out to die."

Raina's jaw sagged. "Are you related to the Black Widow, by any chance?"

"She is my niece."

All the breath whooshed out of Raina as if the woman had slugged her in the stomach. She tried to stand, but was so stunned she staggered and might have fallen had Lakanos not jumped up to steady her.

"I am from Tyrel," Raina managed to choke out. "And if I have this right, you are my great-great-aunt. I am Raina, the second daughter of Charlotte of Tyrel."

The old woman frowned. "Second daughter? Not the first?"

"Nay. My sister, Arianna, yet abides in Tyrel. I ran away from home two years ago, and the Mages of Alchizzadon cannot replace her as long as I refuse to bear children."

A collective hiss went up at the name *Alchizzadon.*

Cicero looked over at Raina in disgust. "Another one of your female relatives driven out to die? What is the *problem* with your family?"

Lakanos stared in alarm. "What's this about women in your family dying?"

Raina replied, "It's a long story." To the storyteller—her great-great-aunt—she asked, "How did you find your way so far from Tyrel? And how have you lived so long?"

"The blood that makes daughters of Tyrel strong in magic also enhances our life spans, it seems."

"Are all the people here descended from Ariannas?" Raina asked curiously.

"No. Only two Ariannas have found their way to the Thirst according to our oral history—the first one who founded the Veils long ago and myself. We keep a watch every generation for another to walk into the sands, but none have come in a long time."

Raina thought back. "My aunt Ari left Tyrel four years ago. I have no idea where she ended up."

"If she was lucky, she died," the storyteller retorted bluntly. "The Widow of the Wold was the last to escape the clutches of Alchizzadon when she took her long walk."

"What do the mages do with the women of our family?" She was fairly sure she knew the answer, but wanted confirmation.

"Kill them. Capture their spirits and magics."

Lakanos pivoted to face Raina. "Is there evidence to support this claim?"

"You were there," she replied. "You interrupted them trying to bottle my spirit. According to Kadir, they intended to drain my magic and then keep my body—an empty husk—barely alive in some kind of permanent stasis until they use my magic and my body dies permanently."

Lakanos's eyes narrowed to furious slits. "I will be reporting this to Lord Justinius immediately upon my return."

"By all means, please do," she replied.

"How is it you escaped the mages?" her great-great-aunt demanded.

"These gentlemen"—she gestured at Cicero and Lakanos—"and two more brave men, both Mages of Alchizzadon who have already left our company, rescued me. I am in their debt."

"Be welcome among us, Raina of Tyrel. If you wish to stay and make your home with us, we will embrace the third daughter of the sand."

Another one of the elder women bowed deeply, murmuring, "The Wust welcomes you into its ancient and powerful embrace, daughter of Tyrel."

"Thanks be unto thee, but I cannot stay this time. I must cross the Thirst and find my friends."

One of the Veils responded, "We have arrived at the season when you should travel at night and rest during the heat of the day. We will provide you a guide across the Thirst, for you are about to reach the lands of the Saryl."

"And they are . . . ?" Lakanos asked.

"Red lizardmen who live out here. Also, there have been sightings of Gnogadi, the Wandering Stone. And before you ask, he is a stone elemental indigenous to the area. Even we steer clear of him."

"Are you well enough to travel tonight?" Lakanos asked Raina. "You seemed . . . off . . . earlier when we fought the Veils."

Sometimes she forgot how observant he was. "If I get a few hours' sleep, I'll be ready to go. The headaches only get really bad when I try to use my magic."

"Fair enough. I will guard your sleep."

If only he could guard her nightmares.

CHAPTER

22

Gabrielle waited in an agony of impatience at the little inn in the forest while Talissar finalized the plan for breaking into Maximillian's trophy room. Apparently, he had asked someone to help with the heist, and that person was due to arrive at any moment.

There had been quite a debate between Talissar and the young man over whether or not this outside party was to be trusted. They both agreed the person in question was capricious at best and unhinged at worst. Unpredictable as he might be, though, they both reluctantly agreed that the break-in would simply not be possible without his assistance.

Every day of waiting was agony for her. She consoled herself with praying that her children, her husband, and posterity might remember her, succeed or fail, for her bravery in standing up to the evil of the Kothite Empire. Of course, knowing Maximillian, no one would remember that she'd ever existed at all.

On the afternoon of their tenth interminable day at the inn, a knock on her door sent her innards into turmoil. Her guest was a black-skinned nulvari with the pale blond hair and brows of a human and a handsome rake of a fellow. He was tall and athletic, dressed to the nines, his intelligent gaze darting into every corner of the room and taking in every detail. He looked familiar—

"Are you by any chance Acavaro's son?" she asked. "I believe we met some years ago."

He swept into a grand bow, one nicely turned leg displayed to her. "I am, indeed, Your Highness. But for this adventure,

I have decided to call myself the Thief in the Night. Romantic, no?"

"Terribly," she replied dryly.

He asked briskly, "Are you and yours ready to go? I'm eager to get on with biting a pound of flesh out of our resplendent leader's backside."

So this was revenge for him. She didn't like the hectic air that clung to him and said warningly, "I would remind you, our mission is simply to reconnoiter. We get into the trophy room, have a quiet look around, and get out."

"Of course." His dismissive hand wave and breezy reply didn't calm her fears in the least.

"Last I heard, you went away, vowing never to return to court." She vaguely recalled hearing about a spectacular blowup from him some years ago, around the time she'd lost Sir Darius. It had something to do with a nulvari woman. Supposedly, he'd stolen something on a lark and then given it to her as a gift. She'd been caught with it in her possession and accused of being his accomplice in the theft.

There had been quite a scandal over it, and the woman had fled into hiding, which lent credence to rumors that she had been the mastermind behind the whole affair. He'd vowed it was all his fault and demanded to take her punishment, but his powerful parents had intervened and he'd left court under a cloud.

"My old friend Talissar dangled the one bait that would get me to return to court. A chance at revenge against he who wronged my true love."

"Promise me you won't do anything rash. A lot depends on this mission, and I don't need you to get us all caught and killed."

"There are much worse fates in this world than death, I assure you. I have lived them all in the long decades away from my love."

She rolled her eyes at his romantic foolishness. There were plenty of fates worse than being separated from a loved one. And sometimes separation was for the best. It had nigh killed her to send her own children away, but she could not pass up a chance for them to grow up far away from Maximillian, spared from being pawns in the Emperor's political games.

A knock on her door admitted the other members of the party. The thief took one look at Sir Valyri and demanded, "He's not coming with us, is he?"

Gabrielle responded, startled, "That was the plan."

"No. Absolutely not. The Heart knight cannot go with us."

"Why not?"

"Because we're going to be committing a crime, and he's bound to get squeamish at the worst possible moment. He goes or I go. But not both of us."

Gabrielle looked back and forth between the two men in distress. She could see the thief's point. "I am loath to exclude one of our most accomplished warriors from the mission."

The thief snorted. "If we need any warriors at all, we're dead anyway."

Sir Valyri spoke up. "It's fine. I will wait outside the palace and hold a boat for us. That way if we need a fast departure, it will be waiting and ready."

"You're sure you don't mind?" she asked the knight.

"Our new friend makes an excellent point. In truth, I am relieved to avoid the more larcenous aspects of this plan."

The thief murmured, "Shall we go, my lady? I believe the plan calls for you to lead the way."

Already they were off the plan, and they hadn't even gotten started yet.

She nodded regally, assuming the mantle of her royal title, and said formally, "Let us depart. Korgan and Jossa, follow behind the rest of us. I am sorry, but the two of you will have to carry the luggage. It will be assumed that you are servants because of your races, and to do otherwise would attract the wrong kind of attention."

She swept out of the inn into the crisp mountain air, the afternoon sun warm on her cheeks. They walked across a bridle path and down a short road through a stand of pine and birch trees to the shores of the Crystal River. A magnificent barge floated by the dock like a bloated ladies' brooch, crusted in gems and curlicues until the boat itself was barely visible.

The trip down the Crystal River was as gorgeous as she remembered. Every field and forest they passed was manicured within an inch of its life and looked like a pastoral painting. But mostly, she was sick to her stomach with nervous anticipation of the heist to come.

They rounded a great bend in the river, and the Imperial Seat rose before them, its city-sized mass perched upon the White Crown Plaza, a gigantic platform raised many stories above the river by a spectacular fretwork of arches rising like a three-dimensional stained-glass window between the eight mountains making up Thoris's Shield.

At the peak of the Imperial Palace, topping it like a dark crown, was the Eternal Flame itself. She knew from visiting it once that the flame burned in an enormous brazier, never needing fuel or magic to sustain its life-consuming fire. To pass through the Black Flame was to be consigned to the Void for eternity with no possibility of return.

Evening was falling, and torches were being lit all across the Imperial Seat, turning it into a glittering diamond atop its splendid setting.

The palace of His Resplendent Majesty, Maximillian the Third, was the central jewel in an empire spanning the breadth and length of Urth. It seemed to float in the sky, as awe-inspiring as the immortal ruler who occupied it. No matter how many times she gazed upon the soaring edifice, it never failed to amaze her.

Even Korgan gasped in wonder at the sight of bridges, plaza, and palace. "Gor, how does it stay up? So delicate those arches be. Why does the whole city not crash into the lake?"

Gabrielle answered, "It is said that giants grew the arches."

Bekkan commented, "Giant-grown stone is the strongest in existence. Yon arches may look fragile, but if they're giant-made, they'll last forever."

Gabrielle sincerely hoped not. One day, she would love to see the entire palace and everything it stood for come tumbling down.

She checked her train of thought sharply. She dared not rely solely on her Octavium Pendant to shield her thoughts from the prying minds of the powerful Kothites at court. Not only the Emperor but also his archdukes and archduchesses were adept mind readers.

It took nearly an hour to ride the swift currents to the foot of the floating city, and night fell in the meantime, the sky turning violet, then navy, then black, peppered with bright stars.

The Imperial Seat towered over the entire valley like a massive stone cloud. The hair-raising ride in trolley carts up the mountain took nearly a half hour—plenty of time for the approaching supplicant to soak in the immense wealth and power behind the construction of the edifice overhead.

And then there was the breath-stealing walk across a stone footbridge in buffeting winds to the White Crown Plaza. Gabrielle had always thought the approach to the Imperial Seat was designed to terrify and cow visitors. Defiantly, she refused to be afraid of the lofty heights this eve.

At length, she arrived with her motley companions in tow at the great portcullis, which towered some six stories high. Although she was accustomed to the grand scale of the palace, her companions were uncharacteristically silent. Which was just as well. Perhaps the immense audacity it took to rob the Emperor was finally hitting home with them.

"Sir Valyri, if you will announce me," she murmured to the knight. He was her best chance of knowing the proper etiquette of a queen arriving at court. "Tell the steward I wish no honors and prefer to be shown directly to my quarters."

The new plan was for Valyri to separate from the party and head back down to the water, where he would secure a small, fast vessel and see to transferring all of their gear and luggage over to it. And in the meantime, she and the others would engage in a bit of felonious insanity.

Her name caused a stir at the gate, and immediately, a series of servitors rushed forward to greet her. They were taken aback at her lack of baggage and servants, and she made no explanation of her strange and tiny escort. It took nearly a half hour to wind through the palace to the chambers reserved for the king and queen of Haraland.

Blessedly, Regalo was not in residence at the moment. Last she'd heard, he'd gone back home to oversee the recruitment and drafting of the latest batch of soldiers the Empire had requisitioned from Haraland.

A messenger knocked on her chamber doors in a half hour. He was a handsome young man with dark hair and piercing blue eyes. She was sure she'd seen him before, but then the feeling slipped away. He bowed low, holding out his hand in which lay a folded and sealed sheet of parchment.

"Tell me, messenger, does the Emperor dine in-hall tonight?"

"Nay, Your Highness. He hunted with his familiars today and will dine in chambers."

Thank the Lady. She did not think she was up to shielding her thoughts from the Emperor and his cronies throughout one of the interminable feasts in the Great Hall with the entire court assembled. She murmured her thanks, and the runner backed out of the room, bowing.

The note was written in Talissar's elegant hand. He begged the pleasure of calling upon her to pay his respects. If she could receive him later this evening, he would present himself after the supper hour. She sent back a short note that it would be acceptable, as etiquette dictated.

Quickly, she changed into a gown from the supply of clothing she kept at court. It was appropriate to her rank, but was dark and plain enough not to attract attention as she moved stealthily through the palace. *Madness. This entire scheme was utter madness.* This whole venture would boil down to luck. Would Bekkan manage to spot whatever Tyviden had brought back for Maximillian?

Bekkan, Korgan, Jossa, and the thief followed her quietly as she slipped out of her chambers. Although the hour was late, the palace was still reasonably active. The Emperor rarely slept and often preferred to dine late; hence, the entire schedule of the Imperial Seat was skewed to his night-owlish ways.

The Thief in the Night lived up to his moniker and slipped along deserted hallways, blending into the shadows as if born to them. It was eerie how well he could disappear at a moment's notice. She and the others did their more amateurish best to avoid detection, dodging down side corridors when other people approached.

A few people stepped out of doorways too close to avoid, and in those cases, Gabrielle lifted her chin to its most regal tilt and dared them to question her presence in this part of the palace.

The ploy worked until a woman stepping out of a chamber practically beside her was not a servant but a Kothite noble. A high lady, no less. High-Maker Meridine, daughter of Grand Marshal Korovo and Archduchess Quaya, who ruled the Dreaming.

Meridine was leader of the Inovo, a powerful group of artificers who built the Black Ships, arcane ballistas, and any number of the highest-technology machines the Empire possessed.

And she did not step out of that doorway alone.

"Gabby!" her dear friend Sasha cried, rushing forward from the side of her husband, Rafal, to embrace her. Rafal was the ambassador from the Heartland to the Empire.

"What are you doing here?" Gabrielle asked, hoping to forestall her friend from asking the same of her.

"We're all just coming from dinner with His Resplendent Majesty in chambers," Sasha answered. "And you?"

Mentally, Gabrielle winced, praying her Octavium Pendant would hold up to any probing of her mind that Meridine might be doing at this very moment. A heartbeat too late, she answered her friend, "I've got a message from Regalo to deliver to the Emperor's secretaries. Given the late hour, I thought I would just leave it on one of their desks to find in the morning."

Gabrielle swore under her breath, feeling the slight pressure at the edges of her awareness that indicated Meridine was, indeed, poking at her mind.

"May I escort you to your destination?" Meridine offered.

"Certainly not," Gabrielle responded a shade too quickly. She silently cursed herself for her clumsiness. She added hastily, "I would not keep you from your rest. Please enjoy the remainder of your evening."

"When did you get back to court?" Sasha asked.

"Just this evening. Hence the messages to deliver."

Meridine murmured a surprised greeting to the Thief in the Night, who made a flippant reply about being unable to bear not seeing her beautiful face one moment longer and coming back to court to gaze upon Meridine's beauty. Gabrielle prayed he could shield his mind from Meridine's probing.

"I'll walk with you," Sasha said, looping her arm in Gabrielle's, "and we can catch up. My lord, I'll meet you back in our rooms in a little while. Yes?"

Rafal nodded, gesturing politely to High-Maker Meridine to precede him down the hall. "May I escort you to your chambers, my lady?"

Meridine nodded, but Gabrielle thought she detected the faintest of frowns on the Kothite woman's brow. She swore to herself. There was no way to allay Meridine's suspicions without making them worse. Their only option was to brazen out the encounter.

"Tell me what you've been up to, Sasha," Gabrielle said brightly as they headed down the hall away from Rafal and Meridine, Gabrielle's motley entourage in tow.

It took many long seconds, but at last she heard Meridine's heels clicking on the flagstone floors, retreating in the other direction.

The pair turned the corner, and Sasha immediately stopped in the middle of the hall. "What's going on, Gabby? Are you in trouble?"

"I might be."

"How can I help?" Sasha replied immediately.

The thief made a gesture behind Sasha, silently offering to slit her neck. Gabrielle spoke quickly to him. "She's one of us. No violence is necessary."

"Violence?" Sasha exclaimed. "What is going on?"

Gabrielle spoke urgently. "There's no time to explain.

Please don't ask too many questions. But we need to get into the Emperor's trophy room and have a look around."

"Good heavens—"

She cut her friend off, grabbing Sasha by the arm and dragging her down the hallway quickly toward Maximillian's trophy room.

"Gor, that was close back there," Korgan breathed.

The thief mumbled, "Self-important scion prisses."

"Enough," Gabrielle muttered. Never mind that the thief was one of those self-important prisses himself. "Hurry. We're almost there."

"Why are you breaking into the trophy room?" Sasha muttered. "This is insane."

"I know. Please trust me and don't ask any questions," Gabrielle whispered back.

The thief surprised Gabrielle by stopping her just before she turned into the broad gallery that housed their final destination. "There will likely be guards posted. Let me go first and draw them away. Slip into the trophy room while they are absent from their posts, and I will join you when I've gotten rid of the guards."

"What will you do to them?" she asked suspiciously.

He shrugged, but his smile was wolfish, and bloodlust glinted in his dark gaze.

"We're not here to kill anyone!" she exclaimed under her breath. "Do you have any idea how much attention a murder inside the palace would draw? The Emperor would be furious. He would tear open every mind in the palace in search of the killer."

The thief ignored her and slipped around the corner, out of sight.

Swearing under her breath, Gabrielle peeked around the corner.

His voice floated back to her. "Huh. No guards. Arrogant whoreson must think no one would be foolish enough to rob him."

Gabrielle hurried after him. When she reached the thief, who stood in front of the closed doors to the trophy room, she replied sourly, "Or perhaps the protections upon this room are so great that he has no need to post guards."

Jossa stepped forward and examined the door closely. "I have extensive knowledge of warding magics, and I see none upon this door. Can anyone here detect traps?"

The thief grinned. "I might have a bit of skill in that regard. And I can assure you, there are none upon this portal. There's not even a lock on the door. Of course, roaming parties of the Hand come through here every quarter hour or so."

"How soon will one of those patrols be coming by?" Gabrielle asked nervously. The Hand were Maximillian's personally selected and trained bodyguards, fanatics one and all, the fiercest and most capable warriors in the entire Empire. They had a decided tendency to kill first and ask questions later.

"We're within a few minutes of a patrol passing this spot."

She looked both ways in alarm. "No one told me—"

"You had no need to know. In we go." The thief boldly reached for the great bronze door handle and opened the door.

No explosions or warded alarms went off. No traps sent deadly bolts at them. Not even the slightest flash of magic lit the darkness. The room beyond lay still and silent, illuminated only by faint moonlight coming in through the high windows at the far end of the vaulted chamber.

"I hear someone coming," Jossa whispered urgently.

Gabrielle bolted forward into the trophy room with the others close behind. The thief closed the door quickly, easing it shut at the last moment.

They stood frozen just inside the door, holding their collective breath as several pairs of boots marched down the hall and stopped outside the very door they leaned against. She counted each agonizing second in her head. At long last, the boots finally started to move again, marching away at an unhurried pace from their hiding spot.

Gabrielle's heart was pounding out of her chest. She was no good at this stealth stuff. The iron band that often constricted around her chest was making itself known, and she took several slow breaths, holding them as long as she could before exhaling.

Jossa said in wonder, "This place is huge. We'd better split up to hunt for clues to Bekkan's king. Otherwise, we'll still be here in the morning when they open the place up."

Gabrielle nodded and everyone scattered into the deceptively large space. It was so crowded with display cases, tables, stands, and cluttered trophies that the room felt much smaller than it actually was.

"What on Urth are you up to?" Sasha demanded.

"We're looking for whatever Tyviden Starfire brought back from the Sea of Glass."

"Can I help?" Sasha asked gamely.

Gratitude washed over Gabrielle. "If you see anything that looks like it comes from there, tell me."

"Ooh. A scavenger hunt. What fun," Sasha said cheerfully, taking off down one of the long rows of treasures.

Gabrielle wandered the rows of collectibles as well. Her mind boggled at the wealth: huge shelves of books, exotic stuffed beasts, jewelry, fossils, weapons of unbelievable beauty, even gems of every size, color, and composition were collected here.

"This," Bekkan said abruptly from the next row over. She slipped between a set of glassed-in cases and moved to stand beside him in front of a display of minerals.

He was pointing at a fist-sized lump of something black that shone faintly iridescent in the scant light. "What is it?" she asked.

"Septallum. The giant-made metal that runs in my king's veins—" Bekkan started.

The thief appeared at Bekkan's other side, interrupting, "We can discuss its properties later. Take it and move along."

"We're not here to take anything—" she started.

The thief picked up the rock and thrust it into Bekkan's hand. She sputtered as the rokken traded grins with the thief and the two men moved away from her. But that wasn't the plan!

She couldn't exactly argue in here and risk being overheard. Furious and more terrified than ever, she moved deeper into the great room.

"Gor, will ye look at that?" Korgan exclaimed under his breath ahead of her, staring up high on a wall where a pair of swords were mounted next to an empty hanger for a third sword. "Those be the great swords of the dwarven kings—Deep Fang and Battle Brand."

"Where's King Eitrik's sword, Mountain's Edge?" Bekkan asked.

The thief answered, "It was never found. The Emperor has offered a ten thousand gold reward for it, though."

Gabrielle blurted, "That's enough to buy a small kingdom!"

"Aye," the thief answered dryly. "Apparently, he *really* wants to complete the set."

Bekkan's gaze hardened. "As long as I draw breath, my king's sword shall not end up on that wall. By the giants below, I vow I'll find it myself and put it back into his waiting hands."

"Does anybody know what those are?" Jossa asked, pointing at a series of old-fashioned-looking keys hanging from big iron rings.

The thief answered, "Keys to other planes. The milky crystal ones are keys to the dream realm. And those brightly colored ones should lead to the fae realm."

Gabrielle's gaze snapped to the gem-encrusted, whimsically shaped fae keys. What she wouldn't give to use one to go to the Blue Court. To see her children. To hug them and tell them how sorry she was that she couldn't keep them at home and raise them herself. Her gaze drifted to the next ring of keys, made of some cold, black stone that gave off no light whatsoever. It took no great scholarly skill to guess which realm those led to. She shuddered at the Void keys and turned away as Jossa reached out to caress the sparkling fae keys longingly.

A tinkle of crystal made Gabrielle look up sharply. Near the throne room doors sat a table carved entirely of pale jade, and upon it sat a huge bowl of faintly glowing crystals. Korgan was running his fingers through the gems, each varying slightly in hue and shape from its neighbors.

"Those aren't what we seek," she told the dwarf. "They're Mindori mind crystals. The Emperor's chamberlain told me that each one holds the memories and essence of a famous or important paxan."

"There must be five hundred of 'em here!" Korgan exclaimed. He started to put the handful of stones back, but then tilted his head to one side, as if listening. "Ye hear that?" he murmured.

"Hear what?" she asked quickly.

"They're whispering to me."

"What are they say—" She broke off. "Never mind. They're not what we came for."

She turned away, and when she glanced back, Korgan's hand was in his pocket, and he wore a smug look on his face.

Bekkan swore from just beyond Korgan, where the golden doors to Maximillian's private throne room loomed. She knew what must have caught his attention. The Man in Amber, he who stood eternal sentinel beside the doors.

"I know him," Bekkan rasped, his voice rough with grief and rage. "What did they do to him?"

The Man in Amber was as old as Bekkan? That poor man had been trapped in there for *five thousand years*? Appalled, Gabrielle answered, "He's said to be alive, trapped in amber to serve as a reminder to all of what happens to those who resist Koth."

Sasha, who'd been drawn to the commotion, gasped as she spied the Man in Amber. "He looks so much like Rafal!"

Gabrielle studied the face behind the amber prison and started. He did look like Rafal. They could be *brothers*.

"Who is this man?" Sasha demanded. "Surely he's related to my husband."

Bekkan answered, "His name is Inan Domitri, commander of the Order of the Thorn."

Gabrielle could swear she saw joy flare in the unmoving eyes of the Man in Amber, as if he'd heard his name uttered for the first time in a very, very long time. At least the name of his order explained the rose insignia on the man's chest, the thorns on its stems more prominent than usual in depictions of roses.

"What is this Order of the Thorn?" Sasha asked.

Bekkan answered, "They were the personal guards assigned to Princess Raisa."

"Princess who?" Sasha echoed.

Gabrielle answered, "A people called the etheri ruled this continent until the Kothites came about five thousand years ago and conquered them. This princess would have been one of the last members of the royal family of the etheri."

"How does my husband look practically like his twin?"

Gabrielle frowned up at the Man in Amber. "Perhaps Rafal is a descendant of this man."

Bekkan said, "Inan and Raisa were lovers. They had no children, although there were rumors at the time of the invasion by Koth that she carried his child. She never gave birth to that babe, however."

Sasha frowned. "The Heart has protected the bloodline of Rafal's family for a long time. I will speak with our genealogists upon my return to the Heartland," she declared. She paused for a moment, then asked, "Can he hear us?"

The thief answered, "Absolutely. Preservation in amber is performed specifically to keep the subject alive inside the amber sarcophagus. It is traditionally done for the subject's protection until medical care can be obtained."

Sasha said to the trapped man, "Now that I know you are here, I assure you, sir, the Heart will do everything in its power to have you released."

The thief snorted. "If Maximillian's kept him in there this long, what makes you think he'll release this fellow now? The Emperor obviously has some compelling reason for keeping him trapped."

Bekkan stared up at Inan and said to him in a ravaged voice, "I was trapped like you in copper for five thousand years and more, brother, and I have recently been released. I remember you. I know your name. Memory of Inan Domitri lives once more. And I will find a way to get you out of there.

Have hope, my old friend, and be strong." He reached up to lay his hand on the amber just where the trapped man's upheld hand came close to the surface of the stone.

"No!" the thief exclaimed.

But too late. Bekkan's palm closed on the amber.

A surge of energy rolled forth from the stone, filling the trophy room with warm, golden light for an instant, leaving a glittering haze behind Gabrielle's eyelids as she looked away from the dazzling flash.

When she could see again, Bekkan was on his knees in front of the Man in Amber. She rushed forward to his side. "Are you all right?"

"Yes. Fine," he gasped, clearly not all right. "He just sent me a . . . deluge . . . of images. Memories, I think."

As if Bekkan wasn't struggling enough already with sorting out his own memories. Lovely.

"We've got trouble!" the thief called out. "That burst of light has caught someone's attention. The Hand are coming. On the run. Three, no four, of them."

She did not know how he could tell how many guards were coming or how fast, but she believed him. "We must hide!" she whispered frantically.

"They'll know every inch of this place. Our only hope is to brazen it out," the thief retorted.

She couldn't do it! No excuse could explain their presence, pawing through Maximillian's private treasures in the middle of the night. The guards would know they didn't belong here. The Hand would search the party and find the piece of septallum, and who knew what else the others in the party might have shoved into their pockets. Her breath accelerated hard. She would be dragged in front of the Emperor, her mind torn open—her breath became shallow and ineffective—and the whole conspiracy would be revealed.

"Hide!" she gasped.

This was all her fault! She'd told them not to touch anything, but they hadn't listened to her. She should have been more forceful. Used her rank to order them . . .

The room began to spin gently, and bright spots twinkled

behind her eyelids. She stumbled, fetching up hard against Sasha. Her friend steadied her, propping her against the nearest solid vertical object, the Man in Amber.

A surge of awareness rushed through her of another mind, another person's thoughts intruding upon hers. Oddly enough, the presence was comforting. The word *breathe* drifted through her mind. Then, two words. *In. Out.* Was the Man in Amber coaching her on how to manage her shortness-of-breath affliction?

Stunned, she could only watch on as the doors to the trophy room opened and four men rushed into the chamber, swords drawn and torches held high. They were of the Hand, all right. There was no mistaking the gaudy black armor trimmed in gold and red, the Imperial flames climbing their armor in sinuous lines. Not to mention their height and bulk and speed.

Oh, this was not good. Her companions were dead if they engaged these men, which, with their impetuous natures, they surely would. They were all going to be snared and slaughtered like so many helpless creatures.

This was the end.

Time slowed in her mind. A strange peace came over her. The only strong emotion that remained was regret. Regret that she hadn't been able to spend more time with her children over the years. That she hadn't been a better mother to them. Funny how facing death stripped away everything else and left behind only the essential truths.

She closed her eyes tightly, sending out her love to her children. If only she could go to them, to tell them how dearly she held them and how sorely she missed them—

Another flash of light startled her. A great circular cataract opened behind her, the cobalt blue of a hot flame around the edge. An opulent ballroom was visible beyond, populated with dozens of beautifully dressed people of exotic races and shapes and colors she'd never seen before staring back at her, fully as surprised to see her as she was to see them.

A young man and a young woman, both human in appearance, stepped through the portal.

"Who goes there?" the Hand shouted. "On your knees! Hands on your heads!"

Neither young person obeyed the commands. Rather, they looked around, clearly perplexed until their gazes lit on Gabrielle.

"Mother?" the young man asked in disbelief.

"Roland?" she gasped. By the Lady, he had the look of Regalo in face, build, and bearing. *So handsome.* Her baby boy had become a man.

She stepped toward her son, and the soldiers behind her shouted, "Get down or die!"

She looked at the young woman hopefully. "Giselle?"

"Mama." The young woman smiled.

"Take them!" the soldier shouted.

The young woman frowned as Gabrielle gathered all her strength to fling herself in front of her children in a last act of defiance. *The Hand would not kill her babies while she yet lived.* Gabrielle made eye contact with her children and smiled serenely, at peace with giving her life to save theirs, if only to extend theirs for a few seconds more.

Roland murmured loudly just enough to be heard by Gabrielle and her co-conspirators in a tone that brooked no disobedience, "You might want to cover your ears."

Shocked, Gabrielle did as he said, only vaguely managing to question how he was able to compel her to do as he said like that. Her hands came up over her ears just as Giselle opened her mouth and began to sing.

Through her palms, she heard faint strains of a song so hauntingly beautiful it made Gabrielle literally weep. Tears streamed down her face as the song continued, what little she heard of it weaving its way into her soul, leaving it forever changed, charmed, and enchanted, wishing only to listen to that melody forever.

Giselle stopped singing, and Gabrielle cautiously uncovered her ears, stunned to realize that all four soldiers of the Hand lay crumpled on the floor unconscious. "What was that, daughter? It was the saddest and most beautiful thing I have ever heard."

The thief chuckled quietly from behind Gabrielle. "Oh, well done, mademoiselle. Well done, indeed. I have heard tales of the Siren's Song, but never did I think them true until now."

Giselle rushed forward, and Gabrielle flung her arms around her daughter, more tears joining those from the song. Roland joined the embrace, and she hugged them both with all her strength.

At length, Giselle asked, "What's wrong, Mama? Why did you summon us to you?"

Gabrielle lifted her face from her daughter's shoulder to stare at both of her children. "I summoned you?"

"You activated a portal to the Blue Court directly in front of the two of us," Roland affirmed.

"But how? I merely wished to see you both once more before I died to tell you how very much I love you——" Her voice broke on the words.

"Die?" Roland asked quickly.

The thief spoke up. "Thanks to your sister's exquisite voice, we've bought ourselves a few minutes. Those soldiers were about to slay us all where we stood. We still must make our escape. More guards will come when these do not report in."

"Let us go, and quickly," Gabrielle said.

"One moment, Mother," Roland murmured. He stepped back to the cataract of the portal and reached his hand through it briefly. When he pulled his arm back, the portal collapsed with the sound of a bubble popping, and in his hand Gabrielle spied the brightly bejeweled ring of fae keys off the trophy room wall.

They hurried across the large trophy room to the hallway exit. She gasped for air but did her best to keep up with the others. Sasha, bless her, stayed behind to help her along.

Korgan reached the doors first and inched them open. "Hall's clear."

The dwarf slipped outside with Jossa hard on his heels. Next came Bekkan and then Sasha, Gabrielle, and her children. The thief paused to scoop up something that had dropped and rolled away from one of the unconscious soldiers of the

Hand. She didn't stop to wait for him. He could take care of himself.

As they moved into the gallery and hurried away from the trophy room, Gabrielle asked her daughter quickly, "What did you do to those men?"

"I merely sang them to sleep," Giselle answered playfully.

Gabrielle had never heard of such a thing, but she supposed it was possible that her daughter might have learned the trick of it in a fae court.

"And," Giselle added lightly, "I added a verse to my song to erase their memories of the past hour or so. They'll wake up with no recollection of having seen us."

Impressed, Gabrielle squeezed Giselle's hand. "You must tell me how you learned to do that later. When we are safe."

"Where are we?" Giselle asked curiously.

"The Imperial wing of the Imperial palace," Gabrielle murmured.

"I gather we're not supposed to be here?" Roland responded.

"Correct. It's a long story. If we make it out of here alive, I'll be happy to share it with you," she told her son.

They followed the others back the way they'd come and almost reached the main corridor when a lone figure rounded the corner, stopping accusingly in front of them. *High-Maker Meridine.*

"What are you really doing here?" she demanded. "I just asked one of the Emperor's secretaries if they leave their office unlocked of a night, and they do not. You could not leave a message for Maximillian on one of their desks even if that was really what you were up to. If you have fallen under the influence of someone else again, I can help you—"

The thief stepped forward, moving so unnaturally fast that Gabrielle could barely see the blur of motion, and thrust his sword into the woman's belly.

Meridine stared at the thief in shock. "How dare you! What have you done?"

Another lightning-fast movement and the thief's sword slashed across her neck. A thick welling of blood announced the lethality of the strike. The Kothite woman fell to her knees, making gurgling noises that might have been shouts for help had her vocal cords not have been cut.

She pitched forward face-first onto the floor. A pool of blood spread rapidly under her.

It all happened so fast that Gabrielle barely had time to register what she had just witnessed. "Are you mad?" she demanded of the thief as she fumbled in her pouch for a life spell.

Sasha reached forward, hands already glowing with spirit magic, and began to incant a life spell.

"Don't bother," the thief said curtly, knocking Sasha's hands aside. "I've got this."

Except, instead of pouring a life potion down Meridine's eviscerated throat, the thief thrust a large stone vessel forward toward the corpse and yanked off its lid.

The vessel was pointed on the bottom so it could not be set down like a regular jug. It was about half the length of the thief's arm, tall and narrow with long, narrow handles down each side of its even narrower neck.

An amphora.

Surely not.

"No!" Sasha cried.

As the lid opened, a black flame jumped up from the neck of the vessel. Gabrielle recognized it in shock to be one of *those* amphoras. The kind that carried a small portion of the Eternal Flame within them.

"No!" she had time to cry before the thief thrust the amphora and flame out over Meridine's chest.

Even she, with no skill at all in spirit magics, saw the wispy essence of the Kothite's spirit draw toward the flame like smoke to a draft, adhering to the Flame, entangling the two energies, black and white, life and death, Spirit and Void.

And then, just like that, the spirit vanished, blinking out of existence, consumed by the flame. Where Meridine's body had lain in a pool of blood seconds before, there was nothing. *Nothing.* No body. No blood. Not even a dusting of ash. The Kothite High-Maker was simply gone.

The thief slapped the lid back on the amphora, and the hall's torches guttered heavily as if a great wind had passed through.

"What. Did. You. Do?" Gabrielle demanded in a terrible voice. "You've killed us all."

Will enjoyed the barge ride up the river that natives of the Valelands called simply the Lance. It traversed a great valley sandwiched between two snowcapped mountain ranges that was lush with the coming of spring, bursting with pale green buds on trees, new grass sprouting bright green underfoot, and gentle sunshine contrasting with the as yet cool air. He reluctantly conceded that this was as beautiful a place as he'd ever seen, mayhap even more so than his beloved Wylde Wold.

A team of mules pulled their barge upriver at a steady pace, the teams switched out every six hours or so, around the clock. As a result, they made excellent time inland, and the western reaches of the Valelands where the two mountain ranges came together loomed around them when he woke on the morning of the fifth day.

The northern terminus of the Lance was a village named Rondell. It consisted entirely of sturdy wooden buildings with shingled walls and roofs. Doors, window frames, and roof peaks were adorned with intricate wood carvings of animals, trees, seashells, moons, and other fanciful shapes. The streets were tidy, the people rosy cheeked and hearty.

What would it be like to settle in a place like this with Rosana, to raise a family, maybe take up a trade? He could see it clearly in his mind's eye. It would be a good life. Solid. Respectable. Quiet—and that sounded heavenly right about now.

Abruptly, his parents' decision to live in Hickory Hollow made sense. He cursed under his breath. His whole life, he'd railed at them for sticking him out in the middle of nowhere, cutting him off from the rest of the world, withholding opportunities for education and advancement of his talent for magic.

But now, he understood. Too late, but he understood.

"Where to now?" Sha'Li, ever the practical one, asked as they stepped ashore.

Rynn answered, "The best place to get information and hear the local tales is at a pub. Preferably one that draws bards and storytellers."

The barge captain was only too happy to tell them Rondell was home to two pubs. One was mostly an inn catering to travelers off the barges, and the other, the Lusty Maiden, catered to local residents. It was known for tasty ale and the occasional brawl. It was to this pub they headed.

It was afternoon yet, and the Maiden was mostly empty. They ordered food and pints of ale they sipped slowly, nursing them along until the locals started to knock off work and fill the pub. The patrons didn't seem to mind the party of young travelers sitting quietly in the corner near the bard's platform.

Tonight's entertainment turned out to be a gray-bearded singer who played a stringed instrument that he laid across his lap and strummed in time with his songs. He performed harmless songs about love and springtime, and he ended his set with a raucous drinking tune that had the patrons pounding their mugs on the wooden tables and demanding refills.

As he stepped off the stage, Will shouted over the din, "Can we buy you a drink?"

"I'll never say no to free ale," the bard replied, sliding onto a bench beside Rosana, where she moved aside to make room for him.

Will hated it when she batted her long lashes at other men, but the singer was old enough to be her grandfather, and Will tamped down his jealousy.

Rosana chatted up the singer, drawing forth that the man was a native of Rondell, had been a bard for forty years and more, and made a hobby of composing epic lays. Apparently, the local histories were being lost at an alarming rate, and he did his best to preserve them by setting them to music.

Rynn asked, "Have you ever heard of an ancient elf called Eliassan?"

The fellow burst out laughing. "Gads, man. Everyone knows the song of Eliassan and his magic bow."

Rosana asked sweetly, "Will you sing it for us after your break?"

"For you, my lovely, I will. But I'll be needing another ale to whet my whistle first. It's a long and complicated piece, you know."

Rynn dug out the coin to buy the fellow a pint of honeyed mead, a drink that was smoother and easier on the throat by far than the local ale, which was dark and strong.

The singer finished his mead with a smack of the lips, climbed back onto the tiny stage, and commenced singing the lay of Eliassan. The pub went quiet, the patrons listening with rapt attention to the tale.

Will was familiar with the general story of Gawaine's fall, although the singer's song did not name the ancient elven king who fell in battle against the evil troll king. In a dramatic verse, the elven king's bow fell from his dying fingers and was scooped up by a young page, Eliassan, carried away to safety before the trolls could take it. Without a king to defend the land, trolls raged across it, and only the boy Eliassan had the courage to face the cruel invaders. The song described a magic quiver of arrows, where every arrow fired assumed the magical quality necessary to do most harm to its intended target.

Furthermore, the song described how the magic bow never missed its target. Will wondered if that was a function of Eliassan being an accomplished archer or some innate quality of the bow itself. He wouldn't put it past Gawaine to own a bow that never missed.

The song shifted to an attempt by the fae to steal the bow, and the pub's patrons leaned in toward the singer, holding their breath as the dastardly attempt to steal the bow was foiled at the last minute by a beautiful fae woman who'd fallen deeply in love with Eliassan and betrayed her people in the name of love. *A dryad, maybe?*

In a last-ditch effort to take the bow, the song told of a monster unleashed by the fae upon the Valelands to kill Eliassan. In the final verses of the song, Eliassan, by now an old man, defeated the beast, married the fae woman, and lived happily ever after in the ever-greening woods of the Vale.

Cheers, stomping feet, and pounding mugs erupted as the bard fell silent. The innkeeper must be loving this singer as shouts for refills on the ale rang throughout the pub. Rynn signaled for another mead and set it down before the singer.

As the bard hunkered down beside Rosana, he asked, "Did you like my song, fair gypsy maiden?"

"I loved it!" She batted her eyelashes and asked the man, "Where is the ever-greening woods of the Vale you sang of? Oh, I'd so love to visit it and feel the magic of Eliassan's eternal love for his fae lady."

"Surely it is the Wychwold the song refers to. For it is a magical and ancient forest, lush and green all the year round and said to be inhabited by fae creatures."

Will asked a little gruffly, "Have you personally seen any of these alleged fae creatures of which you sang?"

The singer's eyes twinkled. "The monster, no. But the ladies of the woods, I have seen, indeed. It turns out the green ladies of the trees love a good tune and will oft come out to hear me sing when I play in the wood."

Hah. So the fae ladies *were* dryads!

Rynn asked, "Do you know more of the monster that was sent to defeat Eliassan than was mentioned in the song?"

The singer shrugged. "Only that he was a great, terrible, clawed beast that killed many people. He was said to have destroyed entire villages in his rampage before Eliassan caught up with him."

That sounded more like a hungry bear than a magical beast to Will. Testing that theory, he asked, "Did the beast leave any marks behind, tracks or claw marks that might give away its size and shape?"

The singer blinked, surprised. "I have heard a song that

described his paws as being the width of four men's hands and his shoulders half again the height of a man. Let me see. How did the verse go . . ." After a moment, he recited:

> The great beast of the fane came forth
> Furied eyes red with rage and wroth,
> Withers half again the height of a man,
> With claws four times a man's hand span.
> By the new moon's light he came.
> All who fought, he did kill and maim.
> Until Eliassan with his great bow
> Did at long last lay the fae beast low.

Kendrick asked in a tense voice, "Red eyes, you say?"

"Aye. That's how the verse goes."

"And you're sure it was a new moon by which the beast came and not a full moon?" Kendrick challenged.

The singer threw up his hands. "I only recite the verse as I was taught it. I was not there to witness the beast, boy."

Rynn asked in a soothing tone, "What is this fane the verse mentions?"

"Ah, well," the singer answered confidently, "fanes were sacred places to the fae when they roamed these lands long, long ago. All the fanes but one were destroyed long before any living now have memory of them."

"And the last fane?" Will asked.

A shrug from the singer. "Rumor has it a single fane still exists deep in the Wychwold, protected from the eyes of man by fae enchantments and guarded by a beast much like the one Eliassan slew."

"Where exactly in the wold is this place?"

"I'm sure I haven't a clue," the singer answered a bit testily.

Rynn pushed another mug of mead across the table. "Thank you for bearing our interrogation with such good humor, sir. Have another mead. And perhaps you could be persuaded to sing a song or two more?"

The singer chose a rousing song telling of the conquest of Pan Orda by the great Kothite General Tarses, and Will wasn't surprised to see Eben taking particular note of the story tonight. Nor was Will surprised to catch Eben slipping a silver coin into the bard's palm when the song concluded.

Morning brought a blindingly raucous chorus of birdsong. Or mayhap that was the aftereffects of too much ale making the sun so bright and the birds so loud.

The Wychwold lay to the north of the Lance, so it was in that direction they hiked. The terrain was hilly, but not so rugged as to make walking impossible. Broad, well-trodden trails of packed dirt led into the wold, and they followed a northbound one, grateful for the easy going.

The trees here were ancient and huge, a variety of northern species that had not seen the ravages of the Forester's Guild. Many of the towering trunks would have taken everyone in the party clasping hands together to span, and some trees, even then, they would not have encompassed. The undulating ground was covered with a velvet carpet of bright green moss that grew over the low boulders and up the trunks of many trees, as well. A light fog clung to the hollows and valleys they passed even into midday, lending a mystical quality to the place. Dappled sunlight flickered around them, and he breathed deeply of the clean, pine-scented air. A great sense of well-being came over him.

"I like this place," Rosana announced as they stopped to eat lunch.

"Could you see yourself living here one day?" Will asked.

"I could." She added a shade cautiously, "What about you?"

"Me, too."

Rosana's cheeks turned pink, and she looked away shyly. Did he dare hope that she might be hinting that she would look favorably upon a proposal from him? And that she might also be thinking about what a pleasant home this area would make? Hope leaped in his chest, and his steps were so buoyant after the meal that the others badgered him to slow down as he led them through the forest.

They made camp along the trail that night, and the next evening brought them to a prosperous-looking homestead constructed of great logs chinked with stripes of white clay. The owner and his wife invited them to stay the night, offering Will and the others use of their log barn and a pile of clean straw for bedding.

A half dozen children ran around the yard, laughing and shouting as the older ones did chores and the two youngest, boys, fought with wooden swords. Will vaguely remembered doing the exact same thing in his youth.

For her part, Rosana looked wistful.

"Why the sad eyes, Rosie?" he asked her.

"I always wanted to live in a family like this."

"Maybe you'll have your own someday."

She glanced up at him shyly. "That would be wonderful."

Exultation roared through him. She was definitely hinting that she would accept a proposal from him. Now to find the right engagement gift for her. Simple jewelry wouldn't do the trick. He needed to think of something meaningful to both of them. And then they could leave off quests and adventures and build a life like this for themselves. He smiled as he looked around the clearing.

Rynn and Sha'Li went hunting, bringing back a brace of rabbits and a large bird the farmer called a turkey for their supper. Rosana helped the man's wife pluck the bird while Will and the farmer skinned and dressed the rabbits. The domesticity of it all was almost more comfortable than Will could stand.

After supper, Rynn pulled out the skin of mead he'd purchased at the pub in Rondell and poured mugs of it for their hosts. The liquor did its job and loosened the farmer's tongue as the volume of liquid in the skin decreased.

Rynn asked the farmer, "What do you know of the Wychwold fae?"

"I see them from time to time. Mostly up in the hills north of here. Sometimes it's them green witches; other times it's those half-goat fellows they run with."

Satyrs? Will had never seen one in the flesh. Apparently, they had much the same charm effect on female humans as dryads had on human males.

Rynn nodded. "Have you ever spoken with them?"

"Naw. I look away and make haste for home when they come out. They don't cause trouble as long as we leave them alone, but I've no wish to tangle with their magics. It isn't natural, the way they step in and out of solid trees."

Will knew the phenomenon well. It did look strange to see a dryad pass through a solid tree and yet remain solid herself.

Rynn asked, "Have you ever heard of a place particularly dear to the fae in these parts? Maybe a place where they gather?"

"If there's such a place, it would be to the north of here, in the heart of the Wychwold. That's where every fae sighting I've ever heard of has been."

Will asked, "How far from here is the center of the wold?"

"Two, maybe three days' walk, depending on how hale the hiker is."

Kendrick piped up, asking, "Have you ever seen any magical creatures besides dryads and satyrs? Monsters, perhaps? Furry beasts with big claws?"

"Naw, but I've heard of such. Farmer about a day's walk north of here was killed by some strange creature a while back. Way I heard it, four great claws tore him open from belly button to collarbone."

"What did the beast look like?"

"No one saw it. They just found him dead and shredded."

Will was skeptical of the magical monster. A man from the hollow had been attacked by a bear when he was a boy, and his body had looked much as the farmer described. But Kendrick seemed agitated by the description. Did he know something he wasn't sharing with the others? Had Kerryl been up here and created some great, hulking were-creature in this forest and then lost control of it?

When they retired to the barn, Will asked Kendrick, "What do you think of this beast the farmer spoke of?"

"If it's a were-creature, it's not of Kerryl's making. Maybe it's one of the fae beasts the bard in Rondell sang of."

Sha'Li responded, "Yes, but the song only spoke of one beast, and Eliassan killed it."

"Would that we were so fortunate," Rosana retorted. "With our luck, we'll get to this fane place, and there will be ten of them guarding it."

Will laughed. "Have a little faith, Rosie. We've defeated great, hulking monsters before."

"Yes, but we don't have Raina with us anymore to continually heal us," she replied.

Rynn said, "That reminds me. On the barge, I was able to purchase a brace of healing potions." He passed out several healing potions to each member of the party, and Will carefully tucked his away in an inside pocket of his belt pouch, where he would be able to find them easily should he need one.

"And for you, Rosana," Rynn said, "I was able to buy three life potions." He offered them to her with a little bow as she squealed in pleasure. Will gritted his teeth, but at least she didn't throw herself at the paxan and hug him.

A deep bed of straw in the farmer's barn proved to be both warm and comfortable, and they all benefited from a full night's sleep. They barred the barn door from the inside and did not take turns sitting a night watch. Rather, they let the farmer's dogs act as sentries.

As dawn broke the next day, they insisted that the farmer's wife take two gold coins for the food she'd packed for them. Will knew they had given the family nearly enough coin to pay their taxes for the entire year, which would ease the family's lives considerably in the coming months. They would not have to worry about failed crops or one of their children being taken into slavery this year.

With hugs all around, they departed for the heart of the Wychwold, following the detailed instructions the farmer gave them.

The first time they stopped to drink and refill their waterskins at a cold, fast-running stream, Eben crouched beside Will, holding his skin under the water and murmuring, "I'm worried about Kendrick."

Will was aware that Kendrick had barely spoken at all since they left the Sorrow Wold and he'd separated from Kerryl. "I don't know what we're supposed to do about him," Will muttered back. "It's not like we can give him back his were-curse."

"Nor would I if I could," Eben replied quickly.

"Have you tried talking to him?" Will asked. "You know him better than all of us."

"He won't listen to me. Says I'm biased."

Will grunted. "You are. He's your brother, and you want him to be his old self. Thing is, Eben, we've all changed. This quest of ours, it's bigger than any of us."

Eben trailed his fingers in the cold water, a sign of just how worried he was about Kendrick. He never touched water voluntarily.

Will sighed. "You didn't think waking Gawaine would be free, did you? We're all paying a price each in our own way. You've lost more than most of us, and you've just gotten your brother back. Of course you want to hold on to him tightly."

"I'm worried he's going to harm himself," Eben confessed.

"Do you want me to talk to him?"

Eben glanced up, making brief eye contact, then looking away. "You'd better not. He resents the fact that you've still got your connection to Bloodroot."

Will snorted. "Like that's any great blessing. I fight all the time to contain his rage and jealousy. Every day I fear he's going to get the best of me and that I'll cease to exist."

Eben stared at him. "Really?"

Will stood upright, scuffing dead leaves into the stream and watching the rushing torrent carry them away. "Yeah, really," he answered gruffly.

"I never knew. If you ever need help, someone to steady you or for you to pummel, let me know."

His throat tight, Will squeezed the jann's shoulder briefly as he turned away. Eben didn't understand. His urge wasn't to hit someone. His urge was to kill.

* * *

"What have you *done*?" Gabrielle repeated, in a whisper this time, her voice threatening to break over into hysteria.

Sasha was hysterical, wringing her hands and wailing under her breath about Maximillian destroying them all.

The thief answered a touch wildly, "What I've done is kill a Kothite high lady. In Maximillian's private wing of the palace, no less. Let the whoreson chew on that!"

This mission was not supposed to be about revenge! It was not supposed to even catch the Emperor's notice. But the thief had changed that with his impulsive murder. Assuming it was impulsive at all. Suspicion blossomed in her gut. Why had the thief refused to go on this mission if Sir Valyri been along? Did the thief have something like this in mind the whole time?

For his part, Bekkan shrugged, unconcerned. "Only good Kothite is a dead Kothite if you ask me."

Sasha muttered, "They'll know already, Korovo and Quaya. When Kothites create a child, they give part of their own spirits and powers to it. They'll have felt the loss. They *know*."

"You've ruined everything," Gabrielle accused the thief. "Centuries of work. Hundreds of lives sacrificed for *nothing* because of you."

"Shall we debate that later?" the thief responded lightly. "For the moment, I suggest we run."

Curse him to the darkest corner of the Void!

They did run then.

Such was her shock at the murder she had just witnessed that Gabrielle's airways opened wide and she was able to sprint along with the others around the corner and into the main corridor behind Bekkan.

They'd only been running a half minute or so, though, when the thief announced, "I hear someone coming from ahead of us."

They screeched to a halt, every one of them breathing hard. No way would even the most casual observer fail to notice it.

Bekkan looked around quickly. "This way," he said urgently.

He reversed direction and all but plowed into her. "Quick. Back the other way! There used to be an entrance to the servant tunnels behind us."

They'd all raced back the other way perhaps a hundred feet and turned down a poorly lit side hall when Bekkan stopped abruptly, frowning. Gabrielle managed not to run into him, but Korgan did slam into her and nearly knocked her off her feet. Thankfully, Roland's reflexes were fast, and he grabbed her arm in time to keep her upright.

Bekkan ducked into a niche behind a full suit of armor that belonged to some dead Kothite general.

"What are you doing?" she demanded in rising panic.

Bekkan, who'd been feeling along the wall behind the statue, pushed against the wall with both fists, and a door-sized portion of the wall swung inward. *A secret passageway.*

The Emperor was rumored to have an entire network of them, but she'd never met anyone who had been in one or even seen one.

"Quickly, my lady. Everybody inside."

She slid past Bekkan and was followed by Korgan, Jossa, Sasha, Giselle, Roland, and the thief. Bekkan put his shoulder into the panel, sliding it shut as voices drew near.

The darkness was complete, so thick and stifling that her breathing grew quick and labored with panic, and the iron band of fear tightened around her chest once more, even worse than before. *Not now.*

She heard fumbling, and then a spark flashed in the dark.

A small hand torch flared, and Bekkan grinned over it. "What kind of dwarf would I be if I didn't have a torch at hand?"

"Bless you," Gabrielle responded fervently.

Korgan muttered, "Give me a second here. I've got torches enough for the lot of you." Small hand torches were passed around and lit.

The thief raised his torch high, peering down the narrow tunnel. "This place is clean. No dust. It's obviously still used frequently."

Gabrielle said, "If Sasha's right about Korovo and Quaya,

there will be guards crawling all over the palace soon searching for clues as to what happened to Meridine. Questions will be asked. We have to get out of these tunnels, and all of us have to get as far away from here as we can before anyone decides to have a look around inside our minds."

Bekkan turned to peer into the darkness. "Up ahead, there's another passage heading off to our left. I think it leads to the south wing of the palace, where your quarters are, my lady."

Praise the Lady. Her children might yet survive this evening alive. For them, she would press on, air in her lungs or not. She followed Bekkan as he took off down the tunnel. They came to an intersection, and the rokken turned left down another long corridor.

Bekkan paused at another intersection to peer at a bunch of scratch marks on the wall that looked vaguely like runes. "This way." He turned right and went a little way, stopping before a narrow, circular staircase barely wider than Gabrielle's shoulders.

"If I have not lost my bearings, your chambers are at the top of that stair, my lady."

Gabrielle was deeply alarmed to realize that the Emperor or his agents could have been using this passage to spy on her and Regalo for years, and she and her husband had been none the wiser.

"This is where I leave you all," the thief announced. "How do I get to an exit that brings me out near the south bridge of the Imperial Plaza?"

"Take this tunnel to the end and turn right, then take your first left. Go to the end and climb the stairs there. You'll come out next to the south gatehouse."

The thief gave Gabrielle a small bow, touched his brow in a mockery of an Imperial military salute, and raced off down the hall so fast Gabrielle hardly had time to register that he was leaving before he was gone from view.

"Man, that guy's fast," Korgan muttered.

She was more inclined to mutter something along the lines of *good riddance*.

Bekkan turned sideways to go up the stair, and she followed carefully, feeling for each new step with her foot since her skirts were too big to see past. *Stupid court fashions.*

Bekkan halted abruptly in front of her. He whispered over his shoulder, "Were you expecting company tonight?"

"No," she answered, startled.

"Then I'll go first," Bekkan declared, easing his sword out of its sheath at his waist, a feat to accomplish in silence in the confined quarters. "I hear voices."

"No. I'll go first. You're a thousand times more important than I," she disagreed. "And these are my quarters. No one will question me stepping into my own rooms. The rest of you could be accused of breaking and entering."

Which was ironic given how they'd spent the past hour.

"Stay here, all of you. If I am arrested or killed, use the tunnels and make your way out of the palace to safety."

"Nay—" the rokken started.

"Roland and Giselle are my only children," she declared forcefully. "At all costs, keep them safe. You hear me, Bekkan Kopathul? That's a direct order from the Queen of Haraland. Protect Roland and Giselle with your life. All of you protect them with your lives."

She glared down the whole party, putting the full weight of her royal authority behind her stare. Only when every last one of them had looked down or away from her did she nod firmly. "All right, then. Let me pass, Bekkan."

He frowned, but she squeezed past him determinedly. Praying she wasn't in fact about to die, she lifted an old-fashioned door latch and inched the panel open.

As Will led the party deeper into the Wychwold, the trees grew even larger, the moss thicker, the hills steeper, and the mist ever more mysterious. Truly, he was falling in love with this place.

They'd stopped for the night, and he was a little way from their campsite, gathering an armload of wood for a fire, when he heard Rosana scream. He dropped the wood and sprinted for the clearing, yanking his staff free of its strap across his back as he ran.

He burst into the clearing from one side just as Rynn burst into it from the other. A pair of dryads stood there, along with a bare-chested man who, at a glance, appeared to be wearing furred pants, standing on oddly backward bending knees. On closer inspection, the man also had small horns upon his head, shaggy hair around his face, and dark, upward-slanting eyes. *A satyr.*

"Why come ye to these protected lands?" the satyr demanded. "Your kind be not welcome in this place."

Rynn held out his bare hands as if to indicate that he was not armed. Which was laughable. Will had never seen another fighter so fast and deadly with his hands and feet. "We come in peace, brother," Rynn intoned.

Hah. Also not true.

"I am no brother to you!" the satyr snapped.

Rynn answered prettily and with a graceful bow, "Nonetheless, I am brother to you in my love of the natural forest, in my wish for humans to leave it alone, and in my desire for a warm fire and pleasant conversation. Will you not join us and sit a while?"

The dryads cooed and put their heads together, whispering. A giggle, and then one of them said, "We like you. We will sit with you, paxan prince."

Prince? What did they mean by that?

"Have I met you before?" Rynn asked, frowning slightly. "I confess, your beauty so dazzles me that I have lost my memory."

More giggling.

The brightest green dryad said rather regally, "I am Nerra, and this is my handmaiden, Seritsa."

Handmaiden, huh? Did that make Nerra some sort of noble among her kind? Will asked, "Are you acquainted with Lady Elysia of the Thornwold, perchance? I count her among my friends."

The dryad Elysia had helped Will and his friends dodge Anton Constantine and his mercenary army in the Forest of Thorns two summers ago. Apparently, she was some sort of fae princess.

"She is not of the Green Court, as I am, but I know her," Nerra replied. The dryad stared fixedly at Will, who looked back, privately amused. Wait until she figured out he was immune to her charm spells. It always caused consternation among her kind.

"Sit with me, human boy. Tell me all about yourself and what brings you to my grove."

He was happy to oblige, but not because she willed it so. He and his companions rolled several downed logs over to the fire they'd built, and everyone sat down, save the satyr, who stomped around the clearing on hooved feet that rustled in last year's dead leaves. Whether he stood guard or was merely impatient, Will could not tell.

Several more dryads and another satyr appeared in the grove, these darker shades of green, the deep, velvet tones of leaves in the late evening as dusk falls. Without comment, they took places at the fire, as well. Will noted that a half dozen more creatures, some humanoid and some *not*, milled around the edges of the clearing.

They must be near the fane. What else would explain this large gathering of fae creatures?

Following Rynn's lead, Will made small talk and traded pleasantries with the dryads as Rosana and Sha'Li roasted a brace of rabbits and served them to everyone. After dinner, Will took the lead in the conversation, asking, "Perhaps I could ask you a question about your history without giving you offense, Lady Nerra?"

She purred, "Ask, pretty boy."

"Do any fanes still exist in this forest?"

The congenial atmosphere evaporated in the blink of an eye. "Why do you ask?" the dryad asked sharply.

Will looked around at his companions, and they all nodded, indicating that he should answer the question. "My friends and I are on a quest. To complete it, we believe we need to find the last fane in the Valelands. Or at least, we need to discover where it was once located."

"Why?"

"We seek the home of an elf who we believe lived close to the last fane. He was called Eliassan."

"The Trollslayer?" Nerra blurted. "Why do you seek his abode?"

Will checked again with his friends, and again, he received nods all around. "We seek his bow."

That got a hiss from all the light green dryads, and Nerra's satyr surged toward Will as if he would attack. Nerra waved him back, but not before Will jumped to his feet and took up his staff.

"Power down, Will," Rynn muttered.

He sank cautiously to the log as the satyr reluctantly obeyed Nerra's order to back off.

"You are not the first treasure seekers who have come looking for this bow, and you will not be the last, I wager," the dryad said coolly.

Will scowled. "I will take that wager. We need that bow, and we *will* find it."

"For what purpose do you seek it?" the satyr growled, speaking for the first time since they'd come to this clearing.

"We believe it belonged to an ancient king and that part of his spirit might have been imbued into it. We seek to wake that king and need the shard of his spirit that resides in the bow to help restore him."

The dark green dryads traded interested glances among themselves. For her part, Nerra rocked back on the log, staring intently at Will, not as if to charm him but rather to measure the truth of his words. "Have you proof that this is what you do?"

"A friend of ours has proof, but she is not with us at the moment. She holds the Sleeping King's crown, a wreath of eternally living leaves edged in gold. Also, she wears his signet ring, carved from the horn of a unicorn."

The dryad snorted. "And you wish me to believe you and hand over this precious bow simply because you can describe a few items that might have belonged to this supposed king?"

"I've met him myself," Will started hotly. He paused to take a calming breath. "Or at least I've met his dreaming echo. He's trapped in the dream realm in a beautiful grove much like this one. To wake him, he told us to find his regalia and bring it to his physical body on this plane. The bow we seek is part of that regalia."

The dark dryads murmured among themselves, and one said, "Perhaps you should give him that which he seeks, Lady of the Green Court."

"You are Night Court. Stay out of this!" she snapped back. Testament to her power was the fact that the other dryads subsided. They looked annoyed, but they did not challenge Nerra.

Nerra was speaking again. "You may have some of the details correct, but they would be known to others besides yourself. You could simply have overheard them. How am I to believe you?"

"Because I'm telling the truth," he declared.

"Are you willing to put your life where your words are?" she challenged.

"Meaning what?"

"Will you risk death to have this bow?"

"Risk it how?" He'd learned long ago to be cautious of making deals with dryads.

"If you want me to hand over the bow, fight my champion for it." She gestured at the fuming satyr behind her. "Drest is my champion. A duel against him to the death. Winner keeps the bow. What say you, human?"

"How do I know you even have the bow?"

"You come here to my lands, invading my grove, demanding the life's blood of my forest, and you dare to question my word?" Nerra's voice rose in anger with every syllable.

Will raised up his hands to ward off her fury. "You wanted proof from me. Why should I deserve any less from you?"

She did try to charm him then, staring intently into his eyes for many long seconds. At length, he commented mildly, "If you seek to ensorcel me, I am immune to your kind's magics. Elysia and her sisters in the Forest of Thorns found it most frustrating."

The satyr made an angry sound deep in his throat, and Will eyed his possible opponent warily. Drest's inhuman legs looked heavily muscled, and those backward-bending knee joints looked immensely strong. The satyr's human chest was likewise wreathed in massive, supple muscles that promised to be both powerful and fast. He would be a formidable foe.

"I have the bow," she said flatly.

He was inclined to believe her.

"May I consult with my friends in private for a moment?" he asked Nerra.

She nodded her consent, and he moved across the clearing, gesturing for his companions to follow. They huddled close for a murmured consultation. Except before he could ask his friends their opinions, the dark satyr sidled up beside Will. "I've seen Drest fight before. I know his weakness. I can help you. I have a blade he's particularly vulnerable to."

Will frowned. "Thanks be, but no thanks. If I do combat against him, it will be a fair fight."

The satyr snorted, disgusted, and moved away.

"What do you think?" Will asked his friends. "Should I accept Nerra's offer and fight Drest for the bow?"

Sha'Li answered first. "We don't even know if she has it. I do not trust these green tree faeries."

"Neither do I," Rosana chimed in.

"You could take the satyr," Eben declared stoutly.

"Thanks be, brother," Will replied. "But is it worth the risk?"

Kendrick spoke up slowly. "I think that is not the key question. Rather, I think the question we should be discussing is whether or not it is right to accept her challenge."

Kendrick's words struck a chord in Will's gut. His initial impulse had also been to wonder at the honor in killing another being in order to possess the bow. It had been the same impulse that led him to ask for this consultation rather than immediately accepting the challenge.

Will asked Rynn, "Can you read anything of Nerra's motives in offering the challenge to me?"

"Sorry, no. These fae creatures are adept at guarding their thoughts, and even if they were not, their minds are so foreign to mine that I would not trust any reading I got from them."

"Should we vote?" Will suggested.

Everyone frowned doubtfully at that, and no one volunteered an answer.

Will sighed. "If Raina were here, we all know how she would vote."

Rosana looked up at him, her dark eyes serious. "What would Gawaine say if he were here?"

He stared back at her, torn. The aggressive, impatient part of him, perhaps fueled by Bloodroot's pride, believed he could win the fight and take the bow. He'd been trained by the best warriors in the land and was quickly coming into his own.

But that part of him raised by his father to be a knight one day, the part of him trained by his grandfather to honor the De'Vir name, the part of him that had met the Sleeping King and strove to be like him, and most importantly, the part of him that desperately wished to be worthy of Rosana—that part of him doubted the wisdom of accepting a challenge that could only end in death.

Will answered slowly, "Gawaine would flatly refuse to accept the challenge. He was the Mythar, guardian of all the forest creatures. Although they may be fae, they are still creatures of this place."

Silence met his words, but one by one, his friends nodded in agreement. Eben was last, but even he reluctantly acknowledged it would be dishonorable to kill for an item meant to bring life and hope back to this land.

Will turned around to face the dryad. "I am sorry, Nerra. While I appreciate your offer, I cannot accept. Waking the Sleeping King is a quest to restore life, and killing another cannot be part of that. Honor demands that I decline the combat. Is there not another way we can come to some agreement?"

The satyr growled in frustration while Nerra tilted her head to study him. "Tell me more of your meeting with the Mythar."

So she did know who Gawaine was. Will hadn't referred to him as the Mythar at all in their conversation.

Will sat down cautiously on the log beside her. "His grove, although a prison at heart, is very beautiful. We had to overcome an array of great and terrible creatures to reach it . . ."

He warmed to his subject, describing in detail his conversation with the Mythar, the manifestation of Lord Bloodroot in the grove, and how Gawaine had offered him the choice of keeping the treant's heartwood on his person or releasing it.

"Why do you keep the shard of the bloodthorn if it still tries to kill you?" Nerra asked curiously.

"Because it's the right thing to do. For the Great Circle to be restored one day, his spirit must be protected now. Yes, there's a cost to me, and my health has suffered. But maybe someday I can find a way to restore Bloodroot's tree and in so doing repair the Great Circle."

"You wish to be Mythar?" she asked.

"Stars, no! But when he returns to this place and time, Gawaine will have larger problems to deal with than fixing the

Great Circle. That work can be left to people like me and my friends while he overthrows Koth and establishes a new kingdom."

Nerra tilted her head, considering Will thoughtfully. "You speak easily of treason."

He retorted, "I've earned the right. I've lost everything—my family, my home, even my name. All I have left is this quest."

"Your heart is pure, Will Cobb, vessel of Bloodroot."

He doubted that. But if she thought so and it would make her hand over Eliassan's bow, he wasn't about to contradict her.

Nerra bowed her head slowly and said solemnly, "I will give you Eliassan's bow."

"No!" The satyr leaped forward, all but standing in the fire to loom in front of her, oblivious of his fur singeing with a stink of burning hair. "You cannot! You know what giving it away will do to your tree, the entire forest—my lady, what it will do to you!"

Will looked back and forth between the pair as they engaged in a silent battle of wills, the satyr in desperation, the dryad in long-suffering resignation.

"We always knew this day would come," Nerra said heavily. "Maybe we did not know what the reason for it would be. But the bow was never ours. We merely protected it until its true owner returned."

"That tree-infested human is not the bow's true owner!" the satyr shouted.

"Nay, but he will carry it to the Mythar."

"Let me fight him," the satyr urged. "To the death. Winner keeps the bow."

"No, Drest," she replied gently.

The satyr fell to his hocks, burying his face in her lap. "Do not do this!" he cried, his voice muffled.

Will frowned. The satyr's reaction seemed a little excessive. Unless Will was missing something here. Aloud, he inquired, "Why is Drest so distressed, Lady Nerra?"

"No reason—"

"Yes, there's a reason!" the satyr interrupted, lifting his head, his eyes red-rimmed with fury, or perhaps despair. "If you take the bow, her tree will die, and she will die!"

Rosana audibly let out the gasp that echoed Will's mental one. "We cannot kill a dryad tree!" she exclaimed.

It was Nerra's turn to surge to her feet, emerald eyes flashing. "It's not your choice to make, human children. I have made my decision."

"Wait!" a new voice called out strongly, startling the dryad in the act of stepping into her tree and Will and the satyr from lunging after her.

Sha'Li was on her feet, every scale standing up in agitation, making her look ferocious. "What if there's a way to remove the bow and save your tree and your life, lady dryad?"

Everyone was staring at her now, and she glared back, her white Tribe of the Moon mark standing out nearly as brightly as her eyes against her black scales. "I have something. A knife. I took it from Kerryl Moonrunner."

A hubbub erupted at this announcement, Kendrick exclaiming in surprise, Nerra exclaiming at the Moonrunner name, Rosana expressing shock that she'd stolen Kerryl's knife, and Will demanding to know how she'd managed it.

Sha'Li lifted her hands for silence.

Since when had she become so self-assured? Will fell silent along with the others, watching her rummage in her pack. She came up with a long dagger bearing a curved, wicked-looking blade.

"That's Kerryl's!" Kendrick exclaimed.

"You stole it from him?" Will demanded. "How? When?"

"The first night he and Kendrick camped with us. When Vesper attacked them. We came back to camp and both of them were unconscious. Remember?"

Nods all around.

"While you all fussed over Kendrick and Kerryl, I gathered their gear and laid out their bedrolls. That was when I went through Kerryl's bag and found the knife."

"But why did you take it?" Eben asked.

Sha'Li hesitated for a moment and then looked her old

friend directly in the eyes. "Because sometimes doing the right thing requires a good person to do a thing that looks wrong to others. Kerryl had to be stopped from unnaturally separating the dryads from their trees."

Rosana piped up. "Yes, but how can that dagger save Nerra and her tree?"

Sha'Li looked over at Kendrick expectantly.

He answered, "Kerryl said it was a special blade enchanted to sever the link between a dryad and her tree. He used it to set any number of dryads free from their groves in the Thornwold. He was planning to do the same in the Sorrow Wold but ran into a hunter who nearly killed him before Kerryl could set his plan in motion."

"The one we chased off?" Rynn asked.

"Aye," Kendrick answered.

"Let me see it," the dark satyr demanded.

He bent down over the blade Sha'Li held out, but then drew back sharply. "Fae bane," he growled.

"What's that?" Rosana asked.

None of the dryads or satyrs seemed inclined to answer, and Rynn finally explained, "It's an infused iron particularly harmful to the flesh of fae-based creatures. As I understand it, fae bane only comes from the fae home world." The paxan turned to Kendrick. "I gather, then, that Kerryl learned how to activate fae bane's magical qualities?"

"He did." Kendrick elaborated, "Because of its lethal nature, most fae bane is rendered inert by the fae when it is found. It must be awoken before it becomes dangerous."

"And yon blade is awake?" Will asked.

"Oh yes," the dark satyr answered. "Most definitely. It's as thirsty for green blood as any fae bane I've ever felt."

Nerra interjected, "Wait. You say that blade will sever my link to my tree? Won't I die anyway?"

Kendrick shook his head. "I saw him set free at least a half dozen dryads. They all retained their ability to tree walk into particularly old and strong trees. They were also able to pass freely beyond their groves anywhere in the Thornwold. I do not know if any of them traveled farther afield than that or could have if they wished. We didn't stick around long enough to find out. When Anton's mercenaries invaded and attacked the Boki, we left for our safety."

That fierce and bloody battle had nearly overrun Will and his friends. They'd narrowly escaped with their lives.

Drest snorted. "I don't like it. Trying yon blade's magic is not worth the risk to your life, my love."

The dryad smiled sweetly at the angry satyr, laying a green hand softly on his cheek. "My dear, if we can wake the Mythar and restore the Great Circle, think what it would mean to all of our kind."

"The Wychwold will still die," he declared.

Will blinked. "Wait. What?"

The satyr glared across the fire at him. "The life force within the Mythar's bow sustains this entire forest. Why else do you think it is so healthy and verdant? The Drifts of the Thirst encroach from the north, foresters encroach from the south, the salt water of Estarra encroaches from the east, and the heart of Haelos barely beats beneath our feet. The only thing keeping these lands alive is the spirit of the Sleeping King. Take that away and all of this dies."

Will was stunned. They were talking about only a tiny piece of Gawaine's spirit, thousands of years old, trapped in the bow. Yet it could still sustain this entire, vast forest?

"Is this true?" Will asked the dryad.

"It is," she answered soberly. "But," she added more brightly, "if you wake the Mythar, he can heal the entire continent."

A big *if*. Did they dare risk this entire forest, all the creatures living in it, and all the humanoids depending upon it by removing the shard of Gawaine's spirit? Although truth be told, all of that was at risk anyway. If they failed in their quest or if the Empire got wind of their quest, the bow would not matter. Maximillian and the Kothites would lay waste to this land and everyone in it.

"What say the rest of you?" he asked his friends.

Rynn was first to answer. "It's worth a try to sever Nerra's connection to her tree. If that works, we can proceed with removing the bow. Plus, the forest will not die overnight. It will take some time to weaken and wither. We've got a window in which to attempt to wake the Sleeping King. If we fail, we can always bring the bow back here."

Assuming whatever ritual they tried to wake Gawaine didn't destroy the bow. But as a magic user, he kept that observation to himself.

His other friends nodded in agreement.

Will turned to Nerra and Drest. "What say you?"

Nerra looked at her lover. "I could travel the forest runs with you. You could show me all your favorite places."

"And you would not have the safety of your grove to protect you," he growled.

"I have you for that," she purred, petting his muscular arms and back.

The satyr scowled, but Will sensed that the fellow's argument was lost. He sympathized with Drest. He never could say no to Rosana when she really wanted something either.

Will turned to Sha'Li. "Very well, then. Let's give this knife a try. Anyone know how to use it?"

"I do," Kendrick answered reluctantly. He held out his hand, and Sha'Li laid the blade into it.

For a moment, Will fancied he saw a pale, silvery glow about the lizardman girl's hand as she released the blade. He blinked and looked again, but the glow was gone. However, her tribe mark was definitely glowing. She was easy to underestimate, lurking quietly in the background, not saying much about her skills, rarely airing her opinions or thoughts. A natural-born rogue. And what little he knew of the Tribe of the Moon suggested there was much more to the secret group than met the eye.

Kendrick stepped up to Nerra's tree, a magnificent rowan. "Ready?" he asked the dryad.

The satyr wrapped his powerful arms around her protectively, and she huddled in her lover's embrace. She nodded to Kendrick.

Will watched with interest as Kendrick slashed the tree with the blade, a cut traveling all the way around the tree, girdling it. Clear sap welled up, and Nerra cried out in pain. She would have fallen had not Drest been holding her.

"Give me your hand," Kendrick said grimly to her.

She held out a trembling palm, and Kendrick slashed the blade across it as well. An upwelling of green blood darkened her flesh, and she cried out again, this time a keening wail of pain and loss.

Kendrick flung the blade to the ground in distaste. Grief and pain resonated in his voice as he mumbled, "It is done."

Raina woke to a touch on her shoulder. It was Lakanos. She rolled out of the impossibly comfortable pile of cushions and soft-furred throws in which she'd slept.

"I'm sorry to wake you. It goes against my training to let you drive yourself so hard, Emissary. But I defer to the urgency of your quest."

"Thank you for worrying about me. That means more to me than you can know." Precious few people in her life had actually given a care for her wishes or well-being. She'd been born a pawn and used as one for much of her life. At least until she'd run away from home and taken control of her own destiny.

A small, wiry woman stepped forward. "I am Hatma, a scout and hunter among the Veils. Where do you wish to go, daughter of Tyrel?"

"I'm looking for a woman I've heard might live in the Thirst. She's said to be a shaman of some kind. Claims to be from an ancient tribe of elves known as zinnzari. She might have some sort of spider markings or tattoos on her skin."

"Zinnzari? As in Zinn, the Great Spider?" Hatma asked.

"The very same," Raina affirmed.

Hatma frowned. "I have traveled the four corners of this desert, and only one person do I know who might fit the description you give."

"Can you take us to her?" Raina asked eagerly.

"We must go west, then," Hatma declared.

Raina estimated that they'd walked to midmorning when Hatma declared a halt for the day. The tiny woman showed them how to set up the oiled tarps the Veils had given each of them as one-person tents, and then to partially collapse a dune face over the tents to bury them and keep them cool. Sweaty and aching when she finally crawled into her tomb-like shelter, Raina was surprised to find it noticeably cooler than the outside air.

Soon. She could feel herself getting close to the zinnzari. Close to Gawaine himself. The ring on her finger tugged her onward with increasing urgency.

She pulled the flap across the opening and fell into exhausted slumber.

The grove was as cool and green and the desert around her was hot, dry, and lifeless. She smiled joyfully as she looked around for him.

There he was. Across the grove, turning toward her, a smile on his impossibly handsome face. He reached her, lifting her hand to kiss it before drawing her into his arms for a long hug. He was taller than she, and the top of her head barely reached his muscular shoulder.

"I've missed you," she murmured against Gawaine's chest.

"And I you."

"Did you call me to your grove this time, or did I dream my way here?"

He set her away from him but did not let go of her hand. He led her to a pair of bentwood chairs beneath the spreading boughs of a fragrant apple tree perpetually in bloom while songbirds serenaded them from its branchs.

"My, this must be serious if you're bringing me to my favorite spot to talk," she teased. *Except a frisson of worry did chatter across the back of her neck.*

"I did, in fact, summon you here, Raina. Please. Sit."

She sank onto the edge of one of the cushioned seats. "What's wrong?"

"Events are accelerating here in the dream realm."

"How so?"

"Forces that would see me destroyed are on the move, gathering their strength for some kind of strike."

Alarm speared through her. He was only an echo of himself and trapped in this place, easy prey for any who wished to attack him.

"What forces?" she asked, although she feared she knew the answer. *Vesper.*

"An army of phantasms has been assembled, and a dangerous woman in the guise of a child leads it."

"Yes, I've seen her. She recently stole back a piece of her spirit from a friend of mine. Her name is Vesper."

"Her true name is Avilla. She has taken the moniker Vesper so others will not use her true name against her."

Raina remembered him speaking once long ago about the power of true names. She knew nothing of such magics but did not question his assertion.

Gawaine continued, "If she has, indeed, regained a portion of her spirit, that would explain why she's suddenly so powerful."

"What can I do to protect you?" she asked.

"Time grows short for you and your friends to find my physical remains and restore me to my body. Apparently, Vesper seeks my body to possess it for herself."

"Why is she so interested in you all of a sudden?"

"The lure of inhabiting an immortal body must be great for her."

"You are immortal?"

"Obviously not entirely, or I would not have spent the past several thousand years in this place."

"I'm sorry. That was a stupid question."

"No apologies necessary," he said mildly.

They were silent for a time while the birds sang their hearts out overhead.

At length, Raina said, "I'm searching for a zinnzari shaman in hopes that she can tell me where your body lies."

"The zinnzari may be reluctant to help you. They vowed to protect me to the end, and if they think your attempt to wake me might fail, they will block you from trying."

"What if I show them your ring and crown?"

He studied her thoughtfully for a moment. "I expect they

would take them from you. And that could be a problem because then Hemlocke might sense my regalia and seize both ring and crown from them."

"Why doesn't Hemlocke want you to wake?" she asked curiously.

"Dragons generally have complicated motives. In her case, Hemlocke is bound by her vow to Acadia to protect me. But Hemlocke also considers herself the ultimate protector of Haelos, a role she's unlikely to want to relinquish to me. And, of course, there's an element of sibling rivalry to our relationship."

"Siblings? Your sister is a dragon?" Raina exclaimed.

"Not by birth. I'm entirely an elf. But Acadia raised both of us as her own children. We did grow up side by side."

"What's that like? Growing up with a dragon?"

Gawaine laughed a little. "One learns to be nimble when a dragon is learning to control her fire breath."

She shook her head, unable to imagine growing up with a dragon. "So we must find a way to convince the zinnzari we can successfully wake you. That shouldn't be too hard to do once we have all of your regalia."

"Mmm. Therein lies the rub. I do not know if you will have time to find many more pieces of it before Vesper finds my body."

"But if we do not have the whole set, we risk losing you if we try to wake you."

"Indeed."

"How will we know when we have enough parts of your regalia assembled?" she asked in sharp alarm.

He shrugged. "You will have to use your best judgment."

"If we fail, we'll kill you!"

"I'm already dead. I made my peace with that a very long time ago."

"Speak for yourself. I haven't made peace with that idea at all, and I don't plan to!"

He smiled gently. "Sometimes I forget how passionately you humans live your lives."

"This isn't about being human. It's about needing you!"

She broke off, unwilling to elaborate on whether it was she personally who needed him, or whether she spoke in the broader sense of the people and land of Haelos needing him.

He snagged her fingers with his, sitting in silence like that for several long minutes. "If I knew that I could come back to my body and spend the remainder of a normal life span in your company, I would be satisfied with that and think it a life well lived."

She was staggered. It was the first time he'd ever mentioned wanting to be with her for the long term once he woke. He was a king and would have a great nation to restore. And she was just a commoner healer.

He rose to his feet and lifted her to hers, as well. As if he'd picked her doubtful thoughts straight from her mind, he said, "There is much more to you than even you know. Now is not the time to reveal all, but one day you will correctly see yourself as my equal."

She snorted inelegantly and sent Gawaine into peals of laughter. She tried to glare at him, but could not stay annoyed in the face of his amusement.

"While I'm here," she said, "I have a problem. Perhaps you can help."

He sobered immediately. "What's wrong?"

"I went to visit the Mages of Alchizzadon a few weeks ago—"

"Are you mad? They cannot be trusted, particularly where you're concerned." It was the first time she'd heard Gawaine actually sound angry.

"They promised to behave," she tried.

"And they broke their promise, didn't they?"

She looked away from his accusing stare. "A few of them did."

"Tell me what happened."

She winced as he sounded every inch an irritated king who would brook no evasions or glossing over of the facts in the case before him for judgment. She answered, "It turns out there are sharply divided factions with the mages. One faction, more extreme than the others, thought it would be a good idea to perform a ritual on me."

"What sort of ritual?" His voice had gone flat now. Cold. Which was infinitely more alarming than his irritation.

She reluctantly admitted, "They tried to bottle my spirit."

"What?" he exploded. "That would have killed you permanently!"

"I'm aware of that," she said soothingly.

"I'll destroy them—"

She interrupted. "It wasn't all of them. Just a small faction. In fact, two of the other mages rescued me, along with Cicero and a Royal Order of the Sun knight who was a prisoner of the order."

"Are you all right?" he asked curtly.

"Not entirely. There was a backlash—"

Gawaine's hands gripped her shoulders, and a wave of incredibly powerful magic rushed through her. She guessed it might be nature magic, and it felt like some sort of enhanced diagnostic spell to assess her for injuries.

Wordlessly, jaw clenched, he turned her loose and spun on his heel to stalk away from her. He took two full laps around the grove before he finally came to a halt in front of her once more. He wore a resigned expression. "You'd better wake me up soon so I can stop you from taking foolish risks like that again."

She lifted her chin stubbornly. "I'll take whatever risks I deem necessary to properly do my job as a White Heart emissary."

"Perhaps one day I will be in a position to have some say over the risks you take."

As her king, or as someone with a more personal stake in her life? Stunned, she mumbled, "Until then, I shall make my own choices."

That sent him off on another stomp around the grove.

His face was inscrutable when he returned to her. He asked tersely, "How do you feel now?"

"I'm plagued by headaches. And the voices are back. Sometimes the pain and noise are so bad I can barely cast magic."

"The mages' backlash broke down the barrier between you and the spirit echoes from whom you draw your power. For now, I can only suggest you minimize the amount of magic you cast. Perhaps with time, the barrier will restore itself."

It had been a few weeks since the ritual, and if anything, the barriers were getting weaker, not stronger. But given how put out with her he already was about placing herself in harm's way, she wasn't about to admit that right now.

"Are you practicing the exercises I showed you when you first started hearing the voices?" he asked.

"Yes. Every day."

"Keep doing them." He shoved a frustrated hand through his dark hair. *"If only I were with you in physical form. I could heal the breach in a few seconds. But as it is, I can only help you here. Once you leave my grove, the voices and pain will return full force."*

"One day, you will be fully restored," she said softly. *"And until then, I'll manage."*

"Promise me you won't do anything foolhardy or suicidal between now and then."

It was a promise she couldn't keep, so she merely smiled up at him and murmured, *"Take care of yourself."*

The grove started to fade out, and Gawaine called after her, *"Beware the child . . ."*

Gabrielle eased the hidden door open, unsure of exactly where in the Haraland chambers she would pop out. A glimpse of a painting and a bronze wall lamp came into view. The formal receiving room. She eased the door open another few inches and spied a familiar figure. *Talissar.* And he appeared to be conversing with someone. She studied the young man, who was dark-haired and handsome with blue eyes. He definitely looked familiar.

She was so relieved the two men were not soldiers or inquisitors here to arrest her that she all but fell the rest of the way through the opening and into the room.

Talissar and the young man whipped around defensively.

"It's me, Gabrielle!" she cried, hands held well away from her sides with no magic summoned to her fingers.

"What on Urth?" Talissar exclaimed. "Why are you using a secret passage? Was there a problem with your mission?"

She called for Bekkan and the others to join her, and they filed into the salon.

"Lady Sasha?" Talissar exclaimed. "What on Urth?"

Gabrielle explained quickly, "We ran into Sasha and her husband as we were approaching the trophy room. They were with High-Maker Meridine. Rafal escorted Meridine to her quarters while Sasha came with us."

"Where's the thief—" Talissar started. He spied Roland and Giselle, who were last through the door, and finished, "Who are these people?"

"These are my son, Roland, and my daughter, Giselle."

Talissar made a short bow to them, then repeated, "Where's the thief?"

"He continued through the tunnels toward an exit from the palace. It seemed prudent to get him out of the Imperial Seat as soon as possible."

"Why?" the dark-haired, blue-eyed young man with Talissar asked warily.

Gabrielle answered grimly, "The thief murdered Meridine when she came back to check on us as we left the trophy room. Not satisfied to merely kill a high lady," she said over their gasps, "your thief used an amphora of the Black Flame to send Meridine to the Void."

Talissar actually fell into a chair in his shock. Finally, he looked over at the young man and said grimly, "I told you he was a problem."

"So there's no body and no physical evidence?" the young man asked tersely.

Gabrielle was impressed. He'd set aside any immediate emotional reaction to her news and had cut instantly to the heart of the matter. "No. But as Sasha has pointed out, Grand Marshal Korovo and Archduchess Quaya will surely sense their daughter's passing."

"Indeed, they will," the young man said grimly. "Even I cannot protect all of you from Maximillian and Laernan on a rampage with Korovo and Quaya at their backs—"

Gabrielle cut him off, already fully aware of the danger they faced. "We have one play. Everyone in this room must get out of the palace immediately, which means we need a distraction. Meridine said something that gave me an idea. She asked if my mind had been controlled again."

Talissar frowned. He'd been the one who found her years ago dancing in an undignified display in the Imperial gardens, her mind controlled by Tyviden Starfire. It had been that day he'd first placed the Octavium Pendant around her neck to shield her from any more mental assaults.

"What do you have in mind?" the young man asked.

"I'll go to the gardens. Stage a display to make them think

I've been controlled again. When everyone's attention is on me, the rest of you will sneak out of the palace."

The young man stared at her for a long moment, and then began to smile. "We may survive this night after all."

Talissar nodded, more businesslike. "Roland and Giselle, into the bedroom. You'll need more practical traveling clothes. Borrow some from your parents. As for you, my lady—we need to get you out to the gardens. We have only a few minutes before the Hand comes looking for Meridine's killer. For nothing short of outright murder will take down a Kothite."

"What about you?" Gabrielle asked him. "Quantaine is every bit as much at risk as Haraland."

The young one answered, "I have taken special measures to defend my old friend's mind from . . . incursions."

Gabrielle got the impression the word he'd been about to say was *torture*. Mayhap those special measures were also why Talissar seemed to know who the fellow was, and she could not quite seem to remember him.

"Protect my children, both of you," she pleaded. "At all costs, they must get away from here safely."

The young man replied, "I will walk them out of the palace myself tonight. I give you my word that no one will remember them. It will be as if they were never here."

Roland and Giselle ducked into the other room to change, and Gabrielle's legs gave out from under her at last. She crumpled to the floor.

Gentle hands raised her up and led her to a settee. Talissar murmured, "You have been very brave, my lady, and done all the peoples of Urth a great service."

"At what cost?" she whispered, heartbroken. "I have to give up my babies again."

"Think of all the mothers who will not have to suffer the same agony because of you."

She nodded miserably and took the handkerchief he passed her.

"Did you find anything of interest in Maximillian's trophy room?" he asked quietly.

"Bekkan spotted a piece of septallum, and the thief told

him to take it." She added, "I think Korgan may have stolen a handful of Mindori mind gems, and my son took the keys to the fae realm. I tried to talk them out of the thefts, but they wouldn't listen to me."

"Did Jossa take anything?" Talissar asked mildly.

"If she did, I didn't see it."

"We expected as much. Honestly, the theft of the other items will draw attention away from the septallum. It may work to our advantage."

"Are you always so optimistic?" she complained.

Talissar smiled. "I try to make the best of those events I do not control. Like the death of Meridine. With some careful rumor planting, we should be able to cast suspicion on any number of the high lords and ladies."

"How?" she asked, startled.

"It's long past time for Maximillian to relinquish his throne to another Kothite."

She stared at Talissar, aghast. "But . . . but . . . he's *eternal.*"

"You of all people know that's not true. When the twelve Kothites conquered the etheri people, they made a pact that they would take turns ruling the Empire. Maximillian, in a bid to make himself more powerful than his comrades and retain the throne, did something that ended up driving him mad. That was when Ammertus briefly ascended the throne."

"Ammertus? Emperor?" She had to laugh at the improbability of that notion. "How did that go?"

"Not well. It was known as the Dread Reign of Ammertus. In fact, it went so badly that the other members of the Twelve felt obliged to repair Maximillian with the Second Great Forgetting and remove all memory of Ammertus's reign while they were at it."

"They put Maximillian back on the throne?"

Talissar nodded. "The Empire was such a mess after Ammertus they felt only Maximillian could put it back together."

She absorbed all of that in amazement. Given the wonders she'd already heard of lost history from Bekkan and the horrors of the Kothite conquest over the etheri kingdom, she had no trouble believing this wild tale.

Eventually, she asked, "Why would they change leadership now? The conquests of Pan Orda, Mindor, and Haelos are faltering, and all three continents are restless. Why not let Maximillian stay in power until the situation stabilizes somewhat?"

Talissar grinned. "Because unseen forces—namely, us— seem to be pushing events into an ever-greater cycle of unrest. Also, Endellian and her cadre of bored scions are rumbling about wanting a chance at ruling. Of course, the other original Kothites also feel entitled to the throne. If Maximillian doesn't step aside gracefully, any number of contenders for his job could form an alliance and push him out. He may be the most powerful Kothite of the bunch, but even he cannot withstand all of them at once."

"How exactly does Meridine's murder play into this?"

"Quaya is next in line to assume the throne. Honestly, she's not a bad choice, given her skill with dreaming and intuition. The dream realm is in chaos, and that mess threatens to spill over onto Urth at any moment. But the death of her only scion will weaken Quaya. Not only does she lose a powerful force among the scions, but she may also have to siphon off a good bit of her own power to create another heir. I'm told she was close to her daughter, too. She may prefer to withdraw into a period of mourning."

"If not Quaya, then who would take over next?" she asked.

"Korovo and Iolanthe are solidly Maximillian's lackeys. Neither of them would take the throne from him. Our best guess is that Endellian or Ammertus will attempt to seize power. However, several other less-obvious candidates have amassed fewer enemies than those two. Thought Lord Rahl, Prescient Lord Evard, or even Worthy Lady Phendra could emerge from the Twelve as a favorite to replace Maximillian."

"Would any of them make better rulers than he?"

Talissar made a sound of disgust. "I suppose that depends on how you define *better*. Kinder, more temperate, and more humane than Maximillian? Not bloody likely. They're all warped by their infatuation with their own immortality."

She commented wryly, "Meridine's death ought to puncture that balloon a wee bit."

Roland and Giselle emerged from the bedroom, and Gabrielle was out of time with them. Tears streamed down her cheeks. "I can't believe this. I've just found you, and I must let go of you again. I have so much to say to you. So much I want to know of you both—" Her voice gave out, and sobs racked her. She flung herself at her beloved children, hugging them with all her strength.

Giselle whispered, "We love you, too. We know it wasn't easy for you to send us away—" She, too, broke down in tears and could speak no more.

"But we're grateful you did," Roland finished for his sister. "We had a fine childhood, safe and free. Our nurse never let us forget how much love it took for you to let us go."

"When a little time has passed, come home to Haraland. I'll be waiting and watching for you. Your father's life will be complete if he can see both of you again."

"Give him our love," Roland murmured.

Talissar's companion interjected, "Sadly, she will not be able to tell him of this visit lest she endanger your lives. Your brief appearance in the Imperial Seat is just the sort of anomaly that would make Maximillian suspicious."

"I will not let you take away my memory of them," Gabrielle said forcefully.

The young man bowed his head in her direction. "Nor would I try, madam. I have faith in a mother's love for her children to keep you from betraying their visit to anyone."

There was one more round of fast, hard hugs, and then the young man led Gabrielle's children and the others back through the secret doorway and into the tunnels once more.

"Courage, Gabrielle," Talissar murmured.

Gabrielle's legs wanted to give out then, but she had one last job to do. She must provide a distraction that ensured her children's safety.

Talissar stood up to take his leave. "Take comfort in the fact that after this night's performance is over, your work for us will be finished. You will be able to go home. To be with your family. To rest. May the Lady bless you and keep you safe."

As she watched him go, she was startled to realize she felt nearly as hollow and bereft at this parting as she had when saying farewell to her children just a little while earlier. Except she didn't think her work would be finished after tonight. Not by a long shot.

Steeling herself to the task at hand, she recalled the strange compulsion that had drawn her to the Imperial gardens years ago, when Tyviden had, in a childish prank, planted a suggestion in her head to go there from time to time and dance like an undignified hoyden. That memory firm in her mind, she left the Haraland suite and headed down the grand staircase, past the Great Throne Room, and outside into the gardens. She ignored the guards and nodded absently at whatever people she passed in the hallways, praying one of them would say something to someone official about seeing her acting strangely.

The Crown Plaza was a massive, city-sized space. What parts of it that were not filled by the palace itself were landscaped into extensive and magnificent gardens. She strolled across one of the great lawns and stopped to kick off her slippers and go barefoot in the grass. It was cold and wet, and frankly uncomfortable, but she wiggled her toes and pretended to enjoy the sensation.

Dangling her slippers from her fingertips, she headed for the great rose gardens housing row after row of rare and gorgeous varieties of roses. In its own way, this garden was a second trophy room for Maximillian's living treasures.

Blooms shone pale in the moonlight, and a subtle perfume with notes from sweet to spicy wafted to her. She bent down to sniff a half dozen blossoms and then twirled away from each, giggling happily.

It was hard not to look around, not to search for others who might have spotted her. As she recalled, she'd been oblivious to everyone and everything around her on those strange forays into the gardens.

Past the rose garden lay the hundred plots of the Garden

of Nations. Each kingdom of Koth was responsible for planting and maintaining a garden reflective of its own country. Haraland's was colorful and fragrant, a rich variety of flowers crowding together in orderly chaos reminiscent of the vibrant energy of the people of Haraland. She trailed her fingers through the scented clusters of a lilac bush in full bloom, its lavender blooms silver in the moonlight. The lush fragrance of lilac went straight to her head, and it wasn't hard to act a bit drunk on the scent.

A pair of lovers strolled past her, averting their faces. An affair, then. She sang a silly greeting to them and whirled away, skipping deeper into the gardens. The place Talissar had first found her dancing years ago was the Quantaine garden, and she headed there now. Interestingly enough, Lyssandra had chosen to leave her country's plot natural and untrained at all except for a pair of winding dirt trails mulched with pine bark that prevented them from becoming muddy. Supposedly, it was a homage to the ironwood forests of Quantaine. Ironwood was nigh indestructible, and the Imperial Navy's Black Ships were built entirely of the stuff.

It was an isolated part of the gardens of the nations, and her great worry was that no one would be out here at this time of night to spot her and draw attention to her. She needed to create a large enough diversion for her children to escape.

But she'd forgotten that this was the time of night for furtive assignations, and the more isolated corners of the Imperial gardens were favorite destinations for lovers. She spotted at least a half dozen couples in as many minutes.

She threw her arms up and twirled around in carefree abandon, humming a little tune to herself. Were this not such deadly serious business, she might actually be enjoying herself out here. As it was, she silently prayed that her Octavium Pendant would hold up to scrutiny and that all chaos would break loose any second.

"Your Highness! Greetings! Is all well?"

She spun around smiling, her hair falling down from its pins and wisps of it trailing across her face. Perfect. One of Korovo's generals. A royal insider.

"Isn't it wonderful out here?" she cried.

"It is, indeed, a lovely evening. Where are your guards, my lady? Your escort?"

"This is the Imperial Seat. I have no need for guards," she replied, caressing a paper birch tree, its ghostly white bark smooth and cool.

"Sadly, events earlier this evening have proven that not to be true, Your Highness. May I escort you back to the palace?"

"No. I'm fine." She skipped away from the concerned general, moving deeper into the heavy shadows of the Quantaine forest. Off the two main trails lay a few small trails, and it was down one of those she darted now, intentionally losing sight of the general.

There. That should force some sort of search party to head out this way. Regalo of Haraland was far too influential a man to risk having his wife murdered when something or someone at court was obviously influencing her.

Sure enough, it was only a matter of minutes before she heard voices shouting her name in the distance. She plunged off the trails altogether, losing herself in the darkest part of the miniature forest. Vines pulled at her gown, and sharp twigs scratched her bare feet until she was forced to stop and don her slippers. As she looked around, nothing but trees and shadows loomed around her, blocking out the moon entirely. She realized with a start that she actually was lost. Perfect. Anyone who probed her mind would sense genuine confusion from her.

Satisfied with her present predicament, she sat down on a fallen log to wait for someone to find her.

It took only a few minutes for a chorus of shouts to become audible. It sounded like the general had sent out an entire company of the palace guard looking for her. Excellent. *Fly, my beloved children. Fly far from here.*

She let the guards come, fanning out in a line, carrying torches, and when they drew close, she resumed dancing in a little patch of moss.

"I've found her!" a guard shouted. "Your Highness, you need to come inside. It's not safe out here."

"Of course it is." She hummed a tune and danced a little jig to it for good measure.

A half dozen guards converged on her position, and one of them, who acted like a leader, said gravely, "My lady, there has been a death in the palace tonight. I request that you come inside with me and my men now, for your own safety."

"People die all the time. And I'm enjoying the evening." She twirled in a circle, fluffing her skirts around her so they would fly out like a parasol as she spun.

"We have reason to believe this death was a murder."

She stopped spinning, her hair and skirts askew. "Murder? Here? That's ridiculous."

"Nonetheless, it has happened, Your Highness. Your lord husband would be gravely worried if he knew you were out here by yourself."

She laughed gaily. "He would be more concerned if I were out here at this time of night and I was *not* by myself."

The guards grinned reluctantly.

"Please, my lady. Come with us."

She heard the tone of an indirect order creeping into his voice. "Oh, all right. Except I've lost my stockings some-where around here. I laid them down . . ."

It took several minutes more of searching until her white silk stockings were located, draped over the log she'd sat on before. At last, the entire gaggle of guards and she made their way out of the deep woods and back toward the palace.

Once she had daintily picked her way out of the woods and had let the men guide her onto a main path, she asked the head guard, "Who was murdered?"

"It appears that High-Maker Meridine has met her end."

"No! Shocking!" She did not have to feign the emotion. It was shocking to think of. "How are Archduchess Quaya and Grand Marshal Korovo taking the news?"

"She's distraught. He's stoic, but devastated."

Genuine grief speared through her. "I'm so sorry for their loss. It must be terrible for them."

"Indeed."

As they approached the palace from the gardens, an

abnormal number of lights burned in windows throughout the enormous complex of wings and halls. "The place looks like it's in an uproar," she murmured.

"That's an understatement," the guard muttered.

"Oh, dear. And here you and your men are chasing me all over the palace grounds. I don't know what came over me. Thank you so much for finding me and escorting me back to the palace."

The guard made her a short half bow as one of his men opened an uncharacteristically barred door for her. "Several of my men will see you to your chambers along with men from the house guard. The rest of my men and I must return to our posts."

She touched his arm briefly, all the familiarity her rank and his allowed between them, before turning and sweeping into the palace.

Another large phalanx of guards met her at the door, and a harried-looking sergeant at arms assigned a half dozen soldiers to see her up to the Haraland chambers.

It was not hard to act dazed and confused as Kothite functionaries and Kothite lords and ladies hurried through the halls of the palace. She'd never seen the place so stirred up. She could physically feel the mental energy of agitated Kothites zinging through the air as she made her way through the throngs of people toward her rooms.

No one stopped her to specifically poke into her mind, but she had no doubt whatsoever that multiple high lords and a few archdukes did just that. She focused with all her might on the gardens, on the feel of dancing with abandon, that moment of disorientation when she'd realized she was lost.

Let them chew on that.

She made it to her chambers and asked the palace guard to search her rooms before they left her alone for the evening. When they declared the rooms clear, she nodded her thanks and closed the door behind them. And that was when she fell across her bed, buried her face in a pillow, and sobbed out her stress and fear.

* * *

The party did not spend the night with Nerra and Drest. Will led his friends into the forest, well away from the grove. Personally, Will couldn't stand to be close to Nerra's tree after her connection to it had been broken. Bloodroot, on the other hand, seemed aggressively, darkly pleased. Will got the impression a chain of events had been set in motion that excited the tree lord. Which could not be anything good. Bloodroot thrived on death and destruction.

Only minutes after Kendrick severed the dryad's link to the great rowan tree, it had drooped and wilted, losing its color and vibrancy. Leaves had started drifting to the ground, and death had clung to the increasingly bare branches. The entire grove had lost its luster the moment the dryad had been separated from her tree. It was as if the grove's luminous magic expired, a candle snuffed out.

Kendrick was distraught over what he'd done. No amount of reassuring him that the dryad had wanted the separation and that it was worlds better than killing her would console him.

As Will led the party away from the blighted grove, the entire Wychwold felt less alive. It was disturbing to him at a deep and fundamental level of his being. He would have fled the grove all night if the others had let him, but Rosana eventually asked for a halt to eat and sleep, and he'd acceded reluctantly. They set up camp, and he sat morosely by the fire staring into the flames.

Eben came to sit beside him. "Do you feel it, too?" the jann asked.

"Feel what?"

"The change in the forest. The elements feel . . . out of alignment."

"How so?" Will asked curiously.

Eben shrugged. "I don't know. It's just a feeling. Like balance was lost."

"Bloodroot's ready to throw a cursed party in my noggin. And he's the king of balance. He's all about death as the natural and necessary counterbalance to life."

"Yeah, well, that feels like a load of dung to me at the moment," Eben grumbled. "This wold isn't right anymore."

Will didn't know what to say. Intellectually, he agreed with Eben. But in his heart, he had the feeling a great and needed chain of events had been set in motion.

"Did you see the way those dark fae reacted after Kendrick sliced the tree and Nerra?" Eben asked abruptly.

"No. I was focused entirely on Nerra," Will admitted.

"They were all smiles among themselves. While all the other fae were busy weeping and wailing, they gloated like they'd just won a prize."

Huh. What could that be all about? From what little he'd heard about fae over the years, they were best steered well wide of. The politics of his own world were complicated enough. He didn't need to get himself embroiled in theirs, as well.

Eben picked up Eliassan's bow, turning it over in his hands. The firelight danced off its warmly golden wood, making the weapon seem almost alive. It was a double curved great bow and stood nearly as tall as Rosana, its smooth, sinuous silhouette speaking of exceptional quality workmanship.

Experimentally, Eben fashioned a crude arrow, whittling a shaft from a tree branch and fletching it with trimmed leaves tied on with a bit of thread.

Sha'Li said around a mouthful of roasted quail, "They say an archer never misses with Eliassan's bow. See if you can hit that white pine over there." She pointed with a drumstick at a large tree some twenty yards beyond the clearing at the edge of the firelight.

Eben nocked the arrow and drew back the string. Will was surprised to see his powerful friend actually have to strain to pull the bow. Angling the arrow tip up to compensate for its natural drop in flight, Eben loosed the arrow.

With a twang of string and a flash of green too fast for the eye to follow, the arrow flew up into the night. A moment later, Will stared as the arrow quivered in the trunk of the white pine tree, stuck dead center in its trunk about chest high to a man.

"The legends must be true," Eben breathed. "I'm no better

than an average archer, and yet that crude shaft landed exactly where I aimed it."

Rynn commented, "Then you'd best get busy making yourself more arrows. We could use a decent archer."

Rosana spent the evening fashioning a torn waterskin into a quiver for Eben to hold his rough arrows. Sha'Li cut fletches out of the feathers from the brace of quail that had been their supper, and Rynn busied himself rolling an extra bowstring for Eben out of a piece of sinew Rynn pulled out of his pack. Only Kendrick and Will had no craft projects to busy their hands.

Will moved over beside Kendrick, who stared morosely into the fire. "How are you doing? You seem a little down."

Kendrick grunted. "Don't patronize me."

"Okay. Let me rephrase. What's got you in a funk *now*? You look on the verge of slitting your wrists."

Kendrick actually smiled a little at that. "That's better. And the thought has crossed my mind."

That took Will aback more than he let on. Kendrick's despair was worse than Will had realized if he'd actually considered ending his own life. "Well? Spill what's troubling you, then. We don't keep secrets among ourselves out here. Breeds too much festering ill will."

"Of course you keep secrets. Everyone does," Kendrick retorted.

Will didn't feel like debating the point. Particularly since he harbored certain drastic secrets of his own. Like his real name. The identity of his father. The fact that he worried about Bloodroot fully possessing him or driving him mad one day. Or even killing him.

"You're dodging my question," Will persisted. "Why are you moping like a kicked puppy?"

Kendrick picked up a long stick and poked at the fire, sending up a shower of sparks. "I have failed in every way that matters. I have become the worst of Kerryl and lost the best of what I once was, of the man my father taught me to be."

"So you've run around the woods killing Keepers of the

Great Beasts, stealing the scions under their protection, and forcing unwilling humans to merge with them, have you?" Will asked skeptically.

"No, of course not."

"Then you're not the worst of Kerryl Moonrunner." Will kicked a loose ember back into the fire. "For that matter, today you reminded me to take the high ground and not kill the satyr. You helped us choose the honorable course of action, and furthermore, you did the difficult thing that had to be done. You took no joy in freeing Nerra, and your heart was not so hardened that her pain did not affect you. It seems to me you were very much your father's son today."

"Thanks for trying, Will. But"—a long, pained pause—"I am lost. Without my were-gift, I am empty. I am . . . nothing."

Was this how he would be after he was done with Bloodroot and removed the treant's seed from his chest and spirit from his heart? Cold terror coursed through him. He glanced across the fire and spied Rosana, her dark head bent over Eben's partially sewn quiver. No. As long as he had her, he would be all right.

Sha'Li came over to sit by Kendrick's other side. The firelight flickered off her shining black scales, making her look like some sort of elemental being not of this world.

"My kind," she said, touching the crescent moon and star mark on her cheek, "have legends of creatures gifted with were-magics by Lunimar himself."

Kendrick stared at her intently. "How?"

She spoke carefully, obviously trying hard to be comprehensible. "Certain tribe warriors earn such great regard from Lunimar and prove themselves to be so worthy that he grants them powers much like those Kerryl granted you."

"What powers?" Kendrick asked with markedly more interest.

"They have the power to transform at will into a creature, part man and part animal, with enormous strength, resistance to certain forms of magic, special abilities."

"At will?" Kendrick exclaimed. "These were-creatures control their own transformations?"

"Aye. Most of them." Sha'Li hesitated, then continued, "Some of the were-creatures are said to be cursed. They are made by means not of Lunimar himself—by birth as the child of a were-beast, or from the bite of one. The Cursed are slaves to the cycles of the moon and perhaps to their own rage. But the ones Lunimar makes—they're known as the Gifted. And they do, indeed, control when and where they transform to beast and back to human."

"That would be a fine thing, indeed," Kendrick murmured.

"If you miss your gift so greatly, perhaps there is a way to earn it back," Sha'Li said practically.

For the first time since they'd run into Kerryl and Kendrick fighting for their lives in the Sorrow Wold, Will saw real hope light Kendrick's hazel eyes.

"How, Sha'Li? How do I earn it?"

She shrugged. "The legends speak of heroic service as a Tribe of the Moon warrior."

Kendrick was crestfallen.

But she continued, "Have you considered asking it of Lunimar? You have already spent a long time living as a were-boar."

Kendrick stared morosely into the fire. "I was no hero. I was merely Kerryl's slave. A puppet on a string."

Sha'Li made a sound that Will took for disgust. "You protected Kerryl from harm. You were willing to listen to him when no one else would." She shot a damning look around the fire at the others, Eben in particular, but Will was not spared the silent condemnation either.

"You had a chance the first time we found you to renounce your curse, to leave Kerryl, and to return home. Instead, you told us to cure Tarryn, and you stayed with Kerryl to learn more of the threats he perceives. You turned down an opportunity to assume your father's post as landsgrave of Hyland, and instead, you chose to stay out here in the wilderness, risking life and limb to protect all the people of Haelos, and not just those in your father's holding."

"Enough, Sha'Li. I'll not sit here and have you falsely paint me a hero that I am not."

Will commented dryly, "Sha'Li makes a good point, you know. You're not a totally bad guy. Maybe this Lunimar fellow would give you a chance to gain back your lost skills."

"I wouldn't have the first idea how to go about asking some mythic being for such a thing." Kendrick sighed.

"I would," Sha'Li answered quietly.

Will stared at her. She knew how to talk to a being said to be one of the twelve immortal protectors of Haelos? Since when?

She placed a hand on Kendrick's arm. "There is a ceremony—it will summon Lunimar. If he wishes to speak with you, he will come."

"How difficult is this ceremony to perform?" Kendrick asked guardedly.

"Not difficult at all. We'll need a mug or goblet to hold a drink. Something to eat. And a clearing where the light of the moon can reach us."

"Can I watch?" Will asked.

"Me, too," Rosana piped up.

"I'd like to observe if it is not forbidden," Rynn chimed in.

"I'll watch if everyone else is going to," Eben said last of all.

Sha'Li tilted her head. "Normally, the ceremonies are secret and reserved only for tribe members. But we are family, and like Will said before, we do not keep secrets from one another."

Her words cut at Will. He'd never been honest with her. They'd fought together, *died* together, and he'd never found it in his heart to tell her—to tell any of them, not even Rosana—the truth. Yet here Sha'Li was, sharing the deepest secrets of her order with them.

Rosana dug out a wooden mug, which Rynn partially filled from the flask of wine he dug out of his pack. Eben unwrapped a loaf of bread the farmer's wife had baked for them two days ago, and they all trooped into the woods a little way, into a clearing Sha'Li had found for them. She arranged them in a circle in the blue-gray moonlight.

Will listened with interest as she dedicated this gathering to Lunimar and the tenet that he presented. She quickly recited seven oaths, and he tried to remember them all, but failed. They had to do with protecting the innocent, defending the weak, sustaining freedom, and things of that nature, though. All seemingly worthy ideals.

Sha'Li dedicated the food and drink to Lunimar and then invited him to join their gathering. They passed around the mug, and Will dutifully took a sip of the finest wine he'd ever tasted, full-bodied and rich, so dry it all but evaporated off his tongue before he could swallow it. Give Rynn full marks for having excellent taste. The bread was crusty and hard on the outside, yeasty and satin smooth on the inside. Give the farmer's wife full marks for her baking skills.

After they finished eating and drinking, Sha'Li set the mug of wine and plate of torn bread on the ground, then stepped back to join them in their circle. At first, nothing happened, but after a minute or two of uncomfortable silence, Will thought the moonlight might be growing a little brighter.

Surely it was just the strong wine affecting his sight.

No, the light was definitely getting stronger. And one shaft of moonlight in particular was glowing down upon the mug and plate in a visible beam of energy.

And then a man was there. One second he wasn't, and the next he was. Will didn't blink or look away, but he never saw the man take shape. He was just *there*.

Dressed entirely in white, even down to his white boots and the white gloves tucked in his white belt, the man looked around the circle until his gaze landed on Sha'Li. "Greetings, Child of the Moon. Well met."

For her part, Sha'Li seemed struck speechless.

Lunimar—for who else could this person be?—bent down and lifted the mug to his lips. "Very nice," he murmured.

Rynn smiled and said politely, "I'm pleased to learn that the elder beings have discerning palates."

Lunimar threw his head back and laughed, a rich, joyous

sound. When his humor passed, he addressed Sha'Li. "Why have you summoned me here, White Guardian?"

"My friend," she gestured to Kendrick, "has suffered a great loss. He was ritually gifted with the power of the were-boar by a nature guardian, one Kerryl Moonrunner. But through no doing of his own, that power was stripped from him by another being of great power and, I fear, great malice. Kendrick suffers terribly from the loss of that part of himself, and it is my fondest wish that you show him a path by which he might one day regain his gift."

Lunimar turned to face Kendrick. "How did you find living with the were-gift?"

"Difficult at best. Agonizing at worst," Kendrick answered.

"And yet you seek to regain this curse?"

"Through the eyes of my mentor, Kerryl Moonrunner, I saw some of the threats that even now approach this land and these people. How could I not accept the power along with the pain that I might better protect them?"

"A worthy answer." Lunimar stepped forward and laid a hand on one of Kendrick's shoulders. The two men stared at each other for a long time. Will got the feeling some sort of silent interview was being conducted.

At length, Lunimar's hand fell away from Kendrick. "I have seen into your heart, and it is pure. You are worthy of the gifts you were given and which you ask for once more."

Kendrick bowed his head. "Honestly, my lord, I do not think so."

"Which is exactly why I say what I do. Pride has been the downfall of many a powerful warrior."

The words went straight to Will's heart, a warning and advice to live by. If he didn't know better, he would say Lunimar had made the statement specifically to him. He bowed his head, acknowledging and accepting the wisdom.

Which was why he didn't see exactly what happened next. A bright flash of light made him flinch, partly blinded. When he looked up, both Kendrick and Lunimar were bathed in the shaft of moonlight, glowing brightly. As quickly as it had come, the light departed, leaving Will blinking and straining to see in the sudden dark.

Gradually, his night vision returned, and the clearing came into focus once more, a pale shaft of moonlight—no brighter or dimmer than usual—bathed Kendrick, on his knees now beside the mug and plate on the ground. The man in white was gone.

"What in name of Under Urth was that?" Eben demanded, rushing forward to help Kendrick to his feet.

"Your cheek!" Rosana exclaimed.

Will saw Kendrick reach up and brush at something on his face. A mark. A gold crescent overlaid upon a black eight-pointed star. "You're marked, Kendrick! Just like Sha'Li. Well, not just like her. Your mark is gold, where hers is white."

"Does that mean he has accepted me?" Kendrick asked wonderingly.

"It means more than that," Sha'Li said soberly. "It means he has granted your request. That's the mark of the Chosen of the Moon."

"What does that mean?" Kendrick asked.

Sha'Li smiled. "I'm not sure. But I suppose you'll find out."

"Am I a were-creature again?"

She shrugged. "Most tribe members come by their powers gradually, over a period of time. I have never seen Lunimar himself gift someone, though. Maybe you have all the powers of the marked ones, or maybe you still have to earn them."

For the first time in a very long time, Kendrick's shoulders were square, his head held high, as he walked out of that moonlight and back to their campfire. Will followed behind, profoundly relieved. They needed their friend back at full speed if they were to succeed in their increasingly perilous quest.

In a moment of prescience, it dawned on Will that Lunimar had not randomly gifted Kendrick with were-powers. There had to be an urgent purpose behind such a boon.

So much for feeling relieved. What did the greater beings know that he didn't?

CHAPTER

26

To say trekking through the Thirst was rigorous didn't quite capture the exhaustion and discomfort of this journey. Raina's usual headache was supplemented by constant pain from heat, dehydration, and blinding sun during the days. The nights were better, but the sand continually sucked at her feet, weighing down each step and getting inside her boots, rubbing her ankles and soles raw.

Without Hatma, they never would have found the seeps under rocks or tiny oases tucked in deep valleys that kept them supplied with life-giving water. Raina began to forget what green and growing things looked like as the days passed, the vast and unrelenting Thirst around them nothing but sand and more sand.

One night as they stopped to eat and refill their skins at a seep, Hatma commented, "They say that once this place was covered by water. The Estarran Sea used to curve inland all the way to the western end of Iridu. Once I found the skeleton of a great fish in the Silver Sands, uncovered by a sandstorm."

"What are the Silver Sands exactly?" Raina asked.

"Magical sands infused with silver. Changelings who venture into this region often lose their minds. They wander off and die unless they can be convinced to listen to their companions."

"Why changelings?" she asked.

"Unknown" was Hatma's only reply.

The fifth morning of their trek, as they pitched camp in the lee of a dune, Raina broke down and asked their guide,

"How much longer do you think it will take to reach this zinnzari woman?"

"Tonight, if the weather holds."

Lakanos looked up at the sky quickly. "What's wrong with the weather?"

"Storm's brewing," their guide muttered.

Raina looked up at the sky, which was the same dirty color of blue that it had been every day of their trek. "How do you know?"

"I feel it in my bones."

Cicero asked the scout, "How bad does it feel?"

Hatma shrugged. "Bad enough. Sometimes we get lines of storms. Several light storms come through, and just when you think it's cleared up and life can go back to normal, the big one hits."

"Sounds like a hurricane," Lakanos remarked.

"Aye," Hatma agreed.

A sand hurricane? That sounded ominous.

"We should get an early start tonight," Hatma declared.

Lakanos agreed quickly and then helped Raina finish setting up her tent. She wasted no time crawling into it to rest. If they were going to be racing a sandstorm, she would need all her strength tonight.

Indeed, when Hatma reached into Raina's tent a little before sunset, wind whipped around the guide, peppering Raina's skin with sharp grains of sand, a harbinger of things to come. They wrapped their bodies from head to toe, tying shut sleeves and pant legs with lengths of sinew, using their sunshades over their eyes even though dusk was falling. Anything to keep the blowing sand from creeping into their clothes and scouring at the tiniest patch of exposed flesh.

"Drink as much water as you can," Hatma instructed them. "It's easier to carry inside of you than on your back if we have to move fast."

While the three of them complied, guzzling down as much water as they could, their guide continued, "If you get separated from the rest of us, for the Lady's sake, stand still. Do not wander around blind in the storm, or we'll never find you. Hunker down. Use your tarp as a tent. It'll get buried, so every hour or so you'll have to dig a tunnel out to the side, then bending up to the surface so you can get air. Make the bend in the tunnel or the wind will sandblast you to death."

That sounded like a rather unpleasant way to die.

Hatma unrolled a long rope and shocked Raina by actually tying their waists together as she instructed, "Stay close and keep the rope slack so you don't pull each other off your feet."

"I thought you said we would beat the storm to our destination!" Raina shouted to be heard over the howling winds.

"And so we shall if you all can keep the pace I set tonight," Hatma replied.

"This isn't the storm?" she shouted.

Hatma's laughter was carried away on the wind, but Raina got the gist of what the guide thought of that.

Leaning into the wind, Hatma set out, leading the three of them like pets on a leash. How the guide saw where to go or maintained any sense of directional orientation, Raina hadn't the slightest idea. For the most part, she kept her head down, her face turned away from the worst of the blowing sand, and followed the rope blindly. Thankfully, Lakanos's bulk blocked some of the gale. But still, it was unbelievably hard going, every step requiring immense effort and concentration.

They did not stop to eat, but rather chewed on tough dried meat as they slogged along. She was as tired as she'd ever been, and she'd been pretty thoroughly exhausted on several occasions over the past year or two.

Darkness set in, and the world narrowed down to the constant howl of the wind and the shifting sand swirling around her ankles. Sky and sand blended into one, and she moved through it in a daze of fatigue and pain.

All of a sudden, she bumped into something large and hard, oomphing as the breath rushed out of her. Lakanos had stopped in front of her, and she'd run right into him.

"Are you all right?" he shouted back at her.

"Yes! You?"

"Fine. We've reached a cave. Watch your head."

Without his warning, she undoubtedly would have plowed right into the low overhang. She paused to shout the warning over her shoulder to Cicero and then ducked inside. The shock of stillness was palpable.

She shook herself, sending a cascade of sand to the floor of the room-sized cave. Then she unwrapped her head and peeled back the layers of her clothing. More sand piled up at her feet. "There. Much better."

Hatma grinned at her. "You did well for a gai-gee."

"A what?" Raina asked.

"An outsider. Someone not born to the sands. I knew the warriors could keep up with me. But you I was not so sure of."

"The daughters of Tyrel are tough," she declared stoutly.

Cicero grinned. "Or merely too stubborn to know when to stop."

Lakanos found that hilarious and joined the kindari in laughing at her.

Raina shrugged, secretly well pleased with herself. She'd kept up under the most trying of conditions. Glancing around the modest cave, she asked, "Where are we?"

"This cave lies a day's walk from Kahfes, the great cross-roads of the Thirst. It is here I last saw the old shaman you described."

Cicero was wandering around the room, using a hand torch to examine the place. "Someone's been here recently. Looks like they live here. Is there another chamber farther in?"

Hatma smiled. "Well done, wild elf. This is an outer chamber that serves as a buffer against storms and heat. The dwellers of this place make their homes deeper into the rock."

"Ah ha!" Cicero exclaimed. "Clever arrangement."

Raina moved over to the opening he was examining. A broad sheet of rock stood in front of a gap accessible from either side of the big rock. Beyond lay an opening into a much larger cave.

A dozen doorways, these blocked by hanging skins or wooden doors, opened off the central cave. As soon as they entered the space, several men appeared in the doorways, armed with wicked curved swords and hard expressions. But as soon as they spotted Hatma, their demeanors changed entirely. Greetings and thumps on the back were exchanged.

One of them asked, "And who do you bring along with you like a gaggle of lost sheep?"

Hatma made quick introductions all around as Raina and the others continued unwrapping and uncloaking. Raina got down to the White Heart tabard, and an excited exclamation went up. Immediately, a half dozen children and various people with injuries and illnesses came out of the side caves.

Without even stopping to think about it, Raina reached out to the listless toddler who looked the most desperately sick, lolling in his father's arms. She gathered healing and surged it into the child.

And reeled back, clasping her head in agony.

Lakanos reached her side first. "What ails you?" he asked urgently under his breath.

"It's nothing," she managed. Blinking hard, she cleared her head of the searing agony and moved forward to the next child. This time she was more judicious in the amount of magic she summoned, gathering only enough to turn the tide of the child's hacking cough toward healing. Steeling herself as she cast the spell into the child, she managed not to react to the pain this time.

And then she started healing adults. Waves of emotions broke over her. Fear, rage, lust, envy, longing, and grief poured through her until she choked on them, barely able to force words past the feelings to shape her healing. But vividly aware of Lakanos watching her like a hawk, she gritted her teeth and continued healing her way through the cave's denizens.

Before she'd gotten halfway through the adults, she felt like vomiting. It was too much. Her mind and spirit could not contain the excess of feelings and impulses, memories and suffering. She was losing herself in all of it. Losing her mind.

In truth, it was a minor bit of healing for her, and yet she felt on the verge of passing out. She knew full well that if

Lakanos figured out how sick she really was, he would yank her out of this place and march her straight back to Dupree whether she liked it or not.

She was so close to finding Gawaine. She and her friends had been working at this for two years. Not to mention Vesper was closing in on him as well. She had to keep going until they woke the Sleeping King.

It didn't help matters when Lakanos stepped close behind her to mutter, "You're positively gray. What's going on with you? I've heard tales of you casting ten times this much magic without breaking a sweat."

"I'm fine."

His eyes narrowed, and she said quickly, "We've had a hard journey, and I'm a little tired. That's all."

She turned to heal the next person, a man who was suffering from some sort of fever that had him sweating and shivering at the same time. A spell for curing disease was in order—

The next thing she knew, she registered being on her back. In a dark place, the air thick with incense and the smell of smoke. Voices spoke quietly over her head.

"—seen it among my kind before." The voice was female, but old. Raspy.

"How did you fix it?" This voice was male. Deep. Lakanos.

She kept her eyes closed, shamelessly eavesdropping on their conversation.

"My kind were closely tied to the land, and it was from there they drew their magic. The most talented casters not only drew magic but also the thoughts and feelings of the wild creatures to them."

"How did that work out?"

"Some learned to control the feelings. Block them out. Some didn't. Like your girl here."

"What happened to them?"

"They died."

A long pause, then, "Unacceptable. There must be a way to fix her."

"In truth, I'm amazed that the amount of healing she did

earlier didn't drop her where she stood. She should already be dead."

"Mayhap she is strong enough to overcome this affliction."

"Make no mistake about it, warrior. No mage survives this affliction for long. She'll die, and soon."

"There has to be a way to save her!"

"If she stops using magic completely, she'll stop drawing the emotions that overwhelm her."

"She's White Heart."

"You asked how to save her. I answered."

"You never found another way to fix your healers?" Lakanos asked. Raina was surprised at the note of desperation in his voice. He was genuinely worried about her.

Leather squeaked as if someone had shifted position on a hide-covered cushion. "My people have tried everything. Eventually, for some reason, every mage so afflicted casts too much magic and gets lost in the wilding. It's too much for their bodies and minds to handle, and they die."

Raina lay very still, absorbing that news in dismay. Dry fingertips touched her temple, and Raina lurched, surprised, looking up into an ancient face lined with age . . .

. . . and more importantly, lined with faint, red brown lines in the circular scallops of a spiderweb.

"You're zinnzari?" Raina asked.

"I am. And who are you, child?"

"My name is Raina. I need to speak with you urgently and in private." She started to sit up, but a combination of the woman's wiry hand on her shoulder and the sudden return of smashing pain to her skull conspired to force her back down.

"Rest, child. You're not going anywhere soon."

"Where am I?"

"In my hovel. A little dustup is blowing outside, and you need to regain your strength. You know better than to use your magic in your current state, do you not?"

She answered in a small voice, "Yes."

"Good. Then sleep. It'll do you good."

She closed her eyes and dozed until returning voices woke

her once more. Beside the fire, the shaman sat on a low cush-ion covered with some sort of furred pelt. Cicero sat on the floor beside her, and Raina noticed that Lakanos chose to stay by the door, his hand resting on the pommel of his sword. The woman was staring at her, however.

The shaman said, "Hatma tells me you've made a very long journey to find me."

"I have," Raina answered carefully, testing the pain in her skull. Back down to tolerable levels. Thank the Lady. Appar-ently, this had not been the day she killed herself by casting too much magic.

"What brings you to see me, child?"

Gawaine's warning firmly in mind that the zinnzari would likely not be enthusiastic about helping her wake their leg-endary king, Raina took a deep breath. "These past few years, my friends and I have sought to wake the Sleeping King, a man you know as King Gawaine of Gandymere."

The shaman rocked back on her cushion, hissing through the gap left by one of her missing front teeth.

"Please hear me out before you refuse to help me," Raina said quickly. "My companions and I have traveled much of what was once Gandymere in search of clues to his where-abouts and how to wake him. And we've made excellent prog-ress. Now another being seeks him as well, not to wake him but to possess his body and make it her own. Time is short, and we need your help."

"I'm an old lady living in a cave, waiting for death to claim me. I cannot help you."

Raina smiled gently at the zinnzari woman. "You and I both know that's not true."

That seemed to startle the shaman. She picked up a bit of wool braiding, weaving its strands together absently. Raina noticed the woman made a mistake but did not stop to pick out the misplaced knot. Good. The shaman was rattled.

"Last year, my friend Will Cobb and I traveled to the dream realm. There, we found a beautiful grove filled with trees and birds, and the softest green grass you could ever imagine. Can you guess who we found in the grove?"

The shaman held up her hands as if to ward off the rest of Raina's tale.

Raina continued, "We met the dreaming echo of Gawaine. He's been trapped there all this time, waiting for someone to rejoin his spirit to his body. Your king not only lives but is awake on the dream plane. Only his body sleeps, guarded by your kind."

"Enough, child. Stop!"

Raina fell silent.

"The legends say my people will end when he wakes—"

Raina interrupted. "Legends propagated by Hemlocke in order to keep your people from rebelling against her?"

The shaman stared at Raina. "How do you know about the Green?"

"Gawaine told me about her." Raina continued relentlessly, "He also said it is time to wake him, and that your people would likely resist the idea at first. He said you would be afraid to believe me and my friends when we say we have the means and knowledge to wake him."

"Do you? Do you have the means?"

Raina did sit up then, and Lakanos leaped forward to help her, steadying her with a strong arm behind her shoulders and piling folded blankets and skins behind her. "May I have my pouch?" she asked him.

She rummaged in her bag, coming up with Gawaine's crown. She held it out, and the gold edgings on the leaves caught the firelight and glittered bright as sunlight.

The shaman slid off the cushion and to her knees, and then bent over, touching her forehead to the floor in a deep obeisance to the crown of her king. Raina could only imagine what a shock it must be to see a piece of the regalia of a man the shaman's people had waited five thousand years to wake.

Raina held out her right hand, showing the ring she wore on her middle finger. "This is his signet ring."

The shaman rose up onto her knees and took Raina's hand to reverently kiss the ring. "Where did you get these?" the shaman finally managed to ask.

"We found the crown in a cave guarded by the Boki. You might know them as the Night Reavers."

The shaman growled deep in her throat, but Raina cut her off. "They were actually most helpful to us, and many of them died defending us so we could retrieve the crown from its hiding place and journey to the dream realm to meet Gawaine."

"And the ring?" the shaman asked.

"We were led to it by a nature guardian who laid a trail to its hiding place. Shortly thereafter, I met Cerebus—"

"Gawaine's steed lives?" the shaman cried.

"Yes. He was trapped, but we freed him. It is from his horn that this ring is carved. He gave me his blessing to wear it until I can place it on the finger of its rightful owner."

"That explains why you yet live," the shaman declared.

"I beg your pardon?"

"You should be dead already. Mages with your affliction only live to cast magic once or twice before the wild emotions take hold of them. But with my liege's crown in your possession and his ring on your finger, the healing magics in those items must be stabilizing your spirit."

Huh. It made perfect sense now that the shaman said it.

"A warning, child." The shaman continued, "Do not be fooled into believing those items will protect you forever. Eventually, even they will not be able to ward off the wilding. You are in grave danger."

"I'm in grave danger anyway."

"From whom?" Lakanos demanded quickly.

"From Vesper. From Hemlocke if and when she figures out what I'm up to. From the zinnzari themselves if Gawaine speaks true."

Lakanos was suddenly beside Raina, crowding her back, away from the aged shaman.

"Be easy, sir knight," the shaman said. "I will not kill your charge. On that you have my word."

"Thank you for your concern, Lakanos," Raina added. "But she speaks the truth. It will be the zinnzari who guard

Gawaine's body who pose a threat to me. Assuming the dragon guarding him does not incinerate me first."

"Dragon?" Lakanos pivoted slowly to stare at her.

Raina smiled up at him lamely. "Well, yes. Hemlocke is the Green Dragon, and it is she who hid Gawaine's body and has guarded it all these years."

"What have you gotten yourself into, White Heart?" Lakanos blurted.

"It is a quest of utmost importance, I assure you. The safety and survival of Haelos and everyone in it depend on it."

"Treason," he grunted. "That doesn't describe the half of what you're up to."

"Not really, no," she agreed. Full-out rebellion was closer to the truth, but Lakanos prudently didn't say the word aloud.

Raina turned back to the small woman. "Gawaine told me that where I find the zinnzari, there I will find his body. I need you to tell me where I can find the rest of your people."

"I am the last of my kind."

"You lie," Raina said flatly. "I have met the spirit warriors of your kind who still die to this day and join Gawaine in his grove, guarding him into eternity."

"Gads. You really have found him," the shaman breathed.

"Like I said. We've found his spirit. Now we have to find his body and join the two."

"Do you communicate with his spirit?" the shaman asked curiously.

Raina cast an uncomfortable glance in Lakanos's direction. "I dream of him from time to time."

"What does he say about waking him?"

Raina didn't hesitate. "He says time grows short, and it is now or never. If Vesper finds his body before we do, she will steal his body, and he will be destroyed. His last link to this plane will be gone, and even his dreaming echo will be lost."

"Who is this Vesper?" the shaman asked.

"Another spirit trapped upon the dream plane, also seeking escape. However, she has recovered enough of the shards of her spirit that she is very close to breaking out. She is a Kothite, the child of Archduke Ammertus, and very powerful."

"Also very evil," Lakanos added grimly.

Raina stared at him. "You know who she is?"

"Aye."

"How? Memory of her was erased!"

Lakanos pursed his lips. "The Royal Order of the Sun also has its secrets, Emissary."

"Gawaine has spoken to me about great swaths of human memory being lost or stolen. How did your order avoid that?"

"Are you asking as an emissary?" Lakanos asked reluctantly.

"I am if it means you have to answer me!"

He sighed. "I do not *have* to answer you. But I do understand why you have a compelling need to know. Certain members of my order have the means to protect our memories from . . . slipping away."

Raina heard the pause and knew he was glossing over some secret he didn't want to share with her. She let the moment pass without challenging him.

He continued, "We wear a certain gem"—he fished out a chain from under his shirt and showed her a roughly tumbled stone milky green in color and about the size of her thumb—"native to Haelos and imbued with certain protective qualities, one of which is protecting memories."

"You remember Vesper, then?"

"I was not born when she came to Haelos, but I have been taught of her by knights who did know her."

Who knew her. But who didn't fight against her, apparently. "The Heart fought on the side of the Empire, then?"

The shaman looked back and forth between Raina and Lakanos, obviously struggling to follow their shorthand conversation.

"Only the White Heart has the luxury of standing on both sides of the line," Lakanos replied shortly.

"You support Vesper, then?" she challenged.

Good heavens, what had she done? She'd trusted this man and told him everything he needed to know to guide Vesper straight to Gawaine's body. Did she have it in her to stop him somehow? Could she kill him if it came down to that? She might only have one good blast of magic in her before she died, but she might have to use it to stop him.

She wouldn't hesitate to sacrifice herself to save Gawaine. She only wished she knew if she could actually succeed in taking out a knight of his power. He would have spell defenses. Several small attack spells in quick succession, followed by a single big spell. Except she didn't know any killing spells. Would a big enough blast of raw magic take him out?

All those thoughts passed through her head in the single instant it took Lakanos to answer firmly, "I am most definitely not on the side of Vesper. Neither she nor her sire is stable enough to merit support from the Heart."

"What are you two talking about?" the shaman finally interrupted.

"Nothing, madam," Lakanos answered smoothly, bowing a little in the old woman's direction. "I apologize for our obtuseness. It was rude of us." He shot Raina a warning glance as he straightened.

She nodded slightly, acknowledging that now was not the moment to finish their conversation. But they would later. That she silently vowed. Turning her attention back to the shaman, she said, "As my guardian has pointed out, we have been extremely rude. I haven't even properly introduced myself. I am Raina, White Heart emissary, and daughter of Tyrel." That last she added in hopes that it might hold some weight out here in the wilderness where her Heart rank likely meant little or was actually a detriment to her.

"Long ago, I was called Aylinoor. Now people just call me Ayli." The shaman turned away and fussed over serving up bowls of bright yellow stew over rice.

"Is this a big storm?" Lakanos asked conversationally as they all began to eat.

"Pshaw. This is a bare puff of breath. If you want to see a storm, step into a crawling cloud."

"And what's a crawling cloud?" the knight followed up.

"A tainted mist that blows off the Crest." She raised a hand. "It's touched by void magic. Death envelops everything the cloud touches."

Raina was glad to let him carry the conversation, particularly since Ayli seemed taken with him.

"This storm may be nothing, but mark my words. I feel a big one brewing. I'm thinking maybe this little puff of air is running in front of a mist hurricane."

"A mist hurricane?" Lakanos inquired.

"Aye. That's when a crawling cloud and a sand hurricane come in together. They rearrange the whole desert. Move the dunes, bury springs, and uncover great rock outcroppings no one knew were there before."

"Doesn't that disrupt travel routes if the water sources shift?"

"Oh, aye. Something terrible. Takes months after a mist hurricane comes through for the caravans to resume travel through the desert."

"Full caravans traverse the Thirst?" he exclaimed.

"Great long trains of camels carrying goods and riches pass through. That's how this little settlement gets the supplies we can't make for ourselves. We trade water and food to those who pass by this way. Like earlier. Your girl healed us all—everyone pitched in meat or spices or goat milk to this pot to make your supper."

"An efficient way to live," Lakanos commented.

"Brutal and simple. You help me; I help you. You don't help others, they don't help you, and you die."

Lakanos grinned. "What can I do to help you?"

Ayli threw her head back and laughed. "Stars, you make me feel young. That'll go a long way toward getting you what you need, you handsome rascal."

Lakanos spared Raina a single sidelong glance before murmuring, "What I truly need is the location of your zinnzari clansmen. My charge will not stop until she finds them or kills herself trying, and I will be stripped of my knighthood should I fail to keep her safe. Please help me. I'm at my wit's end with her."

Raina sincerely hoped he was overstating both the threat to his knighthood and how frustrated she was making him with her quest.

"What of you, kindari?" Ayli asked Cicero abruptly. "Why do you travel with this strange child?"

"She doesn't have enough sense to look out for herself." A shrug. "My kind look out for the weak and innocent, protecting nature's creatures from harm. The way I see it, she's one of those."

Raina stared at him. She'd never really considered why he'd taken her under his wing and looked out for her the way he had. She'd always stacked it up to him being too honorable to walk away from a young, vulnerable girl on the road alone. But she was no longer vulnerable or alone. And yet, he'd stayed. "Truly, Cicero, why do you put up with me?"

"I believe in your cause, and I believe in you to see it through if you can just stay alive long enough. That is why I lend my sword to your protection."

"Thank you," she said quietly. "I'm sure I do not deserve friends as stalwart and loyal as you."

"Don't go all mushy on me now," he warned.

"Right. No mush." She sniffed loudly and took a wobbly breath.

No more was spoken of the zinnzari that night as the hour grew late and the settlers in the cave doused the fires and crawled into their beds. Even through the rock walls, Raina fancied she heard the wind screaming and felt the raging storm shaking the earth beneath her. As exhausted as she was, sleep was a long time coming.

Morning was hard to distinguish from night with only torchlight illuminating the cave. Raina crawled out of bed and dressed while she assessed her skull this morning. It was back to its usual dull roar.

"How's the storm doing?" she asked Ayli.

"Abating. Another hour or two, and it should be safe for us to go out."

"And where are we going?" Raina asked cautiously.

"You want to find my brethren, don't you?"

"Most assuredly!"

"Then that's where we're going," the shaman declared. On that note, the woman turned her back on Raina and commenced pulverizing some sort of pea-sized seeds into a fine powder using a mortar and pestle held between her knees.

Bless Lakanos for convincing Ayli to help them. Maybe they would beat Vesper to Gawaine after all. And maybe, just maybe, they would succeed in waking him up.

CHAPTER

27

J ustin huddled deeply in the fur-lined cloak Kadir had been wise enough to acquire for him. How could it be spring everywhere else in Haelos and feel like the dead of winter in this corner of the continent? His feet were half-frozen, his hands not far behind, and his nose was definitely frozen all the way through.

"I think this should do it," Kadir said from in front of him, stopping at the crest of a ridiculously high mountain that they'd just spent the past two days climbing, step by painful step.

The air was thin up here, and even as young and strong as he was, he labored to breathe and felt light-headed with even the slightest exertion. "Now what?"

"Now we start a fire and see who it draws."

Justin gratefully dumped the bulky load of wood from his shoulders to the ground. "You think General Tarses is going to magically appear because we light a fire in his mountains?"

Kadir grinned. "It won't be just any fire, my boy. It'll be elemental fire. Ritually enhanced and certain to infuriate any ice-aligned beings in the area."

"It's the infuriating bit that worries me," Justin retorted. He'd heard the legends and songs of General Tarses. The man had conquered an entire continent. He would crush a simple pair of mages.

"Yes, but we know something he'll give his life to hear."

Justin thought Kadir was entirely too optimistic that he was going to get an actual chance to tell Tarses they knew where his children were before the general blasted them off this mountaintop. This wasn't his plan, however. He was just the lowly apprentice.

"Lay a fire while I set up the ritual circle and prepare the components," Kadir ordered.

Justin broke twigs and stacked kindling, sorting the firewood he'd carried up here into piles of increasing size, ready to feed into a fledgling fire. "Ready when you are," he reported.

The sunset was nearly complete, with only a thin slice of its fiery orb skimming along the mountains in the west. And then it disappeared from view. Their plan was to light the fire at night when it could be seen for miles.

Kadir nodded and took a seat in the circle. "Light the fire, Justin."

Using his body to shield the grease-soaked wool from the light breeze up here, he struck the flint, sending sparks into his fire starter. It lit on the second try. He bent over it to blow gently and began feeding in twisted strands of grass. Over the next few minutes, he gradually fed the flame larger sticks of fuel until he had a decent fire crackling merrily. "Fire's steady," he murmured.

"Keep feeding while I start the ritual."

Justin watched with interest as Kadir built a magic dome to contain the wild ritual magics and then summoned more and yet more fire magic to himself beneath the dome. By the time Kadir had finished, the entire interior surface of the dome danced with flames writhing and twisting in a ferocious effort to escape.

As Kadir pointed his hotly glowing hands at the fire, Justin cried, "Don't blast it all at once or you'll explode the fire and send embers everywhere!"

Kadir half opened one eye in disgust, as if to say he knew better than to do such a thing. He began streaming the ritual fire magic into Justin's campfire, and in seconds, a raging bonfire rose to the very top of the ritual dome. Spectacular ribbons of red, green, and purple threaded through the yellow, orange, and blue of the blaze.

"Step out of the circle, boy."

Justin did as he was told, backing away from the flame until his face didn't feel as if it were roasting. Using his pack for a seat, he sat down and leaned back against a boulder, enjoying the coldness of it against his back as the fire heated his front.

The ritual fire was a mesmerizing dance of flames and magic intertwined. The power of it rolled forth into the night, passing through him with unfamiliar vibrations. He had no training in the elemental magics, but after this display, he was tempted to learn how to control this wild magic.

Without warning, something cold and sharp touched his neck just under his chin. A rough voice behind him snarled, "Move and you die!"

"Kadir!" Justin rasped, stretching up and away from the knife at his neck. "We have company."

Ensconced inside his blazing dome of fire, Kadir turned to face Justin and his would-be assassin. "Greetings, Lord of Ice. General Tarses, I presume?"

"Who are you? How dare you bring that magic into my place!"

"We are but a pair of wondering mages seeking audience with the Hand of Winter, who is said to rule these mountains," Kadir answered. Of course that vibrating dome of ritual magic around Kadir gave lie to his description of himself as merely a wandering mage.

"For what purpose do you seek the Hand of Winter?"

His assailant moved far enough away from Justin that he was able to turn his head cautiously to look at his attacker. The man was dressed head to foot in pale armor that looked made of ice. Although, at the moment, firelight glinted off its surface, turning the suit the color of burning blood.

The man wearing the suit was large overall, his face mostly hidden in shadows, but Justin thought he glimpsed pale cheeks, maybe swirled with the elemental tamgas of a jann's skin.

"Come now, General, let us not be coy with each other," Kadir said briskly. "We have traveled a long and arduous path to bring you news of your family."

The man's blade, glittering clear and wet, like ice, came up swiftly. "Now I know you lie." He made a blindingly fast lunge toward the circle.

Kadir never moved. Never changed expression. He merely stared calmly at the man encased in ice. For his part, the warrior stopped just shy of the burning circle, glaring fiercely at the mage seated inside.

It was a long standoff, punctuated only by the occasional snap or crack from the fire. Justin held his breath, not daring to move a muscle, lest the man in ice cut him down where he stood.

Eventually, the man pushed up his visor, revealing the strong, handsome face of a jann in his prime. "Who are you?" he demanded.

"My name is Kadir."

"Have we met?" the warrior asked suddenly.

"Once. When you came to visit the Mages of Alchizzadon, an order to which I and my apprentice, Justin, once belonged."

"Belonged, past tense?"

"Correct. I have parted ways with my order over a minor disagreement."

Justin frowned. Was that all Raina was to him? A minor disagreement over whether or not a young woman should die permanently in the name of the order's research program?

"What do you know of the general's family?" the man demanded, still refusing to identify himself.

Kadir shrugged. "When the general introduces himself to us, we will be happy to speak with him directly. Until then, however, I'm sure he would prefer that we keep our information to ourselves. His family is a matter most personal to him, I'd wager."

The warrior glared at Kadir for several seconds and then unaccountably burst into laughter. "Well played, sir." He sheathed his sword, backed away from the ritual circle, and sat down on a likely boulder. "You can hide in your circle if you like, or you can extinguish the beacon. I have come, and you know full well who I am."

"It is a pleasure to meet you again, General," Kadir said

as the ritual circle faded from view and only a campfire remained, burning cheerfully under the night sky, which was navy blue on its way to black.

Justin stared surreptitiously. That was General Tarses in the flesh? The great conqueror of continents? Personal friend of the Emperor himself? It was hard to imagine that he, a kid from tiny Tyrel, was sitting with someone so important.

"If you have information about my family, speak," Tarses ordered tersely.

"Your children live."

"What?" Tarses leaped to his feet, clearly shocked by the news. "Where? How do you know this?"

"Someone I trust implicitly asked me to pass the message to you."

"What can you tell me of them?"

"I believe your son travels with my source. He seeks to wake an ancient Haelan king and foment rebellion against the Kothite Empire," Kadir answered bluntly.

"Excellent." A fierce smile broke across Tarses's face. He paced back and forth, and as he did so, his expression and tone changed. "Maximillian has overstayed his time on the throne. He needs to go."

Justin was shocked to the core of his being, not only at hearing treason spoken so openly but also with the venom in the general's voice.

Tarses growled, "After all I did for him, the whoreson stripped me of everything. My name, my reputation, my achievements, my honor."

He dared to call Emperor Maximillian such a thing? For a second, Justin wondered wildly if lightning would reach down out of the clear sky and strike them for it.

"As if that was not enough, his lackey killed my wife and children," Tarses's voice rose in anger, "but now you say my children live. I was denied knowing them as they grew, prevented from shaping them into adults, deprived of their love and they deprived of mine—" He broke off, practically shouting.

Tarses breathed hard for several long moments, visibly fighting to calm himself. The ice tamgas on his face actually seemed to be moving across his skin, reflecting his agitation. Then he spoke so coldly Justin physically shivered at the words. "Oh yes. My Emperor has a great deal to answer for. And I shall see to it he does."

"Excellent!" Kadir said brightly. "I was hoping you would feel that way."

The cheerful tone seemed to startle Tarses, whose gaze narrowed suspiciously. "What do you want from me?"

"I want nothing from you. Although I would like you to help your son."

"Why?"

"Because your son is helping my daughter. And I would very much like to see her live."

Justin stared, well and truly dumbfounded. Kadir could only be speaking of Raina. *He* was Raina's father? That certainly explained a lot. Like why he'd let Raina get away when she'd run away from home two years ago. And why he'd rescued her from Elfonse and his cronies when they'd tried to kill her. Why Kadir had recruited Justin and asked him to find Raina and look out for her. Indeed, that explained a great deal.

Tarses was nodding slowly, and Kadir was nodding back, their stares locked in mutual understanding. They were two fathers in agreement that their children would be protected to the limits of both of their considerable abilities. Justin rather pitied whoever got in the way of these two.

"Where's my boy now?"

"My daughter is marked with a scrying rune. The last time I checked, which was yesterday, she was in the Thirst, headed toward Kahfes. I can only assume that your son is with her or plans to rendezvous with her there."

The Thirst was months away from here on foot. Justin mentally groaned at the march that lay ahead of them.

"I cannot bring us directly into Kahfes, but I have access to a gate that can get us close," Kadir declared.

"Close is good enough," Tarses declared.

"When do you wish to leave, General?" Kadir asked.

"I'll summon my warriors. We leave now."

M arikeen listened closely as her superiors received the report from Anton Constantine's messenger.

"—governor's spies report that the same party was seen passing from the Valelands into the Thirst on the night of the new moon, headed toward Kahfes."

That was two days ago. How did Anton send messages hundreds of leagues so quickly? She'd heard of a man who was experimenting with training birds to fly long distances at incredible speeds, carrying messages tied around their legs—

"Marikeen!"

She started and looked up the table at Richard Layheart, leader of the Cabal.

"I need you to go with Anton. Help him find your brother and his companions. Discover what they are tracking, and ensure they don't make off with it. Anton is right. It's high time everyone realizes *we* are the preeminent clearinghouse for magic in Haelos. Henceforth, nothing magical shall be discovered or harvested or mined but that it does not pass to us first."

Anton was a pompous, arrogant thug who thought that enough gold could gloss over his complete lack of civility or nobility. He'd killed the only father she'd ever known, and one day she would kill him. But for now, she would bide her time, smile politely, and make nice with the thug.

"Of course, Richard. It would be my honor to do this service for the Cabal," she answered smoothly. "When do you wish me to leave?"

"As soon as you have gathered what supplies you need for the journey."

"It could take us weeks or even months to find them—"

He cut her off. "I have a magic item that will open a gate to Kahfes. I think the current crisis warrants its use." He added slyly, "And I'll charge Anton for its replacement cost."

The old adage was true. There really was no honor among thieves.

E ben woke up feeling energized and strong, ready to conquer the world. No matter that the journey across the Silver Sands toward Kahfes, in the heart of the Thirst, was nightmarish at best. Ever since he'd come into possession of Eliassan's bow, he'd felt amazingly hale and whole.

The others crawled out of their bedrolls, groaning over sore muscles, cracked lips, headaches, and the general misery of desert travel. Small wind and fire elementals had plagued their journey, rising up out of the sand without warning and attacking viciously. The good news was that Eben was starting to sense the presence of elementals before they manifested. He could only give his friends a few seconds' warning, but that was enough for weapons to be at the ready and defensive positions assumed.

They sat in a circle to break their fast, which was actually supper, and he wolfed down his rations as usual. He asked Sha'Li, who was still eating daintily, "How are you holding up? These Silver Sands aren't messing with your mind?"

Her brow scales lifted and came together in a point over her nose in what he knew to be a frown of mild irritation. "I'm not a changeling. The Silver Sands don't affect me."

He leaned back, propped up on one elbow to stare at her. "What do you mean, you're not a changeling?"

"Are you an elemental?" she shot back.

"No. Jann have an affinity for the elements, but we're not elementals."

"Just so," she declared as if that explained everything.

"But you're part reptile, part human. Doesn't that make you a changeling?"

Sha'Li was on top of him so fast he hardly saw her coming. She tackled him, rolling him onto his back and straddling his chest with her surprisingly powerful legs, pinning him down, hands around his throat. "I'm. Not. Reptile."

Thankfully, she wasn't squeezing his neck too hard nor were her long, sharp claws extended. "Then what are you?"

Up close, her eyes weren't truly black. Dark green and flecks of gold were visible around the edges of her vertical black irises. He reached up to grab her forearms and attempted to peel them away from his throat. He couldn't break her hold without exerting enough force that he might hurt her. Her scaled skin was softer than he'd expected, warm and pliable, not hard or armorlike.

As she leaned over him, an amulet he'd never seen before spilled out of her shirt and dangled between them, hanging from a finely made chain. At a distance of about six inches, he got a good look at it. The piece was made of what looked like nullstone, but instead of carvings upon it, a sinuous line had been cut all the way through the face of the stone. He could look through a slit and see Sha'Li's shirt behind the piece. The amulet looked old, and even he could sense power emanating from it.

She stared down at him until he felt obliged to tease a response out of her. "Don't know what you are, huh?"

"I know. I'm just considering whether or not you deserve to know."

"Aw, c'mon, Sha'Li. We've been friends forever. I'd never do anything to hurt you." He thrashed from side to side playfully, trying to dislodge her from his chest.

"You already have hurt me."

He stilled abruptly beneath her. "How?"

"By believing that I could or would betray you. I know how much Kerryl hurt you. But I could not let you do a wrong thing you would have regretted later. I was trying to protect you."

That night she'd stopped his blade from slitting Kerryl's throat had loomed between them ever since it happened. He'd been so angry at the time he'd been ready to kill her, too.

"Kerryl hurt my brother. And I protect my own."

"I respect your code of honor. It's simple and direct. I like that."

She did? In a rare moment of subtlety, he wondered if it meant that she liked him, too.

"I wish life was always so simple as yours, Eben. But

sometimes the choices we must make are not good or bad, black or white. Sometimes they lie in the gray."

"That's deep. Even for you."

She let go of his neck and gave his shoulder a playful swat. She remained seated on his chest, however. Apparently, she wasn't done having her say with him yet. "Look, Eben. I'm sorry I interfered between you and Kerryl. Well, I'm not sorry I interfered, but I'm sorry I interfered."

He grinned at her garbled words, but he got the point. She was not sorry she'd stopped him from killing Kerryl, but she was sorry she'd angered him. His grin earned him another harder swat on the shoulder.

"Ow!" She was nearly as strong as he was. Not that he was complaining. He'd always been afraid of human girls who seemed so fragile and breakable. He'd never been comfortable around them.

He stared up at her, and she stared back down at him, awareness of each other dawning between them. They'd been friends for two years. But was there more to it than that? Shock poured over him. She loved water. He hated it. She preferred to sneak around in the shadows. He charged straight ahead. He was jann. She was . . . not.

"You never did answer my question, Sha'Li. What are you? I genuinely want to know."

"Are you familiar with how ogre-kin are descended from ogres or troll-kin are descended from trolls? They're not mixed-breed ogre-humans; rather, they're a new race that evolved from the original race."

He nodded. "Like the Boki. Neither orc nor human, but something else."

"Lizardmen are like that."

"What . . . who . . . do you descend from?" But even as he asked the question, he realized he knew the answer.

"Dragons."

She was dragon-kin. Suddenly, she seemed a great deal less reptilian and looked a great deal more like her legendary ancestors. "Why are you called lizardmen, then?"

She shrugged. "It's not what we call ourselves. It is an insult thrown at us by pinkskins."

"I'm sorry."

"For what? For thinking I was part lizard?"

"No. For being mad at you when you stopped me from killing Kerryl. You did the right thing. It just made me angry that you pointed out my loss of control by stopping me. I was embarrassed by my behavior."

"None of us are perfect, Eben. We can only do our best and hope that, in the end, we make a small difference for good."

"There be wisdom in the dragon girl."

Her eyes opened wide in surprise, showing bright whites against her ebony scales for a moment. Another hard swat on his shoulder. "Quit teasing me!"

"I'm not teasing," he replied quietly.

Another long, intense look between them.

And then she jumped up abruptly, holding a hand down to him to help him to his feet. Their palms met, strong fingers clasping, and his breath caught. If he was not mistaken, hers did the same. A quick yank, he was upright, and then she spun away, moving with quick grace before he could say or do anything more.

Well, then. A dragon-kin, huh? His mind filled with that, he followed the others as they set off toward Kahfes and a storm gathered in the west.

R aina pushed back her hood and stared up in wonder at the stone form of a woman warrior holding up the soaring roof of the great cavern of Nhem with her carved hands. The magnificent statue was one of the four great caryatids—pillars carved to look like women—that supported the enormous underground structure.

"Her name is Ghali," Lakanos murmured.

"How can something so beautiful be so strong?" Raina asked.

Cicero answered, "They say no miner has ever been able to even scratch the surface of one of the caryatids of Kahfes. It's illegal to mess with them, but kids try all the time to climb them or chip off a piece as a souvenir. None have succeeded."

The cave of Nhem opened onto the desert, spilling golden light into the night, but the space was so large that before they'd barely ventured into the city within, Raina had lost sight of the outside completely.

It made sense to live below the earth like this, tucked away from the violent storms and heat of the Thirst. In the long journey to reach this great trading center, she'd gained a rich appreciation of just how harsh the desert could be. But she'd never imagined a city could be entirely contained in caves.

Four caves sheltered Kahfes, perched not only on the intersection of overland trade routes but also on the intersection of several great underwaes—navigable underground rivers traversing Under Urth—and at the intersection of several great ktholes, deep underground tunnels of mysterious origin and usage. The city came by its informal nickname, the Cross-roads, honestly.

Kahfes was the capital of the landhold of Hari, situated in the center of the Thirst, bounded by Amadyr and its Silver Sands to the east and Iridu to the west—a strange place of cracked earth, disappearing rivers, and creeping mists. Few were brave enough to venture there, let alone live there.

"Where to, Emissary?" Lakanos asked. He'd reverted to her formal title, no doubt because they were in public and he might be overheard addressing her.

"Is there somewhere around here we can get a drink and a hot meal?" she asked.

"I know a pub called the Desert Rose. It serves excellent food if you like Ordan cuisine. And the silverware is clean," he replied.

"I've never eaten Ordan food. But I'm willing to try. Lead on, sir knight."

Ayli said, "I have friends in Nhem I would like to visit. I'll meet you at the Desert Rose later."

Lakanos turned to their guide. "Please go with her, Hatma, and look after her safety."

The guide nodded, and the two women departed, fading into the crowd of shrouded desert dwellers.

"Want me to follow them?" Cicero murmured.

"No. They'll be fine," Lakanos replied. "With the amount of magic Ayli can cast and Hatma's speed with a knife, I pity anyone who tangles with them."

How did he know how much magic Ayli had or how fast Hatma was? Raina would have asked, but she was distracted as they ducked into the Desert Rose.

The pub was actually a large tavern with rows of long, wooden tables able to seat at least two hundred people. She shed her cloak reluctantly, revealing her White Heart tabard, but the heat pouring forth from the fire in the great hearth gave her no choice. Thankfully, she was not mobbed immediately by locals demanding healing.

"Is there a Heart chapter nearby?" Raina asked as she settled with her back to the room, happy to hide her colors from casual observation.

"Yes. Do you wish to visit it?" Lakanos asked.

"Actually, I'd rather not. I don't have time to get sucked into lengthy Heart business."

"As you wish, Emissary."

Lakanos really was a wonderful bodyguard, patient and nonjudgmental with her. His presence was both reassuring and comforting. "Are you sure there's nowhere else you need to go?" she asked him as they waited for food to arrive. "Surely you have other responsibilities besides babysitting me."

"Once you are safe behind a locked door tonight with Cicero standing guard in my stead, I will slip away to the Heart to make a report to my superiors. They will be eager to know you are safe."

"And interested to hear what you have to say about my recent experience with our mage friends, no doubt," she added.

"No doubt."

Cicero asked, "Why did we come to Kahfes?"

"Besides the fact that both Hatma and Ayli said a big storm was coming and we needed to seek shelter," Raina replied, "if our companions have passed through this region, someone here will have seen them. Everyone in the Thirst passes through the Crossroads. At least that's what Hatma says."

Lakanos murmured, "I asked her to inquire with her contacts after your companions, Emissary. When she returns, mayhap she'll have news for us. Until then, we wait."

Will looked over his shoulder yet again. A strange cloud boiled in the distance, obliterating both horizon and sky. White like a cloud at the top, it faded to beige at ground level where it was picking up and tumbling sand as it boiled forward. It took no great knowledge of weather to see that a massive storm was coming.

The sun must be setting somewhere behind that terrible cloud, for the light faded around them and a bizarre yellow-green twilight turned into full night much earlier than normal.

Every time they topped a dune, a tantalizing glow in the east marked the great crossroads of Kahfes. But the lights ahead were not drawing closer nearly as fast as the storm was overtaking them from behind. A sinking feeling heavy in his stomach, Will realized they would not reach the city's shelter before they were swallowed by the roiling blackness behind them.

Without warning, a large, fast-moving shadow raced toward them from their right, towering three or four man-lengths in height.

He drew his staff in alarm and summoned magic that crackled across his palms tonight as if reacting to the storm drawing near.

"Get on!" a man shouted from within the moving shadow, his words all but torn away by the rising winds.

The shape resolved itself into a sled of some kind with a trio of giant sails attached to a tall mast. Two other men manned lines attached to the swinging booms holding the bottoms of the sails rigid.

"Who are you?" Will demanded.

"Does it matter? If you don't make shelter at Kahfes before that crawling cloud catches you, you're all dead! We don't have much time. I'm cutting it close as it is, and I've stopped to pick you up! Climb aboard and be quick about it if you would live!"

Will helped Rosana clamber over the raised lip of the sled as the others jumped on, and then he tumbled aboard himself. He'd barely hit the deck before the conveyance was under way once more, flying down the face of a dune and zooming up the next.

"What is this thing?" he shouted at one of the crewmen.

"Sandskimmer. The *Last Wind.* Here. Grab this line and help me hold the boom steady."

Will grabbed the rope with both hands and was stunned by the power of the wind vibrating down the sail and into the line.

"Captain Maahes is the best. You're lucky we found you. No other skimmer captain out here would have stopped for you with a storm so close behind us. As it is, we'll barely make Kahfes before the caves are sealed."

The ride was like nothing Will had ever experienced, with wind whipping in his face till his eyes watered and the undulating landscape flying past at an unbelievable speed. The great cloud roiled forward relentlessly behind them, but now it was not gaining on them . . . at least not as much.

They topped a great dune, and a huge, open plain opened out at their feet. The crew let out the skimmer's sails all the way as they zoomed down the last dune, and the sled barely seemed to touch the ground as it lived up to its name, skimming across the flats stretching between them and safety.

The cloud was close now, a growling, rumbling roar behind them, devouring each crest behind them in its turbulent depths. Will look back fearfully and could swear he saw some sort of creature emerge briefly from the wall of the cloud, taking form out of magic and dust, its lower body a whirlwind, its upper body humanoid in shape. Void magic crackled across the being's hands, black and angry. The creature smiled at Will, showing pointed teeth, its eyes glowing dull red, as it extended forward ahead of the cloud, reaching for him.

Will yanked his staff down over his shoulder and aimed at the being, sending a blast of force magic at it. The magic flew erratically, and by lucky happenstance struck the creature full in the chest. It dissipated back into the cloud with a screech audible even over the roar of the cloud.

A tall cave entrance loomed ahead. From each side of it, massive, paneled doors were slowly rolling inward toward one another to seal off the entire cave.

The captain shouted orders, and the crewman Will was helping let out the line to the very last inch. The silken sail overhead strained so hard Will held his breath, expecting it to rip from stem to stern at any moment. The ride became so smooth that he actually thought the runners no longer touched the ground. It was terrifying and exhilarating flying on the breath of the storm.

The storm devoured the plain behind them, seeming to pick up speed as it tumbled over the flat landscape, chasing them with stubborn determination to eat them all.

The door operators must have spotted them, for the blast panels halted with only a narrow opening between them. The *Last Wind* would never fit through that tiny gap, assuming Captain Maahes could even manage to point the skimmer at it as it flew along at the mercy of the howling winds.

Will looked back, and the storm was so close he could almost reach out and touch the violent wall of dust and debris. If he weren't so scared, he'd be hurling his lunch over the side of this vessel. But as it was, his entire body was paralyzed with fear.

"Hang on! This is gonna be close!" Maahes shouted.

The doors loomed. The storm loomed closer.

And then, all of a sudden, they flashed through a tall, narrow opening. Will cringed away from the edge of the sled, convinced the door was going to decapitate him. By some miracle, the entire vessel fit through the gap.

And then Maahes and the crewmen were all yelling, and everyone aboard grabbed the lines and hauled back on them with all their strength. A dock flashed by as the skimmer tipped up onto one skid, careening sideways and throwing up a great rooster's tail of sand as it screeched to a halt mere feet from the back wall of the cave. Slowly, majestically, even, the craft righted itself and came to rest on both skids.

Will drew what felt like the first breath he'd taken since the storm topped that last dune. Behind them, the howl of the storm abruptly cut off as a great clanging thud accompanied the closing of the blast doors.

"Better close than never," the captain declared cheerfully. "Jehan Maahes at your service."

Rynn seemed to be the only member of the party able to summon his voice after the paralyzing panic of the past few minutes. "Thank you for the timely rescue, Captain. May we buy you a drink?"

Will's throat thawed enough for him to guffaw, "One drink?

After that, we'll buy a feast for the whole crew and all the ale you and your men can drink."

That caused much back thumping and laughter, which gave Will time to recover his composure after that close call with certain death.

"To the tavern, boys!" Maahes cried after his men had secured the *Last Wind* and lowered her shredded sails.

And that was when Will's reaction to the last few minutes finally set in. His knees knocked together, and his stomach felt on the verge of turning inside out. He sagged against the cave wall, barely able to stand.

"Buck up, Will," Rosana said jauntily. "That wasn't nearly as bad as a regular sailboat. Let's get some food in you, and your stomach will settle in no time."

Easy for her to say. She'd never experienced a second of seasickness in her life.

Maahes said, "There's a fine spot in Phul, the western cave, where the locals like to eat and drink. It's got gambling parlors and singers. Even has a Diamond. If we're lucky and enough gladiators are stranded here by the storm, the owner might throw together a tournament. Gotta watch out for him, though. Name's Ylvaro. Wandrakin. Wears the coat of an Antillan general he bested. *Never* make a bet with him." The skimmer captain said jovially, "Place is called the Three Veils. A bit pricey, but since you're paying, all's well." Laughing, he slapped Will on the back, and they headed into the great caves of Kahfes while the most violent crawling cloud in recent history howled outside.

Endellian lurched awake, startled to have fallen asleep in a chaise under one of the bejeweled gazebos in the Imperial gardens.

"Ah, she is a vision of loveliness and awakens as gently as a summer breeze to gaze upon me," a smooth male voice said nearby.

Alarmed, her head whipped around—

Vlador Noss stood there, a perfect white rosebud held out to her. She took the flower from him, bemused at how he'd gotten past her guards to approach her this closely. After he'd helped the Man in Amber kill the chamberlain, she'd kept her distance from the Child of Fate.

One thing was undeniable. He was the most accurate seer her father had had since the prophetess Oretia had been killed by Ammertus.

"What prompts you to disturb my rest, Vlador?"

He ignored her question and instead murmured in that rich, mesmerizing voice of his, "Yon flower holds no advantage in beauty over a woman such as you, caught in the first bloom of her life, dewy and radiant, untouched by frost or time."

Her irritation at having her nap interrupted faded in the face of his flattery. "Go on."

"Like that rose, you will open into full bloom and come into your glory. But unlike the rose, you will not wither slowly, fading and dying one sad petal at a time."

She realized with a start that he was prophesying. Vlador was known for his extraordinary bluntness and clarity with his predictions, which was why she'd almost missed this one. Replaying his words in her mind, she asked, "How will I die?"

"I do not see death for you, my princess."

"What do you see?"

"I see a truth as incontrovertible as it is inevitable. But if I dare utter the words aloud, my life is forfeit."

She glanced around. "We are alone. My guards stand well off and cannot hear you. Cover your mouth lest one of them read your lips. But I would hear what you see."

"I see the end of Maximillian. He will put up a great storm of fire and fury, but he will end nonetheless."

Her heart blazed with hope, and her innards clenched with excitement. "When?" she whispered. "How soon?"

"For people like you and me, time is a fluid concept."

"Nail it down for me. I want to know when, *exactly*, your prophecy will occur."

"I cannot tell you that which I do not know. However, I will attempt to find some event or reference within my visions that might give you a reasonably exact time frame."

"As soon as you know, I want to know. Day or night. You'll come to me. Yes?"

He smiled knowingly and bowed deeply. She noticed, not for the first time, how tall and well turned his physique and face were. Too bad Vlador and Laernan were fast lovers. She would have enjoyed sampling his pleasures in her bed. Maybe she still would one day. But for now, she had no wish to cause tension with her brother. If Vlador was right, she might have need of Laernan's services and loyalty soon. Very soon now.

A thousand years and more she'd waited for this chance to seize the throne that was rightfully hers. She'd never entertained any illusions that Maximillian would willingly hand over his power to her. She had always known that if she wanted it, she would have to pry power away from him by trickery or treachery.

So. The portents were aligning, and Oretia's old prophecy of the end of Koth was starting to come true at last. Immense satisfaction coursed through her, along with ferocious determination to have her due.

Yes, indeed. Her long wait was nearly over.

A urelius leaned back in his chair, patting his full belly. "Harun, your cook outdid herself this time. I do believe I might burst."

The landsgrave of Hari, Harun Sandclaw, stroked his wind tamga, which curled around his left ear and onto his scalp, shaved on the left side to display the marking. "I'm sorry you gentlemen have been stranded here by the crawling cloud, but it'll give us time to catch up on what you've been doing since the campaigns."

Aurelius glanced over at Selea, who seemed pained at the idea of days' worth of small talk while the storm blew itself out. "It's been a long time since Mindor and Pan Orda. What about you, Harun? I heard you served in the Cunning Legions of Archduchess Cassamyr of Scythia. Weren't you on the front lines of the fight at the Sultan's Scar?"

"Indeed. I captained the *Sadalcass*, and a faster sand-skimmer there never was . . ."

Aurelius caught Selea's grateful glance as Harun launched into a recitation of every detail of the great battle of the Sultan's Scar. And then, like his nulvari friend, Aurelius tuned out, worrying instead about where his grandson was tonight and praying the boy wasn't caught out in this horrendous storm, audible even through the thick stone walls of the underground.

All the portents said a crisis was coming to a head and that this forsaken place was where the storm would break. The real storm. Not the wind and dust blowing around outside. No, the next storm to come to this land would be of a different kind altogether and would determine its fate for all time.

The storm had finally blown itself out, taking five days and nights to do so. Even the locals were impressed by the rare congruence of a crawling cloud and a major sand hurricane, and everyone was speculating on how dramatically the landscape had changed as a result. A line of scouts was waiting at the great blast doors to head out and remap the Thirst, redrawing the trade routes from water source to water source. Apparently, old oases would be entirely buried and new springs revealed by a storm of this size. The first scouts to come back with passable routes would get hired by the biggest, richest caravans.

Raina followed Cicero as they moved impatiently past the line of scouts and plunged down a broad staircase into the western cave. Phul, she believed it was called. Raina balked, however, when he headed for a huge establishment with a long line of patrons outside betting on the gladiatorial combat apparently taking place inside.

"I have no desire to watch slaves bash each other's heads in for the pleasure of the betting public," she muttered at Cicero.

"Then come into the restaurant of the Three Veils with me instead," he said with unusual good cheer.

Raina ducked inside doubtfully, pausing for a moment to let her eyes adjust—

A fast-moving person slammed into her, nearly knocking her over, and then laid a bone-crushing hug on her.

"Sha'Li?" Raina cried.

"Yes. We're all here. Where have you been?" her friend demanded, laughing and scolding her all at once.

"I ran into a little snag at Alchizzadon—"

"Wait. Come over where we're seated and tell all of us at once." Sha'Li practically dragged her off her feet in her eagerness to show Raina to the others.

A round of hugs, exclamations, introductions, and laughter ensued as she and her friends, old and new, came together. Rynn flagged down a barkeep and asked for a private dining room. The Three Veils had one unengaged at the moment, and Rynn handed over a gold piece that purchased both room and food for the evening.

They piled inside, and everyone took turns telling the tale of their past month of travels over a table piled high with food and drink.

And then it was Raina's turn to introduce Ayli. "Remember the zinnzari shaman Kerryl Moonrunner told us about? I found her."

For her part, Ayli stared at Raina. "Moonrunner? You know him?"

"Yes. He's the one who told us about you and where to look for you."

"Canny old rat," Ayli said fondly.

"Have you known him long?" Kendrick asked her.

"Couple of hundred years," she answered.

Sometimes Raina forgot how long people of other races lived. She frowned. Except . . . She blurted, "How is it Kerryl, a human, has been alive that long?"

"Well, now. Kerryl has done some bad things in his life. And one of those is consuming the life energy of certain creatures to extend his own longevity."

Raina replied, "That's awful!"

Kendrick was quick to respond, however. "He had his reasons. He knows things—has seen things—that others have not. He had to stay alive to prepare for them."

Raina and the rest of the party shared a group eye roll at the familiar refrain.

Eben asked Ayli, "What other bad things did Kerryl do?"

"Well, there's the whole business with Quinton and the Hunter in Green."

"The Tribe of the Moon Hunter in Green?" Sha'Li asked in surprise.

"Aye," Ayli replied. "She loved Kerryl's brother Quinton deeply. But the Hunter in Green cannot forgive Kerryl for taking her lover from her."

Sha'Li leaned forward, asking intently, "Is this Quinton also called the Wild Prince?"

"Why, yes. I believe he is."

"Ah." Sha'Li sat back in satisfaction.

Raina rounded on her. "Who exactly is the Wild Prince?"

"He is a were-wolf. But not just any were-wolf. He is said to hold the spirit of the Great Wolf within him. This story confirms the legend."

Sha'Li turned to Kendrick. "Is Quinton's insanity problem the reason Kerryl used a scion of the boar to create you? Did he learn from his brother that the vessel had to be strengthened before it could handle the power and magic of a great beast?"

Raina interrupted, "Kerryl didn't *use* a scion. He killed it."

Kendrick glared at her, Eben glared at Kendrick, and Sha'Li glared at Eben. Funny how it had taken under two hours for the old arguments between them to resurface.

Ayli intervened. "For all his unorthodox methods, Kerryl did save the Great Wolf. And he showed the Widow of the Wood how to save the scion of Zinn." She added, "It's not as if he got off unscathed. Kerryl lost his wife when the Circle broke. Poor man never was the same after that."

"How and when did the Circle break?" Raina asked.

Ayli studied them all, hesitating to answer. Finally, she mumbled, "If you're going to wake the Sleeping King, you might as well know it all. You'll either handle the truth or lose your minds as fate dictates."

Raina urged her, "Tell us."

"An Imperial Army came to take Haelos. The red-haired Kothite led it—"

"Ammertus?" Rynn interrupted.

"Aye. Just so." Ayli continued, "He brought his daughter, Avilla, with him. She died in the battle that broke the Great

454 • CINDY DEES AND BILL FLIPPIN

Circle. Rumor has it Ammertus shunted her spirit to the dream realm in a last-ditch effort to keep her from dying permanently. But she's become one of the most powerful creatures there."

Raina shuddered. How were they supposed to beat Vesper to Gawaine's body and keep her from possessing it if she was that powerful? First a dragon, and now a Kothite spirit of immense power? She commented wryly, "All we need now is for Anton Constantine to show up."

Hatma spoke up from her spot in the shadows by the door. "Oh, he's here. Got in just before the storm. He's staying in the south quadrant with a dozen or more servants and guards."

Raina and others traded horrified looks.

"How soon will it be safe to leave Kahfes?" Rynn asked, looking to Hatma and Ayli.

The scout answered, "As soon as the great doors open. Conditions won't be ideal for travel, but a person won't die if they know what they're about."

"And when will the doors open?" Will asked.

"Sometime tonight," Hatma answered. "The scouts were lining up to head out when we came here."

Raina swore mentally and joined her friends in pushing back from the table. No words were necessary between them. If Anton was so close behind them and Vesper in front of them, they had to go. Now.

E ben was shocked by the elemental energy swirling in the gritty air as he and his friends slipped through the barely open storm doors and into the last of the storm. The wind buffeting him was not mere air but elemental magic pulling at him aggressively, trying to suck the magic from his bones. Likewise, the sand stinging his facial tamgas was tinged with something dark and deadly. Individual grains sought bare flesh through the chinks in his armor and tiny gaps in his clothing and tore viciously at his skin.

Their party trudged west, across a vast, flat plain that did nothing to slow the attacking gusts. Daylight was breaking behind them before the air finally calmed, the dust settling.

A crystalline stillness came over the Thirst, the sky overhead lightening from black to gray to pink.

No insects or other living creatures disturbed the silence. Only the quiet slide of sand under their feet marked their passing. In the wake of the storm, the peace was immense and filled the vastness of the desert.

A sense of rightness filled him. Kendrick was restored. They would wake the Sleeping King, find Marikeen, and then go home to Hyland as a family.

Hatma murmured from in front of him, "Eben, do you sense any moisture?"

He didn't have to work hard to feel it through the soles of his feet. "A few degrees to the south of our current course. A league or so ahead."

"Excellent. We'll fill up our waterskins and try to get a reading on where the next water might lie before us," the scout murmured.

They hop-skipped to three more seeps before the sun rose high and searingly hot, driving them under a rock overhang to wait out the afternoon heat. Waves of hot air mingled with dust devils—insubstantial beings that danced wildly across the sand, their transparent limbs whirling to and fro in deadly arcs.

"Don't mess with those," Hatma warned them. "They kill the unwary and suck all the moisture from your flesh."

Eben sensed their lust for water even as they disappeared back into the heat mirages from whence they came. He napped through the day, taking his turn at the watch, glad that none of the dust devils came back.

A bright moon lit their night travels, turning the desert to powdered silver. They spent their fifth day of travel at a great oasis their guide called Immunwah. It apparently grew around the roots of a giant tetrakis tree, and hence was able to withstand the ravages of the storms.

They headed due west out of the oasis the following evening. Eben was in the lead, approaching another water source, this one extremely strong, when Hatma grunted beside him.

"What?" he asked her.

"I should have known your quest would bring you here."

"I'm not leading the quest. That madness falls to Will and Raina. I'm merely leading us to water."

"Then how do you explain those?" She pointed west, and on the far horizon he spotted a cluster of spires rising up into the night.

"What are those?" he asked.

"The Towers of Triell. They're said to be dragon-made to stop the Griefalls from splitting the continent all the way to the Estarran Sea."

"And the Griefalls is . . ."

"A great crack in the Urth. It extends for hundreds of miles to the west of the Towers. At its western terminus lies the great Griefall itself, where the Nyghtflume disappears into Under Urth. The Nyghtflume is a massive river that flows down from the Crest, which is a great ring of mountains beyond the Thirst."

He frowned. He didn't sense a great river nearby. "How far away is this Nyghtflume?"

Hatma laughed. "It'll be many hard days' travel before we reach it, if that is where your quest leads you. But let us hope you go elsewhere. A foul river in a foul place is the Nyghtflume."

"How so?"

"The water is poisonous upstream of the great cascade, but the fall purifies it. Beware the waters that bypass the falls and find other routes down into the chasm, though. They are still deadly."

"How are we to drink if we have to traverse this chasm you speak of?"

Hatma snorted. "Carefully."

"How big are yon spires?" he asked suspiciously.

"They tower like mountains over men, hundreds of men's lengths in height."

They looked like toothpicks on the horizon, which meant they were still many leagues away. Eben extended his awareness outward and felt the immense power of the stones, plunging deep into the earth, solid anchors placed there by great magics.

"The great fissure ran right up to the Towers," Hatma explained, "but then it split into two lesser chasms, one running north, and one running south."

Ayli chimed in. "The zinnzari enclave lies beyond the tip of the southern branch on the shores of the great inland sea, Shaelashal."

"We go to Zarva, then?" Hatma asked in surprise.

Raina interjected, "I've been thinking about it. I don't think we should speak directly to the zinnzari."

Eben actually stopped walking and turned to stare at her.

"As we've been getting farther out here, Gawaine's ring is starting to act like a magnet. It's drawing me in a particular direction. Are you feeling anything from the bow, Eben?"

He frowned, concentrating. "I sense a great deal of energy concentrated in that direction." He pointed nearly due west. "Like all the elements rolled into one. But I would not say it pulls me toward it."

Raina nodded nonetheless. "That's the direction the ring is pulling me."

"Then we've got a problem," Hatma said. "To continue in that direction past the Towers of Triell, we'll have to descend into the Griefalls. And there's no way anyone but the most experienced climber can make the descent without dying."

"What about using magic to get down?" Will asked. "I have a feather fall scroll I've been itching to use."

Ayli shook her head. "Magic doesn't work normally in the Griefalls."

Everyone stared at her.

"How not normally?" Raina asked.

"Healing magic still works. But the other kinds are hit or miss. Using magic to get into the crevasse or enhance movement in the crevasse, for example, doesn't."

"How will we get down there, then?" Eben asked practically.

"We could use the ktholes," Hatma answered. "With a group this size, we should be safe."

Should? That didn't sound promising.

They walked for several hours toward the Towers, but the Towers barely grew any larger in size. They stopped to rest and eat, and Ayli regaled the party with stories of a great ruin south of them called Akaram, dominated by ziggurats nearly as tall as the Towers of Triell.

Eben would like to see such a thing. Maybe one day, he would come back this way. Or mayhap on the way home—

Ululating howls erupted from nearby, and Eben scooped up Eliassan's bow and the new quiver of fine arrows he'd purchased in Kahfes. The bandits came at them in a ragged line, seeming to boil up out of the ground like ants pouring out of their mound to defend it.

The fight was challenging to the extent that a lot of bandits attacked them. But with a Heart knight, Kendrick, Will, Rynn, Cicero, and Sha'Li to wield weapons, himself to shoot arrows, Hatma to cast alchemy gases, and Raina, Rosana, and Ayli to cast healing, they formed a highly effective combat unit.

It took perhaps ten minutes to turn the tide of the fight in their favor enough that all the ambulatory bandits fled, disappearing back into the sand as abruptly as they'd appeared. Oddly, Raina didn't do her usual race around the battlefield healing everyone in sight and sending the defeated attackers on their way with stern words of warning to behave themselves.

"Is she all right?" Eben asked Cicero, lifting his chin in Raina's direction.

"The Mages of Alchizzadon did something to her. She hasn't been right since we got her out of there. Complains of headaches and passes out if she heals too much."

Indeed, Raina staggered and went down as the last partially healed bandit shambled off into the sand, and Eben joined the others in rushing over to her.

He was peering down at her in worry as the Heart knight, Lakanos, carefully fed Raina a potion when Rynn murmured, "We've got company. Arm yourselves."

The bandits weren't back, were they? The convention was that once the White Heart took the field, all combatants healed by the order had to retire from the field peacefully and not return. If that rule was broken, the follow-up rule was that the returning fighters would be killed and not healed a second time. He stowed Eliassan's bow and pulled out his long sword and mace. They were more suited to the violent work ahead.

But when he scanned the sand for incoming attackers, he saw nothing.

"Where—" he started.

"Coming in fast from the north," Rynn interrupted.

Eben spied them then. A caravan, if the pack animals and human porters were any indication. They approached in a long, single-file line, and every member of the group was dressed from head to foot in white. They glided across the sand with amazing speed and, as they drew near, were eerily quiet.

Now what?

Anton laughed as the Towers of Triell came into sight at the far edge of the horizon, bare twigs above the sound. "I see where our young quarry is going. You"—he pointed at about half his mercenaries—"follow them at a distance and keep out of sight. I'll cross the Griefalls and will race ahead to Marringat."

"Marrin-who?" the Cabal girl, Marikeen, asked him.

Impudent chit. "Marringat," he answered impatiently. "An old Imperial fort just above the great waterfall at the head of the Griefalls."

"I didn't know there were any Imperial outposts this far into the western wilds," Marikeen commented.

"Just because you didn't know doesn't make it untrue!" he snapped.

Marikeen looked at him steadily with those uncanny, dark eyes of hers contrasting in her pale, water-marked face. Girl gave him the creeps. He made a mental note to have a word with Richard Layheart when he got back to civilization. She was a liability to the current project of building a shadow mage's guild. The girl needed to disappear discreetly.

He gave one last set of orders to his men. "Keep the pressure on them. Don't let them rest or sleep or even eat in peace. I want them to be frazzled wrecks when they get where they're going."

"And where are they going, my lord?"

"You'll see when you get there. That's soon enough for you to know."

Ayli gasped a little and bowed low to the figure at the head of the silent, white-garbed column.

A regal head nod was returned.

"We're honored that you choose to show yourselves to us," Ayli said respectfully.

A male voice answered from within a shroud of white, "We heard the sounds of combat. Is all well here?"

"Yes, these younglings handled a bandit attack with ease."

Eben wouldn't exactly call it easy, but they hadn't been sorely pressed.

"Is that one in need of healing?" the man in white asked, gesturing to where Raina lay.

Rosana rose from her side. "No, sir, she's just overtaxed from healing."

Raina? Overtaxed? Those mages at Alchizzadon must have done something drastic to her.

The man in white stared at Rosana from the slit in his head wrap. In fact, all the people in white were staring at her. Will must have noticed it, too, for he stepped forward to stand protectively at Rosana's side.

"Will you share our fire with us?" Rosana asked the newcomers.

The leader of the white caravan bowed deeply. "It would be our pleasure."

The group, two dozen in all, sat around the campfire and ate as silently as they traveled the Thirst, sliding food up under their veils to eat and not revealing their faces. They must be fugitives, the way they refused to show themselves.

Eben was intrigued to examine the light wooden frames the travelers unstrapped from their boot soles. A webbing of sinew stretched across each frame, providing a sort of ski that attached to the toe of their boot.

One of the caravaners gestured for him to try on a pair. He shuffled around, tripping himself at first, but as soon as he got the hang of the gliding stride required, he could move across the sand without sinking into it at all. Clever.

He took off the sand skis and returned them to their owner with a smile. "Very nice. Smart."

The skin around the eyes of the one he spoke to crinkled slightly. He would take that as a smile.

The only man from the white caravan to speak so far asked, "If you would allow me the honor of a question, healer, how is it you came to be so far from your blood?"

Eben was startled to realize the question had been aimed at Rosana.

"I don't understand," the gypsy replied. "What do you mean, I am far from my blood?"

The white-swathed head tilted, and the white, swirling tattoos visible at the edges of the man's eyes squinted. "You are a daughter of the rose, are you not? Your blood sings loudly to us."

"How's that?" Will asked.

A shrug under a white robe. "We are called to the old blood. Our tie is ancient, but powerful nonetheless."

Rosana glanced at her friends in turn, and Eben shrugged when she got to him. He had no idea what this guy was talking about.

Lakanos asked politely, "What sort of business do you conduct with your most excellent caravan, sir?"

"We carry supplies."

Hatma chimed in. "I have heard legends of the White Caravan, but I was given to understand that one has not been seen in decades."

"We were called."

"By blood?" Rosana asked.

"Aye. Just so."

"Whose blood?" she followed up.

"Of this we cannot speak."

"I thought it was my blood," Rosana responded.

"It is your blood. But not you."

Eben turned that puzzle over in his mind. He said aloud, "So, the blood of a relative of Rosana's calls to you. Where is this person? How will you know where to find him or her?"

Silent stares were the only answer he got.

Rosana tried, "Why do you seek my . . . family?"

"To deliver our goods, of course."

"Do you seek my uncle?" she asked. "Last I saw him, he was traveling the Estarran Sea. How will you find him?"

Palpable frustration rolled off the man in white. He obviously didn't want to talk about any of this, but just as obviously felt obligated to do so with Rosana. He said reluctantly, "We know where to find the one we seek. And he does not move."

"I have another living relative?" Rosana exclaimed eagerly. "Who? Where?"

"You do not know your own blood?" the man exclaimed back.

"I was separated from my family as a baby. Please, tell me what you know."

The man opened his mouth, but no sound came out. He tried again, but still, no sound came. Finally, the man muttered, "I am sorry. I cannot speak of it."

Lakanos and Rynn both reacted strongly to that, trading significant glances with one another. Eben frowned. What was he missing?

The man in white tried again, and words came this time. "We go to the White Tower."

"What is that, and where is it?" Rosana asked.

"I cannot tell you."

"But if I find this White Tower, I'll find more of my blood," Rosana echoed.

"Most assuredly."

Rosana nodded firmly. "Very well. As soon as our work here is finished, I shall seek this White Tower."

"Come with us," the man in white offered. "You may travel as one of us, and we will take you there."

"Uh, *no*." Will didn't sound amused.

Rosana placed a hand on Will's sleeve. "Thank you for the offer, sir, but I am needed here for now. One day, though, I will find the tower, and maybe I will find you when I do."

"Perhaps, white daughter. Perhaps."

And with that, the members of the White Caravan rose silently to their feet, bowed deeply, and moved off into the gathering heat of the day, seemingly unconcerned for the danger of being caught out in midday.

"Strange bunch," Eben commented. "Anyone have any idea what they were talking about?"

Everyone made negative sounds except for Rynn, he noticed. The paxan was silent, looking troubled, as if that odd encounter had made a certain sense to him. But whatever Rynn knew, he obviously didn't want to share.

Eben was intrigued when Hatma led them to the ruin of an old mining settlement about an hour later. Only crude foundations remained. It didn't look like it had been much of a place before, and it looked even less impressive now. They picked their way over the rocks and debris, and he noticed the rocks looked well worked, even and smooth. "Why did this place fail?" he asked.

Hatma shrugged. "Probably because it's haunted." That got everyone's attention. She continued, "We're going underground shortly. Stick close together, and do not believe your eyes if you see strange apparitions."

"You mean ghosts?" Rynn asked.

She stopped in front of a relatively intact structure. It looked like a mine entrance, and turned out to be one, with long steps leading down into the earth through a hatch in the floor. Hatma said, "Yes. I mean ghosts. And there are eidolons and creatures of the dark down here. We will undoubtedly be attacked at some point. Stay close, backs together, and do not let them separate us."

The steps gave way to mining tunnels, which gave way to

wide, high-ceilinged passages containing entire roads that Hatma called ktholes. They looked and felt ancient.

Sha'Li at the very back of the party hissed for silence, and Eben and their friends went still so she could listen. Cicero moved back beside her. At length, Cicero nodded at Sha'Li. They traded hand signals and then moved to join the others.

Cicero murmured, "We're being followed. Close to a dozen people wearing noisy armor, so not in the business of stealth. Probably not bandits."

"Imperial Army?" Eben asked quickly. He'd been followed relentlessly last year by a brace of Imperial hounds trained to hunt elementally aligned people like him. Ever since, he'd had nightmares of the Empire catching wind of him again.

Sha'Li shook her head. "Army types tend to walk in step with one another. This bunch is shuffling along."

"Then who?" he asked.

Will shrugged. "Take your pick. My money's on Anton's boys, though."

"The Kithmar?" Eben retorted. "Oh, I hope it's them. I have a score to settle with them for kidnapping us and murdering my father."

"Kidnapping and murder?" Lakanos exclaimed under his breath. "Anton Constantine's men?"

Rynn nodded at the knight. "Long story. But yes. He's not fond of our little group or of our endeavors."

Sha'Li looked around. "Are there any intersections in this road we travel?"

Hatma replied low, "Not for a while."

Sha'Li shrugged. "Then we move fast until we get to an intersection, and we'll lay false trails when we get there. Buy ourselves time and get far enough ahead to lay an ambush."

Eben grinned at her, liking her thought process.

"Or," Raina responded, "we could simply move fast and stay ahead of them. If they haven't attacked us by now, I doubt they're planning to. Those mining tunnels were much tighter and darker than these passages."

"Party pooper," Sha'Li grumbled under her breath.

Eben caught the comment and grinned at her in commiseration. He preferred her plan, too. Sometimes having a peace-loving White Heart member around was really annoying. However, Raina's plan prevailed, and they moved out fast, racing along the ancient dwarven highway as quickly as the dark and rubble allowed.

Time lost all meaning in the darkness, and Eben had no idea how long they marched. But his feet grew heavy, and his body weary. Every time they stopped to rest and sip at their precious water, Cicero and Sha'Li retreated down the tunnel to listen. And every time they came back, someone was still behind them, not quite harassing them, not quite catching up to them, pressing them as if to intimidate them.

"Do you sense any water nearby?" Hatma asked Eben.

"Very little. Perhaps a seep, far in front of us."

"That should be the Griefalls," she replied.

"Let us hope so. I've had enough of wandering around in the dark, and I'm sick of being followed."

"You and me both," Will replied.

Abruptly, the kthole ended. They emerged into a chasm only slightly less dark than the tunnels. Massive parallel walls of stone towered on each side of them, nearly coming to a point overhead. Only a thin slit of sunlight reached the narrow floor of the valley.

"We almost need torches to light our way," Eben complained.

"Save them. You will need them later," Hatma responded.

Rynn was studying the exit through which they'd just come. "If we blast that bit of rock overhanging the kthole's entrance right there, we can create a rockslide that will block the exit and slow our pursuers."

Will stepped forward, took aim with his staff, and sent a bolt of magic at the overhang. With a crash and a billow of dust, the rocks came down. "There. That should slow them down for a while," Will said in satisfaction.

They set off at a blessedly saner pace. They climbed nearly as much as they walked, for the chasm was heavily littered with rubble that had fallen over the eons from the walls above them. At certain points, the passage was so narrow that Eben's shoulders nearly rubbed against the walls on either side of him. Periodic bouts of claustrophobia made him alternately sweat and shiver. If they were attacked now, they would be hard pressed to defend themselves in these tight quarters.

When the tiny slit of sky visible overhead turned pink and then faded to black, they paused for a few hours to rest, taking turns with half the party napping and the other half standing tense guard. If their pursuers had escaped the tunnel, there was no sign of them. Yet.

But that didn't make him feel any better. He didn't like the sensation of being swallowed up by the earth. Even the tiniest mishap down here could leave them all dead or, worse, buried alive. Only his deep connection to the old, slow magic of the stone around him kept him calm. Frankly, he had no idea how the others were coping down here.

They'd been out of water for nearly twelve hours when they came across the first waterfall. It flowed clear and crystalline down the cliff wall into a pool of inviting water. Had Hatma not warned them of the dangers of tainted water in this place, they would all have rushed forward eagerly to drink from it.

As it was, Sha'Li approached cautiously with an empty waterskin. However, when she attempted to submerge it in the water and her hand touched the liquid, she hissed in pain and blew on her fingers as if they had been burned. Eben saw no damage to her flesh, but the water was clearly as dangerous as advertised.

Rosana took the waterskin from Sha'Li. "Let me try."

Will lurched forward. "Stop! You'll hurt—"

She rounded on him angrily. "When are you going to stop treating me like I'm not capable of doing anything for myself?"

To everyone's shock, Rosana was able to submerge the waterskin into the pool with no apparent ill effect to herself. When the skin was full, she pulled it out, wiped it off, and handed it to Sha'Li, who took it cautiously.

"How did you do that?" Will demanded.

Rosana glanced at Hatma and Ayli and said cautiously, "I have touched Death before and know how to defend myself from it."

Death? Eben watched, worried, as Sha'Li closed her eyes and concentrated upon the water vessel in her hands. Sha'Li's tribe mark seemed to glow a little. It took several minutes, but eventually, she opened her eyes. "It should be safe to drink now."

"What did you do to it?" Raina asked.

"It no longer feels tainted to me," Sha'Li replied.

She hadn't answered Raina's question. Eben sidled over to her and murmured, "Is your hand all right?"

Sha'Li flexed her fingers. "I must have cleansed my flesh of the taint at the same time I cleansed the water."

"You need to have a healer look at you—"

"Are you worried about me? No need. I'm fine."

"Why don't you let the experts decide that?"

She grinned. "When it comes to taints, I am the expert."

"Yes, but I worry about you." Their gazes met, and a strange, nervous feeling tickled his innards. Confused, he turned away. They needed to get out of this strange place, and soon.

Feverish urgency drove Raina forward, in spite of her exhaustion, in spite of her terror of what lay before them, and in spite of whoever was following behind them. The voices were always with her now, and doing even the slightest bit of healing was excruciating. Was this how Will had felt two years ago when he'd first joined with Lord Bloodroot, and the union had slowly poisoned him to death?

At least he'd had Rosana to give a piece of her spirit to him and stabilize his health. Raina had no one who could do the same for her. The Mages of Alchizzadon had succeeded in killing her, after all. It was just happening more slowly than she'd expected. Now it was a race to stay alive long enough to restore Gawaine.

They turned west into the main portion of the great fissure. Although it was wider here and more light reached them, they were also more vulnerable to attack. Mist shrouded the bottom of the chasm, and they had to slow down and move cautiously through the persistent fog. Pools of water lurked behind boulders, waiting to surprise the unwary, and a constant sound of dripping, trickling, and running water echoed around them.

Their first night in the canyon, a wave of black-skinned ogres, who reminded her greatly of the green-skinned Boki, attacked. But when Will ripped open his armor and shirt to reveal Bloodroot's disk on his chest and the network of angry scars radiating outward from it, they disengaged immediately and melted back into the night.

The second night of their trek, more ghostly creatures attacked, monstrous and bestial. Raina had never seen anything like them before. They were accompanied by black-skinned humanoids of some indeterminate race. That fight lasted on and off for an hour as their attackers moved in and out of the fog, striking and retreating, striking and retreating. But eventually, stillness reigned and they came no more.

The next morning, they came across a line of spiked bones that looked distinctly dragon-esque. Hatma wanted to stop and camp in their shadow, using them for protection, but the rest of them voted to move on, away from the disturbing skeleton.

The roar began as a subliminal vibration in Raina's belly and grew over the next several hours into an audible rumble and then a deafening thunder. The mist grew so thick it blocked out first the stars and then the moonlight.

A turbulent shore emerged from the thick fog, and they stopped abruptly at its margin. Sha'Li squatted down to touch the water and frowned. "It's clean. Really clean."

"So we can drink it?" Raina asked. She had to shout to be heard over the roar of the nearby waterfall.

"We can bathe in it," Sha'Li said eagerly.

"I would not recommend doing so," Ayli replied quickly. "The guardians of this place would likely take deep offense at such a sacrilege."

"And who are these guardians?" Will asked.

"The pastors of the King's Tree," the shaman answered.

Raina perked up. "As in our king?"

Ayli nodded solemnly.

Hatma added, "When day breaks, the mist will burn off somewhat, and you will be able to see both the waterfall and the great wake tree."

When dawn finally came, Will woke bleary-eyed. Worse, now they could see the challenge before them. A breath-stealing waterfall crashed down from the top of the chasm to their left, a narrow, raging ribbon of water that churned the lake before them into a roiling cauldron of angry waves and rolls.

He spied a great black hump in the middle of the pool. An island, overshadowed by a massive tree whose roots crawled all over its surface and whose branches spread wider than those of any tree he'd ever seen. It appeared that the impossibly long branches had dropped secondary trunks to support their weight as they grew too far from the main trunk. The effect was a mazelike network of tree trunks that was, in fact, a single organism. That must be the wake tree.

Which meant they were very close now. "This is it," Raina murmured. "The zinnzari will be over there somewhere and not happy to see us."

"How are we to cross the water?" Rosana asked in dismay. "I'm not a strong enough swimmer to survive those currents."

Now that she mentioned it, Will noticed the water was not only turbulent but flowing rapidly around the black mass of the island, presumably racing toward the drain spout into which this entire body of water emptied.

"I'm strong enough," Sha'Li replied, eyeing the water intently. "If we join all our ropes together and I tie one end to my waist, I'll swim it across to the island and tie it off. Then we can use it as a ferry rope for a boat if it's over there. For surely, the zinnzari who guard that place do not swim these waters."

It took them a few minutes to secure all their ropes to one another and for Sha'Li to strip down to a sleeveless shirt and short pants that came to her knees. Eyeing the water, she moved so close to the base of the falls that Will worried she would be caught in the down flow and violently forced under the surface.

She waded into the water, and all of a sudden, the current swept her off her feet and she disappeared from sight.

"Is she all right?" Ayli cried.

Eben answered, "She can breathe underwater. She'll be fine." But as Will and Rynn helped Eben feed out the rope, Will wondered. The rope was spinning out much faster than any humanoid could swim, which meant Sha'Li was caught in the current. They waited anxiously for several long minutes and were nearly to the end of their rope when all of a sudden Sha'Li's head popped up out of the water near the shore of the island.

If he didn't know better, Will would have thought she was drowning. She dragged herself ashore and lay there unmoving. Eben shouted to ask if she was all right, but the noise of the falls was too great. Finally, she lifted her head and looked back at them. Weakly, she lifted one hand and flashed them a thumbs-up.

Eventually, Sha'Li found and dragged back a small skiff, which she secured to the ferry rope and then pulled across the water by hand. Ayli crossed first with Raina and Lakanos. The others took turns riding over in the skiff. Will, Eben, and Rynn went last. The mist thickened as they headed out, and the shore behind them was obscured. As it disappeared from view, though, Will thought he saw something or someone moving along the shore.

He sincerely hoped those were just more of the creatures who seemed to live in this strange place, but he got a sinking feeling those shadows were humanoid. And armed. "I think the people following us have caught up with us," he murmured.

Eben shrugged. "We've got the boat. And I defy anyone other than a lizardman or Merr to survive those currents."

"Still. Let's get moving."

They untied their ferry rope and turned their attention to the island before them. It rose steeply from the shore, rounding out into a domelike crest. Several hundred strides inland, they finally came to the main trunk of the gigantic tree dominating the island. This had to be the King's Tree. Will laid his hand on the trunk and reeled back as it reacted to him with a bolt of recognition. Or perhaps it was reacting to Bloodroot within him. Either way, it hurt.

Without warning, a figure appeared in front of them, an elf who appeared middle aged—which meant he was ancient by human standards—his face covered in a fine fretwork of dark lines that formed a spiderweb. "Well, now. This is a surprise, Ayli," he said.

Clearly not a pleasant one.

Ayli spoke for them. "These children need to speak to the Elder of the Guardians."

"No." The one-word reply was flat, firm, and instantaneous.

Hah. After all they'd done to get here. All they'd sacrificed. An image of his parents' faces flashed through his mind. His home. The normal life he'd left behind. Will replied strongly, "We've spent two years looking for you and have endured grueling hardships along the way. We're not leaving until we finish what we've come to do."

"You must leave. Now."

Raina stepped forward. "What my blunt friend was trying to say is that we have a mutual topic of interest to discuss with you. We can help you achieve your fondest wish, and we want to help you."

The elf's eyes narrowed skeptically as he stared at her. "What wish would that be?"

She held her right fist out, showing the man the creamy white, carved ring upon her middle finger. "Perhaps you recognize this?"

The elf moved swiftly, snatching at the ring. Lakanos lurched forward to block his way, but Raina intervened, saying mildly, "Let him try to remove it from my finger."

The zinnzari reached for the band, but his fingertips had barely grazed the carved unicorn horn before he staggered back, staring at both ring and girl. He whispered, "Who are you?"

"That is what we would like to discuss with you and your companions," Raina replied.

"Follow me."

In a few minutes, they stepped into a small clearing with a half dozen tiny cottages clustered in it. More elves of varying ages, but all heavily armed, stepped outside.

"Show them the ring," their guide said without preamble or introduction.

Raina complied.

"How did this come into your possession, girl?" one of the elves demanded.

Will was amazed. He'd never seen elves be so rude before, completely ignoring all etiquette or social niceties.

Then one of the elves turned on him without warning. "Who are you? Why do I sense strange magics in you?"

"Strange? Me? She's the arch-mage." He pointed at Raina.

His attempt to deflect attention from himself had no effect. All the elves were staring at him now. And frowning. Hands were edging toward weapons.

"Look. We're really here to help you," he tried. "And we hope you can help us. We have no hostile intent. I swear."

"Then why do we sense that in you which is anathema to us?" one of them demanded. "We are sworn to kill you, spawn of the Destroyer."

Raina was surprised when Lakanos, of all people, intervened to save Will from slaughter. "I'm afraid we are not getting off to a good start," he said. "Let us begin again. I am Sir Lakanos of the Royal Order of the Sun, and this is Emissary Raina of the White Heart." The knight quickly introduced all the members of the party, ending with, "And I believe you know the lady, Aylinoor, who was gracious enough to bring us to you."

"The lady you speak of has shunned our society, sir knight. Her introduction is meaningless to us." The elf rounded on Will. "Who are you, boy, and why do you stink of the Betrayer?"

Swords appeared in the hands of the zinnzari. Her friends reacted no less quickly, and in seconds, an armed standoff was in full force.

"Stop!" Raina cried. "My friends and I found the Sleeping King's dreaming echo on the dream plane, and he set us the task of recovering his regalia and bringing it to his body. Unfortunately, forces hostile to him now seek to destroy him. We have come to you to help us wake Gawaine before they succeed."

At the sound of his name, the elves sucked in sharp breaths. "Why should we believe you?"

"Because I'm telling the truth," she answered simply. She reached into her pouch and pulled out Gawaine's crown. Another gasp from the elves.

Eben stepped forward. "And here is his bow." The elves made sounds of disbelief, and Eben added wryly, "Trust me. It's his. I'm no great shot, but I haven't missed a target once since I picked this thing up. It definitely has powerful magical qualities."

An awkward silence fell, and Raina spoke into it. "The land needs its Mythar, and Haelos needs its king. The portents have been read and events foretold. It's time to end your long bondage to Hemlocke and wake your king, children of Zinn."

"Pretty words," the zinnzari scoffed. "But nothing more."

Raina replied, "We're going to wake him with or without your help. If you choose to break your vow to him now, when he most needs you, that's your concern. He will be disappointed that his elite guard abandoned him. As will the spirits of your ancestors."

"You know nothing of our ancestors!"

Will piped up. "We've met their spirits in the grove where they guard their king into eternity. They know full well what goes on here."

"Who do you believe betrayed Gawaine?" Raina asked boldly. "Rudath?"

"Although the troll king slew Gawaine, he was the puppet of another," one of the elves intoned. "Bloodroot, born of death and destruction, destroyed our king. He whispered in Rudath's ear, twisting his mind and inciting him to violence."

Will's hands fisted, and his entire body shook with what looked like rage. On cue, Rosana laid a steadying hand on his arm and whispered something to him. Raina prayed he could hang on to his temper—and the temper of Bloodroot—long enough to get past these stubborn zinnzari.

Will's mouth opened, and a voice nothing like his came out, rough and deep. "Upon my life, I had nothing to do with Rudath attacking Gawaine."

Was that *Bloodroot* speaking? He'd never spoken directly before. Amazement warred with worry for Will. Had he finally been taken over by the treant?

Will-Bloodroot continued, "I admit that I whispered to the greenskin races of the unfairness of their treatment and that the beautiful, flawless elves were better loved by the Great Circle than any others. But never—ever—would I have done anything to harm the Mythar."

Will looked as staggered as the elves.

"Who are you?" one of the zinnzari whispered.

"I am who you think I am. Show them my seed, Will."

Will opened his shirt to reveal the bloodthorn disk grown into his chest and the telltale angry red scars emanating outward from it.

"This human boy acts as my host."

A buzz of consternation broke out among the zinnzari, but thankfully, no one raised a sword to Will's neck.

Bloodroot continued in that gruff, rusty voice, "Never would I unbalance nature or harm the Mythar. My purpose may be death, destruction, and rage, but my result is renewal and rebirth. I vow to you upon my honor and upon the life of my human host I do not lie to you."

"Hey, now," Will protested in his own voice. "Don't be tossing around my life so freely."

Raina was immensely relieved. Her friend was still in his own body.

But then Bloodroot continued, talking over Will's objections, "I never told Rudath to kill Gawaine nor did I ever whisper anything to stir Rudath to such drastic action. I swear. It was not my idea. I did not betray the Great Circle, the Mythar, or you. I joined this boy to help him restore the Great Circle and wake Gawaine."

Raina looked over at the zinnzari hopefully. *Please believe him. Please.* They were so close now. They *had* to wake Gawaine, and soon.

Aurelius looked down over the edge of the waterfall in distaste. The Nyghtflume was no small river, but its fall was so great that it looked like a thin ribbon of white that dissolved into mist far below.

"How are we supposed to get down there?" Selea asked skeptically.

"There's a path, I'm told. Behind the falls."

"And we can't use magic to expedite this? Maybe a series of feather falls?"

Aurelius pulled a face. "If only. I sense great proscribing spells upon this place. No magic to enhance movement would work here."

"Mayhap that is a sign that we're getting close to our goal," Selea murmured.

Aurelius paced along the edge of the cliff and found what they sought only feet from the precarious bank of the river where it plunged over the edge. A notch in the rocks, a step barely wider than his shoulders. He tested it gingerly. "It's wet. Slippery. Be careful."

They started the long descent into the Griefalls. He was too old for this. He'd tried to leave the quest to younger people with fresh legs, quick reflexes, and a burning need for adventure. But he hadn't counted on his own wish for one last moment of glory, his desire to feel young and vital and important. He was insane to be running around out here, facing unknown threats and treacherous climbs best left to the younglings. And yet, he took the next step. And the next.

Will's throat felt like it was ripping free of his neck, the timbre of Bloodroot's voice was so harsh. For that matter, his entire body felt as if it was being torn asunder by the strain of containing Lord Bloodroot's spirit. He realized with a start that he had fallen to his knees. Will struggled to stand upright and was appalled that Rosana and Sha'Li had to help him.

Another zinnzari barged into the clearing, panting. "Intruders come—" He broke off at the sight of their party.

Will spoke up quickly. "Whoever comes is not with us. Only the people you see here have Gawaine's best interest at heart."

"And yet you led our king's enemies to his doorstep!" one of the zinnzari cried over his shoulder as all the zinnzari guardians raced out of the clearing, leaving the party standing alone in the clearing.

"Do we go help them?" Sha'Li asked.

Will shook his head. "We should look for Gawaine's body and protect it."

"Agreed," Raina said quickly. "It must be near here. Not only does the ring feel practically on fire, but the zinnzari would stay close to him."

A quick circuit of the forest around the clearing yielded no sign of Gawaine, however. They'd started a second, wider sweep of the island when they heard sounds in front of them. Someone was talking in low, furtive murmurs.

Will gripped his staff more tightly and hand signaled the others to prepare for combat.

Air currents swirled the mist, stirring it around him, revealing and then hiding the vague outlines of at least two dozen men. He peered through the fog, looking for colors or something to identify them. And then he spied a face that made his blood run cold. He turned back on his friends, plowing into them in his haste to flee.

Anton Constantine.

In the confusion he'd caused, he ordered frantically, "Run!"

S ha'Li, who'd been bringing up the rear of their party, suddenly found herself in the lead as they reversed course and fled from whatever or whoever had panicked Will. She headed into the forest of tree trunks, leaping over small roots and dodging around the big ones. With no destination in mind, she ran blindly, seeking routes that would allow for maximum speed.

Whether it was random chance or some greater force

guided her steps, she couldn't say, but all of a sudden, a clearing of sorts opened up before her. The tree trunks were less dense here, and through them, she glimpsed a large, round carving in the side of an upthrust of the native rock that formed the island.

As she sprinted toward it, she realized it was not a carving but more likely a door. It stood half again as high as a man and was covered with intricate symbols arranged in a spiral pattern that covered the entire giant panel of what had to be nullstone.

Unfortunately, her interest in the door had caused her to run to it, and all her friends had followed her. They fetched up in front of it now, effectively trapped against its unyielding surface.

She ran her hands across its bumpy surface, searching frantically for a handle or latch, but found nothing. As her friends formed a defensive arc behind her, she examined the door more closely, looking for some sort of hidden release mechanism. Nothing.

Lakanos called, "We need to find a more defensible position! Someplace where they can't flank us!"

Will called back, "Over there! That cluster of trees!"

Sha'Li looked where he pointed and spied a U-shaped grouping of the descending tree trunks. If they could all fit in there, their pursuers would only be able to attack through the small front opening, bringing to bear at most four men at a time. It would equalize the odds against them. Their little party could front four of its own fighters, and most of the pursuing force would be neutralized, unable to attack through their own people.

They raced over to the cul-de-sac, reaching it just as a stream of men raced into the clearing. Her blood ran cold as she spied what—who—had made Will panic. Anton Constantine was bringing up the rear of a column of upward of a hundred armed fighters. They moved like soldiers, but none of them wore Imperial colors. No matter. They were the enemy and must not stop her and her friends from getting through that door.

As Will, Rynn, Cicero, and Lakanos stepped into the gap and prepared to fight, Sha'Li glanced back at the door. Something about it looked familiar. She focused on the symbols, and that was when it hit her. The book Kerryl Moonrunner had left for her in that cache in the Angor Swamp last fall!

She fished frantically in her belt pouch and pulled out the small, strange volume. Circular in shape and bound with metal hinges and wooden covers, it was part book and part box. The front cover and first thirty pages of the book were real enough, but behind the parchment leaves had been a small chamber, just large enough to hold the nullstone amulet she now wore around her neck.

Unlike most of the nullstone pieces they'd seen before, carved or inlaid with gold, her amulet was a flat disk that covered most of her palm, its carvings passing all the way through it, forming an intricate shape. It looked as if a razor-sharp quill had written a symbol all the way through the thin stone. She'd spent hours perusing the book's odd, symbolic writing that started at the edge of each page and spiraled toward the center, and she had not found a symbol to match the one on her amulet.

She quickly scanned the door's symbols now, searching for the familiar sinuous shape etched in her amulet.

"Incoming," Will announced.

She turned to face the fight beside Eben. The two of them would jump into the gap when one of their companions was wounded or armor badly damaged. All the fighters would take turns dropping back to receive healing or make quick armor repairs while the others held the line. And in the meantime, Eben pulled out Eliassan's bow and commenced shooting over his friends' shoulders as targets presented themselves to his deadly aim. Ayli and Rosana were already in place, tucked in tightly behind the fighters, using their friends' bodies for protection as they cast protective spells and healing by touch into the fighters.

All in all, they made a lethal door-fighting force. Anton and his mercenaries were going to have their hands full routing them out of this spot.

The first attackers surged forward, and a clash of metal and shouting deafened Sha'Li. Her own claws slithered out, and she bared her teeth aggressively. She'd waited a long time to take a piece of flesh out of Anton Constantine.

Hemlocke shivered as danger rippled across her exquisitely sensitive skin. *Someone touched that which was hers.* It had better not be the zinnzari pastors who served her. How dare they! Surely, they knew death would follow if they made any attempt to enter her lair, home to her greatest treasure of all.

Almost fully awake, she pushed with her great clawed front feet, rising to her haunches and unfurling her wings. Blood flowed into them, rich and hot, bringing strength to tendons and bone, engorging the delicate membranes in between.

Irritated, she swished her tail, once, hard. Coral crumbled into dust, and the bubble around her wavered violently, threatening to collapse.

Alert now, she stretched her awareness outward, encompassing land and sky, plants and creatures, the ebb and flow of life as clear to her as the breath flowing in and out of her lungs. And as fire began to build in her throat, so did fury build in her heart.

Will settled into the rhythm of fighting, instinctively finding the patterns of the battle and spotting the weaknesses of his attackers. He didn't actually like killing people, but the rush of letting his training take over, of flowing from one strike to the next, the cold satisfaction of mowing down those who stood against him was intoxicating. If Bloodroot enhanced that feeling, so be it.

Anton seemed satisfied to throw his men at them, apparently on the assumption that his superior numbers would overwhelm their much smaller force. But Will hadn't set up a door fight for nothing. He and his friends fought Anton's men to a stalemate and made it clear that they could sustain this sort of fight indefinitely. If Raina could just stay conscious and functional behind him and his companions, they could stand here for hours against Anton's men.

The ex-governor was not known for traveling with many healers. The Heart tacitly despised him and few of its members would work for him, and furthermore, Anton was prepared to let his men die where they fell for the most part. To him, soldiers were expendable resources to be used and discarded as needed.

"Alchemy incoming!" Rynn cried from behind Will.

Will managed to dodge the small glass missile aimed at his chest. His movement opened up his left side, however, and he took a nasty cut across his ribs. "Replace me!" he called.

Rynn jumped in front of him as Will dropped back. Hatma ran forward to patch his armor while Rosana cast a healing spell into him.

"How are you doing for healing magic?" he panted.

"Low. Raina can only do a little at a time."

"Does your healing magic heal her?" he asked.

"I don't know."

"Try it. We need her casting at full strength."

Rosana shot him a worried look. "Don't count on it."

He traded grim looks with her. They were in serious trouble then.

As he headed back to the line, he passed Sha'Li dropping back. She'd taken some terrible hacking blow where her neck and shoulder joined and was barely upright.

"Raina!" he shouted. He said to Sha'Li as he raced past her, "See if you can get that door open across the clearing. We can't stay here all day."

Sha'Li staggered and nearly passed out from massive blood loss before a wave of cool, painful healing flowed into her neck.

"Better?" Raina gasped, looking half-dead herself.

"Yes. Thanks. You all right?" she asked. "You look terrible."

"I'm fine. Do you need a magic shield before you head back?" Raina asked in a paper-thin voice.

The girl didn't look capable of lighting a candle with magic, let alone casting a high-level protective spell.

"Save your magic. Will wants me to open that door over there."

"Hurry," Raina urged her before turning away to heal Lakanos, who was bloody and not moving, as if mortally wounded.

Sha'Li moved to the back of the cluster of tree branches and peered over at the door. A few of Anton's men were examining it already, and the way they moved, they were rogues. They looked frustrated, too.

If she didn't look directly at the door, but let it hover at the edge of her peripheral vision, she thought she spied a faint magical gleam about it, like the dim glow of moonlight into the dark of a cold night.

The symbols had to be the key. She pulled out her circular book again and thumbed through the pages, comparing various symbols carved on the door to those in her book. They were very similar in shape and style, clearly the same language or code. Some of them looked vaguely like drawings, while others were collections of slashes, dots, and ink strokes.

In her experience, collections of symbols like this disguised key mechanisms. The right symbols had to be manipulated in the right way, in the right order, to unlock the door. As the thought occurred to her, the tribe symbol on her cheek abruptly felt warm. Startled, she accepted the sign and murmured her thanks to Lunimar.

What order, then? Instead of matching individual symbols, she started looking for matching sequences of symbols in her book to those on the door.

"Hurry, Sha'Li!" Raina called from behind her. "Anton's throwing death poisons, and I can't throw many more life spells."

Frantically, Sha'Li searched the pages of her book. The answer had to be in here *somewhere*.

Justin heard the sounds of combat as they approached the strange, domelike island rising out of the mist and turbulent water. Tarses had created a truly terrifying barge made entirely of clear ice and had ferried his men across a dozen at a time. Justin and Kadir were on the last barge.

Not only could he look straight down into the churning, poisonous depths, but Justin feared that, at any second, the boat would melt or even shatter. He'd never been more glad to set foot back on solid land.

Tarses formed his men and moved out, advancing into the strange forest of dense, leafless tree trunks. To his credit, Tarses led from the front. Kadir stuck to Tarses's heels, and Justin stuck to Kadir's. They followed the shouts and clashing metal to a clearing with a battle raging off to one side of it.

"There's Eben!" Justin shouted, pointing at a beleaguered line of fighters holding a narrow gap between two trees.

Tarses paused for a moment, clearly assessing the battlefield. They stood at the left flank of the attacking force trying to break through the pair of trees.

"Anton Constantine!" Tarses snarled. "I always hated that guy."

And with that, he and his men charged.

Vesper stepped through the portal. Passing through to the material plane, even for a short time, taxed her power to the absolute limit, and she could not sustain it for long. But no way was she missing this, the pinnacle of her achievements, aimed at for the past 150 years.

Her bodyguard, who had stayed with her all this time, loyal to the end, led her forces through the unstable portal. He didn't think it would hold open for long, hence she'd gone through just behind him. Then a stream of phantasms rushed through, pouring out of the cataract as fast as they could jump through.

By her count, several hundred of her elementally powered phantasms made it through the breach before the portal's magic collapsed. The Gaged Man had lined up her army in descending order from strongest to weakest, so those who had made it across to this plane were her deadliest fighters.

"The door!" she called to the Gaged Man. "Over there! We must take it!"

He spied the nullstone door, circular and covered with

dragon runes, and nodded back his understanding. However, a pitched battle of some kind was already under way between them and the door. She stood still and let her minions charge forward around her, crashing into the fight.

A chaotic mêlée ensued, and she shied away from it, terrified of the mortality of the fragile body she inhabited. If it died, she would perish forever. Stars, it was infuriating being forced to exist in this weak state. Just a few more minutes. And then she would find the Sleeping King's body and make it hers.

With his immortal body and her immortal spirit, they would form a being that would make Maximillian himself shake in his boots. Even the dragons themselves would cower before her. And then they would pay for what they'd done to her. They all would pay.

W ill staggered back from the line fight, and Ayli had just trickled the last of her healing magic into him when a great roar made him look up sharply. Somebody had just attacked Anton's forces from the left, hitting them hard.

He craned to see over Eben and Lakanos, and his jaw dropped. Those were elementals. Big ones. Like the ones last year in the Dominion—

Wait a minute. Those were *just* like the ones from last year.

"Rynn!" he shouted. "Are those phantasms on the field?"

The paxan didn't respond immediately, for he was engaged in a lightning-fast fight against a two–long sword fighter who was giving him all the trouble he could handle. Will made his way to Rynn's side, timing his own attack for when both swords were extended forward and unable to snap back to defend against a punishing thrust from his staff. He caught Anton's man under the ribs and drove up into his solar plexus, knocking the wind out of the fellow and forcing him to fall back, gasping and retching.

"The elementals on the right. Are they phantasms?" Will shouted.

Rynn looked across the wild fight. "Yes. Where did they come from?"

"I don't care. They're attacking Anton."

"They'll attack us as soon as they're done with his troops," Rynn warned.

Will grinned. "Yes, but until then, the enemy of my enemy . . ."

Rynn grinned and dived back into the battle.

Thanon stared at the mess before him and didn't have the faintest idea where to begin. His men, a hundred strong, stared along with him, and one of his lieutenants muttered, "Who's who?"

"I have no idea." He reached out with his mind, using his paxan mental powers to feel the combatants, to sense their motives and emotional states. Perhaps he could figure out who was attacking and who defending at the least. From there, perchance he could reason out who wanted what in this sea of clashing weapons, bloodied bodies, shouts, wails, and mayhem.

A mind pushed back against his with such power that he physically reeled from it. "It cannot be . . ."

"Be what, my lord?" one of his men asked.

"I have not felt that mind for nigh on two hundred years." He reached out again, this time with exceeding caution, merely to taste and observe, not to interact with that massive blast of Kothite might.

One of his lieutenants, also a veteran of several hundred years serving in Grand Marshal Korovo's forces, lurched. He looked at Thanon wildly. "What—"

"I feel her, too."

"But . . . she's dead."

He had no explanation for the existence of Ammertus's daughter here. But who else wielded the same mental emanations as Ammertus, layered with the calculating, capricious, female energy of his only daughter, Avilla? She was destroyed 150 years ago. She. Could. Not. Exist.

And yet she lived. Furthermore, she was on this field of battle.

Why, then, had she not simply mind-blasted everyone who opposed her, ordering them all to die?

He scanned the battle frantically in search of her child-sized frame, her long red braids, the same gaudy shade as her father's unruly red hair. Why did he not see her?

He dared not send his men into battle against her. He and they would all die if they chose wrongly who to support in this fight—

His darting gaze halted. Went back to the person he'd just spotted.

His jaw dropped.

What *was* this place?

"Are you all right, my lord?"

His men, almost exclusively paxan and sensitive to emotions and thoughts, were picking up on his mental distress. "I am . . . shocked. Look over there. Who do you see leading that brace of hydesmyn?"

His lieutenant gasped. "Surely not. He died in glorious battle shortly after his return from Pan Orda."

"And yet, there stands a well-formed jann, tall and handsome, wearing ice armor, identical in appearance to every portrait I've ever seen of the Empire's greatest general, ably leading a force of skilled warriors."

At the moment, Tarses's men were being hard pressed by several large elementals on one side and a smaller force of roguish types on the other.

"How can it be anyone but General Tarses?" Thanon demanded.

His mind felt tilted and awhirl. First Avilla, and now Tarses? What cause could possibly bring two such eminent beings back to life and together in this place?

"To General Tarses!" he ordered his men. They waded into the mêlée, slashing their way determinedly toward the legendary Kothite general and Imperial hero.

Sha'Li gave up on the book. She could find no sequence anywhere in its pages that even remotely resembled the symbols on that cursed door. The amulet under her shirt burned her flesh where it rubbed her scales, and she yanked it clear of her collar in frustration. The medallion felt hot in her hand. Odd. Her scales acted as excellent insulators, and she rarely felt heat or cold.

She turned it over and noticed a single row of symbols carved around its edge. She had to turn the thing just right to spot them and did so eagerly now.

Someone bumped into her, and Raina mumbled an apology, then asked, "How're you coming on the door?"

"I'm not!" she snapped.

"Keep trying. I know you can do it."

Sha'Li tilted the amulet and moved to the edge of their little copse of tree trunks, but there wasn't enough light to see by. She spied a bit of filtered sunlight making its way through the wake tree's leaves and the pervasive mist to one side of the great black door.

She had to climb the nearest tree trunk and turn sideways to slip between it and its neighbor, but she escaped their cul-de-sac and picked her way carefully past clusters of fighting to the brighter spot.

Crouching in the shadow of a tree trunk, she held her hand out with the amulet in it. The light illuminated the carvings on its polished surface, and she shifted around so she could look at the amulet and door simultaneously. It was awkward standing thus, but she was able to begin comparing the symbols. This had to be it. Why else would the amulet have heated up on its own?

Rosana had never seen so many fighting so fiercely in the same place at the same time. She'd thought the second incursion of the Boki into Dupree had been bad, but it was a pale shadow in violence and bloodshed compared to this. She was out of mana and resorting to her stash of potions to keep her friends alive.

Raina did what she could, but she could only heal in dribs and drabs that did little to stem the tide of bloodshed and injury around them.

As far as Rosana could tell, no fewer than three separate forces were on the field. And they all appeared to be fighting their way toward the black door while doing their best to keep the others away from the same goal. It reminded her of a giant, deadly game of capture the flag.

She had just turned to check on her frontline fighters when a wave of something dark and sinister rolled through her mind. *What on Urth?* She looked around the grove in alarm, seeking the source of the newest threat.

Through the trees, she glimpsed them coming, dripping wet and creeping low toward the battle. Dark in color, they moved quickly and stealthily. Had they actually come through the Nyghtflume to get here? How had they survived?

But then she felt the wave again, stronger this time, and recognized it. Void magic. These creatures were steeped in it. And for some reason, they drew the same magic out of her. She felt it oozing from her pores along with the rancid sweat of fear.

An urge to summon the black energy to her hands, to blast it in every direction, to rain death and destruction on everyone, nearly overcame her. Gads, it was a seductive call. It was right there. Hers for the taking. No matter that she'd cast all her usual mana already. If she called on that magic, renewed magical power would come to her, flowing from that dark place inside her—

Right. And overcasting would kill her. Not that the void magic cared. It coaxed her to use the power. Kill her foes. Take control of the battle. To rain death upon them all.

She ran up behind Will and shouted to him as he fought, "Void creatures have come out of the river! Beware their magics!"

He grunted an acknowledgment.

Dropping back, she warned Ayli and Raina, "Void magic is on the field! Watch for death spells and wasting diseases cast upon our friends!"

Raina looked where she pointed and gasped. "Are those night trolls?"

"They're trolls, they're black, and they stink of the Void," Rosana replied. "Looks like they've got some nulvari with them, too."

"Tainted, all of them," Ayli declared.

"We have to find a way out of here!" Raina cried. "We'll all die if we stay in the middle of this carnage."

Rosana responded tartly, "We need to get through that door. Open it, slip through, and then lock it behind us so all these other people can kill one another."

Ayli asked tersely as she reached for Cicero to heal him, "Rosana, do you have any healing left?"

"Not really. A potion or two."

"Take Raina and go help your lizardman friend get that door open. Neither of you is doing any good here."

Raina looked crushed, and Rosana spied a spark of rebellion in her friend's blue eyes. She grabbed Raina's hand and dragged her away from the fight. "C'mon."

E ben felt his formidable strength beginning to wane. No matter how many of their foes they killed, more just kept arriving. He had no idea who was who anymore. They were all killing each other indiscriminately as far as he could tell. Not that he was any different. He attacked anyone who raised a sword to him and was in range of his long sword and mace. The entire world had narrowed down to the person on his left and the person on his right. They were his friends, his brothers and sisters in arms. He would die for them, and they would die for him. Everyone else was the enemy.

But then he heard a familiar voice cast water damage, and his head jerked up. He nearly got gutted for his troubles, and he had to refocus on the mercenary before him. Impatient, he took the first opening the man offered and thrust his razor-flanged mace into the man's face. The effect was devastating. The fellow staggered back screaming and spouting blood, weapon dropped and hands plastered over his ruined face.

Eben looked up again, searching for his sister. For surely that had been her clear, calm voice incanting a water spell. He didn't see her, but he did spot a half dozen cloaked, hooded figures with glowing hands moving into the grove in a tight phalanx. *The Cabal.* They didn't wade into the thick of the weapons combat but rather skirted around the edges of the space, apparently headed toward Anton Constantine.

Another flash of water magic. That *had* to be Marikeen.

"Cicero! Take my place!" he shouted.

Eben dashed forward through the gap left by the man whose face he'd slashed. He ducked a polearm that swung at his head and dodged around a cluster of Imperial soldiers surrounding some sort of elemental and pummeling it into the ground.

"Marikeen!" he shouted.

One of the cloaked figures turned toward him momentarily. It was to that one he grimly fought over the next several minutes. The trick was to keep moving forward, not to engage any individuals who took a swing at him but rather to just block the blow and move on.

Eventually, he drew near the cluster of cloaked figures. They seemed to be splitting their magic about equally between casting defensive spells on themselves and attacking people around them. He paused just out of casting range and called his sister's name again. This time one of the cloaked figures separated from the group. Marikeen threw herself into his arms, and they exchanged a short, fierce hug. He pushed back her hood to see her face, and she snatched it back up over her head.

"There's a powerful psionicist on the field," she said quickly. "The hood protects me from her." She led him quickly to one side of the main battle, and they moved behind a large tree trunk out of sight of most of the combatants.

"Come away with me," Eben exhorted. "My friends and I can keep you safe. Kendrick is here, and his curse is cured."

"What curse?"

"Long story. Suffice it to say you will find our brother much changed since you last saw him."

Marikeen replied, "My colleagues are very powerful. I'm safe with them."

"They're not your family. I would die to protect you."

Her hard expression softened. "I know that."

He opened his mouth to argue further that her place was with her family and friends who loved her, but a creature made of fire burning in a vaguely human shape came around the tree just then, and Eben leaped forward to place himself between the elemental and his sister.

"Oh, Eben. Allow me." She raised her right hand and casually flicked a blast of water magic at the creature. It vanished in a great gout of steam, a faint scream all that lingered where it had just stood.

"Nice trick, sister."

They traded grins.

A portion of the battle shifted closer to them, and they were in danger of being swallowed by it. Eben had no choice but to retreat with Marikeen and follow her back to the other mages of the Cabal. They didn't particularly need his protection, but he lent it to them nonetheless, cutting down the occasional fighter who broke through their magical defenses. The amount of magic they cast was astounding. He'd never seen anyone rely solely on magic to wage a battle, and he understood now why people like Will preferred to use a weapon first and reserve magic for special circumstances when it was truly necessary.

"We must find Vesper!" Marikeen shouted to him.

"She's here?" he called back.

"She will be riding in the body of another, but she's here somewhere!"

Possession creeped him out. Anyone here could be carrying the Kothite child's spirit. A group of fighters came toward the mages, but instead of attacking, they wheeled to face off against a group of hydesmyn. The two factions had barely engaged before a stomping earth elemental waded into their midst, stone fists swinging ponderously. All the fighters turned to hack at it.

One of the robed figures of the Cabal called, "Anton! To us!"

On the far side of the elemental, which was not going down easily, a figure waved an acknowledgment. Eben peered through the mêlée and spotted the ex-governor surrounded by a group of rakasha warriors.

He leaned in close to shout in his sister's ear, "He wants to kill me and my friends! He's evil! Anton engineered killing our father—our real father—and his assassins, those white tigers he's fighting with now, killed Leland Hyland!"

Marikeen's dark eyes blazed with cold fury as she turned to stare at him. "You think I don't know that? He will answer to me for his crimes, brother."

"Then come away with me now. Don't fight for him!"

"But, Eben. I fight to get close enough to kill him."

One stood at the edge of the grove, assessing the battle-field, using his host's immense combat experience to do so. A free-for-all mêlée with no established battle lines, at least three separate forces upon the field, if not more.

"What's the prize they fight over?" Two asked in wonder.

Three made a sound of surprise. "You mean there's a point to all this chaos?"

One pointed over the heads of at least five hundred fighters clashing with one another. "Over there. It looks like some sort of large, circular object."

Two tugged his sleeve. "Lift me up a little so I can see it over the crowd."

He bent his knee and helped her climb onto it. She had her look, a brief one, and jumped down. "It's a door. Magical. Might even be a gate to another place. Can't tell from here. We need to take a closer look."

One nodded and gestured for Three to stand at his right shoulder, with Two tucked in close behind them. In a tight wedge, they waded into the battle.

They'd made their way perhaps two-thirds of the way to the black door everyone seemed to be fighting over when they encountered a large concentration of elemental creatures led by a tall human wearing old-fashioned gages on his arms.

Although One did not know him, the Gaged Man nodded at him as if recognizing an ally. Furthermore, the Gaged Man did not set his troops upon the three of them. Shrugging, One joined the Gaged Man's troops in attacking several dozen paxan fighting in a tight Imperial phalanx. He didn't think the Gaged Man's forces were going to break the formation, and he drifted around the edges of the battle, seeking a way past it.

"What are we waiting for?" Two asked briskly. "Let's get to that door. I have business to take care of on the other side of it."

One frowned at Two. That didn't sound at all like her. "Are you all right?" he asked doubtfully.

"Never better." She giggled in a high, girlish voice. "Hurry. I can't stay here forever."

He had no idea what she was talking about, but he knew what he had to do. The compulsion deep inside him that had driven him for all these months spurred him onward now. He turned and plowed into the next soldier standing between him and the black door.

Thanon was struggling to keep his men together in the wild ebb and flow of this chaotic fight. He'd never seen a battle like it. Hundreds of skilled warriors seemed to be attacking anyone and everyone at random. If there was a goal to it all, he had yet to discover it. He'd just felt a great surge of satisfaction from the Kothite on the field a moment ago, but he had yet to spot her.

Yet another group of his men got cut off from the main force, and he had to muster his men to fight through to the isolated pocket of Talons before they all died. They could not continue on like this. Someone had to take control of the battle, containing and shaping it into something manageable. Frankly, he didn't have enough men to do the job or enough experience to know where to begin.

But one man on the field today did. He looked for and eventually found the icy, pale helm of the one he sought and had yet to successfully join. He directed his men to move off toward General Tarses's position.

Thanon and his men ran into a group of black trolls and nulvari casting void magics and were hard pressed for several long minutes. Eventually, a group of ikonesti and hydesmyn attacked the exposed backs of the nulvari and trolls. Pinched between the Thanon's Talons and this new attack, the void users fell back and moved away.

The ikonesti and hydesmyn wheeled to face him and his men.

"Hold your attack!" he ordered his men. Not only did he shout the command aloud, he also projected it forcefully with his mind. His paxan troops could sense the command even if they did not hear the exact words of it.

"I wish to align with General Tarses!" he shouted over the din. "Tell him Commander Thanon and the Talons of Koth offer him their swords!"

There was a brief pause, and the two forces, temporarily at truce with one another, fought off desultory attacks along their margins while the message was relayed.

The force before Thanon parted, and the great general himself strode forward, sheathed in full armor made of ice. Normally, Thanon would take a knee to such a man, but in the midst of combat, such niceties were suspended, though he did briefly bow his head.

"Thanon, is it? I see you wear the mark of Korovo. I trained under him."

Thanon nodded. Excellent. Their men would use similar tactics, and the two forces should integrate easily. He said, "Order must be imposed upon this battle and the chaos corralled. We need one commander on the field on our side of this fight."

"And what do you see being the purpose of this exercise?" Tarses asked.

"I have been following a White Heart emissary for some weeks, and I believe she and her companions are the crux of this fight. As far as I can tell, she and her friends are attempting to get through the door on the far side of the clearing."

"As is everyone else in this place," Tarses replied.

Thanon smiled a little.

"To the door, then," Tarses declared. "Let us make it our goal to take the ground in front of it and defend it against all comers. Once we have control of it, we will decide who to let through."

"I yield to your greater experience. My sword and those of my men are yours to command."

"Form up in a fighting wedge. Swords to the front, spears and polearms in the second rank. Archers and casters behind. Charge!" Tarses ordered the combined force.

Thanon took his place at Tarses's right hand and ran forward, shouting the charge.

Aurelius paused at the edge of the clearing. "Stars above, what a mess."

Selea grunted beside him.

"How are we ever going to find them in this chaos?"

"Look for Will's magic," Selea answered. "Or a healer using mad amounts of magic."

They worked their way around the edges of the battle as much as possible, staying out of the worst of the fighting. Increasingly appalled as he identified the players on the field, Aurelius pressed onward grimly. It wasn't supposed to be like this. They were supposed to quietly find the Sleeping King and wake him in secret. Then the king would have time to raise an army and gather his forces before confronting Koth.

But that was a problem for another day. Right now, they needed to find Will and his companions and make sure they were safe.

A nulvari swung out from behind a tree trunk in front of Aurelius and cast several short, sharp bursts of magic at him. The first one burned through his magical shield, and the second activated an automatic shielding on his armor. But the third one struck him. Reflexively, he captured the magic, using his race's innate skill with trapping and containing magic.

He staggered, weakened by what he identified in shock as shadow magic. Selea's hand shot out to steady him. Using his off hand with shocking speed, Selea slashed the nulvari's throat. Where that dagger had come from, Aurelius couldn't say. But he was grateful for his friend's lethal skills.

A human stepped in front of him threateningly, and Aurelius released the shadow magic he'd just absorbed, casting it clumsily at the fellow. The man didn't duck in time and took the brunt of the dark magic, falling to the ground.

"What was that?" Selea asked. "It didn't look like your usual magic."

"It wasn't."

"Are you all right?"

"No. That shadow magic drained me. Anything much stronger of that same flavor would kill me."

"Then perhaps I should engage any remaining nulvari we encounter," Selea commented.

"Be my guest."

Rynn gaped as a line of green lizardmen appeared off to his right, forming a battle line that looked as if it prepared to sweep into the battle from the right flank. In and of itself, that wouldn't have worried him excessively. The chaos was already complete out here. But he spied three creatures with the lizardmen that made his blood run cold.

They appeared to be giant constructs made entirely of nullstone. Each was ridden by a lizardman. One peeled left, taking a flying leap with what looked like honest-to-goodness nullstone wings into the main body of Tarses's force. A half dozen fighters went down under its claws as it landed in the midst of the tightly bunched troops.

Thanon's Talons closed in around it, but the construct swung club-like fists back and forth, sending the soldiers from the elite unit flying. They were in trouble. Imperial steel wouldn't even scratch nullstone, let alone do significant damage to it.

Rynn started forward with the intent to tell Thanon they would need to use Klangon steel to hit the beast, but the second construct charged just then, cutting off Rynn's path to Thanon. Up close, the construct was reptilian in appearance. It had fins in lieu of arms, and it relied on its tooth-filled mouth for attacks, swinging its head back and forth on a long neck, brandishing its sharp fangs as weapons.

Rynn ducked under a swing of its nullstone tail and then

leaped over it as the tail swung back toward him. The construct was using its open mouth to mow down the humanoids in front of it like weeds in its path.

He lost sight of the third construct and looked around wildly for it. And then he felt the ground rumble beneath his feet. He took off running and found himself barreling headlong into Vesper's massed elemental phantasms. All of a sudden, he was embroiled in a pitched fight for his life as the phantasms swarmed him.

He whirled and kicked and punched, using every ounce of his skill and speed to hold off a half dozen phantasms at once.

The ground beneath his feet began to give way, and he used his extraordinary agility to leap aside just as a great hole opened up and the third nullstone construct burrowed up out of the ground.

The lizardman riding the creature shook himself, sending a rain of dirt down on Rynn, who backed away quickly. He would rather face a dozen phantasms than tangle with that nullstone monster.

Fortunately, in a matter of seconds, the Gaged Man and Vesper's forces had their hands full dealing with the construct, and he managed to slip away, retreating toward the Talons where they were attempting to regroup, repair armor, and heal the worst of their wounds.

He shouted to Thanon, "Use Klangon steel on the nullstone beasts!"

Thanon shouted back, or maybe he was mentally projecting the order at his men and Rynn intercepted it because he was also paxan, "Unseat the rider, but choose your moment! The construct will follow the last order it was given before the rider is taken down. Choose an order you can live with!"

Rynn spun and headed back toward the construct and rider who had burrowed out of the ground. As soon as the lizardman rider gave his beast an order to kill all the trolls or kill all the phantasms, he was going to find himself abruptly separated from his ride.

* * *

S ha'Li turned the amulet this way and that, catching the light on its dark surface so she could see the faint markings along its rim. Glancing up, comparing it to the door itself, she happened to glance through the cutout in the amulet. A dozen symbols on the door were visible through the sinuous hole in her trinket.

Frowning, she intentionally brought the amulet to her eye to gaze at the door through it. Swearing, she all but smacked her forehead in frustration as the trick of the amulet dawned on her. The cutout on it was not a symbol. It was a map. It showed her a linear sequence of symbols to activate on the door, like a code.

"Raina, I need you to go over to the door and push each symbol I describe to you in the correct order."

"Right. Give me a minute to get over there."

While the healer made her way to the door, using her colors to safely pass a group of Imperial soldiers fighting a group of Anton's rogues, Sha'Li continued peering at the door. Which end of the amulet's path to start at? She tried doing it from the top down, pointing and shouting at each symbol she could see through the amulet. They got to the end of the sequence, and Sha'Li ran over to help Raina push on the door.

Nothing.

"Let's try again," Sha'Li panted. "This time we'll work from the bottom up."

Raina nodded grimly.

Sha'Li had to kill a rogue who had, in her absence, camped out in the protected spot Sha'Li had been hiding in. She took a moment to roll the body aside and put the amulet to her eye again.

A groan went up across the battlefield, and she glanced up to see a trio of giant black, stone beasts stomping about, annihilating everything in their paths. She caught sight of Anton's main force and Vesper's forces combining efforts to attack one of the great creatures. Funny how imminent death made fast allies of men who'd been trying to kill each other moments ago.

She turned her attention back to the door. They had to get it open and soon, or she and all her friends were going to die.

"Push that one on the left down by your knee that looks like a house with the door open!"

Raina complied.

"Now move inward one circle in the spiral of symbols and to the right about an arm's length to the one with the three horizontal bars across a box!"

One by one, they worked through the symbols revealed to her by the amulet. They got to the last symbol, and Sha'Li ran forward to push it herself. The stone knob sank several inches into the stone face of the door, and all of a sudden, a crack opened up around the edge of the circular slab of stone.

"You did it!" Raina cried.

"Stay here and don't open it any farther. I'll go get the others," Sha'Li replied. "And then we'll go inside and wake the king."

Hemlocke lurched, stunned. They'd done it. The paltry humans had defeated her defenses. *How. Dare. They.*

She crouched, bunching her mighty muscles, and leaped, bursting through the bubble she'd slept in for the past century and more, exploding up and out of the watery protection of her sea.

Her own proscribing magics in the Griefalls prevented her from transporting herself magically to the door of her brother's prison. Forced to fly, she accelerated and turned northward, skimming aggressively over the surface of the sea. The city of Zarva passed under her nose, and she registered the pale oval faces of humans and lizardmen alike, staring up at her, mouths agape.

In her wake, she both heard and felt the cries. "Hemlocke flies! The dragon is awake!"

Their fear and wonder lent strength to her righteous fury, and she gained altitude, rising above the sands of Iridu, racing northward toward the Griefalls. For five thousand years, she had jealously guarded her greatest and most secret treasure, and no one—*no one*—would take it from her now.

Unleashing a great roar of fury that echoed for miles and turned a swath of the desert beneath her to glass, she pumped her wings several times, hard, rising up high into the sky over the Griefalls. Banking up on her right wing, she executed a barrel roll into a vertical dive that gathered speed until she blazed downward like a burning star falling from the heavens.

Oh no. They would not take her treasure from her . . .

Thanon threw his men at the nullstone construct for a third time, following Tarses's order to at least slow the thing down if it could not be stopped. Tarses's Klangon steel sword damaged the creatures, but at the moment, the general was off dealing with the winged construct, which left Thanon and his men to cope with the finned one, who had just waded into their midst.

If he could just get the thing pointed at one of the other dangerous and hostile creatures on the field . . . and then get the rider to order the construct to attack it instead of his men . . .

He fought a desperate delaying action, risking his life over and over to protect his men as they tried fruitlessly to damage the nullstone beast.

He caught sight of a bright white tabard flashing near the black door, and then he saw Will Cobb join Raina. The gypsy healer and the paxan who ran with Will came into sight as well, gathering at the door. Had they managed to get the thing open, after all?

His attention was drawn back to the battle for several seconds, and he dragged one of his men out of the path of a great nullstone fist smashing through his unit. "Fall back!" he shouted.

Into the gap his men left, one of the black trolls and several nulvari slid forward.

The rider atop the nullstone construct turned his beast toward them and clearly gave it a command to attack them.

"Now!" Thanon ordered his archers urgently. "Take out the lizardman rider!"

A hail of arrows let loose, a half dozen of them piercing

the natural armor of the green lizardman. One lucky shot passed through the rider's throat, and he toppled off his construct, falling to the ground with a thud. Thanon leaped forward himself, swinging frantically, nearly severing the unlucky lizardman's head from his body. One of his other men administered a killing blow to the lizardman's chest.

The nullstone construct lumbered onward, leaving behind his dead rider, chasing the now retreating night troll across the battlefield. Praise the Lady.

Thanon raced over to Tarses's side to report that taking out the rider did, indeed, seem to freeze the nullstone constructs on a single command. He also pointed out that the White Heart emissary and her companions had opened the black door and seemed to be preparing to pass through it.

Tarses nodded tersely and ordered all his forces to fall back and form an arc around the approach to the door. And then he ordered, "Stand your ground or die trying, my friends. No one shall pass through that way but that we let them."

Thanon and his men hacked and slashed their way toward the door, but unfortunately, it seemed that everyone else chose that exact moment to do the exact same thing. The entire battle collapsed in on itself, converging on the black door in a writhing, battling, screaming, bleeding mass of flesh and bone.

"Go in, Raina!" Thanon shouted at the top of his lungs.

She turned, looked in his direction, and made eye contact with him over the mêlée. He waved at her to indicate that she should press forward. She nodded back and gestured for him to join her.

He shook his head and called back, "Go. Tarses and I will hold the line for you until you return!"

Return? Raina did not think that was in the cards for her this day. She would move forward and maybe even wake Gawaine, but there would be no going back for her. The separation between the voices and her sanity was paper thin, and with every healing spell she cast, her grip on life slipped a little bit further. She did her best to meter out her magic in the tiniest possible doses and to rest between castings, but this battle was unbelievable. Even if she had been at full strength, her healing would not have been enough to keep even a portion of the combatants from dying.

"Are we all here?" Will asked urgently.

Raina looked around. Sha'Li, Rosana, Will, Cicero, Rynn. Lakanos had left her side momentarily to beat back someone who'd tried to sneak up behind her, but he would return soon. "Where's Eben?"

Rynn responded, "I see him over there. I'll go get him."

The paxan darted away from their little group.

In his absence, Sha'Li explained, "The door is unlocked. On the other side, there may be traps, so I'll go first. The rest of you stand back at a safe distance. Once I make it through and call back that it's safe to enter, join me, then we will close the door and try to lock it or blockade it from the other side. Yes?"

Everyone nodded in understanding.

A familiar voice said from behind Raina, "Fancy meeting all of you out here. Nice day for a walk, isn't it?"

She whirled, staring at Aurelius and Selea. "What are you doing here?"

"Same thing you are, I imagine. You didn't think we old men were going to let you younglings have all the fun, did you?"

She smiled in gratitude. "You are most welcome here. As you can see, things did not go exactly as we expected. That sandstorm allowed everyone who was following us to catch up."

"Plus a few more players we didn't know about," Selea commented.

"Well, they're all here now," Aurelius retorted. "Where are we on the door?"

"It's open. Rynn is fetching Eben, and then we go inside."

Aurelius shook his head. She thought he might have murmured, "Remarkable," but she wasn't sure.

Rynn and Eben materialized, along with a cloaked and hooded figure. "My sister, Marikeen," Eben explained briefly.

Will nodded. "Welcome, Marikeen. Okay. Let's go."

Sha'Li leaned her shoulder into the door and gave it a good push. Ponderously, the great stone slab gave way a few inches. Rynn, Eben, and Will jumped to help her, and the door opened perhaps the length of Raina's arm.

"That's enough. I can pass through," Sha'Li grunted. She slipped into the darkness beyond and disappeared as the fellows fell back cautiously beside Raina and the others.

Someone bumped into Raina from behind, nearly knocking her off her feet, and she turned around with alacrity to discover that a white tiger rakasha mercenary had slammed into her.

"Sorry, White Heart," he growled. "Healing?"

Frustrated at her requirement to heal everyone, she dribbled a tiny bit of healing magic into one of what had to be Anton's men. But doing even that small amount of magic made the clearing spin. She wavered and had barely managed to right herself when one of Thanon's paxan warriors leaped in front of her and cut down the rakasha she'd just healed. She swore under her breath. It was bad enough to have to heal, but it was worse to waste it for naught.

"Come in!" Sha'Li's muffled voice came out of the crack. "And bring lights."

Aurelius moved forward. "Allow me. I can magically light the space and leave your hands free for whatever comes."

Right. Like more angry guardians determined to kill them all rather than let them wake Gawaine. Her friends passed through the narrow, one-person-wide opening. She paused as she realized Lakanos was engaged in battle with a pair of nulvari.

"Go on!" he shouted. "I'll join you in a minute!"

She turned and slipped inside the chamber. A matching set of symbols decorated the interior side of the door. Excellent. It could be locked from the inside, then.

The chamber itself was huge. It must encompass most of the island. Aurelius's light spell had created soft light throughout what would otherwise have been a black cave. Or series of caves. As she and her friends moved forward, massive tree roots appeared to have grown down through the chamber over the centuries, and dirt clung to the smaller hair roots growing off of the big ones, creating a maze of walls and openings.

"The ring," she blurted. "It feels him. Gawaine's in that direction." She pointed off to their left a bit.

Sha'Li suggested, "You go on. I'll catch up after I close the door and check to make sure it's locked. Otherwise, someone outside will find a way inside." Sha'Li put her shoulder into the door and started to slide it shut inch by ponderous inch. Unable to contain her impatience, Raina moved off, following the lead of Gawaine's ring with the others just behind her. They were only minutes away from finding Gawaine now.

Soon. Very soon, she would meet him in person.

One spied a group of people passing through an opening in the black door and yelled for Two and Three to follow him as he raced toward it frantically. His compulsion to get inside that chamber was almost too much to bear.

Where he came from, One didn't know, but all of a sudden, a large warrior of a man wearing old-fashioned gages upon his forearms appeared at the door and slipped through just behind the jann girl.

One heard a scuffle on the other side of the door, but he jumped through anyway with Two and Three close behind him. A jann girl was just casting some sort of spell upon a jann boy that seemed to command him, and she ran away from the opening with him stumbling along docilely behind her.

A few feet beyond the doorway, a black lizardman girl was fighting the Gaged Man and giving him a hard time of it, too.

Two ordered in a high, childish voice, "Split up. Find the Sleeping King's body, and then come get me immediately. You, too," she ordered the Gaged Man. "And hurry!"

Startled, One complied with the order, which resonated with power deep in his gut. As he started to turn toward the maze of tree roots, he saw a white Royal Order of the Sun tabard with the gold trim of a knight fill the doorway.

He turned back to confront this threat, but an alchemy

globe exploded against the knight's armor, and the fellow went down to the ground. Another figure, a man, leaped over the fallen knight and slipped inside.

Old memory, not quite fully suppressed, supplied a name to him. Anton Constantine. That same part of his mind supplied disdain. Hatred, even. But the order from Two overrode every other consideration.

As Anton disappeared into the shadows and the Gaged Man darted away into the chambers, the black lizardman girl slammed the door shut. One turned and headed into the dimly lit cave. Somewhere in here was the ultimate prize. And he *must* be the one to find it.

Raina moved forward confidently, the ring on her middle finger pulsing with energy. It took them perhaps ten minutes to wind through the maze of smaller roots to a single, massive root perhaps thirty feet across that plunged straight down into the earth.

"The taproot," Will murmured. "This is the heart of the wake tree."

Gawaine's physical body had to be close now. They passed around to the far side of the taproot, and that was when Raina saw the bower. In it was a platform of some kind about waist high. And a man lay resting upon it, hands crossed over his chest. The body was covered in a white shroud made of some silken fabric so sheer and light as to look more like air than solid cloth.

And beneath it, that face . . . so familiar . . . so pale . . . so still . . .

Her heart stopped beating for an instant, and her breath skipped and caught. A cold chill and a hot flash raced through her simultaneously.

Gasps sounded behind her. And then everyone exclaimed all at once, asking if that was the Sleeping King.

"That's Gawaine," she said reverently, moving slowly toward him.

Other small details registered. A throne-like chair sat at

the far side of the bower, placed ideally for someone to sit beside Gawaine's body, contemplating it. Did Hemlocke come to visit her brother, then? Of course, based on Gawaine's description of their relationship, she was as likely to come here to gloat as she was to grieve.

Gawaine's clothing, readily visible through the gossamer shroud, had aged, his tabard turned black, the unicorn rampant upon it a dull, tarnished bronze color. A great diagonal slash marred the cloth from shoulder to hip, but the pieces had been lain together carefully over his torso so the cut was barely noticeable. In his dreaming grove, Gawaine's tabard was emerald green and his unicorn heraldry stitched in thread of gold.

Gawaine's body itself was pristine and looked as if he had not aged a day since being laid here. Raina reverently laid her palm upon his chest, but jerked her hand back.

"What's wrong?" Will asked quickly.

"He's cold. And he has no heartbeat."

"Well, of course not," Rosana said practically. "There's no life in his body. No spirit."

"Let us change that," Aurelius declared.

Rynn spoke up. "The first order of business will be to open Gawaine's prison on the dream plane. There should be some link to his grove here." He looked around the inner chamber they stood in. "Something that's replicated in his grove."

Will said, "The wake tree. There's one just like it, but in miniature, in the grove. Right, Raina?"

She tried to remember the individual trees in the grove, but the only impressions she could call to mind were of Gawaine himself. When she was in his presence, she noticed little else. "If you say so, I'm sure you're right."

Rynn nodded. "If the tree is the link, then it's also the key to the prison. It must be destroyed to release Gawaine's spirit."

Eben eyed the massive trunk doubtfully. "How are we supposed to destroy that? It would take us days or weeks to hack through all of that."

Will laid his hands on the taproot. After a moment, he

replied, "If we cut away a band of the bark all the way around the root, the flow of life from the earth into the tree will be broken. That should kill it. Mind you, it won't turn brown and fall over instantly because trees store energy in their leaves. But if it's a link we're looking to break, that should do it."

Eben pulled out his long sword and drew a line across the rough, hard surface of the root. A thin cut formed, and then healed almost immediately. "Um, how are we supposed to kill a tree that heals itself instantly?"

Kendrick spoke up. "What about Kerryl's dagger? It broke the link between dryads and their trees. Maybe it will break the link between this tree and its equivalent on the dream plane."

Aurelius nodded. "An excellent thought."

Kendrick pulled out the cold iron dagger and drew it across the tree trunk. An upwelling of clear sap ran down the root just like blood would flow from a human wound. Even Raina, who had no great affinity for plants, felt the wake tree's pain.

Kendrick groaned, and the dagger fell from his fingers.

Rosana picked up the weapon and stepped forward, laying the blade against the tree. She murmured in wonder, "I feel its link to the spirit realm. That is where it truly lives. We can kill this manifestation of the wake tree here, and it will not be fully destroyed." With energy and resolve, she commenced slicing a line around the taproot.

It took her several minutes to work her way around the great taproot, but at last, she returned to where she had begun, joining the two ends of her cut into a continuous circle. She finished by stabbing the blade deeply into the root at the spot where the cut began and ended. A great heaving of spirit energy passed through Raina, all but knocking her off her feet. Ayli also staggered, and Rosana did fall to her knees.

The ring on Raina's hand grew warm, and a faint green glow emanated from her pouch all of a sudden. Certainty poured through her. "He comes!" she cried. "Gawaine's spirit is free!"

And that was when all hell broke loose.

* * *

Four figures rushed the group, attacking in a flurry of damaging magic, alchemy globes, and blades. Will raised his staff and started to summon magic, but then stopped, so shocked he forgot what he'd been in the process of doing.

"Mother?" he mumbled. Then louder, "Father? Adrick?"

It could not be. They were *dead*. And yet, here they surely were. Exultation roared through him. They were *alive*. Two years of grief and pain and loneliness fell away like dead leaves shed before the budding of new flowers in spring.

His father leaped at him with a flurry of blows from the white-bladed long sword Will had only ever seen his father wield once. But he knew it to be Ty's sword, Dragon's Tooth. Was this some sort of bizarre way for Ty to show love for his son?

Will had no more time to think, however, because his father was on him. Cripes. He'd forgotten how fast Ty was. Even with the intervening two years' worth of training at the hands of the finest weapon masters in Dupree, Will still was extremely hard pressed to defend himself, let alone launch any kind of attack against his father.

"Where have you been?" he tried.

No answer.

"Why didn't you tell me you were alive?"

Still no answer. In fact, he saw no signs of recognition at all in his father's blank, glassy eyes.

"It's me, Will!" he cried, parrying frantically. "Why are you attacking me? You set me on this quest!"

His father's face remained grim and set, his expression implacable.

"He does not know you!" Aurelius called from behind Will.

"What's wrong with him?" Will called back as he turned and ran, dodging and weaving between the tree roots, using his youth and dexterity to stay a hair's breadth ahead of his father's deadly blade.

"I don't know. Come back to me, and I will backpack you," Aurelius responded. "Between the two of us, mayhap we can slow him down a bit."

Will veered toward the sound of Aurelius's voice. As he raced toward his grandfather, Will heard Selea say urgently, "Kendrick, with me. Adrick is an accomplished fighter in addition to being an outstanding woodsman. I'll need your help to find him and subdue him."

Just as Will careened around a wall of roots, Aurelius pointed off to one side. "Serica went that way. Someone go after her, and look out for her alchemy. She has a fair arm."

"I'm on it!" Cicero called.

"Will, do you need my healing?" Rosana called to him.

"I've got Aurelius. Go help Cicero."

She tore out of the clearing after the kindari.

Will heard metal clanging musically off crystal. Those were Rynn's gauntlets blocking sword blows. The fourth assailant, the Gaged Man, must be attacking him. A female voice Will didn't know shouted an incant for ice damage, and Eben cheered as it hit. That must be Marikeen casting at the Gaged Man.

Something hot slammed into Will's back, knocking him off his feet and sending him tumbling headlong toward Aurelius. Force magic flew over his head as Aurelius answered the attack. Will rolled to his feet, coming up with his staff in hand, facing his father.

"Resorting to magic already, are you?" he taunted his father. "Don't think you can take me with weapons?"

He knew full well the risk of infuriating his father during combat, but if he could taunt Ty into using just weapons, he might stand a chance of distracting his father long enough with swordplay for Aurelius to take him down.

Aurelius fell in behind Will, one of his hands resting on Will's back between his shoulder blades. A protective spell passed over Will's skin. No sooner had it taken effect than Ty blasted Will with a bolt of force damage that would have killed him had it struck home. Aurelius cast another magical shield on him. For the next few seconds, Ty cast and Aurelius countercast as quickly as the two men could draw the power and say the incants, using Will as their target dummy.

It was surreal being the target of his own father's best effort to kill him. He'd spent so long thinking of all the things he would say to his parents if he could but see them one more time, all the questions he had for his father regarding his early training, how he'd become a top-notch battle caster and then had all of it locked away, forgotten until he had need of it.

The barrage of magic ended, and he was, miraculously, still standing. He leaped forward on the attack, taking advantage of Ty's concentration on the magic to finally put his father on the defensive.

Ty darted backward and to the right behind a wall of roots, and Will ran left to cut his father off. As he made the spinning turn, Will glimpsed Sha'Li staggering into the clearing with blood running down the side of her face.

"Is the door closed?" he shouted.

"Aye." She nodded and collapsed.

Anton crouched in the shadow of a broad root, motionless and relying on everyone else's battles to distract them. Tiberius De'Vir—for who else could that outrageously skilled battle caster be?—was fighting his son—for who else could that young man who looked like the very image of his father be?—to a stalemate. Aurelius was helping the son, which was the only reason the boy yet lived. Tiberius had not been called the greatest warrior in Haelos for nothing.

Seeing perhaps his greatest nemeses bashing each other's brains in was one of the most gratifying sights he'd seen in a very long time. He wished them good speed and good deaths.

Off to his right, Anton spied the nulvari assassin Selea Rouge and Hyland's boy, Kendrick, chasing a hydesmyn in and out through the chambers. That hydesmyn was fast and elusive and was giving the pair a hard run.

To his left, the Gaged Man was giving all they could handle to that jann girl from the Cabal and to a jann young man—who had to be her brother if family resemblance counted for anything at all. The Gaged Man's fighting style was old-fashioned, stiff and formal, but he was still a massively skilled fighter.

A kindari elf staring down at the ground moved past him,

clearly hunting the trail of some prey. He recalled seeing the fellow in the company of Raina, the White Heart ingénue, a while back. Never caught his name, though. A gypsy Heart healer followed close behind the elf.

A shout for healing over by the body of the Sleeping King made the gypsy lurch and take off running. Raina came into sight by the body as well as another kindari, an elderly woman whose face was marked with spiderwebs and hands were glowing with white healing magics.

All three healers knelt next to someone who'd gone down. He couldn't see from here who it was. Hopefully it was Tiberius, that traitorous whoreson.

The jann boy and Marikeen came running into the clearing by the king, and then Selea Rouge came out of the trees. The nulvari paused to speak with Aurelius and then went over to the healers to check on whoever was down.

The Gaged Man burst out of the trees just behind the cluster of healers and struck with three lightning-enhanced sword strikes, one to each healer. All three women dropped to the ground. Selea turned with unbelievable speed to parry the swing aimed at him, but instead, a flash of magic came from his right flank and dropped the nulvari like a felled tree.

The Gaged Man leaped off into the maze of chambers just as a paxan burst into sight. The person who'd been down to begin with jumped up and turned out to be a black lizard-man girl. He'd seen her before, but he couldn't place a name to her.

Tiberius raced into the clearing mere seconds after the others left and cast four quick spells, one at each of the downed people—Raina, Selea, the gypsy healer, and the old kindari woman. Given the cold fury on Tiberius's face, Anton ventured to guess that had not been healing he'd cast. In fact, Anton recalled that Tiberius knew no healing spells. He'd always bragged about being in the business of killing his enemies, not fixing them.

Anton had healing potions in his pouch. Not that he had any great interest in using them on this group of children

THE WANDERING WAR • 511

who had been nothing but a pain in his neck for the past two years.

Granted, he would gain favor with Maximillian if he gained favor with the Heart. And he would surely do that if he saved the life of their precious emissary. But spite stilled his hand. Let the emissary die.

What of the king, lying under his shroud? Should he attempt to destroy the body? Or mayhap cast his lot in with the Gaged Man, who'd been the personal bodyguard of Ammertus's beloved daughter?

Ammertus had hung Anton out to dry when the Black Ship captain Kodo had stripped Anton of his governorship of Dupree. Anton's old mentor had declined to speak up for him in any meaningful way at court, and Ammertus had offered no aid, no support to Anton in this entire year of exile. If Ammertus would not help the house of Constantine, then it would not help Ammertus.

Of course, the flip side of that argument was that helping the cause of a Kothite in this battle, even one whom he despised, would still provide a path to redemption at court. The Kothites valued loyalty above all else.

How did General Tarses figure into all of this? Anton had been shocked to recognize the great general on the field of battle outside this place, and he'd been even more shocked to realize Tarses fought on the side of those who wished to wake the Sleeping King. Did Maximillian's favorite know something Anton did not? Or was Tarses as betrayed and angry as he was, working against his liege lord by waking a rival for Maximillian's throne?

Caught in twin dilemmas of whether or not to act and who to support or fight against, Anton opted to stay put, waiting and watching the events unfolding before him a little longer before he made any decisions.

If nothing else, he could always sneak out of here and make his way to the Imperial Seat to report on today's extraordinary events. That alone should garner him a decent amount of goodwill at court.

* * *

Will saw Rosana go down and ran for her as fast as his legs would go. He'd been looking right at her when his father burst into sight, cast a spell at her and the others who were down, and then disappeared back into the trees.

He screeched to a halt beside Rosana and fell to his knees to check her. No pulse. No breath. "She's dying!" he shouted. "Healing!"

Aurelius skidded to a stop beside him. "All the healers lie before you. And, ironically, the professional assassin among us."

Will yanked out the only healing potion he had and started to uncork it, but Aurelius stopped him. "That won't do any good."

"Why not?"

"Because your father cast imprison spells upon these four. No magic of any kind, including potions or poisons, will work on them as long as the imprison is active."

"Then deactivate it!"

"To do that, I would have to drop your father. And by the time we find him and do that, these four will have bled out. We only have about a minute to stop them from dying."

"You're saying we have to let them die?" Will demanded, even though he already knew the grim answer.

"Once they're dead, the magic of the imprison will drop. Then we can renew their lives. But that is our only choice."

Will groaned. "What if one or all of them don't make it back?"

"Then we must be certain they did not die in vain. No one among us can help them in their current state, nor can anyone do them further harm. Come with me. We still have to find your father and find a way to stop him."

"I can't—"

"You must," Aurelius retorted strongly. "You're the only fighter in Haelos who stands even a chance against Tiberius. With me at your back, *maybe* the two of us can stop him. He'll kill the rest of them one by one if we fail."

* * *

Sha'Li sat up, her head pounding, and jolted at the sight of her friends dead beside her. She had some healing, alchemical in nature, but it was not strong enough to revive the dead. The clearing was quiet and empty with no one to help heal her friends. She stood up, blinking away the headache and dizziness that assailed her.

The faintest of noise—whoever'd made it was really very stealthy—was enough to alert her to the presence of someone else. Sha'Li moved off into the shadows quickly as if she intended to stride away in that direction. But instead, she circled back silently and paused in the lee of a great tree root.

It was the petite elven woman who'd jumped through the door while the Gaged Man had attacked. Sha'Li watched her creep toward Gawaine's bier, hand outstretched, a positively avid expression on her face.

Sha'Li leaped forward, letting out a mighty shout as she did so. Her claws slid out of her knuckles with a distinctive *schwing* as she swept forward toward the elf.

For her part, the elf started violently, screamed in a high-pitched voice, dropped something, and fled into the forest of ancient roots. Sha'Li chased after the small figure, pausing only long enough to scoop up the object the elf had dropped.

It looked made of wood and was nearly the size of her fist. It was ovoid in shape with one end slightly pointed. Sha'Li only examined it for a heartbeat before stuffing it in her pouch and giving chase to the elf who had dropped the large seed. Now what was that about? Why had the elf been holding it out toward Gawaine?

Vesper paused, trying desperately not to pant. But it was hard not to in this fragile elven body obviously unused to violent physical activity. She had to get back to Gawaine's body and soon. His spirit was free from its prison and making its way here now, to take possession of his body once more. She had only minutes to possess the body for herself.

But as long as that cursed lizardman was standing guard,

she couldn't just walk up and make the leap into him. She needed help.

Vesper looked around in desperation and was both stunned and delighted to spot a man with a familiar mark upon his forehead creeping toward the Sleeping King. That was the mark of the Coil, an organization long in service to her father. Its leaders had long been among her father's most loyal lackeys. This one would do nicely.

She mustered precious bits of her remaining strength and projected a command outward with her mind, ordering the fellow, Anton Constantine, to do her will and come to her aid.

His resistance to her command was both bitter and angry. His mind whirled with enraged thoughts that he'd intended to help the Kothite anyway and didn't need to be commanded to do it. His main concern seemed to be that now he would not get credit for helping her of his own free will.

Frankly, she couldn't care less. He was an underling. A tool. Nothing more.

"Come to the Sleeping King and protect me with your life," she commanded him imperiously.

Eben and Marikeen had lost touch with the Gaged Man, and a search of the area around the king's chamber yielded no sign of him.

Eben sighed. "We might as well return to the king's body and guard him until some of the others return."

Looking disgusted, Marikeen nodded in agreement. They stepped back into the central clearing, and Eben stared, stunned. A small elven woman and no one other than Anton Constantine himself were approaching the king's body from the opposite direction.

Lifting Gawaine's bow and nocking an arrow as he charged forward, Eben loosed his arrow at Anton's black heart.

The arrow flew true, hungrily seeking his enemy's blood . . . except at the last second, the missile deflected wide to one side as if an unseen hand had reached out and slapped it aside. The elven woman laughed in an odd high-pitched voice entirely unmatched to her body.

Marikeen gasped, "Vesper."

Of course. That was where Eben knew that childish laugh from.

But when he and his sister charged Anton, the laugh cut off abruptly. Rage flooded his mind. Betrayal. Fury that they had turned on her. And just the tiniest hint of fear tinged the mind blast.

"You cannot hurt us!" Marikeen shouted as the elf retreated into the forest of roots. "You're not strong enough!"

Eben prayed that was true. He'd seen evidence of Vesper's powers before, and they had been truly frightening.

"You dare to stand against me?" Anton snarled as their charge brought the two of them close to him.

It hadn't actually been Eben's plan to attack the former governor, but if the man intended to harm Gawaine or take possession of the Sleeping King's body, then Eben would by all means attack him. He and his sister advanced more slowly now as Anton backed away from them.

"You killed our father!" Marikeen snarled beside Eben.

"No, I didn't," Anton snorted.

"Your mercenaries did. On your orders," Eben retorted. "Same difference."

Anton shrugged. "Fine. I concede the point. I killed your precious Hyland. But we all know he was not your father."

Marikeen charged Anton, and Eben was hard pressed to keep up with her. They'd never fought together, and he had no idea which direction she was going to jump, so their tactics were awkward and ill coordinated. Anton, no slouch at combat himself, took advantage of this to pull out a short sword with one hand and gas globes with the other.

Eben blocked an alchemy globe with his mace but took a rather nasty cut from the short sword. He jumped back, swearing. Marikeen should have waited for him to adjust his armor and perhaps heal himself, but instead she charged anew, forcing him to return to the attack well before he was ready.

Anton actually lowered his guard, and Marikeen, not expecting it, barreled into him. Anton slammed his mailed fist into her nose, and she went down hard with blood streaming from her face. Eben leaped over her, and with a furious flurry of sword and mace swings was able to push Anton back far enough for Marikeen to stumble to her feet. But that left Eben face-to-face with an accomplished alchemist. Anton hit him with some sort of poison gas that made Eben violently ill. He struggled mightily to even lift his weapons through the waves of nausea, let alone swing them with any force.

Marikeen fumbled in her belt pouch and emerged with something slender and white. "Do you recognize this, Anton?" she demanded.

"If I'm not mistaken," he drawled, "that is the very antler that slew your precious father, Leland Hyland."

"It's going to slay you, too."

Anton laughed. He *laughed*. Rage filled Eben so full he thought he would explode from it. Ignoring his injuries and illness, he raised his weapon for a mighty charge—

But pulled up short as some sort of . . . smoke . . . emerged from the antler all of a sudden. Anton leaped back, clearly as surprised as Eben. Even Marikeen lurched, dropping the antler on the ground.

The smoke resolved into a human-sized cloud and then quickly coalesced into more solid form. Before his eyes, almost more quickly than he could comprehend, Leland Hyland took shape in front of them.

"What the—" Anton blustered. "What are you?"

Leland glanced back and forth between his children and his enemy. "Is aught amiss that you summoned me, Marikeen?"

"Anton is trying to kill me and Eben."

Leland turned very slowly. Ice-cold fury rolled off of him, and even Anton cringed back from the ghostly figure of Leland Hyland, apparently a spirit warrior. Eben knew well that his father, although slow to anger, was a fearsome man when roused to full rage.

"For Hyland!" Leland roared. "Hope runs free!" And with his motto echoing around him, Leland charged.

Eben fell in on his father's left side while Marikeen jumped close behind her father, using him as a shield so she could cast magic damage at Anton over Leland's shoulder. Anton cursed and fell back before the three of them, spraying alchemy globes inaccurately in between wild swings of his short sword.

It was a lopsided fight, and Anton turned tail and fled from certain death.

"Do we follow?" Leland asked tersely.

"As much as I would like to rid the world of that maggot once and for all," Eben answered regretfully, "protecting the Sleeping King is more important right now."

The fight against Tiberius was hard fought and shifted by tiny degrees as Will's youth and new training in combination with Aurelius's impressive casting skills bit by bit got the better of Tiberius.

Will used an intricate attack, parry, feint, attack sequence that Captain Krugar had shown him, and Aurelius timed a disarming spell to coincide exactly with the second, actual, attack. The result was that Dragon's Tooth clattered to the ground.

Will instantly pressed his advantage. This might be his one and only chance to defeat his father. He unleashed a flurry of blows with his staff, using both ends to pummel his father.

Ty fell back before the onslaught, taking several quick, stumbling steps backward. Wary of overbalancing by pursuing too quickly, Will didn't fall for the trap his father had set for him. Ty tried to force Will to one side with several quick damage spells, but Aurelius was able to replace Will's magical shields as quickly as Ty burned through them.

A flash of movement startled both Will and Ty, and they both jumped away from the incoming attacker. But instead of striking them, the person veered behind Will and scooped up Ty's sword.

Sha'Li.

Bless her. Will had no idea where she'd come from or how

long she'd been watching the fight, but she'd obviously realized the importance of separating Tiberius from his sword.

Ty shouted in dismay and rage and turned on Will then, throwing a blistering barrage of magic at both him and Aurelius. When he had them on full defensive, Ty turned and ran.

Dregs. He had a good head start on Will.

"Leave him," Aurelius said from behind Will. "I'm almost out of mana, and you need to rest."

As soon as Aurelius said the word *rest*, fatigue so ferocious that Will could hardly stand upright under the weight of it slammed into him. Aurelius actually had to wedge a shoulder under Will's armpit to help him back to the king's side.

He dropped to his knees beside the fallen Rosana. "They can be renewed now, can't they?" he asked.

"Aye. But I have no magic left to do it. Your father tapped me out completely with that last attack."

If his father was responsible for Rosana having to resurrect, he would kill Ty.

The thought must have shown on his face, for Aurelius murmured, "Your father is not in his right mind. He would never harm you or anyone you care about. He loves you and your mother more than life."

"There has to be something we can do!" Will cried. "I can't just sit here and watch her die!"

Movement across the clearing made Will reach for his staff defensively. But what he saw when he pushed painfully to his feet made him stare.

"Leland?" Aurelius breathed.

Hyland and his foster children were just stepping into the wide clearing that held the body of a man who could only be the Sleeping King himself when two fighting figures all but knocked them over. A paxan warrior wearing crystal gauntlets and fist fighting in the ancient style was grappling with a heavily armed warrior, tall and thin.

As he turned to address this new threat, the armored man landed a heavy blow in the side of the paxan's head with his metal-gaged forearm. The paxan went down heavily and lay still. Leland couldn't tell if he was unconscious or dead.

Eben shouted and jumped forward, drawing him and Marikeen into a fight with the Gaged Man, whether Leland wished it or no.

Stars, the thin man was fast. He seemed able to fight independently with each hand simultaneously, something Leland had never witnessed. Eben attempted to tie up the man's left-hand sword while Leland fought the fellow's right-hand sword. Marikeen danced back and forth between him and Eben, trying to land elemental magic damage when openings presented themselves. But the Gaged Man steadily drove them backward, across the clearing, past four bodies lying on the ground.

Leland was shocked to recognize the corpses—Selea Rouge, Raina, and Rosana. He didn't know the fourth deceased, an elderly female elf, kindari maybe.

His distraction proved costly because their attacker turned both weapons on Eben for a moment, forcing the jann to retreat quickly and stumble. Marikeen leaped to steady her brother, and Leland jumped forward on the attack once more.

But as he fought, his mind raced. With time, he, Eben, and Marikeen would overwhelm their opponent. But at what cost to the dead lying just behind them? Leland had enough strength left to renew the foursome. But he would have to leave Eben and Marikeen to fight this attacker alone. The pair was doing well, holding their own, even. But he did not think they could beat the Gaged Man without his help.

Selea was one of his dearest friends, and he'd long thought of Raina as the daughter he and his wife should have had. Both of them were *dead*. Time grew short to save them from the dangers of resurrection.

He owed Raina his life. She'd put on the White Heart colors for him when she desperately didn't want to. She was wearing his wife's White Heart tabard, for stars' sake. His wife . . . he knew the choice she would have him make.

"You two have this fight!" he called to Eben and Marikeen. "I believe in you!"

He dropped back and rushed over to the fallen as much as his ghostly form allowed him to hurry. He dropped to one knee beside Raina, placing his hand on her forehead. He murmured the incant for a renewing spell and cast ghostly white magic into her.

Raina's eyes fluttered open, and she jolted when she looked up at him. "You live?" she mumbled.

"Nay, child. I but visit briefly from beyond the Veil. Will you renew your friends or shall I?"

"If you can do it, I would appreciate it," she sighed weakly.

He frowned. She didn't feel right. But rather than address that, he turned to the next body and incanted the magic for renewing life.

Will, who was kneeling beside the young gypsy healer, all but jumped up and down in his urgency to see Rosana healed and alive. Leland cast the spell into her, and her eyes opened. Will dragged her into a smothering embrace, and Leland spied wetness on the boy's cheeks. Poignant longing for his own sweet wife filled him.

Leland moved on quickly to Selea and the elven woman, renewing each of them successfully in turn. Then he said, "Your paxan friend went down a few moments before we came into this clearing. He may be in need of assistance."

A black lizardman girl leaped out from where she'd been lurking in the shadows and raced in the direction he pointed. He hoped she got to the paxan in time. He had put up a valiant fight against the man in the gages. For his part, Leland was too weak to move far from this spot and maintain his current form.

A voice taunted from the woods, "Can't take me by yourself, boy? You'll never be the man I am."

Will Cobb pushed to his feet, a look of determination coming across his young features. Leland would have stopped him, told him he was every bit the man his father had been, but the boy rushed off too quickly for him to say a word. Instead, Leland traded worried looks with the gypsy healer and helped her rise to her feet.

Kendrick ran into the clearing, and Leland's heart swelled with pride as Kendrick spotted him and came over to him. His son had become a man in the past months.

They shared a short, hard embrace, and then Leland murmured, "Eben and Marikeen are in trouble. They fight a tall man in gages. You know how proud I am of you and how much I love you and always will. Go, my son. Do the Hyland name proud."

Thankfully, Kendrick ran for the woods, for no more words would have passed the hot lump in Leland's throat.

Sha'Li darted in the direction Leland Hyland had pointed and found Rynn in a heap on the ground. Cicero was fighting a glassy-eyed hydesmyn just beyond Rynn's prostrate form, and the two were evenly matched. Sha'Li would have helped Cicero, but she didn't know how long Rynn had been down and whether he was bleeding out or even dead.

She checked his neck and was relieved to feel a pulse. Lifting Rynn's head, she poured a healing potion down his throat and waited for it to take effect. In a few seconds, he shuddered and his eyes opened.

"Demons below, that tastes awful!" he declared.

"My granny says it tastes bad so it'll wake a person up."

"It worked." Still making a face, he jumped to his feet.

"You need help, Cicero?" Sha'Li called.

"Nah. I got this."

His opponent scowled and redoubled his efforts.

Rynn said, "Yon hydesmyn is possessed. I can smell it on him from here."

Sha'Li walked beside Rynn as they approached the dueling men. "What does possession smell like?"

"It smells like whatever object was used to bind the phantasm possessing the person to the person."

"What kind of object?"

"Something magical works best. An item of personal importance, and the more indestructible the better. When the binding item is destroyed, the link is broken, and the possession ends."

She frowned and removed the seed from her pouch. "I saw the small, elven woman who traveled with yon hydesmyn carrying this. I sense magic in it. Could it be her binding item?"

Rynn shrugged. "Smash it and see what happens."

Sha'Li dropped the seed onto the ground, rolling it with the heel of her boot onto a flattish stone. She raised her foot and stomped on the seed. Although she nearly succeeded in knocking herself over, the seed was not even scratched.

Rynn frowned and struck the seed with his crystal gauntlet. Still nothing. He said, "We need something heavier and sharper to hit it with."

"I have just the thing." Sha'Li pulled the white-bladed sword out of her belt that she'd taken from Will's father earlier. She raised the weapon over her head in both hands and chopped down on the seed with all her strength.

The explosion as the blade impacted the seed, shattering both blade and seed, knocked her back a good ten feet. It sent Rynn, Cicero, and his opponent flying, as well. A massive wave of magic rolled outward from the broken seed, green in taste and smell and so powerful Sha'Li couldn't breathe through its coating on her skin and inside her lungs. The magic soaked into her body, invigorating her and filling her with such power as she had never imagined possible.

"What was that?" Rynn gasped.

"Where am I?" the hydesmyn asked, confused. "Who are you?" he demanded of Cicero.

"I'm the kindari you've been doing your level best to kill for the last half hour."

"Kill? Why? What have you done to me?"

"Nothing, sir."

Rynn moved forward to stand in front of the increasingly agitated hydesmyn. "May I touch your mind for a moment? You have my word of honor I will do nothing to alter or influence your mind. I merely check to see if you are clear of your late possession."

"Possession! By all means check."

Rynn needed only a few seconds to declare the man free of whatever had been controlling him. "What's your name, sir?"

"Adrick. Yours?"

"Rynn."

"Tell me, Adrick. Are your two companions possessed, as well?"

"No idea."

"Let us go find them. Perhaps you can help us identify what item acts as the binding link of the phantasm possessing them."

Will was knocked off his feet by a huge wave of magical power passing through the underground chamber. It felt like nature magic, but on a scale so far beyond anything he'd ever experienced he hardly recognized it as magic.

Ty also went down, but unlike Will, as he fell, he let out a keening sound that did not sound human in origin.

Will clambered to his feet and rushed over to his father, who was just rolling over slowly onto his back.

"Will? What on Urth?"

"You know who I am?"

"Of course. You're my son! Where are we? And why am I showing myself to you? We're supposed to be following you from a distance and lending support only as you need it while we spy on Governor Constantine and figure out what he's up to."

"You do know that Anton is no longer the governor, don't you?" Will asked, confused.

"What?" Ty squawked.

Aurelius stepped forward. "Whatever was possessing you has obviously fled your mind. That wave of magic must have cleared the creature from you. Anton was deposed nearly a year ago."

"A year? Are you saying I've been possessed for a year? What mayhem have I caused? I have not dishonored the De'Vir name, have I?"

"On the contrary, my son," Aurelius answered soberly. "Your cleverness in secretly teaching your son the ways of the warrior has done you great credit and undoubtedly saved young Will's life."

"On many occasions," Will added.

"Where's your mother? Is she all right?"

Panic rushed through Will. He couldn't lose her again after he'd just found her. Father and son took off running through the maze in search of her before the creature possessing her did anything to permanently harm Serica.

Kendrick attacked and parried alongside his foster siblings, doing everything in his power to keep the full attention of the Gaged Man upon him, Eben, and Marikeen. Kendrick could see Selea Rouge circling around behind the Gaged Man, who truthfully was getting the better of the three of them. Any second now, the assassin would be in position to attack, but he'd better hurry. Kendrick didn't think they could hold off the Gaged Man for much longer.

But then a violent magical wave rushed through the area and smashed into Selea's back, slamming him forward and into the back of the Gaged Man, who crashed to the ground at Kendrick's feet just as Kendrick was knocked over himself. He rolled fast, snatching the Gaged Man's sword and tossing it away. Eben leaped on the Gaged Man, who was still.

Cautiously, Kendrick stood up, and Eben eased off their foe. Last, Selea rose to his feet and rolled over the Gaged Man with his foot. He'd impaled himself awkwardly on his own sword. It had entered his chest at an oblique angle, but appeared to have pierced his heart. He was dying.

As they looked on, he took a final, rattling breath, and died.

"Good riddance," Marikeen muttered.

"What was that wave of energy?" Eben asked.

Selea shrugged. "Let us find Aurelius and ask him."

Vesper was frantic. Time was running out, and nothing was going as she had planned. She was stuck in this fragile body, her bodyguard was nowhere to be found, and that cursed lizardman girl had not only freed Adrick from his possession but in a much more dire development had somehow managed to shatter the unshatterable sword that bound Tiberius to her and had made him her slave all these long months.

Now she only had this elven woman's mortal form and her own wits to rely on.

Gawaine's spirit was drawing close to the chamber—she could feel his dream-touched spirit approaching rapidly. Any minute now, he would enter his body, and her chance for a return to Urth and renewed immortality would be lost.

Racing frantically toward the king's physical body, she slowed only when she heard voices and saw movement ahead. At least her physical host was excellent at moving in silence and stealth.

At least a dozen people were gathered around the king's bier. They were discussing the wave of magic that had ripped through the chamber a few minutes ago.

A solinari who reeked of magic was asking a black lizardman girl, "So you struck this seed with Dragon's Tooth, and both were destroyed?"

"Aye, Guildmaster Aurelius. That was when the wave of nature magic came from the seed."

"So that was nature magic!" a young human exclaimed.

"Yes, Will," the solinari replied. "Extremely powerful nature magic. If I am not mistaken, that was the Seed of Haelos, one of the pieces of the Sleeping King's regalia."

"And I destroyed it?" the lizardman cried in dismay.

"All is not lost, Sha'Li," the one called Aurelius soothed. "I captured a piece of the magic. I can give it back to the king. And I sense a piece of it in you, as well. Your Tribe mark is glowing with exceptional brightness and carrying a green tinge."

The lizardman girl fingered the mark on her cheek.

"I think I caught a piece of the wave, as well," the White Heart healer offered.

Aurelius cast a quick spell that was likely some sort of detection spell. "Why, I believe you did, Raina." He turned to the gypsy healer and cast a spell on her, as well. He frowned but murmured, "You also hold a portion of the nature magic, Rosana."

Raina said, "If I call upon the nature magic now stored within me, do you think I could cast it into Gawaine in the same way I would cast my own magic?"

The solinari nodded. "Yes, indeed. That might just work. All the healers might be able to do that."

The gypsy called Rosana looked back and forth between the boy Will and Gawaine. "If I give you the nature magics within me, they might permanently bond you with Lord Bloodroot. You would never have to be sick or angry or ruled by his violent passions again."

The youth shook his head. "No, Rosana. I can make do as I am. Give it to Gawaine."

"But we could be together—"

The youth pressed his fingers to her lips. "We will yet find a way. But not this way."

Aurelius looked at the old elven woman with spiderweb marks upon her face. "What of you, Ayli? Will you give the magics you absorbed to your king? Will you help us wake him?"

The woman nodded, looking too moved for words.

The solinari said briskly, "Set up a defensive perimeter. The last thing we need now is for someone to attack us and disrupt this ritual."

The jann youth said, "We dropped the Gaged Man over that way. He's dead and won't bother us again."

Dead? Her bodyguard? Panicked, Vesper moved quickly around the clearing toward where the jann had pointed, staying in the shadows and out of sight of the party in the clearing. It took her several long minutes, but she finally found her companion.

Fumbling in the pouch her host body wore, she found a precious renewing potion and poured it down her man's throat. He lurched to life, and she pressed an urgent hand over his mouth to keep him from crying out. After a moment of wildness, he recognized her and nodded up at her.

She crouched down beside him, whispering, "We must stop the ritual to wake the king. I need to borrow your body. I need your strength and combat skill to get close to the Sleeping King and make the leap into him."

For the first time since she'd fled Alchizzadon, Raina felt like her old self again. The voices were firmly controlled, her head pain-free, her magic flowing normally. That burst of nature magic had been powerful indeed. She was so relieved to feel healthy again, she almost wept with joy. This must be how Will had felt when they'd finally stabilized his health after he'd joined with Bloodroot.

Aurelius said, "We have three pieces of the king's regalia and four healers. I would suggest that three of us hold one of the items to help us form a link to Gawaine and that the fourth assist."

Ayli spoke up. "I already have a link to my king, forged through thousands of years of fealty to him by my people. I need no focus item."

"Perfect, then."

Raina passed Gawaine's crown to Rosana while Eben passed Eliassan's bow—Gawaine's bow—to Aurelius. For her part, Raina clutched her fist tight around Gawaine's signet ring, which still clung tenaciously to her middle finger.

She could keep the nature magic for herself. Be healthy and hale. Live a long, full life. Or she could give up the magic to Gawaine and go back to that other state where she would soon go mad and die. *As if there was any question of what she would do.*

"Let us begin," Aurelius intoned.

Raina closed her eyes and concentrated on Gawaine. Good heavens, he was close. His spirit was so close she could practically reach out and touch it. All that was needed was one big spark of energy to complete the joining of body and spirit.

"Call your magic and begin channeling it into the regalia," Aurelius instructed.

Much in the manner of ritual magic, Raina called the green magic and focused it into the ring on her finger. Immediately, the unicorn horn band grew warm and vibrated with excitement. Someone gasped, and she realized the ring was glowing brightly, along with the bow and the crown.

No sooner had she opened her eyes than every bit of the pain and noise and madness pushing at the boundaries of her mind surged forward, all but overwhelming her. And she hadn't even cast any magic!

She wasn't going to beat this. The curse of her magical power was going to get the best of her. But for now, she was determined to see through this ritual.

"Place your item touching his body," Aurelius murmured, staring at the bow in fascination.

As Ayli laid her hands on Gawaine's ankles, Rosana put the crown on his head, and Aurelius wrapped Gawaine's right hand around his bow after all these thousands of years, Raina gave her ring a tug. It came off easily, as if sensing its final destination and approving of it. She slipped the ring on the fourth finger of his left hand, and it shifted imperceptibly in size, widening to fit his larger hand.

Gawaine's hand was cool against hers, but supple and strong, not stiffened with death. As she stared down at it, the magic stored in his ring began to flow into him. His palm warmed faintly to the touch, and his wrist took on a vaguely rosy hue. Blood was starting to flow through his veins.

But it was too slow. It was not enough. They needed more magic, something big to make the final connection between body and spirit. The other three healers must have sensed the same thing because they all started murmuring incants for healing and casting their magics into him.

It was still not enough.

It was going to take her magic—all of it—to wake him.

She didn't hesitate. Her life was a worthy trade for his. She opened the floodgates wide, wider than she'd ever opened them before. The voices surged forward until the noise of them blinded and deafened her. And still she let it flow. She reached out to all the voices, all the echoes, all the spirits in Haelos. And for a moment she felt them all, her connection to each and every one of them, her link the source of her immense well of magic.

Throwing herself into it headlong, she drew all the magic she could summon, not satisfied to let it passively flow through her and into Gawaine. Rather, she sucked it into her lungs in painful, gasping inhalations. She took all the energy of all the living beings of Haelos, channeled it, shaped it, became the magic herself. And then she exhaled every last bit of it out in a great gust of healing magic. Into him.

Blood. Breath. Life.

And as she died, he came to life.

In that single shared instant of in-between, his eyes opened as hers began to close, and they saw each other. Both alive, both dead. Together for one perfect, endless instant.

Joined in magic and spirit, sharing their hopes and dreams, their love and pain, the whole long life they could have had together. Love. Laughter. Children and grandchildren. Dear friends. Struggles and triumphs, a peaceful nation and a healed land. All of it was there in his wise, dark eyes. And she lived it all with him for that one moment out of time.

Then her hand fell away from his, and her legs collapsed out from under her as he sat up, reaching toward her.

The cold, dead ground came up to meet her body, and the blackness of the void wrapped around her spirit, sucking her down, down, down. Into nothing.

Shocked at Raina's collapse, Will belatedly jumped into action as the Gaged Man charged into the clearing, barreling past Rynn and Eben. Rosana screamed something about Raina dying, Ayli screamed something about Gawaine living, and Tiberius and Adrick ran forward toward a small figure that stumbled drunkenly out of the forest.

His mother.

The sight of her froze Will for a costly second as the Gaged Man reached him and took a vicious swing at his knees, attempting to hamstring him. Only Will's long years of training and extreme agility saved him from being crippled. He leaped high over the worst of the blow, but still caught a bad gash on his lower leg. He fell and rolled, coming to his feet well behind the Gaged Man.

Ayli leaped in front of Gawaine to defend him and was gutted for her troubles. She slid off the Gaged Man's bloody sword in a heap of rags and bones on the ground.

Selea swept forward, his dark cloak sailing out behind him, but armed only with daggers, he was not able to close on the Gaged Man and take the ancient warrior down.

The Gaged Man threw magical damage at Marikeen and Kendrick, who charged from his off side, and both of them went down, badly wounded.

They were in big trouble. As far as Will could tell, everyone in the party was tapped out. The healers had just cast everything they had into Gawaine, everyone was injured to some degree or another, and the Gaged Man was a formidable fighter.

Will looked frantically for his father, but Ty was kneeling next to Serica, who lay on the ground in a pool of blood. Panic for his mother slammed through him, but he had no time for it.

Using the metal-clad end of his staff, he walloped the Gaged Man on the back of his helmet hard enough to force the man to turn around and face him. The man bared his teeth in fury and leaped on the attack.

Wounded, out of magic, and armed only with his staff, Will was at a severe disadvantage against a fully armored, magic-wielding, sword-swinging opponent. But by the Lady, he would die rather than let this assailant murder Gawaine.

Will fell back, parrying the blistering flurry of sword swings, drawing the Gaged Man away from Gawaine step by step. As he'd hoped, his friends slid in behind the Gaged Man, forming a living wall between the attacker and Gawaine, who had slid off the bier and had gathered Raina's body in his arms.

The Gaged Man's gaze darted away from Will for an instant. Frantic that his foe would disengage from him and turn back to murder all his friends and Gawaine, Will taunted him. "Afraid you can't take me? I'm bleeding and limping and armed only with a stick, and a great warrior like you can't take me? You're not worthy to lick the dung off my boot if you can't beat me in my current state!"

The ploy worked. The Gaged Man made an aggressive move toward him, and Will fell back a few more paces before the renewed onslaught.

Out of the darkness and tangled tree roots, three elves raced forward, shouting. Will had just enough time to glimpse spiderweb markings on their faces before they attacked the Gaged Man, slashing at him from all sides with swords. Will joined in pummeling the Gaged Man, aiming for the joints in his armor where his flesh would be most vulnerable.

The Gaged Man went down under the attack, letting out a piercing scream of rage and frustration. One of the zinnzari lifted his sword high in both hands over the ancient warrior's body and plunged his sword into the Gaged Man's heart.

"That should do the job," Will commented dryly.

Thanon heard a scream, and his head jerked up. What manner of beast made such a fearsome sound? It went straight to his gut and twisted his innards into knots of abject terror. He projected his mind outward, trying to sense this new threat, and he reeled at the towering fury of the immensely powerful mind that was almost here.

The battlefield was much less chaotic than it had been a half hour ago. Most of the phantasmal forces were defeated and turned to dust. A tight cluster of night trolls and nulvari void casters were still stubbornly holding their ground. Worse, lizardmen seemed to keep pouring onto the island, coming from who knew where, rallying around the one remaining nullstone construct.

Tarses had been forced to lead the attacks on the other two constructs because his Klangon steel sword was one of the only weapons on the field that could damage the incredibly hard creatures.

As for Thanon's men, they were battered and beginning to

show the wear of hard, continuous fighting. His healers were running very low on magic, much lower than he wanted to let on to his enemies. He would not be exaggerating to say the situation was becoming dire.

"Thanon! Report!" Tarses called to him.

He jogged over to where the general directed the battle. At the moment, Tarses was instructing has various subcommanders in how they were going to execute a pincer move upon the night trolls and drive them away from the black door.

"You'll hold the door against the lizardmen, Thanon. Park your men in front of it, let them rest as they can, and don't let anyone through."

"Yes, sir," he responded briskly.

He jogged back to his men, who were grateful to fall back from the main fighting and array themselves in an unmoving line in front of the nullstone door. They bent over, hands on their thighs, breathing hard. His men were even more spent than they'd been letting on. Gratitude and admiration for them coursed through him. They would die to the last man to protect the door Raina had passed through if he told them to.

And that was exactly what he told them to do. Gripping weapons anew and resettling armor into place, they took up guard duty in front of the door.

The scream sounded again, this time much closer and much louder. It grated upon his ears and mind, forcing him to throw up his mental defenses against the agony that shriek induced.

His men flinched but held their ground.

A great shadow swooped out of the mist, passing over the battlefield at high speed, obscuring so much light for that brief moment Thanon could hardly calculate how large the flying creature must be.

The night trolls and nulvari turned as one and ran, literally screaming, for the shore, the fastest of them disappearing into the mist.

The shadow came back without warning, this time from the other direction, with a great whooshing sound of wind. Massive talons reached down out of the mist, grabbing the largest of the trolls and casually crushing them before dropping them. A great, bat-like wing dipped down and swept the nulvari aside like grains of rice on a tabletop. They flew off into the mist, and moments later, Thanon heard splashing and screaming as the violent currents swept them away.

The dragon landed then, her huge claws plunging into the soft ground of the island, great wings spread wide. The lizardmen on the field fell to their knees and plastered their foreheads on the ground, chanting frantically in unison, something about being blessed by the return of the old ones.

Thanon stared in utter shock, gazing upon his first and only dragon in a life that spanned hundreds of years. She stood several times the height of a man, her scaled body glittering every shade of green, her massive, muscular tail twitching in what could only be fury. He did not need to read her emotions to know that she was enraged.

"Why do you come to this place?" she demanded.

He wasn't sure she spoke the words aloud, but they resonated painfully in his mind.

Tarses glanced over at him, and Thanon shrugged back. He had no advice for the general about how to converse with a furious dragon.

"Out of my way," she ordered imperiously. "Attempt to impede me and die."

He blinked, and in the next second, the dragon had been replaced by a shockingly, dangerously beautiful woman. She looked human, and yet he knew without a doubt that she was not. Power poured off her, waves upon waves of it, beyond measuring in scope and scale.

She stalked toward him, and Thanon realized belatedly that the door was her goal. He leaped aside, gesturing for his men to do the same. They all scrambled out of her way, giving her wide berth.

As she drew near, he noted that her human hair was dark, and that green sparks flew off the tips of individual strands as it flowed around her. She wore a form-fitting green dress that was simple and elegant, and her eyes . . . her eyes were mesmerizing. Wide, green, and slightly uptilted, they were impossible to look away from.

Only when she waved her hand and the stubborn nullstone door opened of its own volition before her did he tear his gaze away from her exotic, sharp-edged beauty.

Beyond the door lay a wide chamber that looked to encompass the entire interior of the island. It glowed softly from within, and the dragon, still in human form, strode inside.

Will looked up sharply as a woman moved toward them. She was dressed all in green, her dark hair giving off green lights, and green magic crackling from her fingertips. She stopped a dozen paces from where they were all gathered around Raina's dead body. Not even Gawaine had been able to revive her. Raina was well and truly dead.

The void left by her passing was so vast and painful that he'd gone completely numb inside, his mind lost in blank denial. But he knew that when the feelings came, they were going to be awful beyond measure.

Aurelius had soberly declared her beyond renewing and beyond resurrection. She had apparently completely burned out her spirit channeling all the magic she was capable of into Gawaine.

She'd been so young, so full of dreams, so stubborn and generous. He couldn't believe she was gone. And yet she incontrovertibly was. For now, Will embraced being too devastated for tears, too numb for grief. That would come, but later.

As the stunning, furious woman drew close, Gawaine looked up from where he knelt, cradling Raina's corpse gently in his arms. Will was shocked to see a tear track upon the king's cheek.

The bedraggled, bleeding, exhausted party braced defensively as the woman took an aggressive step forward. But Gawaine said in a weary voice, "Greetings, sister. It has been a long time. How was your nap?"

"Fine! Yours?" she snapped.

Will looked back and forth between Gawaine and the

woman. *Sister?* Could this be . . . Hemlocke? But she was a dragon . . .

If any dragon could take a human form, this would be exactly what he would imagine it to look like. Power and danger and arrogance rolled off the woman in green.

"So! You children couldn't resist meddling, could you?" she snapped. "You have no idea what you've done."

Bloodroot growled inside his chest, and Will frowned, beyond caring right now if he offended a dragon. "Actually, madam, we know exactly what we've done. We've given Haelos its Mythar back, and with him given the continent a chance to heal and be whole. We've given the people of this land their king back, and with him a chance to be free."

"Freedom. Hah! You know not what it means, boy," the dragon retorted.

"Exactly. But we would like to learn."

"Oh, you shall, foolish human. You shall. And in the meantime, you've killed my brother. Well done," she added sarcastically.

"How's that?" Aurelius asked.

"As long as he was here, he was safe. I watched over him, and no one could touch him. But now, he is awake. He no longer falls under my protection. My promise to our mother is fulfilled. You are on your own, brother."

Gawaine did not respond. Instead, he looked down at the body of the girl in his arms and wept.

Which seemed to irritate Hemlocke greatly. She paced from one side to the other and back before stepping forward aggressively enough that he was forced to look up at her. She glared, and Gawaine stared back implacably at her. Will got the distinct impression that they were sharing some sort of psychic communication. Or more accurately, that they were silently arguing with each other.

Hemlocke burst out, "You *loved* her? Since when do you love anything but your precious land?"

Gawaine answered in a voice laced with pain and regret, "Since I met her."

"How fascinating." Hemlocke took a few more steps

forward with sinuous grace that reminded Will of a panther he'd once seen at a fair. The expression in her green eyes was just as predatory, too.

Gawaine rose to his feet as she approached, Raina's limp body still cradled in his arms. Hemlocke stopped directly in front of him, staring down at her.

"She's human," Hemlocke spat.

"She was noble in spirit and kind in heart. And brave. So brave—" Gawaine's voice broke.

Will was close enough to see a distinctly calculating look come into Hemlocke's eyes as she stared at Gawaine's bowed head. Then she reached out, laid her hand over Raina's heart, and closed her own eyes.

Will jumped violently as Raina took a sudden gasping breath. Gawaine moved quickly, laying her on his bier and quickly wadding up his silken shroud under her head.

He placed his hands on either side of her head and stared down at her, concentrating intently for many long seconds. "Come back to me," he murmured aloud at one point.

Another breath, this one deeper. A long exhalation.

Raina's eyes fluttered open.

A gasp went up from everyone followed by exclamations of relief.

Gawaine looked up at Hemlocke, his expression ravaged. He spoke humbly. "Thank you, sister."

"You owe me. And so does she."

Will got the feeling Hemlocke hadn't revived Raina for any altruistic reason at all. She'd done it because she wanted to have some sort of a hold over Gawaine.

Gawaine's gaze narrowed. "I understand."

He obviously thought the same thing of Hemlocke's motives.

"I'll leave you to your human friends and your short life. Don't say I didn't warn you."

And with that, she whirled and leaped upward, transforming in the blink of an eye into a massive, winged green dragon and bursting through the roof of the chamber with an explosion of shattered nullstone, dirt, and splintered wood.

Raina sat up, disoriented. Diffused sunlight streamed down upon her. She'd been in an underground chamber. And then she'd been in a place of shadows and light, a place of spirits.

Gawaine's familiar, beloved face swam before her. He was smiling.

"Oh no." She sighed. "Tell me you aren't dead, too."

"I'm not. I live, thanks to you and your foolish sacrifice."

"I don't understand . . ." If he was alive and she had passed beyond the Veil, how were they communicating?

"You're alive, Raina. My sister, Hemlocke, brought you back."

"How?"

"She's a dragon. Things like death and time are no obstacle to her. She willed you back into your body."

"Why?"

Gawaine's mouth curved in a sardonic smile. "Because she knows how I feel about you and knows you to be a useful weakness."

She frowned. Her mind was still fuzzy, and she wasn't following his reasoning.

Gawaine elaborated. "As long as you live, you are my one point of vulnerability. You are linked to Hemlocke now. She can harm you or destroy you any time she wishes, and she can hold that over me."

"I'm sorry—"

"Never be sorry that you live. I owe my sister a debt of gratitude I can never repay, and I would have it no other way."

He gathered her into a fierce hug made all the sweeter for being entirely real.

"You're truly back?" she murmured against his neck. "And you're well and whole? We got it right?"

"Right enough. I still need to regain quite a bit of strength. But we've got time now." His arms tightened around her, and he murmured low, for her ears only, "All the time in the world."

Raina sighed and laid her head on his chest, reveling in the slow, steady beat of his heart. They'd done it. They'd woken the Sleeping King.